MAEVE BINCHY

Two Complete Novels

MAEVE BINCHY

Two Complete Novels

CIRCLE OF FRIENDS

THE COPPER BEECH

WINGS BOOKS

NEW YORK

This omnibus was originally published in separate volumes under the titles:
Circle of Friends, copyright © 1991 by Maeve Binchy
The Copper Beech, copyright © 1992 by Maeve Binchy

This edition contains the complete and unabridged texts of the original editions.

This 2003 edition is published by Wings Books®, an imprint of Random House Value Publishing, a division of Random House, Inc., New York, by arrangement with Ballantine, a division of Random House, Inc.

Wings Books® and colophon are trademarks of Random House, Inc.

Random House
New York • Toronto • London • Sydney • Auckland
www.randomhouse.com

Printed and bound in the United States of America

A catalog record for this title is available from the Library of Congress.

ISBN 0-517-22202-7

10 9 8 7 6 5 4 3 2 1

To dearest Gordon with all my love

Contents

CIRCLE OF FRIENDS

ONE

—————————————————◆—————————————————

he kitchen was full of the smells of baking. Benny put down her school bag and went on a tour of inspection.

"The cake hasn't been iced yet," Patsy explained. "The mistress will do that herself."

"What are you going to put on it?" Benny was eager.

"I suppose Happy Birthday Benny." Patsy was surprised.

"Maybe she'll put Benny Hogan, Ten."

"I never saw that on a cake."

"I think it is, when it's a big birthday like being ten."

"Maybe." Patsy was doubtful.

"And are the jellies made?"

"They're in the pantry. Don't go in poking at them, you'll leave the mark of your finger and we'll all be killed."

"I can't believe I'm going to be ten," Benny said, delighted with herself.

"Ah, it's a big day all right." Patsy spoke absently as she greased the trays for the queen cakes with a scrap of butter paper.

"What did you do when you were ten?"

"Don't you know with me every day was the same," Patsy said

cheerfully. "There was no day different in the orphanage until I came out of it and came here."

Benny loved to hear stories of the orphanage. She thought it was better than anything they read in books. There was the room with the twelve iron beds in it, the nice girls, the terrible girls, the time they all got nits in their hair and had their heads shaved.

"They must have had birthdays," Benny insisted.

"I don't remember them." Patsy sighed. "There was a nice nun who said to me that I was Wednesday's child, full of woe."

"That wasn't nice."

"Well, at least she knew I was born on a Wednesday . . . Here's your mother, now let me get on with the work."

Annabel Hogan came in carrying three big bags. She was surprised to see her daughter sitting swinging her legs in the kitchen.

"Aren't you home nice and early? Let me put these things upstairs."

Benny ran over to Patsy when her mother's heavy tread was heard on the stairs.

"Do you think she got it?"

"Don't ask me Benny, I know nothing."

"You're saying that because you *do* know."

"I *don't*. Really."

"Was she in Dublin? Did she go up on the bus?"

"No, not at all."

"But she must have." Benny seemed very disappointed.

"No, she's not long gone at all. . . . She was only up the town."

Benny licked the spoon thoughtfully. "It's nicer raw," she said.

"You always thought that." Patsy looked at her fondly.

"When I'm eighteen and can do what I like, I'll eat all my cakes uncooked," Benny pronounced.

"No you won't, when you're eighteen you'll be so busy getting thin you won't eat cakes at all."

"I'll always want cakes."

"You say that now. Wait till you want some fellow to fancy you."

"Do you want a fellow to fancy you?"

"Of course I do, what else is there?"

"What fellow? I don't want you to go anyway."

"I won't get a fellow, I'm from nowhere, a decent fellow wouldn't be able to talk about me and where I came from. I have no background, no life before, you see."

"But you had a *great* life," Benny cried. "You'd make them all interested in you."

There was no time to discuss it further. Benny's mother was back in the kitchen, her coat off and down to business with the icing sugar.

"Were you in Dublin at all today, Mother?"

"No child, I had enough to do getting things ready for the party."

"It's just I was wondering . . ."

"Parties don't run themselves you know." The words sounded sharp but the tone was kindly. Benny knew her mother was looking forward to it all too.

"And will Father be home for the cake bit?"

"Yes, he will. We've asked the people for half-past three, they'll all be here by four, so we needn't sit down to the tea until half-past five, and we wouldn't have got to the cake until your father has the business closed, and is back here."

Benny's father ran Hogan's Outfitters, the big menswear shop in the middle of Knockglen. The shop was often at its busiest on a Saturday, when the farmers came in, or the men who had a half day themselves were marched in by wives to have themselves fitted out by Mr. Hogan, or Mike the old assistant, the tailor who had been there since time immemorial. Since the days when young Mr. Hogan had bought the business.

Benny was glad that her father would be there for the cake, because that was when she might be given her present. Father had said it was going to be a wonderful surprise. Benny *knew* that they

3

must have got her the velvet dress with the lacy collar and the pumps to go with it. She had wanted it since last Christmas when they went to the pantomime in Dublin and she had seen the girls on the stage dancing in pink velvet dresses like this.

They had heard that they sold them in Clerys, and that was only a few minutes from where the bus stopped when it went to Dublin.

Benny was large and square, but she wouldn't look like that in the pink velvet dress. She would be just like the fairy dancers they had seen on the stage, and her feet wouldn't look big and flat in those shoes because they had lovely pointy toes, and little pom-poms on them.

The invitations to the party had been sent out ten days ago. There would be seven girls from school, farmers' daughters mainly from outside Knockglen. And Maire Carroll, whose mother and father owned the grocery. The Kennedys from the chemist's were all boys so they wouldn't be there, and Dr. Johnson's children were all too young so they couldn't come either. Peggy Pine who ran the smart clothes shop said that she might have her young niece stay-ing with her. Benny said she didn't want anyone they didn't know, and it was with some relief that they heard the niece Clodagh didn't want to go amongst strangers either.

Her mother had insisted she invite Eve Malone and that was bad enough. Eve was the girl who lived in the convent and knew all the nuns' secrets. Some people at school said look how Mother Francis never gives out to Eve, she's the real pet; others said the nuns had to keep her for charity and didn't like her as much as they liked the other girls whose families all contributed something to the upkeep of St. Mary's.

Eve was small and dark. She looked like a pixie sometimes, her eyes darting here and there, forever watchful. Benny neither liked Eve nor disliked her. She envied her being so fleet and lithe and able to climb walls. She knew that Eve had her own room in the convent, behind the curtain where no other girl was allowed to step. The girls said it was the room with the round window that

4

faced down the town and that Eve could sit at the window and watch everyone and where they went and who they were with. She never went on holidays anywhere, she stayed with the nuns all the time. Sometimes Mother Francis and Mrs. Pine from the dress shop would take her on an outing to Dublin, but she had never stayed away a night.

Once, when they had gone on a nature walk, Eve had pointed to a small cottage and said that it was her house. It stood in a group of small houses, each separate and surrounded by a little stone wall. When she was older she would live in it all on her own and there would be no milk allowed in the door, and no clothes hangers. She would put all her things on the floor because it was hers to do what she liked with.

Some of them were half afraid of Eve, so nobody denied the story, but nobody really believed it either. Eve was so strange, she could make up tales and then, when everyone had got interested, she would say, "Fooled you."

Benny didn't really want her to come to the party, but for once Mother had been insistent.

"That child has no home. She must come to this one when there's a celebration."

"She *has* a home, Mother, she's got the run of the whole convent."

"That's not the same. She's to come here, Benny, that's my last word."

Eve had written a very neat correct letter saying that she accepted the invitation with pleasure.

"They taught her to write nicely," Eve's father had said approvingly.

"They're determined to make a lady out of her," Mother had said. No one would explain why it seemed so important.

"When it's her birthday she only gets holy pictures and holy water fonts," Benny reported. "That's all the nuns have, you see."

"God, that would turn a few of them over in their graves up

there under the yew trees," Benny's father had said, but again there was no explanation of why.

"Poor Eve, what a start for her," Benny's mother sighed.

"I wonder was she born on a Wednesday like Patsy." Benny was struck by something.

"Why would that matter?"

"She'd be miserable. Wednesday's child is full of woe," Benny parroted.

"Nonsense." Her father was dismissive.

"What day was I born on?"

"A Monday, Monday September eighteenth, 1939," her mother said. "At six o'clock in the evening."

Her parents exchanged glances, looks that seemed to remember a long wait for a first and, as it turned out, an only child.

"Monday's child is fair of face," Benny said, grimacing.

"Well, that's true certainly!" her mother said.

"You couldn't have a fairer face than Mary Bernadette Hogan, spinster of this parish, almost ten years of age," said her father.

"It's not really fair, I mean I don't have fair hair." Benny struggled to fit in with the saying accurately.

"You have the most beautiful hair I have ever seen." Her mother stroked Benny's long chestnut locks.

"Do I really look nice?" she asked.

They reassured her that she looked beautiful, and she knew they had bought the dress for her. She had been worried for a bit but now she was certain.

At school next day, even the girls who hadn't been asked to the party wished her a happy birthday.

"What are you getting?"

"I don't know, it's a surprise."

"Is it a dress?"

"Yes, I think so."

"Ah, go on, tell us."

"I don't know yet, really. I won't have it till the party."

"Was it got in Dublin?"

"I think so."

Eve spoke suddenly. "It might have been got here, there's lots of things in Mrs. Pine's."

"I don't think so." Benny tossed her head.

Eve shrugged. "Okay."

The others had gone away.

Benny turned on Eve. "Why did you say it was got in Mrs. Pine's? You don't know, you don't know anything."

"I said okay."

"Have *you* got a frock?"

"Yes, Mother Francis got one at Mrs. Pine's. I don't think it's new. I think someone gave it back because there was something wrong with it."

Eve wasn't apologetic. Her eyes flashed, she was ready with the explanation before anyone else could make the accusation.

"You don't know that."

"No, but I think it. Mother Francis wouldn't have the money to buy me a new frock."

Benny looked at her with admiration. She softened in her own attack.

"Well, I don't know either. I think they got me this lovely velvet one. But they mightn't."

"They got you something new anyway."

"Yes, but I'd really look great in this," Benny said. "It would make anyone look great."

"Don't think about it too much," Eve warned.

"Maybe you're right."

"It's nice of you to ask me. I didn't think you liked me," Eve said.

"Oh, I do." Poor Benny was flustered.

"Good. Just as long as you weren't told to, or anything."

"No! Heavens no!" Benny was far too vehement.

Eve looked at her with a measured glance. "Right," she said. "See you this afternoon."

They went to school on Saturday mornings, and at twelve-thirty when the bell went they all poured out of the school gates. All except Eve, who went to the convent kitchen.

"We'll have to feed you up with a good meal before you go," said Sister Margaret.

"We wouldn't want them to think that a girl from St. Mary's would eat all before her when she went out to tea," said Sister Jerome. They didn't want to spell it out too much for Eve, but it was a big event, the child they had brought up being invited out to a party. The whole community was delighted for her.

As Benny had walked down the town, Mr. Kennedy called her into the chemist's.

"A little bird told me it was your birthday," he said.

"I'm ten," Benny said.

"I know. I remember when you were born. It was in the Emergency. Your Mam and Dad were so pleased. They didn't mind at all that you weren't a boy."

"Did they want a boy do you think?"

"Everyone with a business wants a boy. But I don't know, I've three of them, and I don't think one of them will ever run this place for me." He sighed heavily.

"Well, I suppose I'd better be . . . ."

"No, no. I brought you in to give you a present. Here's a pack of barley sugar all for you."

"Oh, Mr. Kennedy . . ." Benny was overwhelmed.

"Not at all. You're a grand girl. I always say to myself, there's that little barrel Benny Hogan coming along."

A bit of the sunlight went out of the barley sugar. Moodily Benny tore the corner off the packet and began to eat a sweet.

Dessie Burns, whose hardware shop was next door to Kennedy's, gave her a shout of approval.

"That's it, Benny, like myself, always head in the nosebag. How are you in yourself these days?"

"I'm ten today, Mr. Burns."

"Jaysus isn't that great, if you were six years older I'd take you into Shea's and put you up on my knee and buy you a gin and It."

"Thank you Mr. Burns." She looked at him fearfully.

"What's your father doing over there? Don't tell me he's after hiring new staff. Half the country taking the emigrant ship and Eddie Hogan decides to expand."

Dessie Burns had small piggy eyes. He looked across the street toward Hogan's Gentleman's Outfitters with huge unconcealed interest. Her father was shaking hands with a man—or a boy, it was hard to see. He looked about seventeen, Benny thought, thin and pale. He had a suitcase in his hand. He was looking up at the sign over the door.

"I don't know anything about it, Mr. Burns," she said.

"Good girl, keep your mind out of business, let me tell you it's a heart scald. If I were a woman I wouldn't have the slightest interest in it either. I'd just get myself a fine eejit of a man to keep me in barley sugar all day."

Benny went on down the street, past the empty shop which people said that a real Italian from Italy was going to open up. She passed the cobbler's shop where Paccy Moore and his sister Bee waved out to her. Paccy had a twisted leg. He didn't go to mass, but it was said that the priests came down to him once a month and heard his confession and gave him Holy Communion. Benny had heard that they had sent to Dublin and maybe even Rome for him to have a dispensation, and it wasn't a question of his being a sinner or outside the Church or anything. And then she was home to Lisbeg. The new dog, which was half collie, half sheepdog, sat sleepily on the step loving the September sunshine.

Through the window she could see the table set for the party. Patsy had cleaned the brasses specially, and Mother had tidied up the front garden. Benny swallowed the barley sugar rather than be accused of eating sweets in the public view, and let herself in the back.

"Not a word out of that dog to let you know I was coming," her mother said crossly.

"He shouldn't bark at you, you're family," Benny defended him.

"The day Shep barks for anything except his own amusement there'll be white blackbirds. Tell me did you have a nice day at school, did they make a fuss of you?"

"They did, Mother."

"That's good. Well they won't know you when they see you this afternoon."

Benny's heart soared. "Will I be getting dressed, like in anything new, before the party?"

"I think so. I think we'll have you looking like the bees knees before they come in."

"Will I put it on now?"

"Why not." Benny's mother seemed excited about seeing the new outfit herself. "I'll lay it out for you on the bed. Come up and give yourself a bit of a wash and we'll put it on."

Benny stood patiently in the big bathroom while the back of her neck was washed. It wouldn't be long now.

Then she was led into her bedroom.

"Close your eyes," said Mother.

When Benny opened them she saw on the bed a thick navy skirt, a Fair Isle jumper in navy and red. A big sturdy pair of navy shoes lay in their box and chunky white socks folded nice and neatly beside them. Peeping out of tissue paper was a small red shoulder bag.

"It's an entire outfit," cried Mother. "Dressed from head to foot by Peggy Pine . . ."

Mother stood back to see the effect of the gift.

Benny was wordless. No velvet dress, no lovely soft crushed velvet that you could stroke, with its beautiful lacy trim. Only horrible harsh rough things like horsehair. Nothing in a misty pink, but instead good plain sensible colors. And the shoes! Where were the pumps with the pointed toes?

Benny bit her lip and willed the tears back into her eyes.

"Well, what do you think?" Her mother was beaming proudly.

"Your father said you must have the handbag and the shoes as well, it would make it a real outfit. He said that going into double figures must be marked."

"It's lovely," Benny muttered.

"Isn't the jumper perfect? I'd been asking Peggy to get something like that for ages. I said I didn't want anything shoddy . . . something strong that would stand up to a bit of rough-and-tumble."

"It's gorgeous," Benny said.

"Feel it," her mother urged.

She didn't want to. Not while she still had the velvet feel in her mind.

"I'll put it on myself, Mother, then I'll come and show you," she said.

She was holding on by a thread.

Fortunately, Annabel Hogan needed to go and supervise the shaking of hundreds-and-thousands on the trifle. She was just heading off downstairs when the telephone rang. "That'll be your father." She sounded pleased and her step was quicker on the stair.

Through her sobs, which she choked into the pillow, Benny heard snatches of the conversation.

"She loved it, Eddie, you know I think it was almost too much for her, she couldn't seem to take it all in, so many things, a bag and shoes, and socks, on top of everything. A child of that age isn't used to getting all that much at once. No, not yet, she's putting it on. It'll look fine on her . . ."

Slowly Benny got off her bed and went over to the mirror on the wardrobe to see if her face looked as red and tearstained as she feared. She saw the chunky figure of a child in vest and knickers, neck red from scrubbing, eyes red from weeping. She was not a person that anyone would ever dream of putting in a pink velvet dress and little pumps with pointed toes. For no reason at all she remembered Eve Malone. She remembered her small earnest face warning her not to think about the dress from Dublin too much.

Perhaps Eve knew all the time, maybe she had been in the

shop when Mother was buying all this . . . all this horrible stuff. How awful that Eve knew before she did. And yet Eve had never had anything new, she knew that whatever dress *she* got for today would be a reject. She remembered the way Eve had said "They got you something new anyway." She would never let them guess how disappointed she was. Never.

The rest of the day wasn't very clear to Benny because of the heavy cloud of disappointment that seemed to hang over the whole proceedings. For her anyway. She remembered making the right sounds and moving like a puppet as the party began. Maire Carroll arrived wearing a proper party dress. It had an underskirt that rustled. It had come from America in a parcel.

There were games with a prize for everyone. Benny's mother had bought cones of sweets in Birdie Mac's shop, each one wrapped in different colored paper. They were all getting noisy but the cake had to be delayed until Mr. Hogan returned from the shop.

They heard the Angelus ringing. The deep sound of the bells rolled through Knockglen twice a day, at noon and at six in the evening, great timekeepers as much as reminders to pray. But there was no sign of Benny's father.

"I hope he wasn't delayed ramishing on with some customer today of all days," Benny heard her mother say to Patsy.

"Not at all Mam. He must be on his way. Shep got up and gave himself a good stretch. It's always a sign that the master is heading home to us."

And indeed he was. Half a minute later Benny's father came in full of anxiety.

"I haven't missed it, we're not too late."

He was patted down and given a cup of tea and a sausage roll to bolster him up while the children were gathered and the room darkened in anticipation.

Benny tried not to feel the rough wool of the jumper at her

neck. She tried to smile a real smile at her father, who had run down the town to be here for the big moment.

"Do you like your outfit . . . your first entire outfit?" he called over to her.

"It's lovely, Father, lovely. Do you see I'm wearing it all."

The other children in Knockglen used to giggle at Benny for saying "Father." They used to call their fathers Daddy or Da. But by now they were used to it. It was part of the way things were. Benny was the only one they knew without brothers and sisters, most of them had to share a mam and a dad with five or six others. An only child was a rare occurrence. In fact they didn't know any, except for Benny. And Eve Malone of course. But that was different. She had no family at all.

Eve was standing near Benny as the cake came in.

"Imagine that's all for you," she whispered in awe.

Eve wore a dress that was several sizes too big for her. Sister Imelda, the only nun in the convent who was good with the needle, had been in her sickbed so a very poor job had been done on taking up the hem. The rest of it hung around her like a curtain.

The only thing in its favor was that it was red and obviously new. There was no way that it could be admired or praised, but Eve Malone seemed to have risen above this. Something about the way she stood in the large unwieldy garment gave Benny courage. At least her horrible outfit fitted her, and though it was far from being a party dress, let alone the dress of her dreams, it was reasonable, unlike Eve's. She put her shoulders back and smiled suddenly at the smaller girl.

"I'll give you some of the cake to take back if there's any left over," she said.

"Thanks. Mother Francis loves a slice of cake," Eve said.

Then it was there, the blurry light of the candles and the singing happy birthday and the big whoosh . . . and the clapping and when the curtains were open again Benny saw the thin young man that her father had been shaking hands with. He was far too old for the party. They must have brought him back to tea with the grown-ups who would come later. He was very thin and pale, and he had a cold hard stare in his eyes.

"Who was he?" Eve asked Benny on Monday.

"He's the new assistant come to work with my father in the shop."

"He's awful isn't he?"

They were friends now, sitting on a schoolyard wall together at break.

"Yes, he is. There's something wrong with his eyes I think."

"What's his name?" Eve asked.

"Sean. Sean Walsh. He's going to live in the shop."

"Ugh!" said Eve. "Will he go to your house for meals?"

"No, that's the great thing. He won't. Mother asked him to come to Sunday lunch and he made some awful speech about not assuming, or something."

"Presuming."

"Yes, well whatever it is he's not going to do it and it seems to mean coming to meals. He'll fend for himself he said."

"Good." Eve approved of that.

Benny spoke hesitantly.

"Mother said . . ."

"Yes?"

"If you'd like to come anytime . . . that would be . . . it would be all right."

Benny spoke gruffly as if fearing the invitation would be spurned.

"Oh, I'd like that," Eve said.

"Like to tea on an ordinary day, or maybe midday dinner on a Saturday or Sunday."

"I'd love Sunday. It's a bit quiet here on Sundays, a lot of praying you see."

"Right, I'll tell her." Benny's brow had cleared.

"Oh, there is one thing though . . ."

"What is it?" Benny didn't like the intense look on Eve's face.

"I won't be able to ask you back. Where they eat and I eat, it's beyond the curtain you see."

"That doesn't matter at all." Benny was relieved that this was the only obstacle.

"Of course, when I'm grown up and have my own place, you know, my cottage, I could ask you there," Eve said earnestly.

"Is it really your cottage?"

"I told everyone." Eve was belligerent.

"I thought it might only be a pretend cottage," Benny said apologetically.

"How could it be pretend? It's mine. I was born there. It belonged to my mother and my father. They're both dead, it's mine."

"Why can't you go there now."

"I don't know. They think I'm too young to live on my own."

"Well, of course you're too young to live on your own," Benny said. "But to visit?"

"Mother Francis said it was sort of serious, my own place, my inheritance she calls it. She says I shouldn't be treating it as a dolls' house, a playing place when I'm young."

They thought about it for a while.

"Maybe she's right," Benny said grudgingly.

"She could be."

"Have you looked in the windows?"

"Yes."

"Nobody's gone and messed it all up on you?"

"No, nobody goes there at all."

"Why's that? It's got a lovely view down over the quarry."

"They're afraid to go there. People died there."

"People die everywhere." Benny shrugged.

This pleased Eve. "That's true. I hadn't thought of that."

"So who died in the cottage?"

"My mother. And then a bit later my father."

"Oh."

Benny didn't know what to say. This was the first time Eve

had ever talked about her life. Usually she flashed back with a Mind Your Own Business, if anyone asked her a question.

"But they're not in the cottage, they're in heaven now," Benny said eventually.

"Yes, of course."

There seemed to be another impasse.

"I'd love to go and look through the window with you some-time," Benny offered.

Eve was about to reply when Maire Carroll came by.

"That was a nice party, Benny," she said.

"Thanks."

"I didn't know it was meant to be fancy dress though."

"What do you mean?" Benny asked.

"Well, Eve was in fancy dress, weren't you Eve? I mean that big red thing, that wasn't meant to be ordinary clothes was it?"

Eve's face tightened into that hard look that she used to have before. Benny hated to see the expression come back.

"I thought it was quite funny myself," Maire said with a little laugh. "We all did when we were coming home."

Benny looked around the school yard. Mother Francis was looking the other way.

With all her strength Benny Hogan launched herself off the wall down on Maire Carroll. The girl fell over, winded.

"Are you all right Maire?" Benny asked, in a falsely sympathetic tone.

Mother Francis came running, her habit streaming behind her.

"What happened child?" She was struggling to get Maire's breath back, and raise her to her feet.

"Benny pushed me . . ." Maire gasped.

"Mother, I'm sorry, I'm so clumsy, I was just getting off the wall."

"All right, all right, no bones broken. Get her a stool." Mother Francis dealt with the panting Maire.

"She did it purposely."

"Shush, shush, Maire. Here's a little stool for you, sit down now."

Maire was crying. "Mother, she just jumped down from the wall on me like a ton of bricks . . . I was only saying . . ."

"Maire was telling me how much she liked the party Mother. I'm so sorry," Benny said.

"Yes, well Benny, try to be more careful. Don't throw yourself around so much. Now, Maire, enough of this whining. It's not a bit nice. Benny has said she was sorry. You know it was an accident. Come along now and be a big girl."

"I'd never want to be as big a girl as Benny Hogan. No one would."

Mother Francis was cross now. "That's quite enough Maire Carroll. Quite enough. Take that stool and go inside to the cloak-room and sit there until you're called by me to come away from it."

Mother Francis swept away. And as they all knew she would, she rang the bell for the end of break.

Eve looked at Benny. For a moment she said nothing, she just swallowed as if there were a lump in her throat.

Benny was equally at a loss, she just shrugged and spread out her hands helplessly.

Suddenly Eve grasped her hand. "Someday, when I'm big and strong, I'll knock someone down for you," she said. "I mean it, I really will."

"Tell me about Eve's mother and father," Benny asked that night.

"Ah, that's all long ago now," her father said.

"But I don't know it. I wasn't there."

"No point in raking over all that."

"She's my friend. I want to know about her."

"She used not to be your friend. I had to plead with you to let her come to the party," Mother said.

"No, that's not the way it was." Benny couldn't believe now that this was so.

"I'm glad the child's coming here to her dinner on Sunday," Eddie Hogan said. "I wish we could persuade that young skinnymalinks above in the shop to come too, but he's determined not to trespass, as he calls it."

Benny was pleased to hear that.

"Is he working out well, Eddie?"

"The best you ever saw, love. We'll be blessed with him I tell you. He's so eager to learn he almost quivers like Shep there, he repeats everything over and over again, as if he's learning it off by heart."

"Does Mike like him?" Benny's mother wanted to know.

"Ah, you know Mike, he likes nobody."

"What does he object to?"

"The way Sean keeps the books. God it's simple to understand, a child could do it, but old Mike has to put up a resistance to everything. Mike says he knows everyone's measurements, and what they paid and what they owed. He thinks it's like a kind of insult to his powers to write things down."

"Couldn't you keep the books, Mother?" Benny suggested suddenly.

"No, no, I'd not be able to."

"But if it's as simple as Father says . . ."

"She'd well be able to but your mother has to be here, this is our home, she runs it for you and me, Benny."

"Patsy could run it. Then you wouldn't have to pay Sean."

"Nonsense, Benny," her father said.

But she wasn't to be stopped. "Why not? Mike would like Mother being in there. Mike loves Mother, and it would be something for Mother to do all day."

They both laughed.

"Isn't it great to be a child," said her father.

"To think that the day isn't full already," agreed her mother.

Benny knew very well that her mother's day was far from full. She thought that it might be nice for Mother to be involved in the shop, but obviously they weren't going to listen to her.

"How did Eve's parents die?" she asked.

"It's not a thing to be talking about."

"Why? Were they murdered?"

"Of course not." Her mother sounded impatient.

"Why then . . . ?"

"Lord, why, why, why," her father sighed.

"At school they're always telling us to ask why. Mother Francis says that if you have a questioning mind you get to know all the answers." Benny was triumphant.

"Her mother died giving birth, when Eve was being born. And then a bit later, her poor father, may the Lord have mercy on him, went out one evening with his wits scattered and fell over the cliff into the quarry."

"Wasn't that desperate!" Benny's eyes were round with horror.

"So, it's a sad story, all over long ago, nearly ten years ago. We don't start bringing it all up over and over."

"But there's more to it isn't there . . . there's a kind of secret."

"Not really." Her father's eyes were honest. "Her mother was a very wealthy woman, and her father was a kind of handyman who helped out in the convent, and did a bit of work up at Westlands. That caused a bit of talk at the time."

"But it's not a secret or a scandal or anything." Annabel Hogan's face was set in warning lines. "They were married and everything in the Catholic Church."

Benny could see the shutters coming down. She knew when to leave things.

Later she asked Patsy.

"Don't ask me things behind your parents' back."

"I'm not. I asked them, and this is what they told me. I just wanted to know did you know any more. That's all."

"It was before I came here, but I heard a bit from Bee Moore . . . Paccy's sister, she works in Westlands you see."

"What did you hear?"

"That Eve's father did a terrible act at the funeral, cursing and shouting . . ."

"Up in the church, cursing and shouting . . . !"

"Not *our* church, not the real church, in the Protestant church, but that was bad enough. You see Eve's mother was from Westlands, from the big house beyond. She was one of the family and poor Jack, that was the father, he thought they'd all treated her badly . . ."

"Go on."

"That's all I know," Patsy said. "And don't be asking that poor child and upsetting her. People with no parents don't like endless questions."

Benny took this as good advice not only about Eve, but about Patsy herself.

Mother Francis was delighted to see the new friendship developing, but far too old a hand in dealing with children to say so.

"Going down to the Hogans again are you?" she said, sounding slightly put out.

"Do you mind?" Eve asked.

"No, I don't mind. I can't say that I mind." The nun tried hard to conceal her enthusiasm.

"It's not that I want to be away from here," Eve said earnestly.

Mother Francis felt an urge to take the child in her arms as she used to do when Eve was a baby given into their care by the accident of her birth.

"No, no of course child, strange though this place is, it is your home."

"It's always been a lovely home."

The nun's eyes filled with tears. "Every convent should have a child. I don't know how we're going to arrange it," she said lightly.

"I wasn't a nuisance when I arrived?"

"You were a blessing, you know that. It's been the best ten years St. Mary's ever had . . . you being here."

Mother Francis stood at a window and watched little Eve go down the long avenue of the convent out to Sunday lunch on her own with the Hogans. She prayed that they would be kind to her, and that Benny wouldn't change and find a new friend.

She remembered the fights she had to keep Eve in the first place, when so many other solutions were being offered. There was a cousin of the Westwards in England who would take the child, someone who would arrange Roman Catholic instruction once a week. The young Healys who had come to start the hotel were reported to be having difficulty in starting a family. They would be happy to have Eve in their home, even after their own children came along, if they did. But Mother Francis had fought like a tiger for that small bundle that she had rescued from the cottage, on the day she was born. The child they had reared until some solution could be found. Nobody had seen that Jack Malone's solution would involve throwing himself over the quarry one dark night. After that there had been no one with better claim to Eve than the nuns who had reared her.

It was the first of many Sunday dinners in Lisbeg for Eve. She loved coming to the house. Every week she brought something which she arranged in a vase. Mother Francis had shown her how to go up the long windy path behind the convent and pick catkins and wild flowers. At the start she would rehearse arranging them with the nun so that she would do it well when she got to the Hogans, but as the weeks went by she grew in confidence. She could bring armfuls of autumn colors and make a beautiful display on the hall table. It became a ritual. Patsy would have the vases ready to see what Eve would bring today.

"Don't you have a lovely house!" she would say wistfully and Annabel Hogan would smile, pleased, and congratulate herself on having brought these two together.

"How did you meet Mrs. Hogan?" she would ask Benny's father. And "Did you always want to run a business?" The kinds of questions Benny never thought to ask but was always interested in the answers.

She had never known that her parents met at a tennis party in a county far away. She had never heard that Father had been apprenticed to another business in the town of Ballylee. Or that Mother had gone to Belgium for a year after she left school to teach English in a convent.

"You make my parents say very interesting things," she said to Eve one afternoon as they sat in Benny's bedroom, and Eve marveled over being allowed to use an electric fire all for themselves.

"Well, they've got great stories like olden times."

"Yes . . ." Benny was doubtful.

"You see the nuns don't have."

"They must have. Surely. They can't have forgotten," Benny said.

"But they're not meant to think about the past, you know, and life before Entering, they really start from when they became Brides of Christ. They don't have stories of olden days like your mother and father do."

"Would they like you to be a nun too?" Benny asked.

"No, Mother Francis said that they wouldn't take me, even if I did want to be a nun, until I was over twenty-one."

"Why's that?"

"She says it's the only life I know, and I might want to join just because of that. She says when I leave school I have to go out and get a job for at least three years before I even think of Entering."

"Wasn't it lucky you met up with them," Benny said.

"Yes. Yes, it was."

"I don't mean lucky that your mother and father died, but if they had to wasn't it great you didn't go somewhere awful."

"Like in stories with wicked stepmothers," Eve agreed.

"I wonder why they got you. Nuns usually don't get children unless it's an orphanage."

"My father worked for them. They sent him up to Westlands

to earn some money because they couldn't pay him much. That's where he met my mother. They feel responsible I think."

Benny was dying to know more. But she remembered Patsy's advice.

"Well, it all turned out fine, they're mad about you up there."

"Your parents are mad about you too."

"It's a bit hard sometimes, like if you want to wander off."

"It is for me too," Eve said. "Not much wandering off above in the convent."

"It'll be different when we're older."

"It mightn't be," Eve said sagely.

"What do you mean?"

"I mean, we have to show them we're terribly trustworthy or something, show them that if we *are* allowed to wander off, we'll wander back in good time."

"How could we show them?" Benny was eager.

"I don't know. Something simple at the start. Could you ask me to stay the night here, for one thing?"

"Of course I could."

"Then I could show Mother Francis that I'd be back up in the convent in time for mass in the chapel, and she'd get to know I was to be relied on."

"Mass on a weekday?"

"Every day. At seven."

"No!"

"It's quite nice. The nuns sing beautifully, it's nice and peaceful. Really I don't mind it. Father Ross comes in specially and he gets a lovely breakfast in the parlor. He says the other priests envy him."

"I didn't know that . . . every day."

"You won't tell anyone will you?"

"No. Is it a secret?"

"Not a bit, it's just that I *don't* tell anything you see, and the community likes that, they feel I'm part of them. I didn't have a friend before. There wasn't anyone to tell."

Benny smiled from ear to ear. "What night will you come? Wednesday night?"

"I don't know, Eve. You don't have any smart pajamas or anything to be going to stay with people. You don't have a good sponge bag, things that people who go visiting need."

"My pajamas are fine, Mother."

"You could iron them, certainly, and you have a dressing gown." She seemed to be faltering. "A sponge bag though?"

"Could Sister Imelda make one for me. I'll do extra clearing up for her."

"And what time will you come back?"

"I'll be at my *prie dieu* in time for mass, Mother."

"You won't want to get up that early if you're visiting people." Mother Francis's face was soft.

"That's what I'd want, Mother."

It was a great evening. They played rummy with Patsy in the kitchen for a long time because Mother and Father went across the road to Dr. and Mrs. Johnson's house. It was a supper to celebrate the christening of their new baby.

Eve asked Patsy all about the orphanage, and Patsy told more details than she had ever told Benny. She explained how they used to steal food, and how hard it was when she came to the Hogans, her first job, to realize she didn't have to take any stray biscuit or a fistful of sugar and put it into her apron.

In bed that night Benny said in wonder, "I don't know why Patsy told us all that. Only the other day she was saying to me that people with no parents didn't like being asked questions."

"Ah, it's different with me," Eve said. "I'm in the same boat."

"No you're not!" Benny was indignant. "Patsy had nothing. She had to work in that awful place and get nits and steal and be beaten for wetting the bed. She had to leave there at fifteen and come here. It's not a bit like you."

"No. We are the same, she has no family, I don't. She didn't have a home like you do."

"Is that why you told her more than you told me?" Benny had been even more astounded at the questions Patsy felt free to ask. Did Eve hate the Westwards who were so rich for not taking her into the big house? Eve didn't, they couldn't, they were Protestants, she explained. Lots more, things Benny wouldn't have dared to ask.

"You don't ask things like that," Eve said simply.

"I'd be afraid of upsetting you," Benny said.

"You couldn't upset a friend," Eve said.

Benny and Eve, who had lived all their lives in the same village, were each amazed at the things the other didn't know about Knockglen.

Benny didn't know that the three priests who lived in the presbytery had been given the game of Scrabble, which they played every night, and sometimes rang the convent to ask Mother Francis questions like how you spelled "quixotic" because Father O'Brien was going to get a triple word score.

Eve hadn't known that Mr. Burns in the hardware shop was inclined to take to the drink or that Dr. Johnson had a very bad temper and was heard shouting about God never putting a mouth into the world that he didn't feed. Dr. Johnson was of the view that there were a lot of mouths, especially in the families with thirteen children, that God had forgotten to feed.

Benny didn't know that Peggy Pine was an old friend of Mother Francis, that they had been girls years ago and that when she came to the convent she called Mother Francis Bunty.

Eve hadn't known that Birdie Mac who ran the sweetshop had a man from Ballylee who had been calling for fifteen years, but she wouldn't leave her old mother and the man from Ballylee wouldn't come to Knockglen.

It made the town far more interesting to both of them to have such insights. Particularly because they knew these were dark secrets not to be shared with anyone. They pooled their knowledge on how children were born, and hadn't any new enlightenments to offer. They both knew that they came out like kittens, they didn't know how they got in.

"It's got something to do with lying down one beside the other, when you're married," Eve said.

"It couldn't happen if you weren't married. Suppose you fell down beside someone like Dessie Burns." Benny was worried.

"No, you have to be married." Eve knew that for certain.

"And how would it get in?" It was a mystery.

"It could be your Little Mary," Benny said thoughtfully.

"What's your Little Mary."

"The bit in the middle of your tummy."

"Oh your tummy button is what Mother Francis calls it."

"That must be it," Benny cried triumphantly. "If they all have different names for it, that must be the secret."

They practiced hard at being reliable. If either said she would be home at six o'clock then five minutes before the hour struck and the Angelus rang she would be back in place. As Eve had anticipated, it did win them much more freedom. They were thought to be a good influence on each other. They didn't allow their hysterical laughing fits to be seen in public.

They pressed their noses against the window of Healy's Hotel. They didn't like Mrs. Healy. She was very superior. She walked as if she were a queen. She always seemed to look down on children.

Benny heard from Patsy that the Healys had been up to Dublin to look for a child to adopt but they hadn't got one because Mr. Healy had a weak chest.

"Just as well," Eve had said unsympathetically. "They'd be terrible for anyone as a mother and father." She spoke in innocence of the fact that Knockglen had once thought that she herself might be the ideal child for them.

Mr. Healy was much older than his wife. It was whispered, Patsy said, that he couldn't cut the mustard. Eve and Benny spent long hours trying to work out what this could mean. Mustard came in a small tin and you mixed it with water. How did you cut it? Why should you cut it?

Mrs. Healy looked a hundred but apparently she was twenty-seven. She had married at seventeen and was busy throwing all her efforts into the hotel since there were no children.

Together they explored places where they had never gone alone. To Floods', the butchers, hoping they might see the animals being killed.

"We don't really want to see them being killed do we?" Benny asked fearfully.

"No, but we'd like to be there at the beginning so that we could if we want to, then run away," Eve explained. Mr. Flood wouldn't let them near his yard so the matter didn't arise.

They stood and watched the Italian from Italy come and start up his fish-and-chip shop.

"Weel you leetle girls come here every day and buy my feesh?" he said hopefully to the two earnest children, one big, one small, who stood watching his every move.

"No, I don't think we'll be allowed," Eve said sadly.

"Why is that?"

"It would be called throwing away good money," Benny said.

"And talking to foreign men," Eve explained to clinch matters.

"My seester is married to a Dublin man," Mario explained.

"We'll let people know," Eve said solemnly.

Sometimes they went to the harness maker. A very handsome man on a horse came one day to inquire about a bridle that should have been ready, but wasn't.

Dekko Moore was a cousin of Paccy Moore's in the shoe shop. He was very apologetic, and looked as if he might be taken away and hanged for the delay.

The man turned his horse swiftly. "All right. Will you bring it up to the house tomorrow, instead," he shouted.

"Indeed I will sir, thank you sir. I'm very sorry sir. Indeed sir." Dekko Moore sounded like a villain who had been unmasked in a pantomime.

"Lord, who was that I wonder?" Benny was amazed. Dekko was almost dead with relief at how lightly he had escaped.

"That was Mr. Simon Westward," Dekko said, mopping his brow.

"I thought it must be," Eve said grimly.

Sometimes they went into Hogan's Gentleman's Outfitters. Father always made a huge fuss of them. So did old Mike, and anyone else who happened to be in the shop.

"Will you work here when you're old?" Eve had whispered.

"I don't think so. It'll have to be a boy, won't it?"

"I don't see why," Eve had said.

"Well, measuring men, putting tape measures round their waists, and all."

They giggled.

"But you're the boss's daughter, you wouldn't be doing that. You'd just be coming in shouting at people, like Mrs. Healy does over in the hotel."

"Um." Benny was doubtful. "Wouldn't I need to know what to shout about?"

"You could learn. Otherwise Droopy Drawers will take over."

That's what they called Sean Walsh who seemed to have become paler, thinner and harder of the eye since his arrival.

"No, he won't, surely?"

"You could marry him."

"Ugh. Ugh. Ugh."

"And have lots of children by putting your belly button beside his."

"Oh, Eve, I'd hate that. I think I'll be a nun."

"I think I will too. It would be much easier. You can go any day you like, lucky old thing. I have to wait until I'm twenty-one." Eve was disconsolate.

"Maybe she'd let you enter with me, if she knew it was a true vocation." Benny was hopeful.

Her father had run out of the shop and now he was back with two lollipops. He handed them one each proudly.

"We're honored to have you ladies in our humble premises," he said, so that everyone could hear him.

Soon everyone in Knockglen thought of them as a pair. The big stocky figure of Benny Hogan in her strong shoes and tightly buttoned sensible coat, the waiflike Eve in the clothes that were always too long and streelish on her. Together they watched the setting up of the town's first fish-and-chip shop, they saw the decline of Mr. Healy in the hotel and stood side by side on the day that he was taken to the sanatorium. Together they were unconquerable. There was never an ill-considered remark made about either of them.

When Birdie Mac in the sweetshop was unwise enough to say to Benny that those slabs of toffee were doing her no good at all, Eve's small face flashed in a fury.

"If you worry so much about things, Miss Mac, then why do you sell them at all?" she asked in tones that knew there could be no answer.

When Maire Carroll's mother said thoughtfully to Eve, "Do you know I always ask myself why a sensible woman like Mother Francis would let you out on the street looking like Little Orphan Annie," Benny's brow darkened.

"I'll tell Mother Francis you wanted to know," Benny had said quickly. "Mother Francis says we should have inquiring minds, that everyone should ask."

Before Mrs. Carroll could stop her Benny had galloped out of the shop and up the road toward the convent.

"Oh, Mam, you've done it now," Maire Carroll moaned. "Mother Francis will be down on us like a ton of bricks."

And she was. The full fiery rage of the nun was something that Mrs. Carroll had not expected and never wanted to know again.

None of these things upset either Eve or Benny in the slightest. It was easy to cope with Knockglen when you had a friend.

TWO

<hr/>

1957

There hadn't been many teddy boys in Knockglen, in fact no one could ever remember having seen one except on visits to Dublin when there were groups of them hanging round corners. Benny and Eve were in the window of Healy's Hotel practicing having cups of coffee so that they would look well accustomed to it when they got to the Dublin coffee-houses.

They saw him pass by, jaunty and confident in his drainpipe trousers, his long jacket with velvet cuffs and collar. His legs looked like spider legs and his shoes seemed enormous. He seemed oblivious of the stares of the whole town. Only when he saw the two girls actually standing up to peer at him past the curtains of Healy's window did he show any reaction. He gave them a huge grin and blew them a kiss.

Confused and annoyed they sat down hastily. It was one thing to look, another to call attention to themselves. Making a show of yourself was high on the list of sins in Knockglen. Benny knew this very well. Anyone could have been looking out the window seeing them being cheap with the teddy boy. Her father maybe, with the tape around his neck, awful sleeveen Sean Walsh, who never said a word without thinking carefully of the possible effect it might have. He could have been looking. Or old Mike, who had called her father Mr. Eddie for years, and saw no reason to change.

And indeed everyone in Knockglen knew Eve as well. It had long been the nuns' ambition that Eve Malone be thought of as a lady. She had even joined in the game herself. Eve didn't want it to get back to the convent that she was trick acting in Healy's Hotel and ogling teddy boys out of the window. While other girls with real mothers resisted all the attempts to gentrify themselves, Eve and Mother Francis studied books on etiquette and looked at magazines to see how nice people dressed, and to pick up any hints on behavior.

"I don't want you to put on an artificial accent," Mother Francis had warned, "nor do I want you sticking out your little finger when you're drinking tea."

"Who are we trying to impress?" Eve had asked once.

"No, look at it the other way. It's who you're trying not to let down. We were told we were mad and we couldn't rear you. It's a bit of human, non-saintly desire to be able to say 'I told you so' to the begrudgers."

Eve had understood that immediately. And there was always hope that the Westward family would see her one day as an elegant lady and be sorry they hadn't kept in touch with the child who was after all their own flesh and blood.

Mrs. Healy approached them. A widow now, formidable as she had always been, she managed to exude disapproval at fifty yards. She could not find any reason why Benny Hogan from the shop across the road and Eve Malone from the convent up the town should not sit and drink coffee in her bay window, but somehow she would have preferred to keep the space for wealthier and more important matrons of Knockglen.

She sailed toward the window. "I'll adjust the curtains—they seem to have got all rucked up," she said.

Eve and Benny exchanged glances. There was nothing wrong with the heavy net curtains of Healy's Hotel. They were as they always were: thick enough to conceal those within while giving a perfect view out.

"Well, isn't that a terrible poor ibex!" exclaimed Mrs. Healy, having identified easily what the girls had been looking at.

"I suppose it's only his clothes really," Eve said in a sanctimonious tone. "Mother Francis always says it's a pity to judge people by the garments they wear."

"Very admirable of her," snapped Mrs. Healy, "but of course she makes sure that the garments of all you pupils are in order. Mother Francis is always the first to judge you girls by the uniforms you wear."

"Not anymore, Mrs. Healy," Benny said happily. "I dyed my gray school skirt dark red."

"And I dyed mine black, and my gray jumper purple," Eve said.

"Very colorful." Mrs. Healy moved away like a ship under full sail.

"She can't bear us being grown up," Eve hissed. "She wants to tell us to sit up straight and not to put our fingers on the nice furniture."

"She knows we don't feel grown up," Benny said gloomily. "And if awful Mrs. Healy knows then everyone in Dublin will know."

It was a problem. Mr. Flood the butcher had looked at them very strangely as they walked up the street. His eyes seemed to burn through them in disapproval. If people like that could see their awkwardness, they were indeed in a bad way.

"We should have a rehearsal, you know go up for a couple of days ahead of everyone else so we won't look like eejits." Eve was hopeful.

"It's hard enough to get up there when we have to. There's no point in asking to go up there in order to waltz around a bit. Can you see them agreeing to that for me at home?"

"We wouldn't call it waltzing around," Eve said. "We'd call it something else."

"Like what?"

Eve thought hard. "In your case, getting book lists and timetables—there's endless things you could say." Her voice sounded suddenly small and sad.

For the first time Benny realized properly that they were going to live separate lives though in the same city. Best friends from the age of ten, now they would go down different roads.

Benny was going to be able to go to University College, Dublin, to study for a B.A. degree because her parents had saved to pay for her. There was no money in St. Mary's convent to send Eve Malone to university. Mother Francis had strained the convent's finances already to provide secondary education for the daughter of Jack Malone and Sarah Westward. Now she would be sent to a convent of the same order in Dublin where she would do a secretarial course. Her tuition fees would be waived in exchange for some light housework.

"I wish to God you were coming to College too," Benny said suddenly.

"I know. Don't say it like that, don't let your voice get drippy or I'll get upset." Eve spoke sharply, but without harshness.

"Everyone keeps saying that it's great, we have each other, but I'd see more of you if you were still in Knockglen," Benny complained. "Your place is miles across the city, and I have to come home on the bus every night, so there'll be no meeting in the evenings."

"I don't think there's much of the nightlife planned for me either," Eve said doubtfully. "A few miles of convent floor to polish, a few million sheets to hem. A couple of tons of potatoes to peel."

"They won't make you do that!" Benny was horrified.

"Who knows what light housework means? One nun's light could be another nun's penal servitude."

"You'll need to know in advance won't you?" Benny was distressed for her friend.

"I'm not in much of a position to negotiate," Eve said.

"But they never asked you to do anything like that here." Benny nodded her head up in the direction of the convent at the end of the town.

"But that's different. This is my home," Eve said simply. "I mean, this is where I live, where I'll always live."

"You'll be able to get a flat and all when you get a job." Benny sounded wistful. She didn't think she would ever see freedom.

"Oh yes, I'm sure I'll get a flat, but I'll come back to St. Mary's, like other people come home from flats on holidays," Eve said.

Eve was always so definite, Benny thought with admiration. So small and determined with her short dark hair and white elfin face. No one had ever dared to say that there was anything different or even unusual about Eve living in the convent, sharing her life with the community. She was never asked about what life was like beyond the curtain where the nuns went, and she never told. The girls also knew that no tales would be told of their own doings. Eve Malone was nobody's spy.

Benny didn't know how she was going to manage without her. Eve had been there for as long as she remembered to help her fight her battles. To deal with the gibes of those who called her Big Ben. Eve had made short work of anyone who took advantage of Benny's gentle ways. They had been a team for years: the tiny wiry Eve with her restless eyes never settling long on anything or anyone; the big handsome Benny, with her green eyes and chestnut brown hair, tied back with a bow always, a big soft good quality bow a bit like Benny herself.

If there had only been some way they could have gone in the doors of University College together and come home on the bus each night, or better still got a flat together, life would have been perfect. But Benny had not grown up expecting life to be totally perfect. Surely it was enough to have got as much as she had.

Annabel Hogan was wondering whether to change the main meal of the day to the evening. There were a lot of arguments for this and a lot against.

Eddie was used to his dinner in the middle of the day. He walked back from the shop and the plate of meat and potatoes was put in front of him with a regularity that would have pleased an army officer. As soon as Shep started his languid stroll out to meet the master at the turn of the road, Patsy began to heat the plates. Mr. Hogan would wash his hands in the downstairs cloakroom and always profess pleasure at the lamb chops, the bacon and cabbage, or the plate of cod and parsley sauce on a Friday. Wouldn't it be a poor thing to have the man close his shop and walk back for a kind of halfhearted snack. Maybe it might even affect his work and he wouldn't be able to concentrate in the afternoon.

But then think of Benny coming back from Dublin after a day in the University: wouldn't it be better if they saved the main meal for her return?

Neither husband nor daughter had been any help. They both said it didn't matter. As usual the burden of the whole house fell on herself and Patsy.

The meat tea was probably the answer. A big slice of ham, or grilled bacon, or a few sausages, and they could put a few extra on Benny's plate in case she felt the need of it. Annabel could hardly believe that she had a daughter about to go to university. Not that she wasn't old enough—she was well old enough to have seen a family through university. She had married late, at a time she had almost given up hope of finding a husband. She had given birth at a time when she thought miscarriages would be all she ever knew.

Annabel Hogan walked around her house: there was always some little thing to be done. Patsy was in the big, warm kitchen, the table covered with flour and crockery, but it would all be swept away and scrubbed by mealtime.

Lisbeg was not a big house, but there was plenty to do in it. There were three bedrooms and a bathroom upstairs. The master bedroom looked out over one side of the front door and Benny's bedroom was on the other. At the back of the house, the dark spare room and the big, old-fashioned bathroom with its noisy pipes and its huge wood-surrounded bath.

Downstairs if you came in the front door (which people rarely did) you would find a large room on each side. They were hardly ever used. The Hogans lived in the back of the house, in the big shabby breakfast room that opened off the kitchen. There was hardly ever a need to light a fire in the breakfast room because the great heat of the range came through. There was a big double door kept permanently open between the two rooms, and it was as comfortable a place as you could imagine.

They rarely had visitors, and if ever anyone was expected the front drawing room in its pale greens and pinks with damp spots over the wall could be aired and dusted. But in the main, the breakfast room was their home.

It had three big red plush armchairs, and the table against the wall had three dining chairs with plush seats as well. A huge radio stood on the big sideboard, and shelves of ornaments, and good china and old books, were fixed precariously to the wall.

Now that young Eve had become such a regular guest in the household, a fourth chair had been found, a cane chair rescued from one of the sheds. Patsy had tied a nice red cushion to it.

Patsy herself slept in a small room beyond the kitchen. It was dark and had a tiny window. Patsy had always told Mrs. Hogan that it was like being dead and going to heaven to have a room of your own. She had always had to share with at least two other people until the day she came to Lisbeg.

When Patsy had walked up the short avenue and looked at the square house with its creeper and its shabby garden, it seemed to her like a house on the front of a calendar. Her small room looked out on the backyard, and she had a window box. Things didn't grow very well in it because it was in shadow and Patsy wasn't much of a gardener, but it was her own, and nobody ever touched it, any more than they ever went into her room.

Patsy was excited as any of them about Benny going to university. Every year on her annual holidays, Patsy paid a dutiful visit of one half day to the orphanage which had reared her, and then she went to stay with a friend who had married in Dublin. She had asked her friend to take her to see where Benny would be a student. She had stood outside the huge pillars of University College, Dublin, and looked at it all with satisfaction. Now she would know where Benny went and studied; she would know the look of the place.

And indeed it was a big step for Benny, Annabel Hogan realized. No more safe trotting to and fro from the convent. It was life in the big city with several thousand other students from all kinds of places, with different ways and no one to force you to study like Mother Francis. It was not surprising that Benny had been as excited as a hen walking on hot coals all summer long, never able to keep still, always jumping up with some further excitement.

It was a relief to know that she was with Eve Malone for the morning, those two could talk until the cows came home. Annabel wished that there had been some way young Eve could have been sent to university too. It would have made things more fair somehow. But things rarely turned out nice and neatly in this life. Annabel had said as much to Father Ross the last time he had come to tea, and Father Ross had looked at her sternly over his glasses saying that if we all understood the way the Universe was run what would there be left for God to tell us on the Last Day.

To herself Annabel thought that it wouldn't interfere with the running of the Universe if enough money could be found somewhere for the university fees and accommodation for Eve Malone, the child that had no home except the big bleak convent with the heavy iron gates.

❦

Mother Francis had asked God very often for a way to send Eve
Malone to university, but so far God had not seen fit to show her
one. Mother Francis knew it must be part of His divine plan, but at
times she wondered had she prayed hard enough, had she examined every possibility. She had certainly been up every road as
far as the Order were concerned. She had written to the Mother
General, she had put Eve's case as persuasively as she could. The
girl's father, Jack Malone, had worked all his life for the convent as
handyman and gardener.

Jack had married the daughter of the Westward family, as unlikely a match as was ever known in the country, but necessary
since a child was on the way. There had been no problem in having
Eve brought up as a Catholic, since the Westwards had never
wanted to know about her at all, and didn't care what faith she was
raised in just as long as they never had to hear her name.

Mother General's view was that enough had been done for the
child already. To provide a university education for her might mark
her out as a favored pupil. Would not others from needy back-
grounds expect the same?

It had not stopped there. Mother Francis had taken the bus to
their convent in Dublin and spoken to the very difficult Mother
Clare who held sway there. With so many young nuns starting
university education in the autumn and lodging in the Dublin convent, was there not a chance that Eve might join them? The girl
would be happy to do housework to earn her place among the
students.

Mother Clare wouldn't even consider it. What an extraordinary suggestion, to put forward a girl—a charity child who was not
a Sister, a novice, a postulant, nor anyone with the remotest intention of becoming a nun—and raise her up above the many Sisters
in the community who were all hoping and praying for a chance of
higher education . . . what would they feel if a girl who had al-

ready been pampered, it seemed, by the convent in Knockglen, were put in to study, over their heads? It would be an outrage.

And perhaps it was outrageous of her, Mother Francis thought sometimes. It was just that she loved Eve as much as any mother could love a daughter. Mother Francis, the celibate nun who had never thought she could know the joy of seeing a child grow up in her care, had loved Eve in a way that might well have made her blind to the feelings and sensitivities of other people. Mother General and Mother Clare were indeed right, it would have been preferential treatment to have financed Eve's university education from the convent funds.

But when all was said and done, Mother Francis wished she could be sure that they would treat Eve well up in Mother Clare's convent. St. Mary's had always been home for Eve; the fear was that she might find the sister house in Dublin more like an institution, and worse still she might find her own role there not that of an honored daughter, but more that of a maid.

When Benny and Eve came out of Healy's Hotel, they saw Sean Walsh watching them from the doorway of Hogan's across the street.

"If you keep talking to me, he might think we haven't seen him," Benny hissed out of the corner of her mouth.

"Not a chance. Look at him standing there with his thumbs in behind his braces, copying the way your father stands."

Eve knew only too well Sean Walsh's expectations: he had a long-term career plan, to marry the daughter of the house, the heir to Hogan's Gentleman's Outfitters, and inherit the lot.

They had never been able to like Sean Walsh, not since the very first day he had turned up at Benny's tenth birthday party. He had never smiled. Not once in all those years had they seen a real smile on his face. There were a lot of grimaces, and a little dry bark sometimes, but never a laugh.

He didn't throw his head back like Peggy Pine did when she

laughed, or giggle into his fist like Paccy Moore; he didn't make big gestures like Mario in the fish-and-chip shop, or even get wheezing and coughing fits like Dessie Burns often did. Sean Walsh seemed watchful the whole time. Only when he saw others smiling and laughing did he give the little barks.

They could never get him to tell anything about the life he had lived before he came to Knockglen. He didn't tell long stories like Patsy did, or wistful tales like Dekko Moore about the time he made harnesses for the Lords of the Soil somewhere down in Meath. Sean Walsh would not be drawn.

"Oh, dear, you don't want to hear my stories," he would say when Benny and Eve plagued him for some information.

The years had not improved him: he was still secretive and insincerely anxious to please. Even his appearance annoyed Benny, although she knew this was unreasonable. He wore a suit that had seen a lot of pressing, and was obviously carefully looked after. Benny and Eve used to tell each other in fits of laughter that he spent hours in his little room above the shop pressing all his ambitions into the suit with a damp cloth.

Benny didn't really believe Eve about Sean having ambitions to marry into the shop, but there was something deeply unsettling all right about the way he looked at her. She had so much wanted to be fancied, it seemed a cruel blow to think that if it ever happened it might only be by someone as awful as Sean Walsh.

"Good morning, ladies." He made an exaggerated bow. There was an insult in his voice, a sneer that he hadn't intended them to notice. Other people had called them "ladies," even that very morning and had done so without any offense. It was a way of acknowledging that they had left school and would shortly start a more grown-up life. When they had been in the chemist's buying shampoo, Mr. Kennedy had asked what he could do for the two young ladies and they had been pleased. Paccy Moore had said they were two fine ladies when they had gone to have heels put on Benny's good shoes. But with Sean Walsh it was different.

"Hallo Sean." Benny's voice was lackluster.

"Surveying the Metropolis, I see," he said loftily. He always spoke slightly disparagingly of Knockglen, even though the place he came from himself was smaller and even less like a metropolis. Benny felt a violent surge of annoyance.

"Well, you're a free agent," she said suddenly. "If you don't like Knockglen you could always go somewhere else."

"Did I say I didn't like it?" His eyes were narrower than ever, almost slits. He had gauged this wrong, he must not allow her to report his having slighted the place. "I was only making a pleasant remark comparing this place to the big city. Meaning that you'll have no time for us here at all soon."

That had been the wrong thing too.

"I'll have little chance of forgetting all about Knockglen considering I'll be coming home every night," said Benny glumly.

"And we wouldn't want to anyway," Eve said with her chin stuck out. Sean Walsh would never know how often she and Eve bemoaned their fate living in such a small town which had the worst characteristic any town could have: It was actually within striking distance of Dublin.

Sean hardly ever let his glance fall on Eve, for she held no interest for him. All his remarks were directed to Benny. "Your father is so proud of you, there's hardly a customer that he hasn't told about your great success."

Benny hated his smile and his knowing ways. He must know how much she hated being told this, reminded about how she was the apple of their eye, and the center of simple boastful conversation. And if he knew, why did he tell her and annoy her still further? If he did have designs on her, and a plan to marry Mr. Eddie Hogan's daughter and thereby marry into the business, then why was he saying all the things that would irritate and upset her?

Perhaps he thought that her own wishes would hardly be considered in the matter. That the biddable daughter of the house would give in on this as she had on everything else.

Benny realized she must fight Sean Walsh. "Does he tell everyone I'm going to College?" she asked, with a smile of pleasure on her face.

"Only subject of conversation." Sean was smug to be the source of information but somehow disconcerted that Benny didn't get embarrassed as he had thought she would.

Benny turned to Eve. "Aren't I lucky?"

Eve understood. "Oh, spoiled rotten," she agreed.

They didn't laugh until they were out of his sight. They had to walk down the long straight street past Shea's pub with its sour smell of drink coming out onto the street from behind its dark windows, past Birdie Mac's sweetshop where they had spent so much time choosing from jars all their school life. Across the road to the butcher's where they looked in the window to see back at the reflection of Hogan's Outfitters and realize that Sean Walsh had gone back inside to the empire that would one day be his.

Only then could they let themselves go and laugh properly.

Mr. Flood, of Flood's Quality Meat Killed On The Premises, didn't appreciate their laughter.

"What's so funny about a row of gigot chops?" he asked the two laughing girls outside his window. It only made them laugh more.

"Get on with you then, do your laughing somewhere else," he growled at them. "Stop making a mock and a jeer out of other people's business."

His face was severely troubled and he went out into the street to look up at the tree which overhung his house.

Mr. Flood had been staring into that tree a lot lately, and worse still having conversations with someone he saw in its branches. The general thinking was that Mr. Flood had seen some kind of vision, but was not ready to reveal it to the town. His words to the tree seemed to be respectful and thoughtful, and he addressed whatever he saw as "Sister."

Benny and Eve watched fascinated, as he shook his head sorrowfully and seemed to agree with something that had been said to him.

"It's the same the whole world over, Sister," he said, "but it's sad it should come to Ireland as well."

He listened respectfully to what he was hearing from the tree, and took his leave. Vision or no vision, there was work to be done in the shop.

The girls only stopped laughing by the time they had reached the convent gates. Benny turned to go back home as usual. She never presumed on their friendship with Eve by expecting to be let into the inner sanctum. The convent in holidays was off-limits.

"No come on in, come in just to see my room," Eve begged.

"Mother Francis? Wouldn't they think . . . ?"

"It's my home, they've always told me that. Anyway, you're not a pupil anymore."

They went through a side door; there was a smell of baking, a warm kitchen smell through the corridors, then a smell of polish on the big stairway, and the wide dark hall hung with pictures of Mother Foundress, and Our Lady and lit only by the Sacred Heart lamp.

"Isn't it desperately quiet in the holidays?"

"You should be here at night. Sometimes when I've come home from the pictures and I let myself in, it's so quiet I'd nearly talk to the statues for company."

They went up to the small room where Eve had lived for as long as she could remember. Benny looked around with interest.

"Look at your wireless, right beside your bed!" The brown Bakelite electric radio, where, like very other girl in the country, Eve listened at night to Radio Luxembourg, was on her night table. In Benny's house, where she was considered a very pampered only child, she had to borrow the kitchen radio and then perch it on a chair because there wasn't any socket near enough to her bed to plug it in.

There was a neat candlewick bedspread and a funny night-dress case shaped like a rabbit.

"Mother Francis gave me that when I was ten. Isn't it awful?"

"Better than holy pictures," Benny said.

Eve opened a drawer in which there were piles of holy pictures, each one bound up with a rubber band.

Benny looked at them fascinated. "You never threw them away!"

"Not here. I couldn't."

The small round window looked down over Knockglen, along the tree-lined drive of the convent through the big gates and down the broad main street of the town.

They could see Mr. Flood fussing round the window of his shop as if he were still worried about what they could have found so amusing in its contents. They saw small children with noses pressed against the window of Birdie Mac's, and men with caps pulled well down over their faces coming out of Shea's pub.

They saw a black Ford Prefect pull up in front of Hogan's and knew it was Dr. Johnson. They saw two men walking into Healy's Hotel, rubbing their hands. These would be commercial travelers, wanting to write up their order books in peace. They could see a man with a ladder up against the cinema putting up the new poster, and the small round figure of Peggy Pine coming out of her dress shop to stand and look admiringly at her window display. Peggy's idea of art was to put as much in the window as could possibly fit without falling over.

"You can see everything!" Benny was amazed. "It's like being God."

"Not really, God can see around corners. I can't see your house, I can't see who's having chips in Mario's; I can't see over the hill to Westlands. Not that I'd want to, but I can't."

Her voice was tight when she spoke of her mother's people in the big house. Benny knew from old that it was a thorny subject.

"I suppose they wouldn't . . ."

"They wouldn't." Eve was firm.

They both knew what Benny was going to say: that there was no chance of the wealthy Westwards paying for a university education for Eve.

"Do you think Mother Francis might have approached them?"

"I'm sure she did, lots of times over the years, and she always got the door slammed in her face."

"You can't be certain," Benny said soothingly.

Eve looked out of the window down the town, standing as she must often have done over the years.

"She did every single thing to help me that anyone could. She *must* have asked them, and they must have said no. She didn't tell me because she didn't want me to feel worse about them. As if I could."

"In a fairy story one of them would ride up the avenue here on a white horse and say they'd been wanting you as part of their lives for years," Benny said.

"And in a fairy story I'd tell him to get lost," Eve said, laughing.

"No, I wouldn't let you, you'd say thank you very much, the fees are this price, and I'd like a nice flat of my own with carpets going right up to the wall and no counting how much electric fire we use." Benny was gleeful.

"Oh yes, and a dress allowance of course, so much a month put into Switzer's and Brown Thomas for me."

"And a holiday abroad each year to make up for not seeing you much over the past while!"

"And a huge contribution to the convent building fund for the new chapel to thank the nuns for doing the needful."

Benny sighed. "I suppose things like that *could* happen."

"As you said, in a fairy story," Eve said. "And what would be the best happening for you?"

"Two men to get out of a van down there in a minute's time and tell my father that Sean Walsh is a criminal wanted for six murders in Dublin and that he has to be handcuffed and out of there this instant."

"It still leaves the business of you having to come home from Dublin on the bus every night," Eve said.

"Listen, don't go on at me. For all that you've been in and out of our house a thousand times you don't know the way they are."

"I do," Eve said. "They idolize you."

"Which means I get the six-ten bus back every night to Knock-glen. That's what being idolized does for you."

"There'll be the odd night surely in Dublin. They can't expect you home every single night."

"Where will I stay? Let's be practical—there'll be no nights in Dublin. I'll be like bloody Cinderella."

"You'll make friends, you'll have friends with houses, families, you know, normal kinds of things."

"When did you and I have anything approaching a normal life, Eve Malone?" Benny was laughing to cheer them up and raise the mood again.

"It'll soon be time for us to take control, seriously." Eve refused to laugh at all.

Benny could be equally serious.

"Sure it will. But what does it mean? You're not going to hurt Mother Francis by refusing to go to this place she's sending you. I'm not going to bring the whole world down on us by telling my mother and father that I feel like a big spancelled goat going to College and having to come back here every night as if I were some kind of simpleton. And anyway, you'll be out of there in a year and you'll get a great job and be able to do what you like."

Eve smiled at her friend. "And we'll come back to this room someday and laugh at the days when we all thought it would be so dreadful."

"We will, we will, and Sean Walsh will be doing penal servitude . . ."

"And the Westwards will have lost all their money and their land."

"And Mrs. Healy will have thrown away her corsets and be wearing a short skirt."

"And Paccy Moore will own a fleet of shoe shops throughout the country."

"And Dr. Johnson will have learned to smile."

"And Mother Francis will be the Reverend Mother General of the whole Order and can do what she likes, and go to see the Pope, and everything."

They laughed, delighted at the thought of such wonders.

THREE

*E*mily Mahon stood in front of the gas cooker and grilled the ten rashers that she served every morning except Friday. Her white blouse hung neatly in the corner of the room. She wore a nylon jacket to make the breakfast lest her clothes get spattered before she went out to work.

She knew that Brian was in a mood this morning. He hadn't a word to throw to a dog. Emily sighed as she stood in the shabby kitchen. Theirs must be the least improved house in Maple Gardens. It was always the same, they say that the shoemaker's children are never shod. So it was logical that the builder's wife would be the only one in the road without a decent kitchen to work in. She had seen the jobs that were done on other people's houses. Kitchens that were tiled so that they only needed a wipe down the walls and a quick mop of the floor. There were units that all fitted together like a continuous counter rather than the cupboards and tables of different sizes that Emily had lived with for twenty-five years. It was useless trying to change him. "Who sees it but us?" was the reply.

Very few visitors came into 23 Maple Gardens. Brian's builder's yard was the center of his social activities, such as they were. The boys, Paul and Nasey, had never brought their friends home, and now they too worked with their father in the yard. That's where fellows called to pick them up, or to take them over to a pub for a pint.

And Nan, the baby of the family, eighteen years old and about to start at university today, Nan had not been one for inviting friends home either.

Emily knew that her beautiful daughter had a dozen friends at school, she had seen her walking down the street when classes were over, surrounded by other girls. She went to the houses of friends, she was invited everywhere, but not one of her schoolmates had crossed the door of Maple Gardens.

Nan was not just beautiful in Emily's eyes. This was the opinion of everyone. When she was a small child people had stopped in the street asking why this little girl with the blond, almost white, curls had never been chosen for the Pears soap advertisement . . . the one where it said "Growing up to be a beautiful lady." In truth Emily did have dreams that one day in a park or on the street a talent scout would stop and see the perfect features and flawless skin of this child and come to the house begging on bended knees to transform her life.

Because if there was anything that Emily Mahon wanted for her little princess, it was a transformed life.

Emily wanted Nan to have everything that she had never had. She didn't want the girl to marry a bullying drunk like her mother had done. She didn't want a life of isolation stuck out here in a housing estate, only allowed to go out to work as a favor. Emily had read a lot of magazines, she knew that it was perfectly possible for a girl with Nan's looks to rise to be the highest in the land. You saw the very beautiful wives of rich businessmen, and the really good-looking women photographed at the races on the arms of well-known people from important families. It was obvious that not all these people could have come from the upper classes. *Their* women were often plain and horsey. Nan was in the running for that kind of life, and Emily would do everything in her power to get it for her.

It had not been hard to persuade Brian to come up with the fees for university. In his sober moods he was inordinately proud of his beautiful daughter. Nothing was too good for her. But that was when he was sober.

And then, during this last summer, Nan had said, "You know, one day he'll break your jaw and then it'll be too late."

"I don't know what you mean."

"He hit you last night, while I was out, when the boys weren't here. I know he did."

"Now you know nothing of the sort."

"Your face, Em. What will you tell them today?"

"The truth. That I got up in the night and walked into an open press."

"Is it going to be like that always? Will he get away with it for the rest of his life?"

"You know how sorry he is Nan. You must know how he'd give any of us the moon after he's been—not himself."

"It's too high a price to pay for the moon," Nan had said.

And now today she was going to start out as a student, this lovely girl that Emily still looked on with awe. Brian had been handsome before alcohol had thickened his face, and she herself had good features, high cheekbones and deep-set eyes. Their daughter seemed to have taken the best features and left the bad ones. Nan had no trace of the coarseness that was in her father's face. Nor did she have any of the pale and slightly apologetic stance of her mother.

As Emily Mahon stood in the kitchen she hoped that Nan would be warm and pleasant to her father this morning. Brian had been drunk last night, certainly, but there had been no dog's abuse out of him.

Emily turned the rashers expertly. There were three for Paul, three for Nasey, and four for Brian. Neither she nor Nan ate a cooked breakfast. Just a cup of tea and a slice of toast each. Emily filled the washing-up bowl with hot soapy water. She would collect their plates to steep when they had finished. Usually everyone left the house around the same time; she liked to have the table cleared before she closed the door behind her, so the place looked respectable when they came in again in the evenings. That way nobody would raise too many objections about Emily going out to work. It had been a battle hard fought.

Nan had been so supportive during the long war waged with Brian. She had listened wordlessly to her father saying, "No wife of mine is going out to work. I want a meal on the table. I want a clean shirt . . ." She had heard her mother say that she could provide these things, but that the days were long and lonely on her own and she would like to meet people and to earn her own money, no matter how small.

The boys, Paul and Nasey, had not been interested, but played the game to win and stuck with their father in the need to have a nice warm house and meals.

Nan had been twelve then, and it was she who had tipped the balance.

"I don't know what you're all talking about," she had said suddenly. "None of you are ever in before six, winter or summer, and so there *will* be a meal. And if Em wants more money and will do all your washing and clearing as well, then I can't see what the fuss is about."

Nobody else could either.

So Emily had worked in a hotel shop since then; her own little world surrounded by nice things: glass and linen and high-class souvenirs for tourists. At first the hotel had been unwilling to employ someone with a young daughter. She would constantly need time off they told her. Emily had been able to look them straight in the eye even then and say that Nan would cause no trouble. And she had been right. It was only Brian who had ever interrupted the even style of her working life by phoning or calling, to ask idiotic questions about things that had already been agreed or arranged, but forgotten through drink.

She called them, as she did every morning. "Breakfast going on the table."

Down they came, her two big sons, dark like their father, square and looking as if they had been manufactured by a toy firm to look like younger versions of a father in a game. Then came Brian, who had cut himself shaving, and was dabbing the blood on his chin. He looked at his wife without pleasure.

"Do you have to wear that bloody garment in the house? Isn't it bad enough going out to work as a skivvy in someone's shop without dressing as a skivvy at home."

"It's to keep my blouse clean," Emily said mildly.

"And you have your clothes draped so that the place looks like a hand-me-down shop," he grumbled.

Nan came in at that moment. Her blond curls looked as if she had just come from a hairdresser rather than from the handbasin in her own bedroom, which was where she had washed her hair this morning. Brian Mahon might have skimped on comfort for the rest of the house, but his daughter's bedroom had the best of everything. A washbasin neatly boxed in, a big fitted wardrobe with even a rail for her shoes in it. Nothing had been spared on Nan's room. Each item was an apology for a drunken bout. She wore a smart blue skirt, and her new navy three-quarter-length coat over her shoulders; a white lacy blouse with a navy blue trimming. She looked like the cover of a magazine.

"That's right, attack Em for leaving her blouse there, but if it's seven of your shirts and seven each of the boys', that's twenty-one shirts ironed for you and there's no word of it being a hand-me-down shop then, is there?"

Her father looked at her in open admiration. "They're going to look twice when you walk in the door of University College," he said. Nan showed no pleasure at the compliment—in fact Emily seemed to think it irritated her.

"Yes, that's all very well, but we never discussed the matter of pocket money."

Emily wondered why Nan brought it up now. If she were to ask her father on her own, he would give her anything.

"There's never been any shortage of pocket money in this house." His face was red and angry already.

"Well, there hasn't been any question of it up till now. Paul and Nasey went in to work for you, so they got a wage from the start."

"A *sort* of wage," Paul said.

"More than any other human would give a lout like you," his father retorted.

Nan continued, "I wanted it to be clear from the start rather than having to ask every week."

"What's wrong with asking every week?" he wanted to know.

"It's undignified," she said shortly.

That was exactly what Emily had felt each week asking for her housekeeping; now she could work out a budget to suit herself.

"What do you want?" He was annoyed.

"I don't know. I'm not really entitled to anything. I'm going to be dependent on you for three or four years. What do *you* suggest?"

He was at a loss. "We'll see."

"I'd prefer if we could decide today. It would get things off to a good start. I'd know what I could buy, how long it would take me to save for something . . . a new dress or whatever."

"I bought you that coat there! It cost me an arm and a leg—it's an ordinary navy coat to me, and it cost as much as a fur."

"It's very well cut, that's why. It will last for years."

"I should hope so," he muttered.

"So you see in order not to have discussions like this all the time, don't you think . . ."

Emily held her breath.

"A pound a week for . . ."

"Fares and lunches, yes, that's fair . . ." She stood looking at him expectantly.

"And what else is there . . . ?"

"Well, I suppose there's cinema, newspapers, books, coffee, going to a dance."

"Another two pounds a week for that?" He looked anxiously at her.

"Oh, that's very generous, thank you. That would be marvelous."

"And what about clothes then . . . ?" He nodded over at the coat that had cost him an arm and a leg.

"I could manage stockings out of what you've given me."

"I want you as well dressed as the next man's daughter."

Nan said nothing.

"What would it cost?" He was like a child now.

Nan looked at him thoughtfully, as if she knew he was in her power now.

"Some people's fathers give them an allowance by the month for clothes. A sum like . . . I don't know . . . twenty . . . but I don't know . . ."

"You'll have thirty pounds a month, nothing is shortchanged in this house." He almost roared it.

Emily Mahon watched Nan start to smile.

"Thank you very much, Daddy, that's more than generous," she said.

"Well"—he was gruff—"I won't have you saying I'm not generous."

"I never said that, never once," she answered him.

"Well, all this business putting me on the carpet . . . implying that I might leave you short."

"In your right mind, Daddy, you'd never leave me short, but I don't want to rely on your always being in your right mind."

Emily caught her breath.

"What do you mean?" He was like a turkeycock now.

"You know exactly what I mean. You're two people, Daddy."

"You're in no position to be giving me lectures."

"I'm not. I'm explaining why I wanted it on a regular arrangement so that I wouldn't have to be annoying you when you're . . . well, when you've had a drink I suppose."

There was a moment's silence. Even the boys wondered what

would happen now. The usual way of coping with their father had been to make no reference to anything untoward that might have happened, for fear of bringing it all upon them again. But Nan had chosen her time and place well.

The silence was broken by Emily.

"Well, that's a very good allowance, there can't be many girls setting off today who'd get that."

"No indeed." Nan was undisturbed by the tension around her. "I mean it, Daddy. And I honestly think that if you are going to give me that much, it's probably easier for you to do it once a month."

"Yes, that's agreed," he said.

"So will I ask you for forty-two pounds today and then not come near you for a month?"

Paul and Nasey looked at each other with widened eyes.

"Forty-two pounds?" Her father seemed astounded.

"You said three pounds a week, and thirty pounds for clothes." She seemed apologetic. "It is a lot, I know."

"I'm not going back on my word." He reached into his back pocket and took out a wad of old notes. He peeled them off.

Emily willed her daughter to show the right amount of gratitude, she prayed that the girl wouldn't take it for granted.

But as usual Nan seemed to know better than everyone what to do.

"I'm not going to go down on my knees and thank you, Daddy, because that would just be words. I'll try to make you proud of me. Make you feel glad you've spent so much to put a daughter through College."

Brian Mahon's eyes misted slightly. He swallowed but could say nothing. "That's it," he said eventually in a hoarse voice. "That's it. Now could a man have a cup of tea in this place does anyone think?"

❦

In a big terraced house in Dun Laoghaire, another household was getting ready for the opening of the university term. Almost a town in itself, Dun Laoghaire was some miles from the center of Dublin, a big harbor where the mail boat came in and left every day for Holyhead bringing the holiday visitors. Full also on the outgoing journeys with emigrants about to seek their fortune in London.

Ever since the days it had been called Kingstown, it had been a lovely place to live; tropical palm trees along the coastline made it seem like somewhere much more exotic than it really was. The sturdy Victorian houses spoke of a time when this was a place of substance and quality. It was healthy too; the two great arms of piers reached out into the sea and were a regular walking spot for anyone in need of a breath of air or some exercise.

It was a curious mixture of staid respectability with overtones of holiday fun. Every year there was a big noisy carnival with its ghost trains and chairoplanes, and yet matrons with shallow baskets did sociable shopping excursions usually ending with coffee in Marine Road and tut-tutting over the state of the borough.

Kit Hegarty moved swiftly around her large house in a quiet road that led down to the sea. She had a lot to do. The first day was always important, it set the tone for the whole year. She would cook them all a good breakfast and make it clear that she expected them to be at the table on time.

She had kept students for seven years now, and was known as one of the University's favored landladies. Normally they didn't like to sanction a digs so far away from the city and the University buildings, but Mrs. Hegarty had been quick to explain how near her house was to the railway station, how short was the train journey into town, how good the bracing sea air.

She didn't need to plead for long; soon the authorities realized that this determined woman could look after students better than anyone. She had turned her big dining room into a study; there each boy had his own place at the big felt-covered table, books could be left undisturbed. It was expected in Kit's house that there would be some period of study after supper, most nights at any rate. And her only son, Frank, studied with them too. It made him feel grown up sitting at the same table as real university students, engineers and agricultural science students, law or medicine, they had all sat and studied around the Hegarty dining table while young Frank was working for his Intermediate and his Leaving Certificate.

Today he would join them as a fully fledged student himself.

Kit hugged herself with pleasure at the thought that she had raised a son who would be an engineer. And raised him all on her own. Joseph Hegarty had been long gone now, his life in England was no concern of hers anymore. He had sent money for a little while, and dates when he was going to be back; and then excuses, and little money. And then nothing.

She had tried not to bring Frank up with any bitterness against his father. She had even left a photograph of Joseph Hegarty in the boy's room lest he should think that his father was being banished from his memory on top of everything else. It had been a heady day when she noticed the photograph no longer in a place of honor, on the chest of drawers, but moved to a shelf where it could hardly be seen, and then facedown, and then in the bottom of a drawer.

Tall, gangly Frank Hegarty didn't need any mythical father's picture anymore.

Kit wondered whether Joseph, if he had stayed around, would have had any views on Frank's motorbike. It was a black 250cc BSA—his pride and joy.

Probably not. He had never been a man to face up to anything unpleasant. And Frank's bike was unpleasant. And dangerous, and it was the only black cloud in her life on this morning when her son started university.

In vain she had pleaded and begged him to use the train. They were only minutes from the railway station, the service was frequent. She would pay for his weekly ticket. He could make as many journeys as he liked. It was the only thing he had ever stood out for.

He had gone to Peterborough and worked long hours in a canning factory only that he could own this bike. Why did she want to take away the one possession that was truly valuable to him? Just because she didn't know how to ride a motorbike or even want to, it was unfair that she should try to stop him.

He was eighteen years and six months. Kit looked at the statue of the Infant of Prague that she kept in the house to impress the mothers of the students who boarded with her. She wished she had a stronger conviction that the Infant of Prague might be any earthly use in keeping her son safe on this terrible machine. It would be nice to have been able to offload your worries onto someone or something like that.

Patsy asked Mrs. Hogan if she'd like her to wet another pot of tea.

"Ah, go on, mam, you'd need tea on a bad day like this," Patsy said encouragingly.

"That would be nice, Patsy." She sank back into her chair relieved.

It hadn't been so wet earlier, when Benny had left for her first day at College. Benny in her navy jumper and white blouse with the navy and gray checked skirt.

"You'll be the belle of the ball," Eddie had said to her, bursting with pride.

"Oh, Father, I won't. I'm so big and drab-looking," Benny had said suddenly. "I'm like some kind of hearse. I caught sight of myself in the mirror."

Eddie's eyes had filled with tears. "Child, you're beautiful," he had said. "Don't talk about yourself like that. *Please.* Don't upset your mother and me."

Annabel had wanted to hug her and tell her that she looked lovely. Big, certainly, but with that lovely glowing skin and all that chestnut hair tied back in a navy and white ribbon, she looked what she was: a girl from a nice family, from a house in the country, whose father ran an established business.

But it wasn't a morning for hugging. Instead she had reached out her hand.

"You are a handsome, lovely girl, and they'll all see that," she said softly.

"Thank you, Mother," Benny said dutifully.

"And what's more, you'll be very, very happy there. You won't be going back to dreary little bed-sitters like a lot of girls have to do, or being half starved in some digs . . ." Annabel sighed with pleasure. "*You'll* be coming home to your own good home every night."

Benny had smiled at her but again it had seemed a little as if it were expected.

The girl was nervous, as any girl would be starting out in a new place, with strangers.

"It'll be a quiet house from now on, mam." Patsy arrived with the teapot and put it on the stand. She placed the quilted cozy on it and patted it approvingly.

"I expect she'll make friends." Annabel was doubtful. There had always been Eve and only Eve; it was going to be a big wrench.

"And will she be bringing them down here to stay do you think?" Patsy's eyes shone at the excitement. She loved speculating.

"I hadn't thought of that. But I'm sure she will. After all she can't possibly stay up in Dublin with people we don't know or have never heard of. She knows that."

Mother Francis in the convent at Knockglen was thinking about Eve as she watched the rain fall steadily on the convent grounds. She would miss her. Obviously she had to go to Dublin and stay in the convent there; this was the only way she could train for a career. Mother Francis hoped that the community in Dublin would understand the need to make Eve feel important and part of the place as they had always done here in Knockglen. Eve had never felt remotely like a charity child, nor had there been any pressure on her to join the Order.

Her father had worked long hours for the convent in his time, he had paid many times over in advance for his child to be housed and educated, had he but known it. Mother Francis sighed and prayed silently that the Lord would look after the soul of Jack Malone.

At times there had been other options. Mother Francis and her old school friend of years ago, Peggy Pine, discussed it long and often.

"I could let her serve her time to me, and make her fit for a job in any shop in Ireland, but we want more than that for her don't we?"

"Not that it isn't a very worthwhile career, Peggy," Mother Francis had said diplomatically.

"You'd love the few letters after her name though, wouldn't you now, Bunty?" Few people on earth called Mother Francis that and got away with it.

And what Peggy said was true. Mother Francis *did* want everything that might help to push Eve up some kind of ladder. She had been such an innocent victim from the start, it seemed only fair to help her all they could now.

There had never been enough money to dress the child properly and even if there had been they didn't have the style or the know-how. Peggy had advised from the wings, but Eve didn't want outside charity. Anything that came from the convent she regarded as her right. St. Mary's was her home.

It was certainly the only place she thought of as home. The three-room cottage where she had been born had lost its interest for Eve as her dislike of the Westwards had grown. When she was a youngster she was forever going up the long path through the convent kitchen gardens, past the briars and brambles, and peering in its windows.

When she was about ten she had even started to plant flowers outside it. Mother Francis had nurtured them behind the scenes, just as she had taken cuttings from the various bushes and plants in the convent garden and made a garden around the stony waste ground, the ugly edge of the cliff where Jack Malone had ended his life.

It was hard to know when this hatred of her mother's family had begun. But Mother Francis supposed it was only natural. A girl brought up in a convent with the whole town knowing her circumstances could not be expected to feel any warmth toward the people who lived in splendor over in Westlands. The man who used to ride around Knockglen as if it were all part of his estate; that was Eve's grandfather, Major Charles Westward. A man who had shown no wish to know his daughter's child. He had not been seen much in recent years, and Peggy Pine—who was Mother Francis's line of communication with the outer world—said that he was now in a wheelchair as a result of a stroke. And that small, dark young man Simon Westward, who was seen from time to time around Knockglen, he was Eve's first cousin. He looked very like her, Mother Francis thought, or maybe she was being fanciful. There was another child, too, a girl, but at some fancy Protestant school up in Dublin, hardly ever seen around the place here.

As Eve's resentment of the family had grown, so had her interest in the cottage dwindled. It stood empty. Mother Francis had never given up hope that Eve would live there one day, with a family maybe, and bring back some happiness to the little house that had known only confusion and tragedy.

And it was such a comforting little place. Mother Francis often sat there herself when she came up to tidy up. It had always been the custom in St. Mary's for the nuns to go anywhere in the grounds to read their daily Office. You were as close to God in the gardens, under the big beech tree, or in the walled garden with its smell of rosemary and lemon balm, as you were in the chapel.

Nobody thought it odd that Mother Francis often went up the path past the blackberries to read her Office up by the cottage. She kept a watchful eye on any leaks that might have sprung. If there was anything she couldn't cope with herself she would ask Mossy Rooney, a man of such silence and discretion that he found it hard to reveal his own name in case it might incriminate someone.

If anyone were to ask whether the cottage was for sale or rent, Mother Francis was always ready with a helpless shrug of the shoulders and say that things hadn't been fully sorted out yet, but that it was in Eve's name and nothing could be done until she was twenty-one. Nobody ever brought the matter up with Eve; and as for Mossy Rooney, who had replaced some of the window frames and the guttering, it would have been pointless asking him for information. The whole town knew he was silent as the tomb, a man of deep thoughts, none of them revealed; or possibly a man of no thoughts at all.

Mother Francis would have loved that old cottage to be Eve's home; she could see in her mind's eye a kind of life where Eve would bring her student friends home from university to stay there for weekends, and they would call to the convent and have tea in the parlor.

It was such a waste of a little stone house with a wooden porch and a view across the county as well as down the craggy rocks of the stone quarry. The cottage had no name. And the way things were it might never have a name or a life of its own.

Perhaps she should have approached the Westwards directly. But the reply to her letter had been so cold. Mother Francis had deliberately written on plain paper, not on the heavily embossed convent paper with Our Lady's name all over it. She had spent sleepless nights composing the right words, words that would sound neither sleeveen nor grasping. Evidently she hadn't found them. The letter from Simon Westward had been courteous, but firm and dismissive. His aunt's family had raised no objections to her daughter being brought up in a Roman Catholic convent, and that was where their interest in the matter ended.

Mother Francis had not told Eve about the letter. The girl had hardened her heart so much; there was no point in giving her further cause.

The nun sighed heavily as she looked back at her sixth-year class, heads bent over their composition books all intent on their essay "The Evils of Emigration." She wished she could believe that

Mother Clare in Dublin would welcome Eve and tell her that the Dublin convent would be her new home for the next year.

It wasn't Mother Clare's style, but God was good, and perhaps she had, for once, been openhearted and generous.

She might have been generous; but on the other hand she probably hadn't been. There had been no word from Eve for a week, which was not a good sign.

Eve's room in the Dublin convent had no bedside table with a small radio on it. There was no candlewick bedspread. A small neat iron bed with a shabby well-washed coverlet, and one lumpy pillow and sheets which were hard to the touch. There was a narrow, poky cupboard and a jug and basin from earlier times but possibly necessary still today since the bathroom was a long way away.

It wasn't like a prison cell, it was like a maid's room, Eve told herself firmly. And in a sense that was how they must view her, a difficult prickly maid up from the country. Worst of all, a maid with airs and graces.

Eve sat on her bed and looked around the room. She could hear the regretful, gentle voice of Mother Francis telling her that life was never meant to be easy and that her best course was to work very hard now and get out of this place in record time. Study her grammalogues in the shorthand, take sharp interest in the bookkeeping, flex her fingers for the typing, practicing over and over. Listen and take notes on office procedure. In a year's time or less she would land herself a good job, and a place to live.

Never again would anyone offer her an iron bed in a dark poky little room.

The Wise Woman would grit her teeth and get on with it, Eve told herself. That was a phrase she and Benny used all the time. What would the Wise Woman do about Sean Walsh? The Wise Woman would pretend that he did not exist. The Wise Woman wouldn't buy another half pound of toffees in Birdie Mac's because she'd get spots. The Wise Woman would do her homework because Mother Francis was on the warpath.

After a week Eve realized that the Wise Woman would also need to be a canonized saint to adapt to the new surroundings.

Mother Clare had suggested a regime of light housework, "to cover all your obligations my dear."

And Eve would admit that she did have obligations. She was getting a free residential course for which others paid handsomely. There was no history of association with this convent as there was with St. Mary's in Knockglen. She would have been eager to help from a sense of justice and also to do Mother Francis credit. But this was different.

Mother Clare's idea of covering obligations centered around the kitchen. She thought perhaps that Eve might like to serve the breakfast in the refectory and clear away, and that she should also leave classes ten minutes before lunch and be back in the refectory to serve soup to the other students when they came in.

In all her years at St. Mary's Eve Malone had never been seen by the other girls to perform one menial task. She had been asked to help behind the scenes as would any girl in her own home. But in front of the other pupils Mother Francis had made an iron-hard rule that Eve must never been seen to do anything which would give her a different status.

Mother Clare had no such qualms. "But my dear girl, you don't know these other pupils," she had said when Eve had politely requested that she should not be put in a public position of a non-fee-paying student.

"And I hardly *will* get to know them if they think I'm there on some different basis to themselves," she had said.

Mother Clare's eyes had narrowed. She sensed trouble in this girl, who seemed to have taken in the entire community below in Knockglen.

"But isn't that the case, Eve? You are here on a different basis," she had said, smiling very sweetly all the while.

Eve knew the battle had to be fought and won there and then before the other students arrived.

"I am happy to cover my obligations in whatever way you suggest Mother, but not in view of my fellow students. Can I ask you to rethink your plans for me."

Two spots of red appeared on Mother Clare's cheeks. This was pure insolence. But Mother Clare had fought many battles since she had taken her vows and she always realized when she was on poor ground. Like now. The community in Knockglen would defend Eve vociferously. Even some of the Sisters here in Dublin might see that the girl had a point.

"I'll tell you tomorrow," she had said, and turned to swish her long black skirts and veil down the polished corridor.

Eve had spent the day wandering around Dublin with a heavy heart. She knew she had visited heavy housework upon herself because of her attitude.

She looked in shop windows and willed herself to think of the days when she would be able to afford clothes like she saw there.

Imagine if you could go in and buy maybe four of the pencil-slim skirts in different colors. They were only twelve shillings and eleven pence each. It didn't matter that they were not great quality, you could have all those colors. And there was cotton gingham at two shillings a yard, you'd have a smashing blouse out of that at six shillings, maybe four of them to go with each of the skirts.

Eve dismissed the swagger coats. She was too short, they were too sweeping, they'd envelop her, but she'd love six pairs of the fully fashioned very sheer nylons just under five shillings each. And tapered slacks in wine or navy; she saw those everywhere. They varied in price, but usually around a pound a pair.

If she had a wallet of money, she'd go and buy them now. This minute.

But it wasn't money for clothes that she wanted. Eve knew that only too well. She wanted a different kind of life entirely. She wanted to study, to spend three, even five, years at university. She was prepared to make sacrifices for it, but there seemed to be no way she could even begin.

There were stories of people putting themselves through college by working during the day and studying at night. But that would still mean the year with the terrible Mother Clare to qualify herself for any kind of work. Eve noticed that almost without realizing it her journey had taken her up through St. Stephen's Green toward the big gray buildings of University College. It was still empty and she wandered at will around the main hall seeing only those involved in administration moving about.

The term would start next week. Lucky Benny would arrive as would hundreds of first-year students from all over Ireland.

Eve realized that there were thousands like herself who would never get there. But their expectations hadn't been raised. They hadn't been encouraged and treated well and led to believe that they had brains and insights like she had. That's what made it so hard.

Eve knew that through these doors next week would come girls who only intended to use university as part of their social life. There would be unwilling students, who didn't want to be here at all, who had other plans and other dreams, but came to satisfy the wishes of parents. There would be those who drifted in and would use the time to make up their minds. She felt a boiling rage about the Westwards, the family who cut off their own flesh and blood, who let her be raised by the charity of the nuns and never bothered themselves to think that she was now of university age.

There was no fairness on earth if someone who would appreciate it and work hard was kept out just because of a greedy, uncaring family who would prefer to forget the child of an unsuitable union rather than make a generous gesture and ensure that some Right was done at the end of the day.

She looked in the glass-fronted noticeboards and read of the societies that would be re-forming when term started, and the new committees and the sports arrangements and the practice times, and the appeals for people to join this group and that club.

And she saw the big staircases leading up to the libraries and the lecture halls. She saw the red plush benches which would be filled with students next week, and she ached to be amongst them. To spend her days reading and writing and finding out more and talking to people, and to spend no time at all trying to outwit awful people like Mother Clare.

The Wise Woman would get on with her life and stop dreaming. Then she thought how tiring it was going to be for the rest of her life trying to be the Wise Woman all the time. It would be great to be the very Unwise Woman on occasion.

Benny took the bus to Dublin on the first day of term with more trepidation than she would ever have expected. At home they had behaved as if she were a toddler going to a first party in a party frock rather than a huge ungainly student eighteen years of age going to university dressed from head to toe in dark clothes.

She could still see the tableau this morning; her father with tears of pride in his eyes—she knew he would go to the business and bore everyone to death with tales about how his wonderful daughter was going to university. Benny could see her mother sitting there stretching her hand out full of what she had been full of for months now: the huge advantages of being able to come home every night by bus. Patsy, looking like the faithful old black mammy slave in a film except that she was white and she was only twenty-five. It had made Benny want to scream and scream.

And she had other worries, too, as she sat on the bus and started her university career. Mother Francis had told her that the bold Eve hadn't written or telephoned, and that all the Sisters were dying to hear from her. Yet Eve had phoned Benny twice in the last week to say that life in the Dublin convent was intolerable and she would have to meet her in Dublin because otherwise she would go mad.

"But how can we meet? Don't you have to stay in that place for lunch?" Benny had asked.

"I've told them I have to go to hospital for tests."

As long as she had known her Eve had hardly ever told a lie. Benny had to tell a lot of little lies in order to be allowed out late or indeed at all. But Eve had been resolute about never lying to the nuns. Things must be very bad in Dublin if she had gone this far.

And then there was Sean Walsh. Naturally she had not wanted to go out with him, but both her mother and father stressed how nice it was of him to take such an interest in the fact that she was going off to university and wanted to take her to the pictures as a treat. She had decided to take what might be the easiest way out and accept. After all, if it were to be something to mark the beginning of a new stage in her life, then she could make it clear that this new life wouldn't involve any further outings with him.

Last night they had gone to the film *Genevieve*. Almost everyone else in the world must have loved it, Benny thought grimly, all over the place people left cinemas humming the tune and wishing they looked like either Kay Kendall or Kenneth More. But not Benny. She had left in a black fury.

All through the film Sean Walsh had put his thin bony arm around her shoulder or on her knee or even on one particularly unpleasant occasion, managed to get his hand sort of around her back under her arm and around her breast. All of these she had wriggled out of, and as they were leaving the cinema he had the nerve to say, "You know, I really respect you for saying no, Benny. It makes you even more special, if you know what I mean."

Respected her! For saying no to *him*? That was the easiest thing she had ever done, but Sean was the type who thought that she enjoyed it.

"I'll go home now, Sean," she had said.

"No, I told your father we'd have a cup of coffee in Mario's. They won't be expecting you."

She was trapped again. If she *did* go home they would ask why the coffee hadn't materialized.

Next to the cinema, Peggy Pine's shop had some new autumn stock. Benny had looked at the cream-colored blouses and soft pink angora sweaters. In order to talk about something that did not have to do with fondling and stroking she spoke of the garments.

"They're pretty, aren't they, Sean," she had said, her mind barely on them. She was thinking instead that once she got to University she would never need to see him again.

"Well, they are, but not on *you*. You're much wiser not to draw attention to yourself. Wear dark colors. Nothing flashy."

There had been tears in her eyes as she crossed the road with him to Mario's and he brought two cups of coffee and two Club milk chocolate biscuits to the plastic-topped table where she waited for him.

"It's an ill wind," he had said.

"What do you mean exactly?"

"Well, that brought Eve off to Dublin and out of your life."

"Not out of my life. I'm going to be in Dublin."

"But not in her world. Anyway, you're grown up now, it's not for you to be as thick as thieves with the likes of *her*."

"I like being as thick as thieves with her. She's my friend." Why do I have to explain this to him, Benny had thought.

"Yes, but it's not seemly. Not anymore."

"I don't like talking about Eve behind her back."

"No, I'm just saying, it's an ill wind. Now that she's gone you won't always be saying that you're off to the pictures with her. I can take you."

"I won't have much time for the pictures anymore. Not with study."

"You won't be studying every night." He had smiled at her complacently. "And don't forget, there's always weekends."

She had felt a terrible weariness.

"There's always weekends," she repeated. It seemed easier somehow.

But Sean had felt like making a statement. "Don't think that it's going to come between us, you having a university education," he had said.

"Not come between us?"

"Exactly. Why should it? There are some men that might let it but I'm not one. I tell you something, Benny, I've always modeled myself a lot on your father. I don't know whether you know this or not."

"I know you work with him, so I'm sure you must learn from him."

"Much more than that. I could learn from any outfitters in the country. I could learn tailoring by sitting at a bench. No, I watch the way Mr. Hogan has faced the world, and I try to learn from that."

"What have you learned in particular?"

"Well, not to be proud for one thing. Your father married an older woman, a woman with money. He wasn't ashamed to put that money into his business, it's what she wanted and he wanted. It would have been a foolish, bullnecked man who would have looked a gift horse in the mouth . . . so I like to see myself in a small way as following in his footsteps."

Benny had stared at him as if she had never seen him before.

"What exactly are you trying to say Sean?" she had asked.

"I'm trying to say that none of it means anything to me. I'm above all that sort of thing," he had said loftily.

There was a silence.

"Just to make my point clear," he had ended.

That had been last night.

Mother and Father had seemed pleased that she had spent time having coffee with Sean.

If that's what they want for me, Benny asked herself, why on God's earth are they allowing me to go to university. If they want to take it all away in the end and match me up with that slimy half-wit, why then take me up to the mountain and show me the world? It was too hard to answer, as was Eve's problem. Eve had said not only was she going to be free for lunch, she would meet Benny off the bus and walk her up to University College. Hanged for a sheep was what Eve had said on the phone.

✦

Jack Foley woke with a start. He had been dreaming that he and his friend Aidan Lynch were on Death Row in some American prison and they were about to die in the electric chair. Their crime seemed to be that they had sung the song "Hernando's Hideaway" too loudly.

It was a huge relief to find himself in the big bedroom with its heavy mahogany furniture. Jack said you could hide a small army in the various wardrobes around the house. His mother had said that it was all very well to mock but she had stood many long hours at auctions all over the city finding the right pieces.

The Foleys lived in a large Victorian house with a garden in Donnybrook, a couple of miles from the center of Dublin. It was a leafy place, professional people, merchants, senior civil servants had lived around here for a long time.

The houses on the road didn't have numbers; they all had names, and the postman knew where everyone lived. People didn't move much once they got to a road like this one. Jack was the eldest of the family and he had been born in a smaller house, but he didn't remember it. By the time he was a toddler his parents had arrived here.

He noticed that in the photographs of his childhood the rooms looked a lot less furnished.

"We were building up our home," his mother had told him. "No point in rushing and getting the wrong type of thing entirely."

Not that Jack or any of his brothers really noticed the house much. It was there for them as it had always been. Like Doreen had always been putting the food on the table, like the old dog Oswald had been there for as long as they could recall.

Jack shook off his dream about Death Row and remembered that all over Dublin today there would be people waking to the first day of term.

The first day of term in the Foley household meant that Jack would put on a college scarf and head into UCD for the first time.

In the dining room of the big Donnybrook house there was a sense of excitement. Dr. John Foley sat at the head of the table, and looked at his five sons. He had assumed they would all enter medicine as he had, so it had been a shock when Jack had chosen law. Perhaps the same thing would happen with the others. Dr. Foley looked at Kevin and Gerry. He had always seen them somewhere in the medical field as well as on a rugby pitch. His eyes fell on Ronan. Already he seemed to have the reassuring kind of manner one associated with being a doctor. That boy Ronan could convince even his own mother that the wounds he got in a playground were superficial, that the dirt on his clothes would easily wash out. That was the personality you needed in a good family doctor. Then there was Aengus, the youngest: his owlish glasses made him look studious and he was the only Foley boy not to be chosen for some kind of team in the school. Dr. Foley had always seen his son Aengus as going into medical research when the time came. A bit too frail and woolly for the rough-and-tumble of ordinary practice.

But then he had been wrong about his eldest son. Jack said he had no wish to study physics and chemistry. The term he had spent at school trying to understand the first thing about physics had been wasted. Nor did he want botany and zoology, he'd be no good at them.

In vain Dr. Foley had pleaded that the pre-med year was a necessary Term of Purgatory before you started the real business of medicine.

Jack had been adamant. He would prefer law.

Not the bar either, but being apprenticed as a solicitor. What he would really and truly like was to do this new degree course for Bachelor of Civil Law. It was like doing a B.A. but all in law subjects. He had discussed it with his father seriously and with all the information to hand. He could be apprenticed to his mother's brother, surely. Uncle Kevin was in a big solicitors' practice: they'd find a place for him. He timed his request well. Jack knew that his father's head was buried as deeply in the world of rugby as the world of medicine. Jack was a shining schoolboy player. He was on the pitch for his school in the Senior Cup final. He scored two tries and converted one of them. His father was in no position to fight him. Anyway it would have been foolish to force someone into a life so demeaning. Dr. Foley shrugged. There were plenty of other boys to follow him down the good physician's route to Fitzwilliam Square.

Jack's mother, Lilly, sat at the far end of the table opposite her husband. Jack could never remember a breakfast when she had not presided over the cups of tea, the bowls of cornflakes, the slices of grilled bacon and half tomato which was the start to the day every morning except Fridays and in Lent.

His mother always looked as if she had dressed up for the occasion, which indeed she had. She wore a smart Gor-Ray skirt, always with either a twinset or a wool blouse. Her hair was always perfectly done, and there was a dusting of powder on her face as well as a slight touch of lipstick. When Jack had spent the night in friends' houses after a match he realized that their mothers were not like his. Often women in dressing gowns with cigarettes put food on kitchen tables for them. The formal breakfast at eight o'clock in a high-ceilinged dining room with heavy mahogany sideboards and floor-to-ceiling windows wasn't everyone else's way of life.

But the Foley boys weren't pampered either; their mother had seen to that. Each of them had a job to do in the mornings before they left for school. Jack had to fill the coal scuttles, Kevin to bring in the logs, Aengus had to roll yesterday's papers into sausage-like shapes which would be used for lighting the fires later, Gerry, who was meant to be the animal lover, had to take Oswald for a run in the park, and see that there was something on the bird table in the garden, and Ronan had to open the big heavy curtains in the front rooms, take the milk in from the steps and place it in the big fridge, and brush whatever had to be brushed from the big granite steps leading up to the house. It could be cherry blossom petals, or autumn leaves or slush and snow.

When breakfast was finished the Foley boys placed their plates and cutlery neatly on the hatch into the kitchen before going to the big room where all their coats, boots, shoes, schoolbags and often rugby gear had to be left.

People marveled at the way Lilly Foley ran such an elegant home when she had five rugby-playing lads to deal with, and marveled even more that she had kept the handsome John Foley at her side. A man not thought to be easy to handle. Dr. Foley had had a wandering eye as a young man. Lilly had not been more beautiful than the other women who sought him, just more clever. She realized that he would want an easy uncomplicated life where everything ran smoothly and he was not troubled by domestic difficulties.

She had found Doreen at an early stage, and paid her over the odds to keep the house running smoothly. Lilly Foley never missed her weekly hairdo and manicure.

She seemed to regard her life with the handsome doctor as a game with rules. She kept an elegant attractive home. She put on not an ounce of fat, and always appeared well groomed at Golf Club or restaurant, as well as at home. This way he didn't wander.

Today when the four younger boys left for school, Jack helped himself to another cup of tea.

"I'll know what you two talk about when you're alone now." He grinned. He looked very handsome when he smiled, his mother thought fondly. Despite reddish-brown hair which wouldn't stay flat, those freckles on his nose, he really was classically good-looking, and when Jack Foley smiled he would break any heart. Lilly Foley wondered would he fall in love easily, or did the rugby take so much time that he would just be satisfied with the distant adulation of the girls who watched and cheered the games.

She wondered would he be as hard to catch as his father had been. What would some wily girl see in him that he would respond to? She had captured his father by promising an elegant uncluttered life-style very different from the neglected unhappy home he had come from. But this would not be the way to lure away her

Jack. He was happy and well looked after in this home. He wouldn't want to flee the nest for a long time yet.

"Are you sure you won't take a lift?" Dr. John Foley would have been proud to drive his eldest son up to Earlsfort Terrace and wave him into his first day at University.

"No, Dad, I told a few of the lads . . ."

His mother seemed to understand. "It's not like school, it's sort of more gradual isn't it. There's no bell saying you all have to be there at such a time."

"I know, I know. I've been there, remember." Dr. Foley was testy.

"It's just that I said . . ."

"No, your mother is right, you want to be with your own friends on a day like this, and the best of luck to you son, may it turn out for you just as well as you ever hoped. Even if you're not doing medicine."

"Ah, go on, you're relieved. Think of all the malpractice suits."

"You can get those in law just as well as medicine. Anyway, there's no reason why they shouldn't pick a law student for the rugby first fifteen."

"Give me a bit of time, Dad."

"After the way you played in the Schools Cup? They're not blind in there. You'll be playing in the Colors match in December."

"They never have freshers for that."

"They'll have you, Jack."

Jack stood up. "I'll be on it next year. Will that do you?"

"All right, if you play for UCD in 1958 that'll do me. I'm a very reasonable, undemanding man," said Dr. Foley.

When Benny got off the bus on the quays, she saw Eve waiting, with her raincoat collar turned up against the rain. She looked cold and pale.

"God, you really will end up in hospital this way," Benny said. She was alarmed by the look in Eve's eyes and the uncertainty of the future.

"Oh, shut up will you. Do you have an umbrella?"

"Do I have an umbrella? We're lucky that I don't have a plastic bubble encasing me, the weather was tested all night, I think. I have a folding mac that makes me look like a haystack in the rain, I have an umbrella that would fit most of Dublin under it."

"Well, put it up then," Eve said, shivering. They crossed O'Connell Bridge together.

"What are you going to do?" Benny asked.

"Anything. I can't stay there. I tried."

"You didn't try very hard, less than a week."

"If you saw it, if you *saw* Mother Clare!"

"You're the one who's always telling me that things will pass, and to make the best of them. You're the one who says we can stick anything if we know where we're going."

"That was before I met Mother Clare, and anyway I don't know where I am going."

"This is Trinity. We just keep following the railings, and up one of the streets to the Green . . ." Benny explained.

"No, I don't mean here. I mean, where I'm going really."

"You're going to get a job and get shot of them as quick as possible. Wasn't that the plan?"

Eve made no reply. Benny had never seen her friend so low.

"Isn't there anyone nice there? I'd have thought you'd have made lots of friends."

"There's a nice lay Sister in the kitchen. Sister Joan, she's got chapped hands and a streaming cold, but she's very kind. She makes me cocoa in a jug while I'm washing up. It has to be in a jug in case Mother Clare comes in and thinks I'm being treated like someone normal. I just drink it straight from the jug you see, no cup."

"I meant among the others, the other girls."

"No, no friends."

"You're not trying, Eve."

"You're damn right I'm not trying. I'm not staying either, that's for good and certain."

"But what will you *do*? Eve, you can't do this to Mother Francis and everyone."

"In a few days I'll have some plan. I won't live in that place. I won't do it." Her voice had a slightly hysterical ring about it.

"All right, all right." Benny was different now. "Will you come home on the bus tonight, back to Knockglen, back to the convent?"

"I can't do that. It would be letting them down."

"Well, what would it be standing shivering round the streets here, telling lies about being in hospital? What'll they say when they hear that? Will we walk through the Green? It's nice, even though it's wet." Benny's face looked glum.

Eve felt guilty. "I'm sorry, I'm really making a mess of your first day of term. This is not what you need."

They had reached the corner of St. Stephen's Green. The traffic lights were green and they started to cross the road.

"Look at the style," Benny said wistfully. Already they could see students in duffel coats, laughing and talking. They could see girls with ponytails and college scarves walking in easy friendship with boys along the damp slippery footpaths up toward Earlsfort Terrace. Some did walk on their own, but they had great confidence. Just beside them Benny noticed a blond girl in a smart navy coat; despite the rain, she still looked elegant.

They were all crossing together when they saw the skid, the boy on the motorbike, out of control and plowing toward the sedate black Morris Minor. It all seemed like slow motion, the way the boy fell and the bike swerved and skidded. How the car tried to avoid it and how both motorbike and car came sideways into the group of pedestrians crossing the wet street.

Eve heard Benny cry out, and then she saw the faces frozen as the car came toward her. She didn't hear the screams because there was a roaring in her ears as she lost consciousness, pinned by the car to the lamppost. Beside her, lay the body of the boy Francis Joseph Hegarty, who was already dead.

FOUR

*E*veryone said afterward that it was a miracle that more people hadn't been killed or injured. It was another miracle that it was so near the hospital, and that the driver of the car, who had been able to step out of it without any aid, had in fact been a Fitzwilliam Square doctor himself, who had known exactly what to do. Clutching a handkerchief to his face, he felt blood over his eye but he assured them it was superficial, he gave instructions which were followed to the letter. Someone was to hold up the traffic, another to get the guards, but first someone was sent down the side lane toward St. Vincent's Hospital to alert casualty and summon help. Dr. Foley knelt beside the body of the boy whose motorbike had lost control. He closed his own eyes to give a silent prayer of relief that his own son had never wanted to ride a machine like this.

Then he closed the eyes of the boy with the broken neck, and placed a coat over him to keep him from the eyes of the students he would never get to know. The small girl with the wound in her temple had a slightly slow pulse and could well be concussed. But he did not think her condition critical. Two other girls had been grazed and bruised, and were obviously suffering from shock. He himself had bitten his tongue from what he could feel in his mouth, probably loosened a couple of teeth and had a flesh wound over his eye. His task now was to get things into the hands of the professionals before he asked anyone to take his blood pressure for him.

One of the injured girls, a big, soft-faced girl with chestnut-colored hair and dark, sensible clothes, seemed very agitated about the one lying unconscious on the ground.

"She's not dead is she?" The eyes were round in horror.

"No, no, I've felt her pulse. She's going to be fine," he soothed her.

"It's just that she didn't have any life." The girl's eyes were full of tears.

"None of you have yet, child." He averted his glance from the dead boy.

"No. Eve in particular. It would be terrible if she weren't all right." She bit her lip.

"I've told you. You must believe me, and here they are . . ." The stretchers had been brought the couple of hundred yards from the hospital. There wasn't even a need for an ambulance.

Then the guards were there, and the people directing the traffic properly and the little procession moved toward the hospital. Benny was limping slightly and she paused to lean on the girl with the blond curly hair that she had noticed seconds before the accident.

"Sorry," said Benny, "I didn't know if I could walk or not."

"That's all right. Did you hurt your leg?"

She tested it, leaning on it. "No, it's not much. What about you?"

"I don't know. I feel all right, really. Maybe too all right. Perhaps we'll keel over in a moment."

Ahead of them on the stretcher was Eve, her face white. Benny had picked up Eve's handbag, a small cheap plastic one which Mother Francis had bought for her in Peggy Pine's shop as a Going to Dublin present a few weeks ago.

"She's going to be fine, I think," Benny explained in a shaky voice. "The man with all the blood on him, the man driving the car, he says she's breathing and her pulse is all right."

Benny looked so worried that anyone would have wanted to take her in their arms and stroke her, even though she was bigger than most people around.

The girl with the beautiful face, now grazed and muddy, the girl in the well-cut navy coat, now streaked with blood and wet mud, looked at Benny kindly.

"That man's a doctor. He *knows* these things. My name is Nan Mahon, what's yours?"

It was the longest day they had ever known.

The hospital machinery moved into action, but slowly. The guards took charge of the dead boy as regards telling his family. They had been through his things. His address was on a lot of his belongings. They had deputed two young guards to go out to Dun Laoghaire.

"Can you tell her it was instantaneous?" John Foley said.

"I don't know," said the young officer. "Can we tell her that?"

"It's true, and it might be some comfort to her," John Foley said mildly.

The older Garda sergeant had a different view.

"You never know, Doctor, many a mother might like to think their son had time to whisper an Act of Contrition."

John Foley turned his head away lest his annoyance be seen.

"And it wasn't his fault, be sure to tell her that," he tried.

"I'm afraid my men can't . . ." the sergeant began.

"I know, I know." The doctor sounded weary.

The nurse said of course they could use the phone, but they should have themselves looked at first. Then they'd be in a position to tell their parents what had happened. It made a lot of sense.

The news was good: minor cuts, nothing deep, anti-tetanus injections just in case, mild sedative for shock.

Eve was a different matter. Cracked ribs and mild concussion. Several stitches at the edge of her eye, and a broken wrist. She would be in hospital for several days, possibly a week. They wanted to know whom to inform.

"Give me a minute," Benny said.

"Well, you must know who it is, you're her friend." The almoner was puzzled.

"Yes, but it's not that easy."

"Well, what about her wallet?"

"There's nothing in it, no next-of-kin or anything. Please let me think, I just want to work out what's best."

Benny was also putting off telling her own parents about the accident, but she had to decide which of the two nuns to talk to on Eve's behalf. Would Eve be furious if Mother Francis heard the whole earning of the lies, the unhappiness and the circumstances that had brought her to the other side of the city and now into a hospital bed?

Would Mother Clare be as bad as Eve had said?

The woman was a nun after all, she must have some redeeming qualities if she were to keep her vows all her life.

Benny's head ached as she tried to work it all out.

"Would it be any help to tell me?" Nan Mahon asked. They had cups of sweet milky tea and they sat at a table.

"It's like a Grimms' fairy tale," Benny said.

"Tell it," Nan said.

So Benny told it, feeling slightly disloyal.

Nan listened and asked questions.

"Ring Mother Francis," she said at the end. "Tell her that Eve was about to ring her today."

"But she wasn't."

"It'll make the nun feel better, and what does it matter what day she was going to ring?"

It made sense. It made a lot of sense.

"But what about Mother Clare?"

"The baddy?"

"Yes, she sounds really awful and she'll crow over Mother Francis, the good one. It's awful to let her in for all this."

"It's much better than ringing the bad one and bringing all the torments of hell down on yourself for nothing."

"I think you're right."

"Good. Will you go and tell that Sister there, she's beginning to think you have delayed concussion or something. And by the way put someone medical on to tell her about Eve's injuries. You'll only frighten her to death."

"Why do you not want to tell your parents?"

"Because my mother works in a hotel shop where they don't really go a bundle on employing married women in the first place, so I don't want to get her all into a fluster for nothing. And my father . . ." Nan paused.

Benny waited.

"My father, that's different."

"You mean he wouldn't care?"

"No, I mean the very opposite, he'd care too much. He'd come in here ranting and raving and making an exhibition of himself, saying that his poor little girl was injured, scarred for life and who was to blame."

Benny smiled.

"I mean it. He's always been like that. It's good and bad. Good mainly because it means I can get what I want."

"And bad?"

"Oh, I don't know. Bad too." Nan shrugged. The confidences were over.

"Go on and ring the Good Sister before we have the starched apron in on us again."

Kit Hegarty was in the big front bedroom, the one she had let to the two brothers from Galway. Nice sensible boys she thought, well brought up by their mother, hung their clothes up neatly, which made a nice change. They wouldn't be much trouble during the year, one doing Agriculture, one studying for a B. Comm. No matter what they said, it was the farmers who had the money. There were a good many farmers' sons going in the doors of University College today for the first time.

She thought of her own son amongst the crowd today. He would walk up those steps with a confidence he didn't feel, she knew that. She had seen so many of the students set out from her door, awkward and anxious, and after a few weeks it was as if they had been studying there all their lives.

It would be easier for Frank because he knew Dublin already. He didn't have to get to know a new city like the boys from the country did.

She heard the front gate squeak open, and as she saw the two young Garda officers look up at the windows and come slowly up her path, Kit Hegarty suddenly knew without any doubt what they were coming to tell her.

Jack Foley had met several fellows from school. Not necessarily close friends, but it was amazing how welcome they were in that sea of faces. And they too seemed glad to see him.

There was an introductory lecture at twelve, but until then there wasn't much to do except get their bearings.

"It's like school without the teachers," said Aidan Lynch, who had paid very little attention to any teacher during his days at school with Jack Foley.

"This is what's meant to be forming our character, remember?" Jack said. "It's like being on your honor to work all the time."

"Which means we don't have to work at all," Aidan said cheerfully. "Will we go round the corner to Leeson Street. I saw armies of beautiful women all heading in that direction."

Aidan was a better authority on women than any of the rest of them so they followed him willingly.

At the corner they saw that there had been an accident. People still stood around talking about it. It was a student, they said, very badly hurt, possibly dead. The blanket was over his face when they carried him away.

He had been on that motorbike, which was in bits over beside the wall. Someone said he was going to be doing Engineering.

Aidan looked at the twisted wreck of steel and metal.

"Jesus, I hope it wasn't that fellow who was canning peas in Peterborough with me during the summer. That's the bike he was getting. Frank Hegarty. He was going to do Engineering."

"There could have been hundreds of people . . ." Jack Foley began, but then he saw the car that had been pulled away from the corner where it had crashed. There was blood and glass all over the road. The car had been moved in order to let the traffic get through.

It was his father's car.

"Was anyone else hurt?"

"A girl. A young girl. She looked very bad," said the man. The kind of man you always find at an accident, full of information and pessimism.

"And the man, the man driving the car?"

"Oh, he was all right. Big fancy coat on him, with a bit of fur on the collar. You know the type. Walked out of the car, giving orders left, right and center, just like a general."

"He's a doctor, he's meant to do that," Jack said defensively.

"How do you know that?" Aidan Lynch was astonished.

"It's our car. You go on and have coffee. I'm going into the hospital to see if he is all right."

He ran across the wet road and over to the hospital entrance before any of them could answer him.

"Come on," Aidan said. "The main thing with women is to be the first person they meet. They love that. It gives you a huge advantage."

✦

It was much easier to tell Mother Francis than Benny had feared. She had been calm and not at all put out about Eve having abandoned all the plans that had been so carefully thought out for her. She had also been very practical.

"Tell me as simply and quickly as you can Bernadette, where does Mother Clare think that Eve is today?"

"Well, Mother . . ." Benny felt as if she were eight years of age again, instead of almost eighteen. "It's a bit awkward . . ." It was partly to do with Mother Francis calling her "Bernadette." It put her straight back in the classroom, in her gymslip again.

"Yes, I'm sure, but the best thing is if I know everything, then I can judge how much has to be said to Mother Clare." The nun's voice was smooth. Surely she couldn't be planning to go along with the lies.

Benny risked it. "I think she thinks that Eve is sort of in hospital already. I think that's what Eve would have been telling you had she been able to give you a ring . . ."

"Yes, of course, she would. Please stop fretting, Bernadette. I am much more concerned that Eve gets well and is aware that we have all made things easier. Can you give me more details . . ."

Biting the corner of her lip Benny haltingly told a tale of mythical blood tests. It was noted crisply.

"Thank you Bernadette. Now can you put me on to someone qualified to tell me about Eve's injuries."

"Yes, Mother."

"Bernadette?"

"Yes, Mother?"

"Ring your father at work first. Say you couldn't get through to your mother. It's easier to talk to men. They fuss a lot less."

"But look at you, Mother, you don't fuss at all."

"Ah, child, I'm different altogether. I'm a nun," she said.

Benny gave the phone to the Sister, and sat down with her head in her hands.

"Was it awful?" Nan was sympathetic.

"No, like you said, it was easy."

"It always is, if you do it right."

"Now, I have to ring my parents. How do I do that right?"

"Well, what are you hiding from *them*?" Nan seemed amused.

"Nothing. It's just that they'll make such a fuss. They think of me as in nappies."

"It all depends on how you begin. Don't say, 'Something terrible happened.'"

"What do I start with, then?"

Nan was impatient. "Maybe you *should* be in nappies," she snapped. Benny felt her heart sink. It was probably true. She was a big baby, soft in the head.

"Hello, Father," she said into the phone. "It's Benny. I'm absolutely fine, Father, I was trying to ring Mother but there was something wrong with the number. Wouldn't it be great to have the automatic exchange?" She looked across at Nan, who was giving the thumbs-up sign.

"No, I'm not actually *in* the College, but I'm just beside it. These people here are very overcareful you know, they just like to cover every eventuality so they asked us all to ring our families even though there isn't a thing wrong . . ."

Sean Walsh ran through Knockglen to tell the news to Annabel Hogan. Mrs. Healy saw him running as she looked from her bow window and knew that something must be amiss. That young man always moved very correctly. He didn't pause as Dessie Burns called out to him from the hardware shop, he didn't notice Mr. Kennedy looking over his glasses at all the bottles and apothecary jars in the window display of the chemist's shop. He ran past the chip shop where he had had coffee with Benny only last night, past the newsagents, the sweetshop, the pub and Paccy Moore's cobbler's shop. Up the short avenue to the Hogans' house; the ground was wet and covered with leaves. If *he* owned this house, he thought to himself, he would give it a good coat of paint, put a smart gate on it. Something more imposing than the way the Hogans had it.

Patsy answered the door. "Sean," she said, without much enthusiasm.

Sean felt his cheeks redden slightly. If he were master of the house, no maid would address a senior employee of the master's by his Christian name. It would be Mr. Walsh, thank you very much, or sir. And she would wear something to show that she was a maid, a uniform, or a white collar and apron anyway.

"Is Mrs. Hogan at home?" he asked haughtily.

"Come in, she's on the phone," Patsy said casually.

"The phone? It's working again?"

"It never wasn't." Patsy shrugged.

She led him into the sitting room. He could hear Mrs. Hogan in the distance talking to someone. They had the phone in the breakfast room off the kitchen. He wouldn't have had it that way. A telephone should be on a half-moon table in the hall. A highly polished table under a mirror, perhaps a bowl of flowers beside it reflecting in the table. Sean had always looked around him when he went into people's houses. He wanted to know how things should be done. For when the time came.

The sitting room had shabby chintz furniture, and faded curtains in the long window alcove. It could have been a very smart room, Sean thought, mentally ticking off the changes he would make. He hardly noticed Patsy, who had come back in.

"She says you're to come out to her."

"Mrs. Hogan isn't coming in here?" He didn't want to be telling the news in the territory where the maid could be involved, but followed obediently to the shabby breakfast room.

"Ah, Sean." Annabel Hogan was polite to him even if her maid wasn't.

"I'm very sorry to be the bearer of bad news, but there's been an accident," he said in the sepulchral tones of an undertaker.

"I know, poor Eve, Mother Francis was on to me about it."

"But Mrs. Hogan . . . Benny was involved in it . . ."

"Yes, but she's not hurt at all, she was talking to Mother Francis and to her father. There was some fault on the phone here or else I was on the phone myself talking to Father Rooney about the Station."

"She got scratches and a sprained ankle." Sean couldn't believe this calm acceptance. He had expected to be the deliverer of the news and then the great consoler, but Mrs. Hogan was making light of it. It was incomprehensible.

"Yes, but she's perfectly all right. She's going to sit there in the hospital, and they'll keep an eye on her and someone will put her on the evening bus, just as she planned. It's only the shock Mother Francis says. Better to let her sit calmly there with people who know all about it."

Sean felt all his thunder being stolen from him.

"I had thought I would drive to Dublin and collect her," he said.

"Ah, Sean, we couldn't ask you to do that."

"She might not like hanging around the hospital, you know, sick people, smells of disinfectant . . . it's early closing and I was going to ask Mr. Hogan for a loan of the car."

Annabel Hogan looked at Sean Walsh's concerned face and at a stroke all the careful, calming work of Mother Francis was destroyed.

"You're very kind Sean, but maybe if it's as bad as that my husband would want to go himself. . . ."

"But Mrs. Hogan, if I might presume, it's very hard to find a place to park the car in the center of Dublin. Mr. Hogan hasn't been used to driving in the city traffic of recent years, and I had planned to go to Dublin to collect the samples of material. You could ask them till kingdom come to put them on the bus, but they never do . . ."

"Will I come with you, do you think?"

Sean Walsh's mind did a slow, careful calculation, then he came to a decision.

"I'll go on my own, Mrs. Hogan, if that's all right. Then you can make all the preparations here."

It had been the right thing to say. Annabel saw herself in the role of getting ready to welcome the invalid home.

Sean smiled as he left the house. This time he didn't run up the main street of Knockglen. He walked on the other side of the road. He nodded to Dr. Johnson, who was coming out of his surgery. He glanced in the window of Peggy Pine's women's outfitters and saw with distaste the pastel colors that Benny had admired last night. Benny was such a big girl, she could hardly have wanted them for herself. Still, it was good that she sought his advice.

He saw that *Monsieur Hulot's Holiday* was coming to the cinema this weekend. That was good. Benny wouldn't be well enough, and Sean didn't like foreign language films. They put him at a disadvantage.

He held his shoulders back. There was no reason for him to feel at a disadvantage. Things were working out fine.

All he had to do now was to let Mr. Hogan know how distressed Mrs. Hogan was and how he had saved the day.

Dr. Foley said he'd just go in and see how that child was in casualty before he left.

"They've canceled my appointments for this morning . . . Maybe you'd walk me down to the Shelbourne for a taxi," he asked Jack.

"I could get one here, and come home with you."

"No, no, you know I don't want that. Stay here in the waiting room will you, Jack?"

Jack moved into the overbright room with the yellow walls. Two girls sat at a table. One of them was a spectacularly pretty blonde; the other, a big girl with long chestnut hair tied back in a bow, had a bandage on her foot. He realized they must have been in the accident.

"Was it terrible?" he asked, looking questioningly at the empty chair, as if asking their permission to sit down. They pulled the chair forward and told him about it. They told him they had heard that the doctor had managed to avoid them all by driving into the lamppost. Only Eve, who had been hit by the moving car, was seriously hurt and even Eve would be out of hospital in a week.

They talked easily. Benny stumbled from time to time, and became tongue-tied when she looked at the handsome boy sitting beside them. Never before had she held a conversation with anyone like this, and she would begin a sentence and not know how to finish it.

Jack Foley's eyes rarely left Nan's face, but she seemed to be unaware of this and talked as if all three of them were equal partners in the conversation. Jack explained that it had been his father driving the car. Nan said that both she and Benny were busy trying to play down their bruises and scratches because it would cause such almighty upheavals in both their homes.

"I don't feel like going in to College now. Do you?" She looked from one to the other. It was as if she knew a solution would be proposed.

"Why don't I take the pair of you for a plate of chips?" Jack asked.

Benny clapped her hands like a child. "I didn't know that what my soul cried out for, well possibly not my soul, but there was a cry there definitely," she said. They both smiled at her.

"I'll just see my father to a taxi and come back for you." He was looking straight into Nan's eyes.

"Where would we go? It's the best offer we've had all day," Nan said.

"He's very nice," Benny said, when Jack had gone.

"He's the College hero before he even gets there," said Nan.

"How do you know?"

"I saw him play in the Schools Cup."

"Play what?"

"He was on the wing." Nan saw Benny's mystification and explained. "Rugby. He really is very good."

"How did you go to a rugby match?"

"Everyone does. It's a kind of social event."

Benny realized that there were going to be a great many areas where she would be at a loss. Rugby matches would only be a very small part of them, and none of these gaps in her knowledge would be helped by continuing to live in Knockglen all her life.

She wished suddenly that she were someone totally different, that she were much smaller and had a small face and tiny feet like Nan had. That she could look up at men rather than over or down at them. She wished her parents lived in the Aran Islands and that there could be no question of her having to go home every night. She felt a sudden desire to dye her hair blond and keep dyeing it every day so that the roots would never show. There was nothing she could do about her size. Even if she were thinner she would still have huge shoulders and great big feet. No operation had been invented to give you small feet.

She looked at them with distaste in their sensible shoes and thick bandage. Her mother had normal feet, her father had, why did Benny's have to be the way they were. At school they had once heard of some animal which had become extinct because of its huge flat feet. Benny hadn't know whether to envy it or be sorry for it.

"Is it hurting much?" Nan had seen Benny studying her foot and thought it must be paining her.

Jack came back at that moment.

"Well," he said to Nan.

She stood up. "I think Benny's foot is hurting her."

"Oh, I'm sorry." He looked at her briefly with a sympathetic smile.

"No, it's fine," she said.

"If you're sure?" He was polite. Perhaps he wanted to go off with Nan on his own. She didn't know. But it would always be like this anyway so there was no point in getting upset about it.

"You were looking at it and frowning," Nan said.

"No, I was only thinking about all those prayers we say for the conversion of China. Do you put three Hail Marys on to the Rosary for it?"

"I think it was the conversion of Russia in ours," Jack said. "But I'm not sure. Just shows you how well I'm able to escape it."

"Well, I can't think why we should be praying for them," Benny said with mock indignation. "They have lovely habits out there. They bind everyone's feet."

"What?"

"Oh yes, as soon as they're born, so there's no problem about people falling over them. Everyone has tiny feet and nice squashed-up bones. So elegant-looking."

Jack seemed to realize she was there for the first time.

"And now chips," he said, looking straight at her. "Four plates, one plate each and one to pick off. And lashings of tomato ketchup."

Then she heard the nurse tell someone that Miss Hogan was out in the waiting room, and there was Sean Walsh coming toward them. Her face fell.

"I've come to drive you home, Benny," he said.

"I told Father I was coming home on the bus," she said, coldly.

"But he gave me the car . . ."

Jack let her hands go and looked politely from the thin-faced boy to the big girl with the red-brown hair.

No introductions were made.

Benny spoke with an authority she didn't know that anyone could have let alone herself.

"Well, I hope you had some other work to do in Dublin, Sean. That you didn't come up specially, because I have to leave now. And I will be home on the bus as arranged."

"What do you have to do? You're to come home. Now. With me." Sean sounded petulant.

"She has to go for some more treatment," Jack Foley said. "I'm just taking her there. You wouldn't want her to miss that."

FIVE

_B_enny knew they would come to meet her off the bus. But she hadn't expected all three of them, not Patsy as well, and not the car. Sean must have driven home with dire tales to have brought such a gathering to the bus stop. Before Mikey had swung the bus around and brought it to a stop she had seen their pale faces in the wet night, the two umbrellas. She felt the familiar surge of irritation mixed with guilt. No one on earth had such a loving family, no one on earth felt so cooped up and smothered.

She walked with a heavy heart to the front of the bus.

"Good night, Mikey."

"Good girl, Benny. Something wrong with your foot?"

"I hurt it," she said, realizing his wife would probably have the tale already.

"It's all this drunken life as a student. That's what it is," he said, roaring with laughter at his wit.

"That's what it is," she repeated in a dull, polite way.

"There she is!" cried her father, as if there had ever been any doubt about her arrival.

"Oh, Benny, are you all right?" Her mother's eyes were wide with anxiety.

"Mother, I *told* Father on the phone. I'm fine. Fine."

"Then why did you have to go back for treatment?" Annabel Hogan had the face of someone who thought that very bad news was being kept from her. "We were very alarmed when Sean told us that they needed to look at you again, and you didn't ring a second time . . . so we were afraid . . ."

Her father's face had lines of worry.

"Sean had no business coming up there for me, interfering and giving orders and upsetting everyone here and there." Benny's voice was calm, but a little louder than normal.

She saw Mrs. Kennedy from the chemist's turn and look at her. That would be a subject for discussion in *their* house tonight, a scene, no less, at the bus stop with the Hogan family of all people. Well, well, well. Hadn't it been a mistake to let that Benny go to Dublin on her own after all?

"He went to set our minds at ease," Benny's father said. "We were very worried."

"No, Father, you weren't. You were quite happy for me to come home on the bus. I talked to you and you were grand, and you said Mother would be grand and then suddenly Sean manages to spoil everything."

"The boy drove the whole way to Dublin on his half day to bring you home and then drove straight back and said you had to see another doctor. Do you blame us for being worried?" Eddie Hogan's face was working with distress: beside him Annabel raked her face for more information. Even Patsy didn't seem convinced that all was well.

"I didn't *want* him to come for me. You never said he was coming. There was nothing wrong with *me*, for God's sake. You *must* see that. I was perfectly all right, but a boy was killed. He was killed in front of my eyes. He was alive one minute and then he was dead with his neck broken. And Eve's in a hospital ward with broken ribs and concussion and all kinds of things. And all Sean Walsh can do is stand like a stuffed dummy in that hospital and talk about me!"

To her horror Benny realized that there were tears pouring down her face, and that a small circle of people was watching her in concern. Two schoolgirls from the convent who had been in Dublin to buy books with one of the young nuns turned to see what was happening. It would be all around the convent before bedtime.

Benny's father decided to act. "I'll get her into the car," he said. "Patsy, will you run down to Dr. Johnson's like a good girl and ask him to come over as soon as he can. Now, Benny, it's all right. It's all right. It's natural, just shock."

Benny wondered was there a condition which might be known as Rage. Because that was definitely what she felt her condition to be. Helpless rage.

Everyone in Knockglen heard about it in record time, but what they heard bore little relation to the facts. Mrs. Healy said that she heard the girls were running and laughing like they had done in Knockglen and they were hit by a car. As a precaution they had both been admitted to hospital, but Sean Walsh had driven up and got Benny discharged. It was a lesson on how to conduct yourself in huge menacing Dublin traffic if you came from a small place like Knockglen.

Mr. Flood was silent and blessed himself a great deal when he heard the news. He said that it was obviously meant as some kind of warning. What kind of a warning he couldn't say, but his family noticed with alarm that he had gone out to consult the tree again. They had hoped that this little habit had died down.

Mrs. Carroll said it was a waste of good money sending girls to university. Not if the grocery was three times the size of Findlaters in Dublin would they send Maire and her sisters there. You might as well take money and shovel it down the drain. What did they do on the very first day except walk under the first vehicle they saw? Maire Carroll, serving in the shop and hating it, felt a firm and vicious sense of satisfaction over the fate of Eve and Benny, but of course she pretended great care and concern.

Bee Moore, who worked in Westlands and was a sister of Paccy Moore the shoemaker, had heard that Eve was dead from horrible injuries and that Benny was in such shock she couldn't be told. The nuns would all be going up to Dublin to collect her body shortly.

Birdie Mac in the sweetshop told people that it took a great amount of faith these days to realize that God was fair-minded. Wasn't it hard enough on that poor child to know no parents, to be totally disowned by her relations up in Westlands, to be brought up an orphan in the convent in secondhand clothes, and sent to a secretarial course when she had her heart set on going to university without being mown down by a car on her first week. Birdie sometimes questioned the fairness of life, having spent overlong looking after an ailing mother and missing her chances with a very suitable man from Ballylee who married another, who wasn't bound to an ailing parent.

Dessie Burns said that there was a lot of truth in the theory that if you fell down drunk, you never hurt yourself, a theory he had tested only too often. It was a girl like Eve Malone, a little pikasheen who wouldn't have had a drink on her at all, that would end up in hospital.

Father Ross said that Mother Francis would take it badly. She felt as much for that girl as if she had been her own flesh and blood. No mother could ever have done more for the girl. He hoped Mother Francis wouldn't get too great a shock.

✦

Mother Francis had acted swiftly when she heard about Eve. She had gone straight to Peggy Pine and waited demurely until the shop was free of customers.

"Do me a great favor, Peg."

"Whatever you want."

"Could you close the shop and drive me to Dublin?"

"When?"

"As soon as you can, really, Peg."

Peggy pulled down the orange sheets of plastic intended to keep the glare off her goods in the window, both in summer when there might have been sunshine and in winter when it was unnecessary.

"Off we go," she said.

"But the business?"

"One thing about you, Bunty, you have the good sense to ask a favor at the right time. You decide to leap over the convent wall and hightail it to England to a new life, and you have the wit to do it on early closing day." She picked up her handbag, rooted for her keys and then put on her tweed coat and closed the door behind her. There were advantages about the Single State. You didn't need to tell anyone what you were doing. Or why.

You didn't even need to ask why.

"Mother Francis!" Eve's voice was weak.

"You're going to be fine."

"What happened to me? Please Mother. The other people just say 'Hush' and 'Rest.'"

"Not much point in saying either of those words to you." The nun was holding Eve's thin hand. "Broken ribs, but they'll knit together. A wrist that's going to be painful for a while, but it will heal. A few stitches. Truly I never lied to you in my life. You're going to be fine."

"Oh, Mother, I'm so sorry."

"Child, you couldn't have stopped it."

"No. About you. Having to find out about me this way."

"I know you were *going* to ring me. Benny told me that. She said you were about to phone."

"I never lied to you, either, Mother. I wasn't going to phone."

"Not immediately, perhaps, but you would have sometime."

"Do you still think any question must be answered?"

"Of course."

"What'll I do Mother, what on earth will I do when I get out of here?"

"You'll come home to get well and then we'll think of something else for you."

"And Mother Clare?"

"Leave her to me."

Jack came in the side door and found Aengus sitting in the cloakroom studying his glasses.

"Oh, Jesus, not *again*."

"It's not my fault, Jack, I don't do anything, I swear I don't. I just went past these fellows and one of them shouted, 'Hey, speccy four-eyes,' and I ignored them like you told me and then they came and took them off and stamped on them."

"So, it's my fault." Jack looked at the glasses; they were beyond repair. Sometimes he had been able to fit the frames back and push in the lenses; not this time.

"Listen, Aengus, don't make a big thing out of it. They've had enough here today."

"Well, what will I say?" Aengus looked naked and defenseless without his spectacles. "I mean I can't say I stamped on them myself."

"No, I know. Listen I'll go in tomorrow and kick the shit of the fellows who did it."

"No, no, Jack, please. That would make it worse."

"Not if I beat them to a pulp it won't. They won't try anything again. They'd be afraid they'd have to deal with me again."

"But they'll know you won't be there all the time."

"I can be there at odd times. You know, just happen to be passing when they're going out of school."

"Wouldn't they think I was a telltale?"

"Nope." Jack was casual. "You're smaller. You have to wear glasses to see, if they don't respect that then you have to bring in reinforcements . . . that's the system."

There was no need for a gong in their household, Lilly Foley said that Holy Mother Church looked after all that for them. As soon as they heard the Angelus ring they gathered from all over the big house to the supper table. Jack's father had asked him not to mention the accident in front of the younger children. He didn't want to go into the fact that someone had died. His father looked pale, Jack thought, his eye slightly swollen; but maybe he wouldn't have noticed it if he hadn't been involved. Certainly none of his brothers saw anything amiss. Ronan was entertaining them; he was a good mimic and this time he was doing a fussy brother in the school trying to get everyone to sit still in the big hall for a lecture. Then he went on to a merciless performance as an inarticulate Garda, who had called to the school to deliver the annual lecture on road safety.

Ronan had picked the wrong day for this story.

Another time his father might have laughed or mildly remonstrated about the cruelty of the imitation. But today Dr. Foley's face was gray and set.

"And whatever his accent or his defects, I don't suppose one of those blockheads making a jeer of him listened to a word he was saying." The voice was harsh.

"But, Daddy . . ." Ronan was bewildered.

"Oh, you can 'But, Daddy' at me all you like—it's not going to bring you, or any of those amadans mocking the poor guard, back to life when they walk out under a ten-ton truck."

There was a silence. Jack watched his brothers look at each

other in alarm, and saw his mother frown slightly down the table at his father.

For no reason Jack remembered something that girl Benny had said earlier in the day. It was something about wishing she had the power to control conversations. If you could do that you could rule the world, she had laughed.

"You mean like Hitler?" he had teased her.

"I mean the reverse of Hitler. I mean sort of patting things down, not stirring them up."

That was the moment when the fabulous Nan Mahon had flashed her eyes. Anyone could pat things down, she had said with a toss of all that blond curly hair. The point was to liven things up. She had looked straight at Jack when she said it.

Nan Mahon turned the key in number 23 Maple Gardens. She had no idea whether there would be anyone home yet. It was six-fifteen. Whoever came in first turned on the electric heater in the hall to take the chill off the house, and then lit the gas fire in the kitchen. They had all their meals at a big kitchen table; there was never any company, so it didn't matter.

The hall was already slightly warm so somebody was home.

"Hallo," Nan shouted.

Her father came out of the kitchen.

"That was a fine message you left. That was a great day's work, frightening the bloody lives out of us."

"What is it?"

"What is it? What is it? Meek as milk! God Almighty, Nan, I've been here for the past two hours without knowing hair nor hide of you."

"I left a message. I said there had been an accident. I wouldn't have, but the hospital said we had to. I left a message at the yard. I told Paul to tell you I was all right. Isn't that what he said?"

"Who'd believe the daylight out of that fool, reading magazines with one hand stuffing his face with another . . ."

"Well, you were out." Nan had taken her coat off and was examining the mud stains. She hung it up carefully on a big wooden coat hanger and began to brush hard at the dried mud.

"Someone was killed, Nan. A boy died."

"I know." She spoke slowly. "We saw it."

"And why didn't you come straight home?"

"To an empty house?"

"It wouldn't have *been* empty. I'd have come back. We'd have got your mother back out of that place."

"I didn't want to get her back, disturbing her when there was nothing she could do."

"She's worried sick too. You'd better ring her. She said she'd stay put in case you came by the hotel."

"No, *you'd* better ring her. I didn't get her worried."

"I can't understand why you're being so callous . . ." He looked at her, bewildered.

Nan's eyes were blazing. "You haven't even begun to *try* to understand . . . you haven't a notion what it was like, all the cars and the blood and the glass and the boy with the blanket over him, and a girl breaking her ribs, and all the hanging about and waiting . . . it was . . . it was . . . just awful." He came toward her, arms outstretched, but she avoided him.

"Oh, Nan, my poor baby," he was saying.

"That is precisely why I didn't want you to come to the hospital. I'm not anyone's poor baby. I only had scratches. I didn't want you making an exhibition of yourself. And of me."

He flinched.

Nan continued. "*And* I didn't ring Em because it's hard enough to get a job in any place as a married woman without having hysterical daughters ringing up crying for Mamma. Em's been working in that kip for six years, since I was twelve. And there *have* been days I'd have liked her at home when I had a headache or one of the nuns had roared at me at school. But I thought of her. You, you never give anyone a thought but yourself. You'd ring her if you couldn't find your socks where you thought they should be."

Brian Mahon's hand was in a fist. He moved closer to where his daughter was starting again to brush the mud from the coat that hung on the side of the kitchen dresser.

"By God, you won't speak to me like that. You may well be upset, but you're not going to get away with treating me like dirt. Your own father out slaving day and night so that you'd have a College education. By God, you're going to take that back or you're going to get out of this house."

Not a muscle of Nan's face moved, her stroke never faltered as she brushed and watched the flakes fall down on the newspaper she had spread beneath. She said nothing.

"Then you'll not stay under my roof."

"Oh, but I will," said Nan. "For the moment anyway."

Mother Francis had been putting off her visit to Mother Clare as long as possible. There had been a deliberately vague telephone call. But it became clear that she would soon have to go out in the rain and get a bus to their sister convent. She had sent Peggy home. It was not a visit she relished making.

Still, she thought, bracing her shoulders, if she had been a real mother she would have had to endure many such problems with a teenage daughter. As a schoolteacher she knew only too well the dance they led their parents. Natural mothers had to put up with a great deal. This was the very thought in her head as she turned the corner of the corridor and back into the waiting room and saw the weeping figure of a woman hunched over and hugging herself in grief.

Beside her stood a pleasant-looking, round, gray-haired woman, unsure of what to do, hesitating about whether to hush the weeping figure or let her cry.

"Frank," the woman sobbed. "Frank, tell me it's not true. Tell me it's someone else, tell me it was just someone that looked like you."

"They're going to get the nurse again," said her companion. "She was fine a minute ago. We have a taxi ordered. I was taking her home with me . . ."

"Was it her son . . . ?" Mother Francis asked.

"Her only child." The woman's eyes were eager but anxious. "I'm her neighbor. She's going to spend the night with me. I've sent my sister in to look after the other lads."

"Lads?"

"She keeps students you see. This was her boy's first day at College."

The nun's face was sad. Beside them, the anguished figure of Kit Hegarty rocked to and fro.

"You see Sister, Mother, I'm the worst one for her. I have everything. A husband, and a family, and Kit has nothing now. She doesn't want to be with the likes of us. She doesn't want anything nice and normal and safe. It's only reminding her of what she hasn't got."

Mother Francis looked at the woman with appreciative eyes. "You're obviously a very good friend Mrs. . . . ?"

"Hayes, Ann Hayes."

Mother Francis was kneeling down beside Frank Hegarty's mother.

She reached out and held the woman's hand.

Kit looked up, startled.

"In a few days, when the funeral's over, I want you to come and stay with me," she said softly.

The ravaged face looked at her. "What do you mean? Who are you?"

"I'm someone like you. I've lost my child in a sense. I could tell you about it, maybe you could advise me. You see, I'm not a real mother. You are."

"I was." Kit smiled a terrible twisted grimace.

"No, you are, you still are, you'll always be his mother, nobody can take that away from you. And all you gave him, all you did for him."

"I didn't give him much. I didn't do much for him. I let him have that bike." She clawed at Mother Francis's hand as she spoke.

"But you had to. You had to give him freedom. That was the greatest gift, that was what he would have wanted most. You gave him the best he could want."

Nobody had said anything like this to Kit all day. Somehow she managed to take a proper breath, not the little shallow gasps she had been giving up to now.

Mother Francis spoke again. "I live in the convent in Knockglen. It's simple and peaceful. And you could spend a few days there. It's different, you see, that's the main thing. It wouldn't have memories."

"I couldn't go. I can't leave the house."

"Not immediately, of course, but whenever you're ready. Ann will look after things for a few days. Ann Hayes and her sister."

Somehow her voice had a hypnotic effect. The woman had become less agitated.

"Why are you offering me this?"

"Because my heart goes out to you. And because my girl was hurt in the same crash . . . she's going to be all right, but it's a shock seeing her so pale in a hospital bed . . ."

"She's going to be all right." Kit's voice was flat.

"Yes, I know. I know you would accept your son to have any injury if you thought he was going to come out."

"Your girl, what do you mean . . . ?"

"She was brought up in our convent. I love her every bit as much as if she were my natural daughter. But I'm no use as a mother. I'm not out in the world."

Through her tears Kit managed something like a real smile.

"I will come, Mother. The convent in Knockglen. But how will I know you? Who will I ask for?"

"I'm afraid you won't have any difficulty in remembering the name. Like your son, I was called after St. Francis."

✦

Mario looked at Fonsie's yellow tie with disapproval.

"You're going to frighten them away."

"Don't be an eejit Mario. This is the way people dress nowadays."

"You no call me eejit. I know what eejit means."

"It's about the only word of English you *do* know."

"You no speak to your uncle that way."

"Listen, Mario, pass me those biscuit tins. If we put the player on top of something tinny it'll sound a bit more like real music."

"Eeet soun horrible, Fonsie. Who will come to hear things so very, very loud?" Mario put his hands on his ears.

"The kids will."

"The kids have no money."

"The old ones wouldn't come in here in a fit anyway."

The door opened and Sean Walsh walked in.

"Now do you see!" Fonsie cried.

At the very same moment Mario said, "Now, what did I tell you!"

Sean looked from one to the other with distaste. It was a place he rarely went, and now he had been twice in twenty-four hours; last night with Benny, and tonight because he was so late and fussed getting back from his useless journey to Dublin. He had not been able to buy himself provisions, both grocery shops were closed. Normally Sean Walsh divided his custom. One day he might patronize Hickey's, beside Mr. Flood; other days he would go to Carroll's, immediately next door to Hogan's. It was as if he were preparing for the day he would be a big man himself in this town and wanted everyone on his side, wanted them all to think of him as a customer. If he had been a drinking man he would have had a half pint in every establishment. It was the way to get on. But tonight there had been no time to get the cheese or sardines or cold ham that made his evening meal; Sean never liked to cook in his bed-sit above the premises of Hogan's lest the smell of food linger and be deemed offensive. He had thought that he might slip in for a quick snack that would keep body and soul together before he went back to his room to brood about the situation that he had handled so badly.

Now it appeared that Mario and his half-wit nephew were making fun of him.

"He's old and he's come in here two times," Mario was saying.

"He's not old, and the word is twice, you gobdaw," the unappealing Fonsie said.

Sean wished that he had gone down to Birdie Mac's and knocked on the door for a bar of KitKat, anything rather than face these two.

"Are you serving me food, or am I interrupting some kind of talent contest?"

"How old are you, Sean?" Fonsie said. Sean looked at him in disbelief. The huge spongy soles making him four or five inches taller than he really was, the hair slicked into waves with some filthy oil, his narrow tie and huge, mauve-colored jacket.

"Are you mad?"

"You tell how old you are." Mario looked unexpectedly ferocious.

Sean felt the whole world had tilted. First Benny had turned her back on him in public and told him to go home without her after he had driven up especially to collect her. Now both men in the chipper. It was one of the rare occasions in his life when Sean Walsh spoke without calculation.

"I'm twenty-five," he said. "Since September."

"There!" Fonsie was triumphant.

"Now!" Mario was equally sure he was right.

"What *is* this?" Sean looked angrily from one to the other.

"Mario thinks the place is for old people. I say it's for young fellows like yourself and myself," Fonsie said.

"Sean is not a fellow, he is a businessman."

"Oh, jaysus, does it matter? He's not on two sticks like most people in the town. What do you want Sean? Rock salmon or cod?"

Patsy had gone for a walk with Mossy Rooney.

He had waited wordlessly in the kitchen until the daughter of the house had been soothed and put to bed. Mossy, a little like Sean Walsh, would have wished that the kitchen and living quarters of the Hogan household were more separate. Then he would have been able to sit down at the table, loosen his shirt collar, his shoelaces, and read the evening paper until Patsy was ready. But the Hogans lived on top of you when you went to that house. There was the master, a man of importance in the town that you'd think would want a house properly run for himself. And the mistress, much older by all appearances than her husband, who fussed too much over that great big daughter.

There had been a great deal of fussing tonight. The doctor had come and given her two tablets to take, he had said there wasn't a thing wrong with her that wouldn't be wrong with any red-blooded girl who had seen a fatal accident. She was shocked and upset and what she needed most was to be allowed to rest, alone.

Mossy Rooney, a man who though he spoke little, noticed a lot, saw the look of relief pass over Benny Hogan's face, as she was sent to bed with a hot water bottle and a cup of hot milk. He saw also the way the Hogans looked after her as she left the kitchen. He had seen that look on the faces of mother ducks when they took their little flocks down to the river for the first time.

If he had been walking out with any other girl in service in the town they could have stayed in on a wet night and talked by the kitchen range, but with the Hogans hovering around he had to bring Patsy out into the rain.

"Would you not like to take your ease indoors on a bad night like this?" Mrs. Hogan had said kindly.

"Not at all, mam, a nice fresh walk would be grand," Patsy said with little enthusiasm.

For a long time Annabel and Eddie Hogan sat in silence.

"Maurice said that we're not to worry about a thing," Eddie said eventually.

Maurice Johnson obviously realized who were the real patients in the house. He had uttered more words of advice to them than to the girl he was meant to be treating.

"It's easy for Maurice to say that. We don't worry about his children," Annabel said.

"True, but to be fair he and Grainne don't worry much about them either."

Kit Hegarty lay in her own narrow bed and heard the foghorn and the town hall clock, heard the occasional sound of a car going past. The sleeping tablets hadn't worked. Her eyes were wide open.

Everyone had been so kind. Nobody had counted the time or the trouble. The boys in the house, ashen-faced at the shock, had offered to leave. Their parents had telephoned from the country. And that little Mrs. Hayes next door, whom she hardly knew, had been a tower of strength, sending her sister in to cook and keep the place going. And the priests in Dun Laoghaire had been great, in and out all evening three or maybe four of them saying nice things and talking to other people, making it seem somehow more normal, drinking cups of tea. But she had so wanted to be left alone for a while.

The only thing that stuck out in a day that seemed to have been a hundred hours of confusion was that nun. The aunt possibly of a girl who had been injured in the accident. *She* had understood that Frank had to have the bike. Nobody else appreciated that. Fancy a nun being able to realize it. And she had been insistent in her invitation. Kit thought that she would go and see her in that convent. Later, when she was able to think.

Judging from all the chatter, everyone in UCD must have got to know each other pretty quickly, Benny thought as she went up the steps the following morning. The main hall was thronged with people standing in groups, there were shouts of laughter and people greeting each other.

Everyone had a friend of some sort.

On another day it might have worried Benny, but not today.

She walked down a stone staircase to a basement where you could hang your coat. It smelled faintly carbolic, like school. Then up to the ground floor again and into the Ladies' Reading Room. This was not at all like school. For one thing nobody seemed to think that a reading room was a place you were meant to read. There were girls fixing their makeup at a mirror over the mantelpiece, or scanning notices on the board—items for sale, extra tuition offered, rooms to share, sodalities to join.

A very confident group laughed and reminisced about their summers abroad. They had been in Spain, or Italy, or France . . . the only thing in common was how little of the language they had learned, how monstrous the children they had had to mind had been, and how late everyone ate their meals in the evening.

They were happy to be back.

Benny soaked it all up for Eve. She would visit her again at lunchtime. This morning she had been pale, still, but cheerful as anything. Mother Francis was going to sort it out. There would be no recriminations.

"I'm going to try to get to College, Benny," she had said, her face blazing with the intensity of it. "I'll only be a few weeks late. I'll get a job, really I will. So you just watch out for everything for me, and take notice, so that I'll catch up."

"Are you going to ask the Westwards?"

"I'm not going to rule it out."

There were always a great many students who took English as a subject in First Arts. The lectures were held in a big hall, confusingly called the Physics Theatre. Benny streamed in with the others. It was so different to the classrooms at school. More like an amphitheatre, with rows of seats in semicircles high up at the back. There were some young student nuns already in place, they were in the front rows, eager and anxious to miss nothing. Benny walked slowly up toward the high seats at the back where she thought she might be more inconspicuous.

From her vantage point she watched them come in: serious-looking lads in duffel coats, earnest women in glasses and hand-knitted cardigans, the clerical students from the religious seminaries in their black suits all looking remarkably cleaner and neater than the other males not bound for religious life. And the girls, the confident, laughing girls. Could they really just be First Years, these troupers in brightly colored skirts, flouncing their hair, aware of the impression they were creating. Perhaps they had spent a year abroad after they left school, Benny thought wistfully. Or even had a holiday job during the summer. Whatever it was, it didn't bear the hallmark of life in Knockglen.

Suddenly she saw Nan Mahon. Nan wore the smart navy coat she had worn yesterday, but this time over a pale yellow wool dress. Tied loosely around the strap of her shoulder bag was a navy and yellow scarf. Her curly hair was back from her face more than yesterday, and she had yellow earrings. As she walked in, flanked by a boy on each side, each competing for her attention, Nan was the object of all eyes. Her eyes roamed the banks of seats, deciding where to sit. Suddenly she saw Benny.

"Hallo, *there* you are!" she cried.

People turned around to see whom she was waving at. Benny reddened at the stares, but Nan had left the two admirers and was bounding up to the back row. Benny was taken aback. She felt sure that Nan would know everyone in UCD in days. It was surprising to be singled out. And so warmly.

"Well, how did it go?" she asked companionably.

"What?"

"You know, you sent the young man packing and he more or less said you'd rue the day. I haven't seen anything so dramatic for years."

Benny was dismissive. "You couldn't get a message through to him. Mercifully he didn't turn up at home. I thought he'd be there, with big cows' eyes."

"He's probably more madly in love with you than ever, now." Nan was cheerful, as if this was good news.

"I don't think he has a notion of what love is. He's like a fish. A fish with an eye to the main chance. A gold-digging goldfish."

They giggled at the thought.

"Eve's fine," Benny said. "I'm going to see her at lunchtime."

"Can I come too?"

Benny paused. Eve was often so prickly even when she was in the whole of her health. Would she like seeing this golden College belle at her bedside?

"I don't know," she said at last.

"Well, we were all in it together. And I know all about her, and the business of Mother Clare and Mother Francis."

For a moment Benny wished she hadn't told the story in such detail. Eve certainly wouldn't like her business being discussed as she lay unconscious.

"That got sorted out," Benny said.

"I knew it would."

"Do you think you could come tomorrow instead?"

SIX

⸺⸺⸺⸺⸺✦⸺⸺⸺⸺

*T*he body of Frank Hegarty was brought to the church in Dun Laoghaire.

Dr. Foley attended the prayers and the Removal service with his eldest son.

Also in the church was Mother Francis, who had found it necessary to spend a little longer in Dublin than she had hoped sorting things out with Mother Clare. Peggy had offered to collect her later. She knew there was some kind of trouble, but didn't ask what it was. She had given her own kind of encouragement to Mother Francis.

"Whatever that one says to you Bunty, remember that her people were tinkers."

"They weren't."

"Well, dealers, anyway. That should give you the upper hand dealing with her."

It hadn't, of course, any more than it should have. Mother Francis had a grim face as she waited in the big church for the funeral party to arrive. She didn't know why she was there; it was as if she wanted to represent Eve.

Nan Mahon went out on the bus to Dun Laoghaire and stood

among the group at the back of the church. She was instantly spotted by Jack Foley, who went to join her.

"That's nice of you, to come all the way out," he said.

"You did too."

"I came with my father. But do you see that group there, those are fellows who worked with him in the summer. That's Aidan Lynch—he was at school with me, and a whole lot more. They were all canning peas together."

"How did they know?"

"His picture was in the paper, and there was some kind of announcement at the Engineering lectures today."

"Where's Benny? Did you see her today?"

"Yes, but she couldn't come tonight. She had to go home, you see, every evening on this one bus."

"That's hard on her," Jack said.

"It's very foolish of her," Nan said.

"What can she do about it?"

"She should make a stand at the outset."

Jack looked at the attractive girl beside him. She would have made a stand, he knew that. He remembered the big soft-featured Benny.

"She stood up to that awful fellow with the white face who tried to take her off with him yesterday."

"If you couldn't stand up to *him* you shouldn't be allowed out," Nan said.

"This is Eve Malone," Benny said as Nan sat on the end of the hospital bed.

She wanted Eve to like Nan, to recognize that Nan could have been anywhere but had chosen to come and see Benny's friend. Benny had heard this fellow Aidan Lynch almost begging Nan to come and have lunch with him.

Nan had not brought flowers or grapes or a magazine; instead she had brought the one thing that Eve truly wanted, a College handbook. All the details of registration, late registration, degree courses, diplomas. She didn't even greet the girl in the bed. Instead she spoke about the matter which was uppermost in Eve's mind.

"I gather you're trying to get into College. This might be of some use to you," she said.

Eve seized it and let her thumb riffle through the pages. "This is just what I need, thank you very much indeed," she said.

Then her brow darkened slightly.

"How did you think of bringing me this?" she asked suspiciously.

Nan shrugged. "It's all in there," she said.

"No, what made you think I'd need it?"

Benny wished Eve wouldn't be so prickly. What did it matter that Nan Mahon knew her hopes? There was no need to be secretive.

"I asked, that's all. I asked what you were doing and Benny said you hadn't enrolled yet."

Eve nodded. The tension was over. She fingered the book again with gratitude and Benny felt a pang of regret that *she* hadn't thought of something so practical.

Little by little Eve was losing her look of wariness. And as Benny watched the girls talk easily she realized they were kindred spirits.

"Will you have it sorted out fairly soon do you think?" Nan was asking.

"I have to go and ask a man for money. It's not easy but it won't get any easier by delaying," Eve said.

Benny was astounded. Eve never talked of her business to anyone and the matter of approaching the Westwards for money was one she had only barely acknowledged to Benny herself. Nan was unaware of this. "Will you play up the being injured bit?" she inquired.

Eve was on the same wavelength. "I might. I've been considering it, but he's the kind of fellow that might regard that as weakness and sniveling. I'll have to work out how to play it."

"What's it all about?" Nan asked with interest.

And as Eve began to tell her the story of the Westwards, the story never spoken aloud to anyone, Benny realized with a shock that Nan was in fact pretending to Eve that she hadn't heard any of this already. She had asked Nan to be discreet, and she certainly had followed the instructions to the letter. And judging by the way Eve was confiding, the instructions had been unnecessary.

It had been harder to deal with Mother Clare than Mother Francis would ever have believed possible. Sometimes Mother Francis talked directly to Our Lady about it and asked for immediate and positive advice.

"I've *said* I was sorry, I've *said* that we will look after Eve from now on, but she goes on and on and says it's her duty to know what plans are being made for the girl. Why can't she just stay out of it? Why, Holy Mother, tell me?"

As it happened, Mother Francis got an answer which she presumed had come from the Mother of God, even though it was spoken by Peggy Pine.

"What that auld rip wants is to be able to prance around like the cock of the walk saying I told you so, I told you so. She wants you to humble yourself, then she'll give up on it and start torturing someone else."

Mother Francis agreed to use the tactics of humbling herself. "You were right all along, Mother Clare," she wrote in the most hypocritical letter she had ever penned. "We were wrong to ask you to take on someone like Eve who had been given a wholly exaggerated set of expectations by our small community here. I can only say that I bow to your wisdom on this as in so many other matters and hope that the Sisters were not unduly inconvenienced by the experiment which you knew was destined to be full of pitfalls."

It had been the right approach. The regular bewildered and hurt interrogations from Mother Clare ceased.

And just in time too. Eve was pronounced fit to leave hospital a week to the day after she had been admitted.

"I'll come on the bus, with Benny," Eve had said on the telephone.

"No, you won't, there's half a dozen people who'll go and collect you. I don't like to ask Peggy again but Mrs. Healy will be going up."

"*Please*, Mother."

"All right, Sean Walsh? No, don't even tell me . . . !"

"I've caused you enough trouble. I'll go with anyone you say though I *would* rather go on the bus."

"Mario?"

"Marvelous. I love Mario."

"All right, we'll see you tomorrow. I'm so glad you're coming home Eve. I missed you."

"And I missed you, Mother. We'll have to talk."

"Of course we will. Wrap up warmly won't you."

When Eve hung up Mother Francis sat for a moment. It was true they would have to talk. Talk seriously.

As she sat there the telephone rang again.

"Mother Francis please?"

"Speaking."

There was a pause.

"Mother, in a fit of generosity you said to me . . . I mean you wondered if I'd like . . . and isn't it odd, in the middle of everything I kept remembering it. I wonder would you think it strange if I *did* come to see you . . . ?"

The woman's voice stopped again hesitantly.

A great smile lit up Mother Francis's face.

"Mrs. Hegarty, I'm delighted to hear from you. This weekend would be lovely. You tell me which bus and I'll walk over and meet you. It's only a couple of minutes from the convent gate. I'm very pleased you're going to come and see us."

She wondered where she would put the woman to sleep. She had thought of her as staying in Eve's room. But there was the extra parlor that they had always been meaning to do up as a guest room. All it needed was curtains. She'd get some material from Peggy and ask Sister Imelda to ask the senior girls to run them up at Domestic Science class. She'd get a bedside light from Dessie Burns and a nice cake of soap in Kennedy's chemist.

"Eve's going home today," Benny reported when she met Nan for coffee in the Annexe as she did every morning.

"I know. She told me last night."

"What?"

"Well, it's at night she really wants people to go in and see her, and you've long gone, so I took a couple of fellows in to cheer her up."

Benny felt a jolt. She knew that Nan and Eve got on well . . . but taking fellows into a hospital bed!

"What fellows?" she asked lamely.

"Oh, you know, Aidan Lynch and some of that gang. Bill Dunne—do you know him?"

"No."

"He's very nice, does Commerce. I bet you know him to see, he's always outside the History Library with a group."

"Did Eve like them coming in?"

"Yeah, she loved it. Did you think she wouldn't?"

"It's just that she's a big edgy sometimes . . . you know on the defensive a bit."

"I never noticed that."

It was true. Eve had seemed much less chippy whenever Nan came in. Nan had a gift of making things simple, everyone went along with her way. Just then four boys approached the table. They were all looking at Nan.

"Would you girls like to come down Grafton Street and get some real coffee? Decent coffee for a change," said the spokesman, a thin boy in an Aran Island sweater.

Nan smiled up at them warmly.

"Thanks a lot, but no, we have a lecture at twelve. Thanks anyway."

"Come on, that's only a big lecture, no one'll miss you." He was encouraged by her smile to think it was only a matter of saying it often enough.

"No, honestly." Nan stopped suddenly as if she had been thoughtless. "I mean I'm only speaking for myself. Benny, do you want to go?"

Benny reddened. She knew the boys didn't want her. It was Nan that had attracted them. But they had nice faces and seemed a little bit lost, like everyone else.

"Why don't you sit down with us?" she suggested with a big smile.

That was exactly what they wanted to do. Chairs and benches were pulled up, names exchanged. School names given. Did they know this person or that? What were they studying? Where were they staying? It was much easier than Benny had thought to be in the middle of a group like this. She had completely forgotten that she was big and that they were boys. She asked eagerly about the societies, and which ones were good, and where were the best dances.

Nan didn't make as much effort, but she was very pleased to hear all the information. Her smile was so bright that Benny could see the boys almost loosening their collars as she turned it toward them.

The boys said that the Debating Society on a Saturday night was great. And then when it was over you could go to the Solicitor's Apprentice or down at the Four Courts. They looked from one girl to the other.

Benny said that unfortunately she had to stay in the country at weekends. As she said it she realized what a death knell it sounded, so she cheered up at once and said that this was only for this term. Maybe things would change then. She looked brightly at the boys and they seemed pleased with her. She knew they were all mad keen for Nan to go with them this Saturday, and Nan wasn't a bit flirtatious.

If she could, she would. She hadn't wanted to go because she didn't know anyone, she said.

"You know us," said the thin boy in the grubby white sweater.

"I do, of course." Nan's smile nearly broke his heart.

Benny knew that it would be a great night. She could see it. Of course, she would be in Knockglen. But her smile was bright. After all, one of the things she had been afraid of was that she wouldn't know how to talk to fellows when she got to College. She didn't have much practice at home. But it seemed to be easy enough, like talking to ordinary people. That was what she must think about. The good side. Not always dwelling on the bad side like having to go home on the bus before the fun began.

When Mario collected Eve in his ice-cream van it was Fonsie who ran lightly up the steps of the hospital to escort the patient to her transport.

"You're to take it easy, you'll remember that." The Sister looked doubtfully at Fonsie as a companion.

"Nothing faster than slow jive." Fonsie leaned back and clicked his fingers slowly. Sister was not amused.

"And you *are* staying in a convent?"

"Don't be prejudiced now," Fonsie warned. "Just because I don't look like your idea of a nun doesn't mean . . ."

"Oh shut up, Fonsie, Mario's nearly having a fit down there in the van."

It was the first time she had seen the outside world for over a week. Eve shuddered when she saw the corner where the crash had taken place. They tucked her up in the van and drove back to Knockglen arguing all the while.

Some arguments she was able to take part in—like having brighter lights and music in the chip shop, like calling the chip shop a "cafe," like having "Island in the Sun" so that you could hear it from the street and it would make you want to come in.

"Make you want to call the Guards more likely," Mario said.

There were other arguments she couldn't contribute to—like whether Mario's brother had been mad to marry an Irish girl, Fonsie's mother, or whether Fonsie's mother had been mad to marry an Italian, Mario's brother. She drifted off to sleep during that particular saga, which she felt would never be solved anyway.

Eve sat up in bed and drank her beef tea.

"Sister Imelda made it. Have a taste?"

Benny sipped some from the cup.

"Patsy told me she heard her in Flood's talking about shin beef, and pointing to her ankle in case she wasn't making herself clear. Mr. Flood was saying 'I know where the shin is, Sister, God forgive me I may not know much but I know where the shin is.' "

"Is Patsy still going out with that dumbo, Mossy?"

"Yes, Mother's terrified she'll marry him."

"Is he that bad?"

"No, we just don't Patsy to marry anyone, because she'll leave."

"A bit hard on Patsy," Eve said. "I feel like the prodigal son. I never had any time for him in the gospel but still it's a nice feeling. The accident saved me, everyone's so sorry for me they forget I told all those lies and was so rude to awful Mother Clare. Listen, I meant to tell you, the most extraordinary thing. The boy that got killed, Frank Hegarty . . . Mother Francis met his mother that day. I don't remember it clearly, but anyway they got talking and she's coming here to stay for a few days. Here to Knockglen."

"Will she stay in Healy's?"

"No, here in the convent would you believe? They've done up one of the parlors as a bedroom."

"Go on!"

"She's coming on the bus today. It's going to be very hard to know what to say to her."

"I know," Benny agreed. "I mean anything could be the wrong thing. She mightn't want to talk about it at all, but then it could be considered callous to start up chats about other things."

"Nan would know what to say," Eve said suddenly.

Benny felt a cold lurch in her heart. It was an unworthy thought, considering how kind Nan was to her and how she included her in everything. But Benny did feel that Nan got *too* much credit for things. Was it right that she would know what to do in every circumstance.

A little wave of pure jealousy came over her. She said nothing. She was afraid it might show in her voice.

Eve hadn't noticed. She was still musing what Nan would do or say.

"I think it's because she doesn't dither, like we do. She always sounds as if she knows what she's doing, whether she does or not. That's the secret."

"I suppose it is," Benny said, hoping the glum, mean note didn't sound in her voice.

"Nan could make anyone do anything," Eve said. "She got them to let us smoke in the ward!"

"But you don't smoke!" Benny was startled.

Eve giggled. "Oh I did for the fun of it, the others all did. It was the principle of the thing."

"What will she do all day? Mrs. Hegarty?" she asked.

"I don't know. Walk around. She's going to feel lonely and odd here."

"She would at home too I suppose," Benny said.

"Have you talked to Sean since?"

"Not really. He was on his high horse last weekend, you know, head turned the other way when he saw me at mass, a fit of the sulks. Unfortunately, that didn't last and he came round last night to discuss the pictures. I'm afraid I used you shamelessly. I said I couldn't make any plans until I knew what you'd be doing."

"*That* didn't please him."

"Well, he said that from what he heard you'd most likely be in Mario's, clicking your fingers with that Fonsie . . . He was full of disapproval."

Eve pealed with laughter.

"I wonder what Fonsie said. He's very funny, really he is. He thinks he's going to be Mr. Big of Knockglen."

"Lord, that wouldn't be hard."

"I know, I told him. But he said I'd missed the point. He said that by becoming a Mr. Big he would make Knockglen big too, he would drag it up with him."

"It can't happen soon enough," Benny said gloomily.

"God, you sound like a cross between Father Rooney and Mrs. Healy with your dire voice," Eve warned her.

"Maybe that's who I am. Maybe my parents were given the wrong baby."

"Boy, would *that* be the wrong baby," Eve said, and that started them off all over again.

Kit Hegarty said she never saw such a lovely room. It was exactly what she wanted. It was small and low-ceilinged and there were no shadows or corners in it to keep her awake at night. She knew she would sleep here as she had not slept since it happened. She would love to do something to help, she said. She hadn't many skills, but she was used to running a house.

Mother Francis was soothing. Not now, later maybe, now she must rest. She showed her the chapel. It was quiet and dark. Two nuns knelt in front of the altar where Mother Francis explained that the Blessed Sacrament was exposed. There would be compline later, if she liked to come and listen to the nuns singing their office.

"I'm not sure . . ."

"Neither am I," Mother Francis said firmly. "It might make you too sad, on the other hand it might be just what you need, to sit in a church with people you don't know and weep for your son.

And there are the glasshouses. I'll show you those. They're not in very good condition. We don't have the money or the people to look after them. Ah, if only you'd known them when Eve's father was alive . . ."

She told the woman the story that was rarely told, the workman and the restless daughter of the Big House, the unsuitable relationship, the pregnancy, the marriage and the birth of Eve and the two deaths.

There were tears in Kit Hegarty's eyes.

"Why are you telling me this?" she said.

"I suppose it's a clumsy attempt to let you know other awful things happen in the world," said Mother Francis.

"Are you not going out tonight?" Annabel Hogan asked as Benny pulled up a chair with them in the breakfast room after supper. "Out" meant out with Sean Walsh. Benny pretended not to realize this.

"No, Eve has to take it easy. She's up and everything and coming down for supper tonight with the nuns and Mrs. Hegarty." Her face was bland.

"I meant, nothing on at the pictures?" her mother asked equally innocently.

"Ah, of course there's something on, Mother. It's meant to be very exciting—about the sound barrier."

"And wouldn't you like to be at that?" her father asked.

"I don't really like going by myself, Father. If we were *all* going now . . ." The Hogans hardly ever went to the cinema.

She knew that they liked to see her stepping out with Sean from time to time. Somewhere in their confused minds they must think it was company for her, entertainment, a date even. And from Sean's point of view, they knew he considered it an honor to take the daughter of the house out for all to see. Somehow it made things nice and orderly. Safe.

Sean wouldn't leave them, go to a better shop in a bigger town if he was happy, and this must be their view, however short-term, and foolish.

"You know we don't go to the pictures," her mother said. "We wondered were you going to go with Sean?"

"Sean! Sean Walsh?" asked Benny as if the town were full of Seans, all of them craving to take her to the cinema.

"You know I mean Sean Walsh." Annabel's voice was sharp.

"Oh no, I don't think it's a good idea to go with him all the time."

"You don't go all the time."

"No, but with Eve not being here, there'd be a danger I could slip into the way of it."

"And what would be the harm of that?"

"Not a bit of harm, Mother, but you know."

"Did he not ask you? He told *me* he was going to ask you." Eddie Hogan looked puzzled. He didn't like things that weren't clear.

"I said no to Sean because I didn't want Sean to think and me to think, and the whole of Knockglen to think, we were a twosome."

It was the first time such a notion had ever been mentioned in their household.

Benny's parents looked at one another at a loss.

"I wouldn't say going to the pictures occasionally is making you into a twosome," Annabel Hogan said.

Benny's face lit up. "That's exactly my point too. I think it's fine to go to the pictures with Sean *occasionally*, but not every week. Occasionally was the very word I said, I think."

Actually the words she had said were "Sometimes, perhaps, but not in the immediate future," and he had looked at her with his cold small eyes, and she had shivered. But there would be little point in trying to explain this to her parents. It was quite enough to have told them as much as she had already told them.

Jack Foley and Aidan Lynch decided to go to the debate on Saturday night. It was held in the big Physics Theatre, and was fairly rowdy, despite the dinner jackets worn by the committee and the visiting speakers.

As they stood at the doorway watching from the sidelines Aidan saw the blond head of Nan Mahon in the center of a sea of male duffel coats. She was laughing, her head thrown back and her eyes sparkling. She wore a white frilly blouse with a rose pinned to the top button, and a black skirt. She was the most attractive girl in the room.

"Look at the lovely Nan," Aidan said, whistling a low envious sound through his teeth. "I asked her to come with me to this and she said she'd rather be free."

"So, she'd rather be free," Jack said, looking at her closely.

"I thought she liked me." Aidan sounded mock desolate.

"No, you didn't. You thought she liked Bill Dunne. In fact *I* thought she liked *me*," said Jack.

"There's enough of them liking you," Aidan grumbled. "No, I thought I was special with Nan. She took me to see her friend in hospital."

"You're a natural hospital visitor." Jack laughed. "Look at Nan over there. She likes everyone."

He looked with a pang of regret at the girl in the center of the crowd.

"What was the friend like in hospital?" he asked Aidan in order to take their minds off lost opportunities with Nan.

"Okay," Aidan said unenthusiastically. "A bit skinny and ready to bite your head off about everything, but all right I suppose." Even as he said it, Aidan realized that it might not sound all that gallant. "Not that I'm exactly an Adonis myself," he added.

"But you are, you are!" Jack Foley said. "Listen, I've had enough of this caper looking at our girl in the middle of that crowd. Will we go for a pint?"

"You're on," Aidan said.

Jack looked long and hard at Nan as they went out of the hall, but if she saw them come in and go out her eyes gave not a flicker of recognition. Jack could have sworn she was looking straight at them but then perhaps there were so many in the crowd at the door she just didn't see them.

Eve was disappointed in the way that Mother Francis had invited Frank Hegarty's mother to stay. It would mean that their talk had to be put off for one thing, and she was restless and eager to know the nun's view on how she should approach the Westwards. She intended only to ask for her university fees. She would find a place to live where she could mind children. It must be possible. Not every single student who went in the doors of University College could have parents with money to pay for everything. There had to be some of them working their way through a degree. Eve had refused to consider a daytime job and night studying. She had heard of course of those who had done it, but the atmosphere was different. The students were older and grayer. They scurried in for lectures and scurried out again. It wasn't just the letters after her name that Eve Malone wanted. It was the life of a student. The life she could have had if things had been different.

She hoped that the Hegarty woman wouldn't stay long in Knockglen, because Eve needed to act soon. She must not malinger in the convent and prove Mother Clare's point about how she was a liability. Also if she were going to aim to be enrolled in UCD this year then she must do so within the next few days. And if there were to be an unpleasant interview with Simon Westward, the sooner it was over the better. She wished she had Mother Francis's attention to herself.

After supper Eve sat in the warm kitchen. Sister Imelda had clucked around for a while getting her some warm milk with a little pepper shaken on top, which was known to cure any condition. The tea towels had been washed and laid out on the Aga. The smell was familiar, it was home; but Eve didn't feel the sense of comfort that the place usually brought her.

Moving quietly as she always did, Mother Francis came in and sat down opposite her. "Don't drink that if it's horrible. We'll pour it away and rinse the mug."

Eve smiled. It had always been the two of them against the world.

"It's all right . . . not something you'd choose, though, if you had a choice."

"You *do* have a choice, Eve, a series of them."

"It means going up to Westlands, doesn't it?"

"If your heart is set on it . . . then yes."

"And what will I say?"

"We can't write a script, Eve."

"I know, but we could try to work out what would be the best way to approach them." There was a silence. "I expect you *have* approached them for me already?" It was the first time Eve had ever mentioned this.

"Not for a long time, not since you were twelve, and I felt that we should ask them in case they might want to send you to a posher boarding school in Dublin."

"And no response?"

"That was different. That was six years ago and there was I, a nun wearing black, covered in beads and crucifixes . . . that's the way they might see it."

"And was that the last time? You didn't ask them about university fees did you?"

Mother Francis looked down. "Not in person, no."

"But you wrote?"

The nun passed over the letter from Simon Westward. Eve read it, her face set in hard lines.

"That's fairly final, isn't it?"

"You could say that, or you could look at it differently. You could say that then was then and now is now. It's you, you can ask them for yourself."

"They might say I never went near them except to ask for money."

"They'd be right."

Eve looked up startled.

"That's not fair, Mother. You know how I felt all these years. I wouldn't lower myself to go to them cap in hand when you had all done so much for me and they had done nothing. It would have been letting the convent down." She bristled at the injustice of the nun's remark.

Mother Francis was mild. "I know that. Obviously I do. I'm trying to look at it from their point of view. There's no point otherwise."

"I'm *not* going to say I'm sorry. I'm *not* going to pretend . . ."

"True, but is there any point in going at all if you go with that attitude?"

"What other attitude is there?"

"There are many Eve, but none of them will work unless . . ."

"Unless . . . ?"

"Unless you mean it. You don't have to cringe and pretend a love you don't feel, you don't have to go up there with a heart filled with hate either."

"What would your heart be full of, going up there?"

"I told you. It's *your* visit."

"Help me, Mother."

"I haven't been much help to you so far. Do this one on your own."

"Have you lost interest in me? And what happens to me?" Eve's chin jutted up as it always did when she was warding off a hurt.

"If you believe that . . ." Mother Francis began.

"I don't. It's just that it's like a series of dead ends. Even if I *do* get the fees I'll have to find somewhere to live, some work."

"One step at a time," Mother Francis said.

Eve looked at her. Her face had that look she used to have years ago when there was some surprise in store.

"Do you have any ideas?" she asked eagerly.

"My last idea wasn't very successful now was it? Go to bed, Eve. You'll need all your strength to deal with the Westwards. Go up there in the late morning. They'll be going to church at eleven."

The avenue was full of potholes, and there were clumps of weeds rising in the middle of what must once have been a well-kept drive. Eve wondered if her father had worked on this very road. Mother Francis had always been vague about Jack Malone when pressed. He had been a good man, a kind man and very loving of his little daughter. That was really the sum total of it. And it was what you *would* tell a child, Eve realized.

And about her mother there was even less information. She had looked very beautiful when she was young. She had always been very gracious, Mother Francis had said. But what else could she say about a gardener and the disturbed daughter of the Big House. Eve was determined that she would not lose her clear-sighted way of looking at her background. She had long realized that there was no mileage in romanticizing her history. She squared her shoulders and approached the house. It was shabbier close up than it looked from the road. The paint on the conservatory was all peeling. The place looked untidy and uncared for. Croquet mallets and hoops were all thrown in a heap as if someone had played a game many months ago, but no one had ever bothered to tidy the set away or to have another game since. There were Wellington boots in the hall, old golf clubs splintering, with their bindings coming undone. Tennis racquets slightly warped stood in a big bronze container.

Through the glass doors Eve could see a hall table weighed down with catalogues and brochures and brown envelopes. It was all so different from the highly polished convent where she lived. A stray piece of paper would never find its way onto the hall table under the picture of Our Lady Queen of Peace. If it did it would soon be rescued and brought to the appropriate place. How extraordinary to live in a house where you could hardly *see* the hall table for all that was covering it.

She rang the bell, knowing that it would be answered by one of three people. Bee, the sister of Paccy Moore, the shoemaker. Bee was the housemaid in Westlands. Or possibly the cook might come to the door if it was Bee's Sunday off. Mrs. Walsh had been in the family for as long as anyone could remember. She hadn't come from Knockglen in the first place and didn't fraternize with the people of the town, even though she was a Catholic and seen at early mass. She was a large woman who looked rather ominous on her bicycle. Or perhaps Simon Westward himself would come to the door. His father was in a wheelchair and reported to be increasingly frail, so he would not appear.

Ever since she could remember, Eve had played a game. It was like not stepping on the cracks in a footpath. It was what Mother Francis would have called a superstition probably. But she had always done it. "If the next bird to hop up in the windowsill is a thrush then I'll get my exam. If it is a blackbird, I'll fail." "If I have to wait until I count twenty-five at the door of the convent in Dublin, I'm going to hate it." For some reason she always felt like doing it at doors.

As she stood outside the unfamiliar door of the place that was once her mother's home, Eve Malone told herself firmly that if Bee Moore, the housemaid, came to the door it would be a good omen, she would get the money. If Simon Westward himself came it would be bad. If it was Mrs. Walsh the thing could go either way. Her eyes were bright as she waited and heard the sound of running feet.

She saw the figure of a schoolgirl, about ten or eleven years old, running toward the door. She reached up to open it and stood looking at Eve with interest. She was wearing the very short tunic that girls in Protestant schools always wore. In the convent everything had to be a bit more droopy and modest. She had her hair tied in two bunches, one sticking out over each ear almost like candles, as if someone was going to pick her up and carry her by them. She wasn't fat, but she was square and stocky. She had freckles on her nose and her eyes were the same dark blue as her school uniform.

"Hallo," she said to Eve. "Who are you?"

"Who are *you*?" Eve asked. She wasn't afraid of anyone in the Big House if they were this size.

"I'm Heather," the child replied.

"And I'm Eve."

There was a pause while Heather tried to work something out.

"Who did you come to see?" she said, after some consideration.

Eve looked at her with admiration. The child was trying to work out whether Eve was for the master or for the staff. She had phrased the question perfectly.

"I came to see Simon Westward," she said.

"Oh, sure, well come in."

Eve walked behind the little figure through the hall, full of dark pictures, hunting prints maybe. It was impossible to see. Heather? Heather? She didn't know of any Heather in the household, but then she didn't really keep up with who was who in this family. If people in Knockglen spoke of them she didn't join in the conversation. Sometimes the nuns mentioned them, but Eve would toss her head and turn away. Once she came upon an article about them in the *Social and Personal* magazine and she had turned the pages on angrily in case she would find out any more about them and their goings-on. Benny had always said that if the Westwards had been *her* family she would have wanted to know everything about them and would probably have made a scrapbook as well. But that was Benny all over. She'd probably have been doing their errands for them by now, and thanking them for everything instead of the guarding the cold indifference that Eve had nurtured for so long.

"Are you one of Simon's girl friends?" the child asked conversationally.

"No indeed," Eve said with no emotion.

They had reached the drawing room. The Sunday papers were

spread out on a low coffee table, a sherry decanter and glasses stood on a silver tray. Over by the window in his wheelchair sat Major Charles Westward, his shoulders sloped down and it was obvious even from a distance that he was not really aware of his surroundings. A rug over his knees had partly slipped to the floor.

This man was Eve's grandfather. Most people hugged their grandfather, they called him Granddad, and sat on his knee. Grandfathers gave you two shilling pieces and took pictures of you on First Communion and Confirmation days. They were proud of you and introduced you to people. This man had never wanted to see Eve, and if he was in the whole of his sense he might have ordered her out of his house, as he had done her mother.

Once upon a time she had thought he might see her from his horse or his car and ask who was that lovely child. She had a look of the family about her. But that was long ago. She felt no sense of loss looking at him, no wish that things had been different. She was not embarrassed by his infirmity nor upset by looking at him closely after the years of rejection.

Heather looked at her curiously. "I'll go and find Simon for you now. You'll be all right here?" she said.

The child's face was open. Eve found it hard to be stiff with her.

"Thanks. Thanks a lot," she said gruffly.

Heather smiled at her. "You don't look like his girl friends usually look."

"No?"

"No, you look more normal."

"Oh good." Despite herself Eve smiled.

The child was still curious. "Is it about the mare?"

"It's not about the mare. I wouldn't know a mare from a five-bar gate."

Heather laughed good-naturedly and headed for the door. Eve surprised herself by giving the information the child had been looking for.

"I'm not one of his girl friends," she called. "I'm one of his cousins."

Heather seemed pleased. "Oh, then you're a cousin of mine too. I'm Simon's sister."

Eve said nothing because of a slight lump in her throat. Whatever she had thought would happen when she went to Westlands it was not this. She would never have believed that any Westward would have been pleased to see her.

Mother Francis told Kit Hegarty that there was no need for her to hurry back to Dublin. She could stay as long as she liked, a week maybe.

"Don't go back too soon. The peace of this place could wear off you if you went back to the city too quickly."

"Ah, that's country people for you. You think Dublin is all like O'Connell Street. We're out in *County* Dublin you see, by the seaside. It's a grand place full of fresh air."

Mother Francis knew that the peace of Knockglen had nothing to do with its being in the country or the city. The advantage was the place was far from the home where Frank Hegarty would return no more.

"Still, stay here awhile and take our air."

"I'm in the way." Kit had sensed Eve's eagerness to have Mother Francis to herself.

"On the contrary. You are very helpful in that Eve needs time to talk to other people before she commits herself to *any* plan. There's no point in she and I going round in circles. Much as I hate it, I realize that she *has* to make up her own mind."

"You would have made a marvelous mother," Kit said.

"I don't know. It's easier one step removed."

"You're not removed. You just manage not to do what all the rest of us wish we didn't do. You don't nag."

"I don't think you were a nagger either." Mother Francis smiled.

"Did you not want to marry and have children?" Kit asked.

"I wanted a wild unsuitable farmer's son that I couldn't have."

"Why couldn't you have him?"

"Because we hadn't a farm of land to go with me . . . or so I thought. If he had really wanted me he'd have taken me, farm or no farm."

"What happened to him?"

"He married a girl who had legs much better than Bunty Brown, and who *did* have a farm to go with her. They had four children in five years, then he found another as they say."

"And what did the wife do?"

"She made a fool of herself the length and breadth of the county. That's not what Bunty Brown would have done. *She* would have thrown him out, started a guesthouse, and held her head high."

Kit Hegarty laughed. "Are you telling me *you* are Bunty Brown?"

"Not any longer. Not for a long time."

"He was a fool not to take you."

"Ah, that's what I said too. I said it for three years. They didn't want to take me in the convent at first. They thought I was just running away, trying to hide from the world."

"And do you regret it, not waiting for a different farmer's son?"

"No, not a bit."

Her eyes were far away.

"And you've had everything in a way," Kit said. "You've had all the joy of children in a school."

"It's true," Mother Francis said. "Every year, new children, every year new young faces coming in." She still looked sad.

"It will work out for Eve."

"Of course it will. She's probably talking to him now."

"Who is she talking to?"

"Her cousin, Simon Westward. Asking him for fees. I hope she doesn't lose her temper. I hope she won't throw it all away!"

Heather had left the room as soon as her brother came in. Simon went over first to the figure in the wheelchair, picked up the rug, and knelt to tuck it in around the old man. He stood up and came back to the fireplace. He was small and dark, with a thin handsome face, dark-eyed, and his brown hair fell into his eyes. He had had to shake it away so often, it was now a mannerism. He wore riding breeches and a tweed jacket with leather cuffs and elbows.

"What can I do for you?" His voice was cold and polite.

"Do you know who I am?" Eve's voice was equally cold.

He hesitated. "Not really," he said.

Her eyes blazed. "Either you do or you don't," she said.

"I *think* I do. I asked Mrs. Walsh. She said you were the daughter of my aunt Sarah. Is that right?"

"But you know of me, surely?"

"Yes, of course. I didn't recognize you coming up the drive, so I asked."

"What else did Mrs. Walsh say?"

"I don't think that's relevant. Now can I ask you what it's about?"

He was so much in command of the situation that Eve wanted to cry. If only he could have looked ill at ease, guilty about his family's treatment of her, confused and wondering what lay ahead. But Simon Westward would always know how to handle things like this.

She was silent as she looked at him. Unconsciously imitating his stance, hands behind her back, eyes unflinching, mouth set in a hard thin line. She had dressed carefully, deciding not to wear her best outfit in case he would think she had put it on specially, or had come from mass. Instead she had worn a tartan skirt and gray cardigan. She had a blue scarf tied around her throat in what she had thought was a jaunty look.

Her glance didn't fall from his stare.

"Would you like a glass of sherry?" he asked, and she knew she had won the first round.

"Thank you."

"Sweet or dry?"

"I don't know the difference. I've never had either." She spoke proudly. There was going to be no aping the manners of her betters from Eve Malone. She thought she saw him raise his eyebrows in surprise that bordered on admiration.

"Then try the sweet. I'll have that too." He poured two glasses. "Will you sit down."

"I'd rather stand. It won't take long."

"Fine." He said nothing, he just waited.

"I would like to go to university this term," she began.

"In Dublin?"

"Yes. And there are a few things standing in the way."

"Oh yes?"

"Like that I cannot afford it."

"How much does it cost in Trinity now?"

"It's not Trinity and you know that well. It's UCD."

"Sorry, I didn't know actually."

"For years Trinity wouldn't let Catholics in, and now when it does, the Archbishop has said it's a sin to go there, so you know it's UCD."

He put his hands out as if warding her off. "Peace, peace," he said.

Eve continued. "And since you ask, the fees are sixty-five pounds a year for three years for a BA, and after that I would like to do a diploma in librarianship so that would be another sixty-five pounds. There would be books to buy. I am talking about one hundred pounds a year."

"And?"

"And I was hoping you would give it to me," she said.

"Give? Not lend?"

"No, give. Because I wouldn't be able to pay it back. It would be a lie to ask for a loan."

"And how will you live there? You'll have to pay for rooms and everything."

"I told you. It's not Trinity. There are no rooms. I'll get a job in a family, earn my keep. I'd be able to do that. It's just the fees I don't have."

"And you think we should pay them?"

"I'd be very glad if you did." Not grateful, Eve told herself firmly, she had sworn she would not use that word. No matter how much Mother Francis had warned her. Glad was the nearest she could get.

Simon was thinking. "A hundred pounds a year," he repeated.

"It would be for four years," Eve said. "I couldn't really start unless I knew I wouldn't have to come and beg for it every year."

"You're not begging for it now," said Simon.

"That's right, I'm not," Eve said. She felt a great pounding in her head. She hadn't known it was going to be remotely like this.

He smiled at her, a genuine smile. "I never beg either, it must be a family trait."

Eve felt a hot flush of anger. Not only was he going to refuse her, he was going to make fun of her as well.

She had known that she might be refused, she thought it would be with apologies cold and distant, closing the door firmly, and this time forever. She had steeled herself against it. There would be no tears. No pleading. Neither would there be recriminations. She had heard enough in the gossip of the town to know that her father had sworn and cursed this family long years ago. She wasn't going to let history repeat itself.

She had rehearsed staying calm. "So what do we do now?" she asked in a level voice. There was nothing arrogant or pleading about it.

"That seems perfectly reasonable," Simon said.

"What?"

"What you ask for. I don't see any reason why not." His smile was very charming.

She felt that to smile back would put her in some kind of danger.

"Why now?" she asked. "Why not before?"

"You never asked me before," he said simply.

"Not personally," she agreed.

"Yes. It's quite different to be asked indirectly, by a religious order who never made any other approach to me."

"What approach might they have made?"

"Oh, I don't know. Hard to say. I can't say I'd have liked them to ask me to tea or to pretend a friendship I didn't feel. But it was rather bald just to ask for money on your behalf as if you hadn't a mind or a voice of your own."

She considered it. It was true. Of course it was also true that she should never have had to ask him or any of the Westwards for what was rightfully hers. And Mother Francis had been sent away twice with a flea in her ear.

But these were not the subjects at issue. And the need was for calm, not for raking up the past.

"I see," she said.

Simon had almost lost interest in it. He was prepared to talk about other things.

"When does term start, or has it started?"

"Last week. But there's late registration."

"Why didn't you register in time?"

"I tried another kind of life. I couldn't bear it."

He must have been used to short answers. It seemed to satisfy him.

"Well, I'm sure you won't have missed very much in a few days. All I ever see in Dublin when I go there is students from both universities drinking coffee and talking about changing the world."

"They might, one day."

"Of course." He was courteous.

She was silent. She couldn't ask him to get the money now, she didn't want to launch into any thanks. The word grateful might slip out. She sipped her sherry thoughtfully.

Their eyes met. "I'll get a checkbook," he said, and went out to the hall. Eve heard him rooting around amongst the papers and documents stacked on the table.

By the window the old man sat silently staring with unseeing eyes at the unkempt garden. Out on the lawn the sister who must have been nearly twenty years younger than her elder brother played with a couple of large dogs throwing them sticks. It was like a foreign land to Eve.

She stood there like the visitor she was, until Simon came back in.

"You'll have to forgive me, I am not saying this in any way to be offensive, but I don't know if your name is Maloney or O'Malone, or what."

"Eve Malone." She spoke without expression.

"Thank you. I didn't want to go out and check with Mrs. Walsh. It was one or the other, ask you or ask her." He smiled.

Eve did not return the smile. She nodded her head slightly. He wrote the check slowly and deliberately, then folded it in half and handed it to her.

Common politeness must make her thank him. The words stuck in her throat. What had she said before, what had been the word which had pleased her? Glad.

She used it again. "I'm glad you were able to do this," she said.

"I'm glad too," he said.

They did not use each other's names, and they knew there was no more to say. Eve put the check in the pocket of her cardigan and stretched out her hand.

"Good-bye," she said.

Simon Westward said exactly the same thing at the same time.

She waved cheerfully at the child, who seemed disappointed to see her go, and walked down the avenue of the house that had been her mother's home with her back straight, because she knew that she was being watched from the house. From the kitchens, from the garden where the dogs were playing, from the drawing room and from a wheelchair.

She didn't let the skip come into her step until she was outside.

In the convent Mother Francis and Kit Hegarty were having lunch in the window of the community dining room, and a place had been set for Eve.

"We didn't wait for you," Mother Francis said, her eyes anxiously raking Eve's face for the answer.

Eve nodded twice. The nun's face lit up.

"I'll go now. I have a lot of things to do. Eve, your meal's in the kitchen. Bring it out and sit here with Mrs. Hegarty like a good girl."

"Perhaps . . ." Kit looked uncertain. "Can't I go and let you two talk."

"No, no, no you've not finished yet, I have. And this is Eve's home and mine. We have years to talk. You'll be going away soon."

Eve brought out her heaped plate of bacon and floury potatoes with a white sauce. She placed it on the table and saw the sad tired face of the older woman watching her.

"Sister Imelda's always trying to fatten me up, but it's no use. When you've got my kind of way of going on it just burns up food."

Mrs. Hegarty nodded.

"I expect you're the same," Eve said. She felt almost lightheaded with relief. She was only making small talk until the lunch was over, until she could run up the road to tell Benny the news, until she could talk to Mother Francis alone when this sad woman went away.

"Yes, I am the same," Kit Hegarty said. "I never rest, I hardly ever sleep. I think about everything too much."

"You've had a lot to think about," Eve said sympathetically.

"Not always. Frank used to say to me that I couldn't sit down, that my eyes were never still."

"People say that to me, too," Eve said, surprised.

They looked at each other with a new interest, the two who had been competing for Mother Francis's time and attention. They didn't think it odd that she hadn't come back to them. They didn't notice that Sister Imelda never came in to take away their plates. As the gray clouds that raced along behind the big banks of convent trees turned black, as the short winter afternoon turned into evening, they talked on.

Their stories fell into place, like pieces of a jigsaw. Eve Malone needed somewhere to live, a place where she could earn her keep. Kit Hegarty needed someone to help her with her guesthouse. She had no heart to stay in it all day now that Frank, the reason for all the work, had gone. They both could see the solution and yet were afraid to voice it.

It was Eve who spoke first. In the convent which had been her home, Eve softened her voice to ask. Eve, who could never ask for a favor, who hadn't been able to form words of thanks for the £400 in her cardigan pocket, was able to ask Kit Hegarty could she come and live with her.

And Kit Hegarty leaned across the table and took Eve's hands in hers.

"We'll make some kind of a life out of it," she promised.

"We'll make a great life out of it," Eve assured her.

Then they went to tell Mother Francis, who seemed very surprised and thought it must be the direct intervention of God.

SEVEN

*B*rian Mahon had been drinking now for several days. Not a real batter, nothing that had involved any violence or a brawl as it sometimes did, but steady drinking. Emily knew that things were shaping up for a fight. And this time it was going to be about Nan's bedroom.

Nan had decided that from now on she would study there in the evenings. She had said it was not possible to study downstairs with the radio on and the family coming and going all the time. Nasey had fixed her up a simple desk and Paul had put a plug on an electric fire. This is where she would work from now on. Emily sighed. She knew that Brian would object as soon as it was brought to his notice. Why had he not been consulted? Who was going to pay for the electricity? Who did Nan think she was?

The answer to the last part was that Nan thought she was a lot too good for Brian Mahon and Maple Gardens. Her mother had ensured that over the years. As she brushed her daughter's golden hair, Emily had always made the girl believe that there would be a better and a different life. Nan had never doubted it. She felt no need to conform to the life-style of a house ruled by an often drunken father.

Nan Mahon was not afraid of her father because she knew

with a certainty which her mother had helped to create that her future didn't lie in her father's kind of world. She knew without arrogance that her beauty would be her means of escape.

Emily wished that there was some way that she could take Brian aside and talk to him in a way that he would listen. Really listen and understand. She could say to him that life was short and there was no point in crossing Nan. Let her work up in the bedroom if that's what she wanted. Be nice—be pleasant about it, then she'd come down and sit with them afterward.

But Brian didn't listen to Emily these days. If he had ever listened to her. She sighed to herself as she opened up the new delivery of Belleek china, and put the packing neatly into a big container under the counter. She arranged the little jugs and plates on a shelf so that they would best catch the eye and began to write out price tags in her meticulous handwriting. Emily Mahon sighed again. It was so easy to run a hotel shop, and so hard to run a family. People didn't realize how often she'd like to make her bed in the corner of this little world, amongst those nice car rugs and cushions with Celtic designs on them. It would be simpler by far than going back to Maple Gardens.

She had been quite right of course. The row had well begun when Emily Mahon let herself into the family home.

"Do you know anything about all this?" Brian roared.

Emily had decided to try and play it lightly.

"Well, I must say that's a great greeting to one of the workers of the world," she said, looking from her husband's hot, red face to Nan's cool and unruffled expression.

"Aw, shut up with that workers of the world crap will you? We all know there isn't a reason in the world for you to be going out to work. Only because you took some figario. If you'd stayed at home and minded your business we wouldn't have all this trouble now."

"What trouble?" Emily was weary.

"Well might you ask what trouble. Sure you don't know what's going on in your own house."

"Why are you picking on Em?" Nan asked. "She's only in the door, she hasn't her coat off, or her shopping-up down."

Her father's face was working. "Don't call your mother by her Christian name, you young pup."

"I'm not." Nan was bored with this argument. "I'm calling her 'M,' short for Mother, Mama, Mater."

"You're dismantling that contraption you have upstairs, and coming back down here to where we have the house heated. You'll study your books in this room like a normal human being."

"Excuse me?" Nan asked. "Excuse my mentioning it, but what kind of study could anyone get in a room like this with people bellowing and shouting."

"Listen to me you impertinent young rossie . . . you'll feel the weight of my hand on you if there's any more of this."

"Ah, Dad, don't hit her . . ." Nasey had stood up.

"Get out of my way . . ."

Nan didn't move. Not an inch did she stir from where she stood, proud, young, confident in her fresh green and white blouse and her dark green skirt. She had her books under her arm, and she could have been a model picture for student fashion.

"Am I breaking my back for you to speak to me like that in front of the family? Am I working to make you into a bad-mannered tinker?"

"I haven't said anything bad-mannered at all, Dad, only that I'm going up to work, to get a bit of peace. So that I'll get my degree eventually, so that you'll be prouder of me than ever."

The words were inoffensive, but Brian Mahon found the tone of his daughter almost more than he could bear.

"Get up there out of my sight then, we don't want to see hair nor hide of you this evening."

Nan smiled. "If you want me to give you a hand Em, just call me," she said, and they heard her light step going up the stairs.

The three students in Mrs. Hegarty's digs were delighted to hear of Eve's arrival. They had felt awkward and unsure of themselves in a place where the son of the house had been killed so tragically. Now at least an attempt at normality was being made.

They liked Eve too, when she appeared. Small, attractive in a wiry kind of way and prepared to put up with no nonsense from the very start.

"I'll be getting your breakfast from now on. Mrs. Hegarty is feeding you like fighting cocks so you get bacon and egg and sausage every day and scrambled eggs on a Friday. But I have a nine o'clock lecture three days a week so I was wondering if you could help me clear and wash those days, and the other days I'll run round after you like a slave . . . pouring you more cups of tea and buttering you more toast."

They went along with her good-naturedly, and they did more than she asked. Big lads who wouldn't have known where the Hoover was kept in their own homes were able to lift it out for Eve on a Tuesday before they went to catch the train to College. They wiped their feet carefully on the hall mat. They said they never again wanted to risk anything like the reception that they got when they had accidentally walked some mud in on top of a carpet that Eve had cleaned. They kept the bathroom far cleaner than they had ever done before Eve had come on the scene. Kit Hegarty told her privately that if she had known how much the presence of a girl would smarten the lads up, she might have had a female student years ago.

"Why didn't you? They'd have been easier."

"Don't you believe it, always washing their hair, wanting the lavatory seat put down, drying their stockings over chairs, falling in love with no-hopers . . ." Kit had laughed.

"Aren't you afraid of any of those thing happening with me?" Eve asked. They got on so well now, they could talk easily on any subject.

"Not a chance of it. You'll never fall for a no-hoper. Hard-hearted little Hannah that you are."

"I thought you said I was like you?" Eve was making bread as she spoke. Sister Imelda had taught her to make soda bread when she was six. She had no idea of the recipe, she just did it automatically.

"Ah, you *are* like me, and I didn't fall for a no-hoper, there was lots of hope in Joseph Hegarty. It's just that as time went on it didn't seem to include me." She sounded bitter and sad.

"Did you make any attempt to find him, you know to tell him about Frank?"

"He didn't want to know about Frank when there was something to tell like when he learned to swim, or when he lost his first tooth, or when he passed his Inter. Why tell him anything now?"

Eve could see a lot of reasons, but she didn't think it was the time or the place.

"Suppose he came back," Eve asked. "If Joe walked in the door one day . . ."

"Funny I never called him Joe, always Joseph. I'm sure that tells us something about him or me. Suppose he came back? It would be like the man coming to read the meter. I gave up looking at that gate years ago."

"And yet you loved him? Or else thought you did?"

"Oh, I did love him. There's no use denying it just because it wasn't returned and didn't last."

"You're very calm about it."

"You didn't know me years ago. Let me see. Around the time you were one or two, if you'd known me then you wouldn't have said I was calm!"

"I've never loved anybody," Eve said suddenly.

"That's because you were afraid to."

"No, the nuns were much more liberal than people think. They didn't fill me with terror of men."

"No, I meant afraid to let yourself go . . ."

"I think that's right. I feel things very strongly like resentment. I resent those bloody Westwards. I hate asking them for money. I can't tell you how much it took to make me walk up there that Sunday. And I feel very protective too, if anyone said a word against Mother Francis or Sister Imelda I'd kill them."

"You look very fierce with that knife. Put it down for God's sake."

"Oh." Eve laughed, realizing she was brandishing the carving knife, which she had used to put a cross on the top of the soda cake. "I didn't notice. Anyway it wouldn't harm anyone. It's as blunt as anything. It wouldn't cut butter. Let's get one of those budding engineers inside there to take it into a lab and sharpen it up for us."

"You *will* love somebody one day," Kit Hegarty said.

"I can't imagine who." Eve was thoughtful. "For one thing he'd have to be a saint to put up with my moods, for another I don't see many good examples, where love seems to have worked out well."

"Have you anything planned on Sunday?" Dr. Foley asked his eldest son.

"What am I letting myself in for if I haven't?" Jack laughed.

"Just a simple answer. If you're busy I'll not bother you."

"But then I might miss something great."

"Ah, that's what life is all about, taking risks."

"What is it Dad?"

"You *are* free then."

"Come on, tell me."

"You know Joe Kennedy, he's a chemist in the country. He wants to see me. He's not well I think. We go back a long way. He wondered if I'd come and call on him."

"Where does he live?"

"Knockglen."

"That's miles away. Don't they have doctors there?"

"They do, but he wants a friend more than a doctor."

"And you want me to come is it?"

"I want you to drive me, Jack. I've lost my nerve a bit."

"You can't have."

"Not altogether, but just for a long wet drive, slippy roads. I'd be very grateful."

"All right," Jack said. "What'll I do while you're talking to him?"

"That's the problem. I wouldn't say there's all that much *to* do there, but maybe you could go on a drive or sit in the car to read the Sunday papers."

Jack's face brightened. "I know. There's a girl that lives there. I'll give her a ring."

"That's my boy. Only a couple of months at University and already there's a girl in every town."

"She's not a girl in that sense. She's just a nice girl," Jack explained. "Have you the phone book? There can't be that many Hogans in Knockglen."

Nan was very excited when Benny said that Jack Foley had rung her.

"Half the girls in College would give anything to have *him* coming to call on them, let me tell you. What'll you wear?"

"I don't think he's coming to call, not in that sense. I mean it's not something to get dressed up for. I won't wear anything," Benny said, flustered.

"That should be a nice surprise for him when you open the door," Nan said.

"You know what I mean."

"I still think you should get dressed up, wear that nice pink blouse, and the black skirt. It is a party when a fellow like Jack Foley comes to call. If he was coming out to Maple Gardens I'd dress up. I'll get you a length of pink ribbon and a black one and you can tie them both round your hair to hold it back. It'll look great. You've got gorgeous hair."

"Nan, it won't look great on a rainy Sunday in Knockglen. Nothing looks great there. It'll just look pathetic."

Nan looked at her thoughtfully. "You know those big thick brown bags, the ones they sell sugar in. Why don't you put one of those over your head and cut two slits for eyes. That might look right."

Annabel Hogan and Patsy planned to make scones, and queen cakes and an apple tart. There would be bridge rolls first with chopped egg on one plate and sardines on the other.

"Maybe we shouldn't overdo it," Benny suggested.

"There's nothing overdone about a perfectly straightforward afternoon tea for your friend." Benny's mother was affronted at the notion that this might not have been their normal Sunday afternoon fare.

They were going to light a fire each day in the drawing room to heat it up for the occasion and after tea had been cleared away Benny's parents would withdraw to the breakfast room, leaving the young people the run of the good room on their own.

"There's not any question of having the run of the place," Benny had begged, but to no avail. "He's only coming here because he has to kill the time," she pleaded. They wouldn't hear of it, a nice young man telephoning courteously several days in advance to know if he could call. It wasn't a matter of killing time. There were a rake of things he could do in Knockglen.

Personally Benny could think of very few. Window-shopping didn't bear thinking about. The cinema wasn't open in the afternoon. Healy's Hotel would pall after half an hour, and Jack Foley wasn't likely to put away an afternoon in Mario's, however entertaining Fonsie might be. The Hogans were the only game in town. Still, it was nice that he remembered her. Benny rehearsed the pink and black ribbon. It looked well. She started wearing it on Friday evening so that the household wouldn't think it was part of the dressing up.

When Sean asked her to the pictures she said no, that since she was having a friend from Dublin she had to stay at home on Saturday and get things ready.

"A friend from Dublin!" Sean sniffed. "And might we know her name?"

"It's a him, not a her," Benny said mulishly.

"Pardon me," Sean said.

"So that's why I can't go you see," she added lamely.

"Naturally." Sean was lofty and knowing.

For some reason that she couldn't explain Benny heard herself saying, "It's just a friend, not anything else."

Sean's smile was slow and cold. "I'm sure that's true Benny. I wouldn't have expected anything less of you. But it's good of you to say it straight out."

He nodded like a self-satisfied bird. As if he were being generous and allowing her to have her own friends until the time came. And a pat on the head for defining that there was nothing but friendship involved.

"I hope it's a very pleasant visit. For all of you," Sean Walsh said, and bowed in what he must have thought was an elegant or a gracious manner. Something he had seen Errol Flynn or Montgomery Clift do, and stored up for a suitable occasion.

Jack Foley was the easiest guest they had ever known in Hogans. He ate some of everything put in front of him. He praised it all. He had three cups of tea. He admired the teapot and asked was it Birmingham 1930s silver. It was. Wasn't that amazing, they said; no, Jack said, that's what his parents' silver was. He just wondered was it the same. He punched Benny playfully like a brother when they talked about University. He said how marvelous it was to have boys and girls in the same classes. He had felt so gauche when he had come there from a single-sex school. Benny saw her mother and father nodding sagely, agreeing with him. He spoke of his parents and his brothers, and the boy Aengus with the glasses, which were always getting broken at school.

He said that the debates were great on a Saturday night, you learned a lot from them as well as having fun. Had Benny been. No Benny hadn't. You see there was this problem about getting back to Knockglen, she said in a flat voice. Oh that was a pity he thought, they really were part of College life. Perhaps Benny could stay with her friend Nan, he sometimes saw her there. They all nodded. Perhaps. Some Saturday.

He was discreet about why his father wanted to meet Mr. Kennedy. It could be anything he said, rugby club business, or new drugs on the market, or old school reunions. You never knew with his father, he had so many irons in the fire.

Benny looked at him with admiration. Jack Foley didn't even look as if he were putting on an act.

The only other person she knew who could do that was Nan. In many ways they would be ideally suited.

"It's nice and fine. Do you think you could show me the town?" he asked Benny.

"We were just going to leave the two of you to . . . er, chat," Benny's mother began.

"I've eaten so much . . . I think I do need a walk."

"I'll get proper shoes." Benny had been wearing flat pumps, like party shoes.

"Get boots, Benny," he called after her. "We're really going to walk off this fabulous tea."

They walked companionably together. Benny in her winter coat, with the pink collar of her smart blouse showing over it. She had put on Wellingtons, and she felt that the cold wind was making her cheeks red, but it didn't matter. Jack wore his purple and green Law Society scarf wound round his neck.

Several people were out walking in the wintry sunshine which would soon turn into a sunset.

"Where will we go?" he asked at the Hogans' gate.

"Through the town out the other side, and up to Westlands. That'll undo the harm of all the apple tart."

"Poor Mr. Kennedy's dying. He wanted to talk to my father about it. He doesn't get much joy out of the local man apparently."

"That's very sad. He's not old," Benny said. "That's where the local man, as you call him, lives." She waved across the road to Dr. Johnson's house, where the children were throwing sticks for a dog.

"I didn't mention that to your parents . . ." Jack began.

"Nor will I, don't worry," Benny said.

They knew the story would travel the length of the one-street town.

Benny pointed out places, and gave a little commentary. Bee Moore called out from the doorway of Paccy Moore's cobbler's shop that there were lovely new skirts arrived into Peggy Pine's.

"They're just right for you, Benny," Bee said, and added, with no sense of offense, "they'd fit an elephant, and there's a great stretch in them."

"Beautiful!" Jack commented, with a grin.

"Ah, she doesn't mean any harm," Benny said.

In Mario's, both Fonsie and his uncle blew extravagant kisses out to Benny. And in Dessie Burns' hardware shop they wondered who could have written "Useful Gift" over a saw. They passed Kennedy's chemist swiftly without saying anything about the man inside sitting talking to Jack's father. Benny took him across to point out some of the finer points of Hogan's Gentleman's Outfitters. And to look out of the corner of their eyes at Mrs. Healy and speculate about her corset.

Jack admired the shop courteously, and said it was very discreet. You'd never know from the outside what it was like on the inside. Benny wondered was that a good thing, but decided it probably was. Country people were different. They didn't like anyone knowing their business.

She asked Jack to keep staring in the window and to notice the reflection of Mrs. Healy across the road watching them beadily from her hotel. Jack heard about Mrs. Healy's corsets, and what amazing structural feats they were. There was a rumor that Mrs. Healy was quite a plump, soft person, but nobody except the late Mr. Healy would have had any proof of this. New and ever-more taxing underpinnings were bought every time she went to Dublin, and there was a rumor that she had once gone to London on a corset-buying spree, but this might only be a rumor.

When she had gone back into her hotel Benny felt it safe to move on. She showed Jack the clean white slabs of Mr. Flood's the butchers. She said that Teddy Flood, his son, didn't really want to work there, but what else could he do. It was hard to be born into the business if you were a boy. Mr. Flood was becoming very odd these days.

Jack said he could see that without being told. It was surely highly questionable to have so many cows and pigs and lambs painted around the wall in a highly colored gamboling state. It must make people feel sensitive about buying them in their very dead condition, and eating them. Benny said that this was nothing. Mr. Flood had always had piteous-looking animals peeping at you from the walls. The real thing was that he now had a fairly permanent vision of something up a tree. A saint possibly, but definitely a nun. It was a source of worry to the family and a cause of great fits of giggling among the customers when he would suddenly pause in sawing or chopping and go out-of-doors for a brief consultation upward.

They passed the church and paused to study the details of the Men's Mission, which would be coming to the church shortly. Benny said that during the two weeks of the Missions little wooden stalls selling prayerbooks and beads, and holy objects and Catholic Truth Society pamphlets did huge business outside the church. Was it the same in Dublin? Jack was apologetic. He didn't really know. He had gone to the Mission of course, but like everyone he and Aidan had always wanted to try and find out which had the lecture on sex. That was the one that was usually packed out, but the Missioners were becoming more and more cunning. They sort of hinted each night that the big sex sermon would be tomorrow and they had crowds coming in every night, in case they missed it.

Benny said that men were much more honest than women really. Girls felt exactly the same but didn't admit it.

She showed him the square where the bus came in. Mikey was just drawing up.

"How's Benny?" he called out.

"Great altogether," Benny said, with her big smile.

They paused in front of the gates of St. Mary's and she pointed out the landmarks to him. The big long lawns, the camogie field, the glasshouse, windy path through the kitchen gardens that went uphill to the quarry path, where Eve had her cottage.

She knew everything and everyone, he told her, and there was a story attached to whatever they saw.

This pleased her. At least he wasn't being bored.

Neither of them saw Sean Walsh looking at them from inside Birdie Mac's sweetshop. Birdie often made tea and toast of a Sunday afternoon and Sean Walsh had taken to dropping in. His eyes were cold as he watched Benny Hogan and the arrogant young pup that she had gone off with that very first day, trick-acting and showing off right outside the convent gates in full view of the town. It didn't please him one little bit.

They stood on the five-bar gate that had a good view down over the Westwards' land. Benny pointed out places to him. The graveyard where all the Westwards lay. The small war memorial in it that had wreaths of poppies in November, because so many of them had died in wars.

"Wasn't it odd to think of them all fighting in those wars when they lived here," she said.

"But that would be their whole culture and tradition and everything," Jack said.

"I know, but when the others would be talking about homeland and fatherland and king or queen and country . . . they'd only be talking about Knockglen."

"Don't knock Knockglen," he said laughing.

"Don't let Fonsie in the chipper hear you say that, he'll be trying to turn it into a hit single. Move over Bill Haley . . . that's Fonsie . . ."

"Where did he get the name?"

"Alphonsus."

"God."

"I know. Didn't you escape lightly, Jack Foley, with your nice normal name."

"And what about you . . . Benedicta was it?"

"No, nothing as exotic. Mary Bernadette, I'm afraid."

"Benny's nice. It suits you."

It was dark as they walked back. The lights were on up in the convent. Benny told Jack of Eve's life there, and the lovely bedroom where you could sit and look down the town.

"Now I have you home safely in good time," she said, delivering him to the door of Kennedy's chemist.

"Will you come in?"

"No, he might be upset."

"Thanks, Benny. It was a lovely visit."

"I enjoyed your being here. Wasn't it lovely for me too."

"Will you come out one night in Dublin?" He spoke suddenly, almost surprising himself.

"Not at night. I'm Cinderella remember. But I'll see you round."

"Maybe a lunch?"

"Wouldn't that be grand?" she said, and walked off down the dark street.

"Poor Joe," his father said after a long silence in the car.

"Has he got cancer?"

"Riddled with it. He's only a couple of months I'd say, from the sound of things."

"What did you tell him?"

"He wanted me to listen."

"Has he no one here who'll do that?"

"No. According to him there's an arrogant, bad-tempered GP, a wife who thinks it's all safe and in the hands of the Little Flower or the Infant of Prague or some such helpful authority and won't brook any discussion on the matter. . . . However, enough's enough. How was your friend? Joe said she was a nice girl, big horse of a girl he called her."

"Isn't it a pity he couldn't have found a better way to describe people."

"Let me get this straight again," Nan said, her eyes wide with disbelief. "He asked you out. I mean he said the words, 'I would like you to come out with me one night,' and you said no?"

"No, I didn't say no, and he didn't ask me out like that."

Nan looked to Eve for guidance. They were all three together waiting for the lecturer to arrive. They sat away from the main body of the students in order to get this matter sorted.

"Well, did he or didn't he?" Eve asked.

"It was like you'd ask a friend. Casual. It wasn't like a date."

"It certainly wasn't if you said no," Eve said dryly.

"Don't go on like that." Benny looked from one to the other. "I swear, if he *does* ask me out I'll go. Now are you satisfied?"

"And where will you stay the night in Dublin?" Eve asked.

"I could stay with you, couldn't I, Nan?"

"Oh yes, sure." The reply was half a second late.

Benny looked to Eve. "Or if there was any problem with that I could stay with you Eve out in Dun Laoghaire."

"Easily." That was said quickly, but of course Mother and Father would never let her stay in a guesthouse full of boys with a woman they didn't know, even if Eve did live there in a semi-work capacity. Benny was philosophical. It wouldn't happen anyway. What were all the plans for?

❦

In the Ladies Reading Room stuck into the crisscross tapes on the notice board was a folded piece of paper. "Benny Hogan, First Arts." She opened it casually. It must be from that pale-faced clerical student who had missed the history lecture and she had promised to give him the notes. Benny had remembered to take carbon paper with her. He could keep the copy for himself. She didn't know his name. He was a worried young man, definitely not strong, his white face made even whiter by the black clothes. She got an odd feeling when she saw that the letter was from Jack Foley. It was like the sudden jolt you get if you touch something too hot or too cold.

> *Dear Benny,*
>
> *I remember you said evenings were difficult at the moment, so what do you say to lunch in the Dolphin? I've never been there but I'm always hearing about it. Would Thursday be good? I remember you saying you didn't have a tutorial or anything on Thursdays. I'll probably see you before then, but if you can't make it or don't want to, can you leave a note in the Porter's Office? I hope I won't hear from you because that means I'll see you in the Dolphin at one-fifteen on Thursday.*
>
> *And thank you for the lovely afternoon in Knockglen.*
>
> *Love Jack.*

Love Jack. Love Jack. She said it to herself over and over. She closed her eyes and said it again. It was possible wasn't it? Just possible that he did like her. He didn't *need* to ask her out, or to remember that she had a free afternoon on Thursdays, or be so kind as to think of lunch. He could have sent a postcard if he wanted to be mannerly, as her father would call it. Jack Foley didn't need to ask her to lunch in a big posh hotel where the high of the land went. He must have done it because he liked being with her, and that he liked her.

She didn't dare to believe it.

Benny heard Nan's infectious laugh in the corridor outside. Hastily she pushed the note deep into her shoulder bag. It seemed a bit shabby considering how enthusiastic Nan and Eve always were on her behalf, but she couldn't bear them giving her advice on what to wear and what to say. And worst of all she couldn't bear them to think that Jack Foley might in fact fancy her, when she so desperately hoped it was true.

EIGHT

$\mathcal{B}$enny decided she would be thin on Thursday week. She would have hollows in her cheeks and a long narrow neck. It would, of course, involve eating nothing. Not easy to do at home where Patsy would put a bowl of porridge, a jug of cream and the silver sugar basin in front of her to start the day. Then there was the brown bread and marmalade. And on either side of her, a parent determined she should have a good start to the day.

Benny realized that you'd need great ingenuity if you were to lose an ounce of weight as a resident of Lisbeg in Knockglen. So she first pretended that she had gone off porridge. In fact she loved it, swimming in cream and dusted with brown sugar. Then she would leave her departure until as late as possible and cry, "Is that the time? I'll take my bread and butter with me."

When no one was looking she would tip it into Dr. Johnson's hen run or drop it into the bin outside Carroll's or Shea's. Then there was lunchtime. She found it beyond human endurance to go into the cafes where the smell of sausage and chips in one kind of place or almond buns in another would drive her taste buds wild.

She told Nan and Eve that she had to work and stayed resolutely in the library all the time.

The stuffiness of the library and no food made her feel head-achy and weak all afternoon. It was another test of will to pass the sweetshops when she knew a packet of Rolos would give her the energy to struggle down to the quays and get the bus. Then back in Knockglen she had to cope with the meat tea as well.

"I had a huge feed up in town today," she'd say apologetically.

"What did you do that for when there's good food waiting for you here?" her mother would reply, puzzled.

Or else she'd try the angle that she didn't feel like it because she was very tired. They didn't like that either. Should they have a word with Dr. Johnson about her? What could be making a normal healthy girl tired? Benny knew that it would be useless to tell them the truth, that she wanted to lose some weight. They would tell her she was fine. They would worry and discuss it endlessly. Meals would become a battleground. It was quite hard enough already to resist slices of Patsy's treacle tart, and to toy with one piece of potato cake when she craved half a dozen. Benny knew that the road to beauty was not meant to be an easy one, but she wondered grimly whether it was such hard going for everyone else.

She wondered should she wear a corset like Mrs. Healy, or better still not like Mrs. Healy's very obvious whalebone. There was the one she had seen advertised. "Nu Back corset . . . expands as you bend, stoop or twist . . . returns to position easily and cannot ride up when sitting." It cost 19/11, almost a pound, and it did seem to promise everything you could dream of. Except of course it didn't hold out any hope for the cheeks and the neck.

Benny sighed a lot. Wouldn't it have been great going to lunch in a smart Dublin place if she were small and neat like Eve was. Or better still if she looked like Nan. If she looked so gorgeous that everyone would look and Jack Foley would be so proud and pleased that he had asked her.

Because Benny was never available for lunch anymore, Nan and Eve often found themselves walking together to one of the cafes near the University. Eve watched with a wry amusement as the boys came to join them wherever they went.

Nan put on an amazing performance Eve thought to herself. She had a practiced charm, but no gush whatsoever. Eve had never known anyone play such a role. But then she asked herself, *was* it a performance. She seemed totally natural and was invariably warm and pleasant to those who approached. Almost regal, Eve thought. It was as if she knew that there would be admiration everywhere and was quite accustomed to coping with it.

Eve was always included in the conversations, and, as she told Kit Hegarty in their easy companionship out in Dun Laoghaire, it was the best introduction you could have to every single male in UCD.

"Of course they do see me as a pale shadow," Eve said sagely. "Like the moon not having any light of its own, it reflects the light of the sun."

"Nonsense," Kit said loyally. "That's not a bit like you to be so humble."

"I'm being practical," Eve said. "I don't mind it at all. There's only one Nan in every generation."

"Is she the sort of College Belle?"

"I suppose so, though she doesn't act it. Not like that Rosemary, who thinks she's at a party all day every day. Rosemary has a foot of makeup on, and she has eyelashes about ten inches long, you wouldn't believe it. She keeps looking up and down so that no one will miss them. I wonder that doesn't make herself dizzy or blind herself."

Eve sounded very ferocious.

"But Nan's not like that?" Kit Hegarty had yet to meet this paragon.

"No, and she's just as nice to awful fellows as she is to real hunks. She spends ages talking to ones that are covered in pimples and can hardly string two words together. Which drives the hunks out of their minds."

"And does she not have her eye on anyone for herself?" Kit

asked. She thought that Eve was seeing far too much of the dazzling Nan and not nearly enough of her old friend Benny Hogan.

"Apparently not." Eve was surprised too. "Because she could have anyone she liked, even Jack Foley, but she doesn't seem to want them. It's as if there's something else out there that we don't know about."

"Martians?" Kit suggested.

"Nothing would surprise me."

"How's Benny, by the way?" Kit's voice was deliberately casual.

"Funny you should ask. I haven't seen her all week, except at lectures, and then only to wave across to."

Kit Hegarty knew better than to probe or criticize, but her heart went out to that big untidy girl with the bright smile, the girl who had been Eve's friend through thick and thin and now seemed to be left out in the cold. It was tough on ordinary moths and insects when a gorgeous butterfly like Nan came onto the scene.

"Eve, are you going to the Annexe?" Aidan Lynch seemed to be everywhere. He had a fawn duffel coat which had seen much better days, long curly hair which fell into his eyes, and dark horn-rimmed spectacles that he always said were plain glass but made him look highly intellectual.

"I wasn't thinking of it, no."

"Could the thought of my company there and back and the distinct possibility that I would buy you a coffee and a fly cemetery make you change your mind?"

"I'd love a fly cemetery," Eve said, referring to the pastries with the black, squashy filling. "I cook breakfast for huge greedy men and I forgot to have any myself today."

"Huge, greedy men?" Aidan was interested. "Do you live in a male harem?"

"No, a digs. I help with the housework to earn my keep." She spoke without self-pity or bravado. For once the jokey Aidan was without words. But not for long.

"Then it's my duty, not just my pleasure to feed you up," he said.

"Nan won't be there. She has a tutorial."

A flicker of annoyance passed over his face. "I didn't want Nan to be there. I wanted you."

"Well recovered, Mr. Lynch." She smiled at him.

"Is there anything more harsh in this life than to be misjudged, and have one's motives entirely misunderstood?" he asked.

"I don't know. Is there?" Eve liked the lanky law student. She had always thought of him as part of Jack Foley's gang. Full of nonsense of course and all that lofty talk. But basically all right.

They walked companionably down the corridor toward the stone stairs that led to the Annexe, the College coffee shop. They passed the Ladies Reading Room on the way. Through the door Eve caught a glimpse of Benny sitting in a chair on her own.

"Aidan, just a minute. I'll ask Benny to come with us."

"No! I asked *you*," he said, petulantly.

"Well, God Almighty, the Annexe is open to everyone in the whole place. It's not as if you'd asked me to a candle-lit dinner for two," Eve blazed at him.

"I would have, but I don't know where they serve them at this time of the morning," he said.

"Don't be a clown. Wait here a second."

Benny's mind seemed far away. Eve touched her shoulder.

"Oh, hallo," she said, looking up.

"Good, you admit you know me. Let me introduce myself. My name is Eve Malone. We met some years ago in . . . where was it . . . Knockglen . . . yes that's where it was!"

"Don't, Eve."

"What is it? Why don't you play with me anymore?"

"I can't tell you."

"You can tell me anything," Eve said, kneeling down beside the chair.

Out in the corridor Aidan Lynch cleared his throat.

"No, go on, there's a fellow waiting for you."

"Tell me."

"I'm on a diet," Benny whispered.

Eve threw back her head and pealed with laughter. Everyone in the room looked over at them. Benny's face got red.

"Now look what you've done," she spat out furiously.

Eve looked into her friend's eyes. "I'm only laughing with relief you great fool. Is that all? Well, I don't think there's any point in it. You're grand as you are, but if you want to, be on one, but don't run away from everybody. I thought I'd done something awful to you."

"Of course not."

"Well, come on, come and have a coffee with Aidan and myself."

"No, I can't bear the smell of food," Benny said piteously. "My only hope is to keep away from where it is."

"Will we have a walk in the Green at lunch then? There's no food there," Eve suggested.

"We might see someone feeding the ducks and I could snatch the bread and run off stuffing it down my throat," Benny said with a hint of a smile.

"That's better. I'll pick you up in the Main Hall at one."

"Don't tell anyone."

"Oh, Benny, honestly!"

"What was all that about?" Aidan said, pleased to see that Eve had returned alone.

"I was letting Benny know where I was going and explaining that if I wasn't back by a stated time she was to ring the guards," Eve said to him.

"Aren't you very droll."

"Well, you're not a great one at taking life too seriously yourself," she said with spirit.

"I knew we were suited, I knew from the very first minute I saw you. In bed."

Eve just raised her eyes, not to encourage him. But Aidan was warming to the theme.

"It will be a nice thing to tell our grandchildren in years to come."

"What?"

Aidan spoke in a child's voice. " 'Tell me, Granddad, how did you and Grandmama meet?' and then I'll say, 'Ho, ho, ho, little boy, we met when she was in bed. I was introduced to her in bed. It was like that way back in the fifties. It was a racy time, ho, ho, ho.' "

"You are an idiot." Eve laughed at him.

"I know. I said we were well suited," he said, tucking her arm into his as they joined the crowds on the stairs down to coffee.

Benny took out a small mirror from her handbag. She put it inside a copy of *Tudor England* and examined her face carefully. Five days with no food to speak of and her face was still round, her jaw was still solid and there was no sign of a long swanlike neck. It would almost make you give up believing in God.

"Are there women after you in College?" Aengus asked Jack Foley.

"I never looked." Jack wasn't concentrating.

"You'd know. They'd be breathing heavily," Aengus explained.

Jack looked up from his notes.

"They would?"

"So I hear."

"Where do you hear this?"

"Well, mainly from Ronan. He was doing a very funny imitation of people in a car, huffing and puffing. He says that girls get like that when they're passionate."

"And where did he see all this that he could be imitating it?" Jack asked, a trifle anxiously.

Aengus was innocent. "I don't know. You know Ronan."

Jack did know his brother Ronan and he had an uneasy feeling that there had been someone in the vicinity when he had been saying good-bye to Shirley the other night. Shirley was quite unlike most of the other girls in UCD. She had been in America for a year, which made her very experienced. She had offered Jack a lift home from the Solicitors' Apprentice dance last Saturday night at the Four Courts. She had her own car and her own code. She had parked right outside his house under a streetlight.

When he had murmured that they might have more shade, Shirley had said, "I like to see what I'm kissing."

Now it looked as if his brother had also seen whatever kissing had been going on.

Jack Foley made a note to leave Shirley alone. Next time it would be Rosemary or even the ice-cool Nan Mahon. No more crazy ladies thank you very much.

Benny ate an apple walking around St. Stephen's Green at lunchtime and felt a little bit better. Eve never spoke of the diet again. Benny knew she didn't even need to warn her not to tell Nan. It wasn't that Nan wouldn't be helpful, she'd be very helpful. It was just that Nan didn't ever need to try. She just was perfect already, and it put her in a different world.

Instead they talked about Aidan Lynch and how he was going to come out to Dun Laoghaire tonight and take Eve to the pictures. He understood that she had to wash up after supper. He'd come out on the train.

"I've missed you a lot, Eve," Benny said suddenly.

"Me too. Why can't you stay in town some evening?"

"You know."

Eve did know. The arguments about the evenings drawing in, the dark nights, it would be such hard work they decided they should wait until Benny had a real date, a real reason to stay in

town. It almost seemed like frittering it away to use a night off just
for the two of them to be together like the old days.

"I'd love it if you'd come home to Knockglen," Benny said.
"And not that I'm twisting your arm, but I know Mother Francis
would too."

"I will," Eve promised. "It's just that I've got obligations too.
It's then that I'm the most help to Kit. I get the Saturday tea over
so quickly it would make your head swim. I keep telling the lads
they have to be on the six-thirty train into town to see the action.
They don't know what I mean but it gets a bit of urgency into
them. Otherwise they'd be dawdling there all night."

Benny giggled. "You're a terrible tyrant."

"Nonsense. I was raised by an army general in St. Mary's,
that's all. Mother Francis would get her way over anything. Then
on Sundays we have this rule. They get a big Sunday lunch, and
there's a plate of salad left under a tea towel for each of them in the
evening, no serving or anything."

"I'm sure she's delighted with you," Benny said.

"I'm a bit of company. That's all."

"Does she ever talk about her son?"

"Not much. But she cries over him at night. I know that."

"Isn't it extraordinary that people can love their children so
much that they kind of live for them?"

"Your parents do. That's part of the problem. Still, it's nice to
know they do," Eve said.

"Yours would have, if they'd stayed round long enough."

"And if they'd been sane," Eve said dryly.

Benny sat beside Rosemary at the history lecture. She had never
really spoken to her before. She wanted to look at Rosemary's
makeup and wondered was there anything she could learn.

As they waited for the lecturer to arrive they talked idly.

"Knockglen?" Rosemary said. "That's the second time I heard
of that today. Where is it?"

Benny told her, and added glumly that it was too far to be accessible and too near to let you live in Dublin.

"Who was talking about it?" Rosemary puckered up her face trying to think. She often applied a little Vaseline to her eyelashes in the privacy of the lecture hall. It was meant to make them grow. She did so openly in front of Benny, who was no rival that must be kept out of beauty secrets.

Benny watched with interest. Then Rosemary remembered.

"I know. It was Jack. Jack Foley. He was saying that a friend of his fancies someone from Knockglen. It's not you by any chance."

"No, I don't think so." Benny's heart was like lead. Rosemary was on such close terms with Jack, and Jack was making a joke out of Knockglen.

"His friend Aidan. You know, goofy Aidan Lynch. He's quite witty actually, it sort of makes up for everything else."

Benny felt her cheeks burning. Is this the way people talked? People like Jack and Rosemary and maybe even Nan for all she knew. Did handsome people have different rules.

"And did Jack approve of whoever Aidan fancied?" she wanted to keep Jack's name in the conversation, however painful it was.

"Oh yes. He said it was a great place. He's been there."

"Really." Benny remembered every moment of the day that Jack Foley had been in her town in her house in her company. She could probably give a transcript like they did in court cases of every word that had been said.

"He's really out of this world," Rosemary confided. "You know, not only is he a rugby star, but he's bright. He got six honors in his Leaving, and he's nice."

So Rosemary had prized out of Jack how well he had done in his exams leaving school, just like she had.

"Are you going out with him?" Benny asked.

"Not yet, but I *will* be, that's my project," Rosemary said.

All during the lecture on Ireland under the Tudors Benny sneaked little looks at her neighbor. It was so monstrously unfair that a girl like Rosemary should have a bar of KitKat in her bag and have no spots and no double chin.

And when had she had all these conversations with Jack Foley? In the evenings probably. Or even the early evenings, when poor Benny Hogan was sitting like a big piece of freight on the bus back to Knockglen.

Benny wished she hadn't eaten the apple. Perhaps what her system had wanted was a complete shock. No food at all after eighteen years of too much food. Maybe the apple had delayed the process.

She looked at Rosemary and wondered was there any hope that she would fail in her project.

"How's work, Nan?" Bill Dunne prided himself on getting on well with women. He thought that Aidan Lynch's reputation was quite unjustified. That was fine at school when everyone was jokey. But in University women were there because they were studious. Or because they wanted people to think they were studious. You couldn't go on trick-acting and making schoolboy jokes to university women. You pretended to take their studies seriously.

Nan Mahon smiled one of her glorious smiles. "I suppose it's like it is for everyone else," she said. "When you like the lecturers, when you enjoy the subject, it's fine. When you don't, it's hell, and there's going to be hell to pay at the end."

The words themselves were meaningless, but Bill liked the tone. It was warm and almost affectionate.

"I wonder could I take you to dinner one night?" he asked.

He had thought this out carefully. A girl like Nan must get asked to hops, and to pubs and to parties and to cinemas all the time. He wanted to move it one grade up the ladder.

"Thank you, Bill." The smile was still warm. "I don't go out very much. I'm a real dull stick. I study a bit during the week, you see. In order to keep up."

He was surprised and disappointed. He had thought dinner would work.

"Perhaps we could dine at a weekend, then. When you're not so tied up."

"Saturdays, I usually go to the debate, and then down to the Four Courts. It's become a bit of a ritual." She smiled apologetically.

Bill Dunne wasn't going to beg. He knew that would get him nowhere.

"I'll catch you at one of those rendezvous then," he said, loftily, refusing to let his pique be seen.

Nan's room became her living quarters. She had an electric kettle there and two mugs. She took her tea with lemon, so there was no need for milk or sugar.

Sometimes her mother came in and sat with her.

"It's peaceful in here," Emily said.

"That's why I wanted it this way."

"He's still annoyed." Nan's mother sounded as if she were about to plead.

"He has no reason to be Em, I am perfectly polite always. He's the one who uses the language and loses control of himself."

"Ah, if only you understood."

"I do. I understand that he can be two different people. I don't have to be dependent on his moods. So I won't be. I won't sit down there wondering when he'll come home and what condition he'll be in."

There was a silence.

"Neither do you, Em," Nan said at last.

"It's easy for you. You're young and beautiful. You've the world ahead of you."

"Em, you're only forty-two. You've a lot of the world ahead of you."

"Not as a runaway wife, I wouldn't."

"And anyway you don't want to run away," Nan said.

"I want *you* to be away from it."

"I will be, Em."

"You don't go out with any young men. You never go out on dates."

"I'm waiting."

"What for?"

"For the Prince, the white knight, the Lord, or whatever it was you said would come."

Emily looked at her daughter, alarmed.

"You know what I meant. Something much better than here. Something far above Maple Gardens. You meet people amongst your friends, these law students, these young engineers . . . these boys with fathers who have big positions."

"That's only the same as Maple Gardens, except a bit more garden and a downstairs cloakroom."

"What do you mean?"

"I haven't held on to this dream just to end up in another Maple Gardens, Em, with another nice fellow who'd turn out to be a drinker like Dad."

"Hush, don't say that."

"You asked me. I told you."

"Yes, I know. But what do you hope to get?"

"What you told me I'd get, anything I wanted."

She looked so proud and confident sitting there at her desk, her mug of tea in her hand, her blond hair back from her brow, her face unruffled by the kind of conversation they were having.

"You could too." Emily felt the belief she had always held in her heart soar back again.

"So there's no point in going out with the people I don't want to live amongst. It's only a waste of time."

Emily shivered. "There could be some very, very nice people in all that number."

"There could, but not what you and I want."

Emily's glance fell on the desk and amongst Nan's books and

files were magazines, *The Social and Personal, The Tatler, Harper and Queens.* There were even books of etiquette borrowed from the library. Nan Mahon was studying a great deal more than First Arts.

Mrs. Healy looked through the thick net curtains and saw Simon Westward getting out of his car. He had his small stocky sister with him. Perhaps he was going to take her into the hotel for a lemonade. Mrs. Healy had long admired the young Squire as she called him. Indeed she had half harbored some little notions about him. He was a man of around thirty, within a few years of her own age.

She was a fine substantial widow in the town, a person of impeccable reputation. Not exactly his social class of course, and not the right religion. But Mrs. Healy was a practical woman. She knew that when people were as broke as the Westwards would appear to be a lot of the old standards might not be as firm as they used to be.

She knew that Simon Westward owed Shea's since last Christmas for the drink he had bought to cover the hunt and what they called the Boxing Day party. Many a traveler came and had a drink in Healy's Hotel and spoke indiscreetly because he would have thought that the lofty and distant landlady had not the remotest interest in the tittle-tattle of the neighborhood.

In most cases they would have been correct, but in terms of the Westwards, Mrs. Healy had always been interested. She had grown up in England where the Big House had always been much more a part of the town. It had never ceased to amaze her that back home again in her native land, it appeared that nobody knew or cared about the doings up at Westlands.

To her disappointment the Westwards went into Hogan's Gentleman's Outfitters across the road.

What could they want there? Surely they would deal in Callaghan's up in Dublin, or Elveryss. But perhaps credit had run out in those places. Maybe they were going to try locally where a man as nice as Eddie Hogan would never ask to see the color of their money before lifting the bale of material down from the shelf and starting to write the measurements into his book.

From the inside of his dark shop, peering through his dark window with its bales of materials and its shutters that never fully opened, Eddie Hogan saw with delight that Simon Westward and his small sister were coming into the premises. He wished he had time to smarten the place up.

"You'll never guess . . ." he began to whisper at Sean.

"I know," Sean Walsh answered back.

"It's very dark," Heather complained, screwing up her eyes to get used to the change from the bright winter sunshine outside.

"Shush." Her brother didn't want her to seem rude.

"This is an honor," Eddie Hogan said.

"Ah good morning, Mr. . . . Hogan, isn't it?"

"Of course it is," Heather said. "It's written outside."

Simon looked annoyed; Heather immediately became repentant.

"Sorry," she muttered, looking at the ground.

"It is indeed Edward Hogan at your service and this is my assistant, Sean Walsh."

"How do you do, Mr. Walsh."

"Mr. Westward." Sean bowed slightly.

"I'm afraid after all that, it's only something rather small. Heather wants to buy a present for my grandfather. It's his birthday. Just a token."

"Ah yes. Might I suggest some linen handkerchiefs." Eddie Hogan began to produce boxes of them, and open a drawer where they were stocked singly.

"He's got more hankies than he knows what to do with," Heather explained. "And he's not great at blowing his nose anyway."

"A scarf, maybe?" Eddie Hogan was desperate to please.

"He doesn't go out, you see. He's very, very old."

"It's a puzzler all right." Eddie scratched his head.

"I thought you might have some sort of geegaws," Simon said, smiling from one man to the other. "It doesn't really matter what. Grandfather isn't really in a position to appreciate anything . . . but . . . you know." With a flick of his head he indicated Heather, who was prowling earnestly around the shop.

Eddie Hogan had now ventured into the whole problem. "Might I suggest Miss Westward, if it's something just to give your grandfather a feeling of pleasure that you remembered him and marked his birthday, you might think in terms of sweets, rather than clothing."

"Yes." Heather was doubtful.

"I know I may appear to be turning business away, but we want to think of what's best for everyone. A little box of jellies possibly. Birdie Mac would wrap it up nicely and you could get a card."

Simon looked at him with interest. "Yes, that's probably much more sensible. Silly of us not to see it. Thanks."

He must have seen the look of naked disappointment on Eddie Hogan's face. "Sorry to have bothered you Mr. Hogan, wasting your time and everything."

Eddie stopped and eagerly looked back at the small dark confident young man.

"It was an honor, as I said, Mr. Westward," he said foolishly. "And maybe now that you've been in our place you'll come back again."

"Oh, undoubtedly." Simon held the door open for his sister and escaped.

"That was very clever of you, Mr. Hogan," Sean Walsh said approvingly. "Putting him under a compliment to us."

"I was only trying to think of a present for the little girl to give her grandfather," Eddie Hogan said.

Thursday arrived. Benny looked at herself in the bathroom mirror. She stared long and hard. There was a possibility that she had lost some weight around her shoulders. Only a possibility, and even if it were true what a useless place to lose it.

She had washed her hair the night before and it looked nice and shiny. The skirt that Peggy Pine had said might crush, did indeed crush. It looked awful. But it was a lovely blue color, not like all the sensible navy and browns that she had worn like a school uniform. The kinds of colors that wouldn't draw attention to you. The blouse looked a bit raggy too, not like the heavy ones she normally wore. But it was much more feminine. If she were sitting across a table from a gorgeous man like Jack Foley he would have nothing to look at except her top. She *had* to have something fancy, not look as if she was a governess or a school prefect.

Her heart soared and plummeted a dozen times as she dressed. He had been so easy and natural that day he was here in Knockglen. But in College it was different. You always heard people talking about him as if he were some kind of Greek god. Even real Holy Marys in her class who spoke of him. These were girls with straight hair, and glasses and shabby cardigans who worked harder than the nuns and seemed to have no time for fellows or a social life, even those kinds of girls knew of Jack Foley.

And he was asking her out today. She'd love to tell Rosemary. She would really adore to see her face. And lots of them, she'd love to go up to Carroll's shop now and kick on the door and tell horrible Maire Carroll who used to call her names at school how well things were turning out. Maire who didn't get called to the Training College like she had thought, and was sulking in her parents' grocery shop, while Benny would be having lunch in the Dolphin with Jack Foley.

Benny folded the flimsy blouse up and put it in her big shoulder bag. She also put in a small tube of toothpaste and a toothbrush, her mother's Blue Grass talcum powder, which she would say she had borrowed by mistake if it were noticed. It was seven thirty-five. In six hours time she would be sitting opposite him.

Please God may she not talk too much and say stupid things that she'd regret. And if she did say stupid things let her remember not to give a great laugh after them.

She felt a flicker of guilt that she hadn't told Eve about the outing. It was the first time she had kept anything from her friend. But there hadn't been time, and she was afraid that Eve would tell Nan—there was no reason not to after all. And Nan would have been great and lent her a nice handbag or a pair of earrings to match her skirt. But she didn't want it all planned and set up. She wanted to do it on her own, and be herself. Or sort of herself. Benny smiled wryly at her reflection. It wasn't exactly her own ordinary self that would walk into the Dolphin in six hours time. It was a starved, overpolished shiny Benny who hadn't given one minute's thought to her books for the last ten days.

"I wish you'd tell me what's wrong with the porridge, Benny." Patsy was on her own in the kitchen when Benny came down.

"Nothing Patsy, I swear."

"It's just that if ever I married I'd want to be able to put a decent pot of porridge for a man and his mother on the stove."

"His mother?"

"Well, I'd have to marry in somewhere wouldn't I? I've nowhere for anyone to marry into."

"Do you fancy anyone, Patsy?"

"Divil a point in yourself or myself fancying anyone. I haven't a penny to bless myself with, and you'd have to be sure he'd be a grand big ox of a fellow the size of yourself," said Patsy cheerfully.

Somehow the morning passed. Benny skipped her twelve o'clock lecture. She didn't want to have to run through the Green, down Grafton Street and round by the Bank of Ireland in order to be in the Dolphin at one-fifteen. She would be able to do it, but she didn't want to arrive flushed and panting. She would walk down slowly and take her ease. Then at the last moment she would change somewhere nearby in the ladies' cloakroom of a pub or a coffee shop and put on more talcum powder and brush her teeth. She would look so relaxed and unfussed.

She pitied the people she saw as she walked slowly through the Dublin streets. They looked gray and harassed. They had their heads down against the wind that blew instead of holding themselves high and facing it as Benny did. They were all going to have dull ordinary things at lunch. Either they would go home on a bus to a house where the radio would be on and children were crying, or they would queue up for a meal in a city restaurant where it would be crowded and the smell of other people's dinners would be unattractive.

She checked herself finally, and decided she was as good as she could be. She should of course have started the diet much earlier. Like maybe three years ago. But there was no point in crying over that.

She had been big and fat when he had met her in Knockglen only a couple of weeks ago. It hadn't stopped him asking her out to a place like this. She looked up at the Dolphin unbelievingly. He hadn't said which part. She knew his letter off by heart. But he must mean the hall.

There were three men in the entrance. None of them was Jack. They were much older. They were wealthy-looking, possibly people who went racing.

She saw with the shock that comes with recognition that one of them was Simon Westward.

"Oh, hallo," said Benny, forgetting she didn't actually know him, just all about him from Eve.

"Hallo." He was polite but mystified.

"Oh, Benny Hogan, from the shop in Knockglen."

She spoke naturally, with no resentment at not being recognized. Simon's smile was warm now.

"I was in your father's shop yesterday."

"He told me. With your little sister."

"Yes, he's a very courteous man, your father. And his assistant . . . ?"

"Oh, yes." Benny wasn't enthusiastic.

"Not the same type of person?"

"Not at all, but you couldn't tell my father that. He thinks he's fine."

"No boys in the family to help him run it?"

"No, only me."

"And do you live in Dublin?"

"Oh, I wish I did. No I go up and down every day."

"It must be exhausting. Do you drive?"

Simon lived in different world Benny decided.

"Only on the bus," she said.

"Still it makes it a bit better if you can have nice lunches in a place like this . . ." He looked around him approvingly.

"This is the first time I've been here. I said I'd meet someone. Do you think I should wait in the hall?"

"The bar, I think," he said, pointing.

Benny thanked him and went in. It was crowded but she saw him immediately over in a corner . . . he was waving.

"There she is!" Jack cried. "Now we're all complete."

He was standing up smiling at her, from the middle of a group of seven people. It wasn't a date. It was a party. There were to be eight people. And one of them was Rosemary Ryan.

Benny didn't really remember much about the part before they went into the dining room. She felt dizzy, partly with the shock and partly with the lack of food over the past few days. She looked wildly to see what the others were drinking. Some of them had glasses of Club Orange, but it could have been gin and orange. The boys had glasses of beer.

"I'd like one of those." She pointed weakly to a beer glass.

"Good old Benny, one of the lads," said Bill Dunne, a boy she had always liked before. Now she would have liked to pick up the heavy glass ashtray and beat him over the head with it until she was perfectly sure he was dead.

They were all chatting easily and happily. Benny's eyes raked the other girls. Rosemary was as usual looking as if she had come out from under the hair dryer and hours of ministration in the poshest place in Dublin. Her makeup was perfect. She smiled at everyone admiringly. Carmel was small and pretty. She had been going out with her boyfriend Sean since they were sixteen or maybe even fifteen. They were known as the College's Perfect Romance. Sean looked at Carmel with adoration and she listened to every word he said as if it were a pronouncement. Carmel was no threat. She would have eyes for nobody, not even Jack Foley.

Aidan Lynch, the long, lanky fellow who had taken Eve to the pictures, was there too. Benny breathed a prayer of relief that she had told nobody about what she had thought was her date. How foolish she would have felt had the story got around. But of course Aidan would tell Eve that Benny was there, and Eve might very reasonably wonder why nothing had been mentioned. She felt cross and hurt and confused.

The other girl was called Sheila. She was a law student. A pale sort of girl, Benny thought, looking at her savagely; pale and rather dull-featured. But she was small. God, she was small. She had to look up at Jack Foley, not over at him like Benny did. She remembered Patsy talking about her needing a big ox of a man. She willed the tears back into her eyes.

None of them had ever been there before. It was all Jack's great plan they said . . . a scheme that would make them well-known, highly respected personages here by the time they qualified. Lots of lawyers and a lot of racing people met there. The thing to do was to establish yourself as a regular.

The words of the menu swam in front of Benny. She was going to eat real food for the first time in ten days. She knew it would choke her.

She was sitting between Aidan Lynch and the wordless Sean when the final seating arrangements had been made. Jack Foley was between Rosemary and Sheila across the table from her. He looked boyish and pleased, delighted with his notion of getting the four boys to pay for a smart lunch in a place like this.

The others were pleased with him too.

"I must say you went out and plucked the best of the bunch for us to be seen with," Aidan Lynch said extravagantly.

Faithless pig, Benny thought to herself, remembering that he had sworn such undying devotion to Eve Malone earlier in the week.

"Only the best is good enough." Jack's smile was warm and included everyone.

Benny's hand was reaching for the butter, but she pulled back. To her fury, Bill Dunne saw her.

"Ah, go on, Benny, hanged for a sheep as a lamb," he said, pushing the butter dish toward her.

"You should see the marvelous teas that go on the table in Benny's house," Jack said, trying to praise her. "I was down there not long ago and you never saw the style. Scones and savories and tarts and cakes, and that was just an ordinary day."

"That's the country for you. They like to feed them up down there. Not like us poor starved Town Mice," Aidan said.

Benny looked around them. The thin blouse with the frills had been no good, nor had the blue skirt. The waft of Blue Grass that she could feel coming from under her arms and down the front of her bra. She wasn't the kind of girl that people would admire and want to protect like they felt about Rosemary Ryan and the little loving Carmel and the pale but interesting Sheila from the Law Faculty. Benny had been brought along only as a jokey person. Someone that they'd all talk to about big feeds and being hanged for a sheep as well as a lamb.

She smiled a brave smile.

"That's it, Aidan. You come down to Knockglen and we'll fatten you all right. You'd be like one of those geese that they stuff so that they'll have nice livers."

"Benny, please." Rosemary fluttered her lashes and looked as if she were going to come over all faint.

But Bill Dunne was now interested. "Yeah, we could be seeing Lynch's Liver on menus."

Jack was entering into it too. "A Knockglen speciality. Fattened fifty miles from Dublin," he said.

"I'd have to go into hiding. They'd want me dead, not alive. God, Benny, what have you got planned out for me."

"But think of what a delicacy you'd be," said Benny. Her cheeks were glowing. Fattened fifty miles from Dublin. Had Jack really said that? Had he meant it as a joke about her? The most important thing was not to seem hurt.

"It's a high price to pay." Aidan was looking thoughtful, as if he were considering it as a serious possibility.

"I think it's all rather awful to joke about raising poor defenseless animals to eat them," Rosemary said, looking fragile.

Benny wished she could remember what Rosemary had ordered. But she didn't need to. Jack did.

"Come on, that's hypocritical," he said. "You've ordered veal chops . . . the calves didn't exactly enjoy getting ready to become that, now did they?"

He smiled at her across the table. The Knight who had come to her rescue.

Rosemary sulked and pouted a little, but when nobody took any notice she recovered.

Rosemary and Sheila competed all during the meal for Jack's attention. Carmel only cared what her Sean thought of this or that item on the menu; they ate little pieces from each other's plates. Benny entertained Bill Dunne and Aidan Lynch as if she had been a hired cabaret. She worked at it until she could feel beads of sweat in her forehead. She was rewarded with their attention and their laughter. She could see Jack straining to join in at times, but he seemed pinioned by the warring women on each side.

The less she tried to seek his attention, the more he tried to engage her in chat. It was obvious that he liked her company, but only as someone who was a load of fun. With a smile that nearly cracked her face Benny knew inside that Jack Foley liked to be where there was laughter, and good times. He wouldn't in a million years have thought of asking someone like Benny out alone.

Simon Westward passed the table.

"See you back in Knockglen sometime," he said to Benny.

"Who's he? He's rather splendid," Rosemary asked. She seemed to be losing slightly on points to Sheila who had the advantage of being able to compare notes about lecturers with Jack. Rosemary must have decided on the making-him-jealous route.

"He's one of the ones we didn't manage to fatten up properly in Knockglen," she said.

The others all laughed at this, but Jack didn't.

"Don't knock Knockglen," he said softly.

He had said that before to her. This time he seemed to be saying something else.

Mossy Rooney worked on the roof of the cottage over the quarry. There had been a high wind and eleven slates had been lifted right off. They probably lay in smithereens now at the foot of the quarry.

He had been asked by Mother Francis to come urgently and repair the damage.

The nun came up and watched anxiously as he worked out what needed to be done.

"It won't be very dear, will it Mossy?"

"Not to you Mother Francis." His face was expressionless as always.

"But you must be paid for your work." She looked worried.

"It won't bankrupt you and the Order," he said.

Never once did he hint that it was odd of the convent to maintain a small house up here that nobody used. By nothing in his tone was there any trace of surprise that a place which had seen two deaths nearly two decades ago was still kept as a kind of shrine for a young rossie who was above in Dublin getting a university education, if you don't mind, and never came next or near the place.

Mossy wasn't a person to speculate about things like that. And even if he were, his mind was too busy. He had another thought in it.

He might ask Patsy to meet his mother. He was collecting information about her first. He didn't want to get into anything he might have to extricate himself from later. . . .

"Simon, will you come and see me at school?"

"What?" He was studying a ledger.

"You heard. You only say 'what' to give yourself time to think," Heather said.

"I can't, Heather. I have far too much to do here."

"You haven't," she grumbled. "You're always going to Dublin. Even to England. Why can't you stop for a day and come and see me. It's awful. You've no idea. It's like a prison."

"No it's not, it's perfectly all right. All school is boring. It gets better when you get older."

"Did yours?"

"What?" He laughed. "Yes, it did. Look, the holidays come quickly. You're having a lovely half-term now, and then you'll be back for Christmas before you know it." His smile was very broad.

"Haven't we any other relations. They only let relations come."

"Not here, you know that."

They had cousins in England and in Northern Ireland. But Simon and Heather and their old grandfather were the only surviving members of the Westward family to live on the big estate in Westlands.

Nobody ever said it, but the crazed crying-out of Jack Malone praying that none of the family should die in their beds seemed to have been heeded. There were very few Westwards about.

❦

"I saw your friend Benny yesterday, I expect she told you," Aidan Lynch said to Eve as he sat patiently in Kit Hegarty's kitchen waiting for the washing up to be finished so that they could go out.

"Take a tea towel, Einstein, and we'll be finished quicker," Eve said.

"She didn't tell you then?"

"Amazingly no. You may find this hard to believe but a day passed by in the forest without a record of your movements being sent by the tom-toms."

"I thought she might have dropped it, after all it isn't every day one goes to the Dolphin?"

"Benny was in the Dolphin?"

"And I was, I was there, don't forget about me."

"It's not easy," Eve admitted.

"Perhaps she was covering up for me."

Eve had lost interest in Aidan's ramblings, she was much more curious as to what Benny had been doing in the Dolphin.

"Was she eating anything?" she inquired.

"Like a horse. She ate everything before her," he said.

"I didn't know you knew Jack Foley," Rosemary said next day to Benny.

"Not very well."

"Well enough for him to go to tea with you in Knockglen."

"Oh, he was just passing through. His father had to see someone."

Rosemary wasn't satisfied. "Are they family friends then?"

"No. It was a nice lunch wasn't it?"

"Yes, it was. Aidan Lynch is an awful eejit, isn't he?"

"I think he's rather nice. He takes a friend of mine to the pictures now and then. She says he's great fun."

Rosemary Ryan did not look convinced.

"Sean and Carmel would make you sick wouldn't they, all that gooey stuff."

"They seem very well settled certainly." Benny's eyes were dancing with mischief.

She knew the next attack would be on Sheila.

"Did you know that one, Sheila, from the Civil Law course before?"

"No." Benny's face was innocent. "She seemed to be very well up in all her studies. I thought they all seemed very fond of her."

Rosemary returned to her notes in disgust. Benny noticed that she had a bar of Fruit and Nut and nibbled at it from time to time. Comfort eating is what that was. Benny knew it well.

Brian Mahon was very drunk on Friday night. Nan heard only some of it. She locked her door and turned on her radio so that she couldn't hear what was being said. She knew her mother wasn't a whore, and so did Paul and so did Nasey. So did her father when he was sober. But when he was drunk he seemed to want to say at the top of his voice that not only was she a whore but a frigid one and that the sooner people realized this the better. Nan also knew that her mother would never leave the home where such humiliations were forced on her with ever greater frequency.

"It's for you, Eve." One of Kit's students answered the phone on Saturday morning.

"Oh, good." Eve hoped it was Benny. Maybe she would go down to Knockglen on the lunchtime bus. Kit had said that she was free to go whenever she wanted.

But it wasn't Benny. It was Nan.

"Can I tempt you out for a walk today?"

"Yes, that would be nice. Will I come in your way and learn a bit of that side of town? I could pick you up."

"No." Nan spoke sharply. Then her voice softened. "Anyway it's much nicer out your side. We could go down the pier. I'll pick *you* up."

"Sure."

Eve felt a vague sense of disappointment. She would have preferred it to be Benny saying she'd meet her off the bus.

Five minutes later Benny rang. But it was too late now.

"Can't you ring Nan and tell her you're coming home?"

"I can't. I don't have her number. Do you?"

"No." Benny too had hoped that Eve would come back.

"You never told me you were at the Dolphin," Eve challenged.

"I was going to tell you all about it."

"Not only that, but threatening to pickle Aidan's liver."

"I had to say something."

"Why?"

"They expected me to."

"They sure as hell didn't expect you to say that," Eve said. "But they seemed to enjoy it. And are you back on your food again?"

"Oh yes. Patsy's making currant bread here. You should smell it."

Nan wore a white pleated skirt and a dark green jacket. The boys who were in the digs looked up with great interest when she came in.

Kit Hegarty too looked at her with interest. She was indeed a striking young woman. Most of all because she seemed so much in control of herself. She spoke in a low clear voice as if she expected that others would listen without her having to make any effort.

She went to Eve's bedroom with her and Kit could hear her exclaiming with admiration.

"A sea view as well. Lord, you are lucky, Eve."

With the familiar feeling of loss she always felt, Kit heard Eve explain, "It used to be Frank Hegarty's room. I wanted to keep some of his things around it, but Kit said no."

"What are you going to wear?" Nan asked.

"Why? It's only a walk on the pier!" Eve protested.

"Everywhere's only a walk somewhere. So that you look nice. That's why."

Kit Hegarty heard Eve sigh, and the door close as she changed into the red blazer and red tartan skirt which really did look nice on her, and went well with her dark coloring.

But Kit in her heart agreed with Eve. It was only a walk on the pier. Nan was making it seem like a public appearance. Maybe that's what she did everywhere.

They walked companionably along with the crowds from Dublin, among people who had come out from Dublin City to walk off the effects of lunch or who were trying to keep children and mothers-in-law entertained.

"Look at those kids," Nan said suddenly, pointing out a crocodile of small schoolgirls walking purposefully with two well-wrapped-up women teachers.

"What about them?" Eve asked.

"Look, one of them's waving at you."

Eve looked over. It was true, one of the small blue-clad figures was making great signs.

"Eve, hallo Eve," she called behind her hand so as not to alert the schoolteachers.

"Who is she?" Nan asked.

"No idea." Eve looked bewildered. The child was wearing a school beret and had a round face, snub nose and freckles. Then Eve saw the two bunches of hair, one on each side of the head like two jug handles.

It was Heather Westward. Simon's little sister.

"Oh hallo," Eve said lamely, and without much enthusiasm.

"Do you live near here?" the girl hissed at her.

"Why?" Eve was wary.

"I was wondering would you come and take me out sometime. Just for a bit?"

Eve looked at her dumbstruck. "Take you out? Where? What for?"

"Anywhere. I'd be no trouble."

"Why me?"

"We can only go out with relations. You're my cousin. Please?"

"I can't. It's not possible."

"Yes, it is. If you phoned the school and said you're my cousin."

"But your brother?"

"He never comes up. He's too busy at home. Trying to organize things."

"Your other relations?"

"I don't have any."

The crocodile, which had been pausing to look at the big mail boat moored at the jetty, was now moving on. The teachers were shepherding them for the off.

"Please," called Heather Westward.

Eve stood there wordlessly looking after them.

"Well?" Nan asked her.

"I suppose I'll have to," Eve said.

"Of course you will."

"She's only a child. You can't disappoint a child," Eve said crossly.

"And it would be foolish. Look at all the housepoints you'd get."

"Housepoints?"

"Well, they'll have to ask you to the Big House especially if you're a friend of Heather's. And they'll owe you. Don't forget that. You won't be going cap in hand anymore."

"I won't go there, anyway, cap or no cap."

"Yes you will," said Nan Mahon firmly. "And what's more you'll take me with you."

NINE

Peggy Pine regarded the arrival of her niece Clodagh as something of a mixed blessing. The girl wore very, very short skirts; she was loud and flamboyant. She had worked for two years in shops in Dublin and spent a summer in London. According to her aunt she felt herself a world authority on dress and the buying habits of the female population.

There was much about her aunt's shop she was going to change.

"She *might* be a nice friend for you," Annabel Hogan said, weighing it up. "But we should wait and see. She might be altogether too flighty for Knockglen, from what Peggy says, and indeed from first impressions."

"Oh, Sean up in the shop is full of disapproval of her," Eddie Hogan observed.

"Then I like her already," Benny chimed in.

"You need a friend now that you don't see Eve anymore," Annabel said.

Benny's eyes flashed. "What do you mean Mother? Don't I see Eve three or four times a week in College."

"But it's not the same," her mother said. "She never comes home here anymore, and she has her own friends out in Dun

Laoghaire in that house she works in. And there's this Nan. You never say Eve anymore, it's always Eve and Nan."

Benny was silent.

"It was only to be expected," her mother consoled. "And you'll make lots of new contacts, where you need them. Round here."

"Who have you asked to the dance?" Bill Dunne asked Jack as they walked out of their lecture together. One of the big College Dress Dances was coming up in a few weeks time.

"I knew your mind wasn't on constitutional law," Jack said.

"We have a written constitution here. No need to upset ourselves about it," Bill said.

"All the more reason, it would appear. I haven't done anything yet. What about you?"

"I was waiting to see who you were going to ask so that I could pick up the crumbs from the rich man's table."

"You're a pain. You're beginning to talk as obscurely as Aidan."

"I think he's all right. He's going to ask Eve Malone, I think, when he gets up enough courage. She's inclined to bite off his head. I'm more interested in knowing what *you're* going to do."

"I wish I knew."

"Well ask somebody," Bill begged, "and leave the field clear for the rest of us."

That was the problem. Whom should he ask? Jack had been vague anytime Shirley phoned. He had been busy disentangling himself there, and Sheila who sat beside him at lectures had dropped fairly heavy hints. But the gorgeous Rosemary Ryan had rung him only last week saying she had two free tickets to a show which meant of course that she had gone out and bought two tickets for a show, but didn't want him to know that.

And Nan Mahon had smiled a lot at him across the Annexe and the Main Hall and places where she had been and he had been. He would like to ask her in many ways. She was so lovely and yet so unattainable.

Suddenly he had an inspiration.

"I know what we'll do," he said to Bill Dunne, banging him on the arm enthusiastically. "We'll ask them all. All the girls we fancy. Tell them to pay for themselves, and then we'll have our pick."

"We couldn't do that!" Bill gasped at the audaciousness of the plan. "It would be very mean. They wouldn't say yes. They'd go with fellows who'd pay for them."

"We could have a little party first." Jack was thinking on his feet.

"Where? You're not going to get girls in evening dress to go into Dwyer's or Hartigan's."

"No, in a house."

"Whose house?"

"Mine, I suppose," Jack said.

"Why can't you just take a girl to a dance like every normal boy," Jack's father grumbled.

"I don't know who to take," Jack said simply and truthfully.

"It's not committing you for life, there won't be a breach of promise action if you take the wrong girl to a dance in your first term."

"I thought that you both might like to use the opportunity . . . ?" Jack looked hopefully from his mother to his father.

"Use it for what, might one ask?" Lilly Foley asked.

"Well, you know, the way you're always saying that you mean to have people in for drinks . . ."

"Yes . . . ?"

"And you know the way you're always grousing that you never meet any of my friends . . ."

"Yes . . . ?"

"I thought you could have a sherry party on the night of the dance, and sort of kill two birds . . . ?"

Jack's smile was very powerful. In minutes it was all agreed.

Rosemary Ryan offered Benny a peppermint. She must be about to divulge some information or do some detective work. Benny wondered which it was. It turned out to be both.

"Jack Foley's asked me to the big dance," she said.

"Oh, that's nice." Benny's heart was like lead.

"Yes, well I did tell you earlier in the term I was sort of making him my project."

"You did indeed."

"I think it's a large party."

"Well, they usually are, I hear," Benny said. She had heard little else in conversations in the Ladies Reading Room and overheard in the cloakrooms and the cafes. People went to the Dress Dances in parties of ten or twelve. The boys decided on the groupings and the girls were their guests. The tickets were about twenty-one shillings, and there was dinner, and everyone danced with everyone else apparently, but with their own special date most of all and at the end.

She had a vain hope that Aidan Lynch might get up a party for it and include her. But then he couldn't really unless she had been asked by some other fellow. Those were the rules.

Rosemary was chewing her pencil as well as the peppermint.

"It's a bit odd though. It's like a big group, and we're all meeting at Jack's house first. I was wondering were you going?"

"Not as far as I know." Benny was cheery.

"You weren't asked?"

"No, not as yet. When were *you* asked?"

"About an hour ago," Rosemary admitted grumpily.

"Oh well, then, there's every hope." Benny wondered did your face break by putting these false smiles on.

❧

After the lecture she met Jack Foley in the Main Hall by chance.

"Just the girl I was looking for. Will you join our group? It's a sort of dutch party for the big dance."

"Lovely," Benny said. "Will we dress in clogs?"

"No, I meant like we all sort of get our own tickets." Jack looked embarrassed.

"That makes much more sense, then we can all be free as birds," she said.

He looked at her surprised.

"Birds?"

"Different kinds of birds. Sparrows, emus, but free," she said, wondering was she actually going mad to be having this stupid conversation.

"You'll come, then?"

"I'd love to."

"And we'll have drinks in my house. I'll write down the address. My parents are having friends of their own age in. Would your parents like to come do you think?"

"No." Her voice was like a machine gun. "No, what I mean is thank you, but they hardly ever come up to Dublin."

"This might be the excuse they need." He was politely courteous. He had no idea how much she would hate them there.

"It's very kind of you, but I think not. However, I certainly would love it."

"That's great," he said, pleased. "We need someone to cheer us up in these dim and dismal days."

"Ah, I'm the one for that," Benny said. "Never short of a word, that's me."

The wind lifted his hair, and his shirt collar stood high around his neck over his navy sweater, coming out over his navy jacket. He looked so handsome she wanted to reach out and stroke him.

His smile seemed as if he had never smiled for anyone else in the world.

"I'm really glad you're going to be there," he said.

"Stop looking as if you're going to your execution," Kit said to Eve. "She's only a child."

"In a big posh Protestant school," Eve grumbled.

"Not at all. It's shabbier than our own, I can tell you."

"Still, full of airs and graces."

"She can't have that many airs and graces. She wouldn't have begged an old misery boot like you to come and see her."

Eve grinned. "That's true. It's just we won't have anything to say to each other."

"Why don't you bring a friend. It might be easier."

"Oh God, Kit, who could I bring on an outing like this?"

"Aidan Lynch?"

"No, he'd frighten the wits out of her."

"Nan?"

"Not Nan," Eve said.

Kit looked up sharply.

There was something about Eve's tone that meant the matter was closed. Mother Francis had warned Kit about this. She said that Eve had areas where nobody followed her.

Eve was now miles away from the conversation. She was thinking about what Nan had said, using the child to get accepted into the life at Westlands.

It wasn't a joke either. She had meant it. She had said that she would go down to Knockglen and stay with Benny if there was a chance of meeting the Westward family socially.

"But they're a senile old man, a kid and Simon, an uppity fellow with an accent you could cut, who wears riding breeches," Eve had exclaimed.

"They're a start," Nan had said perfectly seriously.

It had made Eve shiver to think that someone could be so determined and so cool.

Also so graceful in defeat. When Eve had said that Nan would *never* visit Westlands through her introduction, Nan shrugged.

"Someone else, somewhere else then," she had said, with her easy smile.

Heather had her coat and beret on when Eve arrived at the school. She was received by the headmistress, a woman with hair cut so short, it might have been shaved at the back of her head. How could she have thought this looked attractive, Eve wondered. It was such an old style, so like pictures in school stories of the way schoolmistresses looked in the twenties and thirties.

"Miss Malone. How good of you to arrive so promptly. Heather has been ready since she got up, I do believe."

"Good. Well, we said two o'clock." Eve looked around the parlor. It was so strange to be in a school without pictures of saints everywhere on the walls. No statues, no little Sacred Heart lamps. It didn't feel like a school at all.

"And Heather must return for supper at six, so we like the girls to be back at five forty-five."

"Of course." Eve's heart sank. How could she entertain this child for nearly four hours.

"As you suggested, we telephoned Mr. Simon Westward, but he wasn't at home. We spoke to Mrs. Walsh, the housekeeper, who confirmed that you are indeed a cousin."

"I just wanted to make sure that they agreed. I haven't been in close contact with the family for a long time."

"I see," said the headmistress, who saw only too well. A slightly shabby girl with the surname Malone, that was *indeed* likely to be a relation not in close contact. Still, the housekeeper had said it was all in order.

"Enjoy yourself, Heather, and don't be too much trouble for Miss Malone."

"Yes, Miss Martin. No, Miss Martin," Heather said.

Together they walked down the avenue.

There were no words and yet the silence didn't seem uncompanionable.

Eve said, "I don't know what you'd like to do. What do you normally do when you go out?"

"I've never been out," Heather said simply.

"So what do you think you'd like to do?"

"I don't mind. Honestly. Anything. Just to be out, to be away from it all is smashing."

She looked back at the school as an escaped prisoner might.

"Is it awful?"

"It's lonely."

"Where would you rather be?"

"At home. At home in Knockglen."

"Isn't that lonely too?"

"No, it's lovely. There's my pony Malcolm and my dog, Clara, and Mrs. Walsh and Bee and of course Grandfather."

She sounded enthusiastic when she talked about them all. That big empty house was home. The school full of chattering children her own age and class was prison.

"Would you like an ice cream in a glass?" Eve said suddenly.

"I'd love it. At the end of the afternoon if that would be all right. We have it to look forward to . . . as the crown of the day."

Eve smiled a big wide smile. "Right, the crown of the day it will be. In the meantime we'll have a good walk down to the sea to get up an appetite."

"Can we go near it and feel the spray?"

"Yes, that's the best bit."

Their legs were tired when they reached the Roman Cafe.

"They always stop us from going near the spray when we're out on school walks," Heather said.

"I'll have to tidy you up a bit so that they'll not discover."

"Are you going to have a Knickerbocker Glory?" Heather asked, studying the menu.

"No, I think I'll just have a coffee."

"Is Knickerbocker Glory too dear?" Heather asked.

Eve took the menu. "It's on the dear side, but it is the crown of the day so that's all right."

"You're not just having coffee because of the cost?" Heather was anxious.

"No, truly. I want a cigarette. It goes better with coffee than ice cream."

They sat contentedly. Heather chatted about the games at school, lacrosse and hockey.

"Which did you play?" she asked Eve.

"Neither. We played camogie."

"What's that?"

"Well might you ask! It's a sort of gaelicized version of hockey in a way, or a feminine version of hurley."

Heather digested this with some interest.

"Why didn't we know you before, Simon and I?" she asked.

"I'm sure you must have asked Simon that, the day I came to your house."

"I did," Heather said, truthfully. "But he said it was a long story."

"He's right."

"But it's not a mystery or a crime or anything is it?"

"No," Eve said thoughtfully. "No. It's not either of those things. My mother was called Sarah Westward, and I think she may have been wild or a bit odd or something, but whatever caused it she fell in love with a man called Jack Malone. He was the gardener in the convent, and they were mad about each other."

"Why was that odd?"

"Because she was a Westward and he was a gardener. And anyway they got married, and I was born. And when I was being born my mother died. My father carried me down from the cottage to the convent. The nuns went rushing up to the cottage, but it was too late. They sent for Dr. Johnson and there was a terrible commotion."

"And what happened then?"

"Well, apparently there was some kind of row and a lot of shouting at my mother's funeral."

"Who shouted?"

"My father, I believe."

"What did he shout?"

"Oh, a lot of old rameis . . . rubbishy stuff about some of the Westwards dying in their beds . . . because they hadn't behaved better to Sarah."

"And where was the funeral?"

"In the Protestant church. Your church. She's buried in your family grave. Under the name Westward, not Malone."

"And what happened to the cottage?"

"It's still there. It's mine I suppose. I never use it though."

"Oh, I know I wouldn't either."

"And was Sarah my aunt?" Heather asked.

"Yes . . . your father was her older brother . . . there were five in the family I believe."

"And they're all dead now," Heather said factually. "Whatever your father was shouting at that funeral seems to have worked."

"What happened to your parents?"

"They were killed in India, in a car accident. I don't remember them. Simon does of course, because he's so old."

"How old is he?"

"He's nearly thirty. I wonder. Did he know all about the shouting and everything at the funeral? I suppose he was there."

"He might have been. He'd have been about eleven."

"I'm sure he was." Heather was scraping the bottom of her glass.

"I wouldn't necessarily . . ." Eve began.

Heather looked up and their eyes met. "Oh, I wouldn't tell him all about our conversation," she said. And changing to something that interested her much more, she leaned across the table eagerly. "Tell me, is it true that nuns put on shrouds and sleep in their coffins at night like vampires?"

Eddie and Annabel Hogan were pleased that their daughter had been asked to the dance.

"It's nice that it will be just a group of friends going to it, isn't it?" Annabel sought reassurance. "It's not as if she had a special boy yet that she was keen on or anything."

"In my day the men took the women to dances, paid for them and went to their houses to pick them up," Eddie complained.

"Yes, yes, yes, but who's going to come the whole way down to Knockglen to the door and pick Benny up and then deliver her back again. Don't go saying that now, and making trouble where there isn't any."

"And you're happy enough to let her stay in this boarding-house in Dun Laoghaire?" Eddie looked at his wife anxiously.

"It's not a boardinghouse. There you go again, getting it all wrong. You remember the woman who was down staying with Mother Francis in St. Mary's, whose son was killed. That's where Benny will stay. They'll put another bed in Eve's room."

"Well, as long as you're happy." He patted her on the hand.

Shep sat between them at the fire, and looked up from one to the other as if pleased to see this touching.

Benny was out at the pictures with Sean Walsh.

"I'm happy enough about her going to the dance and staying with Eve, of course I am. I want her to have a great night, some-thing she'll always remember."

"What are you not happy about then?"

"I don't know what's going to happen to her. Afterward."

"You said she'd go back to this house that isn't a real board-inghouse." Eddie was bewildered.

"Not after the dance. After . . . . after everything."

"None of us knows what will happen in the future."

"Maybe we're wrong sending her up there. Maybe she should

have done a bookkeeping course and gone into the shop with you. Forget all these notions of getting a degree."

Annabel was chewing her lip now.

"Haven't we been talking about this since she was born?"

"I know."

They sat in silence for a while. The wind whistled around Lisbeg, and even Shep moved closer to the grate. They told each other they were glad to be indoors on a night like this, in and settled, not out in Knockglen where people were still sorting out their lives. Sean and Benny would be leaving the cinema shortly and going for a cup of coffee at Mario's. Patsy was up with Mrs. Rooney being inspected as a suitable candidate for Mossy. Peggy Pine's niece Clodagh was going through the order books with her aunt. People said that it was a fallacy nowadays that the young didn't work. In fact, some young people couldn't stop working. Look at Clodagh, and Fonsie and Sean Walsh. Between them they would change the face of Knockglen in the next ten years.

"I hope they'll change it into a place we'll like to live in," Eddie said doubtfully.

"Yes, but we won't have all that much longer to live in it. It's Benny we should be thinking about."

They nodded. It was nearly always Benny that they were thinking about anyway, and what the future had in store. They had lived their whole adult lives in a thirty-mile radius of this place. A huge city like Dublin on their doorstep had never affected them.

They simply couldn't envisage a life for their daughter that didn't revolve around Knockglen, and the main street business of Hogan's Gentleman's Outfitters. And, though they hardly dared speak of the matter to each other, they thought too that it might best revolve around Sean Walsh.

Benny looked across the table in Mario's at Sean Walsh. In the very bright light his face looked thin and pale as always, but she could see the dark circles under his eyes.

"Is it hard work in the shop?" she asked him.

"Not hard, exactly, not in terms of physical work . . . or hours . . . just trying to know what's best really."

"How do you mean?"

For the first time ever, Benny was finding it easy to talk to Sean. And it was all thanks to Nan Mahon. Nan, who knew what to do in every situation.

Nan said that Benny should always be perfectly pleasant to Sean. There was nothing to be gained by scoring points off him. She should let him know in a variety of ways that there was no question of ever sharing any kind of life or plans with him, but that he was highly thought of as her father's employee. That way he couldn't fault her, and it would also keep her parents happy.

"I'm sure I'll do it wrong," Benny had said. "You know me. I'll think I'm being pleasant and distant, and I'll end up walking up to Father Ross arranging for the banns to be read out."

But Nan had said it was easy. "Ask him all about himself, sound interested but don't get involved. Tell him things about yourself that you'd like him to know and never answer any question directly, that's the secret."

So far it seemed to be working quite well. Sean sat there in Mario's and, raising his voice to compete with Guy Mitchell on the new record player, he told a tale of how the clothing industry was changing and how men were going to Dublin and buying ready-made suits off the peg, and how the bus from Knockglen stopped so near McBirney's on the quays in Dublin it was as bad as if McBirney's had opened a branch next to Mr. Flood's.

Sean said that it was sometimes hard to convince Mr. Hogan of the need for change. And perhaps not his place to do so.

Benny listened sympathetically with her face and about a quarter of her mind. The rest of her thoughts were on the dance and what she should wear. She was back on her diet again, drinking bitter black coffee instead of the frothy, sugary cups that everyone else in the cafe was having. She moved the chocolate biscuits on the plate around, making patterns of them with the yellow ones underneath and the green ones on top. She willed her hands not to rip one open and stuff it into her mouth.

There were no dresses big enough for her, in any of the shops in Dublin. Well, there *were*, but not the kinds of shops she'd go to. Only places that catered for rich older women. Dresses with black jet beading on them, or dove gray with crossover fronts. Suitable for someone in their sixties at a state banquet. Not for Benny's first dance.

Still, there was plenty of time, and there were dressmakers, and there were friends to help. Nan could probably come up with a solution for this as well as everything else. Benny had asked Nan if she could stay the night in her house after the dance.

Nan hadn't said yes or no. She asked why Benny didn't stay with Eve.

"I don't know. It *is* the place she's working, after all."

"Nonsense. It's her home. You two are old friends, you'd enjoy staying there."

Perhaps this is what Nan meant by not answering any question directly. Certainly Benny hadn't felt even slightly offended. It would be wonderful to know how to deal with people like Nan did.

Sean was still droning on about the need to have a sale. And the dangers of having a sale. Mr. Hogan felt that if a place like Hogan's had a sale it might look to customers as if they were getting rid of shoddy goods. Also what would people who had paid the full price for similar items a few weeks previously think if they saw them reduced now?

Sean saw the reason in this, but he also wondered how you could attract local people to buy their socks and shoes in Hogan's instead of going up to O'Connell Street in Dublin on a day trip and coming home sliding past the door trying to hide the name Clerys on the package?

Benny looked at him and wondered who would marry him and listen to this for the rest of her life. She hoped that this new policy of being polite but uninvolved would work.

"What about next week?" Sean said as he walked her down the town and round the bend of the road to Lisbeg.

"What about it, Sean?" she asked courteously.

"*Jamaica Inn,*" he said triumphantly, having read the posters.

The old Benny would have made a joke and said that Jamaica was a bit far to go on an outing. The new Benny smiled at him.

"Oh, Charles Laughton, isn't it, and Maureen O'Hara?"

"Yes," Sean said, a trifle impatiently. "You haven't seen it, I don't remember it being here before."

Never answer a question directly. "I loved the book. But I think I preferred *Rebecca*. Did you read *Rebecca?*"

"No, I don't do much reading. The light's not very good up there."

"You should have a lamp," Benny said eagerly. "I'm sure there's one in the spare room we never use. I'll mention it to Father."

She beamed such enthusiasm for this helpful idea, and put out her hand so firmly to shake his, that he couldn't press her for a yes or a no about the pictures next week. Nor could he press his cold, thin lips on hers with any dignity at all.

Mother Francis moved around the small cottage. She had been very heartened by Kit Hegarty's report on the meeting between Eve and Heather. Perhaps the way to a reconciliation was opening up after all. The agreement to pay the fees had done nothing to soften Eve's heart to the cold distant family who had treated her mother, her father and herself so shabbily.

In some ways it had almost strengthened her resolve not to give in to them in any way.

If only Mother Francis could get her to stay a night in this cottage, to sleep here, to feel the place was her own. If Eve Malone were to wake in this place and look out over the quarry she might feel she belonged somewhere rather than perching here and there which was what she felt now. Mother Francis had high hopes that she might be able to install Eve by Christmas. But it was work of high sensitivity.

It would be no use pretending that she needed Eve's room in the convent. That would be the worst thing to do. The girl would feel she had been evicted from the only home she knew. Perhaps Mother Francis could say that the older members of the community would like a little outing and that since they couldn't leave the convent grounds perhaps Eve might arrange a tea party for them in her cottage. But Eve would see through that at once.

When Mother Francis and Peggy Pine were young together, Peggy used to say, "It will all come clear in the end."

Mainly it had. This cottage was an area where it had taken a long time for things to come clear.

She was always careful to lock the door with the big key, and put it under the third stone in the little wall near the iron gate. There was a big padlock that Mossy had suggested she put on the gate as well, but it looked ugly and forbidding. Mother Francis decided to risk doing without it.

Nobody came up this way unless they had business here. Either you came through the briar- and bramble-covered paths of the convent or else a steep, unmade track up from the town. If anyone wanted a view of the big stone escarpments they chose a much better and broader way which went up at a gradual incline from the square where the bus turned every day.

To her shock, when she turned around she saw a figure standing only a few feet away.

It was Simon Westward. He had his back to her and was looking out over the dark, misty view. She rattled the gate so that he would hear her and not be startled.

"Oh . . . um, good afternoon," he said.

"Good afternoon, Mr. Westward."

In religious life a part of the day was known as The Great Silence. It meant that nuns did not feel uneasy when there was no conversation. Mother Francis waited easily for the small dark man to speak again.

"Rotten weather," he said.

"Never very good, November." She could have been at a garden party instead of on top of a quarry in the mist and rain with a man she had crossed swords with several times.

"Mrs. Walsh said you come up here a lot," he said. "I told her I didn't feel I'd be quite in place in the convent. I wondered where I might run into you casually, as it were."

"You'd be very welcome in the convent, Mr. Westward, you always would have been."

"I know. Yes, I know."

"But anyway you've found me now."

It would have been more sensible for them to go back into the cottage, but there was no way that she would take him over Eve's doorstep. It would have been the final betrayal. He looked at the house expectantly. She said nothing.

"It's about Eve," he said eventually.

"Oh yes."

"It's just that she very kindly went and took my sister out from school. I'm afraid Heather very probably asked her to do so, in fact I know she did. But anyway Eve took her on a nice day out and is going to again . . ."

"Yes." Mother Francis had cold eyes and a heavy heart. Was he going to ask Eve to stay clear of the family? If so, she would have a heart as hard as Eve's.

"I was wondering if you could tell her . . ."

The nun's gaze didn't waver.

"If you could tell her how grateful I am. I mean truly."

"Why don't you tell her yourself?" Mother Francis felt the words come out of her mouth in a quick breath of relief.

"Well, I would, of course. But I don't know where she lives."

"Let me write it down for you." She began to seek deep in the pockets of her long black skirt.

"Let me. Farmers always have backs of envelopes to scribble things on."

She smiled at him. "No, let *me*. Nuns always have little note-books and silver-topped pencils."

She produced both from the depths of her pockets and wrote with a shaking hand what she thought might be the outline plans for an olive branch.

Clodagh Pine came into Hogan's shop.

"How are you, Mr. Hogan? Do you have a loan of a couple of hat stands?"

"Of course, of course." Eddie Hogan went fussing off to the back of the shop to look for them.

"Opening a millinery section are we?" Sean Walsh said to her in a lofty tone.

"Watch your tone with me, Sean. You don't know what you're dealing with here," she said, with a loud laugh.

Sean looked at her without pleasure. She was pretty, certainly, in a flashy sort of way. But she had her long legs exposed for all to view, in a ridiculously short skirt. She wore a lime green dress with a black jacket over it, a pink scarf, and her earrings, which were long and dangly, were precisely the same green as her dress, and her very obviously tinted blond hair was held up with two black combs.

"No, I probably don't."

"Well, you will," she said.

There were just the two of them standing in the shop. Old Mike was at his tailoring and Mr. Hogan was out of earshot.

"I'll hardly miss you, that's for sure."

"You'd be wise not to." She deliberately misunderstood him. "We can be rivals or friends. It's probably more sensible to be friends."

"I'd say everyone's your friend, Clodagh." He laughed a scorn-ful little laugh.

"You'd be wrong there. A lot of people aren't my friends at all. However my aunt is. I'm doing a major reorganization of her window. Every notice saying 'A Fashion Snip' has already been burned. Wait till you see the new display."

"On Monday, is it?" He was still superior.

"No, genius. This afternoon, early closing day, the only day anyone really looks in your window. And tomorrow we'll let it rip."

"I should congratulate you."

"Yes, you should. It's harder for me coming in than it is for you. I haven't any plans to marry my aunt."

Sean looked nervously at the back storeroom where Eddie Hogan had found some hat stands and was returning with them triumphantly.

"I'm sure your new windows will be a great success," he said hastily.

"Yes, they'll be fabulous," she said. She gave the surprised Eddie Hogan a kiss on the forehead, and was gone in a flash of color, like a bird of paradise.

"I'm not spending hard-earned money on a dress," Eve said with a ferocious scowl when Nan started talking about what they would wear.

She expected Nan to tell her that you are how you look, and that you must expect people to take you or leave you on the way you present yourself. It was one of Nan's theories.

"You're right," Nan said unexpectedly. "Whatever you buy it shouldn't be an evening dress."

"So?" Eve was wrong-footed now. She had expected an argument.

"So what will you do?" Nan asked.

"Kit said I can look through her things, just in case. She's taller than I am, but then so's everyone. I could take the hem up, if I found something."

"Or you could have my red wool skirt," Nan said.

"I don't think so . . ." Eve began, the prickles beginning to show.

"Well, nobody's seen it in college. Red looks great on you. You could get a fancy blouse or maybe Mrs. Hegarty has one. Why not?"

"I know it sounds ungrateful, but I suppose it's because I don't want to wear your castoffs," Eve said straight out.

"But you wouldn't mind wearing Mrs. Hegarty's, is that it?" Nan was quick as a flash.

"She offers them because . . . because she knows I wouldn't mind taking them."

"And what about me? Haven't I got the same motive?"

"I don't know, to be honest." Eve fiddled with her coffee spoon.

Nan didn't plead with her, and she didn't shrug. Very simply she said, "It's there, it's nice, it would look well on you."

"Why are you lending it to me, I mean what's in your mind?" Eve knew she sounded like a five-year-old but she wanted to know.

"Because we're a group of friends going to this dance. I want us to look knockout. I want us to wipe the eyes of people like that stupid Rosemary and that dull Sheila. That's why!"

"I'd love it," Eve said, with a grin.

"Mother, would it be awful if I was to ask you for a loan of money, like to get some material for a dress?"

"We'll buy you a dress Benny. Your first big dance. Every girl should have a new dress from a shop."

"There isn't one to fit me in the shops."

"Don't be full of misery like that. I'm sure there is. You haven't looked."

"I'm not even remotely full of miseries. People don't come in my size until they're old. I don't mind now that I *know*. I used to think people were born with big bones and large frames, but apparently these grow when you're about sixty-eight. You'd better watch it, Mother, it could happen to you."

"And where did you develop this nonsensical theory may I ask?"

"After slogging round every shop in Dublin. Lunchtimes, Mother, I didn't miss my lectures!"

She looked not remotely put out about it, Annabel was relieved to see. Or perhaps she was inside. With Benny it was hard to tell.

There was nothing to be gained by probing. Benny's mother decided to be practical.

"What material had you in mind?"

"I don't know. Something rich . . . I don't know if this is ridiculous, but I saw something in a magazine. She was a biggish woman and it was like tapestry . . ."

Benny's smile was broad, but not totally sure.

"Tapestry?" Her mother sounded doubtful.

"Maybe not. It might make me look like a couch or an armchair."

Annabel wanted to take her daughter in her arms, but she knew she must do nothing of the sort.

"Do you mean brocade?" she asked.

"The very thing."

"I have a lovely brocade skirt."

"It wouldn't fit me, Mother."

"We could get a bit of black velvet let into it, maybe, as panels, and then a top of black velvet and some of the brocade to trim it. What do you think?"

"We couldn't cut up your good skirt."

"When will I ever wear it again. I'd love you to be the belle of the ball."

"Are you sure?"

"Of *course* I am. And it's better than anything you'd buy in the shops."

It was. Benny knew that. Her heart sank though at the thought of what her mother might envisage as a design.

A sudden picture of her tenth birthday flashed before Benny.

The day she thought she was going to get a party dress and had been given that sensible navy blue outfit. The pain of it was as real now as then. But there seemed few alternatives.

"Who'd make it, do you think?"

"Peggy's niece is a great hand with the needle we hear."

Benny brightened. Clodagh Pine looked anything but frump-ish. The project might not be doomed after all.

Dear Eve,

Just a very brief note to thank you most sincerely for your visit to my sister at her boarding school. Heather has written glowingly of your kindness. I wanted to express my appreciation, but to tell you not to feel in any way obligated to this in consideration of any assistance with fees that this family may have given you. I need hardly add that you are very welcome to call at Westlands during the Christmas vacation should you wish to do so.

Yours in gratitude,
Simon Westward.

Dear Simon,

I visit Heather because I want to and she wants me to. It has nothing to do with considerations as you call them. During the Christmas vacation I shall be in residence at St. Mary's Convent, Knockglen. You are very welcome to call there, should you wish to do so.

Yours in explanation,
Eve Malone.

Dear Mr. and Mrs. Hogan,

As Benny may have told you, a group of us are going to the end of term Dress Dance next Friday week. My parents are having a small sherry party in our house in Donnybrook, where we will all gather before setting off for the dance. They asked me to suggest to some of the parents that they might like to drop in for the drinks party should they be in the area. I realize it is rather far away, but just in case there was a chance, I thought I would mention it.

Thank you again for that wonderful afternoon at your home weeks ago during my visit to Knockglen.

Kind regards,
Jack Foley.

Dear Fonsie,

I'm going to have to ask you very firmly to cease writing these notes to me. My aunt thinks there is only one Miss Pine in the world and that she is it. She has read aloud to me your letters about being groovy, and inviting me to where the action is. She has begun to ask me what "turning someone on" is about, and why do people say "It's been real."

I have a healthy respect for my aunt. I have come here to help her modernize her shop and improve her business. I do not intend to spend every morning listening to her reading See you later Alligator at me.

I am perfectly happy to meet you and talk to you, but the correspondence must now cease.

Cordially,
Clodagh.

Dear Mother Francis,

I intend to spend Christmas at St. Mary's in Knockglen for a variety of reasons. I hope this will not unduly disturb the community. I shall be in touch later with full details.

Your Sister in Christ,
Mother Clare.

Lilly Foley was pleased about the party. John would enjoy it. He would like seeing their big house filled with lights and flowers and the rustle of evening dresses, beautiful girls.

Her husband would enjoy playing host to a roomful of hand-some young people. It would make him feel their age.

She was determined it would be just right, and that she herself would look her very best. There was no way he could be allowed to look across at her and think she was drab and gray compared to all the glitter around them.

She would think of her own outfit later. In the meantime she must plan it properly. She could not let Jack know how welcome the excuse was. She would let him and his father know what a wonderful wife and mother she was to cope with his demands.

"Will they want sausages and savories, do you think?" Lilly Foley asked.

"They'll want whatever we give them." Jack had no interest in the details.

"Who'll serve it? Doreen will need help."

Jack looked round the table. "Aengus," he said.

"Can I wear a napkin on my arms?" Aengus asked.

"You'd probably better wear one on your bottom as well," Ronan said.

His mother frowned.

"It's for *your* friends, Jack. I wish you'd pay some attention."

"And for yours and Dad's. Look, aren't the pair of you delighted, you've got those new curtains you've been talking about and you had the gate painted."

"It'd be like you to tell everyone that."

"Of course I won't. I keep telling you that I think it's great all your friends are coming round."

"And all yours!"

"Mine will only be here for an hour or two. Yours will stay all night and disgrace themselves. I'm as well off not to be a witness to it."

"And what about the oldies, as you call them? The parents of your friends."

"I asked Aidan Lynch's parents. You know them already."

"I do." Mrs Foley raised her eyes to heaven.

"And Benny Hogan's parents, the people from Knockglen. But they can't come. They wrote to you remember? It's only going to be people like Uncle Kevin and the neighbors, and all your own crowd. You'll hardly notice my few."

"I wish I knew why you've inflicted this on us," his mother asked.

"Because I couldn't decide which girl to ask, so I asked them all." Jack beamed at her in total honesty.

The weekend before the dance, Eve came home to Knockglen.

"I've left it far too long," she confessed to Benny on the bus on the Friday evening. "But it really was that I didn't want to run out on Kit. Do you think Mother Francis knows that?"

"Tell her," Benny said.

"I will. She said she had a favor to ask of me. What do you think it could be?"

"Let's guess. Help her set up a poteen still in the kitchen garden?"

"I'd be good at that. Or maybe, based on my huge experience beating off the advances of Aidan Lynch, she wants me to give Sixth Year a course of lessons in sex education."

"Or take the older nuns to Belfast on a day excursion to see a banned film."

"Or bring Sean Walsh into the art room and drape a duster over his vital parts and have him for a life class."

They laughed so much that Mike the driver said they put him off concentrating.

"The pair of you remind me of those cartoons of Mutt and Jeff, do you know the ones I mean?" Mikey shouted at them.

They did. Mutt was the big one, Jeff was the tiny one. Mikey was always pretty subtle.

"I can't turn her away," Mother Francis pleaded with Eve in the kitchen.

"Yes you can, Mother, yes you bloody can."

"Eve! Please!"

"No, honestly, you can do anything. You've always been able to do anything you wanted. Always."

"I don't know where you got this idea."

"From living with you, from watching you. You can tell Mother Clare that it damn well won't suit the community to have her here just because her own lot above in Dublin want to be shot of her for Christmas."

"It's hardly a charitable thing to say, or do."

"Since when has that had anything to do with it?"

"Well, we must have raised you under some misapprehension here. Charity is meant to have quite a lot to do with the religious life, actually."

They both laughed at that.

"Mother, I couldn't be in the same house as her."

"You don't *have* to Eve. The rest of us do."

"What do you mean?"

"You have your own house, if you want to use it."

"Another of your ploys!"

"On my word of honor. If you think that I went to all the

trouble to arrange that Mother Clare came here just so that I could maneuver you into that cottage, then you really don't understand anything at all."

"It would be going a bit far, certainly," Eve agreed.

"Well, then."

"No."

"Why? Just one good reason."

"I won't take their charity. I won't live in their bloody grace and favor home like some old groom who broke his back looking after horses for the Squires and gets some kind of bothan and tugs his remaining bit of hair out in gratitude for the rest of his life."

"It's not like that."

"It *is* Mother, it is. She was thrown out, not good enough to walk through their doors, never let back in again. But they didn't want her to die on the side of the road so they gave her that cottage that no one wanted because it was miles from anywhere and in addition, horror of horrors, beside the Roman Catholic convent."

"They liked it, Eve. It was where they wanted to live."

"It's not where I want to live."

"Not even look at it? I go to so much trouble minding it for you, always hoping, I thought you'd be delighted."

Mother Francis looked tired, weary almost.

"I'm sorry."

"I was so sure you'd be so relieved to have a place to escape . . . but I suppose I got it wrong."

"I wouldn't mind having a look Mother. To please you. Nothing to do with them."

"Tomorrow morning, then. We'll go up, the pair of us."

"And my room here . . ."

"Will be your room here until the day you die."

"What do you think?" Benny looked anxiously at Clodagh.

"It's a gorgeous bit of stuff. A pity to cut it up."

"You've seen people going to these places. Will it look all right?"

"When I'm through with it and you it will be a sensation."

Benny looked doubtfully at Clodagh's own outfit, which was a white smock over a mauve polo-neck jumper and what looked like mauve tights. It was very far ahead for anywhere, let alone Knockglen.

"We'll cut the bodice well . . . well down like this."

Benny stood in her slip. Eve sat companionably on a radiator smoking and giving her comments.

Clodagh made a gesture with the black velvet top which implied a startlingly low neckline.

"Cut it where?" Benny screamed. Clodagh gestured again.

"That's what I thought you said. I'd fall into my dinner for God's sake."

"Presumably you'll be wearing some kind of undergarment to prevent this."

"I'll be wearing a bra made of surgical steel . . ."

"Yes, and we must push your bosom right up and in like this."

Clodagh made a grab at her and Benny gave a yell.

"I haven't had as much fun in years," Eve said.

"Tell her, Eve. Tell her my mother's paying for this. She won't let me out like the whore of Babylon."

"It's a dance isn't it?" asked Clodagh. "It's not a function to put forward the cause for your canonization or anything is it."

"Clodagh, you're off your head. I can't. Even if I had the courage."

"Right. We'll give you a modesty vest."

"A what?"

"We'll cut the thing the way it should be cut and mold you into it. Then I'll make a bit of pleated linen or something and a couple of fasteners and we can tell your mother that this is what you'll be wearing. You can take it out as soon as you are outside the city limits of Knockglen."

Clodagh fiddled and draped and pinned.

"Put your shoulders back, Benny," she ordered. "Stick your chest out."

"Jesus, Mary and Joseph, I look like the prow of a ship," said Benny in alarm.

"I know. Isn't it great."

"Fellows love the prows of ships," Eve said. "They're always saying it."

"Shut up, Eve Malone. I'll stick the scissors in you."

"You will not. Those are my expensive pinking shears. Now isn't that something." Clodagh looked pleased.

Even in its rough-and-ready state they could see what she had in mind for Benny. And it looked very good indeed.

"The Wise Woman wouldn't let her mother near the fittings for this dress," Eve said sagely.

"They'll be climbing all over you in this," Clodagh said happily as she began to unpin it.

"Wouldn't that be fantastic," Benny said, smiling delightedly at her reflection in the mirror.

TEN

❖

*I*t's great that you'll be working late tonight," Nan said to her mother. They poured another cup of coffee at the kitchen table. The dance was in the same hotel as Emily's shop. Nan planned to bring her friends in to introduce them and parade their finery.

"You don't have to you know, I can always peep out and see you going into the ballroom."

"But you know that I'd love to Em. I want you to meet them and them to meet you."

Between them, unspoken, lay the certainty that Nan would never bring them home to Maple Gardens.

"Only if it seems right at the time. There might be people there that you don't want to bring into a shop . . . you know."

Nan laid her hand on her mother's.

"No, I don't know, as it happens. What do you mean?"

"Well, we've had such hopes for you . . . you and I, that you'll get out of all this." Emily looked round the small, awkward house. "You mightn't want to be bringing grand people in on top of me in a shop." She smiled apologetically.

"It's a gorgeous shop. And you run it like a dream. I'd be proud to have them see you there," Nan said.

She didn't say that she was not relying on the Aidan Lynches, the Bill Dunnes or the Jack Foleys to take her out of Maple Gardens. She had set her sights much higher than that.

"I wish you'd come in tonight for the drinks bit," Eve said to Kit.

"No, I'd be no good at a thing like that, all falling over my words. I was never any good at social occasions."

"Aidan Lynch's parents are going to be there. You could talk about him!"

"God, Eve, leave me alone. I'd a million times prefer to be here. Ann Hayes and I are going to the pictures. That's much more our style than having cocktails with doctors in Ailesbury Road."

"It's not Ailesbury Road," Eve said defensively.

"It's not far off it." Her face softened. "To be asked is enough. Have you the bed made up for Benny?"

"I have. We won't make a noise and wake you."

"It's easy to wake me. I sleep very lightly. Maybe you'll tell me about it. That outfit is gorgeous on you. I never saw anything like it."

They had a dress rehearsal the night before, with evening bag borrowed from Mrs. Hayes next door, and the good white lacy blouse from Kit's wardrobe starched and pressed until it was like new. Now Kit's surprise gift was produced. Scarlet earrings exactly the same color as the skirt.

"No, no. You can't be buying me things," Eve stammered.

Something in Kit's face reminded Eve that Frank Hegarty might have been dressing up in a dinner jacket this night to go to the dance if things had been different.

"Thank you very, very much," she said.

"You really are very beautiful. Very striking."

"I think I look a bit like a bird," Eve said seriously. "A sort of crazed blackbird with its head on the side before it goes picking for things."

Kit pealed with laughter. "I mean it. I really do," she said.

"You *are* very attractive, mad as a brush of course, but with any luck people might not notice that."

Benny's outfit had been packed in a box in tissue paper. It had been much admired at home. There had been a dangerous moment when Patsy had giggled and said she hoped nobody would snatch Benny's modesty vest away. The Hogans looked at each other, alarmed.

"Why would a thing like that happen?"

Benny had glared at Patsy, who went back to the range in confusion.

"I'd love to see you all dressed up setting out tonight," Benny's mother said. "You and Eve and all your friends."

"Yes, well you could have come up of course to Dr. Foley's. You *were* invited."

Benny felt hypocritical. She would have hated them to have been there.

"Yes, it was very civil of them certainly," Eddie Hogan said. "Repaying the hospitality we gave to that boy."

Benny felt herself wince with embarrassment. How provincial and old-fashioned they were compared to people in Dublin. Then a wave of guilt came over her and she felt protective about them. Why *should* they have the same style and way of going on as people who went to cocktail parties.

"And you'll be home on the morning bus?" her mother said hopefully.

"Maybe the later one. It would be nice to get value out of the visit, and meet the girls for coffee . . . or lunch."

"But you'll ring?" her father asked.

"Of course I will." She was dying to be gone. "Tomorrow morning."

"You'll be fine, up in Dublin," her father said, sounding as doubtful as if she were going to the far side of the moon.

"Don't I go there every day, Father?"

"But not every night."

"Still I'm safe with Mrs. Hegarty, you know that." Oh, please let them let her go.

"And enjoy every minute of it," her mother said.

"I'd better go for the bus, Mother. I don't want to be rushing, not carrying this parcel."

They stood at the door of Lisbeg, Mother, Father, Patsy and Shep. If Shep had known he would have raised his paw to wave. He would have.

"Enjoy the dance, Benny," Dr. Johnson called to her.

Clodagh, already rearranging her now much-talked-of windows in Pine's shop, made marvelous gestures, miming Benny ripping off a modesty vest and exposing enormous amounts of bosom.

Fonsie watched this from across the street with interest.

"Fabulous bird, isn't she," he said.

"There's great talent here in Knockglen," Benny agreed.

"Keep on rocking," Fonsie encouraged her.

Outside Hogan's Sean Walsh was polishing the brasses.

"Tonight's the big night," he said with a slow smile.

Remember Nan's advice. It doesn't hurt to be nice. It often helps.

Benny smiled back. "That's it, Sean," she said.

"I was trying to persuade your father to let me drive them up to that reception he was invited to."

"It wasn't a reception. It was more a few drinks in Dr. Foley's house."

"The very thing. He showed me the letter inviting them. I said it would be a matter of nothing for me to drive them."

"But they refused." She knew her voice was high-pitched now.

"Ah, sure what would that be except to lift the phone and say they were able to come after all? I told them they owed it to themselves to go out once in a while."

"Did you?"

"Yes. And I said when better than on the night of Benny's big dance?"

"What a pity they weren't able to take you up on it."

"The day's young yet," Sean Walsh said, and went back into the shop.

He was only saying it to annoy her. He must have known how much she would hate her parents to be at something like this. She felt slightly faint and leaned against the wall of Birdie Mac's.

Birdie knocked on the window, mouthing at her.

God, Benny thought, this is all I need. She's going to give me some broken chocolate or something now to build me up.

"Hallo, Miss Mac." She tried to make her voice steady. She must try to be sane. Her parents had just said good-bye to her. They had no intention of coming to Dublin. There would have been preparations for a week.

Birdie was at the door. "Benny, I just had a phone call from your mother. She wants me to give her a home perm this morning. I forgot to ask her, does she have a hair dryer at home?"

Birdie Mac looked at Benny anxiously.

"Are you all right child? You're very pale."

"A home perm you say."

"Yes. It's easy for me, I can run down now and wind it on, and then come back later and do the neutralizing. It's the dryer I was wondering about . . ."

"There is a dryer." Benny spoke like a robot.

She moved up to the square without realizing it. She was startled by the hooting of the bus.

"Well, Benny, are you going to get on? Do you need a special invitation?"

"Sorry, Mikey. Are you leaving? I didn't notice."

"No, not at all. We've all day, and all night. Leisure is the keynote in our bus service, never hurry a passenger, that's our motto."

She sat down and looked unseeingly out.

They couldn't have decided to come up to Dublin. Not to the Foleys'. Not tonight.

Rosemary wasn't at her history lecture.

"She's gone to the hairdresser," said Deirdre, a busy, fussy girl who knew everything. "Apparently she's going to the big dance tonight in a party. They're all going to drinks in Jack Foley's house first. Imagine. In his house."

"I know," Benny said absently. "I'm going too."

"You're what?"

"Yes." Benny looked up at the girl's highly unflattering surprise.

"Well, well, well," Deirdre said.

"Nobody's taking anyone. We're all paying for ourselves." She was determined to bring Rosemary down, in some respects anyway.

"Yes, but to be included. Heavens." Deirdre looked Benny up and down.

"I'm looking forward to it." Benny knew she had a grim, despairing look on her face.

In addition to all her anxieties she now feared that her parents would be there, fumbling and apologizing and mainly horrified by the amount of bosom she would be revealing. It was not beyond the possible that they might actually order her out of the room to cover herself. The thought made Benny go hot and cold.

"I suppose it's being friendly with that Nan Mahon that does it," Deirdre said eventually.

"Does what?"

"Gets you invited to lots of places. It's a great thing to have a friend like that."

Deirdre had shrewd, piggy eyes.

Benny looked at her for a moment or two with dislike.

"Yes. I usually choose my friends for that reason," she said.

Too late she remembered how Mother Francis had warned them to beware of sarcasm.

"It's a way to go, certainly," Deirdre said, nodding her head sagely.

✦

The day seemed very long. She met Eve and they went out to Dun Laoghaire on the five o'clock train. There were a lot of office workers going home. And at some of the stations school children in uniform got on. Eve and Benny nudged each other in pleasure to be part of a different world. A world of going to a big Dress Dance, as part of a big, glittering circle.

Kit had sandwiches for them.

"I'm too excited," Eve protested.

"I've been on a diet. I'd better not fall at the last fence," Benny explained.

Kit was adamant. She wasn't going to have them fainting at the dance, and anyway the food had to be digested and turned into fat, and there wouldn't be time for that to happen. There was no fear that Benny would burst through her outfit. Kit had declared the bathroom a no-go area for her lodgers, though she said that was not strictly necessary. Most of them didn't see the need to spend hours in it.

The coffee and sandwiches were on a tray in their room. Kit seemed to understand their need to giggle and reassure each other.

The meal that night was her responsibility she said. Eve wasn't to think of either preparing it or serving it.

They zipped and hooked each other. They held the light at a better angle for the application of eyeliner and eye shadow. They advised on the amount of lipstick blotting, and they dusted a lot of powder over Benny's bosom, which was whiter than her neck and arms.

"Probably everyone's is. It's just we don't get a chance to see them."

Benny's hand flew to her cleavage.

"Don't *do* that. Remember Clodagh says it looks as if you're drawing attention to it."

"It's easy to say that. Specially wearing a smock like she does."

"Come on, now. Didn't she make you look marvelous."

"Did she, Eve? Or did she and I make me look a fool?" Benny looked so troubled and upset, Eve was startled.

"Come on. We're all a bit nervous. I think I look like a horrible bird of prey, but when I try to be objective I think that's probably not so."

"Of course it's not so. You look terrific. You must *know* that. Look at yourself in the mirror for heaven's sake. You're so petite, and colorful." Benny's words were stumbling over each other in their eagerness to convince her small worried friend.

"And so must *you* know you look great. What's wrong? What don't you like?"

"My chest."

"Not again!"

"I'm afraid of what people will think."

"They'll think it's terrific . . ."

"No, not fellows. Ordinary people."

"What kind of ordinary people?"

"Whoever's there first. You know, at the drinks bit. They might think I'm fast."

"Don't be stupid."

Kit called up the stairs.

"Can I come and see you? Mr. Hayes will be here to drive you in, in about ten minutes."

"Come on up and talk sense into my friend."

Kit came in and sat on the bed. She was full of praise.

"Benny's worried about her cleavage," Eve explained.

"She shouldn't be. Let the other girls worry about it, and envy it." Kit said it as one who knew there was no argument.

"But . . ."

"It's not Knockglen. Your parents aren't going to be here." Eve stopped suddenly. "What's wrong?"

"Nothing." Benny's eyes were too bright.

Eve and Kit exchanged glances.

"Mrs. Hegarty, could I use your phone do you think?"

"Certainly," Kit said. "It's a coin-operated one, I'm afraid."

Benny snatched up her handbag and ran downstairs.

They looked at each other in bewilderment.

"What's that about?"

"I've no idea," Eve said. "Something to do with Knockglen. She's ringing home. You can bet on it."

"Hallo, Patsy. It's Benny."

"Oh, are you at the dance yet?"

"Just setting out. Is Mother there, or Father?"

"No, Benny. They're out."

"They're what?"

"They're out. They went out about six o'clock."

"Where did they go?"

"They didn't tell me," Patsy said.

"Patsy, they must have. They always say where they're going."

"Well, they didn't. What did you want them for?"

"Listen, were they dressed up?"

"What do you mean?"

"What were they wearing, Patsy? *Please.*"

"God, Benny I never notice what people are wearing. They had their outdoor clothes on." Patsy was doing her best.

"Are they in Dublin do you think?"

"Surely not. Surely they'd have said?"

"Did Sean Walsh collect them?"

"I don't know. I was out in the scullery."

"You must have noticed something." Benny's voice was very impatient. Patsy got into a huff.

"I'd have noticed plenty had I been told there was going to be a Garda inquiry on the phone," she said, offended.

"I'm sorry."

"It's all right," said Patsy, but it wasn't.

"I'll see you tomorrow and tell you all about it."

"Oh, very nice."

"And if they do come back . . ."

"Well, Mother of God, Benny, I hope they will come back."

"If they do come back, just say I rang to thank them for everything, and the lovely dress and all."

"Sure Benny. I'll say you rang all sweetness and light."

Benny stood in the hall for a few moments to catch her breath.

She would not burden Eve with the whole thing. She would put her shoulders back and her chest forward. She would go to this party. If her parents turned up she would tell them she had lost the modesty vest. That it had blown away when she took it out of the parcel. She would be fun and make jokes and be jolly.

Even if her parents said mortifying things to people like Rosemary, if they made crass remarks about hospitality being repaid, she would hold her head up high.

Nobody would know that in these hoops of steel which were meant to be called an uplift brassiere there was a heart of lead surrounded by a lot of wavy, nervous, fluttery feelings.

The doorbell rang and she answered it. A man in a hat and overcoat stood there.

"I'm Johnny Hayes, to drive two ladies into Donnybrook," he said and, looking at the expanse of bosom approvingly, he added, "though it wouldn't take much to make me drag a grand armful like yourself into the car and head off for the Dublin mountains."

Now that it had started Lilly Foley was beginning to enjoy herself. Jack had been right. It was indeed well time they gave a party, and this was an ideal occasion. Their neighbors could admire the young people heading off to the dance. The house could be filled with young men in dinner jackets and girls in long, sweeping dresses without it looking pretentious. That was the style these big houses were meant for, Lilly Foley told herself. But she didn't tell her husband or sons. They had a habit of sending her up over what they called her notions. If Lilly Foley liked to see cars draw up in their tree-lined road and hear the sound of long dresses swishing up the steps to the hall door, then she kept that little pleasure to herself.

An early arrival was Sheila, one of Jack's fellow students. To Lilly Foley she had been a fairly constant voice on the telephone, wanting to go over some notes with Jack. Now here in the house she was an attractive girl, in a yellow and black dress, overeager to impress Lilly thought, busy explaining that she had an uncle a judge and a cousin a Senior Counsel so that she was practically born to be a barrister. Soon, a young couple, Sean and Carmel, arrived, who talked animatedly to each other and no one else. Lilly was pleased to see Bill Dunne . . . a personable and easygoing young man. He made a nice antidote to that Aidan Lynch, whose antics she had never understood and whose parents both had voices like foghorns.

She looked proudly at Jack, who was extraordinarily handsome in his rented dinner jacket, welcoming people in and laughing his easy laugh. He had an arm around first this girl and then another. You'd need to be a better detective than Lilly Foley considered herself to know which of them he liked most. The very pretty but rather over made-up girl, Rosemary, had allowed her glance to fall only briefly on Lilly before turning the full-voltage charm on Dr. Foley.

Aengus was extremely solemn in his duty as waiter. He stood at the foot of the stairs with his glasses gleaming, his new spotted bow tie resplendent. He felt the center of attention, the figure that everyone would be aware of as they came in and left their coats in the dining room.

So far it had all been strangers. He was relieved to recognize Aidan Lynch, Jack's friend from school.

"Good evening," Aidan said to him formally. "Are you from a catering agency? I don't remember seeing you much on the social scene around Dublin."

"I'm Aengus," Aengus said, overjoyed not to have been recognized.

"You're very kind to let me use your first name. I'm Aidan

Lynch. My parents have gone ahead into the drawing room and I think are having their drink requirements met by Dr. Foley. Do I give you my order . . . er, Aengus, is it?"

"Aidan, I'm Aengus, Jack's brother." The smile of triumph was wide on his face.

"*Aengus.* So you are. I didn't realize!" Aidan said, smiting his forehead.

"You can have dry sherry, or sweet sherry or a beer or a Club Orange," Aengus said.

"My goodness." Aidan was lost in indecision.

"But only one at a time."

"Ah, that's disappointing. I was just about to ask for them all together in a glass with a dollop of whipped cream on top." He looked saddened.

"Seeing that you're a friend of Jack's I'll ask if you can . . ." Aengus was about to set out for the kitchen where the drink was.

"Come back, you fool. Listen, did a beautiful, small dark girl come in."

"Yes, she's in there. She's with some fellow. She keeps licking his ear and drinking out of his glass."

Aidan pushed past him into the drawing room. How could Eve be behaving like this. Maybe she too had mixed all her drinks. But she was nowhere to be seen. His eyes went round the big room with its warm lights, its huge Christmas tree in the window. He saw a lot of familiar faces, but no Eve.

He came back to Aengus.

"Where is she? Quick."

"Who?" Aengus was alarmed.

"The beautiful dark girl."

"The one licking the fellow's ear?"

"Yes, yes." Aidan was testy.

Aengus had come to the door. "There!" He pointed at Carmel and Sean, who were, as usual, standing very close to each other.

Relief flooded over Aidan.

Carmel and Sean saw him and waved.

"What was all the pointing about?" Carmel asked.

"You look utterly beautiful, Carmel," Aidan said. "Leave this man instantly. I'll give you a better life. You have disturbed my dreams so much . . . come and disturb my waking hours as well!"

Carmel smiled a wise, mature woman-of-the-world smile and patted Aidan's hand.

At the same moment, Aidan heard Eve's voice behind him.

"Well, hallo Aidan. Here you are tongue-tied and wordless as ever."

He turned and looked at her. She looked so good that he got a lump in his throat and for a few seconds he was literally unable to find words.

"You're gorgeous," he said. Very honestly and unaffectedly.

Nan had warned Eve not to say that the red skirt was on loan. If it was praised then thank for the praise, Nan had said. Why throw people's compliments back in their faces.

Eve had never spoken to Aidan in anything other than jokey terms. But his admiration had been unqualified.

"Thank you," she said simply.

Then it was as if the mist had cleared and they went back to their old way of going on.

"I'm glad you arrived just when you did, because Carmel was propositioning me here. It's been deeply embarrassing in front of Sean, but what can I do?" Aidan looked at her helplessly.

"It's something you're going to have to cope with all your life. I'd say it's a physical thing, you know the way animals give off scents. It couldn't be intellectual or anything."

Eve laughed happily and spun around to the admiring glance of Bill Dunne.

"You look *terrific*," Bill Dunne said to her. "Why don't you dress like that all the time?"

"I was just going to ask you exactly the same question," she laughed up at him.

Bill fixed his tie and smiled foolishly. Aidan looked put out. He spoke hastily to Jack, who was at his elbow.

"I don't know whether this was such a good idea."

"What?" Jack looked at the glass of beer in Aidan's hand. "Is it flat?"

"No. I mean asking all the girls. We thought we'd have them under our control. Maybe we'll lose them all."

"Jack?" Aengus had arrived, looking anxious.

"Aha, Mr. Fixit is here," Aidan said, looking malevolently at the small boy he would never forgive for confusing him so at the outset of the evening.

"Jack, will I bring out the sausages yet? Mummy wants to know is everyone here."

"Nan's not here yet. Wait another few minutes."

"Everyone else is here, are they?" Aidan looked round the room. He didn't like the way Bill Dunne was making Eve laugh. He didn't like the way everyone in the older set seemed to be making his parents laugh too loudly.

"I think so. Look, here's Nan now."

Standing at the door utterly naturally, as if she had entered crowded rooms like this every evening of her life, was Nan Mahon. She had a beautiful lemon dress, the skirt in flowing silk, the top a strapless bodice of thousands of tiny seed pearls on a lemon taffeta base. Her shoulders were graceful, rising from the dress, her hair a mass of golden curls was scooped up into a clasp, also decorated with tiny pearl ornaments. Her skin looked as if she had never known a spot or a blemish.

Jack went over to greet her, and take her to meet his parents.

"Is that Jack's lover, do you think?" Aengus asked Aidan Lynch hopefully. Aidan was the kind of person that sometimes told you unexpected things.

He was disappointed this time.

"You are a remarkably foolish and unwise young man to talk about lovers to boys who have been through a Catholic education and know that such things must be confined to the Holy Sacrament of Matrimony."

"I meant like in the pictures . . ." Aengus pleaded.

"You don't know what you mean, your mind is a snake pit of confusion. Go and get the sausages while you still have a few brain cells left alive," Aidan ordered him.

"They're not all there." Aengus was mutinous.

"Yes, they are."

"No, there's someone in the cloakroom. She's been there since she came in."

"She probably got out the window and left," said Aidan. "Get the sausages or I'll tear the face off you."

Aengus knew it had all been going too well. The bow tie, the attention and people thanking him. Now Aidan Lynch was speaking to him just like he had at school.

He went gloomily out toward the kitchen in search of the party food.

In the hall a big girl was looking at herself in the mirror without very much pleasure.

"Hallo," he said.

"Hallo," she replied. "Am I the last?"

"I think so. Are you Nan?"

"No. She just went in, I heard her."

"They said I couldn't serve the sausages until Nan arrived. She was the only one missing."

"Well, I expect they forgot me," she said.

"They must have," he said comfortingly.

"Are you Jack's brother?"

"Yes, I'm Aengus Foley."

"How do you do. I'm Benny Hogan."

"Do you like sausages?"

"Yes, why?"

"I'm getting some now. I thought you could have a few before you went on, to stock up like."

"Thanks, but I'd better not. I'm afraid of bursting out of my dress."

"You've burst out of most of it already," said Aengus, indicating her bosom.

"Oh God," said Benny.

"So you might as well have the sausages anyway," he said cheerfully.

"I'd better go in," she said.

She straightened her shoulders and trying not to look at the small boy who had thought her dress was ripped open, she held back her shoulders as she had promised Clodagh Pine she would and moved into the drawing room feeling like an ocean liner.

Bill Dunne and John O'Brien saw her first.

"God, is that Big Ben? Doesn't she look fantastic?" Bill said, behind his hand.

"Now, that's what I call a pair of Killarneys," John O'Brien said.

"Why Killarneys?" Bill was always interested in explanations of things.

"It's an expression." John O'Brien was still looking at Benny. "She's not bad-looking at all is she?"

Benny saw none of them. Her eyes were roaming the room to see if in the middle of this happy and confident throng her parents were standing, awkward and ill at ease. Worse, would she find them holding forth on subjects of interest only in Knockglen? Worst of all, would they make a scene when they saw her dress?

But as far as she could see there was no sign of them. She peered and twisted, looking at the backs of people's heads, trying to see if they were hidden in that group of older people, where a man with a very loud laugh stood holding court.

No, they definitely weren't there.

She had seen a Morris Cowley pull away from the footpath just as they arrived. It was driven by one person. It was dark and hard to see either the face or the registration number. It *could* have been their car. That was what had unhinged her. She had fled straight into the cloakroom hissing at Eve to go in without her.

"I'll wait for you," Eve had said, thinking that she was just going to the lavatory.

"If you do, I'll kill you, here and now in front of everyone.

There'll be so much blood your blouse will be the same color as your skirt."

"You've made your point. I'll go in without you," Eve had said.

For fifteen minutes Benny had sat in the Foleys' downstairs cloakroom.

Several times she felt the door handle rattle when a girl wanted to go in and check her appearance. But there was a mirror in the dining room and they made do with that.

Finally, she realized that there were no more sounds of people arriving and she emerged.

She felt foolish now, and a dull flush of anger with Sean Walsh for having tricked her into thinking that her night would be spoiled spread over her face. She felt a sense of rage with the unfortunate Patsy that she hadn't found out where the master and mistress had gone on a rare evening out. But most of all she felt an overpowering sense of annoyance with herself.

Now that she was sure they were not in the room she could ask herself what would have been so very terrible if they had turned up.

Slowly normality came back and she realized she was the center of a lot of very interested attention.

"That's a very classy-looking outfit." Rosemary didn't even bother to disguise her surprise.

"Thanks, Rosemary."

"So, where did you get it?"

"Knockglen." Benny's answer was brief. She wanted to catch Eve's eye and tell her that she was all right again. But Eve had her back turned.

Before she could get to her there were several more compliments. As far as she could see they were genuine. And mainly unflattering in their astonishment.

Still, it was heady stuff.

She touched Eve on the shoulder.

"I'm back," she said, grinning.

Eve turned away from the group. "Am I allowed to talk to you or do you still have some kind of plan to carve me up?"

"That's over."

"Well then." Eve lowered her voice.

"What is it?"

"Every single person in this room is looking at the pair of us. We're a Cinderella story come true."

Benny didn't dare to look.

"I mean it," Eve said. "The glamorpusses like Rosemary and Sheila and even Nan are expected to look great at a dance. You and I are the surprise element. We're going to be danced off our feet. Mark my words."

"Eve, what would the Wise Woman do now?"

"In your case the Wise Woman would get a drink, and hold it in one hand and your evening bag in the other. That way you physically can't start covering up your bosom."

"Don't call it bosom," Benny begged.

"Sister Imelda used to call it the craw. You know, like in a bird. 'Make sure you cover your craw Eve,' she'd say. As if I had one to cover."

"As if any of us took any notice of her."

Nan came up and put her arm into each of theirs. It was no treat for Nan to be admired, and she seemed to see nothing staggering about her two friends having emerged from the chrysalis. She behaved as if she had expected them to look magnificent.

She spoke almost as a cat would purr.

"Now, haven't we knocked those awful Rosemarys and Sheilas into a cocked hat."

They all laughed happily, but Benny would have been happier if there had been any sign that Jack Foley, the handsome young host who was handing around plates with his little brother, had even by a flicker of his eye acknowledged that she was in the room, with most of her bosom bare, and if you were to judge by everyone else's glances, looking very well indeed.

✦

The last car door banged as the young people left. John and Lilly Foley stood on the top step and waved good-bye. Inside there was still a lively drinks party with their own friends, and Aidan Lynch's parents. Lilly knew she looked well. It had taken a lot of time, but she had found exactly the right cocktail dress, glittery without being overdone, dressy without it looking as if she should be going to the dance with the youngsters. It had lilac drapes and she had earrings to match it. Her feet hurt in her new shoes, but no one would know that, certainly not the tall handsome man beside her.

"That was lovely, wasn't it? You were a great host." She smiled at her husband, full of congratulations as if it were he rather than she who had organized everything.

"You're wonderful, Lilly," he said, giving her a kiss on the forehead, and he put his arm round her as they closed the door and rejoined the guests.

All the work had been worth it, just for that.

The ladies' cloakroom was full of excited girls combing and lacquering their hair and flattening their lips out into grotesque shapes in order to apply lipstick. Two women behind a counter took their coats and gave them pink cloakroom tickets which the girls tucked into their bags.

There was a smell of perfume and face powder and a little nervous sweat.

Nan was ready before anyone else, unaware of the slightly jealous glances from others in the room. Suddenly their own strapless dresses looked a bit like something from the metal industry. They became aware of how the firm supports cut into their flesh. How could Nan's hair look so perfect without having to be licked into shape with cans of hair spray? Why didn't she need to dab at her chin and hide spots with tubes of covering paste?

"I'm just going to have a wander round until you're ready,"

she said to Benny and Eve. "Then I'll take you into the shop to meet my mother."

She left gracefully in a sea of other girls who were bouncing or bobbing or running up and down the carpeted stairs. She looked serene.

Nan walked in one side of the hotel bar smiling politely around her as if she were waiting to meet someone.

It was a place with dark oak paneling and red plush seats. By the bar a lot of men stood talking. Drinks here were very much more expensive than in an ordinary Dublin pub. This was a bar where the wealthy met.

You would find county people, up in Dublin for the blood-stock sales, or some kind of land business. There might be stockbrokers, bankers, visitors from England, people with titles. It was not the kind of bar where you could ever come in on your own.

But on the night of a dance in the hotel ballroom, a lone girl looking for her partner would be quite acceptable. Nan stood where the light fell on her and looked around her. It wasn't long before everyone in the place saw her. She was aware without having to look at individual groups that everyone had seen her, and that they were admiring the cool young woman in the exquisite dress with the golden hair who stood confidently at the door.

Just when they had all had sufficient time to look at her, she turned around and with a wave of delight moved off to the foyer, where Eve and Nan were waiting.

"What were you up to?" Eve asked.

"Surveying the talent in the bar," Nan replied.

"Won't there be enough of it at the dance. My God, you're insatiable, Nan Mahon."

"Yes, well less of that to my mother."

Nan led them into the hotel shop where an attractive, rather tired-looking woman sat by the till. She had fair hair too, like her daughter, but it was faded. She had a nice smile, but it was wary. Nan must have got her really striking good looks from her father,

Eve decided. Her father who was hardly ever mentioned at all in Nan's conversation.

Nan did the introductions and they paraded their dresses for her. Emily Mahon said all the right things. She told Eve that the scarlet skirt looked much better on a dark person. It had drained the color from Nan's face. She told Benny that anyone could see at ten miles that this was beautiful expensive brocade, and that the girl who had remodeled it for her must be a genius. She had never mentioned the huge cleavage, which cheered Benny greatly. If anyone else mentioned it she was going to dig out that modesty vest and reinstate it.

"And do any of you have any particular boyfriends tonight?" Emily asked eagerly.

"There's a fellow called Aidan Lynch who fancies Eve a lot," Benny said proudly, and then in order to define things properly for Mrs. Mahon she added, "And everyone fancies Nan."

"I think you're going to have a deal with Johnny O'Brien yourself," Nan said to Benny. "He's been following you around as if you had a magnet somewhere about your person."

Benny knew only too well what part of her person Johnny O'Brien was following around.

Emily was pleased that her daughter had such nice friends. She had rarely met anyone that Nan knew. They had never been invited to the school plays or concerts like other parents. Nan had never wanted her father to know anything about school activities. It had always been her dread as a child that he would turn up the worse for wear at her convent school. To meet Eve and Benny was a big occasion for Emily Mahon.

"I'd offer you a spray of perfume from the tester, but you all smell so lovely already," she said.

They said they didn't smell nearly nice enough. They'd love a splash of something.

They leaned over to Emily, who doused them liberally with Joy.

"The only problem is that you'll all smell the same," she laughed. "The men won't know one of you from the other."

"That's good then," Nan said approvingly. "As a group we'll have made an impact on them. They'll never forget us."

They were aware that a customer had come into the shop and might want to be served.

"We'd better move on Em, we don't want you sacked," Nan said.

"It's a treat to see you. Have a wonderful evening." Her eyes hated to see them go.

"Don't hurry on my account," the man said. "I'm just browsing."

His voice made Eve turn sharply.

It was Simon Westward. He hadn't seen her. He had eyes only for Nan.

As usual Nan seemed unaware that anyone was looking at her. She had probably grown up with those looks of admiration, Eve thought, like she herself had grown up with the sound of the convent bell. It became part of the scenery. You didn't notice it anymore.

Simon did indeed start to browse among the shelves of ornaments and souvenirs, picking some up and examining them, looking at the prices on the boxes.

Emily smiled at him. "Tell me if you want any help. I'm just having a chat here . . ."

She saw Nan frown at her slightly.

"No, honestly . . ." He looked straight at Nan.

"Hallo," he said warmly. "Did I see you in the bar a moment ago?"

"Yes, I was looking for my friends." Her smile was radiant. "And now I found them." She spread her hands out to indicate Eve and Benny.

Out of politeness he moved his eyes from Nan to acknowledge them.

"Hallo," Benny grinned. Simon looked at her startled. He

knew her from somewhere certainly, but where? A big, striking girl, very familiar.

He looked at the smaller dark girl. It was his cousin Eve.

"Well, good evening Simon," she said slightly mocking. It was as if she had the advantage of him. She had already recognized him and had been watching while he ogled her friend.

"Eve!" There was warmth in his smile. Swift warmth.

Now he remembered who Benny was also. She was the Hogan girl.

"Small world, all right," Eve said.

"Are you all going to a dance?"

"No, heavens no. This is just our casual Friday night out. We dress up a lot in UCD you know. Not scruffy Trinity students shuffling round in duffel coats." Her eyes danced, taking the sharpness out of her response.

"I was just going to compliment you and say you all looked splendid but if it's like this every Friday, than I *have* been missing out on the social scene."

"Of course it's a dance, Simon," Benny said.

"Thank you Miss Hogan." He couldn't remember her name. He waited expectantly to be introduced to Nan, but it didn't happen.

"Will you be going to see Heather this weekend?" Eve asked.

"Alas no. I'm going to England actually. You really have been frightfully good to her."

"I enjoy meeting her. She has a lot of spirit," Eve said. "And she'd need it in that mausoleum."

"It's meant to be the best . . ."

"Oh, it's about the only place for you lot to send her certainly," Eve reassured him. But she did imply that if Simon and his lot were less blinkered there would have been many more places to send the child.

Simon let another tiny pause develop, enough for him to be presented to the blond girl if he was going to be. But no move was made.

She didn't stretch out her hand and introduce herself, and he wasn't going to ask.

"I must get on with my purchases and leave you all to enjoy the dance," he said.

"Was it anything in particular?" Emily was professional now in her manner.

"I wanted a gift, a small gift for a lady in Hampshire." His eyes were resting on Nan as he spoke.

"Something particularly Irish?" Emily asked.

"Yes, not too shamrocky though."

Nan had been fiddling with a small paperweight made of Connemara marble. She left it back rather pointedly on the shelf.

Simon picked it up.

"I think you're right." He looked straight into her eyes. "I think this is a very good idea. Thank you so much." He ended the sentence on a rising note, where if anyone was going to give a name it would be given now.

"It's very attractive," Emily said. "And if you like I could put it in a little box for you." His eyes were still on Nan.

"That would be lovely," he said.

Aidan Lynch appeared at the door.

"I know I'm always the specter at the feast, but was there any question of you ladies joining us? It's not important or anything. It's just that the people at the door want to know where the rest of our party is and it's a question that's becoming increasingly hard to answer."

He looked from one to the other.

Nan made the decision.

"We got sidetracked," she explained. "Come on, Aidan, lead us to the ball."

She gathered the other two with her like a hen clucking at chickens.

Benny and Eve said their good-byes, and Nan smiled from the door.

"Good-bye, Em, I'll be seeing you."

She didn't say she'd be seeing her tonight, or at home. Simon watched them as they walked with Aidan Lynch toward the ball-room.

"What a very beautiful girl that is," Simon said.

Emily looked after the three girls and boy walking through the crowded hotel.

"Isn't she?" said Emily Mahon.

They had a table for sixteen on the balcony. Dancing was well under way when they trooped in. Girls at other tables looked up when they saw Jack Foley, and people craned to see who he was with.

They had no luck in guessing. He went in talking to Sean and Carmel.

Boys at the other tables saw with envy that Jack Foley's table had Rosemary *and* Nan Mahon. That seemed too much for one party. College beauties should be spread about a bit. Some of them wondered how that goofy Aidan Lynch always seemed to be in the thick of everything, and one or two asked each other who was the very tall girl with the wonderful cleavage.

At their table the plan of campaign was under way. Everyone was drinking a glass of water from the large jug on the table. Then as soon as it was empty the eight boys would each pour the quarter bottle of gin which they had in their pockets into the jug. For the rest of the evening, only minerals would be ordered. They would ask for more and more Club Oranges, and the gin could be added from the jug.

Nobody could afford hotel prices for spirits. This was the clever solution. But the trick was not to let them remove the jug of so-called water, or worse still, fill it up, thus watering the gin. The table was never to be left empty and at the mercy of waiters.

The bandleader called out that they were to take the floor for a selection of calypsos.

Bill Dunne was first on his feet with his hand out to Rosemary.

She had positioned herself near Jack, but that had been the wrong place. She should have sat opposite him, she realized too late. That way he could have caught her eye. With a hard, forced smile she stood up and went down to join the dancers.

Johnny O'Brien asked Benny. She stood up eagerly. Dancing was something she was good at. Mother Francis had employed a dancing teacher who came once a week and they learned the waltz and the quickstep first, but she had also taught them Latin American dancing. Benny smiled at the thought that girls from Knockglen would probably beat any Dublin girls when it came to doing the samba, the mambo or the cha-cha-cha.

They were playing "This is my island in the sun." Johnny looked with open admiration at Benny.

"I never knew you had such a nice . . ." He stopped.

"Nice what?" Benny asked him directly.

Johnny O'Brien chickened out. "Nice perfume," he said.

It was nice, too, the perfume. It was heady, like a cloud around her. Of course he hadn't meant perfume at all, but he was right. That was nice also.

Aidan was dancing with Eve.

"This is the first time I've been able to hold you in my arms without your beating at me with your bony little fists," he said.

"Make the most of it," Eve said. "The bony little fists will be out again if you start trying to dance with me in your father's car."

"Were you talking to my father?" Aidan asked.

"You know I was. You introduced me to him three times."

"He's all right really. So's my mother—a bit loud but basically all right."

"They're no louder than you are," Eve said.

"Oh they are. They boom. I just talk forcefully."

"They talk more directly, normally. Sentences and everything," Eve said, thinking about them.

"You're very beautiful."

"Thank you Aidan. And you look great in a dinner jacket."

"When are you going to stop fighting this hopeless physical passion you have for me and succumb. Allow yourself to have your way with me."

"Wouldn't you drop dead if I said I would?"

"I'd recover pretty quickly, I tell you."

"Well, it mightn't happen for a while. The succumbing bit I mean. A good while."

"That's the trouble about being brought up by nuns. I might have to wait forever."

"They weren't nearly as bad as everyone says."

"When are you going to take me to meet them?"

"Don't be ridiculous."

"Why not? I took you to meet *my* family."

"You didn't. They just happened to be there."

"You didn't arrange for your nuns to rent motorbikes and roar up to the party. I think that was socially rather inept of you," Aidan said.

"They couldn't make it," Eve explained. "Friday's their poker night and they just won't change for anyone."

Sean and Carmel danced entwined. The music played "Brown skin girl stay home and mind bay-bee."

"Imagine, that won't be long now," Carmel said.

"Another four years," Sean said happily.

"And we've been together four years already if you count the year before Intermediate Cert."

"Oh, I do count that. I couldn't get you out of my mind that year."

"Aren't we lucky?" Carmel said, holding him tighter.

"Very lucky. Everyone in the room envies us," said Sean.

❧

"Wouldn't Sean and Carmel sicken you?" Eve said to Benny as they all went back up the stairs.

"Not much value out of asking them anywhere certainly," Benny agreed.

"They remind me of those animals in the zoo that keep picking at each other, looking for fleas," Eve said.

"Don't Eve," Benny laughed. "Someone will hear."

"No, you know monkeys obsessed with each other. Social grooming I think it's called."

Back at the table Jack Foley and Sheila were sitting. Jack had elected to watch the jug of gin for the first watch. Sheila was pleased to have been chosen to sit with him, but she would have preferred to have been on the dance floor.

Nan came back to the table with Patrick Shea, an architectural student, a friend of Jack and Aidan's from school. Patrick Shea was hot and sweating. Nan looked as if she had been dancing on an ice rink in a cool breeze. There wasn't a sign of exertion on her face.

Benny looked across the table at her admiringly. She was so much in command of every situation and yet her mother was quite shy, and not a confident person at all. Perhaps Nan got it all from her father. Whom she never mentioned.

Benny wondered why Eve hadn't introduced her to Simon. It was rather gauche not to. If it had been anyone else Benny would have made the introduction herself, but Eve was always so chippy about those Westwards.

Still Nan had said nothing and knowing Nan if she had wanted an introduction she would have asked for one.

Johnny O'Brien was offering her a glass of orange. Benny took a great gulp of it thankfully and it was only when she had swallowed it she remembered it was full of gin.

She choked it back and saw Johnny O'Brien looking at her admiringly.

"You're certainly a woman who can hold her drink," he said.

It wasn't the characteristic she would most like to be praised for, but at least it was better than having gagged or got sick.

Rosemary had been looking at her.

"I envy you being able to do that," she said. "I get dizzy after even a little drink."

She looked around her knowing that there would be silent praise and admiration for this feminine trait.

"I'm sure," Benny said gloomily.

"It must be coming from the country," Rosemary said, still with the look of mock admiration. "I expect they drink a lot there don't they?"

"Oh, they do," Benny said. "But differently. I mean when I drink gin in the country it's usually by the neck out of a bottle. It's a rare treat to get it in a glass and mixed with Club Orange."

They laughed as she had known they would.

It was never hard to make them laugh. It was very hard to make them look at you with different eyes though.

Benny looked at Jack, relaxed and happy, leaning back in his chair surveying the scene both around him and down on the tables near the dance floor. He would be the perfect host. He would ask every girl at the table to dance.

She felt an extraordinary urge to reach across and stroke his face, just touch his cheek gently. She wondered was she going mad? She had never known an urge like that before.

He would ask her to dance soon. Maybe now, perhaps the very next dance, he would lean across the table and smile. He would put out his hand toward her and smile with a slight questioning look. She could see it happening so clearly, she almost believed it had happened already.

"Benny?" he might say, just like that, and she'd get up and walk down the stairs with him, hands touching lightly. And then they would just move toward each other.

The bandleader had said that their vocalist would knock strips off Tab Hunter in any singing contest and he would now sing "Young Love" to prove it.

Benny willed Jack to catch her eye and dance three soft slow numbers with her, beginning with "Young Love."

But Rosemary caught his eye first. Benny didn't know how she did it, it might have been something to do with some awful beating of her eyelashes, but she managed to drag his glance over to her.

"Rosemary?" he said in that voice which he should have used to say "Benny?"

Her heart was like a lump of lead.

"Will you risk it Benny?" Aidan Lynch was at her elbow.

"Lovely, Aidan, thank you."

She stood up and went downstairs to the floor where Jack Foley and Rosemary were dancing and Rosemary had put both her arms around Jack's neck and was leaning back a bit away from him as if to study him better.

The dance was a success every year. This year the organizers seemed to think it was better than ever. They measured these things by enthusiasm. The spot prizes went very well.

"First gentleman up with a hole in his sock."

Aidan Lynch won that easily. He pointed out that the part you put your foot in was a hole. They had to give it to him. He got a huge cheer.

"How did you know that?" Benny was impressed.

"A friend of mine was a waiter here once. He told me all the spots."

"What are the other questions?" Benny asked.

"There's one which says 'The first lady up with a picture of a rabbit.' That's easy too."

"It is? Who'd have a picture of a rabbit?"

"Anyone with a threepence. There's a rabbit on the thruppeny piece."

"So there is. Aren't you a genius Aidan?"

"I am Benny, I am, but not everyone apart from yourself and myself recognizes this."

They were welcomed as heroes back to the table and the wine they had won was opened.

"More drink. Aren't you marvelous, Benny," Rosemary said. She had somehow managed to nestle her body into Jack's by leaning against him. Benny wanted to get up and smack her face hard. But fortunately Jack had moved away and the need that she felt to separate them passed.

Some waltzes were announced. Benny didn't want to dance this set with Jack. Waltzes were too twirly, too active. No time to lean against him, to touch his face even accidentally.

The others were starting to go downstairs as the music soared up at them. "Che sarà, sarà, whatever will be, will be."

A tall, handsome boy came over to the table and asked courteously, "May I ask Nan for just one dance please, you have her all evening . . . is that all right? Nan, will you?"

Nan looked up, everyone else seemed to be occupied.

"Of course," she said, and went smiling to the dance floor.

Benny remembered at school when you were picked for teams the awful bit about being the last one to be chosen. Or worse when there was an uneven number and Mother Francis would say "All right Benny you go with that team" at the very end. She remembered the musical chairs and being the first one out. She had an uneasy feeling that it was all going to happen again.

Jack was with Rosemary again! She saw Bill Dunne and another boy, Nick Hayes, talking at the end of the table, miles from where she was. If they had noticed her and come to sit with her or asked them to join her that would have been all right.

Benny sat with a fixed smile on her face, fiddling with the menu which said they would have melon soup, chicken and trifle. She wondered absently had they forgotten it was a Friday. She poured out a fizzy orange drink into her glass and drank it. From the corner of her eye she saw a waiter approaching with a large metal jug about to refill the water jugs on the table.

Benny stood up. "No," she said. "No, they don't want any."

The waiter looked an old man. He looked tired. He had seen too many of these student dances, and danced at none of them.

"Excuse me, miss, let me fill it."

"No." Benny was adamant.

"Even if you don't want any, the ones that did get to dance might want it when they come back," he said.

There was something in the mixed pity and scorn of his speech that brought a sharp sting of tears to her eyes. "They said they didn't *like* any more water. Before they went off to dance. Truly."

She must not make him suspicious either. Suppose he reported something odd about their table.

A great weariness came over her. "Listen," she said to him. "I don't give a damn. They told me they didn't want any more but I don't care. Fill it up if you're set on it. What the hell."

He looked at her uneasily. He obviously thought she was slightly mad, and that it was kind of somebody to have given her an outing.

"I'll go on to the next table," he said hastily.

"Great," Benny said.

She felt awkward sitting on her own. She would go to the ladies'. There was no one to excuse herself to. Nick and Bill were having an animated discussion at the far end of the table; they didn't see her go.

In the lavatory she sat and planned. The next dance would probably be rock and roll. That wasn't what she wanted for her dance with Jack either. She wouldn't catch his eye for this one. She'd wait until it was something lovely and slow again. Maybe they'd have "Unchained Melody." She loved that. Or "Stranger in Paradise." That was nice too. "Softly, Softly" was a bit too sentimental. But it would do.

To her surprise she heard Rosemary's voice at the handbasins outside.

The waltzes couldn't be over yet surely. They normally had three of them.

"He is utterly gorgeous isn't he?" Rosemary was saying to someone. "And he's nice too, not full of himself like a lot of those sporty fellows are if they're any way good-looking."

Benny didn't recognize the other girl's voice. Whoever she was she thought that Jack and Rosemary were together.

"Have you been going with him long?" she asked wistfully.

"No, I'm not going out with him at all. *Yet*, that is," she added menacingly.

"He looked pretty keen out there."

Benny's heart lurched.

"He's a good dancer as well as everything else. The waltz isn't my strong point. I pretended I had turned my ankle. I just wanted to come in here for a rest."

"That was clever."

"Well, you have to use every trick in the book. I said to him that I'd grab him for another dance later because we didn't finish this one."

"You've got no competition."

"I don't like the look of Nan Mahon. Did you see her dress?"

"It's out of this world. But you look just as good."

"Thanks." Rosemary was pleased.

"Where is he now?"

"He said he'd finish off the waltzes with Benny."

Benny's face burned. He had *known* she was a wallflower. He had bloody known. He hadn't deigned to ask her for a full dance, but when ravishing Rosemary walked out on him, he'd get good old Benny for the rest of it.

"Who's Benny?"

"She's that huge girl—from way down the country. He knows her through her family or something. She's always turning up at these things."

"No competition there then?"

Rosemary laughed. "No, I don't think so. Whoever she is, her people must have money. They know the Foleys somehow and she's wearing a very expensive dress. I don't know where she got it, but it's fabulous, brocade and beautifully cut. It takes stones off her. She says she got it in Knockflash or wherever she lives."

"Knockflash?"

"Somewhere, real hick town. She no more got it there than she got it in the Bog of Allen."

Their voices faded. They had freshened themselves up, resprayed their hair, put on more perfume. They were ready to go out again, full of confidence, and face it all.

Benny sat on the lavatory. Ice cold. She was huge. She was no competition for anyone. She was the kind of person someone would come and finish off a dance with but not choose in the first place.

She looked at the small wristwatch her mother and father had given her for her seventeenth birthday. It was five to ten.

More than anywhere in the world she wanted to be sitting by the fire in Lisbeg. Her mother in one chair, her father in another and Shep looking at pictures in the flames and wondering what it was all about.

She would like to be hearing the kitchen door latch go and Patsy come in from her walk with Mossy and make them all a cup of drinking chocolate. She didn't want to be in a place where people said she was huge and no competition and must have lots of money and be a family friend of the Foleys to be invited anywhere. She didn't want to be fighting to save jugs of gin on tables for people who wouldn't dance with her.

But wishing wouldn't get her home out of this humiliating place. Benny decided that she would take the good out of what she had overheard. It was good that her dress looked expensive and well cut. It was good though sad that it was necessary to hear that it took stones off her. It was good that Rosemary wasn't any way sure of Jack. And it was good that he hadn't found her sitting at the table, lonely and abandoned, and now he couldn't feel he had fulfilled his obligation to dance with her. There were lots of good things, Benny Hogan told herself as she took the little piece of cotton wool that Nan's mother had soaked in Joy perfume for them and rubbed it behind her ears.

She would go back and Rosemary would never know that her

cruel dismissive remarks had only served to make Benny feel more positive and confident than ever.

They were making an announcement from the stage that the meal would be served shortly, and thanks to a special dispensation from the Archbishop's House the Friday abstinence need not be observed. There was a huge cheer.

"How did they get that?" Eve asked.

"The Archbishop knows we've all been so good he wants to reward us," Jack suggested.

"No, it's just that chicken's the easiest to serve. You know everyone gets a wing. They breed special chickens for functions, with ten wings," Aidan said.

"But why would the Archbishop want us to have chicken seriously?" Benny asked.

"It's a deal," Aidan explained. "The dance organizers promise not to have dances on Saturday night that might run into the Sabbath day and the Church lets them eat chicken on Fridays."

"You ran away on me." Jack leaned over to Benny just as the soup was being served.

"I what?"

"You ran off. I was looking for you to waltz with me."

"No, I didn't," Benny said smiling. "That was Rosemary that ran off on you. She hurt her ankle. I expect you mix us all up, we all look the same to you."

The people around laughed. Rosemary didn't. She looked at Benny suspiciously. How did she know about the ankle.

Jack used the chance to make a flowery compliment. "You don't all look the same. But you all look marvelous. I mean it." And he was looking straight at Benny when he said it. She smiled back and managed not to make a joke or a smart remark.

There was a raffle during the meal, and the organizers came around to invite Rosemary and Nan to go and sell tickets.

"Why us?" Rosemary said. She didn't want to leave her post. The committee didn't want to explain that it was easier to force people to buy tickets if beautiful women were doing the asking. Nan had stood up already.

"It's for charity," she said. "I certainly don't mind."

Rosemary Ryan looked very annoyed. Nothing had been going her way this evening. Nan had won all the honors in this little incident and that big Benny across the table seemed to be smiling at her in some awful smug knowing way.

"Of course I'll come too," she said, jumping to her feet.

"Mind your ankle," Jack said, and she looked at him sharply. He was probably just being concerned, but there was something about Benny's eyes she didn't like.

The man who thought he was streets ahead of Tab Hunter but just hadn't got the breaks also thought he was a pretty good Tennessee Ernie Ford and went down to great depths in his version of "Sixteen Tons," a song Benny had detested since it had been popular when they were studying for the Leaving Certificate and Maire Carroll had always managed to be singing it when she was near Benny.

Benny was dancing with Nick Hayes.

"You're very light to dance with. It's like holding a feather," he said in some surprise.

"It's easy to dance if someone leads well." She was polite.

He was all right, Nick Hayes, but only all right.

Jack was dancing with Nan.

Somehow it was more disturbing than watching him dance with Rosemary.

Nan didn't make those very obvious little efforts. She really made no play for him at all and that must be maddening to someone like Jack Foley who was used to everyone adoring him. In fact they were very much alike those two. She hadn't really noticed it before.

Both so sure of themselves because they didn't need to fight for anyone's attention like everyone else seemed to have to do. But just because they were so sure they could afford to be nice and easygoing. Those kind of good looks freed you to be whatever kind of person you wanted to be.

"I never see you round anywhere in the evenings," Nick was saying.

"Nobody does much," Benny said. "What kind of places do you go?"

She didn't care where he went. She just wanted to get him talking so that she could take her mind off the awful tune they were dancing to, and think more of Jack.

"I have a car," he was saying right across her happy thoughts of the next dance when surely Jack must choose her.

"I could come and see you in Knockglen sometime. Jack said he had a very nice day when he went to your house."

"He did? Good, I'm glad he enjoyed it." This was hopeful. This was very good indeed. "Maybe you'll come back together one time and I'll try and entertain you both."

"Oh no, that's not the idea. The idea would be to keep you to myself," Nick said with a leer. "One doesn't want Jack Foley getting in on all one's discoveries, does one?"

He was putting on an accent deliberately trying to pretend he was being posh. Somehow it was flat and silly and didn't work. He couldn't make people laugh like Aidan Lynch could, like she herself could.

She tried to dull the pain she felt watching Nan and Jack dance together.

Nick Hayes was looking at her waiting for a response.

"I always hate this song," she said to him suddenly.

"Why, it's quite nice I think."

"The words."

" 'I owe my soul to the company store,' " he sang along with the vocalist. "What on earth's wrong with those words?" he asked mystified.

She looked at him. He genuinely didn't remember the first line—"You load sixteen tons and what do you get?"

He had made no connection.

It was there only in her mind. Nobody else in the room heard the song title and swiveled their eyes to Benny Hogan. She must remember this. And she must remember that both Johnny O'Brien and Nick Hayes were asking her for a date.

These were the things she would remember from the night. As well as the dance with Jack when he asked her.

He asked her at twenty-five to twelve. When they had dimmed the lights and the vocalist had told them that since Frankie Laine hadn't been able to show he would sing Frankie's song. "Your eyes are the eyes of a woman in love." Jack Foley leaned across the table and said, "Benny?"

They danced together easily, as if they had been partners for a long time.

She forced herself not to prattle and chatter and make fifteen jokes.

He seemed to be happy to dance without conversation.

Sometimes, looking over his shoulder she saw people looking at them. She was as tall as he was, so she couldn't have looked up at him to speak anyway, even if she had wanted to.

He drew her a little closer which was great except that she feared the place he had his hand on her back was just the part where the heavy-duty bra ended and there was a small roll of flesh.

God, suppose he held that bit of her—it would be like a life-belt. How could she get him to move his hand up her back. How? These were the things you needed to know in life, rather than what was set out in a syllabus for you.

Mercifully the number ended. They stood beside each other companionably waiting for the next one to start. He leaned over and touched a lock of her hair.

"Is it all falling down?" Benny asked alarmed.

"No, it's lovely. I just pretended it was out of place so that I could touch your face."

How extraordinary that he had wanted to feel her face as she had yearned to touch his all night.

"I'm afraid . . ." she began.

She was going to say "I'm afraid it's a very sweaty face, your finger might get stuck to it."

But she stopped herself.

"What are you afraid of?" he asked.

"I'm afraid other Fridays are going to seem very dull after tonight."

"Don't knock Knockglen." He always said that. It was like a special phrase between them.

"You're right. We have no idea what plans Mario and Fonsie have for the place."

The singer was sorry that Dino couldn't make it so he was going to give his own rendition of the Dean Martin number "Memories Are Made of This."

Benny and Jack drew toward each other, and this time his hand was higher on her back. The devil roll of flesh like a lifebelt was not in evidence.

"You're a marvelous person to have in a party anywhere," he said.

"Why do you say that?" Her face showed nothing of what she felt. None of the despair that he only thought of her as some kind of cabaret.

"Because you are," he said. "I'm only an ignorant old rugby player. What do I know of words?"

"You're not an ignorant old rugby player. You're a great host. We're all having a great night because you got us all together and invited us to your home." She smiled and he gave her a little hug. And when he had held her tight he didn't release her again.

Into her ear he whispered, "You smell absolutely lovely."

She said nothing. She didn't close her eyes. It looked too confident. She didn't look around and see the envious glances as she was held by the most sought-after man in the room. She just looked down. She could see the back of his dinner jacket, and the way his hair curled at the back of his neck. Pressed close to her she could feel his heart beating, or maybe it was her heart. She hoped it was his, because if it was hers it seemed a bit overstrong.

Even when the third song, "The Man from Laramie," was over Jack didn't suggest going back to the table. He wanted the next dance.

Benny blessed that dancing teacher who used to drive around in a battered old car teaching the tunic-clad girls of Ireland to dance. She blessed her with all her heart as she and Jack did stirring versions of "Mambo Italiano" and "Hernando's Hideaway." Laughing and flushed they came back to the table. Sheila wasn't even pretending to listen to Johnny O'Brien and Rosemary looked distinctly put out. Nan caught Benny's eye and gave her a discreet thumbs-up sign. Eve sitting across the table with Aidan Lynch's arm loosely round her shoulder gave her a huge grin of solidarity. They were on her side.

"We thought we'd lost you for the night," Nick Hayes said waspishly.

Neither Benny nor Jack took any notice. Aidan Lynch had won yet another spot prize—this time a huge box of chocolates which were opened. Carmel was busy feeding Sean with the soft-centered coffee ones he liked.

Rosemary foolishly grabbed the box to offer it to Jack.

"You must have one before they're all gone," she said. But her movement was too swift and she spilled them all.

Benny looked on. It was the kind of thing she would normally have done. How perfect that it should be Rosemary who did it tonight.

"You owe me another dance for the one we didn't finish," Rosemary said as people tried to retrieve the chocolates.

"I do indeed. I wasn't going to let you forget it," Jack said gallantly.

His fingers were still touching Benny's slightly. She was sure he had been going to dance with her again.

Then suddenly and unbelievably the last dance was announced. They wanted to see everyone on the floor for "California Here I Come."

Benny could have cried.

Somehow, yet again, she had lost the high ground to Rosemary Ryan. She was going to have the last dance with Jack. Nick had his hand out to her, and so had Johnny O'Brien. She thought she saw a look of regret on Jack's face. But she must have imagined it, because when she and Johnny O'Brien took to the floor Jack and Rosemary were whirling around both laughing. Though she couldn't be sure, she thought she saw him push some of the hair out of Rosemary's eyes as he had done to her.

She kept a happy smile on her face for Johnny O'Brien as she clicked through her brain the possibilities that Jack Foley was just a fellow who liked everyone, and said nice things to every single woman he met. Not out of devious cunning, but because he genuinely did feel that every woman had some attraction for him.

This *must* be the case, Benny thought, because the way he had held her when they were dancing together was suspiciously like the way he held Rosemary when everyone was dancing to "Goodnight Sweetheart, see you in the morning."

There was a lot of excitement at the door where the photographers gathered to take snaps. They gave out little pink cards with the address of the places where the small prints could be inspected next day.

Benny was leaving just as Jack called.

"Here," he called. "Benny, come here and let's pose for posterity."

Hardly able to believe that he had called her, she leapt to his side.

Just then Nan came down the steps.

"Nan too," he said.

"No, no," she moved away.

"Come on," he said, "the more the merrier."

The three of them smiled at the flash. And then with a lot of calling good night, and see you, and wasn't it great, they were all in the cars that Jack had organized. Nick Hayes was to drive Benny, Eve and Sheila home because they all lived on the south side. The others were in a couple of miles of the city center.

Nan was going with Sean and Carmel.

Rosemary, to her great rage, had a lift with Johnny O'Brien, who lived in the same road.

Kit had left sandwiches for them and a note saying that she had been out late playing cards so not to wake her until morning.

They crept up to bed.

"He's really nice, Aidan Lynch," Benny said as they got undressed. "I mean really nice. Not just all jokes and playing the fool."

"Yes, but he talks like the goons nine-tenths of the time. It's like having to learn a new language understanding him," Eve complained.

"He seems very fond of you."

"I ask myself what can be wrong with him then. Hereditary insanity maybe. His parents are like town criers. Did you hear them?"

Benny giggled.

"And what about you and Jack? You were doing great."

"I thought I was." Her voice was heavy and sad. "But I wasn't really. He's just a dreamboat who's nice to everyone. He likes to be surrounded by the whole world, and have the whole world in a good humor."

"It's not a bad way to be," Eve said. She lay in her bed with her arms folded behind her neck. She looked so much more cheerful and happy than she had a few short months ago.

"No, it's not a bad way to be. But it's not a good thing to hitch your star to. I must keep remembering that," Benny said.

Next morning they were woken by Kit.

"There's a call for you, Benny."

"Oh God, my parents." She leapt out of bed in her nightie.

"No, not at all. A young man," Kit said, raising her eyebrows in approval.

"Hallo Benny. It's Jack. You said you were staying with Eve. I asked Aidan for the phone number."

Her heart was beating so strangely now, she thought she might fall down.

"Hallo, Jack," she said.

"I was wondering if you'd like to have lunch," he said.

She knew what lunch was now. Thank God. Lunch was a lot of people gathered together in a crowd around a table, with Benny entertaining them.

He certainly was someone who liked all his friends around him all the time. Benny was glad that she had identified that last night to Eve. That she hadn't allowed herself to build up any hopes.

She paused for a couple of seconds before she accepted. Only because she was thinking it all out.

"I meant on our own," he said. "This time just the two of us."

ELEVEN

*E*ddie and Annabel Hogan had raised their eyebrows at each other in surprise as Patsy banged around the kitchen getting breakfast and muttering to herself. They had no idea what it was about.

They could decipher parts of her muttering . . . in all the years she had been in this house she had never been spoken to like that, shouted at, given dog's abuse. Mutter, mutter, crash, crash.

"Probably had words with Mossy," Annabel whispered as Patsy went out to give some scraps to the four hens in their little wire-covered run.

"If so, she must be the first who ever had. I never knew such a silent man," Eddie whispered back.

They had managed to get the information that Benny had telephoned from Dublin shortly before she went to the dance while they had gone for a walk.

Dr. Johnson had said that Annabel should take more exercise and form the routine of a regular walk. Last night they had taken Shep on a long and invigorating journey half a mile out along the Dublin road. So they had missed the call.

"It was only to say thank you for the dress again, is that all Patsy?" Annabel asked, yet again.

"That's what she said it was," Patsy said darkly.

Benny's parents were mystified.

"She was probably overexcited," Eddie said, after a lot of thought.

"She was that all right," Patsy agreed.

Clodagh Pine told her aunt they should stay open at lunchtime.

"Child, you'll have us all in the County Hospital if we work any more."

Peggy couldn't believe that she had thought this niece of hers was going to be a lazy lump. Already she had increased the turn-over of the shop significantly, and despite her own appearance, which was to say the least of it eccentric, she had managed not to alienate any of the old customers either.

"But look at it, Aunt Peg. When else would people like Birdie Mac be able to come down and look at cardigans? When would Mrs. Kennedy come over and see the new blouses? Mrs. Carroll closes the grocery for lunch. She doesn't spend the whole lunch hour eating by the look of her, thin string of misery that she is. Wouldn't she walk down and see what the new skirts are like?"

"It might seem a bit unfair somehow. Unfair on the others." Peggy knew her thinking was confused.

"Tell me, Aunt Peg, have I missed something in my walks up and down Knockglen? Are there several women's draperies, open and competing with us? Is there a whole circle of women running shops like ours thinking that we're a bit sharp opening at lunch-time?"

"Don't be impertinent," Peggy said.

"Seriously. Who would object?"

"They might think we were anxious to make money. That's all." Peggy was defensive.

"Oh, gosh, wouldn't that be dreadful. And there you were all those years not trying to make a penny. Trying to lose it. How could I have been so stupid?" Clodagh put on a clowning face.

"We'll be dropping off our feet."

"Not when we get another girl in we won't."

"There'd never be the call for it."

"Go over the books with me today and you'll see."

Mrs. Kennedy looked without pleasure on the picture of Fonsie who stood in her shop.

"How's the drugs business, Mrs. K?" he asked. He always winked slightly at her as if she were engaged in something shady.

"What can I do for you?" she asked in a clipped voice.

"I'm looking for a nice fancy cake of soap."

"Yes . . . Well." She managed to suggest that it was not a moment before time.

"For girls, like," Fonsie said.

"A gift?" She seemed surprised.

"No, for the new ladies' room," Fonsie said proudly.

He had spent a long time persuading Mario that they should do up the two outhouses as toilets. And make the female one look attractive. Girls liked to spend time painting themselves and doing their hair. Fonsie had driven out to an auction and bought a huge mirror. They put a shelf underneath it. All they needed now was a couple of nice towels on a roller and a bit of smart soap to start off with.

"Would Apple Blossom be a bit too good for what you had in mind?" Mrs. Kennedy brought out what was called a gift pack of soap.

Fonsie made a mental note to tell Clodagh to stock soaps and talcs. Sneak them in before Peggy could protest that they were taking business from the chemist. Mrs. Kennedy was an old bat, and a bad old bat at that. She didn't deserve to have the monopoly on the town's soap.

She wouldn't have, not for much longer.

But in the meantime. . . .

"That's precisely what we need, Mrs. Kennedy, thank you so

much," he said with a great beam, and handed the money across the counter without even wincing at the cost.

Sean Walsh saw from the shop window that Mrs. Healy across the road was polishing the brass sign for the hotel. She was looking at it critically. He wondered had it been defaced, she was frowning so much. There was nobody in Hogan's so he strolled across the road to see what was happening.

"It's hard to get in and out of the letters," Mrs. Healy said. "Bits remain in there clogging them up."

"You shouldn't be doing this, Mrs. Healy, it's not fitting," he said. "A member of your staff should do the brasses."

"You do the ones across the road. I've seen you," she countered.

"Ah, that's different. It's not my place, across there."

"Not yet," said Mrs. Healy.

Sean ignored this. "You must have somebody, Mrs. Healy, one of the kitchen maids."

"They're so unreliable. Just standing chatting to people instead of getting on with it." Mrs. Healy seemed quite unaware that this is what she was doing herself.

"If you like, I'll do yours when I'm doing ours," Sean offered. "But early in the morning, before anyone would see."

"That's extraordinarily kind of you." Mrs. Healy looked at him surprised as if wondering why he would do this. She prided herself on being able to understand human nature. Running a hotel you met all sorts and you had to make judgments about people. Sean Walsh was a difficult person to categorize. It was obvious that he had his eye on the daughter of the house. A big strong-willed girl with a mind of her own. Mrs. Healy thought that Sean Walsh would be wise to make some contingency plans. Just because she was a large girl who might not get many offers, Benny Hogan, once she had her degree from Dublin, might well hightail it off somewhere else. Leaving Sean Walsh's plans in tatters.

❦

Mother Francis was pleased that it was a nice bright Saturday morning and not drizzling with rain like it had been most mornings in the week.

She would go up to the cottage for an hour when school finished and see what else needed to be done. Sometimes she told herself that she was like a child with a dolls' house. Perhaps all the aching that a woman out in the world might have for her own home was coming to the surface. She hoped that this wasn't going to threaten the whole basis of her vocation to the religious life. You were meant to put your own home and family behind you and think only of your calling. But there was nothing in any rules that said you couldn't help to build up a home for an orphan who had been sent by the intervention of God into your care.

Mother Francis wondered how her orphan had got on at the dance last night. Kit Hegarty had phoned to say that Eve looked splendid. Mother Francis wished it hadn't been in a borrowed skirt, no matter how elegant and how rich a red.

She wished that class would be over and she could release the girls who were dying to escape anyway and go to Mario's cafe and look in the very much changed windows of Peggy's shop. Wouldn't it be wonderful if she could just ring the bell now, at eleven-thirty in the morning, and shout, "You're free."

The children would remember it all their lives. But undoubtedly it would get to the ears of Mother Clare. Her heart sank again as it always did at the thought of her sister in religion. If Mother Clare hadn't been coming they might have invited Kit Hegarty for Christmas. They couldn't now. Mother Clare would say they were turning a religious house into some kind of boardinghouse.

In two and a half hours she would be taking the key from its place in the wall and going into the cottage, polishing the piano and covering the damp stain on the wall with a lovely gold-colored wall hanging.

One of the missionary Sisters had brought it from Africa.

They had all admired it, but it wasn't a holy picture. It didn't really seem suitable to put it up in the convent. Mother Francis had kept it carefully. She knew just where it would be useful. And may be she might get some gold-colored material somewhere and Sister Imelda could run up a couple of cushion covers too.

Eve was almost bouncing up and down on her bed when she heard about the invitation to lunch.

"I *told* you, I *told* you," she kept saying.

"No, you didn't. You said he *looked* as if he was enjoying dancing with me. That's all."

"Well, you thought he looked as if it was Purgatory on earth and that he was making eyes at people over your shoulder to rescue him."

"I didn't quite think that," Benny said. But she had almost thought it.

When she had played the whole thing over in her mind again and again, those six lovely dances they had together, she was torn between believing that they were as enjoyable for him as they were for her, and that they were a simple courteous duty. Now it looked as if he really had liked her. The only problem was what to wear to the lunch.

Only the old castoff clothes of yesterday were available. You couldn't wear a ball gown and expose your bosom on a November Saturday. So much the pity!

"I have seventeen pounds. I could lend you some if you wanted to buy something," Eve offered.

But buying was no use. Not for Benny. They simply didn't have the clothes in her size.

If it had been Eve they could have run up Marine Road in Dun Laoghaire to Lee's or McCullogh's and got something in two minutes. If it were Nan all she would have to do was open a cupboard and choose. But Benny's clothes, such as they were, were fifty miles away in Knockglen.

Knockglen.

She had better ring her parents. And find out where they had been. And tell them it would be the evening bus, and say something to Patsy.

She got the coins and went back down to the phone.

They were delighted to hear from her and pleased that the dance had gone well, and wanted to know what had been served for supper. They were very startled to hear about the dispensation to eat meat. They had been out for a walk when she telephoned last night. It was very good of her. And had the party in the Foleys' house been nice? And had she explained again how grateful they were to be asked?

Benny felt her eyes misting.

"Tell Patsy I have a pair of stockings for her as a present," she said suddenly.

"You couldn't have chosen a better time to give her something," Benny's mother said in a low, conspiratorial voice. "She's been like a weasel all day. A weasel with a head cold if you ask me."

Eve said that Kit would find a solution to the clothes problem. Kit had an answer for everything.

"Not about huge clothes." Benny was gloomy.

But she was wrong. Kit said that one of the students who stayed in the house had a gorgeous emerald-green jumper. She'd borrow it off him. Say it needed a stitch or something. Boys never noticed that kind of thing. If he wanted to wear it today he bloody couldn't. That was all. Then Kit would sew a nice lacy collar of her own on it and lend Benny her green handbag. She'd be dressed to kill.

Fonsie wanted Clodagh to be the first to see the new ladies' cloakroom.

"God, it's lovely." She was full of admiration. "Pink towels, pink soap, and purple curtains. It's fabulous."

He was anxious about the lighting. Was it too bright?

Clodagh thought not. If they were old people, who didn't want to see wrinkles, then yes, have it subdued. But they'd be young. Let them see the worst in their faces.

Clodagh wished she could get her aunt to install two fitting rooms. Peggy said that it wasn't needed in somewhere like Knockglen. People could take things home on approval. If they didn't like them they could bring them back.

This was uneconomic and with the increased volume of stock they carried, hard to organize. There was a storeroom that Clodagh had her eye on. All it needed was light mirrors, carpet and bright curtains. They sighed, Clodagh and Fonsie, at the uphill battles with their relations.

"Will we go and have a drink in Healy's?" Fonsie said, suddenly.

"I don't know. I said I'd unpack a whole lot of stuff that came in this morning."

"To celebrate my new bathrooms and to plan your new fitting rooms," he pleaded.

They walked companionably up the street, Clodagh in her short white wool dress worn over a pair of baggy mauve trousers and mauve polo-necked jumper. Great white plastic hoops of earrings dangled under a man's tweed hat with a ribbon of mauve and white on it.

Fonsie's spongy shoes made no sound on the footpath. His red crushed-velvet jacket was bound in a yellow braid, his shirt neck was open and a red thin string like a tie hung down on each side of the collar. His dark red trousers were so tight that it appeared every step would cause him pain in most of his body.

On Saturdays at lunchtime the bar in Healy's Hotel was like a little club. Eddie Hogan would call in for a drink and meet Dr. Johnson coming back from his rounds. Sometimes Father Ross would appear, and if Dessie Burns was off the drink he would sip a Club Orange loudly and know he was welcome in their midst.

Mr. Flood hadn't been in much recently. The visions he had been seeing were preoccupying him. He had been seen standing in his garden looking thoughtfully up at the tree. Mr. Kennedy when he was alive had been a regular. His wife would not have dreamed of coming in his stead. Sometimes Peggy had gone in for a swift gin and vermouth with Birdie Mac.

Clodagh and Fonsie paused at the entrance to the bar, they didn't want to join the group of old people and yet it would have been rude to ignore them.

As it happened they didn't have to make the decision.

Suddenly between them and the room stood the well-corseted figure of Mrs. Healy.

"Can I do anything for you?" She looked from one to the other without hiding her distaste.

"Very probably, but I think we'll confine it to just having a drink at the moment." Fonsie laughed and ran his hand through his mop of dark and well-greased hair.

Clodagh giggled and looked down.

"Yes, well, perhaps Shea's or somewhere might be nice for a drink," Mrs. Healy said.

They looked at her in disbelief. She could not be refusing them entrance to her hotel?

Their silence unsettled her. Mrs. Healy had been expecting a protest.

"So maybe we could see you, here, when you are . . . um . . . more appropriately dressed," she said, with an insincere smile on her lips, but nowhere near her eyes.

"Are you refusing to serve us a drink, Mrs. Healy?" Fonsie said in a very loud voice, intended to make every head in the place look up.

"I'm suggesting that perhaps you might present yourself for a drink in garb that is more in tune with the standards of a town like this and a hotel of this caliber," she said.

"Are you refusing us because we are the worse for drink?" Clodagh asked. She looked over to the corner where two farmers were celebrating a small field bought and sold and were distinctly the worse for wear.

"I think out of respect for your aunt, who is one of our most valued customers, you might mind your tongue," Mrs. Healy said.

"She's joking Clodagh. Don't mind her," Fonsie said, trying to push past.

Two spots of red on Mrs. Healy's face warned everyone that she most certainly was not joking.

Fonsie said that there were four men in the bar without ties, and he was perfectly willing to close his tie if it meant he could get a half pint of Guinness.

Clodagh said that if any of her garments offended Mrs. Healy she would be very happy to remove them one by one until she was in something acceptable like a vest and knickers.

Eventually they tired of the game. With exaggerated shrugs and put-on bewildered expressions, they left the bar. They both turned at the door with the sad, bloodhound faces of condemned criminals, but their laughter could be heard all the way down the corridor and out into the street.

The group in the corner looked at each other in some alarm. The main problem was Peggy, one of the town's most respected citizens. How would she take to her niece being refused entrance to the hotel? The little group of people that Mrs. Healy cherished in her hotel looked down furtively.

Mrs. Healy spoke in a steady voice. "One has to draw the line somewhere," she said.

Lilly Foley said that Aidan Lynch's terrible parents never knew where to draw the line.

Jack asked why they hadn't stopped serving drink, then the Lynches would have gone home. That apparently had been done early on. The bottles had been physically taken away from Aengus, but they had still stayed on and boomed.

"It irritated your father," Lilly told Jack.

"Why didn't he do something about it then, like saying 'Good

God, is that the time?' " Jack saw no problems in the tardy Lynch parents.

"It's a woman's place to organize these things. It was left to me. As things always are." Lilly Foley seemed put out.

"But apart from that it was a great party. Thanks a lot." Jack grinned at her.

It mollified her a bit. She noted that her son had been on the phone already asking some girl out to lunch. She couldn't hear which one, but she assumed it was the glamorous Rosemary, who kept boasting of her relations in the Law, or the very beautiful girl, Nan, in the dress with all the little pearls on it. The girl who had said hardly anything, but was still the center of attention.

Lilly looked affectionately at her eldest son. His hair was tousled, he smelled of Knight's Castille soap, he had eaten a huge breakfast and read the sporting pages of two newspapers. He had given Aengus half a crown for all his help at the party.

Lilly knew that like his father before him Jack Foley was a heartbreaker, and would be one until the day he died.

He had said the name of the restaurant as if everyone knew it. Carlo's. Benny had heard of it. It was down near the quays, her old stamping ground getting on and off the bus from Knockglen. It was small and Italian, and she had once heard Nan say she had been there in the evening and they had candles in wine bottles like you saw in the pictures.

Much too early as usual, she went into a big store and examined the cosmetics. She found a green eye shadow and smeared some on each lid.

It was exactly the same color as the veterinary student's enormous jumper that she was wearing. The shop assistant urged her to buy it, insisting that it was often hard to find exactly the right shade when you were looking for it and you should seize the hour.

Benny explained that it wasn't her sweater. It was borrowed

from a fellow. She wondered why she needed to tell so much to strangers.

"Maybe he'll lend it to you again," said the girl in the short pink nylon coat whose job was to sell cosmetics.

"I doubt it. I don't even know who he is. His landlady pinched it for me."

Benny knew she was sounding very peculiar but conversation of any kind made her feel less anxious. It filled that great empty echo chamber of anxiety she felt about the lunch that lay ahead.

It had been so easy when she smelled of Joy and when she was able to be in his arms. It would be quite different now, in a green sweater across a table. How would she smile and attract him, and hold him. There must have been something about her that appealed to him last night. It couldn't have been all naked bosom, could it?

"Do you think I could have a spray of Joy perfume without buying any?" she begged the girl.

"We're not meant to."

"Please."

She got a small splash. Enough to remind him of last night.

Carlo's had a small door. That was a poor start. Benny hoped it wouldn't have those awful benches, those kinds of church pew seats that were popular now. They were desperately hard to squeeze into. Even though it was bright out on the street, with a cold, wintry sun picking everything out sharply, it was dark and warm inside.

She gave her coat to the waiter.

"I'm to meet someone here," she said.

"He is here already."

That meant that Jack must be well known in this place, she thought with a wave of disappointment. Maybe he came every Saturday with a different girl.

"How do you know it's the right person?" she asked the waiter anxiously. It would be humiliating to be led to the wrong table in front of everyone and for Jack to have to rescue her.

"There is only one person here," the waiter said.

He stood up to greet her.

"Don't you look lovely and well rested considering the night that was in it?" he said admiringly.

"That's the good bracing air of Dun Laoghaire," she said.

Why had she said that? There were words like "bracing" you didn't say. They reminded people of big, jolly girls on hikes. Like the word "strapping."

But he hadn't made any unfortunate word associations. He still seemed quite admiring.

"Whatever it is, it works. Our house is full of the-day-after feeling, glasses and ashtrays piled up in the kitchen."

"It was a lovely party, thank you very much."

"It was fine. Aengus sends you his regards. He was very taken with you."

"I think he thought I was mad."

"No. Why should he think that?"

It had been the wrong thing to say. Why had she said it? Bringing herself down, why couldn't she have asked about Aengus?

The waiter came and fussed over them. He was a kindly man, like a thinner version of Mario. Benny wondered was he any relation. There couldn't be that many Italians working in Ireland.

Benny decided to ask him.

"Do you have a relative working in Knockglen?"

He pronounced the name of her home town over and over, rolling it around, but his eyes narrowing suspiciously.

"Why do you think I have relations in Knocka Glenna?"

"There's an Italian there, called Mario."

Benny wished the purple and red sunburst carpet would open up at her feet and suck her into it, then close over her head.

Jack rescued her. "It's probably a bit like, do you know my uncle Mo in Chicago?" he said. "I'm always doing that."

She couldn't imagine him ever doing it. Was there any way at all of trying to get back some of the magic of last night.

They hadn't even begun the lunch and already he must have

regretted asking her. She had talked about the bracing air of Dun Laoghaire, reminding him of fat ladies on postcards. She had assumed that his younger brother must think she was mad. She had engaged the waiter in an endless and confused dialogue about whether he knew another Italian living miles away. What a great fun person she was. And there wasn't even anybody in the restaurant to distract him, to make him feel that the outing had any excitement at all. Benny wished she were back in the Dolphin Hotel with half of Dublin there and all the Rosemarys and Sheilas and even Carmel and Sean picking at each other and feeding each other bread rolls.

Anything was better than this catastrophic setting.

"Isn't it super to have it to ourselves," Jack said at that moment. "I feel like a sultan, or some millionaire. They do—you know —ring up restaurants and say they want to book all the tables so that they won't be disturbed."

"They do?" Benny asked eagerly.

At least it was conversation and he seemed to be making the best of the place being empty.

"Well, I did it today of course! Carlo, we need the whole place to ourselves . . . a pianist possibly, no. Well, all right. Just a few violinists at the table later. Just don't let any hoi polloi in, no awful Dubliners having their lunch or anything sordid like that."

They laughed and laughed just like last night.

"And what did Carlo say?"

"He said, 'For you Messter Foley anything you like, but only eef the Signorina ees lovely.' "

The words were bitten back. She was about to say, "Well, we fell down on that one, didn't we?"

She was going to put herself down for fear of thinking that she might actually believe herself to be acceptable. But something warned her it wasn't the right thing to do. She put her head on one side and smiled at him.

"And then you arrived and he saw you were very beautiful, so he has now put a House Full sign on the door," Jack said.

"Is that Carlo who's serving us do you think?" Benny asked.

"No idea," Jack said. "He looks much more like a man who has a secret cousin in Knockglen, but didn't want anyone to know."

"I must remember every detail of this place to tell Mario about it," Benny said, looking happily around.

"You're lovely, Benny," Jack said, and laid his hand on hers.

Clodagh told her aunt that she had been barred from Healy's. It didn't matter all that much because it wasn't a place she planned on visiting much anyway, but she felt that Peggy should know from her before anyone else told her.

"What were you doing the pair of you?" Peggy asked.

"I'd tell you if we *were* doing anything you know that. But as it happened we just walked in. She decided she didn't like the look of us."

"She can't do that under the Innkeepers Act."

"I think she can. Management reserves the right and all that. We thought you ought to know, you and Mario, but honestly Fonsie and I don't care. That's the truth."

The truth also was that Peggy and Mario did care. Very much. Neither of them liked the way that the young people dressed, in fact it was a source of great common grumbling between them. But to be refused service in the town's only hotel. That was something else. That was war.

It wasn't long before Mrs. Healy discovered how the lines were being drawn. Mr. Flood, who was having one of his clear spells where he neither saw nor mentioned the nun in the tree who had been visiting him with messages, said that it was time that someone had taken a stand. Those two were an abomination. He had read in the papers that there was an international movement to take over the civilized world, and that its members knew each other by these kinds of garish clothes. It was no accident that Fonsie and Clodagh had gravitated to each other, he said, nodding his head sagely. Mrs. Carroll was with Mrs. Healy too. The sooner this very undesirable influence in the town was stamped on the better. Neither of these two young people had parents to deal with them, relying only on a maiden aunt and a bachelor uncle. No wonder they had run wild.

Mrs. Carroll of the grocery said that her own daughter Maire, who was working in the shop and doing bookkeeping by correspondence course, had often been drawn to the bright lights in the cafe, and to the garish clothes in what had once been a respectable window. Mrs. Healy had been quite right to make her point.

Mrs. Kennedy on the other hand took a different view. She was heard to say that Mrs. Healy had a cheek. She hadn't even been born in Knockglen. Who did she think she was, making rules and regulations for the people of the town? Mrs. Kennedy said that there were many unsavory people seen in the corner of Healy's bar on a Fair Day and when commercial travelers had too much to drink and knew they could always get a drink in the hotel. Mrs. Kennedy, who had never liked the young widow and thought that her own husband used to spend too many evenings there, was outraged that she should think of refusing a drink to a niece of Peggy Pine, no matter how unwisely the poor girl garbed herself.

Birdie Mac wasn't sure. She was a timid woman who had lived all her life looking after an aged mother. She had neither wanted to do this or not wanted to. It was just that Birdie was unable to make a decision. She had never made her own mind up about anything. Even though she was a friend of Peggy's, she also listened to what Mrs. Carroll said. Even though Mario was a good customer and bought biscuits from her every day, she still agreed with poor Mr. Flood that Mario's nephew was going too far altogether and how could it be stopped unless somebody shouted stop.

She didn't like Mrs. Healy personally, but she admired her courage in running a business so well in a man's world, instead of retreating humbly behind the counter of a sweetshop, which was all that Birdie had been able to do in terms of independent living.

Dr. Johnson said that Mrs. Healy was free to serve or refuse whosoever she wanted. Father Ross wouldn't be drawn at all. Paccy Moore told his cousin Dekko that Mrs. Healy had two bunions, one on each foot. That was his only comment. It was taken to be support for Clodagh and Fonsie.

Eddie and Annabel Hogan discussed it for a long time over their Saturday lunch. There were ways of course that Clodagh and Fonsie had misunderstood Knockglen and gone too far. They both looked as if they were in fancy dress almost all of the time. But they were hard workers, it couldn't be denied, and that was their great saving grace. If they had been standing smoking on the corner there would have been no sympathy for them.

But nobody could accuse either of them of being idle. And in Knockglen that would cover a multitude of sins, like dressing so mutinously.

"If someone came into your shop, you'd serve them no matter how they were dressed, wouldn't you Eddie."

"Yes, but if they had manure on their boots I'd ask them not to walk it in," he said.

"But they weren't walking anything in," Annabel Hogan said. She had always thought that Mrs. Healy had a special smile for the men and nothing nearly so warm for their wives. And also Clodagh had made such a lovely dress for Benny it would be hard not to be on her side. All that brocade had looked so well, there were little bits of chestnut color in it, just like Benny's hair, and that beautiful dash of white at the front, that pleated insert over the bosom. It had given the whole thing such a classy touch. So elegant and ladylike, and not at all the kind of thing you'd ever have thought Clodagh would have dreamed up.

Mother Francis heard about the scene in the hotel as well. Peggy drove up to the convent that afternoon for tea and advice.

"Rise above it, Peggy. Rise right above it."

"That's not easy to do if you're out in the world, Bunty."

"It's not easy to do if you're inside a convent either. I have that Mother Clare descending on me for Christmas. Imagine trying to rise above that."

"I'll never go in there for a drink again."

"Think carefully, Peggy, think. If you do want a drink where will you go? The spit and sawdust in Shea's maybe? The pokey little snugs of the other places? Don't do anything rash."

"God, Bunty, for a nun you've a great knowledge of all the bars in town," said Peggy Pine admiringly.

They talked about the dance, and how wonderful Aidan had been. No other table had won so many spot prizes. And there had been an incident Jack told her where a girl fainted at another table and when they had loosened her clothes and tried to revive her two bread rolls had fallen out of her bra. Jack laughed good-naturedly at this. Benny thought of how the girl must be feeling today, and how she would never be able to remember the dance with anything but shame.

"Oh, go on, it *is* funny," he said. She knew she must see the lighthearted side.

"Yes, and full of crumbs, very scratchy I'd say." She felt like Judas to this girl she didn't even know, but she was rewarded with the smile.

"Not anything you'd ever need, Benny," he said, smiling at her across the table.

"Everyone's different." She looked down, very, very embarrassed.

"You're different in a good way," he said.

At least the veterinary student, whoever he was, had a nice floppy jumper. You couldn't see the outline of her breasts. She looked at her front relieved. What could she say now to change the subject?

The door opened and another couple came in. Jack shrugged.

"I said only people from Napoli could come, and then only if they stayed quiet." He looked at them warningly.

They were a pair of middle-aged Dubliners. Cold and shivery.

"Probably civil servants having an affair," Benny whispered.

"No, two school inspectors planning to make everyone fail the Leaving Certificate next year," he countered.

Most of the time it was easy to talk to him. He was so normal and relaxed, and there really was nothing in his manner that made her feel anxious. It was just herself. Benny realized that she had spent years sending herself up and playing the fool. When it came to the time to play the romantic lead, she didn't have a clue. And worse, she wasn't at all sure that was the part she was actually being cast to play. She wished she could read his signals, and understand what he was saying.

If only she could know then she could respond.

The ice cream was offered. The waiter explained cassata, a beautiful Neapolitan ice cream he said, lovely bits of fruit and nuts chopped up in it, some candied peel, some macaroons. *Bellissima*.

Something told Benny that the right thing was to have it, not to talk of diets or calories, or waistlines.

She saw Jack's face light up. He'd have some too.

The waiter saw them smile at each other.

"It's a very dark afternoon. I light a little candle to give you light to see each other when you talk," he said.

Jack's open shirt over his navy sweater was a pale pink. It looked beautiful in the candlelight. She felt again that urge to stroke him. Not to kiss his lips or press against him, just to reach out and rub her hand softly from his cheek to his chin.

She had drunk only one glass of wine. It couldn't be some drink-crazed feeling.

Benny watched as if it was happening to someone else as she leaned across and stroked his face softly three times.

The third time he caught her hand and held it to his lips.

He kissed it with his head bent over it so that she couldn't see his eyes.

Then he gave it back to her.

There was no way he was making fun of her, or making a silly extravagant gesture like Aidan might.

Nobody would hold your hand like that kiss it for such a long time unless they wanted to.

Would they? Would they?

Dessie Burns said that Mrs. Healy could be a bit uppity in herself, and there had indeed been times when she had spoken to him more sharply than was called for. But to be fair, there had been a question of drink involved and perhaps there were those who would say that the woman had been within her rights. There was nothing more scrupulously and boringly fair than Dessie Burns when he was on the dry.

And when all was said and done that young Fonsie was a pup, and a pup needed a good spanking now and then if he was to grow into a good dog, so that's all that had happened. Fonsie had been told he couldn't walk around this town as if he owned it. Who was he? The nephew of an Eyetie, with no sign of the Eyetie mother and the Dub father since the day he'd set foot in the place. That was a young lad without a background, without a history, in Knockglen. Let him take things more slowly. And as for Peggy's niece, she was a sore trial with the getup of her. Maybe this would make her settle down.

Mario said that he would go up and stand on the step of Healy's Hotel and spit in the door and then spit out the door, and then he'd come home and spit at Fonsie.

Fonsie said that none of this would advance them, they should instead go to Liverpool and buy a beautiful secondhand Wurlitzer jukebox that he had seen advertised there.

Mario developed a most unexpected loyalty to Fonsie. Having denounced him to everyone in the town individually and generally he now said that his sister's child was the salt of the earth, the mainstay of Mario's old age and the shining hope for Knockglen.

He also said with a lot of pounding on whatever surface was

near that he would never drink in Healy's again. Which, considering he had never drunk there anyway, was a threat more powerful in the utterance than the deed.

Simon Westward came into Healy's that afternoon to inquire if they did dinners.

"Every day, Mr. Westward." Mrs. Healy was delighted to see him in the place at last. "Might I offer you a little something on the house to celebrate your first visit to us?"

"Very kind of you . . . er . . . Mrs. . . . er . . ."

"Healy." She looked rather pointedly at the hotel sign.

"Ah yes, how stupid of me. No, I won't stay for a drink now. You do do dinners. That's wonderful. I wasn't sure."

"Every day from noon until two-thirty."

"Oh."

"Do those hours not suit you?"

"No, I mean they're perfectly fine hours. I was thinking of dinner in the evening."

Mrs. Healy always prided herself on being ready when Opportunity came to call.

"Up to now Mr. Westward we have merely served high teas, but coming up to the Christmas season and thereafter we will indeed be serving dinner," she said.

"Starting?"

"Starting next weekend, Mr. Westward," she said, looking him straight in the eye.

The waiter thought they must have a Sambuca. It was a little Italian liqueur. This was with the compliments of the house. He would put a coffee bean in it and set it alight. It was a wonderful drink to have at the end of a lunch on a winter's day.

They sat there and wondered would the disgruntled couple get one too, or was it only for people who looked happy.

"Will we see you next weekend?" the waiter asked eagerly. Benny could have killed him. She was doing so well. Why must the waiter bring up the subject of another date.

"Certainly another time, I hope," Jack said.

They walked along the quays, which had often looked cold and wet to Benny, but this afternoon there was a glorious sunset, and everything had a rosy light.

The secondhand booksellers had wooden stands of books on display outside.

"It's like Paris," Benny said happily.

"Were you ever there?"

"No, of course I wasn't." She laughed good-naturedly. "That's me, just showing off. I've seen the pictures and I've been to the films."

"And you're studying French of course, you'd be able to take it in your stride."

"I doubt that. Great chats about Racine and Corneille in English would be more my line."

"Nonsense. I'll be depending on you to be my guide when I'm playing in the Parc des Princes," he said.

"I bet you will," she said.

"No, that's me showing off. I'll never play for anyone if I keep eating like I did last night and today. I'm meant to be in training. You'd never know it."

"You're lucky you didn't have practice today. You often do on Saturdays, don't you?"

"We did. I skipped it," he said.

She looked at him suddenly. The old Benny would have made a joke. The new Benny didn't.

"I'm glad you did. It was a lovely lunch."

She had her overnight bag in a shop near the bus stop. The woman handed it over the counter to her and together they walked toward the bus.

"What will you do tonight?" he asked her.

"Go to Mario's cafe and tell people about the dance. What about you?"

"No idea. Hope there are some invitations when I get home." He laughed lazily, the kind of man who didn't have to plan his own life.

He passed her zippered bag onto the bus. Benny willed Mikey not to make any smart-aleck remarks.

"There you are, Benny. I knew we didn't have you yesterday. The weight in the bus was lighter altogether," he said.

Jack hadn't heard, or if he had heard he hadn't understood Mikey's mumblings. That's what she told herself as she sat and looked out at the darkening city and the beginnings of the country-side.

She had danced close to Jack Foley, who had then invited her out to lunch. She had said nothing too stupid. He had said he'd see her in the Annexe on Monday. He had kissed her hand. He had said she was lovely.

She was absolutely exhausted. She felt as if she had been carrying a heavy weight for miles and miles in some kind of contest. But whatever contest it was, and whatever the rules, it looked as if she had won.

TWELVE

*H*eather wanted to know all about the dance and mainly what they had for pudding. She was stunned that Eve couldn't remember. She found it beyond comprehension that there could be too much else happening to remember pudding.

She broke the news that Simon said he was going to join them on their outing.

"I didn't know anything about this," Eve said annoyed.

"I didn't tell you in case you wouldn't come." Heather was so honest that it was hard to attack her.

"Well, if you have him . . ."

"I want you," Heather said simply.

Simon arrived in the car.

"Think of me as the chauffeur," he said. "You ladies are in charge."

Almost immediately he gave them his own plan for the afternoon. A drive through County Wicklow and afternoon tea in a rather nice hotel he knew.

Eve and Heather had been planning to take the train to Bray, go on the bumpers and have ice creams with hot butterscotch sauce. Eve was pleased that Simon's outing sounded so dull and tame compared to her own. She knew which Heather would have preferred.

But Heather was a dutiful sister, and she saw far too little of Simon already. She gave a mild show of enthusiasm. Eve after a deliberate pause did the same.

Simon looked from one to the other. He knew that this was second best. He was very cheery and answered all Heather's questions about her pony, about Clara's puppies, about Woffles the rabbit.

He explained that Mrs. Walsh was still as silent and as majestic on her bicycle as ever. That Bee Moore was upset over some young man she had wanted and he had turned his attentions to Another. Eve had to put her hand over her face when Heather's questioning revealed the man to be Mossy Rooney and Another to be Patsy.

"How's grandfather?" Heather asked.

"The same. Come on, we're boring Eve."

"But he's Eve's grandfather too."

"Absolutely."

The subject was closed. Eve knew he wanted something. She had no idea what it was.

At teatime he brought it up.

"That was a remarkably beautiful girl, your friend."

"Which friend?"

"In the shop. At the dance. The blond girl."

"Oh yes?"

"I was wondering who she is?"

"Were you?"

"Yes, I was." He was short now.

For ages afterward Eve hugged herself with delight and congratulation that she had managed not to answer such a direct question with any kind of response that would please him. And yet she had remained perfectly polite. For the girl who used to speak so unguardedly, whose temper was a legend in St. Mary's, it was a triumph.

"Who is she? Oh, she's a student at UCD, doing First Arts, like about six hundred of us."

Her smile had told Simon Westward that this was all he was going to get.

The veterinary student was a nice boy called Kevin Hickey. He was very polite and he thanked Mrs. Hegarty for having taken his new green sweater to sew a tape on the back of it in case he wanted to hang it up with a loop. He had thought you should fold them, or put them on a clothes hanger, but still, it was very nice of her. He might wear it tonight. It was a great color. When he picked it up he thought there was a faint smell of perfume, but he must have imagined it. Or else it was Mrs. Hegarty's perfume. Kevin Hickey's mother was dead. It was nice to live in a house where there was a kind woman looking after him. He had asked his father to send her a turkey for Christmas. It would come by train, wrapped in straw and tied well with string.

He smelled his green jumper again. There was definitely some cosmetic. Maybe if he hung it up in the fresh air by the window it would go away.

He heard the gate opening and drew back. He wouldn't like Mrs. Hegarty to see him airing the jumper. But it wasn't Mrs. Hegarty back from her shopping. It was a dark-haired man he hadn't seen before.

The door bell rang and rang, so Kevin ran down to answer it. Mrs. Hegarty was out, he said. The man wanted to wait. He looked respectable. Kevin was at a loss.

"It really is all right." The man smiled at him. "I'm an old friend."

"And what's your name?"

"It's Hegarty also, as it happens."

As Kevin went back upstairs he turned and saw the man who was sitting in the hall pick up the picture of Mrs. Hegarty's son who had died. Possibly he was a relation.

✦

Sheila noticed that Jack ran off immediately after his law lectures these days. No hanging around and chatting. No little jokes, just off like an arrow. Once or twice she asked him why he needed to run so fast.

"Training." He had smiled at her with that boyish kind of laugh which meant he knew he would be forgiven anything.

Sheila decided that he must be seeing that Rosemary Ryan in First Arts.

She inquired from Carmel if that was true. It was easy to talk to Carmel because she wasn't really playing in the same game, she was so preoccupied with Sean that other people were only a vague background to her.

"Rosemary and Jack? I don't think so," Carmel said, after a lot of thought. "No, I haven't seen them together at all. I've seen Jack in the Annexe a couple of mornings, but only talking to Benny Hogan."

"Ah, well, that's all right, so," said Sheila with some relief.

Benny and Patsy were friends again. It had taken the promised stockings plus a tin of French Moss talcum powder and an explanation that her nerves were overwrought because she was frightened of going to the dance. Once Patsy had come round she was as usual a strong champion of the daughter of the house.

"What did you have to be frightened of? Aren't you a fine big girl who shows all the signs of being well fed and well looked after all her life?"

That was one of the things that Benny feared was only too obvious. But it was hard to explain to small, stooped Patsy who had been brought up without enough to eat in an orphanage.

"How's your romance?" she asked instead.

"He's not much with the words," Patsy complained.

"But the words he does say? Are they nice?"

"It's very hard to know with men what they mean," Patsy said sagely. "You'd need someone standing at your shoulder saying this means this, and this means the other."

Benny agreed fervently. When Jack Foley said he had missed her at a party did he mean that he had looked around and thought it would be lovely if only Benny had been there. Had he thought it all evening, or only once? And if he missed her that much why had he gone to it? At the party in Jack's house Aengus had asked Benny if she was one of the ones who was always phoning looking for Jack. She had decided that she would never be one of those. It had worked so well the way things were. Or had it? Patsy was right. With men it was impossible to know what they meant. Nan used to say they never meant anything, but that was too depressing to contemplate.

Mrs. Healy had been disappointed not to see Sean Walsh arriving full of support for her predicament. She knew his distaste for Fonsie and Clodagh and the kind of life-style they represented. But then Sean was not a customer in Healy's Hotel. It had something to do with not presuming she imagined. Not putting himself forward, styling himself as Mr. Hogan's equal when he was in fact a hired hand.

It was nice to see that kind of respect but sometimes Sean carried it too far. Like polishing the brasses, like living in a cramped room over the shop. He seemed to be biding his time and maybe he might bide it too long.

"You should invite young Sean Walsh in for a drink with you sometime," she suggested to Eddie Hogan.

Eddie's honest face told her what she already knew. "I've asked him a dozen times, but he won't come in with me. I don't think he's a drinking man. Weren't we blessed the day he arrived in Knockglen?"

Emily Mahon marveled at the way her daughter kept her clothes and her room. Every garment was sponged and hung up when it was taken off. Her coats and jackets always looked as if they had come straight from the dry cleaners.

The shoes had newspapers stuffed in the toes and stood on a small rack by the window. She polished her belts and handbags until they gleamed. On the wash handbasin in her room were samples of soaps that Emily had been able to get her through the hotel. There was a book on How to Apply Makeup. Nan Mahon didn't rely on weekly magazines or Sunday newspapers to teach her style. She did the thing thoroughly.

Emily smiled affectionately as she saw the books on etiquette that Nan studied as well as her university texts. She had once told her mother that anyone could talk to anyone if they knew the rules. It was a matter of learning them.

The book was open at a section telling you how introductions are made.

"Marquesses, Earls, Viscounts, Barons and their wives are introduced as Lord or Lady X, Honourables as plain Mr." Imagine if Nan was in a world where such things would be of use to her. But then it wasn't all that far beyond the possible. Look at the way she had looked at that dance. People who weren't even part of the student crowd were admiring her. She might very well end up in twinset and pearls on the steps of a big house, with dogs beside her and servants to do her work.

It had always been Emily Mahon's dream for her daughter. The only problem was what part would she play in it. And it didn't bear thinking about how little a part Nan's father might be expected to take in any such life-style.

If Nan were to get there it was easy to see that she would no longer be any part of Maple Gardens.

Rosemary Ryan wore far too much makeup for the daytime. Benny could see that quite clearly now. There was a ridge at the side of her jaw where it stopped.

She was also brighter than people gave her credit for. When

she was with a crowd she always simpered and played the dumb blonde, but in tutorials she was sharp as a razor.

"What are you going to do when this is over?" she asked Benny.

"Go to the Annexe." Benny was meeting Jack. She hoped Rosemary wouldn't come too. "I have to meet a whole lot of different people," she said hastily, to discourage her.

"No, I meant this. All of this." Rosemary waved a vague hand around the University.

"Do a postgrad diploma and be a librarian, I think," Benny said. "What about you?"

"I think I'll be an air hostess," Rosemary said.

"You don't need a degree for that."

"No, but it helps." Rosemary had it worked out. "It's a great way to get a husband."

Benny didn't know whether she meant doing a degree was a good way of being an air hostess. She didn't like to ask. It was such a strange coincidence that Rosemary should say that, because only the day before Carmel had asked Nan would she think of joining Aer Lingus. She had the looks and the style. And she'd meet lots of men.

"Only businessmen," Nan had said, as if that settled it.

Carmel's eyes had narrowed. Her Sean was doing a B.Comm. and was aiming hard to be a businessman.

"Carmel says Nan doesn't think it's a good job." Rosemary was probing. "Do you think Nan's going out with Jack Foley?"

"What makes you think that?"

"I don't know. He hasn't been sighted much. I wondered was he holed up with someone mysterious."

"I see him from time to time," Benny said.

"Oh, that's all right then." Rosemary was pleased. "He's around. He hasn't been snatched away from under our noses. What a relief!"

❧

Kit Hegarty let herself in and found her husband, Joseph, sitting in the kitchen.

She put her shopping on the floor and steadied herself with a hand on the kitchen chair.

"Who let you in?" she asked.

"A boy with freckles and a Kerry accent. Don't say anything to him. He interrogated me and asked me to sit in the hall."

"Which you didn't."

"I was cold."

"Did you tell him who you were?"

"Just that my name happened to be Hegarty. Sit down, Kit. I'll make you a cup of tea."

"You'll make me nothing in my kitchen," she said.

But she did sit down and looked at him across the table. He was fifteen years older than he was the day he had taken the mail boat out of their lives.

How long had she cried herself to sleep at night wanting him to return. How often had she played the scene where he would come back and she would forgive him. But always in that version Francis would be young and would run toward them both, arms outstretched, crying out that he had a Daddy and a real home again.

He was still handsome. His hair had only little bits of gray, but he looked shabbier than she remembered, as if he were down on his luck. His shoes weren't well polished. They needed to be taken to a cobbler's. His cuffs were not frayed exactly, but thin.

"Did you hear about Francis?" she said.

"Yes."

The silence hung long between them.

"I came to tell you how sorry I was," he said.

"Not sorry enough to see him ever, to care to be involved in his life when he had a life."

She looked at him without hate, the man who had abandoned them. She had been told that he had gone to live with a barmaid. At the time somehow that had made it worse, more humiliating

293

that the woman was a barmaid. It was such an obvious kind of thing to do. Now she wondered why the woman's job had been remotely important.

She thought of all the questions she had parried and eventually answered while her son grew up asking about his father, and wondering why he didn't have what everyone else at the Christian Brothers' school had in their homes.

She thought of the day Francis had got his Leaving Certificate and run home with the results, and how she had an urge to find her long-lost husband that day—only a few months ago—and tell him that the child they had produced together would go to university.

In those long nights when she had not been able to find any sleep and thoughts had run scampering around in her head, she remembered with relief that she hadn't raised the hopes of this philandering husband and led him to believe that he had fathered a university student.

She thought of all this as she looked at him sitting in her kitchen.

"I'll make you tea," she said.

"Whatever you think."

"Did she throw you out?" Kit asked. She asked because he hadn't the look of a man who was cared for by a woman, not even a woman who had been brassy and taken him, even though she must have known he had a wife and child in Ireland.

"Oh, that all ended a long time ago. Years and years ago."

It had ended. But he had not come back. Once gone he was truly gone. Somehow that was sadder than the other. For years she had seen him in some kind of domesticity with this woman. But in fact he might have been living alone, or in digs or bed-sitters.

That was worse than leaving her for a grand passion, however ill-advised. She looked at him with a look of great sadness.

"I was wondering . . ." he said.

She looked at him, kettle in one hand and teapot in the other.

He was going to ask, could he come back.

❦

Nan wanted to know if Eve had taken Heather out at the weekend. She often inquired about Heather, Eve noticed, rarely about the digs and Kit or the convent and Mother Francis.

She said they went to Wicklow and it had been wet and misty, and they went to a hotel where tea and sandwiches cost twice what real food like ice cream and butterscotch sauce would cost.

"You must have gone in a car to a place like that," Nan said.

"Yes." Eve looked at her.

"Did Aidan drive you?"

"Lord, I couldn't let Aidan near her. He's quite frightening enough for our age. He'd give a child nightmares."

Nan left the subject of Aidan Lynch.

"So who did?"

Eve knew it was ridiculous not to tell her. She'd get to know someday. It was like being an eight-year-old, having secrets at school. Anyway it was making too much of it all.

"Her brother Simon drove us," she said.

"The one we saw in my mother's shop at the dance, and you didn't introduce me."

"The very one."

Nan pealed with laughter. "You're marvelous, Eve," she said. "I'm so glad I'm your friend. I'd really hate to be your enemy."

Most of the cottages on the road up by the quarry behind the convent were fairly dilapidated. It was never a place that anyone would really seek out to live. It had been different when the quarry was operating, in those days there had been plenty of people wanting to live there. Now there were very few lights burning in windows. Mossy Rooney lived in a small house there with his mother. There had been rumors that Mossy had been seen with building materials and a consequent speculation that he might intend building an extra room at the back. Could this mean that he had plans to marry?

Mossy was not a man to do things in a hurry. People said that Patsy shouldn't count her chickens too soon.

Sean Walsh sometimes went for a walk up that way on a Sunday. Mother Francis would nod to him gravely and he always returned the greeting very formally.

If he ever wondered what the nun was doing pushing her way past the dark green leaves of the wild fuchsia and rolling up her sleeves to polish and clean he never gave any sign of his curiosity. Neither did she pause to think why he walked there. He was a lonely young man, not very attractive to speak to. She knew that Eve had always disliked him. But that might just have been a childish thing, a loyalty to Benny Hogan, who had some kind of antipathy toward her father's assistant.

She was surprised when he addressed her. With a long preamble of apology he asked if she knew who owned the cottages and whether they might perhaps belong to the convent. Mother Francis explained that they had once belonged to the Westlands estate, and had devolved somehow to various quarry workers and others. Politely with her head on one side in her inquiring manner she wondered why he wanted to know.

Equally courteously Sean told her that it had been an idle inquiry but the nature of small towns being what it was, perhaps an inquiry that might remain confidential between the two of them.

Mother Francis sighed. She supposed the poor fellow who had scant hope of making much of a living in Hogan's might be looking to the day when he could buy a house for himself and start a family, and that he was realistic enough to start looking up on this wild craggy road where nobody would really live by choice.

Benny hated going into the Coffee Inn. The tables were always so small. She was afraid that her skirt or her shoulder bag would swoop someone's frothy coffee off onto the floor.

Jack's face lit up when he saw her. He had been holding a seat with some difficulty.

"These awful country thicks wanted to take your stool," he hissed at her.

"Less running down the country people," Benny said. She glanced up and saw with a shock that the three students who had lost the battle for the seat were Kit Hegarty's students, the boys who lived where Eve worked. And one of them, a big fellow with freckles, was wearing his lovely emerald-green sweater.

Aidan Lynch asked Eve to come home and meet his parents.

"I've met them," Eve said ungraciously, handing him another dinner plate to dry.

"Well, you could meet them again."

Eve didn't want to meet them again; it was rushing things. It was saying things that weren't ready to be said like that Eve was Aidan's girl friend, which she wasn't.

"How is this relationship going to progress any further?" Aidan asked the ceiling. "She won't get to know my family. She won't let me near her body. She won't go on a date with me unless I come out to Dun Laoghaire and do the washing up after all the culchies first." He sounded very sorry for himself.

Eve's mind was on other things. Aidan could amuse himself for hours when he was in one of his rhetorical moods. She smiled at him absently.

Kit was out. For the very first time since Eve had been in the house, what was more, there was no message.

Kevin, the nice freckled vet student whose jumper had been purloined for Benny's date, had said that Mrs. Hegarty had gone out with a man.

"Everyone goes out with men," Aidan had interrupted. "It's the law of nature. Female canaries go out with male canaries. Sheep go out with rams. Women tortoises go out with men tortoises. Only Eve seems to have reservations."

Eve took no notice. She was also thinking about Benny. Almost every day for a week now Benny had met Jack Foley, either in the Annexe or the Coffee Inn or a bar. She said he was very easy to talk to. She hadn't put a foot wrong yet. Benny's face had looked as if someone had turned on a light inside when she talked about Jack Foley.

"And of course this Eve that I have the misfortune to be besotted with . . . she won't even stay in Dublin for the Christmas parties. She's leaving me on my own for other women to have their way with, and do sinful things with my body."

"I have to go to Knockglen, you idiot," she said.

"Where there will be no parties, where people will go out and watch the grass grow and see the rain fall and moo cows will walk down the main street swishing their foul tails."

"You've got it so wrong," Eve cried. "We'll be having a *great* time in Knockglen, down in Mario's every evening, and of course there'll be parties there."

"Name me one," Aidan countered.

"Well, I'll be having one for a start," Eve said, stung.

Then she stood motionless with a dinner plate in her hands. Oh God, she thought. Now I have to.

Nan rang *The Irish Times,* and asked for the Sports Department. When she was put through she asked them to tell her what race meetings would be held before Christmas.

Not many, she was told. Things slackened off coming up to the festive season. There'd be a meeting every Saturday, of course, Navan, Punchestown, run-of-the-mill things. But on St. Stephen's Day it would all get going again. The day after Christmas there'd be Leopardstown and Limerick. She could take her pick of those. Nan asked them what did people who usually went racing do when the season slackened off. In a newspaper people are accustomed to being asked odd questions on the phone. They gave it some consideration. It depended on what kind of people. Some might be saving their pennies, some might be out hunting. It depended.

Nan thanked them in the pleasant unaffected voice that had never tried to imitate the tones of another class she wanted to join. An elocution teacher at school had once told them that there was nothing more pathetic than people with perfectly good Irish accents trying to say "Fratefully naice." Nothing would mark you out as a social climber as much as adopting that kind of accent.

They sat in a cafe in Dun Laoghaire, Mr. and Mrs. Hegarty. Around them other people were doing ordinary things, like having a coffee before going to an evening class in typing, or waiting for the pictures to start.

Ordinary people with ordinary lives and nothing bigger to discuss than whether the electric fire would eat up electricity or if they could have two chickens instead of a turkey for Christmas Day.

Joseph Hegarty fiddled with his spoon. She noticed that he didn't take sugar in his coffee now. Perhaps the woman had put him off that. Perhaps his travels had taken him to places where there were no sugar bowls on the table. He had left one insurance company and gone to another. He had moved from that to working with a broker, to having a book himself, to working with another agent. Insurance wasn't the same, he told her.

She looked at him with eyes that were not hard, or cold. She saw him objectively. He was kindly and soft spoken as he had always been. In those first agonized months after he had left that was what she had missed above all.

"You wouldn't know anyone here anymore," she said haltingly.

"I'd get to know them again."

"It'd be harder to find insurance work here than there. Things are very tight in Ireland."

"I wouldn't go back on that. I thought maybe I could help you . . . build up the business."

She thought about it, sitting very still and with her eyes down so that she wouldn't meet the hope in his. She thought of the way he would preside over the table, make the place seem like it was run by a family. She could almost see him giving second helpings, making boys like Kevin Hickey laugh, being interested in their studies and their social lives.

But why had he not done that for his own son? For Francis Hegarty who might still be alive this day if he had had a firm father who would brook no nonsense about a motorbike.

"No, Joseph," she said, without looking up. "It wouldn't work."

He sat there very silent. He thought about his son, the son who had written to him all these years. The son who had come to see him during the summer, on a weekend from canning peas. Frank, the boy who had drunk three pints with his father and told him all about the home in Dun Laoghaire and how maybe his mother's heart was softening. But he had never told his mother about the visit or the letters. Joseph Hegarty would keep faith with the dead boy. Frank must have had his reasons, his father would not betray him now or change his mother's memory of him.

"Very well, Kit," he said. "It's your decision. I just thought I'd ask."

The Westwards were in the telephone book. The phone was answered by an elderly woman.

"It's a personal call for Mr. Simon Westward from Sir Victor Cavendish." Nan spoke in the impersonal voice of a secretary. She had taken the name from *Social and Personal.*

"I'm sorry, Mr. Westward isn't here."

"Where can Sir Victor find him, please?"

Mrs. Walsh responded immediately to the confident tone that expected an answer.

"He's going to have lunch in the Hibernian I believe," she said. "Perhaps Sir Victor could telephone him there."

"Thank you so much," Nan said, and hung up.

"I want to give you your Christmas present today," Nan said to Benny in the Main Hall.

"Lord, Nan, I didn't bring anything in for you." Benny looked stricken.

"No, mine is a treat. I'm taking you to lunch."

She would listen to no refusals. Everyone deserved to have lunch in the Hibernian at least once in their life. Nan and Benny were no exceptions. Benny wondered why Eve wasn't being included.

They met Bill Dunne and Johnny O'Brien as they were crossing St. Stephen's Green.

The boys suggested a Christmas drink. When that was turned down, they came up with chicken croquette and chips in Bewley's with sticky almond buns to follow. Laughing, Benny said they were going to the Hibernian.

"You must have a pair of sugar daddies then," Bill Dunne said crossly to hide his disappointment.

Benny wanted to tell them that it was Nan's treat, but she didn't like to. Perhaps Nan mightn't want to admit that it was just the two of them. She looked hopefully at her friend for some signal. But Nan's face gave no hints of anything. She looked so beautiful Benny thought, again with a pang. It must be amazing to wake up in the morning and know your features were going to look like that all day, and that everyone who saw your face would like it.

Benny wished that Bill Dunne didn't look so put out. On an ordinary day it would have been lovely to have gone to Bewley's with him. Jack was up at the rugby club all afternoon. She would love to have been with Bill and Johnny in many ways. They were

Jack's people. They were part of his life. She felt disloyal to Nan and her generous present. And wasn't it marvelous to go inside the Hibernian for something better than walking through its coffee lounge to the ladies' cloakroom at the back which was all she had ever done before.

Eve had no lectures in the afternoon. She couldn't find either Benny or Nan. Aidan Lynch had invited her to join his parents, who liked to combine an hour of Christmas shopping and four hours of lunch several times in the weeks leading up to the festive season. She had declined, saying it sounded like a mine field.

"When we're married we'll have to see them you know, invite them over for roast lamb and mint sauce," he had said.

"We'll face that when we come to it in about twenty years time," Eve had said to him grimly.

You couldn't put Aidan Lynch off. He was much too cheerful, and totally confident that she loved him. Which of course she didn't. Eve didn't love anybody, as she had tried to explain. Just very strong affections for Mother Francis and Benny and Kit. Nobody had ever shown her why love was such a great thing she told him. Look what it had done for her mother and father. Look how boring it made Sean and Carmel. Look at the way it had wrecked Kit Hegarty's life.

Thinking about Kit made her think that that was where she would go, home to Dun Laoghaire. Kit had looked very strange in the last couple of days. Eve hoped that she wasn't sick, or that the man who had come back hadn't been who Eve feared it had.

She took the train out to Dun Laoghaire and let herself in. Kit was sitting in the kitchen with her head in her hands. Nothing had been touched since Eve had left that morning. Eve hung up her coat.

"Sister Imelda had a great saying. She used to believe that there was no problem on the face of the earth that couldn't be tackled better with a plate of potato cakes. And I must say I agree with her."

As she spoke she took the cold mashed potato from the bowl, opened a bag of flour and dropped a lump of butter on the frying pan.

Eve still didn't look up.

"Not that it solved everything, mind you. Like I remember when nobody would tell me why my mother and father were buried in different churchyards. We had potato cakes then, Mother Francis and I. It didn't really explain it, or make me feel better about it. But it made us feel great eating them."

Kit raised her head. The casual voice and the ritual actions of cooking had soothed her. Eve never paused in her movements as Kit Hegarty told her the story of the husband who had left and come back and been sent away again.

Nan had spotted Simon Westward the moment that she and Benny were led into the dining room. The waiter had been intending to put two such young-looking female students away in a corner, but Nan asked could they have a more central table. She spoke like someone who had been there regularly. There wasn't any reason why she shouldn't get a better table.

They studied the menu and Nan asked about the dishes they couldn't understand.

"Let's have something we never had before," she suggested.

Benny had been heading for lamb because it looked nice and safe. But it was Nan's treat.

"Like what?" she asked fearfully.

"Brains," Nan said. "I never had those."

"Wouldn't it be a bit of a waste. Suppose they were awful?"

"They wouldn't be awful in a place like this. Why don't you have sweetbreads or guinea fowl or snipe."

"Snipe? What's that?"

"It's with game. It must be a bird."

"It can't be. I never heard of it. It's a belt, taking a snipe at someone."

Nan laughed. "That's taking a swipe you idiot."

Simon Westward looked up just then. Nan could see him from the corner of her eye. She had been aware that he was at a table with a couple, a very tweedy older man and a younger, horsey-looking woman.

Nan knew that she had been seen. She settled back into her seat. All she had to do now was wait.

Benny struggled with the things they didn't know on the menu.

"I could have scampi, I don't know that."

"You know what it is. It's a big prawn in batter."

"Yes, but I've never tasted it, so it would be new to me."

At least she had got out of brains and sweetbreads and other strange-sounding things.

"Miss Hogan. Don't you dine in the best places?" Simon Westward was standing beside her.

"I hardly ever go anywhere posh, but anytime I do you're there." She smiled at him warmly.

He didn't even have to look inquiringly across the table before Benny introduced him. Very simply, very correctly.

In Nan's books of etiquette she would have broken no rule, not that she had ever read them.

"Nan, this is Simon Westward. Simon, this is my friend Nan Mahon."

"Hallo, Nan," said Simon, reaching for her hand.

"Hallo, Simon," said Nan, with a smile.

"You were out with a sugar daddy. I heard," Jack accused her laughingly next day.

"No, indeed I wasn't. Nan took me to the Hibernian for lunch, as a treat. A Christmas present."

"Why did she do that?"

"I told you. A Christmas present."

Jack shook his head. It didn't add up.

Benny bit her lip. She wished now that she hadn't gone. In fact she wished at the time that she hadn't gone. She had ordered potatoes with the scampi and hadn't known that you were meant to have rice until she saw surprise on the waiter's face. She had asked for a little of everything from the cheeseboard instead of just picking two cheeses, which is what other people did. She had asked for nice frothy cappuccino coffee and was told gravely that it wasn't served in the dining room.

And there was something about Simon and Nan that made her uneasy too. It was as if they were playing some game, a game that only they understood. Everyone else was outside.

And now here was Jack implying that Nan must have had some kind of ulterior motive to take her to lunch.

"What's wrong?" He saw her looking distressed.

"Nothing." She put on her bright smile.

There was something very vulnerable about it. Jack could see Benny as what she must have been like when she was about four or five pretending that everything was all right even when it wasn't.

He put his arm around her shoulder as they walked across at the traffic lights between Stephen's Green and Grafton Street.

All the shops were done up with Christmas decorations. There were lights strung across the street. A group of carol singers shivering in the cold were starting "Away in a Manger." The collection boxes were rattling. Her face looked very innocent. He felt a need to protect her from all sorts of things. From Bill Dunne who said that a big girl like that with an enormous chest would turn out to be a great court. From drunks walking round with bottles in their hands wild-eyed and with wild hair. He wanted to keep her on the footpath so that the busy Christmas traffic wouldn't touch her, and from the small children with dirty faces who would wheedle the last pennies of her pocket money from someone gentle like Benny Hogan. He didn't want her to go back to Knockglen on the bus this afternoon, and to be there for nearly three weeks of the holidays.

"Benny?" he said.

She turned her face to him to know what he wanted. He held her face in both his hands and kissed her very softly on the lips. Then he drew away and looked to see the surprise in her eyes.

He put his arms around her then, standing right at the top of the busiest street in Dublin and held her to him. He felt her arms go round him and they clung to each other as if it were the most natural thing in the world.

THIRTEEN

*F*onsie had a new black velvet jacket for Christmas. Clodagh had made him a set of lilac-colored button covers, and a huge flouncy handkerchief to put in his breast pocket.

He startled most of Knockglen by moving very deliberately up the church to receive Communion in this outfit.

"He has added blasphemy to the list of his other crimes," Mrs. Healy hissed at the Hogans, who were sitting near her.

"He must be in a State of Grace, otherwise he wouldn't go," Annabel said. She thought Mrs. Healy was making too much of this vendetta. She envied Peggy and Mario for having such lively young blood in their businesses. If only Benny and Sean had made a go of it, then perhaps the dead look of failure might not hang around the door of Hogan's, while the other two establishments went from strength to strength. She looked at Eddie beside her. She wondered what he was praying about. He always seemed genuinely devout, as if he were talking to God when they were in the church, unlike herself. Annabel found that being at mass seemed to concentrate her anxieties about daily life rather than raise her nearer to God. Benny wasn't praying. That was for sure. Nobody who was praying had such a strange faraway look on their face.

Annabel Hogan was fairly sure that her daughter was in love.

Clodagh Pine looked at her friend Fonsie with pleasure. He really did look smart. And he *was* a smart fellow. She had never thought she would meet anyone remotely like Fonsie when she was banished to Knockglen in a foolish effort to quieten her by sending her to a backwater. And her aunt had been very good to her also, much better than Clodagh had dared to hope. She had been generous with her praise for the developments, while at the same time resisting each new one that came along. Once she had accepted an idea Peggy Pine would get the bit between her teeth and run with it. Like the smart home knits which were now attracting people to come to Dublin.

Like the idea of designer labels with the word "Pine" on them.

All had added greatly to the shop's turnover. And the place looked smart and lively. It had been a success for both of them.

Clodagh decided that she would not outrage the sensitivities of Knockglen so for Christmas Day mass she wore a short herringbone tweed coat with a black leather belt. She wore high black boots and a black leather beret pulled down the side of her head. It would have looked really good with big chunky flashy earrings. But for Christmas mass Clodagh showed restraint. She was unaware that her aunt knelt with her head in her hands and asked the Mother of God why a girl so good and helpful as Clodagh should dress like a prostitute.

Sean Walsh knelt stiffly. He had the look of someone who was poised waiting for a blow. He looked rigidly in front of him, lest he be caught gazing around.

Sean had been invited to Christmas lunch at the Hogans' this year. Other Christmases he had gone home to his own people, a world of which he spoke not at all, in a town which no one could remember because Sean Walsh had never referred to it. But this year he had persuaded Mr. Hogan to stay open late on Christmas Eve and not close at lunchtime, as they had done in other years.

Most people had a few presents still to buy on Christmas Eve, Sean reasoned. And if Hogan's wasn't open they could always buy men's handkerchiefs in Peggy Pine's, or boxes of cheroots in Birdie Mac's, or masculine-smelling soaps in Kennedy's. All those places would now be open to catch the trade. Knockglen was changing fast.

"But you can't do that," Mr. Hogan had pleaded. "You'll miss your bus home."

"There's not going to be much of a Christmas there anyway, Mr. Hogan," Sean had said apologetically, knowing that now an invitation would have to be forthcoming.

Sean was looking forward to sitting at Christmas lunch with the Hogans as if he were a person of status. He had bought a dried flower arrangement for Mrs. Hogan, something that could stand on her table all year, he would say. And a talcum powder called *Talc de Coty* for Benny. It was 4/11, a medium-range talcum powder, something that would please her, he thought, without embarrassing her by its grandness.

She had been pleasant this morning, smiled at him very affably and said she was glad he was coming to lunch and that they'd see him about one o'clock in Lisbeg.

He had been pleased to be told what time they expected him. He was wondering if he should have gone back with them after mass. It was as well to have it pointed out to him.

Benny had realized that since Sean was inevitable, she might as well be polite about it. Patsy told her that her mother and father had been worried in case she'd make a fuss.

"It's only lunch. It's not a lifetime," Benny had said philosophically.

"They'd be well pleased if it was a lifetime."

"No, Patsy, you can't be serious. Not anymore. Surely not anymore. Once they may have thought about it."

"I don't know. You can't lay down laws for what people think and hope."

But Patsy was wrong. Benny knew that her parents couldn't have any hopes that she should consider Sean Walsh. Business was poor. Money was tight. She knew this. And she knew that they couldn't have embarked on the whole costly business of letting her have a university education unless they had hopes of better things for her. If they believed she would marry Sean Walsh and that he would run Hogan's, they would have tried to force her into doing a secretarial course and bookkeeping. They would have put her into the shop. They would never have let her near a world that had all it had in it. The world that had given her Jack Foley.

The mass in the convent was always a delight. Father Ross loved the pure clear voices of the younger nuns in the choir. There was never coughing or spluttering or fidgeting when he said mass in the chapel of St. Mary's. The nuns chanted responses and rang the bells perfectly. He didn't have to deal with sleepy or recalcitrant altar servers. And there was nothing like the amazing and highly disrespectful fashion show to which the parish church in Knockglen had been treated this morning. Here everybody was in the religious life except of course young Eve Malone, who had grown up here.

His eyes rested on the small dark girl as he turned to give the final blessing *Ite Missa Est.*

He saw her bow her head as reverently as any of the sisters when she said, *"Deo Gratias."*

He had been worried to hear that she was going to live in that house where her mother had died, out of her senses in childbirth, and where her poor father too had lost his life. She was too young a child to have a place on her own, with all the dangers that this might involve. But Mother Francis, who was an admirably sensible woman, was in favor of it.

"It's only up the garden, Father," she had reassured him. "In a way it's part of the convent. It's as if she never left us at all."

He looked forward now to his breakfast in the parlor. Sister Imelda's crisply fried rashers, with triangles of potato cakes, which would make a man forget everything in the world and follow its smell and its taste wherever it led.

Mrs. Walsh the housekeeper at Westlands cycled back from Knock-glen. Mr. Simon and Miss Heather would go out to church at eleven-thirty. The old gentleman hadn't gone to any service for a long time. It was sad to see him so feeble in his chair and yet at times he would remember very clearly. Usually things best forgotten. Sad incidents, accidents, disasters. Never happy times, no weddings, christenings or festivities.

Mrs. Walsh never spoke of her life in the big house. She could have had a wide audience for tales of the child sitting talking to Clara about the puppies, to Mr. Woffles about his Christmas lettuce and to the pony about how she was going to become a harness maker and invent something softer than the bit for his poor tender mouth.

Mrs. Walsh had warned Bee Moore that she didn't want to hear any stories coming from her reporting either. People were always quick to criticize a family which was different to the village. And the Westwards were a different religion, a different class and also a different nationality. The Anglo-Irish might consider themselves Irish, Mrs. Walsh said very often, to make her point more firmly to Bee Moore. But of course they were nothing of the sort. They were as English as the people who lived across the sea. Their only problem was that they didn't realize it.

Mr. Simon, now, he had his eye on a lady from England, from Hampshire. He was going to invite her to stay. But not in Westlands. He was going to put her up at Healy's Hotel, which was his way of saying that he hadn't made his mind up about her enough to have her in the house.

Mrs. Walsh cycled back to cook the breakfast and thought that Mr. Simon was ill-advised. Healy's Hotel was no place to put a rich woman from Hampshire in. It was a place with shabby fittings and cramped rooms. The lady would not look favorably on Mr. Simon and on Westlands, and on the whole place. She would go back to Hampshire with her thousands and thousands of pounds.

And the object of the invitation surely had been for her to stay and marry into the family, bringing more English blood and even more important, bringing the finances the place needed so desperately.

Mother Clare looked at Eve with a dislike she barely attempted to conceal.

"I'm pleased to see that you have recovered from all your various illnesses, such as they may have been," she said.

Eve smiled at her. "Thank you, Mother Clare. You were always very kind to me. I am so sorry that I didn't repay it properly at the time."

"Or at all," sniffed Mother Clare.

"I suppose I repaid it in some form by getting myself out of your way." Eve was bland and innocent. "You didn't have to think about me anymore and try to fit me into your world, just out of kindness to Mother Francis."

The nun looked at her suspiciously, but could find no mockery or double meaning in the words.

"*You* seem to have got everything you wanted," she said.

"Not everything, Mother." Eve wondered whether to quote Saint Augustine and say that our hearts were restless until they rested in the Lord. She decided against it. That was going over the top.

"Not every single thing, but a lot certainly," she said. "Would you like me to show you my cottage? It's a bit of a walk through the briars and everything, but it's not too slippy."

"Later, child. Another day, perhaps."

"Yes. It's just I didn't know how long you were staying . . ."
Again her face was innocent.

Last night, as on so many Christmas Eves, she had sat and
talked with Mother Francis. This time even telling the nun a little
about Aidan Lynch and the funny quirky relationship they had.

Mother Francis had said the worst thing about Mother Clare's
visit was that it seemed to be open-ended. She couldn't ask the
other nun when she was going to leave. Eve had promised to do it
in her stead.

Mother Clare did not like to be asked her plans so publicly.

"Oh . . . I mean . . . well," she stammered.

"What day *are* you going Mother Clare, because I want to be
sure I can show it to you. You brought me into your home, the least
I can do is bring you into mine."

She forced Mother Clare to give a date. Then by an amazing
surprise it turned out that Peggy Pine was driving to Dublin that
day. The departure was fixed.

Mother Francis flashed a glance of gratitude to Eve.

A glance of gratitude and love.

Patsy had had a watch from Mossy for Christmas. That meant only
one thing. The next present would be a ring.

"Eve says she thinks he's building onto the back of the
house," Benny said.

"Ah, it's hard to know with Mossy," Patsy said.

They set the table with crackers, and crisscross paper decorations as they had done every year as long as Benny could remember.

Around the house they had paper lanterns. The Christmas
tree in the window had had the same ornaments on it for years.
This year Benny had bought some new ones in Henry Street and
Moore Street in Dublin.

She felt a lump in her throat when her father and mother

examined them with pleasure as if they were anything except the most vulgar red and silver tatty objects you could come across.

They were so touched at anything she did for them, and yet she was the one who should be thanking them. You didn't need to be Einstein to see that the business was not doing well. That it was a struggle for them to keep going and to give her what they did. And yet there was no way to tell them that she would one million times prefer to do what Eve was doing, to work her own way through College, staying in a house helping with the work, or minding children.

Anything at all, including being down on her hands and knees cleaning public lavatories. If it meant that she didn't have to come back to Knockglen every single night, if it meant that she would live in the same town as Jack Foley.

"Poor Sean. He won't be any trouble?" Benny's mother spoke in a question.

"And I couldn't let him work all day yesterday and not ask him for a bite to eat today, seeing that he missed his bus home?" Benny's father's remark was a question too.

"Will he ever get a place to live himself, you know a house here?" Benny asked.

"Funny you should say that. There's talk that he's above on the road over the quarry looking at this place and that. Maybe that's what's on his mind."

"He'll have his job cut out for him saving enough for a house with what he's paid above in the shop." Eddie Hogan was regretful.

He didn't need to say because they all knew it, that there wasn't a question of Sean being underpaid. It was just that the takings were so poor there wasn't much to pay anyone at all out of it.

Everything happened at the same time. Sean Walsh knocked on the front door which nobody ever used, but he thought that on Christmas Day things would be different. Dessie Burns arrived at the back door as drunk as a lord saying that he only wanted a stable to sleep in, just a stable. If it was good enough for Our

Savior, it would be good enough for Dessie Burns, and perhaps a plate of dinner brought out to him wouldn't go amiss. Dr. Johnson came roaring out of his avenue to borrow Eddie Hogan's car. "Of all bloody times of that thoughtless bastard up in Westlands to go and have a turn it has to be bloody Christmas Day just as I was putting my fork in the bloody turkey," he roared, and drove off in the Hogan's Morris Cowley.

Birdie Mac arrived agitated saying that Mr. Flood, who had normally seen one nun in the tree above his house now saw three and was out with a stick trying to attract their attention and get them to come in for a cup of tea. Birdie had been down to Peggy Pine to ask her advice and Peggy had been something akin to intoxicated and told her to tell Mr. Flood to get up in the tree with them.

And Jack Foley rang from Dublin, braving the post office, which hated connecting calls on Christmas Day unless they were emergencies.

"It is an emergency," he had explained.

And when Benny came on the line he said that it was the greatest emergency in his whole life. He wanted her to know how much he missed her.

Patsy went for a walk with Mossy, when everything had been cleared away. This year for the first time, Benny suggested that they should all take part in the washing up. They opened front and back doors to let out the smells of food. Benny said it was hardly tactful to the hens to let them smell the turkey dinner, but perhaps hens had closed off sections of their minds on this subject. Sean didn't know how to react to this kind of chat. He debated several attitudes and decided to look stern.

The big grandfather clock in the corner ticked loudly as first Eddie Hogan and then Annabel fell asleep in the warm firelight. Shep slept too, his big eyes closing slowly and unwillingly as if anxious not to leave Benny and Sean to talk on their own.

Benny knew that she could sleep too, or pretend to. Sean would regard this not as the rudeness it was, but as some kind of sign that he was a welcome intimate in their home. Anyway she was too excited to sleep.

Jack had phoned from his own house where he said they were all playing games and he had sneaked away to tell her that he loved her.

Benny was as wide-awake as she ever had been. She longed for better company than Sean Walsh, and yet she felt sorry for him. Tonight he would go back to that small room two floors above the shop. Nobody had telephoned to say they missed him. She could afford to be generous.

"Have another chocolate, Sean." She offered the box.

"Thank you." He even managed to look awkward eating a simple thing like a sweet. It went slowly down his neck. There was a lot of swallowing and clearing his throat.

"You look very . . . um . . . nice today, Benny," he said, after some thought. Too much thought for the remark that resulted.

"Thank you Sean. I suppose everyone feels well on Christmas Day."

"I haven't particularly, not up to now," he confessed.

"Well, today's lunch was nice, wasn't it?"

He leaned across from his chair. "Not just the lunch. *You* were nice, Benny. That gives me a lot of hope."

She looked at him with a great wave of sympathy. It was something she never thought would happen. Within an hour two men were declaring themselves to her. In films the women were able to cope with this, and even play one off against the other.

But this was no film. This was poor, sad Sean Walsh seriously thinking that he might marry into the business. She must make sure that he realized this was not going to happen. There had to be words somewhere that would leave him with a little dignity and make him realize that things would not be improved by his asking again. Sean was of the old school that thought women said "No" when they meant "Yes," and all you had to do was ignore the refusals until they became an acceptance.

She tried to think how she would like to hear it herself. Suppose Jack were to tell her that he loved someone else, what would be the best way for her to find out? She would like him to be honest, and tell her directly, no apologies, or regrets. Just the facts. And then she would like him to go away and let her digest it all on her own.

Would it be the same for Sean Walsh?

She looked into the changing pictures and leaping flames of the fire as she spoke. There was a background of her parents' heavy breathing. The clock ticked, and Shep whimpered a little.

She told Sean Walsh her plans and her hopes. That she would live in Dublin, and she had great hopes that it would all work out.

Sean listened to the news impassively. The part about the person she loved caused him to smile. A crooked little smile.

"Would you not agree that this might be just what they call a crush?" he asked loftily.

Benny shook her head.

"But it's not based on anything, any shared hopes or plans, like a real relationship is."

She looked at him astounded. Sean Walsh talking about a real relationship as if he would have the remotest idea what it was.

She was still humoring him. "Well, of course you're right. It might not work out, but it's my hope it will."

The smile was even more bitter. "And does he, this lucky man, know anything about your infatuation. Is he aware of all this . . . hope?"

"Of course he is. He hopes too," she said, surprised. Sean obviously thought that she just fancied someone from afar like a film star.

"Ah well, we'll see," he said, and he sat looking into the fire with his sad pale eyes.

Patsy had been up in Mossy's house for the evening wearing her new watch and going through a further inspection by Mossy's mother. Mossy's married sister and her husband had come in to give the encounter even further significance.

"I think they thought I was all right," she told Benny, with some relief.

"Did you think *they* were all right?"

"It isn't up to me to be having opinions you know that, Benny."

Not for the first time Benny wanted to find the orphanage where Patsy had grown up with no hope and no confidence and strangle everyone in it. Patsy wanted to know what time Sean Walsh had left, because she saw him walking around up on the quarry path at all hours. He had looked distraught, she reported, as if he had something on his mind.

Benny wanted to know no more of this. She changed the topic. Were there lights on in Eve's cottage, she wanted to know.

"Yes, it looked lovely and cozy. She had a little Christmas crib in the window with a light in it. And there was a tree too, a small tree with lots of things hanging on it."

Eve had told Benny about the crib, a gift from the convent, and every single nun had made a decoration for the tree as well. Angels with pipe cleaners and colored wool. Stars made out of foil wrapping paper, little pom-pom balls, little figures cut out of Christmas cards and given a stiff cardboard backing. Hours of work had gone into those presents.

The community was alternatively proud and sad that Eve had moved to her own house. But they had grown used to her being in Dublin. In those first weeks they had missed her running through the convent, and sitting up in the kitchen talking to them.

And as Mother Francis said it was only at the other end of the garden.

Mother Francis never said that to Eve herself. She always stressed that the girl must come and go, using the ordinary path when she wished. It was her house and she must entertain whom she liked.

When Eve asked about having a party, Mother Francis said

she could have half the county if she pleased. Eve admitted ruefully that she seemed to be having half of Dublin. Because of her boasting they all thought Knockglen was the place to be.

Mother Francis said that this was only the truth and wondered how Eve was going to cope. She wondered what Eve was going to do about food for half of Dublin.

"I've brought a lot of stuff. Clodagh and Benny are going to come in on St. Stephen's Day and help."

"That's great. Don't forget Sister Imelda would always love to be asked to make pastry."

"I don't think I could . . ."

"You know, I believe they eat sausage rolls all over the world, including Dublin. Sister Imelda would be honored."

Clodagh and Benny were up at the cottage early.

"A soup, that's what you want," Clodagh said firmly.

"I don't have a big pot."

"I bet the convent does."

"Why did I take this on, Clodagh?"

"As a housewarming. To warm your house." Clodagh was busy counting plates, making lists and deciding where they would put coats. Benny and Eve watched her with admiration.

"That one could rule the world if she was given a chance," Eve said.

"I'd certainly make a better stab at it than the eejits who are meant to be in charge," said Clodagh cheerfully.

The Hogans were surprised to see Sean Walsh come in through the gate of Lisbeg on St. Stephen's Day.

"We didn't ask him again, today?" Annabel asked, alarmed.

"I didn't, certainly. Benny may have." Eddie sounded doubtful.

But nobody had invited Sean Walsh. He had come to have a

discussion with Mr. Hogan about business. He had taken a long walk last night up around the quarry and he had sorted everything out in his head. Sean Walsh had a proposition to put to Mr. Hogan, that he should be taken on as a partner in the firm.

He realized that there wasn't sufficient cash flow to make him a more attractive salary offer. The only solution would be to invite him to be a full partner in the business.

Mario looked on as Fonsie backed the station wagon up to the door and loaded the record player into the back.

"We go back to the peace and the quiet?" he asked hopefully.

Fonsie didn't even bother to answer. He knew that nowadays anything Mario said was more in the nature of a ritual protest than a genuine complaint.

The cafe was unrecognizable from the run-down place it was when Fonsie had arrived in town. Brightly painted, cheerful, it was attracting all kinds of clientele that would never have crossed its doorstep in the old days. Fonsie had seen that there was an opportunity for morning coffee for an older set, and he had gone all out to get it. This was the time of day when the younger set, the real customers, were tied up at school or working, so the place was almost empty.

Fonsie placed old-style music and watched with satisfaction while Dr. Johnson's wife, and Mrs. Hogan, Mrs. Kennedy from the chemist and Birdie Mac all took to call in for a coffee that was cheaper than Healy's Hotel in an atmosphere that was distinctly less formal.

And as for the youngsters, he had plans for a magnificent jukebox which would pay for itself in six months. But there would be time enough to explain that to his uncle later. In the meantime he just said that he was lending the player they had to Eve Malone for her party.

"That's a better place to play it than here," Mario grumbled.

"Up on the quarry is good. It will only deafen the wild birds that fly around in the air."

"You won't stay too late at this party now, will you?" Benny's father was looking at her over his glasses.

It made him look old and fussy. She hated him peering like that. Either look through them or take them off, she wanted to shout with a surge of impatience.

She forced a reassuring smile onto her face.

"It's the only party there's ever been in Knockglen, Father, you know that. I can't come to any harm, just up at the back of the convent garden."

"That's a slippy old path through the convent."

"I'll come back by the road then, down through the square."

"It'll be pitch-dark," her mother added. "You might be better coming through the convent."

"I'll have plenty of people to come back with me. Clodagh or Fonsie, Maire Carroll even."

"Maybe I could walk up that way myself about the time it would be ending. Shep, you'd like a nice late night walk wouldn't you?"

The dog's ears pricked up at the thought of any kind of walk.

Please let her find the right words. The words that would stop her father walking out in the dark out of kindness and peering through the window at Eve's party, wrecking it for everyone, not only Benny.

Please could she say the right thing that would stop him in this foolish well-meant wish to escort her safely home.

Nan would know how to cope with this. What would Nan do? Nan always said stick as close to the truth as possible.

"Father, I'd rather if you didn't come up for me. It would make me look a bit babyish, you know, in front of all the people from Dublin. And it's the only party that's ever been given in Knockglen and maybe the only one that ever will be. Do you see how I don't want to be taken there and collected as if I were a child?"

He looked a bit hurt, as if a kind offer had been refused.

"All right, love," he said eventually. "I was only trying to be helpful."

"I know, Father, I know," she said.

This Christmas Nan's father had been worse than usual. The festive season seemed to bring him no cheer. The boys were almost immune to him. Paul and Nasey spent very little time in Maple Gardens.

Emily tried to excuse him. She spoke of him apologetically to Nan.

"He doesn't mean it. If you knew how full of remorse he is after."

"I do," Nan said. "I have to listen to it."

"He'll be so sorry he upset us. He'll be like a lamb today," Em pleaded for understanding.

"Let him be like anything he likes, Em. I'm not going to be here to look at it. I'm going to the races."

She had rehearsed this outfit over and over. It seemed to be just right. The cream camel-hair suit with the dark brown trimmings, the hat that fitted so perfectly into the blond curly hair. A small, good, handbag and shoes that would not sink in the mud. She went to the races on the bus, along with other Dubliners going on a day out.

But while they talked form and record and likely outsiders, Nan Mahon just sat and looked out of the window.

She had very little interest in horses.

It didn't take her long to find him, and position herself in a place where she could be seen. She stood warming her hands at one of the many coal braziers placed around the enclosure. She appeared to concentrate very much on the heat as she saw him from the corner of her eye.

"How lovely to meet you again, Nan Mahon," he said. "Where is your supporting group of ladies?"

"What do you mean?" Her smile was warm and friendly.

"It's only I never see you without a great regiment of women in tow."

"Not today. I came with my brothers. They've gone to the Tote."

"Good. Can I bear you off to have a drink?"

"Yes. I'd love that, but just one. I must meet them after the third race."

They went into the crowded bar, his hand under her elbow guiding her slightly.

There were smiles here and there and people calling to him. She felt confident that she was their equal. There were no pitying looks. Not one of those people would ever know the kind of house she had left this morning to get here on the bus. A house where drink had been spilled, where a lamp had been broken, where half the Christmas pudding had been thrown against the wall in a drunken rage. These people accepted Nan as an equal.

Eve looked around her little house with pleasure.

The oil lamps were lit and they gave a warm glow. The fire burned in the grate.

Mother Francis had left what she called a few old bits and pieces around the place. They were exactly the kind of thing that Eve wanted. A big blue vase in which she could put the wild catkins she had gathered. A handful of books to fill a corner shelf. Two slightly cracked china candlesticks for the mantelpiece, an old coal scuttle polished and burnished.

In the kitchen on the old range there were saucepans which must have come from the convent. Nothing much useful had been left from her parents' time.

Only the piano. Sarah Westward's piano. Eve ran her fingers over it and wished yet again that she had paid attention and tried to learn when Mother Bernard had been giving her lessons. Mother Francis had wanted so much for Eve to share what must have been a great love of music. Her mother had a piano stool stuffed with sheet music, and books and scores in a cupboard. They had been neatly tidied and kept free of damp by Mother Francis over the years.

When the piano tuner came to the school he was always asked to do a further chore and had been led through the kitchen gardens up the path to the piano which he always told Mother Francis was twenty times better than anything they had in the music room of St. Mary's.

"It's not ours," Mother Francis used to say.

"Then why am I tuning it?" he used to ask every year.

Eve sat down at the fire and hugged herself.

As in so many things, Mother Francis had been right. It was very nice to have a place of your own.

The Hogans had decided not to talk to Benny yet about Sean Walsh's proposition. Or ultimatum.

It had been very courteously couched, but there was no question about it. If he were not invited to be a partner in the business he would leave, and it would be known why he left. Nobody in Knockglen would think that he had been fairly treated. Everyone knew what his input had been, and how great his loyalty.

Sean did not need to spell out what would be the future for the business if he were allowed to leave. As it was, he was the one holding it together. Mr. Hogan had no real business sense in terms of what today's customers wanted. And old Mike in the shop wasn't going to be any help to him in that regard.

They would talk to Benny about it, but not now. Not since she had put herself out to be polite and courteous to him during the Christmas meal. She might flare up again and they didn't want to risk that.

"Has Sean been asked to the party above in Eve's cottage?"

Eddie asked, although he knew that there was no question of the boy having been invited.

"No, Father."

To Benny's relief the telephone rang. But it was startling to have someone call at nine o'clock in the evening. She hoped that it wasn't Jack to say he wasn't coming.

Benny answered it. Nan Mahon was on the line, pleading, begging that she could come to stay tomorrow night for the party. Nan had said that she didn't think she would be able to come to Knockglen when the party was first mentioned. What had changed her mind? A lot of things, apparently. She would explain everything when she arrived. No, she wouldn't need to be met on the bus. She'd be getting a lift. She'd explain all that later too. No, no idea what time. Could she say she'd see Benny at the party?

Next morning, on the day of the party, Benny went up early to Eve's cottage to tell her the news.

Eve was furious.

"What does she think she's doing, announcing her arrival like some bloody old king from the olden days."

"You did ask her to the party," Benny said mildly.

"Yes, and she said no."

"I don't know what *you're* bellyaching about. It's just one more for the party. I'm the one who was dragging beds all night with Patsy and checking that there's no dust on the legs of the furniture in case Nan does a household inspection."

Eve didn't know why she was annoyed. It was, on the face of it, unreasonable. Nan was her friend. Nan had lent her that beautiful red skirt for the dance. Nan had advised Eve on everything from how to put on eyeliner to putting shoe trees in every shoe every night. The others would be delighted to see her. It would make the party go with an even bigger swing. It was strange that she felt so resentful.

They sat having coffee in the kitchen of Eve's home, the two of them puzzling out who was giving Nan a lift. Benny said it couldn't be Jack because he was coming in a car with Aidan and Carmel and Sean. They knew it wasn't with Rosemary Ryan and Sheila, still deadly rivals and driving discontentedly with Bill Dunne and Johnny O'Brien.

Benny was thinking about Jack and how after tonight surely Rosemary and Sheila would have to give up their hopes of him, once they had seen how he and Benny felt about each other. To say straight out that he had missed her. To say it on the phone on Christmas Day. It was the most wonderful thing that could have happened.

Eve's brow was furrowed. She wished she could think that Nan was just coming for the party. She felt sure that it was in order to wangle an invitation to Westlands. Which she would not get from Eve and that was for sure and for certain.

Heather came to call wearing her hacking jacket and little hard hat.

"You look as if you've just got off a horse," Eve said.

"I have," and Heather proudly showed her pony tied to the gate.

It was eating some of the bushes within its reach. Eve leapt up in panic. Those were her only decoration, she said, and now this terrible horse was hoovering it all up. Heather laughed, and said nonsense, her beautiful pony was only nuzzling. He wouldn't dream of eating anything between meals. Benny and Eve went out and stroked the gray horse, Malcolm, the light of young Heather's life. They kept away from the mouth with the big yellow teeth and marveled at how fearless Heather seemed to be. Heather had come to help. She thought she would be useful in setting up the games and was very perplexed when there seemed to be no games to set up. No ducking for apples like at Halloween. Heather was at a party where they had advertisements all cut out of papers, just the word. The thing that was being advertised was cut out. Everyone had a pencil and paper and the one who got most of them right won.

In desperation they suggested she blow up balloons. That pleased her. She had plenty of breath, she said proudly. As she sat in an ever-increasing heap of green, red and yellow balloons Heather asked casually if Simon had been invited to the party.

"No, it's not really his kind of party," Eve said. "And besides, he'd be very old for it."

She wondered why she was making excuses for not inviting this man for whom she had felt nothing but dislike all her life. But then who could ever have foreseen the way things would turn out. That she would be very fond of his younger sister, and that she would have been settled in this house where she had vowed never to live. The day might well come when her cousin Simon Westward could cross this door, but not for a long time yet.

Jack Foley was recognized as the expert on Knockglen. He had been there before after all. He knew Benny's house. He had been given clear instructions on how to get to the quarry road. You came in like the bus to the square and took a hilly path that had no signpost on it, but looked as if it were leading to a farmhouse.

There was another way through the convent, but you couldn't take the car and Eve had been adamant that there was to be no horseplay anywhere near her nuns.

Aidan wanted them to go and have a look at the convent first. He stared out of the passenger seat at the high walls and the big wrought-iron gate.

"Imagine being brought up in a place like that. Isn't it a miracle that she's normal," he said.

"But *is* she normal?" Jack wanted to know. "She does appear to fancy you, which doesn't augur well for her state of mind."

They wound their way up the perilous path. The curtains were pulled back in the cottage and they could see firelight, and oil lamps, a Christmas tree and balloons.

"Isn't it gorgeous," breathed Carmel, whose plans for the future when Sean was an established businessman now widened to include a small country cottage for weekends.

Jack liked it too.

"It's away from everywhere. You could be here and nobody know a thing about it."

"Unless of course the sounds of 'Good Golly, Miss Molly' were coming out of every window," Aidan Lynch said happily, leaping from the car and running in to find Eve.

Clodagh had brought a clothes rails and hangers up from the shop. It meant that Eve's bed wouldn't be swamped with people's garments and there would be room for the girls to sit at the little dressing table to titivate themselves.

Benny was in there doing a final examination of her face when she heard Jack's voice. She must not run out and fling herself into his arms as she wanted to. It was more important than ever now that she let him make the first move. A man like Jack used to having girls throw themselves at him would not want that.

She would wait, even if it killed her.

The door of Eve's bedroom opened. It was probably Carmel, coming in to dab her face and say something cozy about Sean.

She looked in the mirror and over her shoulder she saw Jack. He closed the door behind him and came over to her, leaning his hands on her shoulders and looking at her reflection in the mirror.

"Happy Christmas," he said in a soft voice.

She smiled a broad smile. But she was looking at his eyes not her own so she didn't know how it looked. Not too broad and toothy she hoped.

Clodagh had covered a strapless bra in royal blue velvet to look like one of those smart boned tops, and then put a binding of the same material down a white cardigan.

Naturally Benny had worn a blouse under it when she left Lisbeg, but the blouse had been removed and was folded neatly to await the home journey.

He sat on the edge of Eve's bed, and held both her hands.

"Oh, I really missed you," he said.

"What did you miss?" She didn't sound flirtatious. She just wanted to know.

"I missed telling you things, listening to you telling things. I missed your face, and kissing you." He drew her toward him, and kissed her for a long time.

The door opened and Clodagh came in. She was dressed from head to foot in black lace with a mantilla and a high comb in her hair. She looked like a Spanish dancer. Her face was powdered dead white and her lips were scarlet.

"I was actually coming to see if you wanted any assistance with your dress Benny, but it appears you don't," Clodagh said, without seeming the slightest confused by the scene she had walked in on.

"This is Clodagh," mumbled Benny.

Jack's face lit up as it did when he was introduced to any woman. It wasn't that he was eyeing them up and down. He didn't even try to flirt with them. He liked women. Benny remembered suddenly that his father was like that too. At the big party in their house Dr. Foley had been pleased to greet each new girl who was presented to him. There was nothing but warmth and delight in his reaction. So it was with Jack. And tonight when all the others arrived he would be the same.

It must be a wonderful thing to be so popular she thought, to be able to please people just by being there.

Clodagh was explaining to Jack how she had got the lace in an old trunk upstairs in the Kennedys' house. Mrs. Kennedy had told her she could go and rummage there and she had found marvelous things altogether. In return she had made Mrs. Kennedy four straight skirts with a pleat in the back. It was amazing with all the plumage available that some people still wanted to dress like dowdy sparrows.

Jack put his arm around Benny's shoulders.

"I've hardly seen any sparrows in Knockglen. You're all pretty exotic birds to me."

Together with his arm around her shoulder and followed by Clodagh in her startling black and white they came out of Eve's room and in full view of Sheila and Rosemary, of Fonsie and Maire Carroll, of Bill Dunne and Johnny O'Brien, they joined the party.

Without Benny Hogan having to maneuver it one little bit, they joined the party as a couple.

There never had been a party like it. Everyone agreed on that. From Fonsie's wonderful solo demonstrations to the whole place on its feet, from Guy Mitchell and "I never felt more like singing the Blues." The soup had been a magnificent idea. Bowl after bowl of it disappeared, sandwiches, sausage rolls and more soup. Eve served it from the big convent cauldron, her face flushed and excited. This was her house. These were her friends. It couldn't be better.

Only during the supper did she remember that Nan hadn't arrived.

"Perhaps she didn't get a lift after all." Benny was on a cloud of her own.

"Did we tell her how to find the house?"

"Anyone in Knockglen would tell her where you live," Benny squeezed Eve's arm. "It's going wonderfully isn't it?"

"Yes. He can't take his eyes off you."

"I don't mean that. I mean the party."

Benny did mean that of course as well. Jack had been at her side all night. He had had a few dances with the others as a matter of form, but for the most of the night he was with her, touching, laughing, dancing, holding, swaying, including her in every conversation.

Rosemary Ryan watched them with some bewilderment for the first few dances.

"I didn't know anything about you and Jack," she said, as she and Benny were having a glass of punch.

"Well, I did tell you I met him from time to time in the Annexe."

"That's right. You did."

Rosemary was quite fair-minded. Benny had said she was meeting Jack. If Rosemary read nothing into it then it was her own fault.

"You do look very well," she said grudgingly, but again struggled to be just. "Have you lost a lot of weight or put on more makeup or what?"

Benny didn't even react. She knew that whatever it was, Jack seemed to like it. And he didn't care who else knew. Benny had thought that somehow it would have had to be a secret about them.

Aidan asked Eve for a pound of sugar.

"What do you want that for?"

"I read that if you put it in the carburetor of a car, then the car won't start."

"How about trying to find some discovery that would make it start. That seems to me to be the better invention," Eve said.

"You're wrong. I want Jack's father's car never to start again. Then we can stay here in this magical place and never go away."

"Yeah, terrific. And I'll have to put up Sean and Carmel for the night as well," Eve said.

"If I stayed, would you take me to meet the nuns tomorrow?" Aidan asked.

Eve told him that there was no question of his staying, at any time, but least of all now when Mother Clare was below watching every move. Or indeed maybe outside in the fuchsia bushes with a torch, for all they knew. But she was glad that he liked the place. And when the weather got finer, he might come and spend a whole day. Aidan said they would probably be spending much of their adult life here. During the long vacations when he was called to the Bar. They would want to escape here with the children, away from the loud booming voices of his parents.

"And what about my job?" Eve asked, entertained in spite of herself by the fantasy.

"Your job will of course be to look after me, and our eight fine children, using your university education to give them a cultured home background."

"You'll be lucky, Aidan Lynch." She pealed with laughter.

"I have been lucky. I met you Eve Malone," he said, without a trace of his usual jokey manner.

Bill Dunne was the first to see Nan when she came in the door. Her eyes were sparkling and she took in the scene around her with delight.

"Isn't it wonderful," she said. "Eve never said it was anything like this."

She wore a white polo-neck jumper and a red tartan skirt, under a black coat. She carried a small leather case with her, and asked to be shown to Eve's bedroom.

Benny called to the kitchen to let Eve know that Nan was here.

"Bloody hell, we've finished the soup," Eve said to Aidan.

"She won't expect it, not at this hour," he soothed her.

It was a late hour to arrive. Eve had thought she heard a car pull away down the path a few moments ago, but she had told herself she was imagining it.

Still someone must have left Nan at the door. It was raining outside and Nan looked immaculate. She could not have climbed up that path in this weather.

Eve put some sausage rolls and sandwiches on a plate, and took them through the sitting room, skirting Fonsie and Clodagh, who were doing such a spirited rendering of the Spanish Gypsy Dance that everyone had formed a circle to clap and cheer. She knocked on the door of her own bedroom in case Nan was changing, but she was sitting down at the dressing table exactly as she was; Rosemary Ryan was sitting on the bed, telling the mystery-of-the-year story. Jack Foley and Benny Hogan, of all people, were inseparable.

"Did you know?" Rosemary was asking insistingly.

"Yes, sort of." Nan didn't sound as if it mattered very much. Her mind seemed to be elsewhere.

Then she saw Eve. "Eve, it's fabulous. It's a jewel. You never told us it was like this."

"It's not always like this." Despite herself, Eve was pleased. Praise from Nan was high praise.

"I brought you something to eat . . . in case you were changing," she said.

"No, I'm all right like this." Nan hadn't thought of changing.

She was of course all right in whatever she wore. It wasn't very dressy. All the others had put on the style. Parties weren't so run-of-the-mill that you went in a jumper and skirt. But on Nan it looked beautiful.

They all went into the room. Nan loved it. She was busy stroking everything, the polished oil lamps, the wonderful wood in those shelves, the piano. Imagine having a piano of your own. Could she see the little kitchen?

Eve took her through and down the stone step. The place was covered with pots and pans and debris. There were boxes and bottles and glasses. But Nan saw only things she could praise. The dresser, it was wonderful. Where did it come from? Eve had never asked. And that lovely old bowl. It was the real thing, not like horrible modern ones.

"I'm sure a lot of those things came from your mother's home," she said. "They have a look of quality about them."

"Yes, or maybe they bought them together." Somehow Eve felt defensive about her father, and the thought that there could be no look of quality attached to him.

Nan said she was too excited to eat. It was marvelous to be here. Her eyes were dancing. She looked feverish and restless. Everyone in the room was attracted to her, but she was aware of none of them. She refused any offer to dance, saying she had to take it all in. And she wandered around touching and admiring, and sighing over it all.

She paused by the piano and opened it to look at the keys.

"Weren't we all very unlucky that we never learned to play?" she said to Benny. It was the first time Benny had ever noticed Nan Mahon sounding bitter.

"Are you ever going to dance, or is this tour of inspection going to go on all night?" Jack Foley asked her.

Suddenly Nan seemed to snap out of it. "I'm being appallingly rude, of course," she said, looking straight at him.

"Now, Johnny," Jack said to Johnny O'Brien. "I knew that all you had to do was wake her out of the trance, and it would work. Johnny says he's been asking you to dance for ten minutes and you can't even hear him."

If Nan was disappointed that Jack had not been inviting her to dance there was no way that anyone would have known. She smiled such a smile at Johnny that it almost melted him into a little puddle on the floor.

"Johnny, how lovely," she said, and put her arms straight around his neck.

They were playing "Unchained Melody," a lovely slow smoochy number. Benny was so pleased that Jack hadn't left her for Nan just as Fonsie had put that one on. It was one of her favorite songs. She had never dreamed that she would dance to it, here in Knockglen with the man she loved, who had his arms wrapped around her, and seemed to love her too. In front of all her friends.

They put more turf and logs on the fire, and when one of the oil lights flickered down, nobody bothered to replace it.

They sat around in groups or in twosomes, the evening drawing to a close.

"Can anybody play that beautiful piano?" Nan asked.

Amazingly Clodagh said that she could. Fonsie looked at her in open admiration. There was nothing that woman couldn't do, he told people proudly.

Clodagh settled herself at the keys. She had a repertoire that staggered them. Frank Sinatra numbers that they all joined in, rag-time solos, and she even got people to sing solos.

Bill Dunne startled them all by singing "She Moved Through the Fair" very tunefully.

"That was a well-kept secret," Jack said to him as they clapped him to the echo.

"It's only when I'm out of Dublin and can't be sent up by all you lot that I'd have the courage," Bill said, red with pleasure from all the admiration.

Everyone said that Knockglen had not been properly praised up to this, and now that they knew where it was they'd be regular visitors. Fonsie told them to come earlier next time, when it was opening time in Mario's, soon to be Ireland's premier stylish cafe. Trends had to start somewhere and why not Knockglen?

Eve was sitting on the floor next to one of her two rather battered armchairs; on Clodagh's advice they had draped bed-spreads over the shabby furniture. It looked exotic in the flickering light.

She thought she should get up and make more coffee for the departing guests, but she didn't want it to end, and the way Aidan had his arm around her and was stroking her, he didn't want to make any move to go either.

Nan sat on a tiny three-legged stool, hugging her knees.

"I met your grandfather today," she said suddenly to Eve.

Eve felt a cold shock run through her. "You did?"

"Yes. He really is a charming old man, isn't he?"

Benny felt she wanted to move away from Jack's arm and go over and support Eve physically. In some way she wanted to be a barrier between her and what Nan was saying.

Please may Eve not say anything brittle or hurtful. Let her just mumble for the moment. Let there not be a scene now to end the party on a sour note.

Eve might have read her mind.

"Yes. How did you meet him?" Although she knew. She knew only too well.

"Oh, I met Simon at the races yesterday and we got talking. He offered me a lift if I was going to this part of the world. So we got here a bit early . . . and, well, he took me to Westlands."

If they had got here so bloody early, Eve thought, then Nan might have been on time rather than turning up when the supper was finished.

She didn't trust herself to say any more. But Nan had in no way finished with the subject.

"You could really see what he must have been like before. You know very upright and stern. It must be terrible for him to be like that in his chair. He was having his tea. They serve it beautifully for him. Even though he's sometimes not able to manage it."

She had been there since teatime. Since five o'clock and she hadn't bothered to come next or near them until after nine in the evening. Eve felt the bile rise in her throat.

Nan must have sensed it. "I did keep asking Simon to drive me up here, but he insisted on showing me everything. Well, I suppose you've been over it dozens of times."

"You know I haven't." Eve's voice was dangerously calm.

Only Benny and Aidan who knew her so well would have got the vibrations.

Aidan exchanged a glance with Benny. But there was nothing he could do.

"Well, you must Eve. You must let him take you all through the place. He's so proud of it. And he describes it so well, not boasting or anything."

"Where's this?" Sheila always liked to hear of places that were splendid and people that were important.

"Eve's relations, up at the big house. About a mile over . . . that way . . . is it?" Nan pointed with her arm.

Eve said nothing. Benny said that it was more or less that way. Benny also wondered did anyone want coffee, but they didn't. They wanted to sit dreamily with low music on the player and to chat. And they wanted Nan to have the floor. There was something about the way her face was lit up by the fire and by the place she was talking about . . . they wanted her to go on.

"He showed me all the family portraits. Your mother was very beautiful, wasn't she Eve?" Nan spoke in open admiration. There was nothing triumphalist about her having been there, about her having been taken on a tour and shown the picture that had not been shown to Eve on her one visit.

Nan had always said that Eve should bury her differences. Nan would have thought that Eve knew what her mother looked like.

"You must have had quite a tour." The words nearly choked her.

"Oh yes. The trouble was getting away."

"Still, you managed it," Aidan Lynch said. "Fonsie, if we're not going to be given cells in the convent for the night, which I was distinctly promised, I think we should have something to loosen up our limbs for the journey home. What would you suggest, man?"

Fonsie had long realized that Aidan was a fellow spirit. He leapt to his feet and flipped through a few record covers.

"I think it comes down to a straight contest between Lonnie Donegan 'Putting on the Style' and Elvis being 'All Shook Up' man," he said, after some thought.

"Man, let's not insult either of those heroes. Let's have them both," Aidan said, and he went around the room clapping his hands at people to get them going.

Benny had followed Eve to the kitchen.

"She doesn't understand," Benny said.

Eve clutched hard with both her hands at the sink.

"Of course she does. How often have we talked about it?"

"Not to her. Seriously not to her. With Nan we usually pretend things are fine. Otherwise she gets you to change them. Remember?"

"I'll never forgive her."

"Yes, of course you will. You'll forgive her this minute, otherwise it will change everything about the party. It was the most wonderful party in the world. Truly."

"It was." Eve softened. Inside she saw Aidan beckoning to her.

Everyone was on the floor. Benny went back. Jack and Nan were dancing, laughing happily, neither of them knowing that anything was amiss.

FOURTEEN

———————————◆———————————

Dear Mr. and Mrs. Hogan,

*Thank you very much for my lovely visit to Knockglen.
You were both so hospitable to me I felt very welcome. As I
said to you, I think your house is beautiful. You have no idea
how lovely it is to come and stay in a real Georgian house.
Benny is very lucky indeed.*

*You very kindly asked me if I would come back again
sometime. Nothing would give me more pleasure. My regards
to Patsy, also, and thank her for the lovely breakfasts.*

*Yours sincerely,
Nan Mahon.*

Eddie Hogan said to his wife that there were some people in life for
whom it was a real pleasure to do the smallest thing, and that
Benny's friend Nan was one of them.

Annabel agreed completely. They had never met a more
charming girl. And such perfect manners too. She had given Patsy
half a crown when she was leaving. She was a perfect lady.

Dear Kit,

The more I think of it, the more I realize that it was ridiculous of me to assume that I could just walk in years later and take up as if nothing had happened. Considering the way I treated you and how little I gave you and Frank over the years you would have had every reason to throw me out on my ear.

But you were very calm and reasonable, and I'll always be grateful for that.

I just wanted you to know that I have always had an insurance policy for you, in case anything happened to me, so that you and our son might have had something good to remember me by. I wish you all the luck and happiness that I didn't bring to you myself.

Love, Joe.

Kit Hegarty folded the letter from the man that everyone else had called Joe. She had never called him anything but Joseph. Meeting him had been so different to the way she thought it would have been. She had intended to hurl everything at him if she ever saw him again. But in fact he was just like a distant friend who was down on his luck. He gave no address. She couldn't even acknowledge the letter.

Dear Mother Francis,

My sincerest thanks for being invited to spend the Holy Feast of Christmas with you and the community in St. Mary's. Thank you also for arranging the lift back to Dublin with your friend Miss Pine. An outspoken person, but no doubt a good Christian with a heavy cross to bear in that niece that she has.

I was very pleased to see that Eve Malone has settled

*down and begun to repay some of the work our Order has
put into her education. It was gratifying to see that she
studies so hard.*

>   *Your sister in Christ,*
>   *Mother Mary Clare.*

Mother Francis smiled grimly as she read the letter, particularly the part about how they had "invited" Mother Clare. But it was wonderful that she had been able to forewarn Eve of the surprise visit that Mother Clare had intended to pay. Mossy Rooney had come along quietly with his cart and removed all the bottles and boxes. The cottage was flung open to the winter air to clear the fumes of smoke and drink from the previous night.

Mother Clare, to her great rage, had discovered Eve sitting blamelessly studying instead of what she had hoped to find as the aftermath of a party, and would have found had it not been for Mother Francis.

>   *Dear Sean,*
>
>   *As you asked me to do I am confirming in writing that
>   I intend to invite you to become a partner in Hogan's
>   Gentleman's Outfitters. I shall arrange with Mr. Gerald
>   Green of Green and Mahers, Solicitors to come to Knockglen
>   and we will formalize the details early in the New Year.*
>   *I look forward to a successful partnership in 1958.*
>
>   *Yours sincerely,*
>   *Edward James Hogan.*

Mrs. Healy read the letter carefully, word by word, and then nodded approvingly at Sean Walsh. It was never any harm getting these things in writing she told him, with the best will in the world people could always go back on what they said. And not a word against Eddie Hogan. He was the nicest man you'd meet in a day's walk, but it was time someone realized Sean Walsh's worth, and acknowledged it.

Eddie Hogan died on Saturday at lunchtime. After he had finished his cup of tea and queen cake, he stood up to go back to the shop.

"If Sean has his way, there'll be no closing for lunch. . . ." he began, but he never finished the sentence.

He sat down on the sofa with his hand to his chest. His face was pale and when he closed his eyes his breathing was strange. Patsy didn't need to be asked to run across the road for Dr. Johnson.

Dr. Johnson came in his shirt sleeves. He asked for a small glass of brandy.

"He never takes spirits, Maurice, you know that!" Annabel's hand was at her throat in fear. "What is it? Is it a kind of fit?"

Dr. Johnson sat Annabel Hogan down on the chair. He handed her the brandy.

"Sip it slowly, Annabel, that's the girl."

He saw Patsy with her coat on as if to go for Father Ross.

"Just a little drop at a time. It was totally painless. He never knew a thing."

The doctor beckoned Patsy over.

"Before you get the priest, Patsy, where's Benny?"

"She's in Dublin for the day, sir. She went up to meet Eve Malone. They were going to a special lecture, I think she said."

"Get Eve Malone to bring her back," said Dr. Johnson. He had managed to take a rug and cover the figure of Eddie Hogan, who lay on the sofa looking for all the world as if he were taking a quick nap before he went back to the shop.

Annabel sat rocking to and fro, moaning in disbelief.

Dr. Johnson went to the door after Patsy.

"No need to tell that bag of bones in the shop yet."

"No sir."

Dr. Johnson had always disliked Sean Walsh. He could almost

see him picking one of the best black ties from the stock and combing his thin lank hair. He could visualize him putting on the correct expression of grief before he came to offer his condolences to the widow, and her daughter.

Whenever they found her.

Benny and Jack walked hand in hand over Killiney Hill. It had been one of those cold, crisp winter afternoons, which was going to end soon. Already they could see the lights of Dun Laoghaire twinkling far below them, and then the great sweep of Dublin Bay.

They would meet Aidan and Eve later in Kit Hegarty's house. Kit had promised them all sausages and chips before they went into the town on the train to the Literary and Historical Debating Society. Tonight the motion was going to be about sport, and Jack had half threatened to speak. He said he didn't know whether he needed huge encouragement and masses of support, or if it would be easier to speak quietly one night on his own when there were no friends to hear him make a fool of himself.

Not since the great dance before Christmas had Benny been able to spend a night in Dublin. Jack had been increasingly impatient.

"What am I going to do with my girl always miles away, it's like having a pen friend," he had complained.

"We see each other in the day." But her throat had narrowed in fear. He sounded cross.

"What's the use? It's at night I need you to go to things."

She had wheedled this Saturday by pretending there was a lecture, and asking if she could tack the night on as well.

And she had another worry. He was very insistent that she go for a weekend to Wales with him.

His team were going to play a friendly match. There would be lots of people going. He really wanted her to go.

"It's not normal," he had fumed. "Anyone else could go. Rosemary, Sheila, Nan, they all have families who'd realize that if they're old enough to have a university education they're old enough to be let out on a simple boat trip for two days."

She hated him saying her family weren't normal. She hated them for not being normal enough to let her go.

Soon it was more dark than it was day. They came down the springy turf together and walked along the Vico Road looking down at Killiney Bay, which people said was meant to be as beautiful as the Bay of Naples.

"I'd love to go to Naples," Benny said.

"Maybe they'll let you when you're about ninety," Jack grumbled.

She laughed, though she didn't feel like it.

"Race you down to the corner," she said, and laughing they ran down to the railway station where they caught a train to Dun Laoghaire.

As soon as Kevin Hickey opened the door to them Benny knew something was wrong.

"They're in the kitchen," he said, refusing to meet her eye. Behind him she saw the tableau of Kit and Eve and Aidan waiting to give them some very bad news.

It was as if everything had stopped. The sound of the traffic outside, the clocks ticking, the seagulls over the harbor.

Benny walked forward slowly to hear what they were going to tell her.

Shep seemed to be in everyone's way, all the time. He was looking for Eddie, and there seemed to be no sign of him. Almost everyone else in Knockglen seemed to be in and out of Lisbeg, but no sign of the master.

Eventually he went out and lay down beside the hen house; only the hens were behaving normally.

Peggy Pine arranged two big trays of sandwiches. She also asked Fonsie to collect drink from Shea's.

"I think your man is going to get some at Healy's."

"Well, your man will be too late then," Peggy said, taking ten pound-notes from her till. "We'll have paid cash. There's nothing he can do about that."

They smiled at each other. The one bright spot in a dark day being the thought of besting both Sean Walsh and Mrs. Healy at the same time.

By teatime everyone in the town knew. And everyone was shocked. By no standards was Eddie an old man, they speculated happily. Fifty-two at most, at the very most. The wife was older. Maybe not even fifty. They tried to work it out. And not a man for the drink, and not a day sick. Hadn't he and his wife taken to going on healthy walks recently. Didn't that show you that your hour was marked out for you and it didn't really matter what you did, you couldn't put it off once it came.

And such a gentleman. Never a harsh word out of him. Not a one to make a quick shilling here and there, he'd not hurry a farmer who hadn't paid a bill for a while. Not one to move with the times, the windows of Hogan's hadn't changed much in all the time he was there. But such a gentleman. So interested in everyone who came in and their family and their news. All the time in the world for them. And he kept poor Mike on there too, long after he might have needed him.

The prayers that were added on to the family rosary that evening for the repose of Eddie Hogan's soul, were prayers that were warm and genuine. And prayers that people said were hardly needed. A man like Eddie Hogan would have been in heaven by two o'clock.

Eve had managed to ward off Sean Walsh's attempts to come to Dublin to collect Benny.

She had also managed to say that Benny was at a lecture where it was impossible to disturb her, because it was a kind of field trip. Nobody knew where they had gone. They would have to wait until she came home at six o'clock.

"They're never bringing her father to the church tonight?" Eve had said.

It was unthinkable that Benny would not be there when her father's body was brought to lie overnight in Knockglen parish church.

"They might have done, if they had known where to find Benny." Sean sounded aggrieved.

Jack said he'd get his father's car.

"They might need it." Benny's face was wan and empty. "They might need it for something important."

"There's nothing more important than this," said Jack.

"Will we go with them?" Aidan Lynch asked Eve.

"No," Eve said. "We'll go down by bus tomorrow."

She could hardly bear to look at Benny's face as she sat looking unseeingly in front of her.

From time to time she said "Dead" in a low voice, and shook her head.

She had spoken to her mother on the phone, her mother had sounded sleepy, she said. That too seemed hard to accept.

"They gave her a sedative, to calm her down. It makes her feel sleepy," Kit explained.

But none of it many any sense to Benny, no matter what tablet you took. It couldn't make you feel sleepy. Not when Father had died. Died. No matter how many times she said it, it wouldn't sink in.

Mr. Hayes next door drove them in to the Foleys' house.

Jack's mother was at the door. Benny noticed that she wore a lovely woollen suit with a cream blouse underneath. She had earrings on, and she smelled of perfume.

She gave Benny a hug of sympathy.

"Doreen has packed you a flask of coffee and some sandwiches for the car journey," she said.

She made it sound as if Knockglen was at the other side of Europe.

"We're both very, very sorry," she said. "If there's anything at all we can do . . ."

"I think I'd better get her on the road." Jack cut short the sympathies.

"Were they going out somewhere tonight?" Benny asked.

"No. Why?"

He was negotiating the early Saturday evening traffic in Dublin, and trying to get out toward the Knockglen road.

"She looked all dressed up."

"No, she didn't."

"Is she like that all the time?"

"I think so." He was surprised, glancing over at her.

She sat in silence for a while, staring ahead. She felt very cold and unreal.

She wished over and over the most futile wish. That it could be this morning. If only it were eight o'clock this morning.

Her father had said that it was going to be a nice bright day.

"Isn't it a pity you have this lecture now. You could have had a great day here in Knockglen, and maybe yourself and Shep would have come up and got me out of the shop early for a bit of a walk!"

If only she had the time again. There'd have been no lies about lectures that didn't exist. There'd have been no shame at accepting his praise for her eagerness to study.

She'd have canceled everything, just to have been there, to have been with him when he began to leave this life.

She didn't believe it was so instant that he didn't know. She would like to have been in the room.

And for her mother too. Mother, who never had to make a decision of her own . . . being alone to handle everything.

Benny's eyes were dry but her heart was full of shame that she hadn't been there.

Jack couldn't find any good words. Several times he almost had the right thing. But always he stopped.

He couldn't bear it any longer. He pulled into the side of the road. Two lorries hooted at him angrily, but he was parked now up on a grass verge.

"Benny, darling," he said, and put his arms around her. "Benny, please cry. Please cry. It's awful to see you like this. I'm here. Benny cry, cry for your father."

And she clung to him and wept and wept until he thought that her body would never stop shaking with the sobs and the grief.

They were all like characters in a play, Benny thought. People moving offstage and onstage all evening. One moment she would look and there was Dekko Moore talking earnestly in the corner, the small teacup and saucer looking ridiculous in his large hands. Then she would glance again and in that corner Father Ross was standing mopping his brow as he listened to the visions of poor Mr. Flood and wondered how best to cope with them.

In the scullery Mossy Rooney stood not wanting to form part of the main gathering that spread through the whole house, but ready when Patsy called him to help. On the stairs sat Maire Carroll, whom Benny had so disliked at school. Tonight, however, she was sympathetic and full of praise for Benny's father. "A very nice man with a word for everyone."

Benny wondered wildly what kind of a word her father would have been able to dredge up for the charmless Maire Carroll.

Her mother sat in the middle, accepting the sympathy, and she was the most unreal figure of all. She wore a black blouse that Benny had never seen before. She worked out that Peggy must have produced it from the shop. Mother's eyes were red, but she was calmer than Benny would have thought possible, considering.

The undertakers had told her that Father was lying upstairs. Jack went up with her to the spare room, where candles burned and everything seemed to have been miraculously tidied and covered. It didn't look like the spare bedroom at all. It looked like a church.

Father didn't look like Father either. One of the nuns from St. Mary's was sitting there. It was something they did, go around to people's houses when someone died and sit there by the body. Somehow it made people more calm and less frightened to see the figure of a nun keeping guard.

Jack held her hand tightly as they knelt and said three Hail Marys by the bed. Then they left the room.

"I don't know where you're going to sleep," Benny said.

"What?"

"Tonight. I thought you could stay in the spare room. I forgot."

"Darling, I have to go back. You know that. I have to take the car back for one thing . . ."

"Of course, I forgot."

She had thought that he would be there with her, standing beside her for everything.

He had been such a comfort in the car, when she had wept on his shoulder. She had begun to assume that he would always be there.

"I'll come back for the funeral. Obviously."

"The funeral. Yes."

"I should go soon."

She had no idea what time it was. Or how long they had been home. Something inside her told her that she must pull herself together now. This minute, and thank him properly for his kindness. She must not allow herself to be a drag.

She walked him out to the car. It was a blowy night now, the dark clouds were scudding across the moon.

Knockglen looked very small and quiet compared to the bright lights of Dublin they had left . . . some time ago. She didn't know how long ago.

He held her close to him, more a brotherly hug than any kind of kiss. Perhaps he thought it was more suitable.

"I'll see you on Monday," he said softly.

Monday.

It seemed so far away. Imagine her having thought he was going to stay for the weekend.

Eve and Aidan came on Sunday.

They walked down from the bus down the main street.

"That's Healy's Hotel. Where I wanted you to stay."

"Until I reminded you I am an impoverished student, who has never spent a night in a hotel in my life," Aidan said.

"Yes, well . . ."

She showed him the Hogans' shop with the black-rimmed notice in the window. She told him about how nice Birdie Mac in the sweetshop was, and how horrible Maire Carroll in the grocery was. From time to time Aidan turned and looked back up at the convent. He had wanted to be invited there first, but Eve had refused. They hadn't come on a social call, she said, they had come to help Benny. There would be time later to meet Mother Francis and Sister Imelda and everyone.

They passed Mario's cafe, which even when closed on a Sunday radiated cheer, and life and excitement.

They turned the corner at the end of the street and went to Benny's house.

"It's awful only going to people's houses when they're dead," Aidan said suddenly. "I'd like to have come here when he was alive. Was he nice?"

"Very," Eve said. She paused with her hand on the gate.

"He never saw any bad in anyone, and he never saw anyone grow up either. He always called me Little Eve. He always thought Benny was nine, and he saw no harm in that Sean Walsh, who'll be lording it inside."

"Will I deal with Sean Walsh, make verbal mincemeat of him?" Aidan asked eagerly.

"No, Aidan, thank you, but that wouldn't be what's required."

It was an endless day, even with Eve and Aidan there. Benny had a headache that she thought would never leave her. There had been so many wearying encounters. Mrs. Healy, for example, wanting to know if there was any way she had offended the family.

No? Well, she was certainly glad to hear that, because she had been so ready and eager to supply the drink that would be needed and then was told that her participation would not be necessary. And then Benny had to cope with old Mike from the shop. There had been words said, words that Mr. Eddie had not meant the way that Mr. Walsh thought he had meant them.

Mr. Walsh? Yes, Mike had been told that it wasn't fitting for a partner to be called Sean anymore, even though Mike had been head tailor when Sean Walsh had come in as a schoolboy.

Benny had been coping with Dessie Burns, who was in that perilous state of being off the jar but threatening to go back on it at any moment because if there was one thing a man should not be it was doctrinaire, and with Mario, who said that in Italy people would cry, cry and cry again over the death of a good man like Eddie Hogan, not just stand in his house talking and drinking.

And then the church bells began to toll. So often in Lisbeg they heard the bells and it just meant the Angelus, or time for mass, or someone else was being brought to the church. Benny put on her black lace mantilla and walked with her mother behind the coffin up the street, where people had come to their doors and to stand outside their businesses on the cold Sunday afternoon.

And as she walked past their shop her heart grew heavier. It would be Sean's shop from now on. Or Mr. Walsh as he would want people to call him.

She wished she could talk to her father about old Mike and ask him what was going to happen. The procession paused momentarily outside Hogan's. And then moved on. She could never talk to her father again about his shop or about anything. And he was powerless now to do anything about the shop he had loved so much.

Unless of course she were to do something herself to try and sort it out.

Aidan Lynch was introduced to Mother Francis.

"I have appointed myself guardian of Eve's morals while she is at university," he said solemnly.

"Thank you very much." Mother Francis was formally grateful.

"I hear nothing but good of the way you brought her up. I wish I'd been left to a convent." His smile was infectious.

"There might have been more problems with you," the nun laughed.

Mother Francis had thought it was very sensible for Aidan Lynch to spend the night in Eve's cottage, while Eve slept at the convent. Everyone liked the thought of Eve being back under their roof again, and her bedroom was going to be there forever. This had been a promise.

Eve showed Aidan how to rake the range.

"I think when we're married we might have something more modern," he grumbled.

"No, surely with the eight children we can have them stoking it, going up the chimney even."

"You don't take me seriously," he said.

"I do. I just believe in child labor that's all."

Back in the convent, having cocoa with Mother Francis in the kitchen, it was impossible to believe that she had ever left these walls.

"A very nice young man," Mother Francis said.

"But basically a Beast of course, like you told us all men were, ravening beasts."

"I *never* told you that."

"You hinted at it."

They were more like sisters these days than mother and daughter. They sat companionably in the warm kitchen and talked of life and death and the town and Mr. Flood's visions and how hard everything was on poor Father Ross. Because if the vision in Fatima was true and everybody believed it, why could they not make the leap of imagination and believe it might all be true in Knockglen?

Possibly because Mr. Flood the butcher was such an unlikely person to be visited by a holy nun in a tree. Or even on the ground according to Mother Francis.

The funeral mass was at ten o'clock. Benny and her mother and Patsy went to the church in the black mourners' car provided by the undertaker.

As she linked arms with her mother up the aisle to sit in the front row, Benny was aware of the people who had come to pay their respects. Farmers had come yesterday, in their Sunday suits, they would be out in their fields on a weekday morning. Today she saw men in suits, commercial travelers, suppliers, people from two parishes away. She saw her father's cousins, and her mother's brothers. She saw standing in a comforting crowd her own circle of friends.

There was Jack, so tall that everyone in the church must have seen him. He wore a black tie and he turned around to see them coming. It was almost like being at a wedding, where people turn around to see the bride . . . the thought came and went.

Bill Dunne had come, too, which was very nice of him, and Rosemary Ryan. They stood beside Eve and Aidan, their faces full of sympathy.

And Nan was there, in a black blazer and a pale gray skirt. She wore gloves and carried a small black bag. Her mantilla looked as if it had been made by a dress designer to sit in her blond hair. Everyone else wore a mantilla that looked like a rag, or a headscarf. Clodagh wore a hat, though. A big black straw hat. It was her only concession to mourning colors. The rest of her outfit was a red and white striped coat dress, considerably shorter than Knockglen would have liked.

But then it was hard to please Knockglen since there was also disapproval for Fonsie's coat—a long one like De Valera would wear except it had a huge velvet collar and small finishings of fake leopard skin at the pockets, collars and cuffs.

Mother looked very old and sad. Benny glanced at her from time to time. Sometimes a tear fell on Mother's missal, and once or twice Benny leaned over and wiped it away. It was as if Mother hadn't noticed.

Mercifully, Sean Walsh had not presumed upon them too much. Startled by the rebuff over obtaining supplies from Healy's Hotel, he had been more cautious in his overtures than Benny had dared to hope. He had not sat anywhere near them now in the church, in the role of a chief mourner. She must keep her head and not let him take over. His style was so different to her father's, his humanity so little in comparison.

Benny wished she had someone who could talk it through with her, someone who really understood. Her glance fell on Jack Foley, whose face was stony in its sympathy. But she knew she wouldn't burden him with it.

The tedious in-fighting over a small shabby country shop. Nobody would bother Jack Foley with all that.

Not even if she loved him, and he loved her.

Outside the church, the people of Knockglen talked to each other in low voices. They commented on the group of young people down from Dublin. Must be friends of Benny, they deduced.

"Very handsome-looking couple that tall boy and the blond girl. They're like film stars," Birdie Mac said.

Eve was nearby.

"They're not a couple," she heard herself saying. "The tall boy is Jack Foley . . . he's Benny's boyfriend. He and Benny are a couple."

She didn't know why she said it, or why Birdie Mac looked at her so oddly. Perhaps she had just spoken very loudly.

Or it didn't seem suitable to talk of Benny having a boyfriend at a time like this.

But in fact she thought Birdie didn't believe her.

As they walked to the open grave past the headstones Eve stopped and pointed out a small stone to Aidan.

"In loving memory of John Malone," it said.

It was nicely kept, weeded and with a little rose tree.

"Do you do this?" he asked.

"A bit, mainly Mother Francis, wouldn't you know."

"And your mother?"

"Across the hill. Over in the Protestant graveyard. The posh one."

"We'll go and see hers too," he promised.

She squeezed his hand; for one of the few times in her life she was without words.

They were very good to her, all Benny's friends. They gave her great support. They were courteous to the people of Knockglen and helpful back at the house after the funeral.

Sean Walsh thanked Jack for coming, as if Jack were there somehow as an act of respect to Hogan's Outfitters. Benny gritted her teeth in rage.

"Mr. Hogan would have been very honored by your presence," Sean said.

"I liked him very much when I did meet him. I came to tea here with Benny months and months ago." He smiled at her warmly, remembering the day.

"I see." Sean Walsh, to Benny's disappointment, now did see.

"You didn't stay overnight did you?" Sean asked loftily.

"No, I didn't. I came down this morning. Why?"

"I heard that one of Benny's friends did stay, up in the cottage on the quarry."

"Oh, that was Aidan." Jack was easy. If he tired of Sean and this pointless conversation he didn't show it, but he managed to maneuver Benny away.

"That's the creep, isn't it?" he whispered.

"That's how it is."

"And he had notions of you."

"Only notions of the business, which he more or less got without having to have me as well."

"Then he lost the best bit," Jack said.

She smiled dutifully. Jack was going to be off soon, she knew. She had heard him tell Bill Dunne that they had to be out of Knockglen by two at the latest. He had asked Bill to make the move.

She made it easy for him. She said that he had been a tower of strength, and everyone had been wonderful to come all that distance. She begged him to get on the road while there was still plenty of daylight.

They were all going to squeeze into Bill Dunne's car. There had been four coming down, but they were going to try and fit Eve and Aidan in as well.

Benny said that was terrific, rather than have them just hanging on waiting for a bus.

She smiled and thanked them without a quiver in her voice.

It was the right way to be, she could see Jack looking at her approvingly.

"I'll ring you tonight," he promised. "About eight. Before I go out."

"Great," she said, eyes bright and clear.

He was going out. Out somewhere on the night of her father's funeral.

Where could he be going on a Monday night in Dublin?

She waved at the car as it went around the corner. It didn't matter, she told herself. She wouldn't have been there anyway. Last Monday night when Father was alive and well, Benny Hogan would have been safely back in Knockglen by eight o'clock.

That's the way things had always been, and would always be. She excused herself from the group of people downstairs, saying she was going to lie down for twenty minutes.

In the darkened room she lay on her bed and sobbed into her pillows.

Selfish tears, too, tears over a handsome boy who had gone back to Dublin smiling and waving with a group of friends. She cried for him as much as for her father, who lay under heaps of flowers up in the graveyard.

She didn't hear Clodagh come in, and pull up a chair. Clodagh still wearing her ludicrous hat, who patted Benny's shoulders and soothed her with exactly the words she wanted to hear.

"It's all right, it's all right. Everything will sort itself out. He's mad about you. Anyone can tell. It's in the way he looks at you. It's better he went back. Hush now. He loves you, of course he does."

There was an enormous amount to do.

Mother was very little help. She slept a lot of the time, and dozed off, even in a chair. Benny knew that this was because Dr. Johnson had prescribed tranquilizers. He had said she was a woman who had focused her whole life around her husband. Now that the center had gone she would take a while to readjust. Better let her get used to things gradually, he advised, not make any sudden changes or press her for decisions.

And there were so many things to decide, from tiny things like thank-you letters, and taking Shep for a walk, and Patsy's wages, to huge things like had Sean Walsh been made a partner yet, and could the business survive, and what were they going to do for the rest of their lives without Father?

Mr. Green, the solicitor, had come to the funeral, but said that there would be ample opportunity for them to discuss everything in the days that followed. Benny hadn't asked him whether he meant Sean Walsh to be in on the discussions or not.

It was something she wished she had said at the time. Then it would have been a perfectly acceptable question as someone distressed and not sure of what was going on. Afterward it looked more deliberate, and as if there was bad feeling. Which there wasn't —except on a personal level.

It was extraordinary how many of Nan's sayings seemed to be precisely appropriate for so many situations. Nan always said that you should do the hardest thing first, whatever it was. Like the essay you didn't want to write, or the tutor you didn't want to confront with an unfinished project. Nan was always right about everything.

Benny put on her raincoat on the morning after the funeral and went to see Sean Walsh in the shop.

The first thing she had to do was to avoid old Mike, who started to shuffle up to her with every intention of finishing the conversation he had begun in her house. Briskly and loudly so that Sean could hear she said that she and her mother would be very happy to talk to Mike later, but for the moment he would have to excuse her, she had a few things she wanted to get settled with Sean.

"Well, this is nice and businesslike." He rubbed his hands together in that infuriating way, as if he had something between his palms that he was trying to grind to a powder.

"Thank you for everything, over the weekend." Her voice was insincere. She tried to put some warmth into it. He *had* stood long hours greeting and thanking. It wasn't relevant that she hadn't wanted him there.

"It was the very least I could do," he said.

"Anyway, I wanted you to know that Mother and I appreciated it."

"How *is* Mrs. Hogan?" There was something off-key about his solicitude, like an actor not saying his lines right.

"Fairly sedated at the moment. But in a few days she will be herself again and able to participate in business matters."

Benny wondered, did Sean have this effect on other people. Normally, she never used words like "participate."

"That's good, good." He nodded his head sagely.

She drew a deep breath. It was something else Nan had read. That if you inhaled all the air down to your toes and let it out again it gave you confidence.

She told him that they would arrange a meeting with the solicitor at the end of the week. And until then perhaps he would be kind enough to keep the shop ticking over exactly as he had been doing so well over the years. And out of respect to her father she knew that there would be no changes made, no changes *at all*; her head inclined toward the back room where old Mike had gone fearfully.

Sean looked at her astounded.

"I don't think you quite realize . . ." he began. But he didn't get very far.

"You're quite right. I *don't* realize." She beamed at him as if in agreement. "There are whole areas of the way this business has been run, and the changes in it that are planned and under way, that I know nothing about . . . that's what I was saying to Mr. Green."

"What was Mr. Green saying?"

"Well, nothing, obviously, on the day of a funeral," she said reprovingly. "But after we have talked to him then we should all talk."

She congratulated herself at her choice of words. However often he played the conversation over to himself again he wouldn't be able to work out whether he was included in the conversation with the lawyer or not.

And he would not discover the huge gap in Benny's own information.

She didn't know whether in fact he was a partner in the business yet, or whether the deed of partnership might not have been signed.

She had a distinct feeling that her father had died before matters were completed, but another even stronger feeling, that there was a moral obligation to carry out what had been her father's wishes.

But Benny knew that if she were to survive in the strange clouded waters that she was now entering, she must not let Sean Walsh know how honorably she would behave to him. Even though she disliked and almost despised him, she knew that Sean had earned the right to be her father's successor in the firm.

Bill Dunne said to Johnny O'Brien that he half thought of asking Nan Mahon to the pictures.

"What's stopping you?" Johnny asked.

What was really stopping him, of course, was the thought that she would say no. Why invite rejection. But she wasn't going out with anyone else. They knew that. It was odd, considering how gorgeous she was. You'd think that half the men in College would want to take her out. But perhaps that was it. They *wanted* to, and yet did nothing about it.

Bill decided to invite her.

Nan said no, she didn't really like the cinema. She was regretful, and Bill didn't think she had closed the door.

"Is there anything you would like to go to?" he asked, hoping he wasn't making himself too humble, too pathetic.

"Well, there is . . . but I don't know." Nan sounded doubtful.

"Yes? What?"

"There's a rather posh cocktail party at the Russell. It's a sort of pre-wedding do. I'd like to go to that."

"But we weren't invited." Bill was shocked.

"I know." Nan's eyes danced with excitement.

"Bill Dunne and Nan are going to crash a party," Aidan said to Eve.

"Why?"

"Search me."

They thought about it for a while. Why go to a place where you might be unwelcome? There were so many places where Nan Mahon could just walk in and everyone would be delighted. She looked like Grace Kelly people said, confident and beautiful without being flashy. It was a great art.

"Maybe it's the excitement," Aidan suggested.

It could be the fear of being caught, the danger element like gambling.

Why else would you want to go to a wedding party with a whole lot of horsey people from the country, neighing and whinnying, Aidan asked.

Once Eve knew it was that kind of party she knew immediately why Nan Mahon wanted to go. And why she needed someone very respectable and solid like Bill Dunne to go with her.

Jack Foley thought it was a marvelous idea.

"That's only because you don't have to do it," Bill grumbled.

"Oh, go on. It's easy. Just keep smiling at everyone."

"That would be all right if we all had your matinee idol looks. Advertising toothpaste all over the place."

Jack just laughed at him.

"I wish she'd asked me to escort her. I think it's a great gas."

Bill was doubtful. He should have known there would be trouble involved once he had dared to ask out someone with looks like Nan Mahon's. Nothing came easy in life.

And it was all so mysterious. Who on earth would want to go to a thing like that, where they'd know nobody and everyone else knew everyone.

Nan wouldn't explain. She just said that she had a new outfit and thought it would be a bit of fun.

Bill offered to pick her up at home, but she said no, they'd meet in the foyer of the hotel.

The new outfit was stunning. A pale pink sheath dress with pink lace sleeves. Nan carried a small silver handbag with a silk pink rose attached to it.

She came in without a coat.

"Better in case we have to make a quick getaway," she giggled.

She looked high and excited, like she had looked when she came into Eve's party in Knockglen. As if she knew something nobody else did.

Bill Dunne was highly uneasy going up the stairs loosening his collar with a nervous finger. His father would be furious if there was any trouble.

There was no trouble. The bride's people thought they were friends of the groom's, the groom's thought they were on the bride's side. They gave their real names. They smiled and waved, and because Nan was undoubtedly the most glamorous girl in the room it wasn't long before she was surrounded by a group of men.

She didn't talk very much, Bill noticed. She laughed and smiled and agreed, and looked interested. Even when asked a direct question she managed to put it back to the questioner. Bill Dunne talked awkwardly to a dull girl in a tweed dress who looked over at Nan sadly.

"I didn't know it was meant to be dressy-uppy," she said.

"Ah. Yes, well." Bill was trying to imitate Nan's method of saying almost nothing.

"We were told it was a bit low-key," the tweed girl complained. "Because of everything, you know."

"Ah yes, everything," Bill mumbled desperately.

"Well, it's obvious isn't it? Why else wouldn't they wait until spring?"

"Spring. Indeed."

He looked over her head. A small dark-haired man was talking to Nan. They looked very animated, and they hardly seemed to notice that anyone else in the room existed.

Lilly Foley looked at herself in the mirror. It was hard to believe that those lines would not go away. Not ever.

She had been used to little lines when she was tired, or strained. But they always smoothed out after a rest. In the old days.

In the old days, too, she didn't have to worry about the tops of her arms, whether they looked a little crepey and even a small bit flabby.

Lilly Foley had been careful about what she ate since the day her glance had first fallen on John Foley. She had been thoughtful, too, about what she wore, and even, if she were honest, about what she said.

You didn't win the prize and keep it unless you lived up to the role.

That's why it was heartbreaking to think that that big overgrown puppy dog of a girl Benny Hogan should think that she had a chance with Jack. Jack was so nice to her, he had his father's manners and charm. But obviously he couldn't have serious notions about a girl like that.

He had driven her down to Knockglen and gone to the funeral out of natural courtesy and concern. It would be sad if the child got ideas.

Lilly had been startled to hear Aidan Lynch talking of Benny and Jack as if they were a couple.

At least Benny had the sense not to keep telephoning him like other girls did.

She *must* realize that there could be nothing in it.

Benny sat at the kitchen table and willed the phone to ring. She was surrounded by papers and books.

She intended to understand all about the business before talking to Sean and Mr. Green at the end of the week. She could ask no help and advice from old Mike in the shop and her mother was not likely to be any help either. Benny had bought a box of black-bordered writing paper. She had listed the people who sent flowers, hoping that her mother would write a short personal note to each of them. She had even addressed the envelopes.

But Annabel's hand seemed to feel heavy and her heart listless. She never managed more than two letters a day. Benny did them herself eventually. She ordered the Mortuary Cards, with little pictures of her father, and prayers on them which people would keep in their missals to remind them to pray for his soul. It was Benny, too, who had ordered the black-rimmed cards printed with a message of gratitude for the sympathies offered.

Benny paid the undertaker, and the gravediggers, and the priest, and the bill in Shea's. She paid everyone in cash as she had drawn a large sum from the bank in Ballylee. Fonsie had driven her there in his van.

"Wait till we get Knockglen on the map," Fonsie had said. "Then we'll have a bank of our own, not having to wait till the bank comes on Thursdays as if we were some one-horse Wild West outpost."

The man in the bank in Ballylee had been most sympathetic, but also slightly uneasy about advancing the sum.

"I'm meeting Mr. Green the solicitor on Friday," Benny reassured him. "Everything will be put on a proper footing then."

She hadn't imagined the look of relief on the banker's face.

She realized that she hadn't the first idea about how her father had run his business all these years, and she had only had a few days to find out.

As far as she could see it was a matter of two big books and a till full of pink slips.

There was the Takings Book. Every item was entered in that as it was received. Some of them were pitiably small. The sale of collar studs, sock braces, shoehorns, shoe-polishing brushes.

And then there was the Lodgement Book, a big brown leather volume with a kind of window in the front of it. It was ruled in three columns: Checks, Cash and Other. "Other" could mean postal orders or in one case dollars from a passing American.

Each Thursday her father had queued up with others when the bank came to town. The bank signature at the end of each week's lodgement was the receipt and acknowledgment that the money had been put in the account.

In the till there were always pink raffle tickets, books that had been sent on spec by Foreign Missions, ideal for tearing off to write out what had been taken out. Each time there was a sum listed and a reason. "Ten shillings: petrol."

It was Wednesday, early closing day. She had lifted both books from the shop and put them into a large carrier bag.

Sean had remonstrated with her saying that the books never left the premises.

Benny had said nonsense. Her father had often pored over the ledgers at home, and her mother wanted to see them. It seemed a small comfort at a time like this.

Sean had been unable to refuse.

Benny didn't even know what she was looking for. She just wanted to work out why the business was doing so badly. She knew that there would be seasonal highs and lows. After the harvest when the farmers got paid for the corn they all came and bought new suits.

She wasn't looking for discrepancies, or falsification.

Which was why she was so surprised when she realized that the Takings Book and the Lodgement Book didn't match up. If they took so much a week, then that much should have been lodged, apart from the small pink tickets called Drawings from the Till, which were very insignificant.

But as far as she could see by reading it and adding everything laboriously, there was a difference between what was taken and what was lodged, every single week. Sometimes a difference of as much as ten pounds.

She sat looking at it with a feeling of shock and despair. Much as she disliked him and wished him a million miles away from Knockglen, she did not even want to think for a moment that Sean Walsh had been taking money from her father's business. It was so unlikely for one thing. He was such an overrespectable person. And for another, if he was to be made a partner why steal from his own business? And most important of all, if this had been going on for months and months, and maybe years, why was Sean Hogan living in threadbare suits in a cramped room two floors above the shop. She sat numbed by the discovery, and hardly heard the telephone ring.

Patsy answered it and said that a young man was looking for Benny.

"How are you?" Jack was concerned. "How's everything?"

"Fine. We're fine." Her voice sounded far away.

"Good. You didn't ring."

"I didn't want to be bothering you." It was still unreal. Her eyes were on the books.

"I'd like to come down." He sounded regretful, as if he were going to say he couldn't. She didn't want him here anyway. This was too huge.

"No, heavens no. Please." She was insistent, and he knew it. He seemed cheered.

"And when will you come back up to me?"

She told him she should have things sorted out in some way by next week. Maybe they could meet for coffee in the Annexe on Monday.

Her lack of pursuit was rewarded. He really *did* seem sorry not to see her.

"That's a long time away. I miss you, you see," he explained.

"And I miss you. You were wonderful, all of you, to come to the funeral."

When he was gone from the phone he went from her mind too.

There was nobody she could ask about the books.

She knew that Peggy, Clodagh, Fonsie and Mario would understand. As would Mrs. Kennedy, and many other businesspeople in the town.

But she owed it to the memory of her father not to reveal him as an incompetent bungler, and she owed it to Sean Walsh not to mention a word of her suspicion until she knew it was true.

"Why won't you let me take you home?" Simon asked Nan after dinner.

It was the second time they had met that week after the extraordinary coincidence of their meeting at the cocktail party.

Nan looked at him and spoke truthfully.

"I don't invite anyone home with me. I never did."

She sounded neither apologetic nor defiant. She was saying it as a fact.

"Might one ask why?"

She smiled at him mockingly. "One might, if one was rather pushing and curious."

"One is." He leaned across the table and patted her hand.

"What you see is the way I am, the way I see myself. And how I feel and the way that I am always going to be. Were you, or anyone to come home with me, it would be different."

For Nan it was a long speech about herself. He looked at her with surprise and some admiration.

He realized that she was from somewhere in north Dublin. He knew her father was in building. He had thought that perhaps they lived in a big nouveau riche house somewhere. They must have money. Her clothes were impeccable. She was always at the best places. He felt quite protective about her wish to keep her home life to herself, and her honesty in saying that this was what she was doing.

He told her gently that she was a silly. He didn't feel ashamed of *his* home, a falling-down, crumbling mansion in Knockglen, a place that had seen better days, where he lived with underpaid retainers, a senile grandfather and a pony-mad little sister. It was a pretty weird background to introduce anyone into. Yet he had invited her there after Christmas. He held his head on the side quizzically.

Nan was not to be moved. It was not a pleasure for her to bring her friends home. If Simon felt uneasy about this, then perhaps they had better not see each other again.

As she had known he would, he agreed to dismiss the matter from their conversation and their minds.

In a way he was actually relieved. It was better by far than being paraded at a Sunday lunch and having expectations raised.

Heather was very bad at needlework at school. But after a conversation with Dekko Moore, the harness maker in Knockglen, she had decided that she should try to be good at it. He said that she might have a future for herself making hunting attire for ladies, and that they could be sold through Pine's or Hogan's.

It was Heather's project for the new term to learn to sew properly.

"It's awful things like cross-stitch, not real things like clothes," she grumbled to Eve. It was Heather's twelfth birthday and the school allowed her to spend the evening out with a relation just as long as she was back by eight.

They had a birthday cake for her in Kit's house and everyone clapped when she blew out the candles. The students liked Heather, and her overwhelming interest in food.

They discussed the teaching of sewing in schools and how unfair it was that boys never had to learn cross-stitch.

"At least you don't have to make big green knickers with gussets in them like we did at school," Eve said cheerfully.

"Why did you have to make those?" Heather was fascinated by tales of the convent.

Eve couldn't remember. She thought it might have had something to do with wearing them over their ordinary knickers and under their tunics when they were doing handstands. Or maybe she was only making that up. She really didn't know. She was annoyed with Simon for not taking his sister out on her birthday and only sending her a feeble card with a picture of a crinoline lady on it. There were hundreds of nice horsey birthday cards around that he could have got.

But more than that, she was worried about Benny. There was some problem, some worry about the business. Benny had said she couldn't talk about it on the phone, but she'd tell all next week.

It was something she had said at the end that wouldn't go out of Eve's mind.

"If you ever say any prayers, Eve, prepare to say them now."

"What am I to pray for?"

"Oh, that things will turn out all right."

"But we've been praying for that for years," Eve said indignantly. She wasn't going to start praying for unspecified things, she told Benny.

"The Wise Woman would leave them unspecified for a bit," Benny had said.

Benny didn't sound very wise or very happy.

"Simon's got a new girl friend," Heather said chattily. She knew Eve was always interested in such tales.

"Really? What happened to the lady from Hampshire?"

"I think she's too far away. Anyway this one's in Dublin, so Bee Moore told me."

Ah, Eve thought, that's going to be one in the eye for our friend Nan Mahon and her notions.

Then the thought came to her suddenly. Unless of course it *is* Nan Mahon.

---

FIFTEEN

*B*enny returned the account books to the shop very early on the following morning. She took Shep with her for the outing. The dog looked around hopefully in case Eddie might come out of the back room beaming and clapping his hands, delighted to see his dear old dog arriving for a visit.

She heard a footstep on the stair and realized that she had not been early enough. Sean Walsh was up and dressed.

"Ah, Benny," he said.

"I should hope so too. We wouldn't want anyone else letting themselves in. Where'll I leave these for you, Sean?"

Was she imagining it or did he eye her very closely? He took both books and laid them in their places. It was a good three quarters of an hour before the shop opened.

The place smelled musty and heavy. There was nothing about it that would encourage you to spend. Nothing that would make a man feel puckish and buy a bright tie or a colored shirt when he had always worn white. She looked at the dark interior and wondered why she had never taken the time to notice these things when her father was alive, less than a week ago, and talk to him about them.

But she knew why. Almost immediately she answered her own

question. Her father would have been so pleased to see her taking an interest, it would have raised his hopes again. The whole subject of a union with Sean Walsh would have been aired once more.

Sean watched her looking around her.

"Was there anything in particular . . ."

"Just looking, Sean."

"There'll have to be great changes."

"I know." She spoke solemnly and weightily. That was the only language he understood, heavy pontificating phrases. But she thought a look of alarm came into his eyes as if her words had been menacing.

"Did you find what you were looking for in the books?" His glance never left hers.

"I wasn't looking for anything, as I told you I just wanted to familiarize myself with the day-to-day workings before I met Mr. Green."

"I thought your mother wanted to see them." His lip curled a little.

"She did. She understands much more than any of us realized."

Benny didn't know why she had said this. Annabel Hogan knew nothing of the business that her dowry had helped to buy. She had deliberately stayed away from it, thinking it to be a man's world where the presence of a woman would be an intrusion. Men didn't buy suits and get measured in a place with a woman around it.

Suddenly Benny realized that this had been the tragedy of her parents' life. If only her mother *had* been able to get involved in the shop how different things would have been. They would have shared so much more, their interest in Benny would not have been so obsessive. And her mother, in many ways a sharper, more practical person than Eddie Hogan, might have spotted this discrepancy, if such it was, and headed it off long ago. Long before it looked as serious as it looked now.

❧

Emily Mahon knocked on the door of Nan's bedroom and came in carrying a cup of tea.

"Are you sure you don't want any milk in it?"

Nan had taken to having a slice of lemon instead. It was puzzling for the rest of the family, who poured great quantities of milk in their tea, which they drank noisily from large mugs.

"It is nice, Em. Try it," Nan urged.

"It's too late for me to change my ways, and no point in it either—not like you."

Emily knew that her daughter had found a special person at last.

She knew from the amount of preparation that went on in the bedroom, from the new clothes, the wheedling money from her father and mainly from the sparkle in Nan's eyes.

On the bed lay a small petal hat. It matched exactly the wild silk dress and bolero in lilac trimmed with a darker purple. Nan was going to the races today. An ordinary working day for most people, a studying day for students, but a day at the races for Nan.

Emily was on late shift; they had the house to themselves.

"You'll be careful, love, won't you?"

"How do you mean?"

"You know what I mean. I don't ask you about him because I know you think it's bad luck, and we wouldn't want to be meeting him anyway, lowering your chances. But you will be careful?"

"I haven't slept with him, Em. I haven't a notion of it."

"I didn't mean only that." Emily had meant only that, but it seemed a bit bald to hear it all out in the open.

"I meant, careful about not neglecting your College studies, and not going in fast cars."

"You meant sleeping, Em." Nan laughed affectionately at her mother. "And I haven't, and I won't, so relax."

❧

"Are you and I going to keep teasing each other forever, or will we give in to ourselves and go to bed together soon?" Simon asked Nan as they drove to the race meeting.

"Are we teasing each other? I didn't notice."

He looked at her admiringly. Nothing threw her. She was never at a disadvantage.

And she looked really beautiful today. Her photograph would probably be in the papers. Photographers always looked for somebody classy as well as the ladies with silly hats. His companion was exactly the girl they would seek out.

They got stuck with a lot of people as soon as they went into the Enclosure. At the parade ring Molly Black, a very bossy woman with a shooting stick, looked Nan up and down with some care. Her own daughter had once been a candidate for Simon Westward's interest. This was a very different type of girl for him to parade. Handsome certainly. A student by all accounts, living in Dublin, and giving nothing away whatsoever about herself or her background.

Mrs. Black moaned about the decree from Buckingham Palace abolishing the debutantes' presentation at court.

"I mean, how will anyone know who anyone is once that goes?" Molly Black said, staring at Nan with gimlet eyes.

Nan looked around for Simon, hurt he wasn't at hand. She resorted to her usual system, answering a question with another.

"Why are they abolishing it, really, do you think?"

"It's obvious. You have to be presented by someone who was herself presented. Some of these are on rather hard times, and they take a fee from really dreadful businessmen to present their ghastly daughters. That's what caused it all."

"And did you have someone to be presented?" Nan's voice was cool and her manner courteous.

She had hit home.

"Not my immediate family, no, obviously," said Mrs. Black, annoyed. "But all one's friends, one's friends' children. It was so nice for them, such a good system. They met like-minded people until all this crept in."

"But I suppose that it's easy to tell like-minded people, to recognize them, do you think?"

"Yes it is, quite easy." Molly Black was gruff.

Simon was at her elbow again.

"Having a most interesting conversation about doing the Season with your little friend here," Mrs. Black said to him.

"Oh good." Simon moved them away.

"What a battle-ax," he said.

"Why do you bother with her then?"

"Have to." He shrugged. "She and Teddy are everywhere. Guarding their daughters from fortune hunters like myself."

"Are you a fortune hunter?" Her smile was light and encouraging.

"Of course I am. You've seen the house," he said. "Come and let's have a very large drink and put a lot of money we can't afford on a horse. That's what living is all about."

He took her by the arm and led her across the grass through the crowds into the bar.

The meeting with Mr. Green was very low-key. It was held in Lisbeg. Benny had woken her mother up enough to attend by strong coffee and a stern talking-to.

Her mother must not ask that things be put off, or postponed until later. There was no later, Benny insisted. Hard as it was on all of them, they owed it to Father to make sure that things didn't end in a giant muddle.

Benny had begged her mother to recall any conversations about Sean's partnership. The letter existed, the letter saying that the intention was there. Had there been anything at all that made her think it had been formalized?

Wearily, Annabel said that Father had kept saying there was

no need to rush things, that they'd wait and see, that everything got done in time.

But had he said that about things in general, or about Sean's partnership?

She really couldn't remember. It was very difficult for her to remember, she complained. It seemed such a short time since Eddie Hogan had been alive and well and running his own business. Today he was buried and they were meeting a solicitor to discuss business dealings that she knew nothing of. Could Benny not be more patient and understanding?

Patsy served coffee in the drawing room, aired and used now because of the stream of sympathizers who had filled the house. There were just the three of them. Benny said they would telephone Sean Walsh and ask him to join them after a suitable period.

Mr. Green told them what they already knew, which was that the late Mr. Hogan, despite numerous reminders, suggestions and cautions, had made no will. He also told them what they didn't know, which was that the Deed of Partnership had been drawn up and prepared ready for signature, but it had not been signed.

Mr. Green had been in Knockglen as was his wont on four Friday mornings in January, but on none of these occasions had Mr. Hogan approached him with a view to signing the document.

On the one occasion that Mr. Green had reminded him of it, the late Mr. Hogan had said that he still had something to think about.

"Do you think he had discovered anything that made him change his mind? After all he did write that letter to Sean before Christmas." Benny was persistent.

"I know. I have a copy of the letter. It was sent to me in the post."

"By my father?"

"I rather think by Mr. Walsh."

"And there were no hints or feelings . . . Did you get any mood that the thing was wrong, somehow?"

"Miss Hogan, you'll have to forgive me for sounding so formal, but I don't deal in the currency of feelings or moods. As a lawyer I have to deal in what is written down."

"And what is written down is an intent to make Sean Walsh a partner, isn't that right?"

"That is correct."

Benny had no proof, only an instinct. Possibly in the weeks before his death her father, too, had noticed that they seemed to be lodging less than they took. But there had been no confrontation. Had there been a face-to-face accusation he would have told his wife about it, and Mike in the office would have heard every word.

Perhaps her father had been waiting to find proof, so this is what she, too, must do.

Like her father she would ask to delay the partnership agreement, by saying that it was hard to know who should be the parties to it.

Mr. Green, who was a cautious man, said that it was always wise to postpone any radical change until well after a bereavement. They agreed that now would be the time to have Sean Walsh to the house.

Fresh coffee was brought in when Sean arrived.

He explained that he had closed the shop. It was impossible to allow Mike to remain in control. He was a man who had given untold service in the past, no doubt, but as Mr. Hogan used to say, poor Mike wasn't able for a lot in today's world.

Her father used to say that, Benny remembered, but he had said it with affection and concern. He had not said it with the knell of dismissal echoing around it.

The arrangement was that for the moment everything would carry on as it was. Did Sean think that they needed to employ somebody on a temporary basis? He said that all depended.

Depended on what, they wondered? On whether Miss Hogan was thinking of abandoning her university studies and coming to work in the shop with him. If that were to happen, then there would be no need to employ a casual.

Benny explained that nothing was further from her father's

dreams. Her parents were both anxious that she should be a university graduate, but she would nonetheless take a huge and continuing interest in the shop. She almost kicked her mother into wakefulness and a few alert statements that she would do the same thing.

Very casually and with no hint of anything being amiss, Benny asked if the very simple bookkeeping system could be explained to them. Laboriously Sean went through it.

"So what's in in the Takings Books should be more or less as what's in the Lodging Book each week." Her eyes were round and innocent.

"Yes. Give or take the Drawings," he said.

"Drawings?"

"Whatever your father took out of the till."

"Yes. And the little pink slips, they say what those were, is that right?"

"When he remembered." Sean's voice was sepulchral and trying-not-to-speak-ill-of-the-dead. "Your father was a wonderful man, as you know, but forgetful in the extreme."

"What might he have taken money out for?" Benny's heart was cold. There would never be any proof, not if this was believed.

"Well, let me see." Sean looked at Benny. She was wearing her best outfit, the new skirt and bolero top that she had been given as a Christmas present.

"Well, maybe for something like your clothes, Benny. He might have taken money out to pay for an outfit without remembering to sign a Drawings slip."

She knew now that she was defeated.

Kevin Hickey said that his father was coming up from Kerry and wondered could Mrs. Hegarty recommend a good hotel in Dun Laoghaire?

"God, Kevin, you pass a dozen of them yourself every day," Kit said.

"I think he wanted your choice rather than mine."

Kit suggested the Marine, and she booked it for him.

She supposed that Kevin's father would like to see the house where his son lived all through the academic year, and urged the boy to bring him round for a cup of tea during his visit.

Paddy Hickey was a big, pleasant man. He explained that he was in machinery in the country. He had a small bit of land, but there wasn't the streak of a farmer in any of them. His brothers had all gone to America, his sons had all done degrees in something, but none of them in agriculture.

Like all Kerrymen he said he put a great emphasis on education.

Kit and Eve liked him. He talked easily about the boy of the house who had died and asked to see a picture of him.

"May he rest in peace, poor young lad who never got a chance to know what it was like down here," he said.

It was awkward but affecting. Neither Kit nor Eve felt able to say anything in reply.

He thanked them for giving his son such a good home, and encouraging him to study.

"No hope he's getting anywhere with a fine-looking young girl like yourself?" he asked Eve.

"Ah no, he wouldn't look at me," Eve said, laughing.

"Besides, she has a young law student besotted about her," Kit added.

"That must leave you lonely here, sometimes, Mrs. Hegarty," he said. "When all the young folk go out of an evening."

"I manage," Kit said.

Eve realized that the man was revving up to ask Kit Hegarty out. She knew that Kit herself was quite unaware of this.

"You do manage," Eve said. "Of course you do. And people want you everywhere, but I'd love you to go out and be silly, just once."

"Well, talking of being silly," said big Paddy Hickey. "I don't suppose there's a chance you'd accompany a poor lonely old Kerry widower out for a night on the town."

"Well, isn't that *great*," cried Eve, "because we're all going out tonight, every single one of us."

Kit looked startled.

"Come back for her about seven o'clock, Mr. Hickey. I'll have her ready for you," Eve said.

When he was gone Kit turned on Eve in a fury.

"Why are you behaving like that? Cheap and pushy. It isn't at all like you."

"It's not like me for me, but by God I'd need it for you."

"I can't go out with him. I'm a married woman."

"Oh yes?"

"Yes, I am. No matter what Joseph did in England I'm married anyway."

"Oh, belt up Kit."

"*Eve!*"

"I mean it. I really do. Nobody's asking you to commit adultery with Kevin's father you great fool, just go out with him, tell him about your living encumbrance across the channel if you want to. I wouldn't personally, but you will. But don't throw a decent man's invitation back in his face."

She looked so cross that Kit burst out laughing.

"What'll I wear?"

"That's more like it." Eve gave her a big squeeze as they went upstairs to examine both of their wardrobes.

"I was wondering would you consider Wales a sort of break . . ." Jack asked Benny hopefully.

"No, it's too soon."

"I just thought it could be a change. They always say that's a good thing."

Benny knew what he meant. She longed to go to Wales with him. She longed to be his girl, on a boat sailing out from Dun

Laoghaire to Holyhead. She longed to be sitting beside him on a train, and meeting the others and being Benny Hogan, Jack Foley's girl, with everything that that implied.

And she knew that a change could clear her head of the thoughts and the suspicions that buzzed around in it.

She had tried to get her mother to make a visit. To go to her brothers and their wives. They had been very solicitous at the funeral. But Annabel Hogan told Benny sadly that they had never approved of her marrying Eddie all those years ago, a man younger than she was with no stake in any business. They had thought she should have done better for herself. She didn't want to go to stay in their homes, large country places, and tell them tales of a marriage which had worked for her but which they had never thought anything of.

No, she would stay in her home and try to get used to the way things were going to be from now on.

But Benny didn't want to explain all this to Jack. Jack wasn't a person to weigh down with problems. The great thing was that he seemed so glad to see her. He took no notice of the admiring glances coming at him from every corner of the Annexe. He sat on his hard wooden chair and drank cup after cup of coffee. He had two fly cemetries, but Benny said she had gone off them. In fact her whole being cried out for one, but she was eating no cakes, bread puddings, chips or biscuits. If she had not had Jack Foley to light up everything for her, it would have been a very dull life indeed.

Nan was delighted to see Benny back at lectures.

"I had no one to talk to. It's great to see you again," she said.

Despite herself, Benny was pleased.

"You had Eve. Lord, I envy the two of you being here all the time."

"I don't think Eve is too pleased with me," Nan confided. "I've been going out with Simon you see, and she doesn't approve."

Benny knew that was true: Eve did not approve, but then it would have been the same with anyone who went out with Simon. She felt that he should have made some effort to make provisions for his cousin once he was old enough to understand the situation.

And she felt that Nan had been sneaky. Eve always claimed that Benny had been dragged to the Hibernian with the express purpose of making the introduction. Benny thought that was impossible, but there were some subjects on which Eve was adamant.

"And where does he take you?" Benny loved to hear Nan's cool comments on the high life that Simon Westward was opening up.

She described the back bar in Jammets, the Red Bank, the Bailey and Davy Byrne's.

"He's so much older, you see," Nan explained. "So most of his friends meet in bars and hotels."

Benny thought that was sad. Imagine not going to where there was great fun, like the Coffee Inn, or the Inca or the Zanzibar. All the places she and Jack went to.

"And do you like him?"

"Yes, a lot."

"So why do you look so worried. He obviously likes you if he keeps asking you to all these places."

"Yes, but he wants to sleep with me."

Benny's eyes were round. "You won't, will you?"

"I will, but how? That's what I'm trying to work out. Where and how."

Simon as it turned out had decided where and how. He had decided that it was going to be in the back of a car parked up on the Dublin mountains. He said it was awfully silly to pretend that they both didn't want it.

Nan was ice cool. She said she had no intention of doing anything of the sort in a car.

"But you do want me?" Simon said.

"Yes, of course I do."

"So?"

"You have a perfectly good house where we can be comfortable."

"Not at Westlands," Simon said.

"And most definitely not in a car," said Nan.

Next day Simon was waiting at the corner of Earlsfort Terrace and Leeson Street as the students poured out at lunchtime, wheeling bicycles, or carrying books. They moved off to digs, flats and restaurants around the city.

Nan had said no, when Eve and Benny asked her to come to the Singing Kettle. Chips for Eve and black coffee for strong-willed Benny.

They didn't see her eyes dart around as if she knew someone would be waiting for her.

They didn't notice as Simon stepped out and took her hand.

"How amazingly crass I was last night," he said.

"Oh, that's perfectly all right."

"I mean it. It was unpardonable. I wondered if you might come down to a pretty little hotel I know for dinner and we might stay overnight. If you'd like to."

"I'd like to, certainly," Nan said. "But sadly I'm not free until next Tuesday."

"You're making me wait."

"No, I assure you."

But she was indeed making him wait. Nan had worked out the safe period, and next Tuesday was the earliest she dared go to bed with Simon Westward.

Clodagh was sitting in her back room sewing. She had a glass door and could see if there was a customer who needed personal attention. Otherwise her aunt and Rita, the new young girl they had taken on, could manage fine without her.

Benny came in and sat beside her.

"How's Rita getting on?"

"Fine. You've got to choose them, quick enough to be of some use. Not so quick that they'll take all your ideas and set up on their own. It's the whole nature of business."

Benny laughed dryly.

"I wish someone had told that to my father ten years ago," she said ruefully.

Clodagh went on sewing. Benny had never brought up the subject of Sean Walsh before. Even though it had been a matter of a lot of speculation in the last weeks. Just after Christmas there had been talk of him becoming a partner. Those who drank in Healy's Hotel said Mrs. Healy spoke of it very authoritatively. Clodagh, since the day she had been barred from Healy's, made it her business to find out everything that went on there, and all subjects discussed at its bar.

She waited to hear what Benny had to say.

"Clodagh, what would happen if Rita was taking money from the till?"

"Well, for a start I'd know it at the end of the day, or else the end of the week."

"You would?"

"Yes, and then I'd suggest cutting off her hands at the wrist, and Aunt Peggy would say we should just sack her."

"And suppose you couldn't prove it?"

"Then I'd be very careful Benny, so careful you wouldn't believe it."

"If she had put it in a bank someone would know?"

"Oh yes. She wouldn't have put it in a bank, not around these parts. It would have to be in cash somewhere."

"Like where?"

"Lord, I'd have no idea, and I'd be careful I didn't get caught looking."

"So you might have to let it go if you couldn't prove it."

"Crucifying as it would be, I might."

Benny heard the warning in her voice. They both knew they were not talking about the blameless Rita out in the shop. They each realized that it would be dangerous to say any more.

Jack Foley said he'd ring Benny when he got to Wales. They were staying in a guesthouse. He was going to share a room with Bill Dunne, who was going for the laugh and a beer.

"You won't need me at all," Benny had said, laughing away her disappointment that she couldn't be there.

"Fine though Bill Dunne is and everything, I don't think there's much comparison. I wish you were coming with me."

"Well, ring me from the height of the fun," Benny said.

He didn't ring. On night one, or night two, or night three. Benny sat at home. She didn't take her mother up to Healy's Hotel to try out one of their new evening dinners, at Mrs. Healy's invitation.

Instead she stayed at home and listened to the clock ticking and to Shep snoring and to Patsy whispering with Mossy while her mother looked at the pictures in the fire and Jack Foley made no phone call from the height of the fun.

Nan packed her overnight bag carefully. A lacy nightie, a change of clothes for the next day, a very smart sponge bag from Brown Thomas, with talcum powder and a new toothbrush and toothpaste. She kissed her mother good-bye.

"I'll be staying with Eve in Dun Laoghaire," she said.

"That's fine," said Emily Mahon, who knew that wherever Nan was going to stay it was not with Eve in Dun Laoghaire.

❧

Bill Dunne ran into Benny in the Main Hall.

"I'm meant to bump into you casually and see how the land lies," he said.

"What on earth do you mean?"

"Is our friend in the doghouse or isn't he?"

"Bill, you're getting worse than Aidan. Talk English."

"In plain English, your erring boyfriend, Mr. Foley, wants to know if he dares approach you, he having not managed to telephone you."

"Oh, don't be so silly," Benny said, exasperated. "Jack knows I'm not that kind of girl going into sulks and moods. He knows I don't mind something like that. If he couldn't phone he couldn't."

"Now I see why he likes you so much. And why he was so afraid that he'd upset you," Bill Dunne said admiringly. "You're a girl in a million, Benny."

Heather Westward didn't really like the thought of Aidan coming on their outings, but that was before she got to know him. Soon Eve complained that she liked Aidan more than she liked Eve. His fantasy world was vastly more entertaining than her own.

He told Heather that he and Eve were going to have eight children, with ten months between each child. They would marry in 1963 and keep having children until late 1970.

"Is that because you're Catholics?"

"No, it's because I want something to occupy Eve during my first hard years at the Bar. I shall be in the Law Library all day and night in order to make money for all the Knickerbocker Glories that these children will demand. I shall have to work at night in a newspaper as a sub-editor. I have it all worked out."

Heather giggled into her huge ice cream. She wasn't absolutely sure if he was being serious. She looked to Eve for confirmation.

"That's what he thinks now, but actually what's going to happen is that he's going to meet some brainless little blonde who'll flutter long lashes at him and giggle, and he'll forget all about me and the long-term plan."

"Will you mind?" Heather spoke as if Aidan wasn't there.

"No, I'll be quite relieved really. Eight children would be exhausting. Remember how Clara felt with all those puppies?"

"But you wouldn't have to have them all at the same time?" Heather took the matter seriously.

"Though it would have its advantages." Aidan was reflective. "We'd get free baby things, and you could come and help with the baby-sitting, Heather. You'd change four while Eve changed the other four."

Heather laughed happily.

"I wouldn't want a brainless little blonde, honestly," Aidan said to Eve. "I'm no Jack Foley."

Eve looked at him astonished. "Jack?"

"You know, the Wales outing. It's all right. It's all right, Benny's forgiven him. Bill Dunne says."

"She's forgiven him for not phoning her. She doesn't know anything about a brainless blonde that should be forgiven."

"Oh . . . I don't think it was anything really . . ." Aidan backtracked.

Eve's eyes glinted.

"Well, only a ship that passed in the night, or the evening, a blonde, silly Welsh ship. I don't know for God's sake. I wasn't there. I was only told."

"Oh, I'm sure you were told, and all the gory details."

"No, really. And Eve, I wouldn't go and say anything to Benny."

"I'm her friend."

"Does that mean you will or you won't?"

"It means that you'll never know."

Nan settled herself into Simon's car.

"You smell beautiful," he said. "Always the most expensive of perfumes."

"Most men don't recognize good perfume," she complimented him. "You are very discerning."

They drove out of Dublin south through Dun Laoghaire, past Kit Hegarty's and past Heather's school.

"That's where my sister is."

Nan knew this. She knew that Eve went there on Sundays when Simon did not. She knew that Heather was unhappy there and would much prefer a day school within reach of her beloved pony and dog and the country life she loved so much, pottering around Westlands. But she didn't let Simon know that she knew any of this.

With Simon she was determined to play it cool and distant. To ask little and seem to know little of his family and home life, so that he would not feel justified in prying into hers. Later, when she had really captivated him, then it would be time for him to get answers to his questions.

And by then he would know her well enough to realize that a drunken father and a messy family would form no part of the life that she led.

She believed that she had flirted with him for long enough and that she was timing it right to go to this hotel with him tonight.

She had looked the hotel up in a guidebook, and knew all about it. Nan Mahon would not arrive anywhere, even at a hotel to lose her virginity, unprepared and uninformed about the social background of the place.

He smiled at her a crooked lopsided smile. He really was most attractive, Nan thought, even though he was smaller than she would have chosen. She didn't wear her really good high-heeled shoes when she was out with him. He was very confident of her, as if he had known that this day would come sooner rather than later.

In fact that thought must have been on his mind.

"I was very glad when you agreed to come to dinner and let us spend a whole evening together instead of rushing away at a taxi rank," he said.

"Yes, it's a lovely place, I believe. It has marvelous portraits and old hunting prints."

"Yes. How do you know that?"

"I can't remember. Someone told me."

"You haven't been there with any of your previous boyfriends."

"I've never been to a hotel with *anyone.*"

"Come on now."

"True."

He looked slightly alarmed. As if the thought of what lay ahead was now more arduous and complicated than he had supposed. But a girl like Nan would not go ahead with something like this unless she intended it.

And when she said she had never been to a hotel with a chap, she might be speaking the literal truth. But a girl like this must have had some kind of experience, whether it was in a hotel bedroom or a sand dune. He would not face that problem until he had to.

There were candles on the table, and they sat in a dark dining room with heavy oil paintings of the hotelier's stern ancestors.

The waiter spoke respectfully like an old retainer, and they seemed to recognize Simon, and treat him with respect.

At the next table sat a couple. The waiter addressed the man as "Sir Michael." Nan closed her eyes for an instant. In many ways being here was better than being in Westlands. He had been right.

It was like a stately home, and they were being treated like the aristocracy. Not bad for the daughter of Brian Mahon, builders' provider and drunk.

Nan had not been telling him any lies, Simon realized with surprise and some mild guilt. He was indeed the first man she had gone to a hotel with in any sense of the word. She lay there with the moonlight coming through the curtains and catching her perfect sleeping face. She really was a very beautiful girl, and she seemed to like him a lot. He drew her toward him again.

Benny knew that Sean Walsh's partnership could not be postponed forever. If only she could get her mother to take an interest in the matter. Annabel woke heavy and leaden from a sleep that had been gained through tablets. It took her several hours to shake off the feeling of torpor.

And when she did the loneliness of her position came back to her. Her husband dead before his time, her daughter gone all day in Dublin and her maid about to announce an engagement to Mossy Rooney, and only holding up the actual date out of deference to the bereavement in the family.

Dr. Johnson told Benny that these things took time. Sometimes a lot of time, but eventually, like Mrs. Kennedy in the chemist's, if the wife could be persuaded to take an interest in the business they would recover.

Dr. Johnson looked as if he were about to say something and thought better of it.

He had always hated Sean Walsh. Benny wondered could it have been about him.

"The problem is Sean, you see," she began tentatively.

"When was it not?" Dr. Johnson asked.

"If only Mother was in the shop and properly there, taking notice . . ."

"Yes, I know."

"Do you think she'll ever be able to do that? Or am I just running after a pipe dream."

He looked affectionately at the girl with the chestnut hair, the girl that he had watched grow from the chubby toddler into the big awkward schoolgirl and now fined down a bit he thought, but still by anyone's standards a big woman. Benny Hogan may have had more comforts than some of the other children in Knockglen whose tonsillitis and chicken pox and measles he had cured, but she had never had as much freedom.

Now it looked as if the chains that bound her to home were growing even stronger.

"You have your own life to live," he said gruffly.

"That's not much help, Dr. Johnson."

To his own surprise he heard himself agreeing with her.

"You're right. It isn't much help. And it wasn't much help saying to your mother stop grieving and try living. She won't listen to me. And it was no help at all, all those years ago, telling Birdie Mac to put her mother into a home, or telling Dessie Burns to go to the monk in Mount Mellary who gets people off the jar. But you have to keep saying these things. Just to stay sane."

As long as she had known him Benny had never known Dr. Johnson to make such a speech. She stared at him openmouthed.

He pulled himself together. "If I thought it would get that long drink of water Sean Walsh out of your business and miles from here, I'd give Annabel some kind of stimulant to keep her working in there twelve hours a day."

"My father had an undertaking to make Sean a partner. We'll have to honor it."

"I suppose so." Dr. Johnson knew that this was so.

"Unless there was any reason my father didn't sign the deed." She looked at him beseechingly. It was the smallest hope in the world that Eddie Hogan might have confided his suspicions to his old friend Maurice Johnson. But no. With a heavy heart she heard Dr. Johnson say gloomily that he didn't know any reason.

"It's not as if he was the kind of fellow who'd ever be caught with his hand in the till. He hasn't spent tuppence on himself since the day he arrived."

Sean Walsh was having his morning coffee in Healy's. From the window he could see if anyone entered Hogan's.

Mike could cope with an easy sale, or measuring a regular customer. Anything more difficult would have to be monitored.

Mrs. Healy sat beside him. "Any word of the partnership?"

"They're going to honor it. They said so in front of the solicitor."

"So they might. It should be done already. Your name should be above the shop, for all to see."

"You're very good to have such a high opinion of me . . . um . . . Dorothy." He still thought of her as Mrs. Healy.

"Nothing of the sort Sean. You deserve to make more of yourself. And be seen to be what you are."

"I will. One day people will see. I move slowly. That's my way."

"Just as long as you're moving, not standing still."

"I'm not standing still," Sean Walsh assured her.

"When can I see you again?" Simon said as he dropped Nan off outside University College.

"What do you suggest?"

"Well, I'd suggest tonight, but where could we go?"

"We could go for a drink anywhere."

"But afterward?"

"I'm sure you know some other lovely hotels." She smiled at him.

He did, but he couldn't afford them. And he couldn't take her to Buffy and Frank's place where he stayed when he was in Dublin. And she wasn't going to take him to her home. A car seemed out of the question, and Westlands was off-limits as far as he was concerned.

"We'll think of something," he promised.

"Good-bye," Nan said.

He looked after her with admiration. He hadn't met a girl like this in a long time.

"Benny, you look awful. You haven't even combed your hair," Nan
said.

"Thanks a bundle, that's all I need."

"It *is* what you need, actually," Nan said. "You've got the most
handsome man in college panting after you. You can't turn up
looking like a mess."

"I'll comb my hair then," Benny said ungraciously.

The most handsome man in College was not panting after her.
He was looking like a guilty sheep, every time he met her he apologized for the whole Wales thing. Benny had said he must forget it,
these things happened. And she wasn't making an issue of it, so
why should he.

She had even arranged to stay in town this Friday, and suggested they have an evening together. She had asked Eve if she
could stay in Dun Laoghaire. She had told Patsy that she would be
gone and she had explained to her mother that she needed one
night a week in Dublin. That everyone got over a loss in their own
way, and her way had to be spending time with her friends.

Her mother's eyes, dull and listless, had clouded as if this was
one further blow.

Worst of all, Jack said that Friday wasn't a good night for him.
They had a meeting in the rugby club, and then they'd all go for a
drink afterward.

"Make it another night," he said casually. Benny had wanted
to smack him very hard. He was as thoughtless as any child.

Why did he not realize how hard it was for her to arrange
anything at all? Now she had to go and unpick everything she had
arranged. Eve, Kit, Patsy, her mother. Bloody hell, she wouldn't.
She'd stay in Dublin anyway that night and maybe go to the pictures with Eve and Aidan. They had asked her often enough, and
to have a curry afterward.

They were still whistling the theme tune of *Bridge on the River Kwai* when they arrived at the Golden Orient in Leeson Street. They met Bill Dunne coming out of Hartigan's, and he joined them for the meal.

Aidan took them through the menu as an expert.

Everyone was to order something different, then they could taste four dishes and become curry bores.

"But we all like koftsa," Eve complained.

"Too bad. The mother of my children is not going to be a one-dish lady," Aidan said.

"Where's Jack?" Bill Dunne inquired.

"At a rugby club meeting." Benny spoke casually.

She thought she saw the boys exchange glances, but decided that she was imagining it. All that watching Sean Walsh made her see glances and looks where none existed.

Jack Foley rang, very cross, on Saturday.

"I believe there was a great outing last night. The only night of the week I couldn't get away," he said.

"You never told me. You always said Fridays were marvelous nights in Dublin." Benny was stung by the injustice of it all.

"And so they were for some, Bill Dunne was telling me."

"What night *are* you free next week, Jack? I'll arrange to stay in town."

"You're sulking," he said. "You're sulking over the Wales thing."

"I told you, I understand that you didn't have time to ring me. I am *not* sulking over a phone call."

"Not the phone call," he said. "The other thing."

"What other thing?" asked Benny.

Nan and Simon met three times without being able to do what they both wanted to do, which was to make love.

"What a pity you don't have a little flat in town," he said to her.

"What a pity you don't," she countered.

What they really needed was a small place where nobody would see them, somewhere they could steal in and out of.

It needn't be in Dublin. It could be miles away. Petrol was no problem. Apparently Simon put it all down for the farm. It was complicated, but it was free.

He just needed to be back in Knockglen to fill up.

Nan remembered Eve's cottage by the quarry.

She had seen where Eve put the key under a stone in the wall. Nobody went there. Except sometimes a nun to keep an eye on the place. But the nun wouldn't be keeping an eye on the place at night.

There were only lights in one cottage. Nan remembered that this was the one where a silent man called Mossy lived. She had heard Benny and Eve talking about him once.

"That's the man our Bee Moore wanted for herself, but some other took him away," Simon said, smiling loftily at his local knowledge.

Nan had brought a pair of sheets, pillowcases and two towels. Plus her sponge bag, this time with soap as well. They must leave no trace of their visit.

Simon couldn't understand why they didn't just ask Eve. Nan said this was not even remotely possible. Eve would say no.

"Why? You're her friend. I'm her cousin."

"That's why," Nan said.

Simon had shrugged. They were here so what did it matter. They dared not light the fire or the range. They brought the bottle of champagne to bed immediately.

❧

Next morning it was very chilly.

"I'll have to bring my Primus stove if I can find it," Simon said, shivering.

Nan folded the sheets and towels carefully and put them into the bag.

"Can't we leave them here?" he asked.

"Don't be ridiculous."

Washed briskly in cold water, but as yet unshaved, Simon examined the cottage for the first time.

"She has some nice things here," he commented. "That came from Westlands, definitely." He nodded at the piano. "Does Eve play?"

"No, I don't think so."

He touched other things. This was definitely from the house, and that might have been. He seemed to know even though he was only a child when his aunt had begun the ill-advised marriage, and started to live in this cottage instead of a Big House similar to the one she grew up in.

He laughed at a statue in place of honor on the mantelpiece.

"Who's he, when he's at home," he said, looking at a china figure of a man with a crown and a globe and a cross.

"The Infant of Prague," Nan replied.

"Well, what's he doing on display like this?"

"Probably one of the nuns gave it to her. They do come and clean the house. Why not leave it there to please them when you don't have to look at it yourself," Nan asked.

He looked at her admiringly.

"You're a businesswoman as well as everything else, Nan Mahon."

"Let's go," she said. "It would be terrible to be caught the first time."

"You think there'll be others?" he teased.

"Only if you get your Primus stove going," she laughed.

✦

On the first floor of Hogan's the rooms were big and high-ceilinged. That was where the family that owned the shop formerly used to live. It was where Eddie Hogan and his bride lived for the first year of their marriage. They had bought Lisbeg just before Benny was born.

The rooms on that first floor were still filled with lumber. To the furniture which was already stacked there came extra lumber, old rails not used in the shop, bales empty now from material, boxes. It was not a pretty sight.

The rooms where Sean Walsh had his home for going on ten and a half years were on the floor above that.

A bedroom, another room which could be a sitting room, and a very old-fashioned bathroom with a geyser that looked like a dangerous missile.

Benny had not been up there since she was about eight or nine.

She remembered her father saying that he had asked Sean would he like a key to his own area. But Sean had been insistent that he did not.

If he had taken the money he would not have hidden it in his own rooms. Since that was the first place that would be searched if it ever were found out. It would be pointless for her to search. Pointless and dangerous. She had not forgotten Clodagh's heavy warning.

Things would be quite bad enough if Sean Walsh were not made a partner. There would be an outrage in Knockglen if he were wrongfully accused of stealing from her father. Benny did not relish the thought of hunting in his private rooms for some evidence. But she felt so sure that there must be something, perhaps in the form of a post office book from some faraway branch.

In the beginning as she had plowed through her father's simplistic and even then not very thorough bookkeeping methods, she had only *suspected* that Sean must be taking away a sum of money each week. But now she knew it. She knew it because of one simple lie he had told.

When she had tried to ask him to explain the system of Drawings slips in front of Mr. Green, she had asked for an example. Sean Hogan had pointed to the outfit she wore and suggested that Benny's own clothes might be something that her father drew money from the till to pay for. The thought had raised a lump in her throat.

Until she had looked at the checks that were returned with the bank statement. Her father had paid for every single garment he had bought for her. Clothes she had liked, clothes she had hated, each one paid for in Pine's by check with his slanting writing.

She wished it were all over. That Sean had been unmasked, and that he had left town. That her mother had recovered her spirit and gone in to run the business. And most of all that someone would tell her what exactly had happened in Wales.

Simon brought his Primus stove. Nan brought two pretty china candlesticks, and two pink candles.

Simon brought a bottle of champagne. Nan brought two eggs, and herbs, and bread and butter. She brought some instant coffee powder too. She made them a glorious omelet in the morning.

Simon said it made him feel so excited, they should go straight back to bed.

"We've just remade it with her things, silly," Nan said. Nan never referred to Eve by name.

After a time Simon stopped calling her Eve as well.

"Where does that daughter of yours spend the nights?" Brian Mahon asked.

"You were very drunk a couple of times Brian. I think she was frightened. She goes out to her girlfriend, Eve, in Dun Laoghaire. They all get on together, that Eve and Benny down in Knockglen. They're her friends. We should be glad she had them."

"What's the point of rearing children and having them stay out at night?" he grumbled.

"Paul and Nasey often don't come home. You never worry about them."

"Nothing could happen to them," he said.

"Nor Nan either," Emily Mahon said, with a small silent prayer.

Nan was out three nights a week at least nowadays.

She did hope most fervently that nothing would happen to her beautiful golden daughter.

Mossy Rooney saw lights there one evening. He walked straight by.

Eve Malone must have come home quietly for a night, he thought to himself.

None of his business.

The very next day Mother Francis asked him if he would do a job on the guttering at the cottage. She came up to show him where it was falling away.

"Eve hasn't been back for weeks, the bold child," Mother Francis scolded. "If it wasn't for yourself and myself, Mossy, the place would fall down around her ears."

Mossy kept his peace.

Eve Malone might have wanted to come back to her house without letting the nuns know.

Sean Walsh walked the quarry road at night. It was a place you didn't meet many people. It left him free to think of his plans, his hopes, his future. It was a space where he could consider Dorothy Healy and the interest she showed in him. She was several years older than him. There was no denying that. He had always thought in terms of marrying a much younger woman. A girl in fact.

But there were advantages in a union with an older woman. Eddie Hogan had done so after all. It had never hurt his prospects.

He had been perfectly happy in his life, limited though it was. He had fathered a child.

Sean's thoughts were in a turmoil as he passed the cottage. He wasn't really aware of his surroundings.

He thought he heard music coming from inside. But he must have been imagining it.

After all, Eve wasn't at home and who else would be in there at midnight playing the piano?

He shook his head and tried to work out what length of time Mr. Green the solicitor had in mind when he spoke about the regrettably snail-like process of the law.

Dr. Johnson pulled over his prescription pad across the desk. Mrs. Carroll had always been a difficult person. He felt that she needed the services of Father Ross more than himself, but was it fair to dump all the neurotic moaners onto the local priest and call the whole thing a religious crisis?

"I know I'm not going to be popular for saying so, Dr. Johnson, but I have to say what's true. That cottage up in the quarry is haunted. That woman died roaring and her poor half-witted husband, God be good to him, may have taken his own life, God bless the mark afterward. No wonder a house like that is haunted."

"Haunted?" Dr. Johnson was weary.

"No soul died at peace there. No wonder one of them comes back to play the piano in the night," she said.

Heather rang Westlands. She was coming home next weekend. Bee Moore said that was grand, she'd tell Mr. Simon.

"I'll be going to tea with Eve in her cottage," Heather said proudly.

"I wouldn't fancy that myself. People say it's haunted," said Bee Moore, who had heard that for a fact.

Heather and Eve sat making toast by the fire in the cottage. They had long toasting forks, which Benny had found for them.

She said there were amazing things on the first floor of Hogan's shop, but she didn't like to denude the place entirely in case bloody Sean *was* going to be a partner. So she had just brought something he could hardly sue for through every court in the land.

"Is it definite about the partnership?" Eve wanted to know.

"Sometime, when you have about thirty-five hours . . ."

"I have."

"Not now."

"Do you want me to go away? I could go out to the pony," Heather said.

"No, Heather, it's a long, long story, and it would depress me telling it and depress Eve listening to it. Stay where you are."

"Right." Heather put another of Sister Imelda's wonderful tea cakes on the toasting fork.

"Anything new though?" Eve thought Benny looked troubled.

But Benny shook her head. There was a resigned sort of look on her face that Eve didn't like. As if Benny wanted to get into a big fight over something and lacked the energy.

"I could help. Like the old days. The Wise Woman would let two people tackle it."

"The Wiser Woman might give into the inevitable."

"What does your mother say?"

"Very little."

"Benny, will you have a toasted cake?" Heather's solution for nearly every crisis.

"No. I'm fooling myself that if I don't eat, this fellow will like me more and stop going off with Welsh floozies."

Eve sighed heavily. So someone had told her.

They cycled along cheerfully, Eve saluting almost everyone they passed. Heather knew no one. But she knew fields that would have donkeys at the gate, and a gap in the hedge where you could see a mare and two foals. She told Eve about the trees and their leaves and how her Nature Scrapbook was the only thing she was any good at. She wouldn't mind schoolwork if it was all to do with pressing flowers and leaves and drawing the various stages of a beech tree.

Eve thought how odd it was that two first cousins, with only seven years between them, living only a mile and a half apart, never having met, and one knowing every person who walked the road and the other every animal in every farm.

It was strange to ride up the ill-kept ridge-filled drive of Westlands, with the young woman of the house.

Even though she was no outsider, coming to ask for a hand-out, Eve still felt odd and out of place.

"We'll go in through the kitchen." Heather had thrown her bicycle up against the wall.

"I don't know . . ." Eve began. Her voice was an almost exact copy of Heather's when lunch at the convent was suggested.

"Come on," Heather said.

Mrs. Walsh and Bee Moore were surprised to see her, and not altogether pleased.

"You should have come in at the front when you had a guest," Mrs. Walsh said reprovingly.

"It's only Eve. We had lunch in the kitchen of the convent."

"Really?" Mrs. Walsh's face expressed very clearly that Eve had been unwise to receive the daughter of the Big House so poorly. The very least that might have been arranged was lunch in the parlor.

"I told her you made great shortbread," Heather said hopefully.

"We must make up a nice little box of it sometime." Mrs. Walsh was polite, but cold.

She definitely didn't want Eve Malone on her patch.

From inside the house, Eve heard someone playing a piano.

"Oh, good," Heather said, pleased. "Simon's home."

✦

Simon Westward was charming. He came forward with both his hands out to Eve.

"Lovely to see you here again."

"I didn't really intend . . ." She wanted terribly to tell him that she had no intention of being a casual visitor to his house. She must make him understand that she was doing it to please a child, a lonely child who wanted to share the place with her. But those words were hard to find.

Simon probably had no idea of what she was trying to say.

"It's great you are here now, it's been far too long!" he said.

She looked around her. This was not the drawing room she had been in on her first visit. It was another, south-facing room, with faded chintz and old furniture, a small desk stuffed with papers stood in the corner, a large piano near the window. Imagine one family having so many rooms and enough furniture to fill them.

Enough pictures for their walls.

Her eyes roamed around the portraits hoping to find the one of her mother.

The one she had not known existed.

Simon had been watching her. "It's on the stairs," he said.

"I beg your pardon?"

"I know Nan told you. Come, and I'll show it to you."

Eve felt her face burn. "It isn't important."

"Oh, but it is. A painting of your mother. I didn't show it to you that first day because, it was all a bit strained. I was hoping you'd come again. But you didn't, and Nan did, so I showed it to her. I hope you're not upset."

"Why should I be?" Her fists were clenched.

"I don't know, but Nan seemed to think you were."

How dare they talk about her. How *dare* they, and whether or not she was upset.

With tears stinging at the back of her eyes, Eve walked like a robot to the foot of the stairs where hung a picture of a small dark woman, with eyes and mouth so like her own she felt she was looking in a mirror.

She must have so little of her father about her, if there was so much of Sarah Westward there already.

Sarah had her hand on the back of a chair, but she didn't look relaxed and at peace. She looked as if she were dying for it all to be over so that she could get away. Somewhere, anywhere.

She had small hands and big eyes. Her dark hair was cut short, like the thirties fashion would have dictated. But looking at her you got the feeling that she might have preferred it shoulder-length and pushed behind her ears. Like Eve's.

Was she beautiful? It was impossible to know. Nan had only said that she was in order to let Eve know that she had seen the picture.

Nan. Nan had walked around this house, as a guest.

"Has Nan been back here since then?" she asked.

"Why do you say that?"

"I just wondered."

"No. That was the only day she was at Westlands," he said.

There was something slightly hesitant about the way he said it, but yet she knew it was the truth.

Out in the kitchen they were getting a grudging afternoon tea ready. Eve thought that the food they were eating this day would never end, but Heather was loving it and it would be a pity to spoil it for her now.

Eve admired the pony and the way Heather had cleaned its tack. She admired Clara's puppies and refused the offer of one as guard dog.

"It would be good to look after your property," Heather tried to persuade her.

"I'm not there often enough."

"That's all the more reason. Tell her, Simon."

"It's up to Eve."

"I'm hardly ever there. Only the odd weekend. A dog would die of loneliness."

"But whoever *is* there could walk him."

Heather held an adorable little male puppy up for inspection. It was seven-eighths Labrador, she explained, all the best, but with a little of the silliness taken out.

"No one but me, and Mother Francis from time to time."

"Does she sleep there?" Heather asked.

"Heavens no. So you see no need for a guard dog."

She didn't think to ask why Heather supposed the nun might sleep in her little cottage. She just assumed it was part of Heather's continuing ignorance of convent life. And she didn't notice any change of expression in Simon's face.

Mrs. Walsh came to tell them that tea was served in the drawing room.

Eve walked in to meet her grandfather for the second time in her life.

The grandfather that Nan Mahon had told everyone was so charming and such a wonderful old man. She felt herself pushing her shoulders back, and taking those deep breaths that Nan said were so helpful if you had to do something that was a bit stressful. As if Nan would know!

He looked about the same. Possibly a bit more alert than on the previous occasion. She had heard that he had been taken ill on Christmas Day, and that Dr. Johnson had been summoned, but that it had all passed.

It was touching to see Heather, the child who had grown up with him and who loved him as part of the only life she knew, sit beside him nestling in to him and helping him with his cup.

"No need to cut up the sandwiches for you today Grandfather. They're absolutely tiny. It must be to impress Eve."

The old man looked across at where Eve sat awkwardly in a hard-backed and uncomfortable chair. He looked at her long and hard.

"You remember Eve, don't you?" Heather tried.

There was no reply.

"You do, of course, Grandfather. I was telling you how good she's been to Heather, taking her out of school . . ."

"Yes, yes indeed." He was cuttingly distant. It was as if someone told him that a beggar on the street had once been a fine hard worker.

She could have just smiled and let it pass. But there was something about the way he spoke which went straight to Eve's heart. The temper that Mother Francis had always said would be her undoing bubbled to the surface.

"Do you know who I am, Grandfather?" she said in a loud, clear voice. There was a note of challenge in it that made them all look at her startled, Heather, Simon and the old man. Nobody helped him out.

He would have to answer now or mumble.

"Yes. You are the daughter of Sarah and some man."

"The daughter of Sarah and her husband Jack Malone."

"Yes, possibly."

Eve's eyes blazed. "Not possibly. Definitely. That was his name. You may not have received him here, but he was Jack Malone. They were married in the parish church."

He raised his eyes. They were the same dark almond-shaped eyes that they all had, except that Major Westward's were smaller and narrower.

He looked hard at Eve. "I never doubted that she married the handyman Jack Malone. I was saying that it is possible he was your father. Possible, but not at all as definite as you believe . . ."

She was numb with shock, the words filled with hate seemed to make no sense. His face, slightly lopsided, was working with the effort of speaking clearly and making himself understood.

"You see, Sarah was a whore," he said.

Eve could hear the clock ticking.

"She was a whore with an itch, an itch that many handymen

around the place found it easy to satisfy. We lost so many good grooms, I remember."

Simon was on his feet in horror. Heather sat where she had been, on the little footstool, the one with beaded trimming at her grandfather's feet. Her face was white.

He had not finished speaking.

"But let us not think back over unpleasant times. You may indeed be the child of the handyman Jack Malone. If you wish to believe that then . . . that is what you must believe . . ."

He reached for his tea. The effort of speaking had exhausted him. His cup shook and rattled against the saucer.

Eve's voice was low, and because of that all the more menacing.

"In all my life there has only been one thing I was ashamed of. I was ashamed that my father used a religious occasion, the funeral of my mother, to call down a curse on you. I wished he hadn't chosen a graveyard by a church. I wished he had more respect for the people who had come down to mourn. I even thought that God might have been angry with him for it. But now I know he didn't curse you hard enough, and his wish wasn't answered. You have lived on full of hate and bile. I will never look on your face again. And I will never forgive you for the things you said today."

She didn't pause to see how the others took her departure. She walked straight out of the door, and through the big hall into the kitchen. Without speaking to Mrs. Walsh or to Bee Moore she let herself out of the back door. She got on her bicycle and without a backward glance cycled down the rutted avenue that led from her grandfather's house.

At the window of the drawing room Heather stood, tears pouring down on her face.

When Simon came to comfort her she pummeled him with her fists.

"You let her go. You let her go. You didn't stop him. Now she'll never be my friend again."

Dearest Benny, dearest, dearest Benny,

Do you remember those shaking tempers I used to get at school? I thought they had passed over like spots do, but no. I was so desperately and hurtfully insulted by that devil in a wheelchair out in Westlands that I am not normal to speak to, and I'm going back to Dublin. I haven't told Mother Francis about the row, and I won't tell Kit, or Aidan. But I will tell you when I'm able. Please forgive me for running off, and not meeting you tonight. I've asked Mossy to leave this note in to you, but honestly it's the best thing.

See you on Monday.

Love from a very distraught Eve.

When Mossy handed her the note Benny first thought it was from Sean Walsh, that it was some kind of threat or instruction to back off her investigations.

She was deeply upset to hear of a row bad enough to send Eve away in one of her very black moods. Sorry, too, because that nice child would be caught in the middle of it.

And selfishly she was sorry, because she had hoped to spend the evening telling Eve all about her ever-growing belief that Sean Walsh had been salting away money and to ask her advice about where they should look for it.

When Eve let herself in to the house, Kevin Hickey was in the kitchen.

"Not out, wowing the girls on a Saturday night Kevin?" she said.

She had promised herself that she would be a professional. This was her job, this house her place of work. She would not allow her personal anger to rub off on the guests.

Kevin said, "I did have a sort of a plan, but I thought I'd hang around." He nodded with his head, indicating upstairs toward Kit's room.

"She's had some bad news apparently. Her old man died in England. I know she hated him, but it's a shock all the same."

Eve came into the dark room with two cups of tea and sat beside the bed. She knew Kit would not be asleep.

Kit lay, head propped up by pillows and cushions, smoking. Through the window the lights of Dun Laoghaire harbor were glinting and shining.

"How did you know I needed you?"

"I'm psychic. What happened?"

"I'm not sure. An operation. It didn't work."

"I'm very sorry," Eve said.

"She said it was very unexpected the operation, that he had no idea that there was anything wrong with him. That if ever he were to die she was to ring me and say he had no idea there was anything wrong."

"Who said all this?"

"Some landlady. He had given her fifty pounds in an envelope and said it was for her."

Eve was silent. It was all curious and complicated and messy, like everything Joseph Hegarty seemed to have touched in his life.

"What's worrying you Kit?"

"He must have known he was dying. That's why he came back. He must have wanted to spend the last few weeks here. And I didn't let him."

"No, didn't he make a big point about that. He didn't know."

"He *said* that because of the insurance."

"The what?"

"Insurance policy. He's done what he never did in his life, he's made sure I'm provided for."

Eve felt a big lump in her throat.

"They're going to bury him in England next weekend. They're

extraordinary over there. Funerals aren't the next day. It's at a weekend so people could get there. Will you come with me, Eve? We could go on the boat."

"Of course I will."

Dear Heather,

I have to go to a funeral in England. Kit's ex-husband died. She needs me to go with her. That's why I won't be there on Sunday. Nothing to do with other things. See you the weekend after. Maybe Aidan will come as well.

Just so that you know it's urgent, otherwise I'd come.

Love, Eve.

Heather read the letter silently at breakfast. Miss Thompson, who was the only nice teacher in Heather's opinion, looked at her.

"Everything all right?"

"Yes."

Miss Thompson shrugged and left her alone. You couldn't push adolescent girls for confidences they didn't want to give.

She's never coming again, Heather said to herself over and over. She said it during morning prayers, during mathematics and during geography. Soon it became like the refrain of a song you can't get out of your mind. "She's never coming again."

Miss Thompson didn't remember about the letter, but she did say that she had noticed Heather was extremely quiet and withdrawn during the week. And she went back over it all, as they all had to on Friday night when Heather Westward didn't turn up for supper, and couldn't be found anywhere on the school premises. And she had not turned up at home. It had to be admitted by all those who didn't want to believe it, that Heather had run away from school.

SIXTEEN

*A*s soon as Simon had heard that Eve Malone had gone to England he said that was where they would find Heather.

Eve had not acknowledged his note of apology and explanation that his grandfather's hardening of the arteries made him unstable and unreliable and therefore someone whose opinions and views were best ignored.

Simon wondered had the note been too formal. He had told Nan about it, and to his surprise she had been critical of him. Normally she had been so cool, unruffled and giving so little of herself and her views.

"Why was it such an awful letter?" he had asked anxiously.

"Because it sounds icy, like your grandfather."

"It wasn't meant to be. It was meant to be low-key, to try and bring down the temperature."

"It did that all right," Nan agreed.

On Friday when the school had been in touch he rang Nan.

"You know what you were saying about the letter . . . do you think that's why she took Heather?"

"Of course she didn't take Heather." Nan was dismissive.

"So where is Heather then?"

"She ran away because you were all so awful."

"Why don't you run away then?" He sounded petulant.

"I like awful people. Didn't you know?"

The schoolgirls were frightened. Nothing like this had ever happened before. They were all being asked extraordinary questions. Had they seen anyone come into the school, had they seen Heather leave with anyone else?

Her school coat was gone, her hated school beret left on the bed. Her pajamas and sponge bag had disappeared, her book of pressed flowers, her snaps of the pony and Clara and her puppies. They were normally on display beside her bed where other girls had pictures of their families.

Heather's classmates were asked had she been upset? They hadn't noticed.

"She's very quiet really," said one of them.

"She doesn't like it here," said another.

"She's not much fun. We don't take much notice of her," said the class bully.

Miss Thompson's heart was heavy.

There had been no sign of Heather on the bus. Mikey said he knew her well. A big thick lump of a child as square as a half door. Of course he'd have noticed her.

She would have had eleven shillings at the most, and possibly a lot less. Heather was known to spend a few pennies on sweets.

By the time Simon arrived at the school they had called the Guards.

"Is it really necessary to have the police?" he said.

The headmistress was surprised. "Since she hadn't gone home and you could throw no light on anywhere she might be . . ."

Miss Thompson looked at Simon with some dislike.

"And we have assumed that there was nothing for her to run

home to apart from her pony and her dog, and she didn't go there anyway, we thought you would have wanted us to call in the Guards. It would be the normal thing for anyone to do, the normal thing to do."

Simon looked at her miserably. Until now he hadn't realized how far from normal poor Heather's life had been.

He would make it up to her, when they got her back from England, which was undoubtedly where Eve had taken her.

At the guesthouse in Dun Laoghaire, the Guards and Simon found three students holding the fort. Mrs. Hegarty had gone to England to a funeral. Eve Malone had gone with her. Yes, of course they had left an emergency number where they could be contacted.

Mrs. Hegarty had said she would ring anyway next morning to see if they had managed their breakfasts.

It was now eleven o'clock on a Friday night. The mail boat would not yet have arrived at Holyhead. Mrs. Hegarty would not be in London until seven in the morning. She and Eve would take the mail train to Euston.

There was a discussion about telephoning the Guards in Wales to look for Heather.

There was some doubt on the part of the two Guards who were busy taking down details.

"You're absolutely sure this is where your sister is, sir?" they asked again.

"There's nowhere else she could be." He was sure of that.

"Did anyone see Mrs. Hegarty and Miss Malone off at the boat?" one Guard asked.

"I did." The boy who said he was Kevin Hickey, veterinary student, was spokesman.

"And were they accompanied by a twelve-year-old girl?"

"You mean Heather?"

Simon and the Guards had not explained the purpose of their inquiries.

"Was she with them?" Simon asked.

"Of course not. That's the problem. Eve was worried because she was going to this funeral. She was afraid Heather wouldn't understand that she simply *had* to go away."

Eve had left a box of chocolates which she had instructed Kevin to deliver to the school on Sunday, with a note from Eve.

"Could you give them to her, if you're connected?" he asked Simon.

They asked to see the note.

It was simple and to the point.

"Just to show I haven't forgotten you. Next week, *you* choose where we go. Love Eve."

Simon read it and for the first time since his sister's disappearance had been discovered tears came to his eyes.

On Saturday morning there could hardly have been anyone in Knockglen who didn't know about it. Bee Moore had done her fair share of telling, and Mr. Flood, who had been one of the early recipients of the news, had been out consulting with the nuns in the tree, but finding to his disappointment that there was no heavenly message about Heather.

"I had hoped she might have been in heaven. Well, her kind of heaven," he said, remembering that he mustn't lose sight of the fact that the Westwards were Protestants.

Dessie Burns said there'd be a fine reward for anyone who found her, and mark his words she was kidnapped, and what's more kidnapped by someone in the know.

Paccy Moore said that the chances of being kidnapped by anyone in the know were slim. If you knew anything about the Westwards you'd know they could hardly pay their bills. If the poor child had been kidnapped it was by some gombeen Dubliner who thought that she was wealthy because she had a posh accent and came from a big house.

Mrs. Healy said to Sean Walsh that they'd be singing a different song up at Westlands now. They had always been so distant and different, and things that happened to ordinary people never happened to them.

Sean wondered why she had turned against them. And Mrs. Healy said it wasn't a matter of that so much as being slightly peeved. Mr. Simon Westward had implied that he would be having the most important of people to stay at the hotel in the near future, if they had evening dinners. Mrs. Healy had put on those dinners, but Mr. Westward had never partaken.

"But other people have," Sean Walsh said. "You've made your profit on them, that's all that matters."

Mrs. Healy agreed, but you didn't like to be hopping and jumping like people in a gate cottage just for the whims of the aristocracy.

She said as much to Mrs. Kennedy from the chemist's, who looked at her thoughtfully, and said that it was a sad thing to have a hard heart when there was a child's life at stake, and Mrs. Healy changed her tune drastically.

Clodagh told the news to Peggy Pine. Clodagh thought that a man in a raincoat had offered poor Heather a whole box of chocolates in Dun Laoghaire harbor.

Mario said that all the men of Knockglen should go out and beat the hedges with sticks looking for her.

"You see too many bad films," Fonsie complained.

"Well, where do you think she is, Mister Smartie Pants?" Mario inquired.

"I see too many bad films too. I think she went for that bloody horse of hers, and rode off into the sunset."

But it was one of the many theories that didn't hold up because the horse was still up in Westlands.

Peggy Pine went up to the convent to talk to Mother Francis.

"Eve was on the phone from London," Mother Francis said. "I could hear her grinding her teeth from there. Apparently they thought she had taken Heather with her. I dread to think what she'll do when she gets back."

"But Eve would never have done that."

"I know, but there was some kind of row up in Westlands last week, needless to say Miss Malone didn't tell *me* anything about it. . . . Lord, Peggy, where would that child be?"

"When you think about running away you think about running to somewhere you were happy." Peggy Pine was thoughtful. It didn't get them much further.

Heather had never seemed to be all that happy anywhere.

Sister Imelda had started the thirty days prayer. She said it had never been known to fail.

"The poor child. I never met a girl who was as appreciative. You should have heard her telling me how much she enjoyed toasting my tea cakes up in Eve's cottage."

Suddenly Mother Francis knew where Heather was.

She reached into the gap in the wall and as she suspected the key wasn't there.

Mother Francis moved softly to the front door of Eve's cottage. It was closed. She peeped in the window and saw a large box on the table. There was something moving inside it, a cat she thought first, a black cat. Then she saw it was a bird.

A wing of black feathers came at an awkward angle out of the box.

Heather had found a wounded bird and had decided to cure it. Not very successfully by all appearances. There were feathers and bits of torn-up newspaper everywhere.

Heather, flushed and frightened-looking, was trying to get a fire going. She seemed to be using only sticks and bits of cardboard. It would flare for a moment, and then die down.

Mother Francis knocked on the window.

"I'm not letting you in."

"All right," Mother Francis said unexpectedly.

"So there's no point in staying. Seriously."

"I brought your lunch."

"No, you didn't. It's a plot. You're going to rush me as soon as I open the door. You have people out behind the wall."

"What kind of people? Nuns?"

"The Guards. Well, maybe nuns as well, my brother. People from school."

Mother Francis sighed.

"No, they all think you're in London. That's where they're looking for you as it happens."

Heather stood on a stool and looked out of the window. There did not seem to be anyone else.

"You could leave the lunch on the step."

"I could. But it would get cold, and I'll need the dish for Sister Imelda, and it means I don't get any."

"I'm not coming home or anything."

Mother Francis came in. She left a covered dish and the big buttered slices of bread on the sideboard.

She looked first at the bird.

"Poor fellow. Where did you find him?"

"On the path."

Gently Mother Francis lifted the bird. She kept up a steady stream of conversation. It was only a young crow. The young often fell from the high trees. Some of them were quite clumsy. It was a myth to believe that all birds were graceful and could soar up in the air at will.

The wing wasn't broken, she told Heather. That was why the poor thing had been trying so hard to escape. It had just been stunned by the fall.

Together they felt the bird and smiled at the beating of the little heart and the anxious bird eyes not knowing what fate was in store for it.

Mother Francis gave it some bread crumbs, and then together they took it to the door.

After a few unsteady hops it took off in a low lopsided flight just clearing the stone wall.

"Right, that's the wildlife dealt with. You get rid of all those feathers and newspapers and put back this box in the scullery. I'll see to lunch."

"I'm still not going back, even if you did help me with the bird."

"Did I say a thing about going back?"

"No, but you will."

"I won't. I might ask you to let them know you're safe, but that's all."

Mother Francis got the fire going. She explained to Heather about the dry turf, which stood leaning against the wall. She showed her to make a little nest of twigs and get that going with a nice crackling light before putting on the turf. Together they ate Sister Imelda's lamb stew, and big floury potatoes, and dipped their bread and butter into the rich sauce.

There was an apple each and piece of cheese for afterward. Mother Francis explained that she couldn't carry much more, because the path was quite slippy and anyway she didn't want to arouse suspicion about where she was going.

"Why did you come for me?" Heather asked.

"I'm a teacher you see. I imagine I know all about children. It's a little weakness we have."

"There's nothing you can do."

"Ah now, we never know that till we've examined all the possibilities."

Eve rang Benny from England. She said she had spent more time making cross-channel phone calls than she had spent being any help to Kit. The whole thing was so infuriating she was going to tear off Simon Westward's affected little cravat and tie it round his thin useless neck and pull it hard until he was blue in the face and only when she saw his tongue and eyeballs protruding would she stop pulling.

"You're wasting time," Benny said.

"I am. I suppose there's no news is there?"

"Not that we've heard."

"I've just had an idea where she might be. It's only an idea," said Eve.

"Right. Who will I tell. Simon?"

"No, go on your own. Just go up as if you happened to be passing, and if the key isn't there you'll know she's inside. And Benny, you know how comforting you can be. She'll need that. Tell her I'll sort it out when I get back."

On her way up the town Benny thought that she might buy some sweets. It would break the ice if Heather *was* there and needed to be talked out of the place. She had no money, but she knew that her credit would be good in Birdie Mac's.

As she passed the door of Hogan's she suddenly thought of the Drawings slips. She could sign a pink piece of paper and write "£1 miscellaneous goods" on it. Why should she, from one business premises in the town, ask credit from Birdie in another.

Sean watched her carefully.

"There, I think that's in order, isn't it?" She smiled brightly.

"You've taken a great interest in the mechanics of the business," he said.

She knew he had something to hide. She *knew* it. But she must be careful. She continued in her same cheery tone.

"Oh well, one way or another I'll have to be much more involved from now on," she said.

He repeated the phrase with an air of wonder.

"One way or another?"

She shouldn't have said that. It implied that there might be doubt over his partnership. She had told herself so often to be careful. Best now to play the role of someone who was not the full shilling.

"Oh, you know what I mean, Sean."

"Do I?"

"Of course you do."

She almost ran from the shop. In and out of Birdie's and up to the square. She had better not go through the convent, even though it was quicker. The nuns would see her and ask her what she was up to.

Eve wanted this done on the quiet.

They had been over a lot of ground, Mother Francis and Heather Westward. The school in Dublin and the games and the other girls having lots of family coming to see them and houses to go to at weekends.

And how much Heather loved Westlands and how horrible Grandfather had been to Eve, and the fear that Eve might not come again.

And how nice it would be if there was a school that she could cycle to every day.

"There is," Mother Francis said.

There were some areas that had to be argued through. Mother Francis said that there wouldn't be any effort made to convert Heather to Catholicism because the main problem these days was keeping those that were already in the flock up to the mark.

And there would be no idols of the Virgin Mary to bow down to and worship. There would however be statues of the same Virgin Mary around the school to remind anyone who wished to be so reminded of the Mother of God.

And there would be no need for Heather to attend religious doctrine classes, and she need have no fear that history would be taught with an emphasis on the Pope being always right and everyone else being wrong.

"What was it all about, the split?" Heather asked.

"The Reformation do you mean?"

"Yes. Was it about your side worshipping idols."

"I think it was more about the Real Presence at mass. You know, whether Communion is truly the Body and Blood of Jesus, or just a symbol."

"Is that all it was about?" Heather asked, amazed.

"It started that way. But it developed, you know the way things do."

"I don't think there should be all that much fuss then."

Heather seemed greatly relieved that the doctrinal differences of three hundred years appeared to be so slight. They were just shaking hands on it when there was a knock on the door.

"You said you didn't tell anyone." Heather leapt up in dismay.

"Nor did I." Mother Francis went to the door.

Benny stood there with her speech ready. Her jaw dropped when she saw the nun and the angry little figure inside.

"Eve rang. She wondered whether Heather might have been here. She asked me to come and . . . and well . . ."

"Did you tell anyone?" Heather snapped out the question.

"No, Eve particularly said not to." The face relaxed.

Mother Francis said she had to be going now before the community assumed that she too was a missing person and started broadcasting appeals for her on the wireless.

"Are they doing that for me?"

"Not yet. But a lot of people are very worried and afraid that something bad might have happened to you."

"I'd better tell them . . . I suppose."

"I could if you like."

"What would you say?"

"I could say that you'll be back later this afternoon, that you'll be calling in to the convent to borrow a bicycle."

She was gone.

Benny looked at Heather. She pushed the box of sweets over to her.

"Come on, let's finish it. We'll tear through it, both layers."

"What about the man who fancies Welsh women, the one you're getting thin for?"

"I think it's too late."

Happily they ate the chocolates. Heather asked about the school and who were the hard teachers and who were the easy ones.

Benny asked about her grandfather and whether he knew all the awful things he had said.

"Did she tell everyone?" Heather looked ashamed.

"Only me. I'm her great friend."

"I don't have any great friends."

"Yes, you do. You have Eve."

"Not anymore."

"Of course you do. You don't understand Eve if you'd think a thing like that mattered, she didn't want to like you in the first place because she had all the bad memories about that old business years ago. But she did, and she always will."

Heather looked doubtful.

"Yes, and you can have me, too, if you want me, and Eve's Aidan as a sort of circle of friends. I know we're way too old for you, but until you make your own."

"And what about the man who goes off with thin Welsh people? Is he in the circle?"

"On the edges," Benny said.

In a way that was more true than she meant it to be. She had met Jack twice during the week, and he had been rushing. There was a lot of training, and hardly any time to speak alone.

He had been very contrite about some still unspecified incident during the friendly match they played in Wales. Some girls had come to the club, and it had all been a bit of fun, a laugh, nothing to it. Tales had been greatly exaggerated. In vain Benny tried to tell him that she had heard no tales so nothing could be made better or worse because there had been no stories to exaggerate.

Jack had said that everyone was entitled to a bit of fun, and he never minded her jiving away in Mario's when he wasn't around. It had been highly unsatisfactory.

There was an uneven number of sweets, so they halved the last one, a coffee cream.

They tidied up Eve's house and damped the embers of the fire. Together they left and replaced the key in the wall.

422

Mossy nodded to them gravely as he passed by.

"Who was that?" Heather whispered.

"Mossy Rooney."

"He's broken Bee Moore's heart," Heather said disapprovingly.

"Not permanently. She's going to be Patsy's bridesmaid when the time comes."

"I suppose people get over these things," Heather said.

Mother Francis handed Heather Eve's bicycle.

"Off you go. Your brother will be waiting for you. I said he should let you go home on your own pedals."

The nun produced Heather's small bag of possessions, her Nature book, her pajamas, the photographs of the horse and dog and the small sponge bag. She had wrapped them neatly in brown paper and twine and clipped them on to the back of the bicycle.

Benny and Mother Francis watched her cycle off.

"You guessed! Eve always said you had second sight."

"If I have then I'd say you have some big worry on your mind."

Benny was silent.

"I'm not prying."

"No, of course not." Benny's murmur was automatic politeness.

"It's just being what people laughingly call out of the real world . . . I hear a great deal about what goes on amongst those who are in it."

Benny's glance was inquiring.

"And Peggy Pine and I were school friends years ago, like you and Eve . . ."

Benny waited. Mother Francis said that if it was of any use to Benny she should know that Sean Walsh had enough money, from whatever source, to think himself able to buy one of the small cottages up in the quarry road. Cash deposit.

Benny's mother said that Jack Foley had rung. No, he hadn't left a message. Benny thought harsh things about Heather Westward for having taken her out of the house when the call came. And she wished that she had not run so readily to do Eve's bidding.

But then Eve would have done the same for her. And if he loved her and wanted to talk to her, he would ring again.

If he loved her.

Nan's mother came to say that there was a Simon Westward on the phone.

Nan's tone was cold.

"Did I give you my phone number?" she asked.

"No, but that's irrelevant. Heather's home."

"Oh, I am glad. Where was she?" Nan was still wondering how he knew where to telephone. She had been adamant about not telling anyone how to contact her.

"She was in Eve's cottage, as it happens."

It had been a distinct possibility that Nan and Simon might have been there also. The thought silenced them both for a moment.

"Is she all right?"

"She's fine, but I can't leave. I have to sort her out."

Nan had been ironing her dress for the last hour. It had complicated pleats in the linen. Her hair was freshly washed and she had painted her toenails a pearly pink.

"Yes, of course you must stay," she said.

"Oh good. I thought you'd be annoyed."

"The main thing is that she's safe."

There was no hint of the rage that Nan was feeling. His tone was so casual.

Simon said that apparently Heather had been very unhappy at the school in Dublin. Nan sighed. Eve had been saying this for months. Heather had probably been saying it for years, but Simon had not listened. There were just a few schools that were suitable for his sister and she would jolly well have to learn to like the one she was in. That had been his attitude.

"So maybe tomorrow?" He was confident and sure.

"Sorry?"

"Tomorrow, Sunday night. Things will have sorted themselves out here . . ."

"And?"

"And I was hoping you might come down . . . for the night?"

"Well, I'd love to." Nan smiled. At last he had invited her. It had taken some time, but he was inviting her to Westlands. She would be given a guest room. She was going there as Mr. Simon's young lady.

"That's marvelous." He sounded relieved. "You get the last bus. I'll go to the cottage and set things up for us."

"The cottage?" she said.

"Well, we know Eve's in England."

There was a silence.

"What's wrong?" he asked.

"Suppose Heather decides to call again?"

"No, by heavens, she'll get a strict talking-to about respecting other people's property."

He saw no irony in this at all.

"I think not," she said.

"Nan?"

She had hung up on him.

Joseph Hegarty had made a few, but not many, friends during his years in England. They had gathered to speak well of him after his funeral.

In the back room of a bar they sat, an ill-assorted group. A landlady who had been fond of him, whenever he didn't have the rent, he always did so many repairs around the house, it was twenty times better than having a lodger, she confided. Eve could see the pain in Kit's face. That Joseph Hegarty should be without the rent was bad enough, but that he should do plumbing and carpentry for a strange woman in England rather than in his own house in Dun Laoghaire was even worse.

If the barmaid was amongst the group she did not declare herself. The whole thing had such an unreal atmosphere about it, Eve felt that they were taking part in some play. Any moment the curtain would fall and they would all start talking normally again.

The only clue to why Joseph Hegarty might have stayed so long in this twilight world where he touched so little on people around him came from Fergus, a Mayo man, who said he was a friend.

Fergus had left a long time ago. There had been no row, no one thing that drove him out of his smallholding in the west of Ireland. He just felt one day that he wanted to be free and he had taken a train to Dublin, and then the boat.

His wife was now dead, his family grown. None of them wanted anything to do with him, and in many ways it was for the best. If he had gone back, he would have had to explain.

"At least Joe saw his son last summer. That was the great thing," he said.

Kit looked up startled.

"No, he didn't. Francis never saw him since he was a child."

"But didn't he write to him and all?"

"No." Kit's voice was clipped.

Eve went to stand beside Fergus the Mayoman at the bar later.

"So he did keep in touch with his son then?"

"Yes, I think I was out of order. The wife is very bitter. I shouldn't have said . . . I didn't know."

"In time she'll be glad. In time I'll tell her properly. And maybe she'll want to talk to you." She took out a diary and a pen. "Where would you be . . . if we wanted to get in touch?"

"Ah, now, that's hard to say." The look in the eyes of Fergus became wary. He wasn't a man who liked to plan too far ahead.

There was a discussion with the man from the insurance, and

some documents to sign. Eve and Kit went to Euston and took the train to Holyhead.

For a long time Kit Hegarty looked out of the window and the land where her husband had lived for so long.

"What are you thinking about?" Eve asked.

"About you. You were very good to come with me. Several people thought you were my daughter."

"I seem to have been on the phone most of the time." Eve was apologetic.

"Thank God it turned out all right."

"We don't know that yet. They're a weird bunch. They could send her back there. I hate being beholden to them, I really do."

"You don't have to be," said Kit. "The first thing I'm going to do when I get the insurance money is to give you a sum. You can walk back up that avenue, and throw it back. Throw it on the floor."

Patsy said that with all their talk about teaching them to work in a house the orphanage had been very bad at teaching them to sew.

Mossy had said that his mother was expecting Patsy to have made a lot of things for her hope chest, like pillowcases, and hemmed them herself.

She was struggling away in the kitchen. The trouble was that often she pricked her fingers and the nice piece of linen got stained with blood.

"He's mad. Can't you buy grand pillowcases for half nothing up in McBirney's in Dublin?" Benny said indignantly.

But this wasn't the point. Apparently Mrs. Rooney expected a suitable bride for Mossy to be able to turn a hem properly and sew dainty stitches. Patsy had to try harder and put up with all this nonsense because she had nothing else to bring to the marriage. No family, no bit of land, not even her father's name.

"Does it have to be hand done? Couldn't it be on a machine?"

Benny was worse than useless, her own stitching was in big loops, irregular and impatient.

"What's the difference? We haven't a machine that works."

"We'll ask Paccy to mend it. Let's look on it as a challenge," Benny said.

Paccy Moore said that a horse with heavy hooves must have been using the sewing machine, and that if you had a fleet of highly paid engineers they wouldn't be able to put it back in working order. Tell the lady of the house to throw it out, was his advice. And surely they must have had an old one years ago, one of those nice firm ones that people like Benny and Patsy couldn't break.

They went sadly back to Lisbeg. There wasn't much point in telling the lady of the house anything. The listless manner hadn't changed. They *did* have an old sewing machine somewhere with a treadle underneath. Benny remembered seeing it once, even playing at it. But it was useless to talk to Mother. She would try to remember and then say that her headache was coming back.

But Benny hated to see Patsy, who had started life with so little, continue in this struggle to please.

"You see, I can't have bought ones Benny. The old rip gives me the material herself, just to make sure."

"I'll ask Clodagh to do them for you. She loves a challenge too," said Benny.

Clodagh said they should both be shot for not knowing how to do a simple seam. She showed them on the machine.

"Go on, do it yourselves," she urged.

"There isn't time for that. You do it and we'll do something in return for you. Tell us what you want us to do."

"Ask my aunt to lunch and keep her there all afternoon. I want to rearrange everything in the shop: if I knew someone was looking after Peg I could get a gang in to help me. When she comes back it'll be too late to change it."

"When?"

"Thursday, early closing day."

"And you'll do all these pillowcases and some sheets and two bolster cases?"

"It's a deal."

Jack Foley said he was going to skip lectures on Thursday and they'd go to the pictures.

"Not Thursday. Any other day."

"Bloody hell. Isn't that the day you don't have lectures?"

"Yes, but I have to go back to Knockglen. There's this great scheme . . ."

"Oh, there's *always* some great scheme in Knockglen," he said.

"Friday. I can stay the night in Dublin."

"All right."

Benny knew she would have to do something to try and smooth down Jack's ruffled feelings. She was very much afraid it might involve doing something more adventurous in the car than they had done already.

As Patsy said, at least three times a day, men were the divil.

Nan had taken a risk in hanging up on Simon. She had also left the phone slightly off the hook in case he called again. She went angrily up to her room and lay on her bed. The freshly ironed dress hung on its hanger, her pink nails twinkled at her, she really should go out somewhere and get value from all this primping and preening.

But Nan Mahon didn't want to arrange a meeting with Bill Dunne, or Johnny O'Brien, or anyone. Not even the handsome Jack Foley, who had been prowling discontentedly since Benny was never around.

Benny. Simon must have got her telephone number from Benny. He had probably pleaded with her and said it was urgent. Benny was very foolish, Nan thought. A handsome man like Jack

Foley should not be left on his own in Dublin. All very well to say that the Rosemary Ryans and Sheilas knew he was spoken for. But when it came to it people often forgot loyalties. There were things more immediate than that.

"You're very cross," Heather said.

"Of course I am. Why couldn't you have told us how awful it was."

Heather had, many times, but nobody had listened. Her grandfather had looked away dreamily, and Simon had said everyone hated school. You just had to grin and bear it. Mrs. Walsh had said that in her position she had to have a suitable education meeting the people she would be meeting socially later on, not the daughters of every poor fellow down on his luck which is what you'd meet in a village school.

She hadn't expected Simon to be so annoyed. He had been on the phone to someone and had come back in a great temper.

"She hung up on me," he had said, several times.

At first Heather had been pleased to see him distracted, but she realized that it wasn't making their conversation about her future any easier.

"Mother Francis will talk to you about the school," she began.

"That's all that bloody woman wants. First they got Eve, and now they want you."

"That's not true. They took Eve because nobody else wanted her."

"Oh, they have *you* well indoctrinated, I can see that."

"But who did want her, Simon? Tell me."

"That's not the point. The point is that we have planned an expensive education for you."

"It'll be much cheaper here, much. I asked. It's hardly anything."

"No. You don't understand. It's not possible."

"*You* don't understand," Heather said, twelve years of age and confronting him with her fists clenched. As she told him that she would run away every single time she was sent back to that school her eyes flashed and she reminded him suddenly of the way Eve had looked that day she came to Westlands.

Jack seemed to have got over his bad temper. On Thursday morning he took Benny to coffee in the Annexe. She ate a corner of one of his fly cemeteries in order to prevent him from overdosing on them, and being pronounced unfit to play in the next match.

He put his hand over hers.

"I am a bad-tempered boorish bear, or bearish boor, whichever you like," he had apologized.

"It won't be long now. I'll have everything sorted out, I swear," Benny said.

"Days, weeks, months, decades?" he asked, but he was smiling at her. He was the old Jack.

"Weeks. A very few weeks."

"And then you'll be able to romp shamelessly around Dublin with me, giving in to my every base wish, and physical lust."

"Something like that," she laughed.

"I'll believe it when I see it," he said, looking straight at her. "You do know how much I want you, don't you?"

She swallowed, not able to find the right words. As it happened, she didn't need to. Nan had approached.

"Is this a Sean–Carmel impersonation, or can I join you for coffee?"

Benny was relieved. Jack went back to the counter to collect it.

"I'm not interrupting anything am I, seriously?" Nan was marvelous. You could actually ask her to take her coffee off and join another group. Nan wouldn't mind. She was a great apostle of the solidarity between girls. But in fact it was much better not to walk any farther down a path of discussing sex.

"I wanted Benny to come to *Swamp Women* but she's stood me up," Jack said, in a mock mournful voice.

"Why d'ya not go to *Swamp Women* with the nice gentleman, honey?" Nan asked. "I sho would in yore place."

"Then come with me," Jack suggested.

Nan looked at Benny, who nodded eagerly.

"Oh, please do Nan. He's been talking about *Swamp Women* for days."

"I'll go and keep him from harm," Nan promised.

On their way to the cinema they met Simon Westward.

"Have you been avoiding me?" he asked curtly.

Nan smiled. She introduced the two men. Anyone passing by would have thought they made an extraordinarily handsome tableau standing there, two of them in College scarves, the third small, and very county.

"We're going to *Swamp Women*. It's about escaped women prisoners and alligators."

"Would you like to join us?" Jack suggested.

Simon looked up at Jack, a long glance.

"No, thanks all the same."

"Why did you ask him to come with us? Because you knew he wouldn't?" Nan asked.

"Nope. Because I could see how much he fancied you."

"Only mildly I think."

"No, seriously I think," Jack said.

Because Nan knew that Simon would have turned to look after them, she took Jack's arm companionably.

Benny went back to Knockglen on the bus in high good humor. Jack was cheerful again. He did say he wanted her, he couldn't have been more explicit. And now she didn't even have to worry about him being left high and dry. Nan had gone to the silly film with him.

All Benny had to do now was keep Peggy Pine entertained while unmentionable things went on in her shop. She knew that Fonsie, Dekko Moore, Teddy Flood and Rita were all poised. Peggy must be kept off the scene until at least five o'clock.

When she got into Lisbeg Benny was pleased to see that Patsy had made a good soup, and there were plain scones to be served with it. Mr. Flood had sent down a small leg of lamb, there was the smell of mint sauce made in a nice china sauce boat.

Mother wore a pale gray twinset with her black skirt, and even a small brooch at the neck. She looked more cheerful. Probably she needed company, Benny realized. She certainly seemed a lot less listless than on other days.

Peggy drank three thimblefuls of sherry enthusiastically, and so did Mother. Benny had never known Clodagh's aunt in better form. She told Mother that business was the best way to live your life, and that if she had her time, and her chances, all over again she would still think so.

She confided to them, something that they already knew which was that she had been Disappointed earlier in life. But that she bore the gentleman in question no ill will. He had done her a service in fact. The Lady he had chosen did not have the look of a contented person. Peggy Pine had seen her from time to time over the years. While she in her little shop was as happy as anything.

Mother listened interested, and Benny began to have the stirrings of hope that Peggy might be able to achieve for Mother what she had not been able to do. Peggy might make Annabel Hogan rediscover some kind of reason for living.

"The young people are the hope you know," Peggy said.

Benny prayed that the transformation taking place in the shop at this moment would not be of such massive proportions as to make Peggy withdraw this view.

"Ah, yes, we've been blessed with Sean Walsh," Annabel said.

"Well, yes, as long as you'll be in there to keep the upper hand," Peggy warned.

"I couldn't be going in interfering. He did fine in poor Eddie's time."

"Eddie was there to be a balance to him."

"Not much of a balance I'd be," Annabel Hogan said. "I don't know the first thing about it."

"You'll learn."

Benny saw the dangerous trembling of her mother's lip. She hastened to come in and explain to Peggy, that things were a little bit up in the air at the moment. There had been a question of Sean being made a partner and that should be cleared up before Mother went into the shop.

"Much wiser to go in before the deed is signed," Peggy said.

To her surprise Benny saw her mother nodding in agreement. Yes, it did make sense to go in and be shown the ropes. It didn't look as if she was only going in afterward to make sure they got an equal share.

And after all they might need more hands around the shop, so Sean if he was going to be a partner would prefer an unpaid one to someone who would need a wage. She told an astonished Benny and Patsy that she might go in on Monday for a few hours to see how the daily routine worked.

Peggy looked pleased, but not very surprised.

Benny guessed that she may have planned the whole thing. She was a very clever woman.

Nan and Jack came out of the cinema.

"It was terrible," Nan said.

"But great terrible," Jack pleaded.

"Lucky Benny. She's back in Knockglen."

"I wish she didn't spend so much time there."

They had a cup of coffee in the cinema cafe and he told her how hard it was to have a girl friend miles away.

What would Nan do if she had a chap down in Knockglen, at the far end of civilization.

"Well, I do," Nan said.

Of course the guy in the cavalry twill and the plummy accent.

But Jack had lost interest. He wanted to talk about Benny and how on earth they could persuade her mother to let her live in Dublin.

He wondered was there any hope that she could have a room in Nan's house. Nan said there was none at all.

They said good-bye at the bus stop outside the cinema. Jack ran for a bus going south.

Simon stepped out of a doorway.

"I wondered if you were free for dinner?" he said to Nan.

"Did you wait for me?" She was pleased.

"I knew you wouldn't see *Swamp Women* round a second time. What about that nice little hotel we went to in Wicklow. We might stay the night."

"How lovely," Nan said, in a voice that was like a cat purring.

It was a marvelous night in Knockglen.

Peggy Pine absolutely loved the changes in the shop. The new lighting, the fitting rooms, and the low music in the background.

Annabel Hogan had called on Sean Walsh and said that she hoped to come and join him in the shop on Monday and that he would be patient with her and explain things simply. She mistook his protestations as expressions of courtesy and insisted that she turn up at 9:00 A.M. on the first day of the week.

Mossy Rooney said that his mother thought that Patsy was a fine person and would be very happy for them to go to Father Ross and fix a day.

And best of all Nan Mahon telephoned Benny and said that *Swamp Women* was the worst film she had ever seen, but that Jack Foley obviously adored Benny and wanted nothing but to talk about her.

Tears of gratitude sprang to Benny's eyes.

"You're so good, Nan. Thank you, thank you from the bottom of my heart."

"What else are friends for?" asked Nan as she packed her little overnight bag and prepared to meet Simon for their visit to Wicklow.

Sean Walsh was in Healy's Hotel.

"What am I going to do?"

"Let her come in. She'll tire of it in a week."

"And if she doesn't?"

"You'll have someone to help you do the errands. It makes it harder for her to refuse you the partnership. She can't be avoiding your eye and the issue if she's working beside you."

"You're very intelligent . . . um . . . Dorothy," he said.

Rosemary Ryan knew what was going on everywhere. Eve said she was like those people during the war who had a map of where their troops were and their submarines and they kept moving them about like pieces on a board.

Rosemary knew Jack had been to the pictures with Nan. She was checking that Benny knew.

"Aren't you the silly-billy to go off and leave your young man wandering around unescorted," Rosemary said.

"He wasn't unescorted for long. I sent him to the pictures with Nan."

"Oh, you did. That's all right." Rosemary seemed genuinely relieved.

"Yes, I had to go back to Knockglen and he had declared an afternoon off for himself."

"You spend too long down there." Rosemary was trying to warn her about something.

"Yes, well, I'm staying in town tonight. We're all going to the dance at the Palmerston rugby club. Are you coming?"

"I might. I have ferocious designs on a medical student. I'll send out a few inquiries to know whether he'll be there or not."

What could Rosemary be warning her about? Not Nan, that was clear. Everyone knew that Nan was besotted with Simon Westward. Sheila had given up on him. There was nobody else. Perhaps it was just that he was getting used to being on his own at social occasions. Perhaps by staying so long in Knockglen Benny was letting Jack think that he was free to ramble, and there might have been a bit of rambling, possibly the Welsh type of rambling . . . that she didn't know about. Benny dragged her mind back to Tudor policy in Ireland. The lecturer said that it was often complicated and hard to pin down since it seemed to change according to the mood of the time. What else is new, Benny wondered? Jack, who had been so loving about her when talking to Nan, was annoyed again now.

He had thought she was going to stay in town for the weekend apparently and had made plans for Saturday and Sunday too. But Benny had to go back to prepare her mother for work on Monday. If he couldn't understand that, what kind of friend was he? Eve would say he wasn't meant to be a friend. He was meant to be a big handsome hunk who happened to fancy Benny. But there had to be more to it than that.

Eve and Kit discussed plans.

They would put a handbasin in each bedroom, and build an extra lavatory and shower. That would stop the congestion on the landings in the morning.

They would have a woman to come in and wash on Mondays. They would have the house rewired, some of those electrical installations didn't bear thinking about.

They would be able to charge a little more if the facilities were that much better. But the real benefit would be they needn't keep students they didn't like. The boy who never opened his bedroom window, who had Guinness bottles under the bed and who had left three cigarette burns in the furniture would be given notice to mend his ways or leave. Nice fellows like Kevin Hickey could stay forever.

For the first time in her life Kit Hegarty would have some freedom.

"Where does that leave me?" Eve asked lightly. "You won't need me now."

But she knew Kit did need her. So she spoke from a position of safety.

They had decided after reflection that the money would not be cast back on the drawing room floor of Westlands. It would be put for Eve in a post office account. Ready to be taken out and thrown, the moment Eve wanted to.

They danced at the rugby club and Benny realized there were people who came here every Friday night and that all of them knew Jack.

"I love you," he said suddenly, as they sat sipping Club Oranges from bottles with straws. He pushed a damp piece of hair out of her eyes.

"Why?" she asked.

"Lord, I don't know. It would be much easier to love someone who didn't keep disappearing."

"I love you too," she said. "You delight me."

"That's a lovely thing to say."

"It's true. I love everything about you. I often think about you and I get a great warm feeling all over me."

"Talking about great feelings all over us, I have my father's car."

Her heart sank. Once in the car it was going to be very, very hard to say no. Everything they had been told at school, and at the Mission, and in all those sermons on Purity, made it seem like a simple choice. Between Sin and Virtue. You were told that Virtue was rewarded, that Sin was punished, not only hereafter, but in this life. That boys had no respect for the girls who gave in to their demands.

But nobody had ever told anybody about how nice it felt, and how easy it would be to go on, and how cheap you felt stopping.

And about how you feared greatly that if you didn't go ahead with what you both wanted to do, then there would be plenty more who would.

People of the temperament and lack of scruples up to now only discovered in Wales.

"I hope we didn't drag you away from each other too early." Eve spoke dryly as they settled down to sleep in Kit Hegarty's.

"No, just in time I think," Benny said.

It had been the opportune demands of Aidan and Eve to let them into the car before they froze to death out of discretion.

"Why can't you stay the weekend?" Eve, too, seemed to be warning her about something. It was like a message that she was getting from everyone. She should stay around.

But there was no way that she could stay, no matter how great the danger. Things were at a crossroads in Knockglen.

"Have you a cigarette?" she asked Eve.

"But you don't smoke."

"No, but you do. And I want you to listen while I tell you about Sean Walsh."

They turned on the light again, and Eve sat horrified as the tale of the money and the suspicions and the partnership was unfolded.

The hopes that Benny's mother might find a life of her own in the shop, the support that would be needed. Eve listened and understood. She said that it didn't matter how much temptation was thrown into Jack Foley's path, some things were more important than others, and Benny had to nail Sean Walsh, no matter what.

Eve said she'd come down herself and help to search for the money.

"But we can't go into his rooms. And if we were to get the Guards he'd hide it."

"And he's such a fox," Eve added. "You'll have to be very, very careful."

There was now a Saturday lunchtime trade at Mario's, toasted cheese slices and a fudge cake with cream. The place was almost full as Benny walked past.

She went in to admire Clodagh's drastic changes. There were half a dozen people examining the rails and maybe four more in the fitting rooms.

Between them Clodagh and Fonsie had brought all the business in the town to their doorsteps. There were even people who might well have gone to Dublin on a shopping trip browsing happily.

"Your mother's in great form altogether. She's talking of shortening her skirts, and smartening herself up."

"Mother of God, who'll shorten her skirts for her? You're too busy."

"You *must* be able to take up a simple hem. Didn't you say you had a sewing machine somewhere?"

"Yes, but I don't know where it is in the lumber and rubble up in the shop."

"Up in the Honourable Sean Walsh's territory?"

"No, he's right upstairs. The first floor."

"Ah, get it out Benny. Get someone to drag it down to your house. I'll come round for ten minutes and start you off."

"It mightn't be working," Benny said hopefully.

"Then your mother'll have to look streelish won't she?"

Benny decided she'd go back to the shop and see if the machine really was there and looked in workable condition before she asked Teddy Flood or Dekko Moore or someone with a handcart to help her home with it.

Sean wasn't in sight in the shop. Only old Mike saw her go upstairs.

She saw the sewing machine behind an old sofa with the springs falling out. It couldn't have been used for nearly twenty years.

It looked like a little table. The machine part was down in it. Benny pulled, and up it came, shiny and new-looking as well it might be, considering how little use it had had. It was quite well made she thought, with those little drawers on each side, probably for spools of thread and buttons and all the things that sewing people filled their lives with.

She opened one of the little drawers. It was stuffed with small brown envelopes, pushed up one against the other. It seemed an extraordinary way to keep buttons and thread. She opened one idly and saw the green pound notes, and the pink ten-shilling notes squeezed together. There were dozens and dozens of envelopes, old ones addressed to the shop, originally with invoices, each with its postmark. With a feeling of ice water going right through her body, Benny realized that she had found the money Sean Walsh had been stealing from her father for years.

She didn't remember walking home. She must have passed Carroll's and Dessie Burns' and the cinema as well as Pine's and Paccy's and Mario's. Maybe she even saluted people. She didn't know.

In the kitchen Patsy was grumbling.

"Your mother thought you must have missed the bus," she said. Benny saw her preparing to put the meal on the table.

"Could you wait a few minutes, Patsy? I want to talk to Mother about something."

"Can't you talk and eat?"

"No."

Patsy shrugged. "She's above in the bedroom trying on clothes that stink of mothballs. She'll run them out of the shop with the smell of camphor."

Benny grabbed the sherry bottle and two glasses and went upstairs.

Patsy looked up in alarm.

In all her years in this house she had never been excluded from a conversation with the mistress and Benny. And never would she have believed that there was any subject that needed a drink being brought to the bedroom.

She said three quick Hail Marys that Benny wasn't pregnant. It was just the kind of thing that would happen to a nice big soft girl like Benny. Fall for a baby from a fellow who wouldn't marry her.

Annabel listened white-faced.

"It would have killed your father."

Benny sat on the side of the bed. She chewed her lip as she did when she was worried. Nan had said she must try to get out of the habit. It would make her mouth crooked eventually. She thought about Nan for a quick few seconds.

Nan wouldn't pause to care about her father's business. Not if it was being robbed blind by everyone in it. It was both terrible and wonderful to be so free.

"I wonder if Father knew," Benny said.

It was quite possible that he had his suspicions, but that being Eddie Hogan he had put them away. He wouldn't have opened his mouth unless he had positive proof. But it was odd that he had delayed the partnership deal. Mr. Green had said he was surprised that it had not been signed. Could Father have had second thoughts about going into partnership with a man who had his hand in the till over the years?

"Your father would not have been able to bear the disgrace of it all. The Guards coming in, a prosecution, the talk."

"I know," Benny agreed. "He'd never have stood for that."

They talked as equals sitting in the bedroom that was strewn with the clothes Annabel had been trying on to wear on her first day in the shop. Benny didn't urge her to make decisions and Annabel didn't hang back.

Because they were equals they gave each other strength.

"We could tell him we know?" Annabel said.

"He'd deny it."

They couldn't call the Guards, they knew that. There was no way that they could ask Mr. Green to come in, climb the stairs to the first floor and inspect the contents of the sewing machine. Mr. Green wasn't the kind of lawyer you saw in movies who did this sort of thing. He was the most quiet and respectable of country solicitors.

"We could ask someone else to witness it. To come and see it."

"What good would that do?" Annabel asked.

"I don't know," Benny admitted. "But it would prove it was there in case Sean were to shift it and hide it somewhere else. You know, when we speak to him."

"*When* we speak to him?"

"We have to, Mother. When you go in there on Monday morning, he has to be gone."

Annabel looked at her for a long time. She said nothing. But Benny felt there was some courage there, a new spirit. She believed that her mother would face what lay ahead. Benny must find the right words to encourage her.

"If Father can see us, it's what he'd want. He'd want no scandal, no prosecution. But he wouldn't want you to stand beside Sean Walsh as a partner knowing what we know now."

"We'll ask Dr. Johnson to witness the find," Annabel Hogan said, with a voice steadier than Benny would ever have believed.

❦

Patsy said to Bee Moore that evening that you'd want to have the patience of a saint to work in Lisbeg these days. There was that much coming and going, and doors being closed, and secrets, and bottles of sherry and no food being eaten and then food being called for at cracked times.

If this is what it was going to be like when the mistress went up into the shop then maybe it was just as well she was going to marry Mossy Rooney and his battle-ax of a mother and be out of it.

Patsy remembered Bee's former interest in Mossy and altered her remarks slightly. She said she knew she was very lucky to have been chosen by Mossy and was honored to be a part of his family. Bee Moore sniffed, wondered again how she had lost him to Patsy. She said that things were equally confusing in her house. Everyone in Westlands seemed to have gone mad. Heather had started in St. Mary's and was bringing what Mrs. Walsh called every ragtag and bobtail of Knockglen back up to the house to ride her pony. The old man had taken to his bed, and Mr. Simon was not to be seen, though it was reliably reported that he had been in Knockglen at least two nights without coming home. Where on earth could he have stayed in Knockglen if he hadn't come home to his own bed in Westlands. It was a mystery.

Maurice Johnson said that he was a man whom nothing would surprise. But the visit of Annabel Hogan and her daughter, and its reason, caught him on the hop.

He listened to their request.

"Why me?" he asked.

"It's you or Father Ross. We don't want to bring the Church into it. It's involving sin and punishment. All we need is someone reliable."

"Let's not delay," he said. "Let's go this minute."

There were two customers in the shop when they went in. Sean looked up from the boxes of V-necked jumpers that he had opened on the counter.

There was something about the deputation that alarmed him. His eyes followed them as they went to the back of the shop toward the stairs.

"Is there anything . . ." he began.

Benny paused on the stairs and looked at him. She had disliked him ever since she had first met him, and yet at this moment she felt a surge of pity for him. She took in his thin greasy hair and his long white narrow face.

He had not enjoyed his life or enriched it with the money he had taken.

But she must not falter now.

"We're just going to the first floor," she said. "Mother and I want Dr. Johnson to see something."

She saw the fear in his eyes.

"To witness something," she added, so that he would know.

Dr. Johnson went down the stairs quietly. He walked through the shop, his eyes firmly on the floor. He didn't return Mike's greeting. Nor did he acknowledge the figure of Sean standing there immobile with a box in his hands. He had said to the Hogans that he would confirm that in his presence they had removed upward of two hundred envelopes each containing sums of money varying from five to ten pounds.

There had been no gloating in the downfall of a man he had never liked. He looked at the little hoard in tightly screwed-up brown envelopes. The man was buying himself some kind of life, he supposed. Had he thought of wine, or women, or song when he had stashed Eddie Hogan's money away? It was impossible to know. He didn't envy the two women and their confrontation, but he admired them for agreeing to do it at once.

❦

They sat in the room and waited. They knew he would come upstairs. And both of them were weak with the shock of their discovery and the shame that they would have to face when Sean came up
to meet them.

Neither of them feared that he would bluster or attempt to
deny that it was he who had put the money there. There was no
way now for him to say they had made it up. Dr. Johnson's word
would be believed.

They heard his step on the stair.

"Did you close the shop?" Annabel Hogan asked.

"Mike will manage."

"He'll have to a lot of the time from now on," she said.

"Have you something to say? Is there some kind of accusation?" he began.

"Let's make it easy," Annabel began.

"I can explain," Sean said.

They could hear the Saturday afternoon noises of Knockglen,
people tooting their car horns, children laughing and running by,
free from school since lunchtime. There was a dog barking excitedly, and somewhere a horse drawing a cart had been frightened.
They sat, the three of them, and heard him whinnying until someone calmed him down.

Then Sean began to explain. It was a method of saving, and
Mr. Hogan had understood, not exactly agreed, but acknowledged.
The wages had not been great. It was known that Sean did the
lion's share of the work. It had always been expected that he
should build a little nest egg for himself.

Annabel sat in the high-backed chair, a wooden one they had
never thought of bringing to Lisbeg. Benny sat in the broken sofa,
the one she had pulled out to find the sewing machine. They
hadn't rehearsed it, but they acted as a team, neither of them said a
word. There were no interruptions or denials. No nods of agreement or shaking of the head in disbelief. They sat there and let him
form the noose around his neck. Eventually his voice grew slower,

his hand movements less exaggerated. His arms fell beside his sides, and soon his head began to hang as if it were a great weight.

Then he stopped altogether.

Benny waited for her mother to speak.

"You can go tonight Sean."

It was more decisive even than Benny would have been. She looked at her mother in admiration. There was no hate, no revenge, in her tone. Just a simple statement of the position. It startled Sean Walsh just as much.

"There's no question of that, Mrs. Hogan," he said.

His face was white, but he was not now going to ask for mercy, or understanding, or a second chance.

They waited, to hear what he had to say.

"It's not what your husband would have wanted. He said in writing that he wanted me to become a partner. You have agreed that with Mr. Green."

Annabel's glance fell on the table full of envelopes.

"And there is no one to confirm or deny that this was an agreement."

Benny spoke then. "Father would not have liked the police, Sean. I know you would agree with that. So Mother and I are going along with what we are sure would be his wishes. We have discussed this for a long time. We think he would have liked you to leave this evening. And that he would like us to speak to no person of what has happened here today. Dr. Johnson, as you need hardly say, is silent as the grave. We only asked him here to give substance to our request that you leave, without any fuss."

"And what'll happen to your fine business when I leave?" His face had become crooked now. "What's to become of Hogan's, laughingstock of the outfitting business? Will it have its big closing-down sale in June or in October? That's the only question."

Agitated and with his features in the form of a smile he walked around rubbing his hands.

"You have no idea how hopeless this place is. How its days are numbered. What do you think you'll do without me? Have old

Mike, who hasn't two brains to rub together, talking to the customers and God blessing them, and God saving them, like Barry Fitzgerald in a film? Have you, Mrs. Hogan, who don't know one end of a bale of material from another? Have some greenhorn of an eejit serving his time from some other one-horse town? Is this what you want for your great family business? Is it? Tell me, is it?"

His tone was becoming hysterical.

"What did we ever do to you that makes you turn on us like this?" Annabel Hogan asked, her voice calm.

"You think you were good to me. Is that what you think?"

"Yes. In a word."

Sean's face was working. Benny realized she had never remotely suspected that he could feel so much.

He told a tale of being banished upstairs to servants' quarters, being patronized and invited to break bread from time to time with the air of being summoned to a palace. He said that he had run the business single-handed for a pittance of a wage and a regular pat on the head. The cry that they would be lost without Sean Walsh, said often enough to render it meaningless. He said that his genuine and respectful admiration for Benny, the daughter of the house, was a matter of mockery, and had been thrown back in his face. He had been honorable and would have been proud to escort her to places even when she was not a physically beautiful specimen.

Neither Annabel nor Benny allowed a muscle to move in the face of the insults.

He had not intruded, imposed or in any way traded on his position. He had been discreet and loyal. And this was the thanks he was getting for it.

Benny felt a great sadness sweep over her. There was some sincerity in the way Sean spoke. If this was his version of his life, then this was his life.

"Will you stay in Knockglen?" she asked unexpectedly.

"What?"

"After you leave here?"

Something clicked then. Sean knew they meant it. He looked at them, as if he had never seen either of them before.

"I might," he said. "It's the only place I've really known you see."

They saw.

They knew there would be talk. A lot of talk. But on Monday the shop would open with Annabel in charge. They had only thirty-six hours to learn the business.

Mrs. Healy agreed to see Sean in her office. Even given his usual pallor, she thought he looked bad, as if he had just had a shock.

"May I arrange to have a room here for a week?"

"Of course. But might I ask why?"

He told her that he would be leaving Hogan's. As of now. That he would therefore be leaving his accommodation there. He was vague in the extreme. He parried questions about the partnership, denied that there had been any fight or unpleasantness. He said that he would like to transfer his belongings across the road at a time when half the town wouldn't be watching, like when they were gone home to their tea.

Fonsie saw him of course, saw him carrying one by one the four cardboard boxes that made up his possessions.

"Good evening, Sean," Fonsie said gravely.

Sean ignored him.

Fonsie went straight back to tell Clodagh.

"I think I see a love nest starting. Sean Walsh was bringing twigs and leaves and starting to build it across in Healy's."

"Was he moving across, really?" Clodagh didn't seem as surprised as she should be.

"In stealth and with lust written all over him for Dorothy," Fonsie said.

"Well done, Benny," said Clodagh, closing her eyes and smiling.

♥

Maire Carroll had come up to the convent to ask for a reference. She was going to apply for a job in a shop in Dublin. As Mother Francis struggled to think of something to say about Maire Carroll that was both truthful and flattering, Maire revealed that Sean Walsh had been seen taking all his belongings and going to live in the hotel.

"Thank God, Benny," Mother Francis breathed to herself.

Sunday was the longest day that any of them had worked. It had an air of unreality because the shutters were closed so that nobody should know they were there.

They would have looked a very strange crew to anyone who saw them. Patsy in her overalls scrubbing out the small room which had been filled with the results of a thousand cups of ill-made tea. Old Mike said that they took it in turns to make the tea and open the biscuits. The place had all the signs of it. The electric ministove had been brought down from Sean's quarters upstairs. From now on there would be proper tea, and even soup or toast made.

Hogan's was going to change.

And to help it change, Peggy Pine and Clodagh were there, as was Teddy Flood.

To none of them had any explanation been given apart from the fact that Sean Walsh had left, and they were in need of some advice. Clodagh said one business was the same as another. If you could run one you could run the lot, and she always hoped she might be seconded to get a steel works or a car plant on its feet.

Mike, who had never been the center of such attention, was asked respectful questions. It was the general opinion that Mike must be addressed slowly, and his answers weighed with the same deliberation that he gave them.

To fuss Mike would be counterproductive. Let him think there was all the time in the world.

Let him wander down no lanes of regret about Mr. Eddie and no tight-lipped mutterings about that Sean Walsh who wanted to be called Mister.

Slowly they pieced it together, the way the business was run. The people who had credit, and those who didn't. The way the bills had been sent out, the reminders. The salesmen who came with their books for orders. The mills, the factories.

Haltingly Mike told it all. They listened and worked out the system, such as it was.

A thousand times Annabel Hogan cursed herself for not taking an interest and forming a part of the company when her husband was alive. Perhaps he would have liked it? It was only her own hidebound feelings that had kept her at home.

Benny wished that she had come to help her father. If only she could have had the time over again, then she would have spent Saturday afternoons here with him, learning about his life at work.

Would he have been proud of her and pleased that she was taking such an interest? Or would he have thought that she was a distraction in the all-male world of a gentleman's outfitters? It was impossible to know. And anyway she had avoided the shop a lot because of Sean Walsh.

As they toiled on working out which bales of material were which, Benny let her mind wander. Could her parents seriously have expected her to marry Sean just because he had been helpful in the business? And even worse, suppose she had gone along with their views? Promised herself to him, allowed his disgusting advances and been engaged to him now? Think then how impossible it would have been once they discovered his theft. The mean, grubbing, regular stealing from a kind employer who had wished him nothing but well.

Patsy had heated up the soup and served the sandwiches. They sat companionably and ate them.

"Is it wrong of us, do you think, to work on a Sunday?" Mike was fearful about the whole thing.

"*Laborare est orare,*" Peggy Pine said suddenly.

"Could you translate for those of us without the classical education, Aunt?" Clodagh asked.

"It means that the Lord thinks working is a form of prayer," Peggy said, wiping away the crumbs and settling down to writing out proper sales tickets which Annabel could understand.

They had opened up the back door of the shop late on Saturday night so they could come and go by the lane at the rear of the premises.

The sun shone on the disused backyard with its rubbish and clutter.

"You could make a lovely conservatory here," Clodagh said, admiringly.

"What for?" Benny asked.

"To sit in, you clown."

"Customers wouldn't want to sit down, would they?"

"Your mother and you."

Benny looked blank.

"Well, you are going to live here, aren't you?"

"Lord no. We'll be living in Lisbeg. We couldn't live over the shop."

"Some of us do, and manage fine," Clodagh said huffily.

Benny could have bitten off her tongue. But there was no point in trying to take it back now.

Clodagh didn't seem a bit upset.

"Good for you if you can," she said. "I thought the object of all this was to try and turn this place round. You won't do that if you don't put some money into it. I assumed you were going to sell your house."

Benny wiped her forehead. Was there ever going to be any end to all this? When could she get back to living an ordinary life again?

Jack Foley telephoned Benny from nine in the morning until noon.

"She can't be at mass *all* bloody morning," he grumbled.

Benny telephoned Jack at home.

She got his mother.

"Is that you, Sheila?" she asked.

"No, Mrs. Foley. It's Benny Hogan."

She heard that Jack was out and not expected back until late. He had left quite early.

"I thought he was down in your neck of the woods, actually," Mrs. Foley said.

She made it sound like a swamp with alligators in it. Like the film Benny hadn't seen.

She forced her voice to be light and casual. No message. Just to say that she had rung for a chat.

Mrs. Foley said that she'd write it down straightaway. She managed to make it sound as if the name of Benny Hogan would be added to a long list of those who had already telephoned.

It was over, and she longed to celebrate. Everything she had wanted for the shop since the day Father had died had been achieved. They had had huge support from their friends in Knockglen. Sean had been rendered unimportant.

It was a night of triumph, she wanted to tell Jack all about it. The awful bits and the funny bits, the look on Sean's face, Patsy making more and more tea, and sandwiches. Old Mike getting surges of energy like Frankenstein's monster. Peggy Pine showing her mother how to ring up a sale. She wanted to tell him that from now on she wouldn't be needed so desperately at home. She would be free to spend several nights a week in Dublin.

She had a terrible foreboding that she had left it all too late. That she had been away too long.

SEVENTEEN

⟵─────────────────◆─────────────────⟶

*B*rian Mahon said that it was great to be spending all that money paying fees for a university student when she didn't get up for her bloody lectures.

Emily said he should hush. That was unfair. Nan worked very hard, and it was rare the girl had a lie-in.

"When she *is* in the house it would be nice to see her, just now and again," he said.

Nan told them that she stayed with Eve out in Dun Laoghaire, on the occasions when she didn't come home. Her father said it was a pity that woman in the guesthouse didn't pay her fees and buy her clothes for her.

But he had to meet a man who had come in on the boat to the North Wall. He'd be down in a dockers' pub. There was a deal about a consignment.

Emily sighed. There might be a deal about a consignment, but there would also be a day's drinking. When he had gone she went upstairs.

Nan was lying on her bed with her arms folded behind her head.

"Aren't you well?"

"I'm fine, Em. Honestly."

Emily sat down on the stool opposite the dressing table.

There was something troubled in Nan's face, some look she had never seen before. It was surprise mixed with indecision.

Nan had never known either, not since she was a little girl.

"Is it . . . Simon?"

Normally Emily never mentioned his name. It was almost like tempting fate.

Nan shook her head. She told her mother that Simon was most devoted and attentive. He was down in Knockglen. She'd be seeing him for dinner tomorrow night. Emily was not convinced. She shook her head as she went downstairs, tidied away the breakfast things, put on her smart blouse and set out for work.

As she stood at the bus stop she wondered what was wrong with her daughter.

Back in her bedroom Nan lay and looked ahead of her. She knew there was no need to have sent the specimen to Holles Street Maternity Hospital. Her period was seventeen days late. She was pregnant.

Eve and Kit were up early. They had builders arriving and they wanted to show them from the beginning that this was a house with rules, a house like they had never known before.

They had left bags of cement and sand in the backyard the night before. The name on the sacks was Mahon.

"You must tell Nan that we're putting a few shillings into her father's pocket," Kit said.

"No, Nan wouldn't like to hear that. She doesn't want to be reminded of her father and his trade."

Kit was surprised.

Nan always seemed remarkably unpretentious for such an attractive girl. You never caught her stealing a look at herself in the mirror, or blowing about the people she had been out with.

Eve had liked her so much at the beginning, but had been very resentful of Nan taking up with the Westwards.

"You're not still bearing a grudge against her because she went out with Simon Westward are you?"

"A grudge? Me?" said Eve, laughing. She knew that most of her life had been spent bearing grudges against the family that had disowned her.

And anyway Kit had used the wrong tense. Nan was still going out with Simon. Very much so.

Heather had been on the phone, squeaking with excitement about her life in the convent and how funny and mad and superstitious everyone was.

"I hope you don't *say* any of that," Eve said sternly.

"No, only to you. And I have another secret. I think Simon's doing a line with Nan. She rings sometimes, and I know he goes off to meet her, because he packs a bag. And he doesn't come home at night."

Eve was sure that Nan and Simon were Going All the Way. Simon wouldn't be remotely interested in a girl unless she would. It wasn't a sin for him anyway, and he wouldn't take Nan out, no matter how gorgeous she looked, unless he was getting value for it.

Because Eve knew very well that Nan was not someone that her cousin Simon was going to bring home to Westlands.

When she telephoned it was as she had known it would be. The pregnancy test was positive.

Nan dressed carefully and left the empty house in Maple Gardens. She took the bus to Knockglen.

She walked past the gates of St. Mary's Convent and looked up the long avenue. She could hear the sounds of children at play. How strange of Simon to let his sister stay there, amongst all the children of people who worked on the estate.

But from her own point of view it was good. It meant that he was tied more to Knockglen. She could come more frequently to the cottage. And there would be fewer crises about Heather being unhappy and running away from the school where she should be.

She couldn't remember clearly how far it was from the village to Westlands, but decided that it was too far to walk. Knockglen didn't have the air of a place that would have a taxi. She had heard so much bad about Healy's Hotel from Benny, Eve and Simon that she dared not risk asking them to arrange her a lift.

Nan would wait until a suitable car passed by.

A middle-aged man in a green car came into view. She hailed him and as Nan had known he would, he stopped.

Dr. Johnson asked her where she was heading.

"Westlands," she said simply.

"Where else," the man said.

They talked about the car. He explained it was a Morris Cowley. He'd love a Zodiac or even a Zephyr, but you had to know when to draw the line.

"I don't think you do," said the beautiful blond girl, whom Dr. Johnson remembered seeing somewhere before.

She had a slightly high, excited look about her. He asked no questions about her visit.

She said that a lot of people were too timid, they didn't reach for things. He should reach for a Zephyr or a Zodiac, not assume that they were beyond his grasp.

Maurice Johnson smiled and said he would discuss the notion of reaching with his wife and with his bank manager. He could see neither of them agreeing with this view, but he would certainly present it.

He turned in the gates of Westlands.

"Were you going here anyway?" Nan asked, alarmed. She didn't want to clash with another visitor.

"Not at all. But a gentleman, even in a Morris Cowley, always saw a lady right to the door."

She gave him a smile of such brightness, he thought to himself that men like Simon Westward who were knee-high to a grasshopper had all the luck when it came to getting gorgeous women just because they had the accent and the big house.

Nan looked up at the house. It wasn't going to be easy. But

then nothing that was important had ever been easy. She took three deep breaths, and rang at the door.

Mrs. Walsh knew well who Nan Mahon was. She had heard the name on the telephone many times, and even though she discouraged Bee from gossiping, she knew that this girl, who had been in the house a couple of days after Christmas, was a friend of Eve Malone and Benny Hogan's.

But just to keep things as they should be, she asked her name.

"Mahon," Nan said, in a clear, confident voice.

Simon was coming out of the morning room anyway. He had heard the car pull up and draw away.

"Was that Dr. Johnson, Mrs. Walsh? He seems to have driven off without seeing Grandfather . . ."

He saw Nan.

His voice changed.

"Well, hallo," he said.

"Hallo, Simon."

She stood, very beautiful in a cream-colored suit with a red artificial flower pinned to the lapel. Her handbag and shoes were the same red. She looked as if she were dressed to go out.

"Come in and sit down," he said.

"Coffee, Mr. Simon?" Mrs. Walsh asked, but she knew she would not be needed.

"No thanks, Mrs. Walsh." His voice was light and easy. "No, I think we'll be all right for the moment."

He closed the door firmly behind them.

Aidan Lynch came up to Jack in the pub and said that Benny had taught him the Charleston.

It was really quite simple, once you learned to work the two legs separately.

"Yes," Jack Foley said.

And it looked very snazzy, Aidan said, and possibly Benny should give up her notion of becoming a librarian, and be a teacher. After all anyone could check books in and out of a library, but not everyone could teach. Impart knowledge.

"True," Jack Foley agreed.

And so Aidan wondered, how much more was he going to have to go on making inane chat until they could get down to the point, the point being that he and Eve, who were so to speak Love's Young Dream of the University at the moment, leaving Sean and Carmel in the halfpenny place, wanted to know had there been a falling-out between Benny and Jack.

"Ask her," Jack said.

"Eve has. And she says no, it's just that she can never find you."

"That's because she's always looking for me in Knockglen," Jack said.

"Have you been able to . . . you know." Aidan was the old confiding mate now.

"Mind your own business," Jack said.

"That means you haven't. Neither have I. Jesus, what do they teach them in these convents?"

"About people like us, I suppose."

They forgot about women and talked about the match and the way that some people couldn't kick a ball out of their way if it was laid down in front of them.

Aidan hadn't any more information for Eve about Benny. But at least he could report that no new person had come on the scene.

"This is a surprise," Simon said. The small narrow frown that was just a half line between his eyes showed it wasn't entirely a welcome surprise.

Nan had rehearsed it. No point in small talk, and fencing.

"I waited until I was certain. I'm afraid I'm pregnant," she said simply.

Simon's face was full of concern.

"Oh no," he said, moving toward her. "Oh no, Nan no, you poor darling. You poor, poor darling." He embraced her and held her close.

She said nothing. She felt his heart beat against hers. Then he drew away, examining her face, looking to see how upset she was.

"How awful for you," he said tenderly. "It's not fair is it?"

"What isn't?"

"Everything." He waved his hands expansively.

Then he went over to the window and ran his hands through his hair. "This is awful," he said. He seemed very upset.

They stood apart, Nan with her hand on the piano, Simon by the window, both of them looking out the long window at the paddock where Heather's pony stood and across at the fields where the grazing had been let and cattle moved slowly round.

Everything seemed like slow motion, Nan thought. Even the way Simon spoke.

"Will you know what to do?" he asked her. "Will you know where to go?"

"How do you mean?"

"Over all this." He waved a slow wave of his hand vaguely in the direction of her body.

"I came to you," she said.

"Yes, I know, and you were right. Utterly right." He was anxious she should know this.

"I never thought it could happen," Nan said.

"Nobody ever does." Simon was rueful, as if it happened all over the place, to everyone he knew.

Nan wanted to speak. She wanted desperately to say, What do we do now?

But she must give him no chance to say anything hurtful or careless that she would have to respond to angrily. She *must* leave silences. The expression was Pregnant Pauses, she thought with a little giggle that she fought back. Simon was about to speak.

"Nan, sweetheart," he said, "this is about as terrible as it can be. But it will all be all right. I promise you."

"I know." She looked at him trustingly.

And then her ears began to sing a little as he told her of a friend who knew someone and it had all been amazingly simple, and the girl had said that it was much easier than going to a dentist.

And there had been no ill effects. Well, actually Nan had met the girl, but it wouldn't be fair to name names. But she was someone terribly bubbly and well adjusted.

"But you don't mean . . . ?" She looked at him shocked.

"Of course I'm not going to abandon you." He came toward her again and took her in his arms.

Relief flooded through her. But why had he talked about this silly bubbly woman who had been to have an abortion? Had he changed when he saw her stricken face?

Simon Westward stroked her hair.

"You didn't think I'd let you look after it all on your own, did you?" he said.

Nan said nothing.

"Come on now, we both enjoyed ourselves. Of course I'll look after it."

He pulled away from her and took a checkbook out of a drawer.

"I don't know what this chap said, he did tell me a figure, but this should cover it. And I'll get the name and address of the place and everything. It's in England of course, but that's all for the best, isn't it?"

She looked at him unbelieving. "It's your child. You know that?"

"Nan, my angel, it's not a child at all. Not a speck yet."

"You do know that you were the first and there has been nobody else?

"We're not going to upset ourselves over this Nan. It can't be between us. You know that, I know it, we've known it since we went into our little fling."

"Why can't it be? You want to get married. You want an heir for this place. We get on well together. I fit in with your world." Her voice was deliberately light.

But she was playing for everything in this plea. She never thought she would have had to beg like this. He had said he loved her. Every time they made love he called out how much he loved her. It was unthinkable that he was reaching for a checkbook to dismiss her.

He was gentle with her. He even took her hand.

"You know that you and I are not going to marry, Nan. You, of all people, so cool, so reasonable, so sensible. You know this. As do I."

"I know you said you loved me," she said.

"And so I do, I love every little bit of you. I don't deny it."

"And this is love then? A check and an abortion?"

His face looked troubled. He seemed surprised that she took this view.

"And it wouldn't have mattered I suppose if my father was a rich builder instead of a shabby builder."

"It has nothing to do with that."

"Well, it certainly has nothing to do with religion. It's 1958 and neither of us believes in God."

He opened her hand and pressed the folded check into it.

She looked at him in disbelief.

"I'm sorry," he said.

She was still silent. Finally she said, "I'm going back now."

"How will you get home?" he asked.

"I was stupid enough to think I was coming home." She looked around her, at the portraits on the wall, the piano, the view from the window.

Something about her face touched him. She was always so very, very beautiful.

"I wish . . ." he began, but couldn't finish the sentence.

"Do you know someone who would drive me back to Dublin?"

"I will, of course."

"No. It would be too artificial. Someone else."

"I don't really know anyone else . . . anyone that I could ask . . ."

"No. You do keep yourself to yourself. But I know what we'll do. I'll take your car just down to the square," she said. "There'll be a bus soon. You can collect it later in the day."

"Let me at least . . ."

He moved toward her.

"No, please stay away from me. Don't touch me."

He handed her the car keys.

"It needs a lot of choke," he said.

"I know. I've been in it a great many times."

Nan walked down the steps of Westlands. He watched from the window while she got into his car and drove away.

He knew that from the kitchen window Bee Moore and Mrs. Walsh were watching and speculating.

He looked at her with admiration as she started his car and drove down the long avenue without looking back.

She left the keys in the car. Nobody would dare to steal the car of Mr. Simon Westward in this feudal backwater. They'd all be afraid of crossing anyone at the Big House.

Mikey was turning the bus. He'd be going back to Dublin in five minutes, he told her. She paid her fare.

"You could have got a return, it would have been cheaper." Mikey was always anxious to give people a bargain.

"I didn't know I'd be going back," Nan said.

"Life's full of surprises," said Mikey, looking at this blond girl in the cream and red outfit, who looked much too smart for this part of the world anyway.

✦

Bill Dunne saw Benny come into the Annexe. She was looking around, hunting for Jack, but there was no sign of him. She stood in the line with the other students. If Jack had been there he would have kept a table, and she could have gone straight to join him.

Bill waved and said he had an extra coffee. In fact he hadn't begun his own, but it seemed a way of calling her over. She looked very well today, in a chestnut-colored sweater, the exact color of her hair, and a pale yellow blouse underneath.

Bill and Benny talked easily. If she was glancing around for Jack she never mentioned it. And he never showed that he noticed Benny was so easy to talk to. They discussed banning the bomb and if it would ever work. Benny said she was afraid it was like asking boxers to tie one hand behind their backs, or like saying we should go back to bows and arrows once they had invented gun-powder. They wondered would Elvis really join the U.S. Army or was it just a publicity stunt. They talked of Jack Kerouac. Would every single person that he met On the Road have been interesting? Surely some of them must have been deadly bores.

The time flew, and they had to go back to lectures. If Benny was disappointed that Jack Foley hadn't turned up she showed no sign of it. But then women were known to be very good at hiding their feelings. Most people didn't know what they were up to half the time.

Rosemary saw everything and noted it all. She watched Bill and Benny chatting animatedly. They seemed like great friends. Perhaps he was consoling her about Jack. Rosemary had often thought that the feeling was unworthy, but she felt that Jack was too handsome for Benny. She thought it was like a mixed marriage. A Black and a White, a Catholic and a non-Catholic. You heard of those that did work. But the usual rule was that they didn't. It wasn't a view that anyone would agree with so she didn't express it. Anyway people might think she was after Jack Foley for herself. Which oddly enough was not true. She had met a very nice medical student called Tom. He wouldn't be qualified for years, which would give Rosemary time to be an air hostess or something with a bit of glamor in the meantime.

Sean Walsh stood on the quays waiting for the bus back to Knockglen. He had stayed in a men's hostel in Dublin for five days to think things out. During the daytime he had walked through the menswear shops in Dublin trying to see himself working in any of them.

The prospect began to look less and less likely. He would not come armed with a reference. He would be unlikely to be taken on anywhere.

Little by little he began to realize how his horizons had narrowed. The idea of buying his own place, renovating a cottage up over the quarry, was now only a fantasy. The notion of standing at the back door of his own business and watching the town walk by was not one he could hold anymore in his dreams. His name would be over no premises in Knockglen, the town where he had lived for ten years, and which, when all was said and done, he thought of as home.

He was going to go back now with a proposition.

He saw a very good-looking girl get off the bus, a blond girl in a cream suit with red trimmings. He recognized her as the friend of Eve and Benny. The girl who had been at Mr. Hogan's funeral, and had been up at Westlands around Christmastime. She didn't acknowledge him. She looked as if her mind was set on something else entirely.

Sean got onto the bus and looked without pleasure at Mikey, a man who was overfamiliar and with an unfortunate habit of referring to people's physical appearance.

"There you are Sean, with a face as long as a wet week. Is it the return of the Prodigal we see?"

"I wish I understood what you meant, Mikey."

"It's a reference to a story Our Lord told in the New Testament, Sean. A man like yourself nearly eating the altar in the church should know that."

"I am well aware of the parable of the Prodigal Son, but since he was a man who spent his life in wrongdoing, I'm afraid I can't see the similarity."

Mikey looked at Sean shrewdly. His wife had given him some highly colored speculation about what might or might not have happened in Hogan's Outfitters. But obviously Sean Walsh had not run away.

"I was only wondering where the Fatted Calf was going to be killed, Sean," Mikey said. "Maybe they're basting it already down in Healy's Hotel."

Nan let herself into the house that she had left that morning. She took off her cream suit and hung it carefully on a padded hanger. She sponged it lightly with lemon juice and water. She put shoe trees in her red shoes, and she rubbed her red leather bag with some furniture cream, before wrapping it carefully in tissue paper and placing it beside her other four handbags in a drawer. She put on her best College clothes, combed her hair and went out to stand for a second time at the bus stop across the road.

Mrs. Healy had tidied up her office. She placed a big jug of daffodils on the window and two small hyacinths in plastic bowls on the filing cabinet.

She had been to Ballylee to have her hair done.

The new corset was very well fitting. It managed to distribute the flesh very well. So well, in fact, that a tight skirt looked remarkably fine. She wore her high-necked blouse and cameo brooch. The ones reserved for special occasions.

And after all it would be a special occasion this afternoon. She knew that Sean Walsh was coming back today. And that he was going to make a proposal of marriage.

❧

It was lunchtime in the convent, and Mother Francis had her turn on Dinner Duty. That meant she walked up and down keeping order as the girls had their sandwiches. Then she supervised the tidying up of the hall, the careful cleaning and refolding of the greaseproof paper for tomorrow's packed lunch, the airing of the room and the quick exercise in the yard.

She saw a group of the girls explaining to Heather Westward the nature of rosary beads.

"Why do you call them a pair, there's only one?" Heather looked at the necklace of beads.

"They're always called a pair." Fiona Carroll, the youngest of the badly behaved Carroll children from the grocery was scornful.

"What does it mean 'Irish Horn'?" Heather was interested.

"That's just what they're made from." Siobhan Flood, the butcher's granddaughter, dismissed it.

"So what does it *do*?" Heather demanded, looking fearfully at the rosary beads.

She was not at all convinced that it did nothing, that you did things with it, you used it to pray with, that was all. That the spacings on the beads meant that you said ten Hail Marys and then stopped and said a Glory Be and then an Our Father.

"Like the Lord's Prayer?" Heather asked.

"Yes, but the proper way," Fiona Carroll said, in case there should be any doubt about it.

They explained that the whole point was not to say one Hail Mary more than was needed. That was why they were made. Mother Francis had an art of listening to one set of conversations while being thought to be in the middle of others. Her heart was heavy when she heard the explanations being given to the unfortunate Heather.

After all her teaching, this is what they thought. They thought the point of this beautiful prayer to Our Lady was never to let yourself say one more Hail Mary than was necessary.

Wouldn't a teacher be very foolish to think that anything ever got into their heads? Perhaps the Mother of God would be touched and pleased by the innocence of children. Mother Francis would, at this particular lunchtime, have liked to take them out individually and murder them one by one.

Kit answered the phone at lunchtime. It was Eve wanting to know if Benny could stay the night. She knew the answer would be yes, but between them there had always been courtesies like this.

Kit was pleased. She wanted to know was there a dance or an occasion.

"No, there's not." Eve sounded worried. "She said she wants her mother to get used to her being away from home."

"And what about Jack Foley?"

"That's the question I wanted to ask and didn't," Eve said.

Hogan's had closed for lunch. Annabel, Patsy and Mike adjourned to the back room and ate shepherd's pie and tinned beans. Mike said he hadn't felt as well in years. These midday dinners in the shop would build you up for the afternoon. Patsy said it was a grand, handy place to cook. They should move up here altogether.

Nan tried three pubs before she found them. It was nearly closing time. Almost the Holy Hour when the Dublin city pubs closed between half-past two and half-past three.

"Well, look who's here." Bill Dunne was pleased.

"Caught you, Nan. You're on a pub crawl," said Aidan.

Jack as always said the right thing. He said it was great to see her and what would she like.

Nan said she was sick and tired of studying and she had come out to find a few handsome men to take her mind off her books.

They were all flattered to think she had set out to look for them. They sat around her in an admiring circle.

She looked fresh in her pale green jumper with a dark green skirt and jacket. Her eyes sparkled as she laughed and joked with them.

"How goes the romance with Milord?" Aidan asked.

"Who?"

"Come on, Simon."

"I haven't seen him for ages," she said.

Aidan was surprised. Only last night Eve had been fulminating about it all.

"Did it end in tears?" Aidan knew that Eve would demand the whole story from him, not just half-said, half-understood bits of conversation.

"Not a bit. Nothing could come of it. We knew that. He's one world, I'm another," Nan said.

"That's establishment baloney. Just because he's part of the crumbling classes," Bill Dunne said.

"Exactly. And much as I know we should be nice to the crumbling classes, they're a bit hard to take," said Nan.

Bill, Jack and Aidan realized immediately that this Simon was besotted with Nan, but that she had thrown him over because she couldn't go along with all that would be involved if she was to play the game as they wanted to play it at the Big House.

Aidan knew that Eve would be very pleased with this news. Jack knew that Nan was just saying what he knew already. Only a few weeks ago he had seen Simon approach Nan and beg to be taken back into her warmth, while she had been polite and distant. Bill Dunne was pleased that he could report to everyone else that Nan Mahon was in circulation again.

The barman mentioned that drinking-up time had long been exceeded. He looked stern, young law students weren't going to be much help to him if he got an endorsement on his license.

Bill and Aidan drifted back to the University.

Jack dallied and spoke to Nan.

"I don't suppose you'd think of being really bad and coming to the pictures with me."

"Lord no, more Swamp Women!"

"We could look at a paper?"

They bought an *Evening Herald.*

Nan said, "What about Benny?"

"What about her?"

"I mean where is she?"

"Search me," said Jack. There was nothing they could agree on. They walked slowly through the Green debating this one and that, heads close together inside the pages of the newspaper.

It took them a long time to get to Grafton Street. They still hadn't made up their minds. The pubs were open again now. The Holy Hour was well over.

"Let's have a drink and discuss it," Jack suggested.

He had a Guinness. Nan had a pineapple juice.

Jack told her a long, sad saga about Benny never being there. Jack said he knew things were difficult in Knockglen and that Benny was trying to get her mother started in the shop. But he wondered was she taking it all on her shoulders too much.

"She shouldn't stay holding her hand," Nan agreed with him. She explained that she had never felt responsible for her mother, who went out to work every day and didn't need anyone to mind her.

Jack brightened. He had been afraid that he was being selfish. No, Nan told him, it was a sign of how much he liked Benny around that he missed her.

He warmed to this view. Take tonight for example. There was a club dance. Everyone brought a partner. And here would he be, Jack Foley, yet again with no partner.

He looked across at her suddenly.

"Unless, of course . . . ?"

"I wouldn't like to. Benny might . . . ?"

"Oh, come on. Benny won't mind. Didn't she ask us to go to the pictures together?"

Nan looked doubtful.

"You're not worried about your old pal Cavalry Twill are you?"

"I told you, that's long forgotten. He's no part of my life."

"Well then." Jack was easy and somewhat cheered. "Will we meet at the club?"

Carmel was on the Ladies' Committee. It involved helping to prepare the supper for the functions. Sean liked her to be involved. He was Treasurer, of course, and very important. She was buying bread for the sandwiches, when she met Benny, who was trying to turn her back on the sweet counter and make do with an apple.

"It's the Tiffin Bar that's almost reaching out its arms at me from the shelf," Benny said. "Thank God you came in. I was nearly going to buy it."

"It'd be a shame to go back on the Tiffin now," Carmel said.

Benny didn't like the feeling that seemed to hang unspoken that there had been years of wedging chocolate bars down her throat. She bought the apple unenthusiastically.

"It's a pity you're not going to be here tonight," Carmel said. "The party's going to be great. They've given us much more money than usual. We're going to have sponge flans filled with whipped cream and decorated with chocolate flake. Oh, sorry, Benny, but you're not here, so you won't be tempted anyway."

"I am here as it happens. I'm staying with Eve," Benny said.

"Great," said Carmel warmly. "See you tonight."

"Ring him," Eve said. "Ring him and tell him you're in town."

"He knows. He must know. I told him."

"They never listen. Ring him."

Benny said she'd have to talk to that woman, Jack's mother, who always made people sound as if they were looking for autographs instead of trying to speak to her son. Eve said that was nonsense. Benny had only phoned the house once. She must ring now. Jack would be delighted.

From the house in Dun Laoghaire Benny eventually did phone.

"I'm sorry, but he's gone out to the rugby club. They're having some kind of party tonight. He said he'd be late back."

"He can't have known you were in town," Eve said.

"No."

They sat at the kitchen table. Neither of them suggested that Benny should just dress up and go into the club anyway.

Neither of them said it had all been the forgetfulness of men, and that Jack would be delighted to see her.

They concentrated instead on Kit Hegarty, who was going out with Kevin Hickey's father.

"Don't cheapen yourself now, remember," Eve warned.

"He won't respect you," said Benny.

Kit said that it was wonderful to see the high moral tone of the younger generation. She was relieved to know that this was their attitude.

"It's not our attitude for ourselves. We have no restraint at all," Eve assured her. "It's only for you."

"I wish we had no restraint," Benny said gloomily. "We might be better off."

Annabel Hogan had brightened up the shop considerably by taking away some of the wooden panels and surrounds in the window. It did not look nearly so sepulchral and solemn. She had several V-necked jumpers in several colors displayed on stands. For the first time a man coming into Hogan's might be able to browse and choose rather than knowing what he wanted before he came in the door.

It also meant that she could see out much more clearly, without having to peer.

She saw Sean Walsh walk into Healy's Hotel without a backward glance at the business where he had worked for so long.

She knew that he had left his belongings there while he went away to make his plans. Perhaps he had got a job somewhere and he had returned to collect his belongings. Peggy Pine had said that Sean had hopes of Mrs. Healy. Annabel doubted it. Dorothy Healy was no fool. She would know quicker than most that Sean would not have left Hogan's as he did unless there had been an incident. He was no longer an aspiring merchant in the town.

"I'm no longer a person of substance in this town," Sean Walsh said to Mrs. Healy.

She inclined her head graciously. There had been a time when he thought he would have more to offer, something to bring to the request he was going to make. But circumstances had changed.

Her head was angled like a bird considering its options. Sean spoke of his admiration for her. The respect in which she was held. The potential in Healy's Hotel, a potential as yet not fully realized.

He said there was a need for an overseer, someone to look after the daily business, the nuts and bolts, while Mrs. Healy's own flair was used where it was of most use in greeting the customers, and being a presence.

Dorothy Healy waited.

He spoke of his admiration, his gratitude for her interest in him and his career, the affection that he hoped he was correct in thinking had grown between them. He was sorrier than he could ever say that things had not worked out as he would have liked. He had always envisaged himself making this speech, when he was a partner in a business and the owner of a small property on the quarry road.

He spoke a lot of the time with his head hanging, and addressed many of his remarks to Mrs. Healy's knees. She looked at his dead-looking hair, which would be perfectly all right if he used a good shampoo and went to a proper barber. When he looked up at her anxiously, his pale face working with the anxiety of his proposal, she smiled at him encouragingly.

"Yes, Sean?"

"Will you accept my proposal of matrimony?" he said.

"I shall be happy to accept," said Dorothy Healy.

She saw some color flood into his face and join the look of disbelief.

He reached out and touched her hand.

He didn't realize that he was a far likelier prospect now than he had been before.

Mrs. Healy wanted no refurbished cottage up on a path by the quarry.

She wanted no connections with a dying clothing business across the road. She needed a man who could manage the heavy and duller side of the hotel for her. And she knew that since Sean Walsh must have been thrown out because he was found with his hand in the till across the road that he would have to be careful in his new employ.

She had him where she wanted him now.

"I don't know what to say," he said.

But as the afternoon became evening they found a lot to say. Plans were made, big plans and little plans. A jeweler in Ballylee would be visited for a ring. Father Ross would be consulted about a date. Sean would visit Dublin and buy three suits off the peg since he was a stock size. Sean would be declared the manager as of Monday. He would live in the new building which had been erected at the back. Sean hadn't been aware of its purpose. He had thought it some kind of storehouse. Together they looked at it. It had all the makings of a fine family house.

As if Mrs. Healy had known that this would happen one day.

Paddy Hickey was a fine dancer. And he said Kit was light as a feather.

"It was the hand of God that directed my son to your house," he said.

"That and the notice I have up in the University," Kit replied.

"Will you come down to Kerry with me?" he asked.

She looked at his big square handsome face. He was an honorable man, who wouldn't run away from her.

"I might, one day, go down and see the place you're from," she said.

He had told her that his family was reared. That Kevin was the youngest lad. That his place was grand and modern, the kitchen had the best Formica in it, and you could eat your dinner off the tiled floor.

He said he had nice neighbors and relatives who knew all about Mrs. Hegarty the widow in Dublin who had given such a home to Kevin.

"I'm only a recent widow," Kit said.

"Well, I didn't know that, until you told me, and they need never know it, and I suppose Joe Hegarty would be pleased to know that someone was looking after you."

"I never called him Joe, in all the years. I never called him that," she said almost wonderingly.

"Maybe that was part of it all," said Kevin Hickey's father, who had every intention of making this woman his wife.

The mournful sound of the foghorn boomed around Dun Laoghaire Harbor. Eve was so used to it now that she hardly heard it anymore.

But she stirred and looked at her clock with the luminous hands. It was half-past three.

She listened. Benny didn't seem to be breathing the way a sleeping person does. She must be lying there awake.

"Benny?"

"It's all right. Go back to sleep."

Eve turned on the light. Benny was propped up against her pillows in the small camp bed. Her face was tear-stained.

Eve swung her legs out of the bed and reached for her cigarettes.

"It's just that I love him so much," wept Benny.

"I know, I know."

"And he must have gone off me. Just like that."

"It's a misunderstanding. For God's sake, if he was going with anyone else we'd know."

"Would we?"

"Of course we would. You should have rung earlier. You'd have saved yourself all this. You'd be out somewhere in a steamy car trying to keep your clothes on you."

"Maybe I kept them on me too much."

"Stop blaming yourself. You always think it's your fault."

"Would you tell me if you know? Really and truly would you tell me? You'd not keep it from me to be kind?"

"I swear I'd tell you," Eve said. "I swear I'd not let you be made a fool of."

The party was great. Carmel was in the kitchen most of the time and so didn't see the way Jack Foley and Nan Mahon danced together. And how they found everything funny, and hardly talked to anyone else.

Carmel was busy washing plates when Jack Foley got Nan's coat and took her home.

"I'm honored to be allowed to take you home. Bill Dunne and the boys say you never tell them where you live."

"Maybe I don't want *them* to know," Nan said.

They sat outside the door of Maple Gardens and talked. The light of the streetlamp on Nan's face made her look very beautiful. Jack leaned across and kissed her.

She didn't move away when he bent over to kiss her. Instead she clung to him eagerly.

It was very easy to kiss and hold Nan Mahon. She didn't move away and pull back just as you were feeling aroused. He stroked her breast through the lilac silky dress she wore under her coat.

His voice was husky. There was no other sensation outside this car.

When she did pull away she spoke to him, cool and unruffled and different to the woman he had held in his arms, pliant, eager and wrapping herself close to him.

"Jack, don't you think we should talk about Benny?"

"Nope."

"Why not?"

"She's not here." He realized that it sounded too harsh, too dismissive. "What I mean is that anything between Benny and me has nothing to do with this." He reached for her again.

She leaned over and kissed him on the nose.

"Good night, Jack," she said, and vanished. He saw her let herself into the house and the door close behind her.

It was the same ritual of hanging up the clothes, sponging them and brushing them.

Cleaning her face with cream and doing her stretching exercises. Though she might have to change those exercises. Nan lay in her bed and thought about the events of the day. She laid her two hands on her stomach where a lab report had proved what she knew already. That a child was beginning to grow. She did not think about Simon Westward. She would never think about him again, no matter what happened.

She lay in the bedroom that she and her mother had decorated over the years, the years when they had told each other Nan was like a princess, and that she would leave Maple Gardens and find a prince.

Her first attempt had not been very successful.

Nan stared ahead of her unseeingly and thought out the options.

She did not want to go to this person and have something that was less important than tooth extraction. She did not want the sordidity of it, the shabby end of something that had been important. She didn't think it was a speck, as Simon had said. But she didn't believe it was a baby either.

If it were done, then it would all be over, the slate would be clean, she could continue with her studies.

She looked over at her desk. She didn't enjoy them. They took up too much time. They ate into the hours she should have been grooming herself, and preparing for the places to go. She found no great joy sitting in those large musty chalk-smelling halls, or the cramped tutorial rooms. She wasn't academic. Her tutor had told her more than once that she would not make the honors group. What was the point of struggling on doing a pass degree while the kudos was on the honors students?

She could go to England and have the child. She could have it adopted. Take less than a year out of her life. But why have a child to give it away. Go through all that just to make some anonymous couple's dream come true?

If she lived in a remote country village in the west of Ireland, the community might have excused a beautiful girl falling for the Squire and bringing up his child, ashamed but still accepted.

In parts of working-class Dublin, an unexpected child would have been welcomed in the family. The child would grow up believing its granny was its mother.

But not in Maple Gardens. It was the beginnings of respectability for the Mahons and their neighbors. And for Nan and Em it would be the end of the dream.

It looked as if a lot of the options weren't really options after all.

It was too early for morning sickness. But she didn't take any breakfast.

Em looked at her anxiously.

478

"You'll be seeing Simon this evening, is that right?" she asked, hoping to see Nan's face light up.

But she was disappointed.

"I haven't seen Simon for weeks and weeks, Em."

"But I thought you said . . ."

"I'm saying now, and I want you to remember it, I haven't been going out with Simon Westward since just after Christmas."

Emily Mahon looked at her daughter astonished.

But there was something about the set of Nan's jaw that made it seem very important.

Emily nodded, as if she had taken the instruction to heart. It didn't make it any easier to understand. Either Nan had been lying when she told her of the outings to smart places with Simon, or else she was lying now.

Jack came into the Annexe. Benny waved eagerly from a table. She had been holding a chair against all comers, by draping her scarf and her books all over it.

She looked so glad to see him and a lurch of guilt shook him.

Nobody had reported his long hours dancing with Nan to her anyway, he was slightly afraid that Carmel might have seen it as her duty to make sure that Benny was informed.

But Benny's eyes were shining with pleasure to see him.

"How was the party?"

"Oh, you know, these things are always the same. Everyone was fine, very cheerful." There had been two wins to celebrate, some fine playing and thanks to Sean they were in funds. He told her all those details and little about the night itself.

"It was a pity you couldn't have been in Dublin."

"But I was. Remember I said it would be early closing day and Mother was going to have a rest and an early night."

"I'd forgotten," Jack admitted.

There was a pause.

"And of course you didn't know about the party."

"Well, I did, because I ran into Carmel when she was shopping for it. And she told me."

She looked unsure. He felt a heel, not just for holding Nan so close last night, but because Benny had thought he mightn't have asked her.

"I'd have loved you to have been there. I just forgot. Honestly, I'm so used to your not being there. What did you do?"

"I went to the pictures with Eve."

"You should have rung me."

"I did, but it was too late."

Jack hadn't even looked at the message pad this morning. His mother would have written the names of anyone who called.

"Ah, Benny, I'm very sorry. I'm stupid." He banged his head as if it were wood.

He seemed very sorry.

"Well, no harm done," she said.

"I ran into Nan. And since she wasn't doing anything I asked her to come instead. I think she quite enjoyed it."

Benny's smile was broad. Everything was all right. He had genuinely forgotten. He wasn't trying to tell her anything. He wasn't wriggling out. He would have loved her to have been with him last night.

Thank God he had met Nan and invited her.

Now she had nothing to worry about.

EIGHTEEN

*J*ack woke suddenly with his heart pounding. He was in the middle of a very violent dream. It was so real it was hard to shake it off. Benny's father, Mr. Hogan, was standing at the top of the quarry pushing the black Morris Minor belonging to Dr. Foley over the edge.

Mr. Hogan had red burning coals where his eyes should be, laughing while the car bounced to the bottom of the quarry with a crash.

It was the crash that had jerked Jack awake.

He lay there, panting.

Beside him lay Nan, sleeping innocently, her hands folded under her face, a little smile on her lips.

They lay in Eve's cottage, the place he had come for a party just after Christmas.

They had needed somewhere to go, Nan said. This was a perfectly safe place. Nobody ever passed by. The key was in the stone wall.

Nan had been wonderful. So cool and practical, saying they must bring a spirit lamp and perhaps their own sheets and towels.

Jack would never have thought of that. She said they should keep the curtains very tightly drawn and leave the car hidden in the square lest anyone see it. There was a place behind the bus shelter where nobody would think to look.

She was naturally observant.

She had said that she never thought it was possible that she could desire someone so much.

He had been worried about everything, of course, but she said that it would be all right. The alternative was just to go on being a tease. She wanted to love him completely and honestly. It had been so wonderful, compared to that girl in Wales, which had all been just rushed and quick and awkward. Nan's beautiful body was magical in his arms. She seemed to love everything as much as he did.

It must have been awful for her the first time, but she had made no complaint. What excited him most was her calm exterior when they met in College. The cool Nan Mahon looking fresh and immaculate was the same girl who wrapped herself around him and gave him an ecstasy that he had not known could exist.

This was their third visit to the cottage.

He had still not spoken to Benny.

It was just that he didn't know what to say.

There was going to be an Easter pageant at the school. Heather wanted to take part.

"We told your brother that you wouldn't be involved in religious instruction," Mother Francis explained.

"But this isn't religion. It's drama. It's only a play," Heather pleaded.

It had been an exercise in spirituality intended to give the children some feeling of the message of Easter by reenacting the Passion of Our Lord. Mother Francis sighed.

"Well, who'll explain it to your brother. Will you, or will I?"

"I don't think we'll bother him about it. He's like a weasel. Could I be Hitler, please, Mother, please!"

"Could you be *who*?"

"Um . . . Pontius Pilate. I got confused . . ."

"We'll have to see. But first I will have to discuss it with Mr. Westward."

"It's too late," said Heather triumphantly. "He's gone to England today. To Hampshire. To look for a wife."

Mossy Rooney cleared out the back of Hogan's shop, and made the derelict yard look as if it had always intended to be a garden. Benny and her mother decided they must put flowers and even shrubs in it.

Mossy said that they could even have a bit of a garden seat. The place was nice and sheltered.

Patsy had told him that if the mistress had an ounce of sense she'd sell Lisbeg and move into the shop good and proper.

There was plenty of room in it, and what did she want to be rattling around like a tin can in a big empty house?

If they were in the shop it would be easier for Patsy to come and do a bit of daily work. It wouldn't be as heavy and constant as looking after a big house where nobody lived. Annabel Hogan had not admitted it to herself yet, but as she stood beside Benny watering in the fuchsias they had taken at Eve's request from the cottage, she began to think that it might be the wisest course.

In a way it would be nice just to walk upstairs and be home. Or be able to stretch out your feet on the sofa.

But time enough to think of that later. There was more than enough to sort out already.

Benny had been careful not to make the first floor, the lumber room where they had found the money in the sewing machine, a place they didn't visit. Bit by bit she managed to get rid of what had to go. Very gradually she started to ferry things up from Lisbeg. Little by little she and Patsy were transforming that big room into a place where it would be quite possible to sit and spend an evening. They took a wireless, some chairs that did not have the springs protruding. They polished a shabby old table and put place mats on it. Soon they were having their meals up here. Shep spent more time nosing around the lane, prowling the small garden which he regarded as his own exercise yard, and sitting proprietorially in the shop, than he did lording it over an empty Lisbeg.

Soon the shop was beginning to feel like home.

Soon Benny would be able to feel more free.

Dekko Moore asked Dr. Johnson was there a chance that Mrs. Hogan might part with Lisbeg.

Very often customers came in to him, people from big places, loaded down with money, and they often inquired were there any houses of a certain style going to come up on the market.

"Give them a few months, yet," Dr. Johnson said.

"I imagine they'll be moved up above by the end of the summer, but you wouldn't want to rush them."

Dekko said it was extraordinary the way things had gone already. He had gone into the shop to buy a pair of socks the other day, and he had spent a fortune.

Nan and Jack ran down the path from the quarry walk to the square. The Morris Minor was hidden behind the bus shelter. For the third time they were lucky nobody was about. It was only six-thirty in the morning. The car started and they were on the road to Dublin.

"One morning it won't start. And then we're for it," Jack said, squeezing her hand.

"We're very careful. We won't be caught," she said. She looked out of the window as they sped past the fields and farms on their way to Dublin.

He sighed, thinking of the nights and early mornings they had spent in Eve Malone's small bed.

But a part of him felt almost sick at the risk they were taking. Eve would kill them if she knew they were using her house like this. Knockglen was a village. Someone must see them sooner or later.

Knockglen was much more than a village. It was Benny's hometown.

Benny.

He tried to put her out of his mind. He had managed to see her only with other people for the last two weeks, since this amazing explosive thing with Nan had begun. He didn't think that Benny noticed. He made sure that Bill or Aidan or Johnny were there, or else he called over people to join them.

They never went to the pictures alone; on the hard-fought nights that Benny was able to stay in Dublin he made sure they went out in a group. He tried not to include Nan with them, though sometimes Benny brought her along.

Nan told him that she accepted exactly what he said, that whatever happened between them had nothing to do with Jack and Benny. They were two different worlds.

Yes, he had said that in the heat of the moment, but when he saw Benny's trusting face, and laughed at her funny remarks . . . when she turned out on a cold afternoon to watch him at a practice match, when she offered to help Carmel with the sandwiches, when he realized that he actually wanted to be with her alone and to touch her the way he touched Nan, then he felt confused.

It was easy to say that your world was compartmentalized. But in real life it wasn't easy.

Nan must be much more mature than all of them if she could accept that what Jack felt for her was a huge and almost overpowering passion. It had everything to do with desire and very little to do with sharing a life. They didn't talk much in the car, while with Benny they would both find the words stumbling over each other.

Jack felt a great sense of anxiety as the traffic began to build up a little on the road and they approached Dublin. Nan told him nothing of her home and family.

"How do they let you stay out all night?" he had asked.

"How do yours let you stay out all night?" she had replied.

The answer was simple. That he was a boy. Nothing terrible could happen to him, like getting pregnant.

But he didn't say it. He didn't dare to say it out of politeness, and out of superstition.

Nan watched fields turn into first factory premises and then housing estates. They would soon be home. She would ask him to leave her at the corner of Maple Gardens. As soon as his car had disappeared, Nan would go to the bus stop.

She would come into College early and get herself ready for lectures.

Not that her heart was in them. But she couldn't go home. Her father thought she was staying with Eve Malone in Dun Laoghaire, instead of sneaking into Eve's cottage in Knockglen.

It would confuse and worry her mother. Let Jack go home to his house with hot water and clean shirts, and a mildly perplexed mother and a maid putting bacon and egg on the table. He had nothing to worry about, a lover and a patient loving girl friend. From what you read in books it was what all men wanted.

Nan bit her lip as they drove along in silence. She would have to tell him very soon. She could see no other way out.

That night when she lay on her bed she examined the options. This was the only one that looked as if it might possibly work.

She was not going to think about Benny. Jack had said that was his business. It had nothing to do with what was between them. Nan didn't really believe that. But he had said that it was up to him to cope with. She had enough to worry about.

She could not confide in one single person because there was nobody alive who would condone what she was about to do. For the second time in a month she was going to have to tell a man that she was pregnant. And with the unfairness of life, the second one who had no duty or responsibility would probably be the one to do the right thing.

Mossy's mother said that May was nice for a wedding. Paccy Moore said they could have the reception in the room behind his shop. After all, his sister Bee was being the bridesmaid, and Patsy didn't have a home of her own.

It wasn't what Patsy had hoped. The guests coming through the cobbler's shop. But it was either that or let it be known she was coming in with nothing to her mother-in-law's house and have the gathering there.

What she would really have liked was to be able to use Lisbeg, and have the reception in the Hogans' house, but it didn't look likely. The master would only be four months gone. The mistress and Benny spent that much time above in the shop they would have little time and energy to spare for Patsy. She was getting a dress at Pine's. She had been paying for it slowly since Christmas.

Clodagh told Benny about Patsy's hopes. "It may be impossible, I'm not suggesting you do it, it's just that you'd hate to hear afterward and not have realized."

Benny was very grateful to be told. It was bad of them not to have thought of it in the first place. They had assumed that all the running would be made by Mossy's side and didn't even think of suggesting a venue.

Patsy's joy knew no bounds. It was one in the eye for Mossy's mother. She began to get the wedding invitations printed.

"And how's your own romance?" Clodagh inquired. "I believe he was down here the other night."

"God, I wish he had been. I *think* it's going all right. He's always coming looking for me and suggesting this and that, but there's a cast of thousands as well."

"Ah well, that's all to the good. He wants to show you to his friends. And he has friends. That lunatic across the road there has no friends except people who sell pinball machines and jukeboxes. I could have sworn I saw him at Dessie Burns' getting petrol."

"Who? Fonsie?"

"No, your fellow. Oh well, I suppose there's dozens of handsome blokes in college scarves getting petrol in Morris Minors."

✦

"It's not only Mr. Flood who's seeing visions," Benny said to Jack next day. "Clodagh thought she saw you getting petrol in Knockglen the other night."

"Would I have come to Knockglen and not gone to see you?" he asked.

It was a ridiculous question. It didn't even need an answer. She had only brought it up to show him that he was a person there, that he had an identity.

He breathed slowly through his teeth and remembered the shock that he and Nan had got when he realized the petrol gauge was showing empty. They had to fill up there and then. There would be nowhere open when they made their dawn escape.

Another very near miss. He wouldn't tell Nan about it. He hoped Benny wouldn't.

Sean Walsh was taking his early morning walk. These days he was accompanied by the two unattractive Jack Russell terriers with whom he would be sharing his home. They were less yappy and unpleasant if they were wearied by this harsh morning exercise.

He had ceased to look at the houses with the resentment and longing that he had once felt.

Things had turned out very much better than he would have dared to hope.

Dorothy was a woman in a million.

From Eve Malone's cottage he saw two figures emerge. The early sunlight was in his eyes and he couldn't see who they were.

They ran hand in hand, almost scampered down the path that led to the square. He squinted after them. They both looked vaguely familiar. Or perhaps he was imagining it. They must be Dublin people who had rented or borrowed the cottage.

But where were they going?

It was much too early for a bus. There had been no cars in the square.

It was a mystery, and that was something Sean Walsh didn't like at all.

Lilly Foley spoke to her husband about Jack.

"Three nights last week, and three again this week John. You'll have to say something."

"He's a grown man."

"He's twenty. That's not a grown man."

"Well, it's not a child. Leave him be. When he's passed over for a team, or fails an exam, *that's* the time to talk to him."

"But who could he be with? Is it the same girl, or a different one each time?"

"It's a fair distance on the old mileometer I notice, whoever it is." Jack's father laughed roguishly.

He had found a receipt for petrol from Knockglen. It must be that big girl Benny Hogan. Which was a turnup for the books, and where on earth did they go? Her father had died, but her mother was strict. Surely she wouldn't have been able to entertain Jack in her house?

Heather rang Eve. "When are you coming home? I miss you."

Eve felt absurdly flattered.

She said she'd come soon, next weekend or the weekend after.

"It doesn't have to be the weekend."

Eve realized that was true. It didn't.

She was free to leave any afternoon. She could travel on the bus with Benny. She'd have tea with Mother Francis and the nuns and then take Heather up to the cottage. She'd hear at first hand how the plans for the Easter pageant were going. She could go to see Benny's mother and admire the changes in Hogan's. She could call to Mario's to end the evening. Knockglen was full of excitement these days. She might go tomorrow, but she had better check it wasn't a night that Benny was coming to town. It would be silly to miss her.

Benny said they'd skip a lecture and meet on the three o'clock bus. That way they'd have a bit of time. They had sandwiches in the place that the boys liked. The pub with the relaxed view about the Holy Hour.

Aidan, Jack and Bill were there. Rosemary had called in to borrow ten shillings. She needed to have a hairdo in a very good place. Tom the medical student had been harder to pin down than she had hoped. It was time for heavy remedies now, like new hairstyles.

Nobody felt like work, but Eve and Benny refused the offer of being taken to play some slot machines in an amusement arcade.

"I'm getting the bus," said Benny.

"Good-bye Cinderella." Jack blew her a kiss. His eyes were very warm. She must have been mad to worry about him.

Benny and Eve left the pub.

Aidan said that he felt sure those two would be up all night and maybe bopping till dawn in Mario's.

"What?" Jack spilled some of his drink.

He hadn't realized that Eve was going back to her cottage. He had arranged to meet Nan on the quays at six o'clock. They had been planning to go to the very same place.

Nan Mahon walked briskly down toward the river. Her overnight bag contained the usual sheets, pillowcases, candlesticks, breakfast and supper materials. Jack just brought a Primus stove and something to drink.

But this time Nan had packed a bottle of wine as well. They might need it. Tonight was the night she was going to tell him.

Heather was overjoyed to see Eve. As she went through the school hall she called her over excitedly. There was a rehearsal in progress, and she was wearing a sheet. Heather Westward was playing Simon of Cyrene, the man who helped Jesus to carry his Cross.

It was something that Knockglen would not have believed possible a few short weeks ago.

"Are you coming to cheer me on when we do it for real?" Heather wanted to know.

"I don't think cheering you on is what Mother Francis had in mind . . ."

"But I'm one of the good people. I help him. I step forward and lighten his burden," Heather said.

"Yes. I'll certainly come and support you."

"You see, I won't have any relations here like everyone else has."

Eve promised that she would be there when the pageant was performed. She might even bring Aidan so that Heather would have two people. Eve Malone knew very well what it was like to be the only girl in the school who had nobody to turn up with a cake for the sale of work or with applause for the pageants and the plays. That had been her lot all during her years in St. Mary's.

She let Heather get back to rehearsal and said she'd see her later in the cottage. It was time to talk to Mother Francis.

Eve said she had to go down to Healy's Hotel to have a cup of coffee so that she could get a close up look at Love's Young Dream, Dorothy and Sean, Great Lovers of Our Time. Mother Francis said she wasn't to be making a jeer out of them. Everyone was being very restrained, and Eve must be the same.

Hadn't it turned out better than anyone dared to hope, Mother Francis said sternly, and Eve realized that she must have known or suspected something of the secret Benny had told her, the missing money and the terror of the confrontation.

But if she did, it would never be discussed.

Up in her own cottage, waiting for Heather to come pounding up the convent path, Eve looked around.

There was something different. Not just the way things were placed. Mother Francis came here often. She polished and she dusted. Sometimes she rearranged things. But this was different.

Eve couldn't think what it was. It was just a feeling that someone else had been there. Staying there, cooking even. Sleeping in her bed. She ran her hand across the range. Nobody had used it. Her bed was made with the neat corners she had learned at school.

Eve shivered. She was becoming fanciful. All those stories about the place being haunted must have got to her. But on a bright April evening this was ridiculous.

She shook herself firmly and started getting the fire going. Heather would need toast within minutes of her arrival.

Later, down in Healy's Hotel, Eve saw Sean. In his dark manager's suit.

"Might I be the first to congratulate you?" she said.

"That's uncommonly gracious of you, Eve."

Eve inquired politely about when they intended to marry. Was courteously interested in the expansionist plans for the hotel, the honeymoon that would include the Holy City and the Italian lakes, and inquired whether Mrs. Healy was around so that she could express her congratulations and pleasure personally.

"Dorothy is having a rest. She does that in the early evenings," Sean said, as if he were describing the habits of some long-extinct animal in a museum.

Eve stuffed her hand into her mouth to stop any sound coming out.

"I see you've decided to capitalize on your property," Sean said.

Eve looked at him blankly.

"Let your cottage out to people."

"No, I haven't," she said.

"Oh, I'm sorry."

She thought he was maneuvering the conversation around to a point where he would ask her to rent it to him or to let it to someone he knew.

A feeling of revulsion rose in her throat. She decided that this must be nipped in the bud. Sean Walsh must be left under no illusion that her home could be let to anyone, not to anyone for money.

"No, I'm sorry for speaking so sharply Sean. It's just that I never intend to. I'm keeping it for myself and my friends."

"Your friends. Yes," he said.

Suddenly he realized who he had seen coming out of Eve's cottage. It was that blond girl he had seen several times before, most recently getting off the Knockglen bus, on the quays in Dublin.

And the man. Of course he remembered who he was. He was Benny's boyfriend. The doctor's son.

So *that* little romance hadn't lasted long. And there had been precious little said about its being over.

He smiled a slow smile. There was something about it that made Eve feel very uneasy. That was twice this afternoon she had got goose bumps. She must be getting very jumpy. Aidan was right. Eve Malone was a deeply neurotic woman. She felt an overwhelming urge to be away from Sean Walsh and out of his presence.

She jumped up and started to hasten out of the hotel.

"You'll pass on my good wishes to Mrs. Healy." She tried to say Dorothy, but somehow the word wouldn't form in her mouth.

The traffic was bad on the quays. Jack saw Nan but he couldn't attract her attention. She was leaning against the wall, and looking down into the Liffey. She seemed many miles away.

Eventually by hooting and shouting he managed to make her hear him. She walked threading her way confidently between the parked cars in the traffic jam. He thought again how beautiful she was, and how hard it was to resist these nights with her. However, he would have to resist it tonight. His heart nearly stopped when he realized how near they had been to discovery. In future they would have to check and double-check that Eve was not going home mid-week.

It was terrifying enough that time they had seen the man with the dogs, the tall thin fellow that Benny hated so much, the one there had been all the fuss over about getting him to leave.

Nan slipped into the car easily and laid her overnight bag on the backseat.

"Change of plan," he said. "Let's have a drink and discuss it."

It was always something that made Benny smile, that phrase. Nan didn't know it.

"Why?"

"Because we can't go down there. Eve's going home."

"Damn!" She seemed very annoyed.

"Isn't it lucky we discovered." He wanted to be congratulated on the amazing accident that made Aidan reveal this to him.

"Isn't it unlucky that she chose tonight of all nights to go down there."

Jack noticed that Nan never referred to Eve by name.

"Well, it *is* her house," he said with a little laugh.

Nan didn't seem amused.

"I really wanted to be there tonight," she said. Even frowning she looked beautiful.

Then her face cleared. She suggested this lovely hotel in Wicklow. It was absolutely marvelous. Very quiet and people didn't disturb you. It was exactly where they could go.

Jack knew the name. It was a place where his parents had dinner sometimes. It was much too expensive. He wouldn't be able to afford it and he told her so.

"Do you have a checkbook?"

"Yes, but not enough money in the bank."

"We'll get the money tomorrow. Or I will. Let's go there."

"And stay the night. Nan we're not married. We can't." He looked alarmed.

"They don't ask for your wedding certificate."

He looked at her. She changed her voice slightly.

"I've heard of people who've been there, and stayed the night. There was no problem."

As they drove out south past Dun Laoghaire they saw the house where Eve lived with Kit Hegarty.

"Why on earth can't she be there tonight," Nan said.

Jack thought it would certainly be a lot cheaper for everyone if she were.

He dreaded the thought of writing a check that bounced in this hotel, and having to face his mother and father when it all came out.

He wished that Nan could just have faced the fact that this was one night they would have to put off. Benny would have been most agreeable and understanding.

He wished he didn't keep thinking of Benny at times like this. It was as hypocritical as hell.

Benny and Eve met in the square next morning. They sat in the shelter and waited for Mikey to arrive with the bus.

"Why do we call this a square?" Eve asked. "It's only a bit of waste ground really."

"That's until the young tigers get their hands on it. It might be a skating rink next week," Benny laughed.

It was true that Clodagh and Fonsie were tireless in their efforts to change Knockglen. They had even frightened other people into improving their businesses.

Fonsie had gone to Flood's and said that if ever he owned a fine frontage like that he'd have the lettering repainted in gold. Mr. Flood, terrified that somehow it would be taken from him unless he lived up to this young man's expectations, had the signwriters in next day. Clodagh had stood in Mrs. Carroll's untidy grocery and chatted about the food inspectors who were closing shops down all over the place. It was amazing what a coat of paint and a spring clean did to fool them. All the time she pretended she was talking in the abstract. But she could have told Mossy Rooney that he would be called in next day, as indeed he was.

Clodagh told Mossy to put up a fitting for an awning without being asked. Dessie Burns was now stocking various colors of big canvas blinds. Clodagh and Fonsie were going to have their town looking like a rainbow before they finished.

"I suppose they'll get married," Eve said.

"Clodagh says never. There's too many nuptials coming up, she says we'll be sick of weddings. Mrs. Healy and Mr. Walsh, Patsy and Mossy, and Maire Carroll home from Dublin with a fiancé already I gather, unlike the two of us who were very slow off the mark."

They were giggling as usual when they got on the bus. Nothing had changed since they were schoolgirls.

Rosemary was full of smiles. The hairdo had been highly successful, she said. Benny had lent her three shillings. It was counted meticulously back to her. Tom had been very impressed.

"It looks a bit flattened," Benny said, examining the hairdo.

"Yes, I know," Rosemary said delightedly. "I owe Jack a shilling. Will you give it to him for me."

Benny said she would. She'd be seeing him in the Annexe anyway.

Sean and Carmel had a table. Benny joined them with Jack's shilling clutched in her hand so that she wouldn't forget to give it to him.

"Jack was looking for you everywhere this morning," Sean said. Benny was pleased.

"He went and stood outside a Latin lecture, he thought it was yours, but it was Baby Latin."

"Oh, I'm not Baby Latin," Benny said proudly. She was just one step above it. Everyone in First Arts had to do some kind of Latin in their first year. Mother Francis would have killed her if she had gone into the easy option.

Bill Dunne joined them.

"Jack said if I saw you, to say that he'll meet you at one o'clock in the Main Hall," Bill said. "Though if you want my personal opinion you wouldn't touch him with a barge pole. He hasn't shaved. He's like a bear with a sore head. He's not worthy of you."

Benny laughed. It made her feel as high as a kite when Bill Dunne said things like this in front of everyone. It confirmed somehow that she was Jack's girl.

"He's not coming here now then." She had been looking at the door.

"Him come anywhere? I asked him about cars and all for the outing to Knockglen after Easter. He said not to talk to him about cars, outings or Knockglen or he'd knock my head off."

Benny knew that Bill was dramatizing it all, so that he could cast himself in the role of the beautifully mannered nice person and Jack the villain.

Since this was different to the way things were, everyone knew it was a joke. She smiled at Bill affectionately. She knew Jack was longing for the great weekend in Knockglen. It would be even better than Christmas.

Everyone had been planning for it for ages. Sean had been collecting money from people, a shilling now and a shilling then. The fund was building up.

There would be a gathering in Eve's, in Clodagh's, and very possibly something upstairs in Hogan's. The rooms were so big and with high ceilings they positively called out to have a party. Benny had been sounding her mother out. And the signs looked good.

She was pleased that Jack was looking for her.

For the past few weeks he had never wanted to see her on her own.

Benny hoped that he might want them to go off to lunch together, like that time ages ago when they had gone to Carlo's.

Maybe she should take *him* there for a treat. But she'd wait and see his mood. She didn't want to be too pushy.

Bill was right. He *did* look very bad. Pale and tired as if he hadn't slept all night. He still looked just as handsome, maybe even more so. There was less of the conventional College Hero and more of the lead player in some film or theatre piece.

Yes, Jack Foley looked as if he were in a play.

And he spoke as if he were in one too.

"Benny, I have to talk to you. Where can we go that's away from all these people?"

She laughed at him good-naturedly.

"Hey, you were the one who said the Main Hall at one o'clock. I didn't choose it. Did you think it would be deserted and just the two of us?"

The crowds swarmed past them in and out, and just standing around in groups talking, duffel coats over arms now, scarves loosely hanging. The weather was getting too warm for them, but they were the badge of being a student. People didn't want to discard them entirely.

"Please," he said.

"Well would you like to go to Carlo's, you know that lovely place we went . . ."

"*No.*" He almost shouted it.

Everywhere else would be full of people they knew. Even if they were to sit in Stephen's Green, half the University would pass by on its way to stroll down Grafton Street at lunchtime.

Benny was at a loss, and yet she knew she had to make the decision.

Jack looked all in.

"We could sit by the canal," she suggested. "We could get apples for us and some stale bread in case we see the swans."

She looked eager and anxious to please him.

It seemed to distress him still further.

"Oh, Jesus, Benny," he said, and pulled her toward him. A flicker of fear came and went. She felt something was wrong, but then she was always feeling that and it never was.

There was a place near one of the locks where they often sat. There was a bit of raised ground.

Benny took off her coat and laid it down for them to sit on.

"No, no we'll ruin it."

"It's only clay. It'll brush off. You're as bad as Nan," she teased him.

"It's Nan," he said.

"What is?"

"She's pregnant. She found out yesterday."

Benny felt a jolt of shock for her friend. At the same time she felt the sense of surprise that Nan of all people had been going all the way with Simon Westward. Nan. So cool and distant. How had she made love properly? Benny would have thought that she would have been the last person on earth to have found herself in this position.

"Poor Nan," she said. "Is she very upset?"

"She's out of her mind with worry," he said.

They sat in silence.

Benny went over the whole awfulness of it in her mind. A university career in ruins, a baby by the age of twenty. And possibly from the look of sympathy on Jack's face a problem about Simon Westward.

Eve would have been right about him.

He would never marry Nan Mahon from the north side of Dublin, a builder's daughter. And beautiful though she was, the fact that she had given in to him would make him less respectful of her than ever.

"What's she going to do? I suppose she's not going to get married?"

She looked at Jack.

His face was working with emotion. He seemed to be struggling for words.

"She *is* getting married."

Benny looked at him alarmed. This wasn't normal speech.

He took her hand, and held it to his face. There were tears on his face. Jack Foley was crying.

"She's getting married . . . to me," he said.

She looked at him in disbelief.

She said absolutely nothing. She knew her mouth was open and her face red with fright.

He was still holding her hand to his face.

His body was shaking with sobs.

"We have to get married, Benny," he said. "It's my baby."

NINETEEN

*E*ve was in the Singing Kettle when she saw Benny at the door. At first she thought that Benny was going to join them and was about to pull up another chair.

Then she saw her face.

"See you later," she said hastily to the group.

"You haven't finished your chips." Aidan was amazed. Nothing could be that pressing.

But Eve was out in Leeson Street.

She drew Benny away from the doorway where they were in the main path of almost everyone they knew.

Then, leaning against the iron railings of a house, Benny began to tell her the tale. Sometimes it was hard to hear the words, and sometimes she said the same words over, and over and over again.

Like that he said he loved her, he loved Benny. He really did and he wouldn't have had this happen for the world. But there was nothing else that could be done. The announcement would be in *The Irish Times* on Saturday.

Eve looked across the road and saw a taxi letting someone off at St. Vincent's Private Nursing Home. She dragged Benny through the traffic and pushed her into the back of it.

"Dun Laoghaire," she said briskly.

"Are you girls all right?" The taxi driver watched them in the mirror. The big girl look particularly poorly, as if she might get sick all over his car.

"We have the fare," Eve said.

"I didn't mean that," he began.

"You did a bit." They both grinned.

Eve said to Benny that she should rest. There'd be plenty of time to talk when they got home.

Kit was out. She was shopping for a new outfit for Easter when she was going to Kerry as a guest of Kevin Hickey and his father.

They had the kitchen to themselves. Benny sat at the table and through a blur saw Eve prepare a meal for them. She noticed her small thin hands cut deftly through the cold cooked potaoes and trim the rinds from rashers of bacon. She saw thin fingers of bread dipped in a beaten egg.

"I don't want any of this," Benny said.

"No, but I do. I left my whole lunch in the Kettle, remember?"

Eve took a bottle of sherry from inside a cornflake packet.

"It's to hide it from the drinky students," she explained.

"I'm not having any."

"Medicinal," Eve said, and poured out two huge tumblers for them as she placed the big white plates of comfort food in front of them.

"Now start at the very beginning and tell me slowly. Start from when you sat down on the coat by the canal, and don't tell me that he loves you or I'll get up and throw every single thing that's on this table on the floor and you'll have to clear it up."

"Eve, please. I know you mean to help."

"Oh, I mean to help all right," said Eve. Benny had never seen her face looking so grim. Not in all that long war she had waged with the Westwards, not in the fight with Mother Clare or in her hospital bed had she seen Eve Malone's face so hard and unforgiving.

They talked until the shadows got longer. Benny heard Kit let herself in. She looked around at the untidy kitchen and the half-finished sherry bottle.

"It's all right," Eve said gently, "she'll understand. I'll do a quick clear-up."

"I should be going for my bus."

"You're staying here. Ring your mother. And Benny . . . she'll ask are you seeing Jack. Tell her you don't see Jack anymore. Prepare her for it being over."

"It needn't be over. He doesn't want it to be over. He says that we have to talk."

Kit came to the door and looked around her in surprise. Before she could make any protest Eve spoke.

"Benny's had a bit of a shock. We're coping with it the best we can, by eating most of tomorrow's breakfast. I'll go up to the huckster's shop and replace it later."

Kit knew a crisis when she saw one.

"I have to hang up my finery. See you in half an hour to prepare supper. That's if there's any of that left?"

She nodded encouragingly and disappeared.

Annabel Hogan said that was fine. She had a lot of work to do in the shop. It would save them making a supper. She and Patsy would just get something from Mario's. Benny thought bitterly of all the nights she had left Jack Foley to his own devices in Dublin while she had trundled wearily home to keep her mother company. Now she was less in the way staying in Dublin.

"Are you going out with Jack?" Mother asked.

Despite Eve's warning, Benny couldn't do it. She couldn't tell her mother that it was over. Even to say it meant it might be true.

"Not tonight," she said brightly. "No, tonight I'm just going out with Eve."

Benny lay on Eve's bed and bathed her eyes with cold water while Eve served the supper downstairs. The curtains were drawn and she could hear the clatter of plates and cutlery below. Kit had looked in briefly with a cup of tea. She had made no attempt to cheer her or sympathize. Benny could see why she must be such a restful person to live with.

She dreaded the bucketfuls of sympathy that Mother would pour on her, the endless wondering, and speculating and ludicrous little suggestions. Maybe if you wore paler colors or darker colors, perhaps if you went round to his house to talk to his mother. Men like girls who get on well with their mothers.

She wouldn't tell Mother that Nan was pregnant. It demeaned them all somehow.

It put everything on a different level.

They walked, Benny and Eve, for what seemed and felt like hours and miles.

Sometimes they argued, sometimes Benny stopped to cry again. To say that Eve wouldn't be so harsh if only she could have seen Jack's face, and Eve would tighten her lips and say nothing. As they walked up the Burma Road and into Killiney Park, Benny said that it was all her fault. She hadn't understood how a man needs to make love. It's a biological thing, and when they sat by the obelisk and looked down on the bay she said that Jack Foley was the most dishonest cheating man in the whole world, and why in God's name did he keep saying he loved her if he didn't.

"Because he did love you. Or thought he did," Eve said. "That's the whole bloody problem."

It cheered Benny that Eve could find some ray of hope and

sincerity in the whole thing. She thought that Eve had set her heart against him.

"I'm not against him," Eve said softly. "I'm only against the idea of your thinking that somehow you'll get him back."

"But if he still loves me . . ."

"He loves the idea of you, and hates hurting you. That's totally different."

Eve put her small hand over Benny's. She wished she had better words, softer ones. But she knew that Benny mustn't sleep a night in false hopes. She pointed out that there was very little hope in a situation where one party was explaining things to an unbelieving family in Donnybrook and another in Maple Gardens.

"Why didn't I sleep with him? Then we'd be explaining things tonight in Knockglen."

When it was dark and they got back to Dun Laoghaire, Eve said Benny should have a bath.

"I don't feel like going to bed."

"Who said anything about that? We're going out, on the town."

Benny looked at her friend as if she were mad. After these hours of listening and appearing to understand she must have had no realization of how Benny felt, if she suggested going out.

"I don't want to meet anyone now. I don't want to be taken out of myself."

Eve said that wasn't the object of the outing. They were going to go everywhere and meet everyone. They were going to talk about Jack and Nan before it became gossip, and long before it appeared as an engagement announcement in the papers. Eve said that it was the only thing that could be done now. Benny must be seen to hold her head high. She didn't want to live with the sympathy vote for the rest of her life. She didn't want to be written off as someone who was let down. Let nobody be the one to tell Benny the news. Let Benny be the one to tell it everywhere.

"What you are asking is ridiculous," Benny said. "Even if I

could do it, everyone would still see through me. They'd know I was upset."

"But they would never think you had been made a fool of," Eve said, eyes burning. "The one good thing about Jack that came out of all this is that he told you first. He told you before he told his mates and asked them for advice. He gave you the story before he gave it to his parents, to the chaplain. You must use that advantage."

"I don't like to . . . and I suppose I keep hoping that his parents won't let him."

"They will. When they hear the sound of shotguns coming from Nan's family and moral responsibility from the clergy. And he's a man of twenty. In a few months he won't even have had to ask them."

It was a shadowy night. She only remembered patches of it. Bill Dunne asking was it an April Fool? He couldn't believe that Jack was going to *marry* Nan Mahon. If he was going to marry anyone it should have been Benny. He said that three times in front of Benny.

Three times she answered brightly that she was far too busy becoming a tycoon in Knockglen and trying to get an honors B.A. to get married.

Carmel held her hand too tightly and too sympathetically. Benny wanted to snatch it away, but she knew Carmel meant well.

"It could be all for the best, and we'll still be seeing lots of you won't we?"

Sean said that he could be knocked over with a feather. And how was Jack going to manage as a married man, with all those years ahead of him? Perhaps he was going to give up his degree and go straight into his uncle's firm as an apprentice. And where were they going to live? The whole thing was startling in the extreme. Had Jack given any indication of what he was going to live on? And presumably a family was planned. Fairly imminently. Hence the haste. Had Jack given Benny any idea of what he was going to live on? Through clenched teeth Benny said that he hadn't.

Johnny O'Brien said he wondered where they'd done it. It gave the lie to the fact that you couldn't get pregnant in a Morris Minor.

When they lay exhausted in their beds in Dun Laoghaire, Benny said sarcastically that she hoped that Eve had found the evening worthwhile, and that it had served her purposes.

"Most certainly it has," Eve said cheerfully. "Firstly, you're so tired that you'd sleep standing up, and secondly you've nothing to dread going in tomorrow. They know you've survived the news. They've seen you surviving."

Aengus Foley had a toothache. He had been given whiskey on a piece of cotton wool. But not much sympathy and no attention. His mother's voice had been sharp as she asked him to go to bed, close the door and realize that pain had to be borne in this life. It wasn't permanent, it would go, probably at the precise moment they took him to Uncle Dermot the dentist.

They seemed to want to talk to Jack interminably in the sitting room. Twice he had come down to hear what it was all about, but the voices were low and urgent, and even the phrases that he could hear he couldn't understand.

John and Lilly Foley were both white with fury as they stood in their drawing room listening to their eldest son describe how he had ruined his life.

"How could you have been so stupid?" his father said over and over again.

"You can't possibly be a father, Jack, you're only a child yourself," said his mother with tears coming down her face. They begged, they pleaded, they cajoled. They would visit Nan's parents, they would explain about his career. How it couldn't be ruined before it had begun.

"What about her career? That has been ruined no matter what happens." Jack's voice was flat.

"Do you want to marry her?" his father asked, exasperated.

"I don't want to marry her now, in three weeks time, obviously I don't. But she's a wonderful girl. We made love. I was the one who wanted to, and now we have no other option."

The pleas began again. She might like to go to England, and give the child for adoption. A lot of people did that.

"It is my child. I'm not going to give it to strangers."

"Forgive me Jack, but do we know that it is your child? I have to ask you this."

"No, you don't have to ask me, but I'll answer you. Yes, I'm absolutely certain that it's my child. She was a virgin the first night I slept with her."

Jack's mother looked away in disgust.

"And are we also absolutely sure that she *is* pregnant? It's not just a false alarm? A frightened young girl. These things can happen, believe me."

"I'm sure they can, but not this time. She showed me the report from Holles Street. The lab test was positive."

"I don't think you should marry her. Truly I don't. She's not even someone you've been going out with for a long time. Someone you've known, that we've all known, for years."

"I met her on the first day in College. She's been in this house."

"I'm not saying that she's not a very lovely girl . . ." Jack's father shook his head. "You're shocked now and frightened. Leave it. Leave it for a few weeks."

"No, it's not fair on her. If we leave it, she'll think I'm going to change my mind. That I'll be persuaded to . . ."

"And what do her parents think of all this mess . . . ?"

"She's telling them tonight."

❦

Brian Mahon was sober. He sat at his kitchen table wordless as Nan in an even tone explained to her father, mother and two brothers that she would be getting married to Jack Foley, a law student, in three weeks time.

She saw her mother twist her hands and bite her lip. Em's dream lay broken into a thousand pieces.

"You'll do nothing of the sort," Brian Mahon roared.

"I think it would be better for everyone if I did."

"If you think . . . I'm going to let you . . ." he began, but stopped. It was all bluster anyway. The damage had been done.

Nan sat looking at him cool and unflustered, as if she were telling him that she was going to the cinema.

"I suppose you knew all about this." He looked at his wife.

"I deliberately didn't tell Em, so that you couldn't accuse her of covering things up," Nan said.

"And by God there's plenty to cover. He's put you up the pole I suppose."

"Brian!" Emily cried.

"Well, if he has, he'll pay, he'll pay good and proper, for whatever we decide to do." He looked foolish as he sat there angry and red-faced, trying to be the big man in a situation over which he had no control.

"You'll decide nothing," Nan said to him coldly. "I decide. And our engagement will be in *The Irish Times* on Saturday morning."

"Janey Mac, *The Irish Times*," Nasey said. It was the poshest of the three papers, not often seen in the Mahon household.

"While you're living in my house . . . I tell you that I make decisions."

"Well, that's just it. I won't be living here much longer."

"Nan, are you sure that this is what you want to do?"

Nan looked at her mother, faded and frightened. Always living her life in the shadow of someone else, a loud drunken husband, a mean-spirited employer at the hotel, a beautiful daughter whose fantasies she had built up.

Emily would never change.

"It is, Em. And it's what I'm going to do."

"But University . . . your degree."

"I never wanted one. You know that. We both know that. I was only going there to meet people."

They talked, mother and daughter, as if the men didn't exist. They spoke to each other across the kitchen, across the broken dream, without any of the accusations or excuses that would be the conversation of most girls in this situation.

"But it wasn't a student you were going to meet. Not this way."

"The other didn't work, Em. The gap was too wide."

"And what do you expect us to do, coming home with this kind of news . . ." Brian wanted to put a stop to the conversation that he didn't even understand.

"I want to ask you a question. Are you prepared to put on a good suit and behave well for four hours at a wedding, without a drink in your hand, or are you not?"

"And if I'm not?"

"If I even *think* you're not, we'll go to Rome and get married there. I will tell everyone that my father wouldn't have a wedding for us."

"Go on, do that then," he taunted her.

"I will if I have to. But I know you, you'd like to blow and blow and boast to your pals and the people you sell supplies to that your daughter's having a big society wedding. You'd like to hire the clothes, because you're still a handsome man and you know it."

Emily Mahon looked at her daughter in amazement. Unerringly she had gone for the right targets. She knew exactly how to make her father give her a wedding.

Brian would think of nothing else. No expense would be spared.

❦

"Go home with her for the weekend," Kit urged Eve.

"No, she has to do it on her own."

Knockglen was quick to judge, and it was important who began to spread the story. If Benny was there saying to people that her romance with Jack Foley was a thing of the past, then no serious whispers could begin. Benny was going to have to live with enough this summer without having to live with the pity of Knockglen as well. Eve was an expert on avoiding the pity of Knockglen.

Mother was still in the shop. It was after seven, and Benny had only looked in automatically and seen her there. Benny let herself in with the key she carried on her key ring.

"Glory be to God, you put the heart across me."

Annabel Hogan was standing on a chair trying to reach something that had slid away on the top of a cupboard. Annabel was hoping that it was some nice rolls of paper with the name Hogan's on it. Eddie had bought it years ago, but it had proved impractical to cut. It hadn't been thrown out. It might be up here covered with dust.

Benny looked up at her animated face. Perhaps when people were older they did recover from things. It was impossible to believe that this was the same listless woman who had sat by the fire with the book falling from her hand. Now she was lively and occupied, her eyes were bright and her tone had light and shade.

Benny said she was bigger, she'd reach. And true there it were rolls of it. They threw it down on the floor. Tomorrow they would dust it, see if it was usable.

"You look tired. Was it a busy day?" Mother asked. It had been a day of heartache to walk the corridors and sit in lectures while the rumor about Jack and Nan spread like a forest fire. Sheila actually came and offered her sympathy as one would for a bereavement. Several groups had stopped speaking as Benny approached.

But Eve had been right. Better let the other story spread, too, the news that Benny was not wearing mourning. That she had been able to talk about it cheerfully. There had been no sign of either Nan or Jack in College. Benny kept thinking that Jack was going to appear by magic all smiles, tucking his arm into hers, and that the whole thing would have been a bad dream.

Mother knew none of this, of course. But she did realize that Benny looked worn out.

She thought she knew just what would cheer her up.

"Come up and look at what Patsy and I were doing today. We've pulled around a lot of the furniture on the first floor. We thought it would be grand for your party before we get the place painted. Then you could make as much mess as you liked without having to worry about it . . . you could even have some of the boys stay here and the girls stay at Lisbeg . . ."

Benny's face was stony. She had forgotten the party. The great gathering planned for the weekend after Easter. She and Jack had talked of little else as they sat with their groups of friends over the last weeks. And all the time, every night possibly, he was saying good-bye to her and making love with Nan.

She gave a little shudder at how she had been deceived, and how he had said with his eyes full of tears that he couldn't help himself, and he was sorrier than he could ever say. She walked wordlessly up the stairs behind her mother and listened to the animated conversation about the party that would never be.

Gradually, her mother, noticing no response, let her voice die away.

"They are still coming aren't they?" she said.

"I'm not sure. A lot of things will have changed by then." Benny swallowed. "Jack and Nan are going to get married," she said.

Her mother looked at her openmouthed.

"What did you say?"

"Jack. He's going to marry Nan you see. So things might change about the party."

"Jack Foley . . . your Jack?"

"He's not my Jack anymore. Hasn't been for some time."

"But when did this happen? You never said a word. They can't get married."

"They are, Mother. The engagement will be in tomorrow's *Irish Times*."

The look on her mother's face was almost too much to bear. The naked sympathy, the total incomprehension, the struggling for words.

Benny realized that Eve was probably right in this harsh face-saving exercise. Bad as it was now, it would be worse if she had said nothing and her mother had found out through someone else. Like today in College, it was over now, the shock and the pity and the whispering. They couldn't continue indefinitely if Benny seemed to be in the whole of her senses. What was very hard was this pretense that she and Jack had been just one more casual romance, with no hearts broken at the end of it.

"Benny, I'm so sorry. I can't tell you how sorry I am."

"That's all right, Mother. You were always the one to say that College romances come and go . . ." The words were fine, but the tone was shaky.

"I suppose she's . . ."

"She's very excited, certainly, and . . . and . . . everything."

If her mother said the wrong thing now she would lose the little control she still held on to. Please let Mother not embrace her or say something about the fickleness of men.

Being in business for a few weeks must have taught Annabel a great deal about life.

There were just a few headshakes at the modern generation, and then a suggestion that they go home for tea before Patsy sent a search party out to look for them.

After supper she called on Clodagh. She moved restlessly around, picking things up and putting them down again as they talked. Clodagh sat and stitched, watching her carefully.

"Are you pregnant?" Clodagh asked eventually.

"I'm not the one who is, unfortunately," Benny said. She told the tale. Clodagh never put down her needle. She nodded, and agreed, and disagreed and asked questions. At no time did she say that Jack Foley was a bastard, and that Nan Mahon was worse to betray her friend. She accepted it as one of the things that happen in life.

Benny grew stronger as she spoke. The prickling of her nose and eyes, the urge to weep, had faded a little.

"I still believe that it's me he loves," she said timidly at the end of the saga.

"It might well be." Clodagh was matter-of-fact. "But that's not important now. It's what people do is important, not what they say or feel."

She sounded so like Eve, so determined, so sure. In the most matter-of-fact way she said that Jack and Nan would probably make no better or no worse a fist of getting married and having a child than most people did. But that's what they would be. A couple with a child. And then another and another.

Whether Jack still loved Benny Hogan was irrelevant. He had made his choice. He had done what was called the decent thing.

"It was the right thing," Benny said, against her will.

Clodagh shrugged. It might have been, or it might not, but whatever it was it was the thing he had done.

"You'll survive, Benny," she said comfortingly. "And to give him his due, which I don't want to do at this moment, he wants you to survive. He wants the best for you. He thinks that's love."

Late that night at the kitchen table Patsy said that all men were pigs and that handsome men were out-and-out pigs. She said he had been well received and made welcome in this house, and that he was such a prize pig he didn't know a lady when he saw one. That Nan wasn't a lady for all her fine talk. He'd discover that when it was too late.

"I don't think it was a lady he wanted," Benny explained. "I think it was more a lover. And I wasn't any use to him there."

"Nor should you have been," Patsy said. "Isn't it bad enough that we're going to have to do it over and over when we're married, and have a roof over our heads. What's the point in letting them have it for nothing before."

It seemed to shed a gloomy light on the future that lay ahead for Patsy and Mossy. It was almost impossible to imagine other people having sex, but depressing to think that Patsy was dreading it so much.

Patsy poured them more drinking chocolate and said that she wished Nan not a day of luck for the rest of her life. She hoped that her baby would be born with a deformed back and a cast in its eye.

The engagement is announced between Ann Elizabeth (Nan), only daughter of Mr. and Mrs. Brian Mahon, Maple Gardens, Dublin, and John Anthony (Jack), eldest son of Dr. and Mrs. John Foley, Donnybrook, Dublin

"I saw *The Irish Times* this morning," Sean Walsh had made it his business to exercise the two Jack Russells up and down the street until he met Benny.

"Oh yes?"

"That's a bit of a surprise isn't it?"

"About Princess Soraya?" she asked innocently. The Shah of Persia was about to divorce his wife. There had been a lot about it in the press. Sean was disappointed. He had hoped for a better reaction, a hanging of the head. An embarrassment even.

"I meant your friend getting married?"

"Nan Mahon? That's right. You saw it in the paper. We didn't know when they'd be making it official."

"But the man . . . she's marrying your friend." Sean was totally confused now.

"Jack? Of course." Benny was bland and innocent.

"I thought you and he . . ." Sean was lost for words.

Benny helped him. They had indeed been friends, even walking out . . . as people might put it. But College life was renowned
for all the first-year friendships, people moved around like musical
chairs. Sean looked at her long and hard. He would not be cheated
of his moment of victory.

"Well, well, well. I'm glad to see that you take it so well, Benny.
I must say that when I saw them here, around Knockglen, I thought
it was a . . . well, a little insensitive you know. But I didn't say
anything to you. I didn't want to upset anybody."

"I'm sure you didn't Sean. But they weren't here. Not here
around Knockglen. So you were mistaken."

"I don't think so," said Sean Walsh.

She thought about the way he said it. She thought about Clodagh
having seen Jack at Dessie Burns' petrol pump. She thought about
Johnny O'Brien wondering where they did it. But it was beyond
belief. *Where* could they have gone? And if Jack loved her, how
could he have come back to her hometown to make love to someone else?

Somehow the weekend passed. It was hard to remember that when
the phone rang it wouldn't be Jack. It was hard when Fonsie talked
about the party to realize that nobody would come to it. It was
hard to believe that he wouldn't be waiting in the Annexe with
eyes dancing, waving her over, delighted to see her.

The hardest thing was to forget that he had said on the banks
of the canal that he still loved her.

It was easy for Eve and Clodagh to dismiss that. But Benny

knew Jack wouldn't have said it unless he meant it. And if he did still love her none of the other business made sense.

She didn't even allow herself to think about meeting Nan. The day would come, probably next week, when she would have to see her.

There had been conflicting stories. Nan was going to continue and finish her degree, while her mother did the baby-sitting. Or that Nan was going to leave immediately. That she was out already flat hunting. She had kept the cutting from the newspaper. She read it over and over to make it have some meaning.

John Anthony. She had known that. And even more like that the name he took at Confirmation was Michael, so his initals were JAM Foley. She hadn't known that Nan would have been baptized Ann Elizabeth. Probably Nan had been a pet name when she was a beautiful little baby. A baby who could get what she wanted. All the time.

Perhaps she hadn't been able to get Simon Westward, and so she had taken Jack instead. How unfair of Simon not to want Nan. That's what must have happened. Benny raged at him, and his snobbery. Nan was exactly the kind of person that would have livened up Westlands. If only that romance had continued then none of this would have happened.

Benny stood behind the counter in the shop, in order to free her mother and Mike for earnest discussions on new cloth. Heather Westward came in in her St. Mary's uniform.

She had come in to buy a handkerchief for her grandfather. It was a treat because he was so ill, and it would cheer him up. Was there one for under one and six. Benny found one, and wondered should it be wrapped up for him. Heather thought not. He wouldn't be able to open the wrapping paper, maybe just a bag.

"He mightn't even know what it is, but if he does, perhaps it'll make him feel better." She looked at Benny for approval.

Benny thought she was right. She handed over the handkerchief for the old man who had shouted at Eve and called Eve's mother a whore.

He might have done the same if Simon had married Nan.

Suddenly with a jolt Benny wondered if Nan had slept with Simon.

Suppose she had. Just suppose that she had, then this baby might be his, and not Jack's after all.

Why hadn't she thought of it before?

The whole thing that looked as if it could never be solved, might in fact have a solution after all.

She looked wild-eyed at the thought of it. She saw Heather watching her in alarm.

She *must* say it to Jack. She had to. He couldn't be forced to marry someone he didn't love, when it might not be his child. No matter that he had slept with Nan. Benny would forgive him. Like she had forgiven him over that business in Wales. It wouldn't matter, just as long as he loved her.

But the feeling of excitement, the ray of hope, died down. Benny realized that she was clutching at straws. That Jack and Nan must have had this discussion. She wished she could remember how long ago it was that Nan had been talking enthusiastically about Simon, but if it was over for ages . . . then there was no hope.

And anyway Jack wouldn't be foolish enough . . .

He'd know, wouldn't he? Men always did. That's why you had to keep your virginity until you married, so that they'd know it was the first time.

No, it was just a mad, wild hope.

But suppose she believed it to be true. It would only lead to a huge confrontation, and almighty indignation if she were to suggest it to Jack. Imply that Nan was passing off someone else's child on him.

The thought had better go back to where it came from.

Heather was still in the shop. She seemed to be hovering as if about to ask a favor.

"Is there anything else, Heather?"

"You know the Easter pageant. Eve and Aidan are going to

come. It's on Holy Thursday. I was wondering would you like to come too. As part of my group."

"Yes, yes I will thank you." Her mind was still far away.

"I'd have forced Simon to come, but he's in England. He mightn't even be back for Easter."

"What's he doing there?"

"Oh, they think he's going to ask this woman to marry him. She's got pots and pots of money."

"That would be nice."

"We could get the drainage and the fencing done."

"Would you mind, someone else coming in there?"

"No, I'd hardly notice." Heather was practical.

"And this romance with the lady in England . . ." Benny inquired. "Has it been going on for a while or is it new?"

"For ages," Heather said. "It's about time they made some move."

So that was that. The wild little hope that Simon could be drawn into the whole business seemed to have faded.

Benny looked distant and abstracted. Heather had been about to tell her that there had been some great row with Nan. That Nan had come to Westlands about four weeks ago all dressed up and there had been words in the morning room and she had driven Simon's car to the bus and wouldn't let him come with her.

Heather remembered the date, because it was when they were casting for the Easter pageant and she had been very nervous. If she had told Benny then, Benny would have realized that it was the very same day as the party in the rugby club. The one she hadn't gone to, but Nan had. The very night it had all begun.

Nan went to Sunday lunch at the Foleys' to meet the family. She was immaculately dressed, and Lilly thought that they would have no apologies or explanations to make for her on grounds of appearance. Her stomach was flat, and her manner was entirely unapologetic.

She came up the steps of the large Donnybrook house as of right, not as the working-class girl who had been taken advantage of by the son of the house. She spoke easily and without guile. She made no effort to ingratiate herself.

She paid more attention to Dr. Foley than to his wife, which would have been the appropriate attitude of any intelligent girl coming to the house.

She was pleasant, but not effusive, to Kevin, Gerry, Ronan and Aengus. She didn't forget their names or mix them up, but neither did she seek their approval.

Lilly Foley watched her with dislike, this cunning, shrewd girl with no morals who had ensnared her eldest son. There were few ways she could fault the public performance. The girl's table manners were perfect.

At coffee afterward in the drawing room, just the four of them, Nan spoke to them with such a clear and unaffected stance that both of Jack's parents were taken aback.

"I realize what a disappointment all this must be to you, and how well you are covering this. I want to thank you very much."

They murmured startled words denying any sense of disappointment.

"And I am sure that Jack has told you my family are all much simpler people than you are, less educated, and in many ways their hopes for me have been realized rather than crushed. If I am to marry into such a family as yours."

She went on to explain to them the kind of ceremony that she would like to provide and for which her father would pay. A lunch for perhaps twenty or thirty people in one of the better hotels. Very possibly the one where her mother worked in the hotel shop.

There would be minimum speech-making because her father was not a natural orator, and she thought that she would wear an oyster satin coat and dress instead of a long, white dress. She would hope that some of Jack's and her friends would attend. On her side she would provide two parents, two brothers, two business associates of her father and one aunt.

When Jack took her away on their journey for afternoon tea in Maple Gardens, John and Lilley Foley exchanged glances.

"Well?" she said.

"Well?" he answered.

He filled the silence by pouring them a small brandy each. It was never their custom to have a drink like this in the afternoon, but the circumstances seemed to call for it.

"She's very presentable," said Jack's mother grudgingly.

"And very practical. She had the Holles Street report in her handbag, left open for us to see in case we were going to question it."

"And very truthful about her own background."

"But she never said one word about loving Jack," Dr. Foley said, with a worried frown.

In Maple Gardens the table was set for tea. A plate of biscuits with sardines on them, another with an egg mayonnaise. There was a bought Swiss roll and a plate of Jacob's USA assortment. Nasey and Paul were in navy suits and shirts. Brian Mahon wore his new brown suit. It hadn't cost as much as it should have because he had been able to give the man in the shop a few cans of paint for his own house. Cans of paint that hadn't cost anything in the first place.

"There's no need to tell all that to Jack Foley when he arrives," Emily had warned.

"Jesus Christ, will you stop nagging at me. I've agreed to stay away from the jar until after they've been and gone, which is a fine imposition to put on a man who's going to lash out for a fancy society wedding. But still, give you lot an inch and you take a bloody mile . . ."

Jack Foley was a handsome young fellow. He sat beside Nan during afternoon tea. He tried a little of everything. He thanked Mr. Mahon for the generous plans for the wedding. He thanked

Mrs. Mahon for all her support. He hoped Paul and Nasey would be ushers in the church.

"You'd hardly need ushers for that size of a crowd," said Nasey, who thought twenty people was the meanest he ever heard of.

"Who's going to be your best man?" Paul asked.

Jack was vague. He hadn't thought. One of his brothers possibly.

He felt awkward asking Aidan, what with the whole Eve and Nan friendship. And Bill Dunne or Johnny . . . it was all a bit awkward to be honest.

He turned to Nan. "Who'll be the bridesmaid?" he asked.

"Secret," Nan said.

They talked about places to live, and flats. Brian Mahon said that he'd be able to give them the name of builders who did good conversion jobs if they found an old place and wanted to do it up.

Jack said that he would be working in his uncle's office, first as a clerk, and then as an apprentice. He was going to take lessons in bookkeeping almost at once, in order to be of some use in there.

Several times he felt Nan's mother's eyes on him, with a look of regret.

Obviously she was upset about her daughter being pregnant, but he felt it was something more than that.

As Nan talked on cheerfully of basements in South Circular Road, or top-story landings in Rathmines, Emily Mahon's eyes filled with tears. She tried to brush them away unseen, but Jack felt that there was some terrible sorrow there, as if she had wanted something very different for her beautiful daughter.

When they had gone Brian Mahon loosened his collar.

"You can't say too much against him."

"I never said anything against him," Emily said.

"He had his fun and he's paying for it. At least that's to his credit." Brian was grudging.

Emily Mahon took off her good blouse and put on her old one automatically. She tied an apron around her waist and began to clear the table. She could puzzle for a thousand years and never understand why Nan was settling for this.

Nan and she had never wanted cheap bed-sitters, student flats, cobwebby conversion jobs. For years they had turned the pages of the magazines and looked at the places where Nan might live. There was never a moment when they planned a shotgun marriage to a student.

And Nan was adamant about saying that her relationship with Simon Westward was long over. And had never been serious. She was almost too adamant when she was telling her mother how long it had been over.

Brian changed into his normal clothes for going to the pub. "Come on, lads, we'll get a pint and talk normally for a while."

Emily filled the sink with hot water and did the washing up. She was very worried indeed.

Jack and Nan sat in his father's car.

"That's the worst over," she said.

"It'll be fine," he assured her.

She didn't believe the worst was over, and he didn't believe everything would be fine.

But they couldn't admit it.

After all, it was there in black and white in the paper. And the chaplain would be able to give them a date very shortly.

Aidan Lynch said that Sundays weren't the same without Heather.

Eve said that he had been invited to watch Heather in a sheet helping Our Lord to carry his burden. Next week, on Holy Thursday, could he bear to come? Aidan said he'd love it, it would count as his Easter duty. Would they bring a First Night present for Heather?

Eve said that he was worse than Heather. The thing was meant to be some kind of religious outpouring, not a song-and-dance act. Still it was great that he'd come down, and he could even stay the night in the cottage.

"It'll make up for us not having the party," Eve said.

"Why won't we have the party?" Aidan asked.

Rosemary was sitting in the Annexe with Bill and Johnny. She was telling them that Tom, her medical boyfriend, had very healing hands. She refused to listen to ribald jokes on the subject. She said that she had an unmerciful headache and he had massaged it right away.

"I'm very sorry that there'll be no party now, down in Knock-glen," she said. "I was looking forward to Tom coming and meeting you all properly."

"Why won't there be a party?" asked Bill Dunne.

"I never heard anything about it being off," said Johnny O'Brien.

Jack was not at his lectures now. He hadn't officially given up, but he was in his uncle's office all day. Learning the ropes. Aidan was going to meet him at six o'clock.

"He has time to go out and drink pints, has he?" Eve said disapprovingly.

"Listen, he hasn't been sent to Coventry. He's not in disgrace. He's just getting married. That's not the end of the earth," Aidan said.

Eve shrugged.

"And what's more, I'm going to be his best man, if he asks me."

"You're not!" She was aghast.

"He's my friend. He can rely on me. Anyone can rely on a friend."

Nan made an appearance in College. She went to a ten o'clock lecture and then joined the crowds streaming down the stairs to the Annexe.

There was a rustle as they saw her coming to join the queue.

"Well, I'm off now," Rosemary said under her breath to Carmel. "If there's one thing I can't bear, it's the sight of bloodshed."

"Benny won't say anything," Carmel whispered back.

"Yes, but have you seen Eve's face."

Benny was trying to calm Eve down. It was ridiculous to say that Nan didn't have a right to show her face in College. Benny begged Eve not to make a scene. What had been the point of urging her to get over everything publicly if Eve was going to ruin it all now.

"That's quite right," Eve said suddenly. "It was just a surge of bad temper."

"Well, why don't you go now, in case it surges again."

"I can't Benny. I'd be afraid you'd be so bloody nice and ask her all about the wedding dress and offer to knit bootees."

Benny squeezed her friend's hand.

"Go on, Eve, please. I'm better on my own. I won't do any of that. And anyway she won't join us."

Nan went to another table. She drank her coffee with a group she knew from another class.

She looked across at Benny, who looked back.

Neither of them made a gesture or mouthed a word. Nan looked away first.

Nan lay on her bed. Jack was going out with Aidan, which surprised her. She thought that there would be a heavy boycott from Eve's side of things.

But men were easier, more generous at forgiving. Men were

more generous in everything. She lay with her feet raised on two cushions.

If Em had been a different kind of mother, she would have pursued the question she had been skirting around. Emily Mahon knew that her daughter was carrying Simon Westward's child. What she didn't know was why she, the Princess, was going to let this one mistake spoil a lifetime of planning. Emily would suggest going to England, having the child adopted, and starting all over again.

The pursuit, the quest, the path to a better life. But Em didn't know that Nan was tired. Tired and weary of pretending. And that for once she had met someone, a good and honest person, who didn't have a life plan . . . a system of passing black as white. That's what she had been doing. Like Simon had been passing as rich.

Jack Foley was just himself.

When told that a child was his, he accepted that it was. And when it was born, it would be theirs. She could leave university. She had made a good impression on the Foley parents. She could see that. There was a small mews at the end of their garden. In time it would be done up, in more time they would live in a house similar to his parents'. They would entertain, they would have dinner parties, she would keep in touch with her mother.

It would all be a great sense of peace compared to the never-ending contest. The game where the goalposts kept moving, and the rules changing.

Nan Mahon was going to marry Jack Foley, not just because she was pregnant, but because at the age of almost twenty she was tired.

Kit Hegarty had a lemon-colored suit and a white blouse for her trip to Kerry.

"You need some color to go with it. I keep forgetting we can't ask Nan."

"Have you spoken to her at all?" Kit asked.

"Nope."

"God, you're a tough girl. I'd hate to make you my enemy."

The Hayeses next door had come in to wish Kit well. Ann Hayes said what she needed was a big copper-colored brooch and she had the very thing at home.

Mr. Hayes looked at Kit admiringly.

"Lord bless us Kit, but you're like a bride," he said.

"Stop putting so much hope in this. It's only an outing."

"Your Joseph would have been glad for you to meet another fellow. He often said."

Kit looked at him startled. Joseph Hegarty would have said little to the Hayeses, he hardly knew them.

She thanked him, but said as much.

"You're wrong Kit. He did know us. He sent us letters for his son."

Eve's heart chilled. Why did this man have to tell Kit now.

"He wanted to keep in touch with his boy. He wrote every month, giving his address as he moved on from place to place."

"And Francis read these."

"Frank read them all. He went to see him last summer when he was canning peas in England."

"Why did he never say, why did neither of them ever say?"

"They didn't want to hurt you. The time wasn't right to tell you."

"And why is the time right now?"

"Because Joe Hegarty wrote to me before he died. He wrote to say that if you met a good man I was to explain that you must never worry about having deprived your son of his father. Because you didn't."

"Did he know he was going to die?"

"Sure, we're all going to die," said Mr. Hayes, as his wife came back in and pinned the brooch on Kit Hegarty's lapel.

Kit smiled, unable to speak. It was something she had been worrying a lot about lately. When she saw how close Paddy Hickey was to his sons, she wondered had she done wrong letting Francis grow up without knowing a father.

She was glad that it had been explained in front of Eve. It showed how much Eve was part of the family.

The Hayeses were going to keep an eye on the house for two weeks. The outing was going to be much longer than Kit had first thought when it had been described as a weekend. And Eve would be down in Knockglen. Kit was delighted they had decided to go ahead with their party. It would be a further betrayal to admit that there could be no party now. That the stars had gone.

When Carmel's Sean had been organizing the finances, he had given some money to Jack as an advance. Jack was the one with most access to a car. Jack could get them a reduction through a wine merchant. He had been the one who was going to bring the drink. But obviously everything had changed now. And no one liked to remind Jack that he was already in possession of eleven pounds of the communal money.

Carmel's Sean suggested they should forget it. The other boys agreed. Jack had quite enough on his plate without reminding him that he owed the kitty eleven pounds.

Heather was wonderful in the pageant.

Aidan, Eve and Benny were enormously proud of her. She was a stockier, more solid, Simon of Cyrene than was normally shown by artists, but then surely they would have pulled from the crowd someone strong to help in the journey up the hill of Calvary.

Mother Francis had always urged the children to make up their own words.

Heather had been adept at this.

"Let me help you, with that cross, Jesus, dear," she said to Fiona Carroll, who was playing Our Lord with a sanctimonious face.

"It's a difficult thing to carry going uphill," Heather added. "It would be much easier on the flat, but then they wouldn't see the Crucifixion so well you see."

There were tea and biscuits in the school hall afterward and Heather was greatly congratulated.

"It's the best Easter ever," she said, with her eyes shining. "And Eve says I can be a waitress at her party, next week, so long as I go home before the necking starts."

Eve looked at Mother Francis sadly. A grown-up look of collusion, of admitting how children would hang you. Heather was unaware of anything amiss.

"Will your friend be here again?" she asked Benny.

"Which one?"

"The man that took to fancying Welsh girls for a bit, but came back."

"He went off again," Benny said.

"Better leave him to go then," Heather advised. "He sounds a bit unreliable."

Standing there in her sheet, in the middle of the party, Heather had no idea why Eve, Aidan and Benny got such a fit of hysterical laughter, and had to wipe the tears out of their eyes. She wished she knew what she had said that was so funny, but she was glad anyway that it had pleased them all so much.

Everyone was delighted to be going to Knockglen. Not for just a party, but for a series of outings.

They would arrive on the Friday after six o'clock, when there would be drinks in Hogan's, and then they would all adjourn to Mario's for the evening. There were bunk beds and sofas and sleeping bags for the boys in Hogan's shop; the girls were going to stay in Eve's and Benny's houses. Then there would be a great trek to Ballylee for lunch and a walk in the woods on Saturday and back for the main event, the proper party in Eve's cottage.

They all said that the one at Christmas would take some beating. Eve said it would be better than ever now. An April moon, and the blossom out on the hedges and grass instead of mud around. There would be wild flowers all over the disused quarry, it would look less like a bomb site than it had done in winter. No one would slip on the mucky paths this time. They wouldn't need to huddle by the fire.

Sister Imelda was as usual aching to be asked to help with the cooking.

"It's no fun for you Sister if you can't see them enjoying it," Eve pleaded.

"It's probably just as well I don't see all that goes on up there. It's enough for me to be told they like it."

"If Simon and the woman from Hampshire come home that weekend, are you going to ask them?" Heather asked.

"No," said Eve.

"I thought you only hated Grandfather. I thought you and Simon got on well enough."

"We do." Eve was dry.

"If he had married Nan, would you have come to the wedding?"

"You ask an awful lot of questions."

"Mother Francis says we should have inquiring minds," Heather said primly.

Eve laughed heartily. That was true. Mother Francis *had* always said it.

"I might have, if I'd been asked. But I don't think your brother would ever have married Nan."

Heather said it would all depend whether Nan had money or not. Simon couldn't marry anyone poor because of the drainage and the fencing.

He had thought that Nan's father was a wealthy builder in the beginning. She heard a lot of this from Bee Moore, but Bee always had to stop when Mrs. Walsh came in because Mrs. Walsh didn't like gossip.

Heather was helping to tidy up the cottage garden. They had a big sack, which they were filling with weeds. Mossy would take it away later.

They worked easily, the unlikely friends and cousins, side by side.

Eve said that maybe they shouldn't talk too much about Nan over the weekend. She was going to marry Jack Foley shortly. Neither of them would be here. There was nothing hush-hush, just better not to bring the subject up.

"Why?" Heather asked. Eve was a respecter of the inquiring mind. As they dug the dandelions and slashed back the nettles, she told an edited version of the story. Heather listened gravely.

"I think you're taking it worse than Benny," she said eventually.

"I think I am," Eve agreed. "Benny fought all my battles for me at school. And now there's nothing I can do for her. If I had my way, I'd kill Nan Mahon. I'd kill her with my bare hands."

The night before they were all due to arrive Benny lay in bed and couldn't sleep.

She would close her eyes and think that a lot of time had passed, but when she saw the luminous hands of the little pink clock she realized that it had only been ten minutes.

She got up and sat by her window. Out in the moonlight she saw the shape of Dr. Johnson's house opposite, and the edge of Dekko Moore's, where young Heather said she was going to work as a harness maker.

What had Benny wanted when she was Heather's age, twelve? She had grown out of the wish for pink velvet dresses and pointed shoes with pom-poms. What had she wanted? Maybe a crowd of friends, people that she and Eve could play with without having to be home at a special time. It wasn't very much.

And they had got it, hadn't they. A whole crowd coming down from Dublin to herself and Eve. How little you knew when you were twelve. Heather Westward wouldn't want to be a harness maker when she was twenty. She'd forget that this is what she had wanted now.

She couldn't get Jack out of her mind tonight. The weeks in between had passed by without touching her. His face was just as dear as it always was, and never more dear than when he had cried on the canal banks and told her he still loved her and that he wouldn't have had this happen for all the world.

She wondered what he and Nan talked about. Did Nan ever tell him how she had helped Benny to put on makeup, and to use good perfume. How Nan had advised Benny to hold in her tummy and push out her chest.

But it was madness to suppose that they ever talked about her at all.

Or to suppose that either of them even remembered that they had been intending to spend this weekend in Knockglen.

"What are you going to wear?" Clodagh asked her next morning.

"I don't know. I've forgotten. I can't get interested. Please, Clodagh, don't nag me."

"Wouldn't dream of it. See you at Mario's tonight then."

"What about up above the shop first, that's where we're starting."

"If you can't be bothered to get dressed for it, why should I be bothered to go."

"Damn you to hell, Clodagh. What'll I wear?"

"Come into the shop and we'll see," said Clodagh, smiling from ear to ear.

By six o'clock they were coming up the stairs, exclaiming and praising. The huge rooms, the high ceilings, the lovely old windows, the davenport, the marvelous frames on the old pictures.

It was like Aladdin's cave.

"I'd live here if I were you," Bill Dunne said to Benny's mother. "Not that your own house isn't terrific . . ."

"I'm half thinking about it," Annabel Hogan said to him.

Benny felt her heart soar. The groundwork was beginning to pay off. She was afraid to smile too much. Clodagh had sewed her into a very tight country-and-western-type bodice. She looked as if she were going to take out a guitar and give them a song. Johnny O'Brien said that she looked utterly fantastic. Fabulous figure, out-in-out, he said, showing her with his hands. Jack must be mad, he said helpfully.

They were all in high form to cross the street to rock the night away in Mario's.

Eve nudged Benny as Sean Walsh, Mrs. Healy and the two Jack Russells went for an evening constitutional around the town.

Mario was delighted to see them, rather overwelcoming, Fonsie thought, until he heard that Mr. Flood had been in with a message from the nun in the tree saying that his cafe was a den of vice and must not only be closed down, but should be exorcised as well.

Any company other than Mr. Flood looked good to Mario at the moment.

Fonsie's new jukebox, which Mario secretly thought looked like the product of a diseased mind, spat out the music. The tables were pushed back and those who couldn't fit in the cafe watched and cheered from outside.

With a mixture of regret and amazement Mario looked back on the days before his sister's son had come to work with him. The peaceful poverty-stricken days when his till hardly ever rang and most people couldn't have told you there was a chip shop and a cafe in Knockglen.

On Saturday Benny and Patsy fried a breakfast for Sheila, Rosemary and Carmel. Then they went up to the shop and did the same for Aidan, Bill, Johnny and the man who was always called Carmel's Sean.

"I do have an identity of my own," he grumbled when Benny called out to know if Carmel's Sean would like one egg or two.

"In this town if your name is Sean, you'd be wise to give yourself some other handle," Benny said. Patsy got a fit of the giggles. It was magical to be able to mock Sean Walsh in these very premises.

Slowly the day took shape. The journey to Ballylee began. Never had the countryside looked lovelier. Benny turned round in the car twice to point things out to Jack. She wondered would it take her long to remember he wasn't there. And wouldn't ever be there again.

Bill Dunne and Eve got separated from the others as they walked up to see an old folly. A summer house facing the wrong way that a family even more unused to the land than the Westwards were had built.

"Benny's fine over all this Jack business, isn't she?" Bill asked, looking for confirmation.

"Hasn't she plenty of fellows looking for her attention. Of course she's fine." Eve was burningly loyal.

"Has she?" Bill seemed disappointed.

He told Eve that nothing had ever surprised him as much. Jack was inclined to talk, the way fellows do, the way girls did too amongst each other he supposed. He never mentioned a word about Nan. Oh, he used to complain that Benny was a convent girl through and through which presumably meant she wouldn't go to bed with him, despite all his blandishments, and that she wasn't in Dublin enough. But not till the night of the rugby club party did Jack even go out with Nan, he knew that for a fact.

"That was only a few weeks ago," Eve said, surprised.

"Yes, didn't the other business happen very quick." Bill shivered in case talking about it might make him the putative father of someone's child.

"Well, it only takes once, that's what they always say." Eve's voice was light.

"That must have been all it was." Bill was sympathetic.

Eve changed the subject. Bill's line of thinking was dangerously near to her own. That the pregnancy had happened too suddenly.

She had not been able to pinpoint Jack and Nan's first encounter until now, and that night was only a few weeks ago. It was the night she and Benny had gone to the pictures in Dun Laoghaire. Even with Benny's poor mathematics, that was surely too soon for anything to have happened and be confirmed. Surely they would know this. Surely Jack's father, a doctor, would know?

And that meant something almost impossible to believe. It meant that Nan Mahon was pregnant with someone else's child, and had taken Benny's Jack to be its father.

Her mind was racing, but the race came to an abrupt end. The engagement was announced. The marriage date was fixed. This is what Nan and Jack were going to do. It wasn't a melodrama of blood tests, and confrontations. It would go ahead, no matter what.

To cast any suspicions would only raise Benny's hope again and break her heart further.

And then there was the possibility that she could be wrong. Eve had never been sure where Simon and Nan could have made love, and had been forced to dismiss the possibility that they ever had. Westlands was out, Maple Gardens was out, so was a car. Simon had no money for hotels. Nan had no friends. None at all except Benny and Eve. She was having great difficulty in finding anyone to be her bridesmaid.

Eve had been forced reluctantly to believe that they might not have been lovers at all. Which was disappointing, as it meant there was no chance of being able to blame the pregnancy on Simon.

But then if there had been any possibility of doing that surely Nan would have done it. She wouldn't have let a chance like that pass by.

But there had been no tales of any rows with Simon. According to all accounts, or to Nan's account, the friendship had ended amicably a long time ago.

"You're muttering to yourself," Bill Dunne criticized her.

"It's my only unpleasant habit. Aidan says it's a tiny flaw in an otherwise perfect character. Come on, I'll race you up to the folly."

She wanted no more of these buzzings in her mind.

The cottage looked beautiful. It had been well worth it to have Mossy give the door a coat of paint. And the garden was a tribute to Heather's and Eve's hard work. Heather was inside in a white chef's hat made for her by Clodagh and a butcher's apron. It seemed excessive for passing plates of savories, but she felt important in it. The dusk was turning to darkness. The stars were coming out in the clear sky.

Figures came up the path to the party. Teddy Flood, Clodagh Pine, Maire Carroll and her new fiancé, Tom the medical student that Rosemary had such ferocious designs on. A few more from College who were just coming for the night rather than making a whole weekend out of it.

Aidan was explaining that tomorrow was called Low Sunday and that this was probably prophetic with the amount they had eaten, drunk and danced, low would be exactly how they would feel.

"Keep the drink moving will you," Eve said. "I have to carve this beast."

They had a huge joint of pork boned and rolled by Teddy Flood for them. He said you'd be able to cut it like butter. Honestly, it would be like carving a Swiss roll. But Eve didn't want to make a mess of it. She closed the door behind her so that she could be on her own in the kitchen.

And as she prepared the place for herself, the huge carving dish, something that Benny had found in the shop, the plates that were heating in the bottom of the range, she was concentrating so hard that she didn't hear the door open and two extra guests arrive.

Carrying bottles of wine and cans of beer, in came Jack and Nan.

Rosemary was the nearest to the door and therefore the first to see them. She let her arm drop from Tom's shoulder where it had rested all evening to mark clearly lines of possession.

"My God," she said.

Jack smiled his easy smile. "Not exactly. Just his deputy," he said.

Carmel was nuzzling Sean on a bench close by. "You didn't say they were coming," she accused Sean in a whisper.

"I didn't bloody know," Sean snapped back.

Johnny O'Brien was doing a complicated tango step with Sheila.

"Hey, it's the black sheep," he called happily.

Sheila whirled around to see if she could see Benny. She was just in time to see Benny look up from where she and Bill Dunne were sorting the records. And to see the color go out of Benny's face as she dropped three of the records straight from her hands.

"Thank God for the passing of the 78's," said Fonsie, whose record collection would have been the loser.

"There's a surprise," Bill said.

Even though the music of "Hernando's Hideaway" was thumping and thudding itself all round them, Nan and Jack must have felt the silence and the chill.

Jack's legendary smile came to his rescue.

"Now, come on, did you think I'd forgotten I said I'd get the drink?" He laughed. He had put it down on the floor, his hands were wide apart, being held out helplessly in the little gesture Benny knew and loved.

It *must* have been a dream. All of it, and now that he was back it was over.

She felt herself smiling at him.

And he saw the smile. All the way across the room.

"Hallo, Benny," he said.

Now everyone could feel the silence. Everyone except the Johnson Brothers, who were singing "Hernando's Hideaway." Clodagh had dressed Benny in black and white for the party. A big black corduroy skirt, a white blouse with a black velvet trim. She looked flushed and happy at the moment that Jack saw her.

He was walking over to her.

"How's your mother and the shop?"

"Fine, going great. We had a party there last night." She spoke too quickly. She looked over his shoulder. Aidan Lynch had taken the bottles of wine from Nan and laid them on the table. Clodagh was trying to explain to Fonsie out of the corner of her mouth.

Johnny O'Brien, who could always be relied on to say something, if not the right thing, came over and punched Jack warmly on the arm.

"It's great to see you. I thought you were barred," he said.

Aidan poured Jack a drink. "Jack the lad!" he said. "Like old times."

"I thought it would be silly to act as if there was a feud or something." Jack looked only mildly anxious that he had done the right thing.

"What feud would there be?" Aidan asked, looking nervously over at where Nan stood beside the door, hardly having moved since she came in.

"Well, that's what I thought. Anyway I couldn't make off with all the money for the jar."

They both knew it had nothing to do with the drink.

"How are things?" Aidan asked him.

"Fine. A bit unreal."

"I know," said Aidan, who didn't know and couldn't possibly imagine it. He thought it safer to move to different waters.

"And your uncle's office?"

"Crazy. They're all so petty, you wouldn't believe . . ." Jack had his arm upon a tall chest of drawers and was talking easily. Benny had moved slightly away. She felt very hot and then very cold. She hoped she wasn't going to faint. Perhaps she could get some air.

Then she realized that Eve didn't know they were here. She must go into the kitchen and tell her.

Aidan had realized this at the same time. He had moved Fonsie in to talk to Jack and headed Benny off at the kitchen door.

"I'll do it," he said. "Come in to rescue me if I'm not out in an hour and there's no sign of supper."

She gave a watery smile.

"Are you all right?" he asked, concerned.

"I'm okay." For Benny that was like saying she was terrible. Aidan looked around him and caught Clodagh's eye. She moved over to join them.

As Aidan went into the kitchen, Clodagh said, "She can stand there at the bloody door all night. She's got some nerve coming here, I tell you. She got short shrift from me."

"What?"

"She said 'Hallo, Clodagh,' nice as pie. I looked through her. She said it again. 'Do I know you?' is what I said." Clodagh was pleased with her repartee.

"People will have to speak to her."

"Let them. I'm not going to."

And indeed Nan did seem curiously isolated, while Jack was the center of his mates.

Benny looked across the room. Nan's face, serene and beautiful as ever, looked around her in that interested, slightly questioning way. She gave no sign that she might feel unwelcome, ungreeted. She looked perfectly at ease standing just where she had come in, when Aidan had removed the wine bottles from her arms.

She looked at Nan as she had done so often admiringly. Nan knew what to say, how to behave, what to wear. Tonight she was in yet another new outfit, a very flowery print, all mauve and white. It looked so fresh, you'd think it had come straight off a shop rail five minutes ago, not from a long car drive.

Benny swallowed. For the rest of her life, Nan would drive in a car with Jack, sit beside him sharing all the things that *she* had once shared. Tears of disappointment came into her eyes. Why had she not done as he asked, taken off her clothes and lain down beside him, loved him generously and warmly, responded to him, instead of buttoning herself up and moving away and saying they should be going home.

If it were Benny that was pregnant, surely he would have been pleased and proud.

He would have explained to his parents, and to her mother as he had done for Nan. Big tears welled up in her eyes at her own foolishness.

Nan saw and came toward her.

"I haven't been avoiding you," Nan said.

"No."

"I was going to write to you, but then we never wrote each other letters so that would be artificial."

"Yes."

"And it's hard to know what to say."

"You always know what to say." Benny looked at her. "And you always know what to do."

"It was never intended to be like this. I assure you." There was something in Nan's voice that sounded phony. Benny realized with a shock that Nan was lying. Perhaps it was intended to be like this. That this was exactly the way Nan had planned it.

In the kitchen Eve was white-faced.

"I don't believe you," she said to Aidan.

"Put those things down." He looked at the carving knife and fork in her hand.

"Well, they're getting out. They're getting straight out of my house, let me tell you."

"No, they're not, Eve." Aidan was unexpectedly firm. "Jack is my friend, and he is not going to be ordered out. It was always planned that he'd come here . . . he brought the drink."

"Oh, don't be a fool," Eve blazed. "Nobody wanted the bloody drink. If he was that worried about it couldn't he have sent it . . . they're not welcome here."

"They're our friends, Eve."

"Not anymore. Not now."

"You can't keep up these things forever. We've got to get back to normal. I think they were absolutely right to come."

"And what are they doing inside? Lording it over everyone?"

"Eve, please. These people are your guests, our guests in a way since you and I are a couple. Please don't make a scene. It would ruin the party for everyone. They're all behaving fine in there."

Eve went over and put her arms around Aidan.

"You're very generous, much nicer than I am. I don't think we'll work as a couple."

"No, you're probably right. But could we sort that one at another time, not just when they're going to have their supper."

Bill Dunne came through the kitchen to go to the bathroom.

"Sorry," he said as he saw Aidan and Eve in each other's arms. "You wouldn't know where to put yourself these days."

"All right," Eve conceded, "just so long as I don't have to talk to her."

Benny was dancing with Teddy Flood when Eve came into the room. Jack was talking to Johnny and Sean. He was as handsome and assured as ever. He looked delighted to see her.

"Eve!"

"Hallo, Jack." Unenthusiastic, but not rude. She had made a promise to Aidan. Hospitality must never be abused.

"We brought you a vase, a sort of glass jug. It would be nice for all the daffodils and everything," he said.

It was a nice jug. How did someone like Jack Foley do the right thing so often? How did he know she had daffodils, he hadn't been here since Christmas, when there was nothing but holly in bloom.

"Thanks. That's lovely," she said. She moved around the

room, emptying ashtrays, making spaces where the plates could be put down.

Nan stood on her own on the edge of a group.

Eve couldn't bring herself to say any words of greeting. She opened her mouth, but she couldn't find anything to say. She went back to the kitchen and stood at the table leaning on both hands. The rage she felt was a real thing, you could almost take it out of her and see it, like a red mist.

She remembered how Mother Francis, and Kit Hegarty, and many a time Benny, had warned her that this temper wasn't natural. It would only hurt her in the end.

The door opened, and Nan came in. She stood there in her fresh flowery print, the breeze from the window slightly lifting her blond hair.

"Listen, Eve . . ."

"I won't, if you don't mind. I have a meal to prepare."

"I don't want you to hate me."

"You flatter yourself. Nobody hates you. We despise you. That's different altogether."

Nan's eyes flashed now. She hadn't expected this.

"That's a bit petty of you, isn't it? A bit provincial? Life goes on. Aidan and Jack are friends . . ."

She looked proud and confident. She knew she held all the winning cards. She had broken all the rules and yet she had won. Not only was she able to take away her only friend's boyfriend, find somewhere, the Lord knew where, to sleep with him, and then get him to agree to marry her, she was also expecting everything to remain the same as it had been in their social life.

Eve said nothing. She looked at her dumbfounded.

"Well, say something, Eve." Nan was impatient. "You must be thinking something. Say it."

"I was thinking that Benny was probably your only friend. That of every one of us she was the only one who just liked you for being you, not just for being glamorous."

Eve knew that this was pointless. Nan would shrug. If she

physically didn't shrug her shoulders, she would mentally. She would say that these things happened.

Nan would take, she would take everything she saw. She was like a child crawling toward a shining object. She took just by instinct.

"Benny's better off. She'd have had a lifetime of watching him, of wondering."

"And you won't?"

"I'll cope."

"I'm sure you will, you've coped with everything."

Eve realized she was shaking. Her hands were trembling as she filled the jug with water and started to arrange a bunch of flowers that someone else had brought.

"I chose that for you," Nan said.

"What?"

"The vase. You don't have one."

Suddenly Eve knew where Jack and Nan had spent their nights together. Here in this house, in her bed.

They had driven to Knockglen, come up the path, taken her key and let themselves in. They had made love in her bed.

She looked at Nan aghast. That was why she had had the feeling that someone had been in the house. The strange undefined sense of someone else's presence.

"It was here, wasn't it?"

Nan shrugged. That awful dismissive shrug. "Yes, sometimes. What does it matter, now . . ."

"It matters to me."

"We left the place perfect. No one would ever know."

"You came to my house, to my bed, to take Benny's Jack in my bed. In Benny's town. Jesus Christ, Nan . . ."

Now Nan lost her temper, utterly.

"By God, I'm sick of this. I am sick of it. This Holy Joe attitude, all of you desperate to do it, playing around the edges, not having the guts or the courage, confessing it, titillating everyone still further . . ."

Her face was red and angry.

"And don't talk to me about this cottage . . . don't talk as if it was the Palace of Versailles. It's a damp, falling-down shack . . . that's what it is. It hasn't electricity. It has a stove that we couldn't light for fear you'd find the traces. It has leaks, drafts, and it's no wonder they say the place is haunted. It feels haunted. It smells haunted."

"Nobody says my house is haunted." There were tears of rage in Eve's eyes.

Then she stopped. People had said that they heard someone playing the piano here at night.

But that was ages ago. Jack didn't play the piano. It must have been before Jack.

"You brought Simon here too didn't you?" she said.

The memory of Simon playing the piano in Westlands came back to her. That day she had gone up there with Heather, the day the old man had cursed at her and called her mother a whore. Nan said nothing.

"You brought Simon Westward to my bed, in my house. You knew I'd never have let him over the doorstep. And you brought him in here. And then, when he wouldn't marry you, you tricked Jack Foley . . ." Nan was suddenly pale. She looked around her at the door to the room where the others were dancing.

The music of Tab Hunter was on the record player.

"Young love, first love . . ."

"Take it easy . . ." Nan began.

Eve had picked up the carving knife. She started to move toward her, the words came tumbling out. She couldn't control them if she tried.

"I will *not* take it easy. What you have done, by Christ, I won't take it easy."

Nan wasn't near enough to reach the handle of the door to the sitting room. She backed away, but Eve was still moving toward her, eyes flashing and the knife in her hand.

"Eve, stop!" she cried, moving as fast as she could out of

range. She lurched against the bathroom door so hard that the glass broke.

Nan fell, sliding down on the ground, and the broken glass ripped her arm. Blood spurted everywhere, even on to her face.

The dress with mauve and white print became crimson in a second. Eve dropped the knife on the floor. Her own screams were as loud as Nan's as she stood there in her kitchen amid the broken glass, the blood and the meal ready to be served, and the sound of everyone joining in the song in the room next door.

"Young love, first love, is filled with deep emotion."

Eventually someone heard them and the door opened.

Aidan and Fonsie were in first.

"Whose car is nearest?" Fonsie asked.

"Jack's. It's outside the door."

"I'll drive it. I know the road better."

"Should we move her?" Aidan asked.

"If we don't she'll bleed to death in front of our eyes."

Bill Dunne was great at keeping everyone back out of the kitchen. Only Jack, Fonsie and of course Tom, the medical student, in case he knew something the rest of them didn't, were allowed in. Everyone else should stay where they were, the place was too crowded already.

They had opened the back door. The car was only a few yards away. Clodagh had brought a rug and clean towels from Eve's bedroom. They wrapped the towel around the arm with the huge, gaping wound.

"Are we pushing the glass further in?" Fonsie asked.

"At least we're keeping the blood in," Aidan said.

They looked at each other in admiration. Jokers yes, but when it came to the crunch, they were the ones in charge.

Benny sat motionless in the sitting room, her arm around Heather.

"It's going to be all right," she kept saying, over and over. "Everything's going to be all right."

Before he got into the car Aidan came over to Eve.

"Don't let anyone go," he warned. "I'll be back very soon."

"What do you mean?"

"Don't let them crawl away because they think it's expected. Give them something to eat."

"I can't . . ."

"Then get someone else. They need food anyway."

"Aidan!"

"I mean it. Everyone's had too much to drink. For God's sake feed them. We've no idea who'll be in on top of us now."

"What do you mean?"

"Well, if she dies, we'll have the Guards."

"Die! She can't die."

"Feed them, Eve."

"I didn't . . . she fell."

"I know, you fool."

Then the car with Jack, Fonsie, Aidan and a still hysterical Nan left.

Eve straightened herself up.

"I think it's ludicrous myself, but Aidan Lynch says we should all have something to eat, so could you clear a little space and I'll bring it in," she said.

Stricken, they obeyed her. Even though they would never have suggested it, it was exactly the right thing to do.

Dr. Johnson looked at the arm and phoned the hospital.

"We're bringing someone in, severed arteries," he said crisply. The three white faces of the boys looked at him as he hung up.

"I'll drive her," he said. "Just one of you. Which one?"

Fonsie and Aidan stood back, and Jack stepped forward. Maurice Johnson looked at him. His face was familiar. A junior rugby player, he had been in Knockglen before. In fact Dr. Johnson had a feeling that he was meant to be Benny Hogan's boyfriend. There had been talk that she was walking out with a spectacularly handsome young man.

He wasted no time speculating. He nodded to Fonsie and Aidan and drove out of his gate.

It was an endless Sunday. The whole of Knockglen had heard that there had been a terrible accident and an unfortunate girl from Dublin had slipped and fallen, cutting herself on a glass door.

Dr. Johnson had been quick to say that there wasn't any horseplay and everyone seemed to him to be stone-cold sober. In fact he had no idea whether this was true or not, but he couldn't bear the tongues to wag, and Eve Malone to get further criticism for things that were beyond her control.

Dr. Johnson also told everyone in sight that the girl would recover.

And recover she did. Nan Mahon was out of danger on the Sunday night. She had received several blood transfusions and there had been a time when her heartbeat had slowed down, causing alarm. But she was young and healthy. It was wonderful, the recuperative powers of the young.

Sometime on the Monday night, she miscarried. But the hospital was very discreet. After all, she wasn't a married woman.

TWENTY

*I*t was summer before Jack Foley and Nan Mahon had the conversation they knew that they would have to have. After her stay in the hospital in Ballylee she had gone back to Dublin.

That was at her insistence. She had seemed so agitated that Dr. Johnson agreed.

Jack still worked in his uncle's office, but he studied for his first-year examination as well. There was, unspoken, the thought that he might return and do his degree in civil law. Aidan kept the notes from lectures.

Aidan and Jack met a lot, but they never talked about what was uppermost in their minds. Somehow it was easier to chat and be friends if they didn't mention that.

Brian Mahon wanted to sue. He said that by God people were always suing his customers for harmless jackass incidents. Why shouldn't they get a few quid out of it? That girl had to have some kind of insurance, surely?

Nan was very weak but her wound was healing, the livid red scar would fade in time.

Since she had never said aloud to her family that she was pregnant she did not have to report that this was no longer the case. She lay long hours in the bed where she had lain full of dreams.

She would not let Jack Foley come to see her.

"Later," she had told him. "Later, when we are able to talk."

He had been relieved. She could see that in his eyes. She could also see he wished it to be finished, over, so that he could get on with his life.

But she wasn't ready yet. And she had had terrible injuries. He owed her all the time she needed to think about things.

"There's no sign of your fiancé," Nasey said to her.

"It's all right."

"Da says that if he leaves you now because of your injuries, we can sue him for breach of promise," Nasey said.

She closed her eyes wearily.

Heather told over and over the story about the fall and the blood. She knew she would never have such an audience again. They hung on her every word. Heather aged twelve had been at a grown-ups' party wearing a chef's hat, and had seen all the blood. Nobody had taken her home or said she wasn't to look. She didn't tell them that she had felt dizzy and had cried into Benny's chest most of the time. She didn't tell them that Eve had sat white-faced, saying nothing for hours.

Eve took a long time to get over the night. She told only three people about having had the carving knife in her hand.

She told Benny, and Kit and Aidan. They had all said the same thing. They told her she hadn't touched Nan, she was only gripping it. They told her that she wouldn't have, that she would have stopped before she got near her.

Benny said that you couldn't be someone's best friend for ten years and not know that about them.

Kit said she wouldn't have anyone living in the house unless she knew what they were like. Eve would shout and rage. She wouldn't knife someone.

Aidan said the whole thing was nonsense. She had been gripping that knife all evening. Hadn't he asked her to put it down himself. He said the future mother of his eight children had many irritating qualities, but she was not a potential murderess.

Gradually she began to believe it.

Little by little she could go into her kitchen and not see in her mind's eye all that blood and broken glass.

Soon the strained look began to leave her face.

Annabel Hogan said to Peggy Pine that they would never know the full story of the night above in the cottage, no matter how much they asked. Peggy said that it was probably better not to ask any more. To think on more positive things like Patsy's wedding, like whether she should sell Lisbeg and move in over the shop. Once people heard that it might be for sale there were some very positive inquiries, and figures that would make poor Eddie Hogan turn in his grave.

"He'd turn with pleasure," Peggy Pine said. "He always wanted the best for the pair of you."

It was the right thing to say. Annabel Hogan began to look at the offers seriously.

Benny found the summer term at University College was like six weeks in another city. It was so different to everything that had gone before. The days were long and warm. They used to take their books to the gardens at the back of Newman House on St. Stephen's Green and study.

She always meant to ask about these gardens and who looked

after them. They belonged to the University obviously. It was peaceful there and unfamiliar. Not like almost every other square inch of Dublin, which she associated with Jack.

Some nights she stayed with Eve in Dun Laoghaire, other nights they both went home on the bus together. There was a divan couch in Eve's cottage; sometimes she spent the night up there. Mother, absorbed with plans and redecoration, seemed pleased that Benny had Eve to talk to. They called it studying, but in fact it was talking, as fuchsias started to bud, as the old roses began to bloom, the friends sat and talked. They spoke very little about Nan and Jack and what had happened. It was too soon, too raw.

"I wonder where they went," Benny said once, out of the blue. "A couple of people said they saw them here in Knockglen, but where could they have stayed?"

"They stayed here," Eve said simply.

She didn't have to tell Benny that it was without her permission, and that it had broken her heart. She saw tears in Benny's eyes.

There was a long silence.

"She must have lost the baby," Benny said.

"I expect so," Eve said.

She found herself thinking unexpectedly of the curse her father had laid on the Westwards.

And how so many of them had indeed had such bad luck.

Could this have been more of it. A Westward not even to survive till birth?

Mr. Flood was referred to a new young psychiatrist, who was apparently a very kind young man. He listened to Mr. Flood endlessly, and then prescribed medication. There were no more nuns in trees. In fact, Mr. Flood was embarrassed that he should ever have thought there were. It was decided that it should be referred to as a trick of the light. Something that could happen to anyone.

❧

Dessie Burns said that what was wrong with the country was this obsession with drink. Everyone you met was either on the jar or off the jar. What was needed was an attitude of moderation. He himself was going to be a Moderate Drinker from now on, not all this going on tears or going off it totally. The management in Shea's said that it all depended on your interpretation of the word "moderation," but at least Mr. Burns had cut out the lunchtime drinking and that could only be to everyone's advantage.

Knockglen was cheated of the wedding of Mrs. Dorothy Healy and Mr. Sean Walsh. It was decided, they told people, that since the nuptials would be second time around for Mrs. Healy and since Sean Walsh had no close family to speak of, they would marry in Rome. It would be so special, and although they would not be married by the Holy Father they would share in a blessing for several hundred other newly married couples.

"They couldn't rustle up ten people between them who'd come to the wedding," Patsy told Mrs. Hogan.

Patsy was thrilled by the decision. It would mean that her own wedding would now have no competition.

Eve was surprised to get an invitation to Patsy's wedding. She had expected just to go to the church to cheer her on. She realized that of course she and Patsy would be neighbors, up on the quarry path. She assumed that Mossy's mother had heard dire reports of the goings-on at the party, and would look on her as a shameless hussy who gave drunken parties. Eve didn't realize that Mossy told his mother as little as he told anyone else. She was getting increasingly deaf, and since she only knew about the world what he told her, she knew remarkably little.

She knew that Patsy was a good cook, and didn't have a family of her own to make demands, so Patsy would be free to look after Mossy's mother in her old age.

Mother Francis saw Dr. Johnson passing the school in his car. She was looking out of the window, as she often did when the girls were doing a test, and thinking about the town. How she would hate to leave Knockglen, and go to another convent within the Order. Every year in summer the changes were announced. It was always a relief to know that she had another year where she was. Holy Obedience meant that you went without question where Mother General decided.

She hoped unworthily each year that Mother Clare would not be sent to join them. She didn't exactly pray that Mother Clare would be kept in Dublin, but God knew her views on that. Any day now they would know. It was always an unsettling couple of weeks waiting for the news.

She wondered where Dr. Johnson was going, what a strange demanding life, always out to see someone being born or die or go through complicated bits in between.

Major Westward was dead when the doctor arrived. He closed his eyes, pulled a sheet over his head and sat down with Mrs. Walsh. He would phone the undertakers and the vicar, just to alert them, but first someone had better find Simon.

"I telephoned him this morning. He's on his way from England."

"Right then. Not much more that I can do." He stood up and reached for his coat.

"Not much loss," he said.

"I *beg* your pardon, Dr. Johnson?"

He had looked at her levelly. She was a strange woman. She liked the feeling of being in the Big House, even though it was Big rather than Grand. She would probably stay if Simon brought home a bride, grow old here, feel that her own state had been ennobled by her contact with these people.

It wasn't fair of him to be snide about the dead man. He had never liked old Westward, he had thought the man arrogant and ungiving to the village that was on his doorstep. He had found the disinheriting of Eve Malone beyond his comprehension.

But he must not tread on the sensibilities of other people. His wife had told him that a thousand times.

He decided to change his epitaph.

"Sorry, Mrs. Walsh, what I said was 'What a loss, such a loss.' You'll pass on my condolences to Simon, won't you."

"I'm sure Mr. Simon will telephone you, Doctor, when he gets back."

Mrs. Walsh was tight-lipped. She had heard very well what he had said the first time.

Jack Foley's parents said that he was behaving most unreasonably. What were they to think, or indeed to say? Was the wedding on or was it off? Obviously since the urgency had gone out of it and the three-week run-up time had been and gone they could assume that she was no longer pregnant. Jack had snapped and said he couldn't possibly be expected to discuss all this with them at this early stage while Nan was still convalescing.

"I think we can be expected to know whether you now have reason to call off this rushed marriage." His father spoke sharply.

"She had a miscarriage," he said. "But nothing else is clear."

He looked so wretched, they left him alone. After all their main question had been answered, the way they hoped it would be.

Paddy Hickey proposed to Kit Hegarty at a window table in a big Dun Laoghaire hotel. His hands were trembling as he asked her to marry him. He used formal words, as if a proposal were some kind of magic ritual and wouldn't work unless he asked her to do him the honor of becoming his wife.

He said that all his children knew he was going to ask her, they would be waiting, hoping for a yes, like himself. He spoke so long and in such flowery tones that Kit could hardly find a gap in the speech to say yes.

"What did you say?" he asked at length.

"I said I'd love to and I think we'll make each other very happy."

He got up from his side of the table and came round to her, in front of everyone in the restaurant dining room he took her in his arms and kissed her.

Somehow, even in the middle of the embrace he felt that people had laid down their cutlery and their glasses to look at them.

"We're going to get married," he called out, his face pink with pleasure.

"Thank God I'm going off to the wilds of Kerry, I'd never be able to come in here again," said Kit, acknowledging the smiles and handshakes and even cheers of the other diners at the tables around them.

Simon Westward wondered could his grandfather possibly have known how inconvenient was the day he took to die. The arrangements with Olivia were at a crucial stage. He did not need to be summoned to a sickbed. But on the other hand, he would be in a better position to talk to her once he was master of Westlands in name as well. He tried to feel some sympathy for the lonely old man. But he feared that he had brought a lot of his misery on himself.

So, it mightn't have been easy to welcome Sarah's ill-matched husband, a handyman, to the house, but he should have made some overtures of friendship to their child.

Eve would have been a good companion for all those years,

petted and feted in the Big House she would not have developed that prickling resentment which was her hallmark as a result of being banished.

He didn't like thinking about Eve. It reminded him uncomfortably of that last terrible day in Westlands when the old man had lashed out all around him.

And it reminded him of Nan.

Somebody had sent him a cutting from *The Irish Times*, with the notice of her engagement. The envelope had been typed. At first he thought it might have been from Nan herself, and later he decided that it was not her style to do that. She had left without a backward glance. And as far as he could see from his statement, had not cashed that check. He didn't know who had sent the newspaper cutting. He thought it might have been Eve.

Heather asked Mother Francis, would Eve be coming to their grandfather's funeral.

Mother Francis said that somehow she thought not.

"He used to be very nice once, he got different when he got old," she said.

"I know," Mother Francis said. Her own heart was heavy. Mother Clare was going to be sent to Knockglen. It was all very well for Peggy Pine to urge Mother Francis to take the whip hand, and to show her who was master, and a lot of other highly unsuitable instructions for religious life. It was going to disrupt the community greatly. If only there was some kind of interest, some area she could find for Mother Clare to be hived off.

"Are you in a bad humor, Mother?" Heather asked.

"Oh, Lord child, you really are Eve's cousin. You have exactly the same way she had of knowing when anything was wrong. The rest of the school could tramp past and never know anything."

Heather looked at her thoughtfully.

"I think you should put more faith in the thirty days prayer.

Sister Imelda says it's never been known to fail. She did it for me when I was lost, and look at how well it turned out."

Mother Francis worried about sometimes how Heather had latched on to some of the more complicated aspects of the Catholic faith.

Nan asked Jack to meet her.

"Where would you like?" he asked.

"You know Herbert Park. It's quite near you."

"Is that not too far from you?" They were curiously formal.

If anyone saw this handsome couple walking there they would have assumed that this was another summer romance and smiled at them.

There was no ring to give back. There were very few arrangements to unpick.

She told him that she was going to London. She hoped to do a course in dress designing. She wanted to be away for a while. She didn't really know exactly what she did want, but she knew what she didn't want.

She talked flatly, with no light and shade in her voice. Jack fought down the guilty, overwhelming surge of relief, that he was not going to have to marry this beautiful dead girl and spend the rest of his life with her.

When they left the small park with its bright rows of flowers and the pit-pat of people playing tennis they knew that they would probably never see each other again.

The day dawned bright and sunny for Patsy's wedding. Eve and Benny were there to help her dress. Clodagh would be down to see that those two clowns didn't get anything wrong.

Paccy Moore was going to give her away. He had said that if she wanted someone with a proper leg he wouldn't be a bit insulted, and he might make a bit of clatter with the iron going up the church, but Patsy would have no one else.

His cousin Dekko was going to be the best man, and his sister Bee the bridesmaid. It gave the appearance of a family.

The best silver was out despite Patsy saying that a couple of Mossy's cousins might be light-fingered. There were chicken and ham, and potato salad, and a dozen different types of cake, and trifle and cream.

It would be a feast.

Clodagh had plucked Patsy's eyebrows and insisted on doing a makeup.

"I wonder would there be a chance that my mother might see me up in heaven," Patsy said.

For an instant, none of the three girls could find an answer. They found it too moving to think that Patsy would need the support of a mother she had never known, and her easy confidence that this woman was in heaven.

Benny blew her nose loudly.

"I'm sure she can see you, and she's probably saying you look lovely."

"God, Benny, don't blow your nose like that in the church. You'd lift half the congregation out of their seats," Patsy warned.

Dr. Johnson was driving the party up to the church.

"Good girl, Patsy," he said, as he settled Paccy and the bride into the back of his car. "You'll tear the sight out of the eyes of that old rip above."

It was exactly the right remark, the partisan response to show Patsy that she was on the winning team, that Mossy's mother wouldn't even be a starter in the race.

Dessie Burns had abandoned Moderation that morning. He tried to wave a cheery greeting at them from his front door, but it wasn't easy with a bottle in one hand and a glass in the other. He somehow went into a spin and fell down. Dr. Johnson looked at him grimly. That would be his next call, stitching up that eejit's head.

It was a great wedding. Patsy had to be restrained several times from clearing up or going to the kitchen to bring out the next course.

They were waved away at four o'clock.

Dekko was going to drive them to the bus, but Fonsie said he had to drive to Dublin anyway, so he'd take them to Bray.

"Fonsie should be canonized," Benny said to Clodagh.

"Yes, I can see his statue in all the churches. Maybe they'd even make this a special place of pilgrimage for him. We'd outsell Lourdes."

"I mean it," Benny said.

"Don't you think I don't know." A rare look of softness came into Clodagh's face.

That night Mother asked Benny if she'd mind if they sold Lisbeg.

She knew she mustn't appear too eager. But she said thoughtfully that it was a good idea, there'd be money to build up the shop. It was what Father would have liked.

"We always wanted you to be married from here. That's the only thing."

The signs of Patsy's wedding were still everywhere, the silver ornaments from the cake, the paper napkins, the confetti, the glasses around the house.

"I don't want to get married for a long, long time, Mother. I mean that." And oddly she did.

All that pain she had felt over Jack seemed much less now.

She remembered how she had ached all over at the very

thought of him and how she had wanted to be the one leaving to walk up the church to a smiling Jack Foley.

That ache was a lot less painful now.

Rosemary said that they should have a party in Dublin just to show that it wasn't only the socialites in Knockglen who could organize things. A barbecue maybe, the night their exams were over, down by White Rock, on the beach, between Killiney and Dalkey.

They'd have a huge fire, and there'd be sausages and lamb chops and great amounts of beer.

Sean and Carmel would not be in charge this time. Rosemary would do the food, and her friend Tom would collect the money. The boys started contributing.

"Will we ask Jack?" Bill Dunne said.

"Maybe not this time," said Rosemary.

Eve and Benny were going to share a flat next year. The digs in Dun Laoghaire would be closed. They were very excited and kept looking at places now before the vacation so that they'd be ahead of the posse in September.

They were full of plans. Benny's mother would come and stay, maybe even Mother Francis might come and visit. There had been wonderful news from the convent. Mother Clare had broken her hip. Not that Mother Francis *called* it wonderful news, but it did mean that she would need to be near a hospital and physiotherapy, and all the stairs and the walking in St. Mary's wouldn't be advisable. Mother Francis was in the middle of the thirty days prayer when this happened. She told Eve that it was her biggest crisis of faith yet. Could the prayer be *too* powerful?

As they left one flat they had been examining, they ran into Jack.

He looked at Benny.

"Hallo, Jack."

Eve said she had to go, seriously, and she'd see Benny later out in Dun Laoghaire. She was gone before they could say anything.

"Would you come out with me tonight?" he asked her.

Benny looked at him, her eyes went all around the face that she had loved so much, every line, every fold of the skin so dear to her.

"No, Jack, thank you." Her voice was gentle and polite. She was playing no games. "I'm going out already."

"But that's just with Eve. She won't mind."

"No, it's impossible. Thanks all the same."

"Tomorrow then, or the weekend?" His head was on one side.

Benny remembered suddenly the way that his mother and father had stood on the steps of their house that night. His mother watchful and wondering.

Little things that she had learned during the past month about the Foleys made her think that this was always the way things were.

Benny didn't want to wonder and watch over Jack for the rest of her life. If she went out with him now, it would be so easy. They would be back to where they had been before. In time Nan would be forgotten like the incident in Wales had been sort of forgotten.

But she would always worry about the next one.

The next time she just wasn't around, ever smiling, always ready. It was too much to ask.

"No." Her smile was warm.

His face was surprised and sad. More sad than surprised.

He began to say something.

"I only did what . . ." Then he stopped.

"I never meant it to . . ." He stopped again.

"It's all right, Jack," Benny said. "Honestly, it's all right."

She thought she saw tears in his eyes and looked away quickly. She didn't want to be reminded of that day on the canal bank.

❦

The firelight danced and they threw more and more logs on. Aidan had said he wondered were he and Eve leaving the conception of their eight children too late; and she assured him that they weren't, it would be wrong to rush these things. He sighed resignedly; he had known she would say this.

Rosemary was flushed and pretty, and Tom paid her the most extravagant compliments; Johnny O'Brien was in disgrace because he had whirled a blazing log and it had set fire to a great bowl of punch. The blaze had been spectacular, but the drink severely diminished.

Fonsie and Clodagh had come up from Knockglen. It would be a long time before anyone forgot their dazzling jive display on the big flat rock.

Sean and Carmel nuzzled up to each other as they had done from the beginning of time, Sheila from the Law Faculty had a new hairdo and a happier smile. Benny wondered why she hadn't liked her so much in the old days.

It was all over Jack probably. Like everything had been.

The clouds that had been in front of the moon scudded past and it was almost as bright as daylight.

They laughed at each other delighted. It was as if someone had shone a huge searchlight over them, then more clouds came and made it discreet again.

They were tired now from singing and from dancing to the little record player that Rosemary had provided. They only wanted to sing something gentle.

Not anything that would make Fonsie start to dance again. Someone started the song about sailing along on Moonlight Bay. Everyone groaned because it was so awful and old-fashioned, but everyone sang it because they knew the words.

Benny was leaning half against a rock and half against Bill Dunne, who was sitting beside her. Bill was so enjoying the night, and was looking after her, getting her nice bits of burned sausage on a stick and some tomato ketchup to dip it on. Bill was a great friend. You wouldn't have to spend your life watching him and wondering about him. You wouldn't have to spend the night worrying if he was having a good time or too good a time.

She was thinking how comfortable he was when she saw Jack coming down the steps.

It was very dark and to the others it might just have looked like a figure in the distance. But she knew it was Jack coming to join the summer party. Asking to belong again.

She didn't make any move. She watched him for a long time, sometimes he stopped in the shadows, as if doubtful of his welcome.

But Jack Foley would never be doubtful for long. He would know that these were his friends. The long, winding steps were quite a distance from the rocks where they sat around their fire. Probably not very far, but it seemed a long time for him to cross the sand.

Long enough for her to realize how often she had seen his face everywhere. She used to see his face smiling and frowning. She used to see it like Mr. Flood saw visions, up in trees and in the clouds. She used to see it in the patterns of leaves on the ground. When she woke and when she slept there was no other image in the foreground, and not because she summoned it there. It just wouldn't go away.

That was the way it had been for a very long time, when things were good and when things were bleak.

But tonight she would have difficulty in seeing his face. She would have to wait until he came into the firelight to remember what he looked like. It was oddly restful.

They were still in full voice when someone saw Jack. The song didn't stop. They were all exaggerating the words anyway, and laughing. A few people waved to him.

He stood on the edge.

Jack Foley on the edge of things. Nobody waved him into the center of the group. He smiled around him, glad to be back. His nightmares brushed away, his sins, he hoped, forgiven. He seemed happy to be part of the court again. Not even his worst enemy would ever have accused him of having wanted to be king. That's just the way it had turned out.

Across the fire his eyes sought Benny. It was hard to know what he was asking her. Permission to be there? Pardon for everything that had gone before? Or the right to come and hold her in his arms?

Benny smiled the big, warm smile that had made him fall in love with her. Her welcome was real. She looked lovely in the light of the flames, and she did what no one else had done. She pointed him to where the drink was, where the long sticks lay for cooking the food. He opened a beer and moved slightly toward her. That had been an encouragement, hadn't it?

There wasn't much room on the rug where she sat leaning against Bill Dunne and the craggy bit of rock.

Nobody moved over to make space. They assumed he would sit down where he was.

After a few moments Jack Foley did that. Perched on a rock. On the edge.

Bill Dunne, who had his arm lightly around Benny's shoulder, didn't take it away because she hadn't moved as he had thought she might.

The song was over and someone had started "Now Is the Hour." They sang in exaggerated poses and mimes, in funny accents and pretense of huge passion. Benny looked into the fire.

It was peaceful here. There would be other nights like this. More like floating along than racing along. And as she saw the sticks move and huge showers of sparks fly up to the sky over the dark hills she couldn't see Jack's face.

All she could see were the flames and the sparks, and the long shadows out over the sand, and the edge of the sea with tiny bits of white coming in over the stones and the beach.

And the friends, all the friends sitting in a great circle, looking as if they were going to sing forever.

Since they were into sentimentality Fonsie said, they shouldn't overlook "For ever, and ever, my heart will be true . . ."

The voices soared up to the sky with the smoke and the sparks and nowhere in the sky did Benny Hogan see the face of Jack Foley.

And Benny sang with the others, knowing that Jack Foley's face was somewhere with all the faces around the fire, not taking over the whole night sky.

THE COPPER
BEECH

1

Shancarrig School

Father Gunn knew that their housekeeper Mrs. Kennedy could have done it all much better than he would do it. Mrs. Kennedy would have done *everything* better in fact, heard Confessions, forgiven sins, sung the Tantum Ergo at Benediction, buried the dead. Mrs. Kennedy would have looked the part too, tall and angular like the Bishop, not round and small like Father Gunn. Mrs. Kennedy's eyes were soulful and looked as if they understood the sadness of the world.

Most of the time he was very happy in Shancarrig, a peaceful place in the midlands. Most people only knew it because of the huge rock that stood high on a hill over Barna Woods. There had once been great speculation about this rock. Had it been part of something greater? Was it of great geological interest? But experts had come and decided while there may well have been a house built around it once, all traces must have been washed away with the rains and storms of centuries. It had never been mentioned in any history book. All that was there was one great rock. And since *carrig* was the Irish word for rock that was how the place was named—Shancarrig, the old rock.

Life was good at the Church of the Holy Redeemer in Shancarrig. The parish priest, Monsignor O'Toole, was a courteous, frail man who let the curate run things his own way. Father Gunn wished that more could be done for the people of the parish so that they didn't have to stand at the railway station waving goodbye to sons and daughters, emigrating to England and America. He wished that there were fewer damp cottages where tuberculosis could flourish, filling the graveyard with people too young to die. He wished that tired women did not have to bear so many children, children for whom there was often scant living. But he knew that all the young men who had been in the seminary with him were in similar parishes wishing the same thing. He didn't think he was a man who could change the world. For one thing he didn't *look* like a man who could change the world. Father Gunn's eyes were like two currants in a bun.

There had been a Mr. Kennedy long ago, long before Father Gunn's time, but he had died of pneumonia. Every year he was prayed for at Mass on the anniversary of his death, and every year Mrs. Kennedy's sad face achieved what seemed to be an impossible feat, which was a still more sorrowful appearance. But even though it was nowhere near her late husband's anniversary now, she was pretty gloomy, and it was all to do with Shancarrig School.

Mrs. Kennedy would have thought since it was a question of a visit from the Bishop that *she*, as the priests' housekeeper, should have been in charge of everything. She didn't want to impose, she said many a time, but really had Father Gunn got it quite clear? Was it really expected that those teachers, those lay teachers above at the schoolhouse and the children that were taught in it, were really in charge of the ceremony?

"They're not used to bishops," said Mrs. Kennedy, implying that she had her breakfast, dinner, and tea with the higher orders.

But Father Gunn had been adamant. The occasion was the dedication of the school, a bishop's blessing, a ceremony to add to the legion of ceremonies for Holy Year, but it was to involve the children, the teachers. It wasn't something run by the presbytery.

"But Monsignor O'Toole is the manager," Mrs. Kennedy protested. The elderly frail parish priest played little part in the events of the parish, it was all done by his bustling energetic curate.

In many ways, of course, it would have been much easier to let Mrs. Kennedy take charge, to have allowed her get her machine into motion and organize the tired cakes, the heavy pastries, the big pots of tea that characterized so many church functions. But Father Gunn had stood firm. This event was for the school and the school would run it.

Thinking of Mrs. Kennedy standing there hatted and gloved and sorrowfully disapproving, he asked God to let the thing be done right, to inspire young Jim and Nora Kelly, the teachers, to set it up properly. And to keep that mob of young savages that they taught in some kind of control.

After all, God had an interest in the whole thing too, and making the Holy Year meaningful in the parish was important. God must want it to be a success, not just to impress the Bishop but so that the children would remember their school and all the values they learned there. Father Gunn was very fond of the school, the little stone building under the huge copper beech. He loved going up there on visits and watching the little heads bent over their copybooks.

"Procrastination is the thief of time" they copied diligently.

"What does that mean, do you think?" he had asked once.

"We don't know what it means, Father. We only have to copy it out," explained one of the children helpfully.

They weren't too bad really, the children of Shancarrig—he heard their Confessions regularly. The most terrible sin, and the one for which he had to remember to apportion a heavy penance, was scutting on the back of a lorry. As far as Father Gunn could work out this was holding on to the back of a moving vehicle and being borne along without the driver's knowledge. It not unnaturally drew huge rage and disapproval from parents and passersby, so he had to reflect the evilness of it by a decade of the Rosary, which was almost unheard of in the canon of children's penances. But scutting apart, they were good children, weren't they? They'd do the school and Shancarrig credit when the Bishop came, wouldn't they?

The children talked of little else all term. The teachers told them over and over what an honor it was. The Bishop didn't normally go to small schools like this. They would have the chance to see him on their own ground, unlike so many children in the country who had never seen him until they were confirmed in the big town.

They had spent days cleaning the place up. The windows had been painted, and the door. The bicycle shed had been tidied so that you wouldn't recognize it. The classrooms had been polished till they gleamed. Perhaps His Grace would tour the school. It wasn't certain, but every eventuality had to be allowed for.

Long trestle tables would be arranged under the huge copper beech tree which dominated the school yard. Clean white sheets would cover them and Mrs. Barton, the local dressmaker, had embroidered some lovely edging so that they wouldn't look like sheets. There would be jars of flowers, bunches of lilac and the wonderful purple orchids that grow wild in Barna Woods in the month of June.

A special table with Holy Water and a really good white cloth would be there so that His Grace could take the silver spoon and sprinkle the Water, dedicating the school again to God. The children would sing "Faith of Our Fathers," and because it was near to the Feast of Corpus Christi they would also sing "Sweet Sacrament Divine." They rehearsed it every single day, they were word perfect now.

Whether or not the children were going to be allowed to partake of the feast itself was a somewhat gray area. Some of the braver ones had inquired, but the answers were always unsatisfactory.

"We'll see," Mrs. Kelly had said.

"Don't always think of your bellies," Mr. Kelly had said.

It didn't look terribly hopeful.

Even though it was all going to take place at the school, they knew that it wasn't really centered around the children. It was for the parish.

There would be something, of course, they knew that. But only when the grown-ups were properly served. There might be just plain bits of bread and butter with a little scraping of sandwich paste on them, or the duller biscuits when all the iced and chocolate-sided ones had gone.

The feast was going to be a communal effort from Shancarrig and so they each knew some aspect of it. There was hardly a household that wouldn't be contributing.

"There are going to be bowls of jelly and cream with strawberries on top," Nessa Ryan was able to tell.

"That's for grown-ups!" Eddie Barton felt this was unfair.

"Well, my mother is making the jellies and giving the cream. Mrs. Kelly said it would be whipped in the school and the decorations put on at the last moment in case they ran."

"And chocolate cake. Two whole ones," Leo Murphy said.

It seemed very unfair that this should all be for the Bishop and priests and great crowds of multifarious adults in front of whom they had all been instructed, or ordered, to behave well.

Sergeant Keane would be there they had been told, as if he was about to take them all personally to the jail in the big town if there was a word astray.

"They'll have to give some to us," Maura Brennan said. "It wouldn't be fair otherwise."

Father Gunn heard her say this and marveled at the innocence of children. For a child like young Maura, daughter of Paudie who drank every penny that came his way, to believe still in fairness was touching.

"There'll be bound to be *something* left over for you and your friends, Maura," he said to her, hoping to spread comfort, but Maura's face reddened. It was bad to be overheard by the priest wanting food on a holy occasion. She hung back and let her hair fall over her face.

But Father Gunn had other worries.

The Bishop was a thin, silent man. He didn't walk to places but was more inclined to glide. Under his long soutane or his regal-style vestments he might well have had wheels rather than feet. He had already said he would like to process rather than drive from the railway station to the school. Very nice if you were a gliding person and it was a cool day. Not so good, however, if it was a hot day and the Bishop would notice the unattractive features of Shancarrig.

Like Johnny Finn's pub where Johnny had said that out of deference to the occasion he would close his doors but he was not going to dislodge the sitters.

"They'll sing. They'll be disrespectful," Father Gunn had pleaded.

"Think what they'd be like if they were out on the streets, Father." The publican had been firm.

So much was spoken about the day and so much was made of the numbers that would attend that the children grew increasingly nervous.

"There's no proof at all that we'll get *any* jelly and cream," Niall Hayes said.

"I heard no talk of special bowls or plates or forks."

"And if they let people like Nellie Dunne loose they'll eat all before them." Nessa Ryan bit her lip with anxiety.

"We'll help ourselves," said Foxy Dunne.

They looked at him round-eyed. Everything would be counted, they'd be murdered, he must be mad.

"I'll sort it out on the day," he said.

Father Gunn was not sleeping well for the days preceding the ceremony. It was a great kindness that he hadn't heard Foxy's plans.

Mrs. Kennedy said that she would have some basic emergency supplies ready in the kitchen of the presbytery, just in case. Just in case. She said it several times.

Father Gunn would not give her the satisfaction of asking just in case *what*. He knew only too well. She meant in case his foolish confidence in allowing lay people up at a small stone schoolhouse run a huge public religious ceremony was misplaced. She shook her head and dressed in black from head to foot, in honor of the occasion.

There had been three days of volunteer work trying to beautify the station. No money had been allotted by CIE, the railways company, for repainting. The stationmaster, Jack Kerr, had been most unwilling to allow a party of amateur painters loose on it. His instructions did not include playing fast and loose with company property, painting it all the colors of the rainbow.

"We'll paint it gray," Father Gunn had begged.

But no. Jack Kerr wouldn't hear of it, and he was greatly insulted at the weeding and slashing down of dandelions that took place.

"The Bishop likes flowers," Father Gunn said sadly.

"Let him bring his own bunch of them to wear with his frock then," said Mattie the postman, the one man in Shancarrig foolhardy enough to say publicly that he did not believe in God and wouldn't therefore be hypocritical enough to attend Mass, or the Sacraments.

"Mattie, this is not the time to get me into a theological discussion," implored Father Gunn.

"We'll have it whenever you're feeling yourself again, Father." Mattie was unfailingly courteous and rather too patronizing for Father Gunn's liking.

But Mattie had a good heart. He transported clumps of flowers from Barna Woods and planted them in the station beds. "Tell Jack they grew when the earth was disturbed," he advised. He had correctly judged the stationmaster to be unsound about nature and uninterested in gardening.

"I think the place is perfectly all right," Jack Kerr was heard to grumble as they all stood waiting for the Bishop's train. He looked around his transformed railway station and saw nothing different.

The Bishop emerged from the train. He was shaped like an S hook, Father Gunn thought sadly. He was graceful, bending or straightening as he spoke to each person. He was extraordinarily gracious, he didn't fuss or fumble, he remembered everyone's names, unlike Father Gunn who had immediately forgotten the names of the two self-important clerics who had accompanied him.

Some of the younger children, dressed in the little white surplices of altar boys, stood ready to lead the procession up the town.

The sun shone mercilessly. Father Gunn had prayed unsuccessfully for one of the wet summer days they had been having recently. Even that would be better than this oppressive heat.

The Bishop seemed interested in everything he saw. They left the station and walked the narrow road to what might be called the center of town had Shancarrig been a larger place. They paused at the Church of the Holy Redeemer for His Grace to say a silent prayer at the foot of the altar. Then they walked past the bus stop, the little line of shops, Ryan's Commercial Hotel, and The Terrace where the doctor, the solicitor, and other people of importance lived.

The Bishop seemed to nod approvingly when places looked well, and to frown slightly as he passed the poorer cottages. But perhaps that was all in Father Gunn's mind. Maybe His Grace was unaware of his surroundings and was merely saying his prayers. As they walked along Father Gunn was only too conscious of the smell from the River Grane, low and muddy. As they crossed the bridge he saw out of the corner of his eye a few faces at the window of Johnny Finn Noted for Best Drinks. He prayed they wouldn't find it necessary to open the window.

Mattie the postman sat laconically on an upturned barrel. He was one of the only spectators since almost every other citizen of Shancarrig was waiting at the school.

The Bishop stretched out his hand very slightly as if offering his ring to be kissed.

Mattie inclined his head very slightly and touched his cap.

The gesture was not offensive, but neither was it exactly respectful. If the Bishop understood it, he said nothing. He smiled to the right and the left, his thin aristocratic face impervious to the heat. Father Gunn's face was a red round puddle of sweat.

The first sign of the schoolhouse was the huge ancient beech tree, a copper beech that shaded the playground. Then you saw the little stone schoolhouse that had been built at the turn of the century. The dedication ceremony had been carefully written out in advance and scrutinized by these bureaucratic clerics who seemed to swarm around the Bishop. They had checked every word in case Father Gunn might have included a major heresy or sacrilege. The purpose of it all was to consecrate the school, and the future of all the young people it would educate, to God in this Holy Year. Father Gunn failed to understand why this should be considered some kind of doctrinal minefield. All he was trying to do was to involve the community at the right level, to make them see that their children were their hope and their future.

For almost three months the event had been heralded from the altar at Mass. And the pious hope expressed that the whole village would be present for the prayers and the dedication. The prayers, hymns, and short discourse should take forty-five minutes, and then there would be an hour for tea.

As they plodded up the hill Father Gunn saw that everything was in place.

A crowd of almost two hundred people stood around the school yard. Some of the men leaned against the school walls, but the women stood chatting to each other. They were dressed in their Sunday best. The group would part to let the little procession through and then the Bishop would see the children of Shancarrig.

All neat and shining—he had been on a tour of inspection already this morning. There wasn't a hair out of place, a dirty nose or a bare foot to be seen. Even the Brennans and the Dunnes had been made respectable. They stood, all forty-eight of them, outside the school. They were in six rows of eight, those at the back were on benches so that they could be seen.

They looked like little angels, Father Gunn thought. It was always a great surprise the difference a little cleaning and polishing could make.

Father Gunn relaxed, they were nearly there. Only a few more moments then the ceremony would begin. It would be all right after all.

The school looked magnificent. Not even Mrs. Kennedy could have complained about its appearance, Father Gunn thought. And the tables were arranged under the huge spreading shade of the copper beech.

The Master and the Mistress had the children beautifully arranged, great emphasis having been laid on looking neat and tidy. Father Gunn began to relax a little. This was as fine a gathering as the Bishop would find anywhere in the diocese.

The ceremony went like clockwork. Monsignor O'Toole's chair was placed just to one side. The singing, if not strictly tuneful, was at least in the right area. No huge discordancies were evident.

It was almost time for tea—the most splendid tea that had ever been served in Shancarrig. All the eatables were kept inside the school building, out of the heat and away from the flies. When the last notes of the last hymn died away Mr. and Mrs. Kelly withdrew indoors.

There was something about the set line of Mrs. Kennedy's face that made Father Gunn decide to go and help them. He couldn't bear it if a tray of sandwiches fell to the ground or the cream slid from the top of a trifle. Quietly he moved in, to find a scene of total confusion. Mr. and Mrs. Kelly and young Madeleine Ross stood frozen in a tableau, their faces expressing different degrees of horror.

"What is it?" he asked, barely able to speak.

"Every single queen cake!" Mrs. Kelly held up what looked from the top a perfectly acceptable tea cake with white icing on it, but underneath the sign of tooth marks showed that the innards had been eaten away.

"And the chocolate cake!" gasped Madeleine Ross, who was

white as a sheet. The front of the big cake as you saw it looked delectable, but the back had been propped up with a piece of bark, a good third of the cake having been eaten away.

"It's the same with the apple tarts!" Mrs. Kelly's tears were now openly flowing down her cheeks. "Some of the children I suppose."

"That Foxy Dunne and his gang, I should have known. I should have bloody known." Jim Kelly's face was working itself into a terrible anger.

"How did he get in?"

"The little bastard said he'd help with the chairs, brought a whole gang in with him. I said to him 'all those cakes are counted very carefully.' And I did bloody count them when they went out."

"Stop saying bloody and bastard to Father Gunn," said Nora Kelly.

"I think it's called for." Father Gunn was grim.

"If only they could have just eaten half a dozen. They've wrecked the whole thing."

"Maybe I shouldn't have gone on about counting them." Jim Kelly's big face was full of regret.

"It's all ruined," Madeleine Ross said. "It's ruined." Her voice held the high tinge of hysteria that Father Gunn needed to bring him to his senses.

"Of course it's not ruined, Madeleine. Get the teapots out, call Mrs. Kennedy to help you. She's wonderful at pouring tea and she'd like to be invited. Get Conor Ryan from the hotel to start pouring the lemonade and send Dr. Jims in here to me quick as lightning."

His words were so firm that Madeleine was out the door in a flash. Through the small window he saw the tea-pouring begin and Conor Ryan happy to be doing something he was familiar with, pouring the lemonade.

The doctor arrived, worried in case someone had been taken ill.

"It's your surgical skills we need, Doctor. You take one knife

I'll take another and we'll cut up all these cakes and put out a small selection."

"In the name of God, Father Gunn, what do you want to do that for?" asked the doctor.

"Because these lighting devils that go by the wrong name of innocent children have torn most of the cakes apart with their teeth," said Father Gunn.

Triumphantly they arrived out with the plates full of cake selections.

"Plenty more where that came from!" Father Gunn beamed as he pressed the assortments into their hands. Since most people might not have felt bold enough to choose such a wide selection they were pleased rather than distressed to see so much coming their way.

Out of the corner of his mouth Father Gunn kept asking Mr. Kelly, the Master, for the names of those likely to have been involved. He kept repeating them to himself, as someone might repeat the names of tribal leaders who had brought havoc and destruction on his ancestors. Smiling as he served people and bustled to and fro, he repeated an incantation—"Leo Murphy, Eddie Barton, Niall Hayes, Maura Brennan, Nessa Ryan, and Foxy Bloody Dunne."

He saw that Mattie the postman had consented to join the gathering, and was dangerously near the Bishop.

"Willing to eat the food of the Opium of the People, I see," he hissed out of the corner of his mouth.

"That's a bit harsh from you, Father," Mattie said, halfway through a plate of cake.

"Speak to the Bishop on any subject whatsoever and you'll never deliver a letter in this parish again," Father Gunn warned.

The gathering was nearing its end. Soon it would be time to return to the station.

This time the journey would be made by car. Dr. Jims and

Mr. Hayes, the solicitor, would drive the Bishop and the two clerics, whose names had never been ascertained.

Father Gunn assembled the criminals together in the school. "Correct me if I have made an error in identifying any of the most evil people it has ever been my misfortune to meet," he said in a terrible tone.

Their faces told him that his information had been mainly correct.

"Well?" he thundered.

"Niall wasn't in on it," Leo Murphy said. She was a small, wiry ten-year-old with red hair. She came from The Glen, the big house on the hill. She could have had cake for tea seven days a week.

"I did have a bit, though," Niall Hayes said.

"Mr. Kelly is a man with large hands. He has declared his intention of using them to break your necks, one after the other. I told him that I would check with the Vatican, but I was sure he would get absolution. Maybe even a *medal*." Father Gunn roared the last word. They all jumped back in fright. "However, I told Mr. Kelly not to waste the Holy Father's time with all these dispensations and pardons, instead I would handle it. I told him that you had all volunteered to wash every dish and plate and cup and glass. That it was your contribution. That you would pick up every single piece of litter that has fallen around the school. That you would come to report to Mr. and Mrs. Kelly when it is all completed."

They looked at each other in dismay. This was a long job. This was something that the ladies of the parish might have been expected to do.

"What about people like Mrs. Kennedy? Wouldn't they want to . . . ? Foxy began.

"No, they wouldn't want to, and people like Mrs. Kennedy are *delighted* to know that you volunteered to do this. Because those kinds of people haven't seen into your black souls."

There was a silence.

"This day will never be forgotten. I want you to know that. When other bad deeds are hard to remember this one will always be to the forefront of the mind. This June day in 1950 will be etched there forever." He could see that Eddie Barton's and Maura Brennan's faces were beginning to pucker, he mustn't frighten them to death. "So now. You will join the guard of honor to say farewell to the Bishop, to wave goodbye with your hypocritical hearts to His Grace whose visit you did your best to undermine and destroy. *OUT."* He glared at them. *"OUT* this minute."

Outside, the Bishop's party was about to depart. Gracefully he was moving from person to person, thanking them, praising them, admiring the lovely rural part of Ireland they lived in, saying that it did the heart good to get out to see God's beautiful nature from time to time rather than being always in a Bishop's Palace in a city.

"What a wonderful tree this is, and what great shade it gave us today." He looked up at the copper beech as if to thank it, although it was obvious that he was the kind of man who could stand for hours in the Sahara Desert without noticing anything amiss in the climate. It was the boiling Father Gunn who owed thanks to the leafy shade.

"And what's all this writing on the trunk?" He peered at it, his face alive with its well-bred interest and curiosity. Father Gunn heard the Kellys' intake of breath. This was the tree where the children always inscribed their initials, complete with hearts and messages saying who was loved by whom. Too secular, too racy, too sexual to be admired by a Bishop. Possibly even a hint of vandalism about it.

But no.

The Bishop seemed by some miracle to be admiring it.

"It's good to see the children mark their being here and leaving here," he said to the group who stood around straining for his last words. "Like this tree has been here for decades, maybe even centuries back, so will there always be a school in Shancarrig to open the minds of its children and to send them out into the world."

He looked back lingeringly at the little stone schoolhouse and the huge tree as the car swept him down the hill and toward the station.

As Father Gunn got into the second car to follow him and make the final farewells at the station, he turned to look once more at the criminals. Because his heart was big and the day hadn't been ruined he gave them half a smile. They didn't dare to believe it.

2

Maddy

When Madeleine Ross was
brought to the church in Shancarrig to be baptized she wore an
old christening robe that had belonged to her grandmother.
Such lace was rarely seen in the Church of the Holy Redeemer
—it would have been more at home in St. Matthew's parish
church, the ivy-covered Protestant church eleven miles away.
But this was 1932, the year of the Eucharistic Congress in Ireland. Catholic fervor was at its highest and everyone would
expect fine lace on a baby who was being christened.

The old priest did say to someone that this was a baby girl
not likely to be lacking in anything, considering the life she was
born into.

But parish priests don't know everything.

Madeleine's father died when she was eight. He was killed in
the war. Her only brother went out to Rhodesia to live with an
uncle who had a farm the size of Munster.

When Maddy Ross was eighteen years old in 1950 there were
a great many things lacking in her life: such as any plan of what
she was going to do; such as any freedom to go away and do it.

Her mother needed somebody at home and her brother had gone, so Maddy would be the one to stay.

Maddy also thought she needed a man friend, but Shancarrig was not the place to find one.

It wasn't even a question of being a big fish in a small pond. The Ross family were not rich landowners—people of class and distinction. If they had been, then there might have been some society that Maddy could have moved in and hunted for a husband.

It was a matter of such fine degree.

Maddy and her mother were both too well off and not well enough off to fit into the pattern of small-town life. It was fortunate for Maddy that she was a girl who liked her own company, since so little of anyone else's company was offered to her.

Or perhaps she became this way because of circumstances.

But ever since she was a child people remembered her gathering armfuls of bluebells all on her own in the Barna Woods, or bringing home funny-shaped stones from around the big rock of Shancarrig.

The Rosses had a small house on the bank of the River Grane, not near the rundown cottages but further on toward Barna Woods, which led up to the Old Rock. Almost anywhere you walked from Maddy Ross's house was full of interest, whether it was up a side road to the school, or past the cottages to the bridge and into the heart of town, where The Terrace, Ryan's Commercial Hotel, and the row of shops all stood. But her favorite walk was to head out through the woods, which changed so much in each season, they were like different woods altogether. She loved them most in autumn when everything was golden, when the ground was a carpet of leaves.

You could imagine the trees were people, kind big people about to embrace you with their branches, or that there was a world of tiny people living in the roots, people that couldn't really be seen by humans.

She would tell stories half wanting to be listened to and half to herself—stories about where she found golden and scarlet branches in autumn and the eyes of an old woman watching her through the trees, or of how children in bare feet played by the big rock that overlooked the town and ran away when anyone approached.

They were harmless stories, the Imaginary Friend stories of all children. Nobody took any notice, especially since it all died down when she went off to boarding school at the age of eleven. Shancarrig school was much too rough a place for little Madeleine Ross. She was sent to a convent two counties away.

Then they saw her growing up, her long pale hair in plaits hanging down her back, and when she got to seventeen the plaits were wound around her head.

She was slim and willowy like her mother, but she had these curious pale eyes. Had Maddy had good strong eyes of any color she would have been beautiful. The lightness somehow gave her a colorless quality, a wispy appearance, as if she wasn't a proper person.

And if anyone in Shancarrig had thought much about her, they might have come to the conclusion that she was a weak girl who had few views of her own.

A more determined young woman might have made a decision about finding work for herself, or friends. No matter how complex the social structure of Shancarrig, you'd have thought that young Maddy Ross would have had some friends.

There were cousins, of course, aunts and uncles to visit. Maddy and her mother went to see families in four counties, always her mother's relations. Her father's people lived in England.

But at home she was really only on the fringe of things. Like the day they had the dedication of the school, the day the Bishop came.

Maddy Ross stood on the edge with her straw sunhat to keep the rays of the sun from her fair skin. She watched Father Gunn bowing his way up the hill toward the school. She watched the elderly Monsignor O'Toole in his wheelchair. But she stood slightly apart from the rest of Shancarrig as they waited for the procession to arrive.

The Kellys with their little niece Maria, all of them dressed to kill. Nora Kelly should have worn a hat like Maddy had, not a hopeless lank mantilla that made her look out of place in the Irish countryside.

Still it would be nice to belong somewhere, like the Kellys did. They had come to that school and made it their own. They were the center of the community now while Maddy, who had lived here all her life, was still on the outside.

She accepted her plate of cakes, thinking it looked as if it had been arranged that way deliberately.

Mrs. Kelly looked at her speculatively.

"I think the time has come to get a JAM," she said.

Maddy was mystified. "I hardly think you need any more," she said, looking at her plate.

"A Junior Assistant Mistress," Mrs. Kelly explained, as if to a five-year-old.

"Oh, sorry."

"Well, do you think we should talk to your mother about it?"

Maddy began to wonder was the heat affecting all of them.

"I think she's a bit set in her ways now . . . she mightn't be able to teach," she explained kindly.

"I meant you, Miss Ross."

"Oh. Of course. Yes, well . . ." Maddy said.

It proved how little she must have been planning her life. She had *no* immediate plans.

There had been much talk that year of visiting Rome. It was the Holy Year. It would be a special time. Aunty Peggy had been, the pictures were endless, the stories often repeated, the lack of good strong tea regretted over and over.

But Mother could never make up her mind about little things like whether to have strawberry jam or gooseberry jam for tea, so how could she make up her mind about something huge like a visit to Rome. The autumn came, the evenings started to get cooler, and everyone agreed that there would be grave danger of catching a chill.

It was just as well they hadn't gone to all the trouble of getting passports and booking tickets. And as Mother often said, you could love God just as well from Shancarrig as you could from a city in Italy.

Maddy Ross had been disappointed at first when the often discussed plans looked as if they were coming to nothing. But then she didn't think about it anymore. She was good at putting disappointments behind her, there had been many of them even by the time she was eighteen.

Her best friend at school, Kathleen White, hadn't even told Maddy when she decided to enter the convent and become a nun. Everyone else in the school knew first. Maddy had been shaking with emotion when she challenged Kathleen with the news.

Kathleen had become unhealthily calm, too serene for her own good.

"I didn't tell you because you're so intense about everything," Kathleen said simply. "You'd either have wanted to join with me or you'd have been too dramatic about it. It's just what I want to do. That's all."

Maddy decided to forgive Kathleen after a while. After all, a Vocation was a huge step. Obviously Kathleen had too much on her mind to care about the sensibilities of her friend. Maddy wrote her long letters forgiving her and talking about the commitment to religious life. Kathleen had written one short note. In two months time she would be a postulant at the convent. She could neither write nor receive letters then. Perhaps it would be better to get ready for that by not beginning a very emotional correspondence now.

And there had been other disappointments that summer. At the tennis club dance Maddy had thought she looked well and that a young man had admired her. He had danced with her for longer than anyone else. He had been particularly attentive about glasses of fruit punch. They had sat in the swinging seat and talked easily about every subject. But nothing had come of it. She had gone to great trouble to let him know where she lived and even found two occasions to call at his house. But it was as if she had never existed.

Sometimes when Maddy Ross went for her long, lonely

walks up the winding tree-covered hill to the Old Rock that stood guarding the town she felt that she handled everything wrong. It was all so different to things that happened to girls in the pictures.

Maddy had always known that there wouldn't be the money to send her to university, so she had thought it just as well that she didn't have any burning desire to be a professor, or a doctor or lawyer. But there was nothing else that fired her either. Other girls had gone to train as nurses, some of them had done secretarial courses and gone into the bank or big insurance offices. There were others who went to be radiographers, or physiotherapists.

Maddy, the girl with the long pale hair and the slow smile that went all over her face once it began, thought that sooner or later something would turn up.

Probably at the end of the holidays.

Mrs. Kelly had been serious on that hot day, and in the very first week of September, Mr. and Mrs. Kelly from the school came to see Mother.

Shancarrig's small stone schoolhouse was a little way out of the town. That was to make it easier for the children of the farmers, it had been said. Mr. and Mrs. Kelly had come as newly marrieds to the school in answer to Father Gunn's appeal. The last teachers had left in some disarray. Maddy had heard stories about drinking and dismissals, but as usual only a very edited version of events, filtered through her mother. Mother never seemed to grasp the full end of any stick.

Mr. and Mrs. Kelly were a strange couple. He was big and innocent-looking, like a farmer's boy. She was small and taut-looking, her mouth often in a narrow line of disapproval.

Maddy Ross had looked at her more than once, wondering what it was about Mrs. Kelly that had attracted the big simple good-natured man by her side. They were only about ten years older than she was.

She wondered if Mrs. Kelly had looked about her and then, finding nobody more suitable, settled for the teacher. She certainly looked as if something had displeased her. Even when they came uninvited to see Mother they both looked as if they were going to issue some complaint.

Maddy found nothing odd about their asking Mother rather than asking her. After all, it was the kind of thing Mrs. Ross would have a view on. Perhaps she thought her daughter Madeleine was intended for something more elevated than working in Shancarrig School. It was better to sound out the opinions before making a direct approach.

But Mother thought it would be an excellent idea. *Fallen straight into their laps* was the way she described it when the cousins came to supper the following day.

"And won't Madeleine need to be trained to teach?" the cousins asked.

"Nonsense," said Mother. "What training would anyone need to put manners on unfortunates like the young Brennans or the young Dunnes."

They agreed. It wasn't a real career like the cousins' children were embarking on, one in a bank, one was doing a very advanced secretarial course, with Commercial French thrown in, which could lead to any kind of a position almost anywhere in the world.

To her surprise Maddy loved it.

She had neither the roar of Mr. Kelly nor the confident firm voice of his wife. She spoke gently and almost hesitantly, but the children responded to her. Even the bold Brennan children, whose father was Paudie Brennan drunk and layabout, seemed easy to handle. And the Dunnes, whose faces were smeared with jam, agreed quite meekly to having their mouths wiped before class began.

There were three classrooms in the little schoolhouse, one for Mrs. Kelly's class, one for Mr. Kelly's, and the biggest one for Maddy Ross. It was called Mixed Infants and it was here that she started the young minds of Shancarrig off on what might be a limited kind of educational journey. There would be some, of course, who would advance to a far greater education than she had herself. The young Hayes girls, whose father was a solicitor, might well get professions, as might little Nuala Ryan from the hotel. But it was only too obvious that the Dunnes and Brennans would say goodbye to any hopes of education once they left this school. They would be on the boat abroad or into the town to get whatever was on offer for children of fourteen years of age.

They all looked the same at five, however. There was nothing except the difference of clothing to mark out those who would have the money to go further and those who would not.

Before she had gone into the school Maddy Ross barely noticed the children of her own place. Now she knew everything about them, the ones that sniffled and seemed upset, the ones who thought they could run the place, those that had the doorsteps of sandwiches for their lunch, those who had nothing at all. There were children who clung to her and told her everything about themselves and their families, and there were those who hung back.

She had never known that there would be a great joy in seeing a child work out for himself the letters of a simple sentence and read it aloud, or in watching a girl who had bitten her pencil to a stub suddenly realize how you did the great long tots or the subtraction sums. Each day it was a pleasure to point to the map of Ireland with a long stick and hear them chant the places out.

"What are the main towns of County Cavan? All right. All together now. Cavan, Cootehill, Virginia . . ." all in a singsong voice.

There were two cloakrooms, one for the girls and one for the boys. They smelled of Jeyes Fluid, as the Master obviously poured it liberally in the evenings when the children had left.

It would have been a bleak little place had it not been for the huge copper beech which dwarfed it and looked as if it was holding the school under its protective arm. As she had felt safe in Barna Woods as a child, Maddy felt safe with this tree. It marked the seasons with its coloring, its flowers, and its leaves.

The days passed easily, each one very much like that which had gone before. Madeleine Ross made big cardboard charts to entertain the children. She had pictures of the flowers she collected in Barna Woods, and she sometimes pressed the flowers as well and wrote their names underneath. Every day the children in Shancarrig School sat in their little wooden desks and repeated the names of the ferns and foxgloves, cowslips and primroses and ivies. Then they would look at the pictures of St. Patrick and St. Brigid and St. Colmcille and chant their names too.

Maddy made sure that they remembered the saints as well as the flowers.

The saints were higher on Father Gunn's list of priorities. Father Gunn was a very nice curate. He had little whirly glasses, like looking through the bottom of a lemonade bottle. Now the school manager was a frequent visitor—he had to guard the faith and morals of the future parishioners of Shancarrig. But Father Gunn liked flowers and trees too, and he was always kind and supportive to the Junior Assistant Mistress.

Maddy wondered how old he was. With priests, as with nuns, it was always so hard to know. One day he unexpectedly told her how old he was. He said he was born on the day the Treaty was signed in 1921.

"I'm as old as the State," he said proudly. "I hope we'll both live forever."

"It's good to hear you saying that, Father." Maddy was arranging a nature display in the window. "It shows you enjoy life. Mother is always saying that she can't get her wings soon enough."

"Wings!" The priest was puzzled.

"It's her way of saying she'd like to be in heaven with God. She talks about it quite a lot."

Father Gunn seemed at a loss for words. "It's wholly admirable, of course, to see this world only as a shadow of the heavenly bliss our Father has prepared for us but . . ."

"But Mother's only just gone fifty. It's a bit soon to be thinking about it already, isn't it?" Maddy helped him out.

He nodded gratefully. "Of course, I'm getting on myself.

Maybe I'll start thinking the same way." His voice was jokey. "But I have so much to do I don't feel old."

"You should have someone to help you." Maddy said only what everyone else in Shancarrig said. Monsignor O'Toole was doddery now. Father Gunn did everything. They definitely needed a new curate.

And it wasn't as if the priests' housekeeper was any help. Mrs. Kennedy had a face like a long drink of water. She was dressed in black most of the time, mourning for a husband who had died so long ago hardly anyone in Shancarrig could remember him. A good priests' housekeeper should surely be kind and supportive, fill the role of mother, old family retainer, and friend.

It had to be said that Mrs. Kennedy played none of these roles. She seemed to smolder in resentment that she herself had not been given charge of the parish. She snorted derisively when anyone offered to help out in the parish work. It was a tribute to Father Gunn's own niceness that so many people stepped in to help with the problems caused by Monsignor O'Toole being almost out of the picture, and Mrs. Kennedy being almost too much in it.

Then the news came that there was indeed a new priest on the way to Shancarrig. Someone knew someone in Dublin who had been told definitely. He was meant to be a very nice man altogether.

About six months later, in the spring of 1952, the new curate arrived. He was a pale young man called Father Barry. He had long delicate white hands. He had light fair hair and dark, startling blue eyes. He moved gracefully around Shancarrig, his soutane swishing gently from side to side. He had none of the bustle of Father Gunn, who always seemed uneasily belted into his priestly garb and distinctly ill at ease in the vestments.

When Father Barry said Mass the shaft of sunlight seemed to come in and touch his pale face, making him look more saintly than ever. The people of Shancarrig loved Father Barry and in her heart Maddy Ross often felt a little sorry for Father Gunn, who had somehow been overshadowed.

It wasn't *his* fault that he looked burly and solid. He was just as good and attentive to the old and the feeble, just as understanding in Confession, just as involved in the school. And yet she had to admit that Father Barry brought with him some new sense of exhilaration that the first priest didn't have.

When Father Barry came to her classroom and spoke he didn't talk vaguely about the missions and the need to save stamps and silver paper for mission stations, he talked of hill villages in Peru where the people ached to hear of Our Lord, where there was only one small river and that dried up during the dry seasons leaving the villagers to walk for miles over the hot dry land to get water for the old and for their babies.

As they sat in the damp little schoolhouse in Shancarrig Maddy and Mixed Infants were transported miles away to another continent. Some of the Brennans had broken shoes and torn clothes, they even bore the marks of a drunken father's fist, but they felt rich beyond the dreams of kings compared to the people in Vieja Piedra, thousands of miles away.

The very name of this village was the same as their own. It meant Old Rock. The people in this village were crying out to them across the world for help.

Father Barry fired the children with an enthusiasm never before known in that school. And it wasn't only in Maddy Ross's class. Even under the sterner eye of Mrs. Kelly, who might have been expected to say that we should look after our own first before going abroad to give help, the collections increased. And in Mr. Kelly's class the fierce master echoed the words of the young priest, but in his own way.

"Come out of that, Jeremiah O'Connor. You'll want your arse kicked from here to Barna and back if you can't go out and raise a shilling for the poor people of Vieja Piedra."

When he gave the Sunday sermon Father Barry often closed his disturbing blue eyes and spoke of how fortunate his congregation were to live in the green fertile lands around Shancarrig.

The church might be full of people sneezing and coughing, wearing coats wet from the trek across three miles of road and field to get there, but Father Barry made their place sound like a paradise compared to its namesake in Peru.

Some of them began to wonder why a loving God had been so unjust to the good Spanish-speaking people in that part of the world, who would have done anything to have a church and priests in their midst.

Father Barry had an answer for that whenever the matter was raised. He said it was God's plan to test men's love and goodness for each other. It was easy to love God, Father Barry assured everyone. Nobody had any problem in loving our heavenly Father. The problem was to love people in a small lonely village miles away and treat them as brothers and sisters.

Maddy and her mother often talked about Father Barry and his saintliness. It was something they both agreed on, which meant they talked about him more than ever. There were so many subjects which divided them.

Maddy wondered would there be the chance for them to go out to Rhodesia to Joseph's wedding. Her brother was marrying a girl from a Scottish family in Bulawayo. There would be nobody from the Ross side of the family. He had sent the money, and the wedding was during the school holidays, but Mrs. Ross said she wasn't up to the journey. Dr. Jims had said that Maddy's mother was fit as a fiddle and well able to make the trip. In fact, the sea journey would do nothing except improve her health.

Father Gunn had said that family solidarity would be a great thing at a time like this and that truly she should make the effort. Major and Mrs. Murphy who lived in The Glen, the big house with the iron railings and the wonderful glasshouses, said that it was a chance of a lifetime. Mr. Hayes the solicitor said that if it were his choice, he'd go.

But Mother remained adamant. It was a waste, she said, to spend the money on a trip for such an old person as she was.

She would soon be getting her wings. She would see enough and know enough then.

Maddy was becoming increasingly impatient with this attitude of her mother's. The wings theory seemed to apply to everything. If Maddy wanted a new coat, or a trip to Dublin, or a perm for her light straight hair, her mother would sigh and say there would be plenty of time for that and money to spend on it after Mother had gone.

Mother was in her fifties and as strong as anyone in Shancarrig, but giving the aura of frailty. Maddy did the housework, because until Mother had got her wings there would be no money to spend on luxuries like having a maid. Maddy's own wages, as a Junior Assistant Mistress, were so small as to be insignificant.

She was twenty-three and very restless.

The only person in the whole of Shancarrig who understood was Father Barry. He was thirty-three and equally restless. He had been called to order for preaching too much about Vieja Piedra, by no less an authority than the Bishop. He burned with the injustice of it. Monsignor O'Toole, the parish priest, was doting, and knew nothing of what was being preached or what was not. Father Gunn must have gone behind his back and complained about him. Father Gunn was only a fellow curate, he had no authority over him.

Father Brian Barry roamed the woods of Barna, swishing angrily against the bushes that got in his way. What right had men, the pettiest and most jealous of men, to try to halt God's work for dying people, for brothers and sisters who were calling out to them?

If Brian Barry's own health had been better, he would have been a missionary priest. He would have been amongst the people of Vieja Piedra, like his friend from the seminary, Cormac Flynn, was. Cormac it was who wrote and told him at first hand of the work that had to be done.

In the Church of the Holy Redeemer there was a window dedicated to the memory of the Hayes family relations who had gone to their eternal reward. There had been many priests in that family. On the window were written the words *The Harvest Is Great but the Labourers Are Few*. There it was, written in stained glass, in their own church, and the mad parish priest and the selfish, complacent Father Gunn were so blind they couldn't see it.

In one of these angry walks Father Barry came across Miss Ross from the school, sitting on a tree trunk and puzzling over a letter. He calmed himself for a minute before he spoke. She was a gentle girl and he didn't want to let her know the depth of his rage and resentment in the battle for people's souls, and all the obstacles that were being put in his way.

She looked up startled when she saw him, but made room on the big tree stump for him to sit down.

"Isn't it beautiful here. You can often find a solution in this place, I think."

He reached through the slit in his cassock to take cigarettes out of his pocket and sat beside her without speaking.

Somehow, she seemed to understand the need for silence. She sat, hugging her knees and looking out ahead of her, as the summer afternoon light came in patches between the rowan trees and beeches that made up Barna Woods. A squirrel came and looked at them, inquisitively looking from one to the other before he hopped away.

They laughed. The tension and the silence broken, they could talk to each other easily.

"When I was young I'd never seen a squirrel," Father Barry said. "Only in picture books, and there was a giraffe on the same page so I always thought they were the same size. I was terrified of meeting one."

"When did you?"

"Not until I was in the seminary . . . someone said there was a squirrel over there and I urged everyone to take cover . . . they thought I was mad."

"Well, that's nothing," she encouraged him. "I thought guerrilla warfare was sending gorillas out to fight each other instead of people."

"You're saying that to make me feel good," he teased her.

"Not a bit of it. Did they all laugh or didn't any of them understand?"

"I had a friend, Cormac. He understood. He understood everything."

"That's Father Cormac out in Peru?"

"Yes. He understood everything. But how can I tell him what's happening now?"

As the shadows got longer they sat in Barna Woods and talked. Brian Barry told of his anguish over the work that had to be done and the burden of guilt he felt about the people of this place that seemed to call to him, but what did he do about Obedience to superiors? Maddy Ross told of her brother, Joseph, who had sent the money and expected his mother and sister to come and be there for the happiest day of his life.

"How can I find the words to tell him?" Maddy asked.

"How can I find the words to tell Cormac there'll be no more support from Shancarrig?" asked Father Barry.

That was the day that began their dependence on each other —the knowledge that only the other understood the pressures, the pain and the indecision. The very thought that somebody else understood gave each of them courage.

Maddy Ross found herself able to write to Joseph, and say that she would love to come to his wedding, but that Mother did not consider herself strong enough to travel. It meant a lot of silences and sulks at home, but Maddy weathered it. She assembled a simple wardrobe and made her bookings.

Eventually her mother relented and began to show some enthusiasm for the trip. She didn't take this enthusiasm to the point of going with her daughter, but at least the stony silences ended and the atmosphere had cleared.

Father Barry too showed courage. He spoke directly to Father Gunn, and said that he accepted the ruling of the diocese that there was not to be exceptional emphasis on the missions in general or on one mission field in particular. He agreed that other themes such as tolerance and charity on a home front and devotion to Our Blessed Lady, Queen of Ireland, be brought to the forefront.

He also said that in his spare time, if he could run sales of work, he could set up charitable projects in aid of Vieja Piedra. He felt sure that there could be no objection. To this Father Gunn, with a sigh of pure relief, said that there would be no objection.

In the summer of 1955 Maddy Ross and Brian Barry wished each other well, she on her journey to Africa, he on his fund-raising efforts so that Cormac Flynn would not be let down. When they met again in the autumn they would tell each other everything.

"We'll meet in the woods with the giant squirrels," said Father Barry.

"Watching out for the military gorillas," laughed Maddy Ross.

They were both looking forward to the meeting even as they were saying goodbye.

They were very much changed when they met again. They knew this just from the briefest meeting in the church porch after ten o'clock Mass. Father Barry was rearranging the pamphlets that the Catholic Truth Society published, which were in racks for sale, but were always mixed up whenever he passed them by. The problem was that everyone wanted to read "The Devil at Dances" and "Keeping Company," but nobody wanted to buy them. Copies of these booklets were always well thumbed and returned to some position or other.

He saw Madeleine come out with her mother. Mrs. Ross spent a lengthy time at the Holy Water font, blessing herself as if she were giving the Urbi et Orbi blessing from the papal balcony in Rome.

"Welcome back, stranger. Was it wonderful?" He smiled at her.

"No. It couldn't have gone more differently than was planned."

They looked at each other, both surprised by the intense way the other had spoken. Father Barry looked over at Mrs. Ross, still far enough away not to hear.

"Barna Woods," he said, his eyes dark and huge.

"At four o'clock," Maddy said.

She hadn't felt like this since gym class back at school, where they did the wall bars and all the blood ran to her head, making her feel dizzy and faint.

When she found herself deliberating over which blouse to wear she pulled herself up sharply. He's a priest, she said. But she still wore the striped one, which gave her more color and didn't make her look wishy-washy.

When her mother asked her where she was going, she said she wanted to pick the great fronds of beech leaves in Barna Woods. They could put them in glycerine later and preserve them to decorate the house for the winter.

"I'll look for some really good ones that have turned," she explained. "I might be some time."

She found him sitting on their log with his head in his hands. He told of a summer where everything he had done for Vieja Piedra had been thwarted, not just by Father Gunn, who had turned up dutifully at the bring-and-buy sale, at the whist drive, and the general knowledge quiz, but the interest simply wasn't there. And since he could no longer use the parish pulpit to preach of the plight of these poor people he didn't have the ears and the hearts of the congregation any more. His face was troubled. Maddy felt there was more he wasn't telling. She didn't push him. He would tell what he wanted to tell. Now he asked her about her, had her brother Joseph been delighted to see her.

"Yes, and no." Her brother's fiancée was of the Presbyterian faith and had only agreed to be married in a Catholic church to please Joseph. Now that his mother wasn't coming to the wedding, Joseph had decided that he shouldn't put Caitriona through all this since, really and truly as long as it was Christian, one service was the same as another in the eyes of God.

So Maddy had gone the whole way to Africa to see her brother commit a mortal sin. There had been endless arguments, discussions, and tears on both their parts. Joseph said that since they hardly knew each other their tie as brother and sister was not like a real family. Maddy had asked why then had he paid for her to come out to see him.

"To show people that I am not alone in the world," he had said.

Oh yes, she had attended the ceremony, and smiled, and been pleasant to all the guests. She had told her mother nothing of this. In fact, she was worn out remembering to say Father McPherson rather than Mr. McPherson, which was the name of the Presbyterian minister who had married the young couple, in a stiflingly hot church under a cloudless sky—a church with no tabernacle, and no proper God in it at all.

They walked together to find the kind of sprays she wanted. She explained that she had made a sort of excuse to her mother for going to the woods. Then she wished she hadn't said that— it might appear to him as if she needed an excuse for something so perfectly innocent as a meeting with a friend.

But, oddly, it struck a chord with him.

"I made an excuse too, to Father Gunn and Mrs. Kennedy of course. I told him that I wanted to make a couple of parish calls, the Dunnes and the Brennans. Both of them are sure to be out, or at any rate unlikely to invite me in."

They looked at each other and looked away. A lot had been admitted.

Speaking too quickly, she told him about how you preserved flowers and leaves, and how the trick was to put very few in a vase with a narrow opening.

Speaking equally quickly, he nodded agreement and perfect understanding of the process, and said that parish calls were an imposition on the priest and the people, everyone dreaded them, and how much better it would be to spend your life in a place where people really needed you rather than worrying had they a clean tablecloth and a slice of cake to give you. His face looked very bitter and sad as he spoke and she felt such huge sympathy for him that she touched him lightly on the arm.

"You *do* a great deal of good here. If you knew how much you touch all our lives."

To her shock his eyes filled with tears.

"Oh, Madeleine," he cried. "Oh God, I'm so lonely. I've no one to talk to, I've no friends. No one will listen."

"Shush, shush." She spoke as to a child. "I'm your friend. I'll listen."

He put his arms around her and laid his head on her shoulder. She felt arms around her waist and his body close to hers as he shook with sobs.

"I'm so sorry. I'm so foolish," he wept.

"No. No you're not. You're good. You care. You wouldn't be you unless you were so caring," she soothed him. She stroked his head and the back of his neck. She could feel his tears wet against her face as he raised his head to try to apologize.

"Shush, shush," she said again. She held him until the sobs died down. Then she took out her handkerchief, a small white one with a blue flower in the corner, and handed it to him.

They walked wordlessly to their tree trunk. He blew his nose very hard.

"I feel such a fool. I should be strong and courageous for you, Madeleine, tell you things that will console you about your brother's situation, not cry like a baby."

"No, you *do* make me feel courageous and strong, really Father Barry—"

He interrupted her sharply. "Now, listen here, if I'm going to cry in your arms, the least you can do is call me Brian."

She accepted it immediately. "Yes, but Brian, you must believe that you have helped me. I didn't think I was any use to anyone, a disappointment to my mother, no support to my brother . . ."

"You must have friends. You of all people, so generous and giving. You're not locked up in rigid rules and practices like I am."

"I have no friends," Madeleine Ross said simply.

••• •••

That afternoon there wasn't time to tell each other all their millions of things still to tell—like how Brian had a letter from his great friend Cormac Flynn in Peru saying for heaven's sake not to be so intense about Vieja Piedra, it was just one place on the globe—Father Brian Barry hadn't been born into the world thousands of miles away with a direct instruction to save the place single-handed.

Father Brian Barry had been more hurt than he could ever express by that letter. But when he told Maddy and she tumbled out her own information about Kathleen White and how she had begged Maddy, her friend, not to write to her so intensely, they saw it as one further common bond between them.

She learned about his childhood—his mother who had always wanted a son a priest. But who had died a month before his ordination and never received his blessing.

He heard of life with a mother who was becoming increasingly irrational—of a life lived more and more in fantasy—in a world where her cousins were people of great wealth and high breeding—where all kinds of niceties were important, the wearing of gloves, the owning of a coach and horses in the old days, the calling with visiting cards. None of it had any basis in reality, Maddy said, but Dr. Jims said it was harmless, lots of middle-aged women had notions and delusions of grandeur, and those harbored by Mrs. Ross were no worse that a lot of people's, and better than most.

Their meetings had to be more and more conspiratorial. Maddy would stay late in the school, decorating her window displays. Father Barry would call with some information for the Kellys and happen to see her in the classroom. The door would be left open. He would sit on the teacher's desk, swinging his legs. If Mrs. Kelly were to look in, and her anxious face seemed to look everywhere, then she would see nothing untoward.

But when they walked together in Barna Woods away from the eyes of the town they walked close together. Sometimes they would stop by chance at exactly the same time and she would lay her head companionably on his shoulder, and lean against him as they peeled the bark from a tree or looked at a bird's nest hidden in the branches.

Night after night Maddy lay alone in her narrow bed remembering that day he had cried and she had held him in the woods. She could remember the way his body shook and how she could hear his heart beat against her. She could bring back the smell of him, the smell of jelly beans and Gold Flake tobacco, of Knight's Castile soap. She could remember the way his hair had tickled her neck and how his tears had wet her cheeks. It was like seeing the same scene of a film over and over.

She wondered did he ever think of it, but supposed that would be foolishly romantic. And for Father Barry . . . for Brian . . . it might even be a sin.

Because of this new center to her life Maddy Ross was able to do more than ever before. She could scarcely remember the days when the time had seemed long and hung heavily around her. Now there weren't enough hours in the week for all that had to be done. She had long back hired young Maura Brennan from the cottages, a solemn poor child who loved stroking the furniture, to do her ironing and that worked out very well. Now on a different day she got young Eddie Barton to come and do her garden for her.

Eddie was a funny little fellow of about fourteen, interested in plants and nature. He would often want to talk to her about the various things that grew in her garden.

"What do you spend the money on?" she asked him one day. He reddened. "It doesn't matter. It's yours to spend any way you like."

"Stamps," he said eventually.

"That's nice. Have you a big collection?"

"No. To put on letters. Father Barry said we should have a pen friend overseas," he said.

It was wonderful to think how much good Father Barry was doing. Imagine a boy with wiry sticky-up hair like Eddie, a boy that would normally be kicking a ball up against a house wall, or writing messages on a wall, now had a Catholic pen friend overseas. She gave him extra money that day.

"Tell him about Shancarrig, what a great place it is."

"I do," Eddie said simply. "I write all about it."

When Eddie got flu and his mother wouldn't let him out, Foxy Dunne offered to do the chore.

"I believe you're a great payer, Miss Ross," he said cheerfully.

"You won't get as much as Eddie, you don't know which are flowers and which are weeds." She was spirited and cheerful herself.

"Ah but you're a teacher, Miss Ross. It'd only take you a minute to show me."

"Only till Eddie comes back," she agreed.

By the time Eddie was better and came back to fume of the desecration he claimed Foxy had done in the garden, Foxy had got himself several odd jobs, mending doors, fixing locks on an outhouse. Her mother didn't like having one of the Dunnes around the place in case he was sizing it up for a job for himself or one of his brothers.

"Oh Mother! They shouldn't all be tarred with the same brush," Maddy cried.

"You're nearly as unworldly as Father Barry himself," said her mother.

There had once been a Dramatic Society in Shancarrig, but it had fallen into inactivity. There was some vague story behind this, as there was behind everything. It had to do with the previous teacher having become very inebriated at a performance and some kind of unpleasantness was meant to have taken place. Nellie Dunne always said she could tell you a thing or two about the playacting that went on in this town. It was playacting in every sense of the word, she might say. But though she threatened, she never in fact did tell anybody a thing or two about what had gone on; and whatever it was had gone on long before Father Gunn had come to Shancarrig. And Monsignor O'Toole wasn't likely to remember it.

Maddy thought that very possibly the members of whatever it had been were sufficiently cooled to start again. She was surprised and pleased at the enthusiasm—Eddie Barton's mother said she'd help with the wardrobe, you always needed a professional to stop the thing looking like children playing charades. Biddy, the maid up at The Glen, said that if there was any call for a step dance she would be glad to oblige. It was a skill which her position didn't give her much chance to use, and she didn't want to get too rusty. Both Brian and Liam Dunne from the hardware shop said they would join, and Carrie who looked after Dr. Jims' little boy said she'd love to try out for a small part, but nothing with too many lines. Sergeant Keane and his wife both said it was the one thing they had been waiting for and the Sergeant pumped Maddy's hand up and down in gratitude.

So Maddy started the Shancarrig Dramatic Society and they were always very grateful for the kind interest that Father Barry took in their productions. Nobody thought it a bit odd that the saintly young priest with the sad face should throw himself wholeheartedly into anything that was for the parish good. And, of course, the proceeds went to the charity of the missions in South America. And it was just as well to have Father Barry, everyone agreed, laughing a little behind Father Gunn's back, because poor Father Gunn, in spite of his many other great qualities, didn't know one side of the stage from the other, while Father Barry could turn his hand to anything. He could design a set, arrange the lighting, and best of all, direct performances. He coaxed the townspeople of Shancarrig to play everything from *Pygmalion* to *Drama at Inish*, and the Christmas concerts were a legend.

Only Maddy knew how his heart wasn't in any of it.

Only she knew the real man, who hid his unhappiness. Soon she found she was thinking of him all the time, and imagining his reaction to the smallest and most inconsequential things she did. If she was telling the story of the Flight into Egypt to the Mixed Infants at school, she imagined him leaning against the door smiling at her approvingly. Sometimes she smiled back as if he were really there. The children would look around to see if someone had come in.

Then at home, when she was preparing her mother's supper, she would decorate the plate with a garnish of finely sliced tomato, or chopped hard-boiled egg and fresh parsley. Her mother barely noticed, but she could see how Brian Barry would respond. She would put words of praise in his mouth and say them to herself.

She spent her time in what she considered was a much more satisfactory relationship than anyone else around her. Mr. and Mrs. Kelly, the teachers in the school, were locked in a routine marriage if ever she saw one. Poor Maura Brennan of the cottages, who married a flash harry of a barman, was left alone with her Down syndrome child to rear. Major Murphy in The Glen had a marriage that defied description. They never went anywhere outside their four walls. In any other land they would have been called recluses, but here, because The Glen was the big house, they were admired for their sense of isolation.

There was nobody that Madeleine Ross envied. Nobody she knew had as dear and pure a love as she had known, a man who depended on her utterly and who would have been lost to his vocation if it had not been for her.

And then one night all of a sudden, when she least expected it, came a strange thought. It was one of those sleepless nights when the moon seemed unnaturally bright and visible even through the curtains, so it was easier to leave them open.

Maddy saw a figure walking past going to the woods. She thought first that it was Brian, and she was about to slip into some clothes and follow him. But then she saw at the last moment that it was Major Murphy, on goodness knew what kind of outing. It was easy to mistake them, tall men in dark clothes. But Brian was asleep in the presbytery, or possibly not asleep, maybe looking at the same moon and feeling the same restlessness.

That was when it came to Maddy Ross that Father Barry should leave Shancarrig.

He could no longer be wasted passing plates of sandwiches, rigging up old curtains, praising a tuneless choir, welcoming yet another bishop or visiting churchmen. There was only one life to be lived. He must go and live it as best he could, serving the people of Vieja Piedra. The whole notion of there being only one life to live buzzed around in her head all night. There was no more sleep now. She sat hugging the mug of tea, remembering how her brother, Joseph, had said those very words to her, all that while ago when she had gone to Rhodesia for his wedding, about there being only one chance to live your life.

And Joseph, who had been given the same kind of education as she had, and who came from the same parents, had been able to seize at the life he wanted. Joseph and Caitriona Ross had children out in Africa. Sometimes they sent pictures of them, outside their big white house with the pillars at the front door. Maddy had never told her mother that these little children weren't Catholics and might not even have been properly baptized. She and Brian had agreed that it was better not to trouble an already troubled mind with such information.

If Joseph Ross had only one life, so had Maddy Ross and so had Brian Barry. Why couldn't Father Brian leave and go to South America? After a decent interval Maddy could leave too and be with him.

For part of the night as she paced the house she told herself that things need not change between them. They would be as they were here, true friends doing the work they felt was calling across the land and sea to them. And Brian could remain a priest. Once a priest always a priest. He wouldn't have to leave, just change the nature and scope of his vocation.

And then as dawn came up over Barna Woods, Maddy Ross admitted to herself what she had been hiding. She acknowledged that she wanted Brian Barry to be her love, her husband. She wanted him to leave the priesthood. If he could get released from his vows by Rome, so much the better. But even if he could not, Maddy wanted him anyway. She would take him on any terms.

It was a curious freedom realizing this.

She felt almost light-headed and at the same time she stopped playing games. She took her mother breakfast on a tray without fantasizing what Brian would say if he had been standing beside them looking on. It was as if she had come out of the shadows, she thought, and into the real world.

She could barely wait to meet Brian. No day had ever seemed longer. Mrs. Kelly had never been sharper or more inquisitive about everything Maddy was doing.

Why was she putting greetings on the blackboard in different languages? Spanish. And French, no less. Wasn't it enough for these bonehead children to try and learn Irish and English like the department laid down without filling their heads with how to say *Goodday* and *Goodbye* in tongues they'd never need to use?

Maddy looked at her levelly. Normally, she would have seen Brian in her mind's eye standing by the blackboard, congratulating her on her patience and forbearance, and then the two of them wandering together in Barna Woods crying, *Buenos días, Vieja Piedra*, we are coming to help you.

But today she saw no shadowy figure. She saw only the small quivering Mrs. Kelly, who was wearing a brown and yellow striped dress and looked for all the world like a wasp.

Maddy Ross was a different person today.

"I'm putting some phrases in foreign languages on the blackboard Mrs. Kelly because, despite what you and the Department of Education think, these children may well go to lands where they use them. And I shall put them on the blackboard every day until they feel a little bit of confidence about themselves instead of being humble and content to remain in Shancarrig pulling their caps and saying *Good morning* in Irish and English until they are old men and women."

Mrs. Kelly went red and white in rapid succession.

"You'll do nothing of the sort, Miss Ross. Not in the timetable that is laid down for you."

"I had no intention of doing it in school time, Mrs. Kelly."
Maddy smiled a falsely sweet smile. "I am in the fortunate position of being able to hold the children's interest *outside* school
hours as well as when the bell rings. They will learn it before or
after school. That will be clearly understood."

She felt twenty feet tall. She felt as if she were elevated above
the small stone schoolhouse and the town. She could hardly
bear the slow noise of the clock ticking until she could go to
Brian and tell him of her new courage, her hope, and her belief
that they had only one chance at life.

She met him at rehearsal under the eyes of the nosey people
in town.

"How is your mother these days, Miss Ross?" he asked. It
was part of their code. They had never practiced it; it just came
naturally to them, as so much else would now.

"She's fine, Father, always asking for you, of course."

"I might drop in and see her later tonight, if you think she'd
like that."

"She'd love it, Father. I'll just let her know. I'm going out
myself, but she'd be delighted to see you, like everyone."

Her eyes danced with mischief as she said the words. She
thought she saw the hint of a frown on Brian Barry's face, but it
passed.

Miss Ross left the rehearsal and she imagined people thinking that she was a dutiful daughter, and very good also to the
priest, to go home and prepare a little tray for her mother to
offer him. As Maddy walked home, her cheeks burning, she
thought that she had been a bloody good daughter for all her
life, nearly thirty years of life in this small place. And come to
think of it she had been good to the priest too. Good for him
and a good friend. Nobody could blame her for wanting her
chance at life.

She sat in the wood and waited on their log. He came gently
through the leafy paths. His smile was tired. Something had
crossed him during the day; she knew him so very well, every
little change, every flicker in his face.

"I'm late. I had to go into your mother's," he said.

"What on earth for? You know I didn't mean . . ."

"I know, but Father Gunn said to me, this very morning, that he thought I should see less of you."

"What!"

Brian Barry was nervous and edgy. "Oh, he said it very nicely, of course, not an accusation, nothing you could take offense at . . ."

"I most certainly do take offense at it," Maddy blazed. "How dare he insinuate that there has been anything improper between us. How *dare* he!"

"No, he didn't. He was very anxious that I should know he wasn't suggesting that." He walked up and down as he talked, agitated, and anxious to get over the mildness of the message, the lack of blame and the motive behind it. It was just that Father Gunn wanted to protect them both from evil minds and idle wagging tongues. In a place this size when people had little real news to speculate about they made up their own. It would be better for Father Barry not to be seen so obviously sharing the same interests as Miss Ross, for both of them to make other friends.

"And what did you say, Brian?" Her pale eyes had flecks of light in them tonight.

"I said that he had a very poor opinion of people if he thought they would give such low motives to what was an obvious and proper friendship." But it was obvious that Brian Barry had not found his own answer satisfactory. He looked confused and bewildered. She had never loved him more. "I am sorry, Maddy. I couldn't think of what else to say." He had never called her Maddy before, always Madeleine like her mother did.

She moved over to him and closed her arms around his neck. He smelled still of cigarette smoke, but his soap was Imperial Leather now, and he hadn't been eating jelly beans. It was the chocolate cake given to him, Maddy realized, by her mother.

"It was perfect," she whispered.

He looked very startled and moved as if to get away.

"What was perfect?" he asked, his eyes large and alarmed.

"What you said. It is a proper friendship and a proper love . . ."

"Yes . . . well . . ." He hadn't raised his arms to hold her.

She moved nearer to him and pressed herself toward him, "Brian, hold me. Please hold me."

"I can't Maddy. I can't. I'm a priest."

"I held you years ago when you had no friend. Hold me now; now that I have no friend and they are trying to take you away." Her eyes filled with tears.

"No, no, no." He soothed her as she had stroked him all that time ago. He held her head to his shoulder and comforted her. "No, it's not a question of being taken away . . . it's just . . . well, you know what it is."

She snuggled closer to him. Again she could hear his heart beat in the way she had remembered so often from that first time. He was about to release her so she allowed sobs to shake her body again. He was so clumsy, and tender at the same time. Maddy knew that this was her man, and her one chance to take what life was presenting.

"I love you so much, Brian" she whispered.

The answering words were not there. She changed direction slightly.

"You are the only person who understands me, who knows what I want to do in the world, and I think I'm the only person who knows what is best for you." She gulped as she spoke so that he wouldn't think the storm was over, the need for consolation at an end. In the seven years since they had first held each other in these woods times had changed; when he offered her a handkerchief now, it was a paper tissue, when he sat down beside her on their log to smoke it wasn't the flakey old Gold Flake, it was a tipped cigarette.

"You've been better to me than anyone in the world. I mean that." His voice was sincere. He *did* mean it. She could see his brain clicking through all the people who had been good to him, his mother, some kind superior in the seminary possibly. She was the best of this pathetic little list. That was all. Why was she not his great love? She would have to walk very warily.

"I have wanted the best for you since the day I met you," she said simply.

"And I for you. Truly."

This was probably true, Maddy thought. Like he wanted the best for the people of Vieja Piedra, wanted it in his heart but wasn't able to do anything real and lasting about it.

"You must go there," she said.

"Go there?"

"To Peru. To Father Cormac."

He looked at her as if she were suggesting he fly to the moon. "How can I go, Maddy, they'll never let me."

"Don't ask them. Just go. You've often said that God isn't worried about some pecking order and lines of obedience. Our Lord didn't ask permission when he wanted to heal people."

He still looked doubtful. Maddy got up and paced up and down beside him. With all the powers of persuasion she could gather she told him why he must go. She played back to him all his own thoughts and phrases about this small village where people had died waiting for someone to come and help them, where they looked up to the mountain pass each day hoping that a man of God would come, not just to visit but to stay amongst them and give them the Sacraments. She could see the light coming to his eye, the magic was working.

"How would I get the fare to go there?" he asked.

"You can take it from the collection." To her it was simple.

"I couldn't do that. It's for Vieja Piedra."

"But isn't that exactly where you would be going? Isn't that why we're raising this money, so that they'd have someone to help them?"

"No, I don't believe that would be right. I've never been sure about the end justifying the means . . . remember we often discussed that." They had, here in this wood, sitting in her classroom, having coffee after the rehearsals for the plays.

She looked at him, flushed and eager in the middle of yet another moral dilemma, but not moved by the fact that he had held her close to him and felt her heart beat, her hair against his face, her eyelashes on his cheek. Was he an ordinary man or had he managed to quell that side of himself so satisfactorily that it didn't respond anymore? She had to know.

"And when you go you can write and tell me about it . . . until I come there too."

His eyes were dark circles of amazement now. "You come out there, Maddy? You couldn't. You couldn't come all that far and you can't be with me. I'm a priest."

"We have only one life." She spoke calmly.

"And I chose mine as a priest. You know I can't change that. Nothing will change that."

"You can change it if you want to. Just like you can change the place you live." There was something in the direct simple way she spoke that seemed to alarm him. This was not the overexcitable intense Maddy Ross he had known, it was a serious young woman going after what she wanted.

"Sit down, Maddy." He too was calm. He squatted in front of her, holding both her hands in his. "If I ever gave you the impression that I might leave the priesthood, then I must spend the rest of my days making up for such a terrible misunderstanding. . . ." His face was troubled as he sought some response in hers. "Maddy, I am a priest forever. It's the one thing that means anything to me. I've been selfish and impatient and critical of those around me, I don't have the understanding and generosity of a Father Gunn but I do have this belief that God chose me and called me."

"You also have the belief that the people of Vieja Piedra are calling you."

"Yes, I do. If there was a way to go there I *would* go. You have given me that courage. I won't take the money that the people of Shancarrig raised. They didn't raise it for their priest to run away with."

The moon came up as they talked. They saw a badger quite nearby, but it wasn't important enough for either of them to comment on. Brian Barry told Madeleine Ross that he would never leave his ministry. He had few certainties in life. This was one of them. In vain did Maddy tell him that clerical celibacy was only something introduced long after Our Lord's time, it was more or less a civil service ruling, not part of the constitution. The first apostles had wives and children.

"Children." She stroked his hand as she said the word.

He pulled both hands away from her and stood up. This was something he was never going to think about. It was the sacrifice he had made for God, the one thing God wanted from his priests: to give up the happiness and love of a wife and family. Not that it had been hard to give up because he had never known it, and now he was heading for forty years of age so it wasn't something he would be thinking of, even if he weren't a priest.

"A lot of men marry around forty," Maddy said.

"Not priests."

"You can do anything. Anything."

"I won't do this."

"But you love me, Brian. You're not going to be frightened into some kind of cringing life for the rest of your days by a silly warning from Father Gunn, by Mrs. Kennedy spying, by a promise made when you were a child . . . when you didn't know what love was . . . or anything about it."

"I still don't really know."

"You know."

He shook his head and Maddy could bear it no more. She reached out for him and kissed him directly on the lips. She moved herself into his arms and opened her mouth to his. She felt his arms tighten around her . . . he stroked her back and then because she pulled away from his clasp a little he stroked the outline of her breasts. She peeped through her closed eyes and saw that his eyes were closed too.

They stood locked like this for a time. Eventually he pulled away.

They looked at each other for moments before he spoke. "You've given me everything, Maddy Ross," he said.

"I haven't begun to give you anything," she said.

"No but you have, believe me. You've given me such bravery, such faith. Without you I'd be nothing. You've given me the courage to go. Now you must give me one more thing . . . the freedom."

She looked at him with disbelief. "You could hold me like that and ask me never to be in your arms again?"

"That is what I'm begging you. *Begging* you, Maddy. It was my only sure center. The only thing I knew . . . that I was to be a priest of God. Don't take that away from me or all the other things you have given will totter like a house of cards."

This man had been her best friend, her soul mate. Now he was asking her permission and her encouragement to leave her life entirely, to step out of it and away from Shancarrig to the village that they had both dreamed about and prayed for and saved for all these years.

Such monstrous selfishness couldn't be part of God's plan. It couldn't be part of any dream of taking your chance in life. Maddy looked at him, confused. It was all going wrong, very very wrong.

He saw her shock, he didn't run away from it. He spoke very gently.

"Since I came to Shancarrig and even before it I've known that women are stronger than men. We could list them in this town. And I know more than you because I hear them in the Confessional. I'm there at their deathbeds when they worry not about their own pain but about how a husband will manage or whether a son will go to the bad. I've been there when their babies have died at birth, when they bury a man who was not only a husband but their means of living. Women are very strong. Can you be strong and let me go with your blessing?"

She looked at him dumbly. The words would not come, the torrent of words welling up inside her. She must be able to explain that he could not be bound by these tired old rules, these empty vows made at another time by another person. Brian Barry was different now, he had come into his kingdom, he was a man who could love and give. But she said none of these things. Which was just as well because he looked at her and the dark blue of his eyes was hard.

"You see, I want to go with your blessing, because I'm *going* to go anyway."

••• •••

They didn't meet again in Shancarrig without other people being present.

There were no more walks in the woods, no visits to the classroom. The rehearsals had to do without the kind help of Father Barry, Shancarrig Dramatic Society was told. He had been told to take it easy. Somehow that was the hardest place, the place she missed him most. They had started these plays together, she didn't know how she would have the heart to continue. In fact, she feared the whole organization would fall apart without him.

The Shancarrig Dramatic Society continued to thrive without Father Barry. In many ways his leaving gave them greater scope. They were able to do more comedies. They had never liked to suggest anything too lighthearted when Father Barry was there, he was so soulful and good it seemed like being too flippant in his presence.

In the weeks that seemed endless to Maddy the society decided to enter an All Ireland contest for the humorous one-act play.

"Poor Father Barry. He'd have loved this," said Biddy from The Glen, who was going to play a dancing washroom woman in the piece.

"Go on out of that, we'd be doing a tragedy if Poor Father Barry was here. Not that I wish the man any harm, and I hope whatever's bothering him gets better."

The rumor was that he had a spot on his lung. Heads nodded. Yes, it was true he did have that color, the very pale complexion with occasional spots of high color that could spell out T.B. Still, the sanatorium was wonderful and anyway it hadn't been confirmed yet.

He didn't avoid her eye, Maddy realized. He was totally at peace with himself, and grateful to her that she had nodded her head that day in Barna Woods and left without trusting herself to speak a word.

He thought she had seen his way was the only way.

The days were endless as she waited to hear that he had gone. It was three whole months before she heard what she had been waiting for. Father Gunn visiting the school in his usual way had asked her pleasantly if she could drop in at the presbytery that evening. Nothing in his face had given a hint of what was to be said.

When she arrived she was startled to see Brian sitting in one of the chairs. Father Gunn motioned her to the other.

"Maddy, you know that Father Barry is going to Peru?"

"I knew he wanted to." She spoke carefully, but smiled at Brian. His face was alive and happy. "You mean, it's settled? You're going to be able to go, officially?"

"I'm going with everyone's blessing," Brian said. His face was full of love, love and gratitude.

"The Bishop is very understanding and when he saw such missionary zeal he said it would be hard not to encourage it," said Father Gunn.

It had always been impossible to see Father Gunn's eyes through those glasses, but they seemed more opaque than ever. Maddy wondered had Father Gunn told the Bishop that Vieja Piedra alone and on Church business was infinitely preferable to another alternative.

"I hope it's every bit as rewarding for you as you and I have always believed it would be." Her voice choked slightly.

"I wanted to thank you, Maddy, for all your help and encouragement. Father Gunn has been so wise and understanding about everything. When I told him that I wanted you to be the first to know he insisted that we invite you here, to tell you that it has all finally gone through."

Maddy looked at Father Gunn. She knew exactly why she had been invited to the presbytery, so that there could be no tearful farewells, implorings, and highly charged emotion in Barna Woods, or anywhere on their own.

"That's very kind of you, Father," she said to the small square priest, in a very cold tone.

"No, no, and I must just get some papers. I'll leave the two of you for a few minutes." He fussed out of the room.

Brian didn't move from his chair. "I owe it all to you, Maddy," he said.

"Will you write?" she asked, her voice dull.

"To everyone, a general letter in response to whatever marvelous fund raising you do for me. . . ." He smiled at her winningly as he had smiled at so many people. As he would smile at the poor Peruvians in the dry valley, who had been calling out for him. She said nothing.

And for the first time in seven years they sat in silence. They willed the time to pass when Father Gunn would have found his letters and returned to the sitting room of the presbytery. The sitting room door had been left open.

The farewells were endless. Father Barry wanted no present, he insisted. He didn't need any goodbye gift to remind him of Shancarrig, its great people, and the wonderful years he had spent here. He said he would try to describe what the place was like, their namesake on the other side of the world.

He cried when they came to see him off at the station. Maddy was in the back of the crowd. She wanted to be sure he was actually going. She wanted to see it with her own eyes. He waved with one hand and dabbed his eyes with the other. Maddy heard Dr. Jims saying to Mr. Hayes that he was always a very emotional and intense young man. He hoped he would fare all right in that hot climate over there.

And the time went by, but it was like a summer garden when the sun has gone, and although there's daylight there's no point in sitting out in it. More children came and went in Mixed Infants. They left Miss Ross and went up to Mrs. Kelly. They still learned how to say *Bonjour* and *Buenos días* in their own time. Maddy Ross had won that victory hard from Mrs. Kelly, she was not going to give it up.

The fund raising continued, but Ireland was changing in the

sixties. There was television for one thing . . . people heard about other parts of the world where there was famine and disaster. Suddenly Vieja Piedra was not the only place that called to them. Sometimes the collections were small that went in the money order to the Reverend Brian Barry at his post office box in a hill town some sixty-seven miles from Vieja Piedra.

Yet his letters were always grateful and warm, and there were stories of the church being built, a small building. It looked like a shed with a cross on top, but Father Barry was desperately proud of it. Pictures were sent of it, badly focused snapshots taken from different angles.

And then there was the wonderful help of Viatores Christi, some lay Christians who were coming out to help. They were invaluable, as committed in every way as were the clergy.

Maddy heard the letters read aloud, and wondered why could Brian Barry not have become a lay missionary. Then there would have been the same dream and the same hope but no terrible promise about celibacy.

But she cheered herself up. If he had not been ordained as a priest, he would never have come to Shancarrig, she would never have known him, never have had her chance in life.

There had been five years of walking alone in Barna Woods, five plays in Shancarrig Dramatic Society, five Christmas concerts, there had been five sales of work, whist drives, treasure hunts. There had been five years of raffles, bingo, house-to-house collections. And then, one day, Brian Barry telephoned Maddy Ross.

"I thought you'd be home from school by now." He sounded as if he were down the road. He couldn't be telephoning her from Peru!

"I'm in Dublin," he said.

Her heart gave an uncomfortable lurch. Something was happening. Why had the communication not been through Father Gunn?

"I want to see you. Nobody knows I'm home."

"Brian." Her voice was only a whisper.

"Don't tell anyone at all. Just come tomorrow."

"But why? What's happened?"

"I'll tell you tomorrow."

"Tomorrow? All the way to Dublin, just like that?"

"I've come all the way from Peru."

"Is anything wrong? Is there any trouble?"

"No no. Oh Maddy, it's good to talk to you."

"I haven't talked to you for five years, Brian. You have to tell me why are you home. Are you going to leave the priesthood?"

"Please, Maddy. Trust me. I want to tell you personally. That's why I came the whole way back. Just get the early train, will you? I'll meet you."

"Brian?"

"I'll be on the platform." He hung up.

She had to cash a check at the hotel. Mrs. Ryan was interested as usual in everything. Maddy gave her no information. Her mind was too confused. She knew there would be no sleep tonight.

For five years she had slept seven hours a night.

But tonight she would not close her eyes. No matter how tired and old she might look next morning, Maddy knew that there was no point in lying in that same bed where she had lain for years, seeking sleep.

Instead she examined everything in her wardrobe.

She chose a cream blouse and a blue skirt. She wore a soft blue woolen scarf around her neck. It wasn't girlish but it was youthful. It didn't look like the aging schoolteacher grown old in her love for the faraway priest.

Maddy smiled. At least she had kept her sense of humor. Whatever he was going to tell her, he would like that.

He didn't seem to have got a day older. He was boyish, even at forty-five. His collar was up, so she couldn't see whether he still wore his roman collar, but she had told herself not to read anything into that. Out in the missions priests wore no clerical garb and yet they were as firmly priests as ever they had been.

He saw her and ran to her. They hugged like a long-separated brother and sister, like old friends parted unwillingly, which is probably what they were. She pulled away from him to see his face, but still he hugged her. You can't kiss someone who is hugging the life out of you.

The crowd had thinned on the platform. Some caution seemed to seep back into him.

"There was no one from home on the train, was there?"

"Where's home?" She laughed at him. "In all your letters you say Vieja Piedra is home."

"And so it is." He seemed satisfied that they weren't under surveillance. He tucked her arm into his and they walked to a nearby hotel. The lounge was small and dark, the coffee strong and scalding. Maddy Ross would remember forever the way it stuck to the roof of her mouth when Brian Barry told her that he was going to leave the priesthood and marry Deirdre, one of the volunteers. It was like a patch of red-hot tar in her mouth. It wouldn't go away as she nodded and listened and forced her face to smile through tales of growth, and understanding and love and the emptiness of vows taken at an early age before a boy was a man, and about a loving God not holding people to meaningless promises.

And she heard how there was still a lot to be decided. Deirdre and he had realized that laicization took such a long time, and brought so much grief, destroying the relationships of those who waited.

But in South America the clergy had understood the core values. They had gone straight to the heart of things. They knew that a blessing could be given to a union of which God would patently approve. What was the expression that Maddy herself had used so many years ago? Something about thinking in terms of the constitution rather than in petty civil service bylaws.

And he owed it all to Maddy. So often he had told that to Deirdre, who wanted to send her gratitude. If Maddy hadn't proved to him that he could be courageous and open up his heart to the world and to love, this might never have happened.

"Did you ever love me?" Maddy asked him.

"Of course I love you. I love you with all my heart. Nothing will destroy our love, not my marrying Deirdre or you marrying whoever you will. Maybe you have someone in mind?" He was roguish now, playful even. She wanted to knock him down.

"No. No plans as yet."

"Well, you should, Maddy." Gone was the lighthearted banter, now he was being serious and caring. "A woman should get married, and have children. That's what a woman should do."

"And have you and Deirdre decided to have children?" She tried to put the smile back in her voice. It was so easy to let a sneer creep in instead, to let him know how she could sense that Deirdre was already pregnant.

"Eventually," he told her, which meant imminently.

He was going to leave Vieja Piedra, and they were going to a place further down the coast of Peru. He would teach in a town, there was just as much work needed there, but they had found a native-born priest, a real Peruvian, to look after the valley of Vieja Piedra. He talked on. Nothing would be said to Father Gunn. The fund raising would take a different style. Nothing would be said to anyone really. In today's world you didn't need to explain or to be intense. It was a matter of seizing what good there was and creating more good. It was taking your chance when it was offered.

The only person who *had* to be told face-to-face was Maddy. That's why he had taken Deirdre's savings to come back and tell her, to thank her in the way that a letter could never do for having put him on this road to happiness.

"And did Deirdre not feel afraid that once you saw your old love you might never return to her?" Maddy's tone was light, her question deadly serious.

But Brian hastened to put her anxieties at rest. "Lord no. Deirdre knew that what *we* had wasn't love. It was childlike fumblings, it was heavy meaning-of-life conversation, it was

part of growth, and for me a very important part." He wanted
to reassure her about that.

The train back to Shancarrig left in fifteen minutes. Maddy
said she thought she should take it.

"But, you can't go *now*, you've only been here an hour." His
dismay was enormous.

"But you've told me everything."

"No, I haven't told you anything really. I have only skimmed
the surface."

"I have to go back, Brian. I would have, anyway, no matter
what you told me. My mother hasn't been well."

"I didn't know that."

"Of course you didn't. You didn't know a great many things,
like Mrs. Murphy in The Glen died, and that Maura Brennan
brings her poor son around with her and he sits in every house
in Shancarrig while she cleans floors and does washing. There
are many many things you don't know."

"Well, they don't tell me. *You* don't tell me. You don't write at
all."

"I was ordered not to. Don't you remember?"

"Not ordered, just advised."

"To you it was the same once."

"If you'd wanted to write to me enough you would have," he
said, head on one side, roguish again.

She closed her mind to his disbelief that she would return on
the next train. He had thought she would spend the whole day,
if not the weekend, in Dublin with him. What was he to do
now? No relations were meant to know he was back.

"Did I do the wrong thing coming back to tell you?" He was
a child again, confused, uncertain.

She was gentle. She could afford to be. She had a lifetime
ahead of her with little to contemplate except why her one stab
at living life had failed. She reached out and held his hand.

"No, you did the right thing," she lied straight into his face.
"Tell Deirdre that I wish you well, all of you. Tell her I went
back to Shancarrig on the train with my heart brimming over."

Maeve Binchy

It was the only wedding present she could give him.

And she held the tears until the train had turned the bend and until she could no longer see his eager hand waving her goodbye.

3

Maura

When the time came for Maura to go to school any small enthusiasm that there had ever been in the Brennan family for education had died down. Maura's mother was worn out with all the demands that were made on her to dress them up for this May Procession and that visit from the Bishop. Not to mention Communions and Confirmations. Mrs. Brennan had been heard to say that the Shancarrig School had notions about itself being some kind of private college for the sons and daughters of the landowning gentry rather than the National School it was, and that nature had always intended it to be.

And the young Maura didn't get much encouragement from her father either. Paudie Brennan believed that schools and all that were women's work and not things a man got involved with. And since Paudie Brennan was not a man ever continuously in work he couldn't be expected to take an interest financially and every other way in each and every one of his nine living children and Maura came near the end of the trail. Paudie Brennan had too much on his mind what with a leaking roof missing a dozen slates, and a very different and worrying kind of slate altogether above in Johnny Finn Noted for Best Drinks, what time was there to be wondering about young Maura and her book learning?

Maura had never expected there to be an interest. School was for books, home was for fights. The older brothers and sisters had gone to England—the really grown-up ones. They went as soon as they were seventeen or eighteen. They came home for holidays and it was great at first, but after a day it would wear off, the niceness, and there would be shouting again as if the returned sister or brother was an ordinary part of the family, not a visitor.

One day, Maura knew, she would be the eldest one left at home—just herself and Geraldine left. But Maura wasn't going to England to work in a shoe factory like Margaret, or a fish shop like Deirdre. No, she was going to stay here in Shancarrig. She wouldn't get married but she would live like Miss Ross, who was very old and could do what she liked and stay up all night without anyone giving out or groaning at her. Of course, Miss Ross was a schoolteacher and must earn pots and pots of money, but Maura would save whenever she started to work, and keep the money in the post office until she could have a house and freedom and go to bed at two in the morning if the notion took her.

Maura Brennan often stayed on late at school to talk to Miss Ross, to try and find out more about this magnificent life-style in the small house with the lilac bushes and the tall hollyhocks, where Miss Ross lived. She would ask endless questions about the dog or the cat. She knew their names and ages, which nobody else at school did. She would hope that one day Miss Ross might drop another hint or two about her life. Miss Ross seemed puzzled by her interest. The child was in no way bright. Even taking into account her loutish father and timid uneducated mother, young Maura must still be called one of the slower learners in the school. Even the youngest of that Brennan string of children, Geraldine with the permanent cold and her hair in her eyes, was quicker. But Maura was the one who hung about, who found excuses to have meaningless little conversations.

One day Miss Ross let slip that she hated ironing.

"I love ironing," Maura said. "I love it, I'd do it all day but the one we have is broke, and my Da won't pay to have it mended."

"What do you like about it?" Miss Ross had seemed genuinely interested.

"The way your hand goes on and on . . . it's like music almost . . . and the clothes get lovely and smooth, and it all smells nice and clean," Maura said.

"You make it sound great. I wish you'd come and do mine."

"Of course I will," said Maura.

She was eleven then, a square girl with her hair clipped back by a brown slide, she had a high forehead and clear eyes. In a different family in another place she might have had a better chance, a start that would have brought her further along some kind of road.

"No, Maura, you can't, child. I don't want the other children to see you rating yourself as only fit to do my ironing. I don't want you making little of yourself before you have to."

"How could that be making little of myself?" The question was without guile. Maura Brennan saw no lack of dignity in coming to the teacher's house to do household chores.

"The others . . . they don't have to know, Miss Ross."

"But they do, they will. You know this place."

"They don't know lots of things, like that my sister Margaret had a baby in Northampton. Geraldine and I are aunts, Miss Ross. Imagine!" Maura had told the family secret easily, as if she knew that there was no danger that Miss Ross would pass on this titbit. There was the same simplicity as when she had spoken of ironing.

"Once a week, and I'll pay you properly," Miss Ross had said.

"Thank you, Miss Ross, I'll put it in the post office." It was the beginning for Maura Brennan. She warned young Geraldine not to tell anyone. It would be their secret.

"Why has it to be a secret?" Geraldine wanted to know.

"I don't know." Maura was truthful. "But it has."

So if ever Mrs. Brennan asked what was keeping Maura above at the school, Geraldine said she didn't know. It seemed daft to her, all this sucking up to Miss Ross. It wasn't as if Maura ever got anywhere at her books. She was slow and was always asking people to help her, Leo Murphy or Nessa Ryan, girls from important families, big houses. Geraldine would know better than to talk to them or their like, but Maura was half daft a lot of the time.

When Maura started doing the ironing Miss Ross gave her a doll as well as the money. She said she had seen Maura admiring it and even taking off its crushed pink dress and giving it a good press. Anyone who thought that much of a doll should have it. Maura always told Geraldine it was on loan. Miss Ross had lent it to her until the time Miss Ross married someone and had children of her own.

"Sure Miss Ross is a hundred. She'll never marry and have children," Geraldine cried.

"People have them at all ages. Look at Mammy, look at St. Elizabeth."

Geraldine wasn't so sure of her ground on St. Elizabeth, but she knew all about their mother. "Mammy started having them and she couldn't stop. I heard her telling Mrs. Barton. But after me she stopped all of a sudden." Geraldine was nine and she knew everything.

Maura wished she had those kinds of certainties.

The doll sat on a shelf in their bedroom. It had a china face and little china hands. When Geraldine wasn't there to laugh at her Maura would hug it and speak reassuring words, saying that the doll was very much loved. Sometimes Miss Ross gave Maura things to wear, a nice colored belt once, a scarf with a tassel.

"I never wore them in the school, no one would know."

"But what would I mind if they knew?" Again the question

was so honest and without guile that Miss Ross seemed taken aback.

"I wish I could help you with your lessons, Maura. I wish I could, but you don't really have the will to concentrate."

Maura was eager to reassure her. "I'll be fine, Miss Ross. There's no point in trying to put things into my head that won't go in, and what would I need with all those sums and knowing poems off by heart. It wouldn't be any use to me at all."

"What's to become of you, though . . . off to England like Deirdre and Margaret with no qualifications . . . ?"

"No, I'm staying here. I'm going to get a house like this one, and have it the way you do, lovely and shiny and clean, and colored china on a dresser and a smell of lavender polish everywhere."

"It'll be some lucky man if you are going to do all that for him."

"I won't be getting married, Miss Ross." It was one of the few things she had ever said with conviction.

Her sister Geraldine believed her too, over this.

"Why don't you go the whole hog and be a nun?" Geraldine wanted to know. "If you're so sure you're not going to get a fellow, hadn't you better be in a convent, singing hymns and getting three meals a day?"

"I can still pray in a house of my own. I'll have a Sacred Heart lamp on a small wooden shelf, and I'll have a picture of Our Lady, Queen of May on a small round table with a blue tablecloth and a vase of flowers in front of it."

She didn't say that she was going to buy a chair for the doll too.

Geraldine shrugged. She was twelve now, and much more grown up than her sister of fourteen, who would be leaving school this year. Geraldine's Confirmation was coming up and between wheedling and complaining she and her mother had managed to get Paudie Brennan to put up money for a lovely Confirmation dress. This was the first item of clothing that had ever been bought new to celebrate the Confirmation of any of his nine children. The dress hung on the back of the bedroom

door and had been tried on a dozen times. Maura had managed
to persuade Geraldine to keep the hair from hanging over her
eyes.

Geraldine was going to look gorgeous on her Confirmation
day. She had written to her sisters and brothers in England
telling them of this event and, getting the hint, they had sent a
pound note or a ten-shilling note in an envelope with a couple
of lines scrawled to wish her well. Maura hadn't done that and
she looked with envy at the riches coming in. It took a lot of
ironing in Miss Ross's house to make anything like that amount
of money.

Three days before Confirmation, Paudie Brennan, on a serious drinking bout, found himself short of ready cash and, deciding that the Lord couldn't possibly be concerned what
clothes young Christians decked themselves in for Confirmation ceremonies, managed to take the new dress to a pawn-
broker in the big town and raise the sum of two pounds on it.

The consternation was terrible. In the middle of the shouting,
tears, and accusations being hurled backward and forward,
Maura realized that this was all that would happen. Bluster and
hurt, disappointment and recriminations. There was no question of anyone getting the dress back for Geraldine. That kind of
money could not appear by magic. Credit had been arranged in
the first place to buy it. There was no possibility of more funds
being made available.

"I'll get it for you," Maura said simply to a red-eyed near
hysterical Geraldine who lay on her bed railing at the unfairness of life and the meanness of her father.

"How can you get it? Don't be stupid."

"I have that saved. Just get the ticket from him. We'll go on
the bus, but you must never tell them, never never."

"Where will they think we got the money? They might say
we stole it." Geraldine didn't dare to believe that there was a
way out.

"Da's not going to be able to say much one way or the other
after what he did," said Maura.

On the day, Paudie Brennan was dressed and shaved and his neck squeezed into a proper shirt collar for the visit of the Bishop. It was a sunlit day, and the children from Shancarrig looked a credit to their school, people said, as they gathered for the group photograph outside the cathedral in the big town. Geraldine Brennan, resplendent with her shiny blond hair and her frilly white dress, caught the eye of a lot of people.

"You have dressed her like a picture. She's a credit to you," said Mrs. Ryan, of Ryan's Hotel. Her own daughter Catherine looked far less resplendent. It was easy to see that she was mystified and even put out that the young Brennan girl, daughter of a known layabout and drunk, should look so well.

"Ah, sure, you have to do your best, Mrs. Ryan, ma'am," Maura's mother said. Maura felt her heart harden. If her Mam had been the one in charge, Geraldine would have stood there in some limp handout dress that had been begged from a family who might not have used all its castoffs. There had been no word of apology from her father, no question of any promised repayment from Geraldine. No questions, no interest.

Any more than anyone had asked what Maura would do when she left school in a few short weeks time. She wouldn't be going to the convent in the town like Leo Murphy and Nessa Ryan. There were no plans for her to go into the technical school. She wasn't smart enough to be taken on as a trainee in one of the shops, or the hairdressing salon.

Maura was going to work as a maid, the only question was where and this, she realized, was something she would have to work out for herself as well as everything else. Maura would really have liked a job where she could live in. In a lovely big house, with beautiful furniture in it. Somewhere like The Glen, where Leo Murphy lived.

She would call and ask them had they a place. It wasn't fair to ask Leo at school and embarrass her in case the answer was no. Or she could possibly get a place in the kitchens of Ryan's Commercial Hotel, or as a chambermaid. She wouldn't like that as much. There was nothing beautiful to touch and polish.

"Are you thinking about your own Confirmation, Maura?" Father Gunn from Shancarrig was standing beside her.

"Not really, I'm afraid, Father. I was thinking about where I'd go to work."

"Is it time for you to leave school already?" He was a kindly man with very thick glasses that made him look vaguer and more confused than he was. It seemed impossible for him to believe that another of Paudie Brennan's brood was ready for the emigrant ship.

"It is. I'll be fifteen soon," Maura said proudly. Father Gunn looked at her. She was a pleasant open-faced child. Not a pretty face like the one being confirmed today, but still easy enough on the eye. He hoped she wouldn't fall for a child the way the elder sister had in Northampton. There were few secrets kept from a priest in a small community.

"You'll be needing a reference, I suppose." He sighed, thinking of the numbers of young people that he had written about, praising their honesty and integrity to anonymous English employers.

"I suppose they'll all know me in Shancarrig," she said. "I'll be looking for a job as a maid, Father. If you hear of anyone, I'm great at cleaning altogether."

"I will, Maura, I'll keep my eyes open for you." He turned away, feeling unexpectedly sad.

Maura went first to the back door of The Glen and waited patiently as the dogs raced around her, barking the news of her arrival, but nobody came to see what was her business. She had seen two figures sitting in the front room. Surely they must have heard. After a lot of thought she went around to the front and Leo, tall and confident, came running down the stairs.

"Maura, what on earth are you doing?" she asked.

"I came wondering do your parents want anyone to work for them in the house, Leo," she said to the girl who had been sitting beside her in school for eight years.

"Work?" Leo seemed startled.

"Yes, like I have to have a job working somewhere, and this is a big house. I wondered . . . ?"

"No, Maura."

"But, I know how to turn out a room . . ."

"There's Biddy here already."

"I meant as well as Biddy, under her of course."

Leo had always been nice at school. Maura couldn't understand why she spoke so brusquely. "It wouldn't work. You couldn't come here and clear up after me."

"I have to clear up after someone. Wouldn't your family be as nice as anyone else's? Let me ask them, Leo." She didn't say that the place could do with a clean. She didn't plead. She had always been quick to recognize when something was impossible. And a look at Leo Murphy's face told her that this was now the case.

"Right then," she said cheerfully, "I had to ask."

She knew Leo was standing at the door with the dogs as she walked down the avenue. Maura thought that she should have been allowed to talk to the people of the house, rather than being sent off by her own schoolfriend. Still, Leo had the air of being the one who made the decisions in that house. They mightn't have hired her if they knew Leo disapproved.

Imagine being able to make the decisions at nearly fifteen. But then Maura told herself that that's what she was doing herself. There were very few decisions made in Brennans by anyone except herself.

Maura went then to Mrs. Hayes. Mr. Hayes was a solicitor so the Hayes family was very wealthy. They had a big house covered with Virginia creeper, and a lovely piano in the drawing room. Maura knew this because Niall Hayes went to the same school. He was very nice. He told her one day how much he hated the piano lessons that his mother arranged for him twice a week, and Maura told him how much she hated going to the pub to tell her father his dinner was ready on Saturday and Sunday lunchtimes. It was a kind of bond between them.

But Mrs. Hayes didn't want a young girl, she told Maura. She'd need someone older, someone trained.

She went to Mrs. Barton, Eddie Barton's mother, who ran a dressmaking business, but Mrs. Barton said it was hard enough to put food on the table for herself and Eddie, without trying to find another few shillings for a child to be playing at pushing a brush around the floor. She had said it kindly, but the facts were the facts.

And Dr. Jims said that he had not only Carrie to look after his son but there were many good years left in Maisie as well. So, everything now depended on going to the Ryans in the hotel. Maura had left that till last because she thought Mrs. Ryan was very strong-willed. She was a woman whom it might be easy to annoy.

She got the job, chambermaid. Mrs. Ryan said she hoped Maura would be happy, but there were three things they should get straight from the start—Maura was not to speak to Nessa just because they knew each other at school—Maura was to live on the premises, they didn't really want her going back to the cottages every night—and lastly, if there was a question of flirting or making free with any of the customers, there would be words with Father Gunn about it and Maura would leave Shancarrig without a backward glance.

It suited Maura not to live at home. Her father was increasingly difficult these days. Geraldine had her friends in and out of the place, giggling in the bedroom. It would be nice to have a place of her own, a small room certainly, like a nun's cell, but all to herself.

Maura began work at once, and in her time off she did the ironing still for Miss Ross and she polished silver for Mrs. Hayes, sitting quietly in the kitchen on her afternoon off from the hotel. She never spoke to Niall when he came home on holidays from his boarding school. Nobody would ever have known they had been school friends and even companions in a kind of a way too. If Niall ever saw her there, he didn't seem to take any notice.

Not even as the years passed and Maura Brennan developed a small waist and began to look altogether more attractive. If you were born square and dull-looking in appearance, you didn't ever think that things would change. Maura knew that her sister Geraldine was pretty, but she didn't feel jealous. It was good that Geraldine had got a job up in the sawmills, they liked someone nice with a bright smile around the office. Maura never thought that it was bad luck to have been square and making beds behind the scenes in a hotel.

In fact, she was so used to being square and dull-looking, she was quite unaware that she had changed and had begun to look very attractive indeed.

The men who came to stay in Ryan's Commercial Hotel noticed, though. Maura had many an occasion to raise her voice sharply and speak in clear firm tones when men asked for an extra blanket, or complained about some imaginary fault in their rooms, just in order to give her a squeeze.

By the time she was eighteen years old, Mrs. Ryan suggested to her husband that they put her behind the bar. She'd be able to attract custom. To their surprise Maura refused. She'd prefer to continue the work she was doing, she had no head for figures. She would need a lot of smart clothes if she was to be in the public eye. She would be happier making beds and helping in the kitchen.

"At least, wait on the tables," Mrs. Ryan asked. But no, if her work was satisfactory she would prefer to keep in the background.

Breda Ryan shrugged. They had tried to better her, a girl from the cottages, poor Paudie Brennan's child, and yet she wouldn't seize the opportunity. Mrs. Ryan had always thought that if the whole wealth of the world was taken back and divided out equally, giving the same amount to each person, you'd find in five years that the same people would end up having money and power and the same people would end up shiftless and hopeless. In a changing world, she found this view very comforting.

Maura didn't want to change because her life suited her just the way it was. She had three square meals a day. She could even choose what she wanted to eat in a hotel, which she mightn't have been able to do in a private house. She had the excuse which she could give her mother and father that the hotel needed her night and day. As a barmaid or waitress she might be expected to live out. And she wanted nothing to interfere with her savings and her plans.

Whenever she took the children she minded for walks she would always go the same way, past the places that she would buy when she had the money. There was the little gate lodge to The Glen. It was totally disused. People had lived there once, but now the ivy grew in the windows. That would be her first choice. Then there was the little house near where Miss Ross lived. It was painted a wishy-washy gray, but if Maura had it she would paint it pink and have window boxes full of red geraniums on each side of the hall door.

There wasn't much time for talking to friends these days. Not if you had to save as hard as Maura did. And she didn't go dancing—dances cost money, lots of money. First you had to buy something to wear, then the price of the bus fare to the town, and the admission to the dance hall, and the minerals. It would run away with your savings.

Maura had never been to a dance by the time her young sister Geraldine was ready to leave Shancarrig and join their sisters in England.

"Come on, just as my goodbye," Geraldine had urged.

"I've nothing to wear."

The sisters had remained friendly over the years as Maura had worked on in the hotel and Geraldine had worked in the sawmills in the office.

"I've plenty," Geraldine said.

And indeed she had, Maura discovered. The bedroom they had once shared would never have held a second bed these days, with all the clothes strewn around it. Maura looked in wonder. "You must have spent everything you earned on these," she said.

"Don't be mean, Maura. There's nothing worse than a mean woman," Geraldine said.

Was she mean? Maura wondered. It would indeed be terrible to be a mean woman. Yet, she didn't think she was mean. She gave a pound a week out of her wages to her mother and she always brought a cake or a half pound of ham when she came home to tea. She seemed to be giving Geraldine the price of the cinema for as long as she remembered. All she had been careful about was not spending on herself.

But perhaps that too was mean.

She fingered the dresses on the bed. A taffeta dress with shot silk in green and yellow colors, a red corduroy skirt, a black satin with little bits of diamante at the shoulders. It was like an Aladdin's cave.

"Do all your friends have clothes like this?" she asked.

"Well, Catherine Ryan from the place you work, she'd have different things. You know, well-cut, awful-looking garments you wouldn't be seen dead in. Some people have a ton of stuff. We swap a bit. What'll you wear?"

Maura Brennan wore the black satin with the diamante decorations and set out for the dance in the big town. She looked at herself in the mirror of the ladies' cloakroom. She thought she looked all right. It was hard to tell what fellows would like, but she thought she'd get asked up to dance and not be left a fool by the side of the wall.

The first man who came over was Gerry O'Sullivan, the new barman in Ryan's Hotel.

"Well, don't tell me you're the same girl that I see in the kitchen in the back of beyond where we work," he said, stretching out his arms to her.

And then the night flew by. They danced everything, sambas and tangos, and rock and roll, and old-time waltzes. She couldn't believe that it was time for the national anthem.

"I have to find my sister and her friends," she said.

"Aw, don't give me that. I've the loan of a car," he said.

He was very handsome, Gerry O'Sullivan, small and dark with black hair and an easy laugh. But there was no question of it. They had all given five shillings to get their lift there and back in a big van.

"I'll see you tomorrow in the hotel," she said, thinking that might cheer him up. She was wrong.

"Tomorrow you won't be looking like this, you'll be dressed like a streel and emptying chamber pots," he grumbled, and went off.

Maura said very little on the way home. Geraldine's friends passed around a bottle of cider, but she shook her head. She supposed he was right, that was the way she dressed and that was what she did for a living.

"I'll write from England," Geraldine said. Maura knew she wouldn't, any more than the others had.

··•••·

A few days later Gerry O'Sullivan found her alone.

"I only said that because I was so mad wanting to be with you. I had a very bad mouth and I'm sorry." He was so handsome and so upset. Maura's face lit up.

"I didn't mind a bit," she said.

"You should have minded. Listen, will you come to the dance again, on Friday? I'll bring you there and back. Please?" She looked doubtful, because this time she literally didn't have anything to wear. Geraldine had taken her wardrobe across the sea to England. "I'll be very nicely mannered all night long," he said with a grin. "And it's Mick Delahunty's Show Band and he won't be back this way for a good bit."

She decided she could take the cost of one party dress from her savings. And the following week she took another, and the price of shoes and nice bag. She'd never have her house at this rate, Maura told herself. But she found herself saying that you only live once. Gerry O'Sullivan told her that she was the loveliest girl in the dance hall.

"Don't be making a jeer of me," she said.

"I'll show you I'm not making a jeer of you." Gerry was indignant. "I'll not dance with you and see how you'll be swept

away . . ." Before she could say anything he picked a girl from
the waiting line and began to dance.

Red-cheeked and unsure, Maura was about to step aside but
from three directions arms were stretched out and faces offered
a dance. She laughed, confused, and picked the nearest one. He
had been right. She *was* the kind of girl men danced with.

"What did I tell you," he murmured in the back of the car
that night. He seemed excited by the thought of other men
wanting Maura and not being able to have her. His own intention of having her had now become a near reality. No protestations were going to be any use, and in honesty Maura didn't
want to protest any further.

"Not in the car, please," she whispered.

"You're right." He seemed cheerful. Too cheerful, in fact.
From his pocket he took out one of the hotel keys.

"Room Eleven," he said triumphantly. "There'll be no one
there. We'll be fine as long as we keep the light off." Maura
looked at him trustingly.

"Will it be all right?" she asked in a whisper.

"I'll not let you down," Gerry O'Sullivan said.

She knew he spoke the truth. She knew it again five months
later, after many happy visits to Room Eleven and even Room
Two, when she told him she was pregnant.

"We'll get married," he said.

Father Gunn agreed that it should be as speedily as possible.
His face seemed to say that it would be no better or worse than
a lot of marriages he was asked to officiate at with speed. And
at least in this case they seemed to have a deposit for a house,
which was more than you might have hoped for in some cases.
Father Gunn talked about it to Miss Ross.

"It could be a lot worse, I suppose," he said.

"She'll never settle in a poor house. She wanted to be well
away from the cottages. She had her eyes on great things," the
teacher said.

"Well, faith and she should have her eyes on being grateful
the fellow married her and putting her mind to raising the child
and being glad they have a roof over their heads." Father Gunn

knew he sounded like a stern old parish priest from thirty years ago, but somehow the whole thing had him annoyed and he didn't want to hear any fairy stories about people having their eyes set on great things.

Maura decided to work until the day before the wedding. She looked Mrs. Ryan straight in the eye and refused to accept any hints about the work being tiring in her condition. She said she needed every penny she could earn.

Mrs. Ryan was cross to be losing a hardworking maid, and at the same time having an attractive barman marry beneath him because of activities obviously carried out under her own roof. She began to look more sternly at her own daughters, Nessa and Catherine, lest anything untoward should happen in their lives.

Nessa, the same age as Maura, had been all through Shancarrig School with her. "What should I give her as a present?" she said to her mother.

"Best present is to ignore it and the reason for it," Mrs. Ryan snapped.

This reaction ensured, of course, that Nessa would go to great trouble to find a nice present. She rang Leo Murphy up in The Glen. Maura, putting away mops and buckets in the room at the end of the corridor, heard Nessa on the phone.

"Leo, she *was* in our class. We have to do something. Of course it's shotgun. What else could it be? You choose something, anything at all. Poor Maura, she expects so little."

That's not true, Maura thought as she put away the cleaning equipment. She didn't expect so little, she expected a lot and mainly she got it. She had wanted to stay in Shancarrig rather than emigrating like the rest of her brothers and sisters, and here she had stayed. She had wanted the one handsome man that she ever fancied in her life, and he had wanted her. He was standing by her now and marrying her.

She had got more than she expected. She certainly hadn't thought that she would be having a baby and yet there was one on the way. The very thought of it made her pleased and excited. It took away the ache of sorrow about the place they would be living.

With Gerry and a baby it wouldn't matter anyway.

Leo Murphy and Nessa Ryan gave her a little glass-fronted cabinet.

She couldn't have liked it more. She stroked it over and over and said how lovely it would look on a wall when she got her own treasures to put in.

"Have you any treasure yet?" Nessa asked.

"Only a doll. A doll with a china face and china hands," Maura said.

"That'll be nice for the baby . . ." Leo gulped. "If you ever have one, I mean," she said hastily.

"Oh I'm sure I will," Maura said. "But the baby won't be let play with this doll. It's a treasure, for the lovely cabinet."

She could see that the girls thought their money had been well spent, and she was touched by how much they must have given for it. As part of her continuing fantasy about a house, Maura used to look at furniture and price it. She knew well that this cabinet was not inexpensive.

Maura hoped that Geraldine would come home from England. She even offered her the fare, but there was no reply. It would have been nice to have had her standing as a bridesmaid, but instead she had Eileen Dunne, who said she loved weddings and she'd be anyone's bridesmaid for them. And with a great nudge that nearly knocked Maura over she said she'd do godmother as well, and laughed a lot.

Gerry's brother came to do the best man bit. His parents were old and didn't travel, he said.

Maura saw nothing sad or shabby about her wedding day.

When she turned around in the church she saw Nessa Ryan, Leo Murphy, Niall Hayes, and Eddie Barton sitting smiling at her. She was the first of their class to get married. They seemed to think this was like winning some kind of race rather than having been caught in a teenage pregnancy. When they went to Johnny Finn's for drinks Mr. Ryan from the hotel came running

643

in with a fistful of money to buy them all a drink. He said he came to wish them well from everyone in Ryan's Commercial Hotel.

There was no word of the haste or the disgrace or anything. Maura's father behaved in a way that, for Paudie Brennan, could be called respectable. This week he happened to be friendly with Foxy Dunne's father, so the two of them had their arms around each other as they sang tunelessly together in a corner. If it had been one of the weeks when they were fighting, things would have been terrible—insults hurling across Johnny Finn's all afternoon.

And Father Gunn and Father Barry were there smiling and talking to people as if it were a real wedding.

Maura didn't see anything less than the kind of wedding day she had dreamed about when she was at school, or when reading the women's magazines. All she saw was Gerry O'Sullivan beside her, smiling and saying everything would be grand.

And everything *was* grand for a while.

Maura left her job in the hotel. Mrs. Ryan seemed to want it that way. Possibly there would be social differences now that Maura was the wife of the popular barman, instead of just the girl from the cottages cleaning the floors and washing potatoes. But Maura found plenty of work, hours here and hours there. When it was obvious that she was expecting a child many of her employers said they would be lost without her. Mrs. Hayes, who hadn't wanted her in the start, was particularly keen to keep her.

"Maybe your mother could look after the child, and you'd still want to go out and work?" she said hopefully.

Maura had no intention of letting any child grow up in the same house as she had herself, with the lack of interest and love. But she had learned to be very circumspect in her life. "Maybe indeed," she said to Mrs. Hayes and the others. "We'll have to wait and see."

It seemed a long time to wait for the baby, all those evenings on her own in the little cottage, sometimes hearing her father going home drunk, as she had when she was a child. She polished the little cabinet, took out the doll and patted the bump of her stomach.

"Soon you'll be admiring this," she said to the unborn baby.

It was Dr. Jims Blake who told her about the baby boy. The child had Down syndrome. The boy, who was what was called a mongol, would still be healthy and loving and live a full and happy life.

It was Father Gunn who told her about Gerry, and how he had come from the cottage to the church and told the priest he was going. He took the wages owing to him from the hotel, saying his father had died and he needed time off for the funeral. But he told Father Gunn that he was getting the boat to England.

No entreaties would make him stay.

Maura remembered always the way that Father Gunn's thick round glasses seemed to sparkle as he was telling her. She didn't know if there were tears behind them, or if it was only a trick of the light.

People were kind, very kind. Maura often told herself that she had been lucky to have stayed in Shancarrig. Suppose all this had happened to her in some big city in England where she had known nobody. Here she had a friendly face everywhere she turned.

And of course she had Michael.

Nobody had told her how much she would love him because nobody could have known. She had never known a child as loving. She watched him grow with a heart that nearly burst with pride. Everything he learned, every new skill—like being able to do up his buttons—was a huge hurdle for the child, and soon everyone in Shancarrig got used to seeing them hand in hand walking around.

"Who's this?" people would ask affectionately, even though they knew well.

"This is Michael O'Sullivan," Maura would say proudly.

"I'm Michael O'Sullivan," he would say and, as often as not, hug the person who had asked.

If you wanted Maura to come and clean your house, you took

Michael as well. And as they walked from job to job each day Maura used to point out the houses that she loved to her son— the little gate lodge, even more covered with brambles and choked with nettles, that stood at the end of the long avenue up to The Glen, and there was the one near Miss Ross which she was going to paint pink if she ever bought it.

At night she would take the doll with the china hands and face out from its cabinet and the two cups and saucers she had been given by Mrs. Ryan. There was a little silver plate, which had EPNS on the back, that Eileen Dunne had given when she stood as godmother to Michael. She said that this meant it wasn't real silver, but since the *S* stood for silver Maura thought it deserved a place in the cabinet. There was a watch, too, one that belonged to Gerry. A watch that didn't go, but might go one day if it were seen to, and would hang on a chain. When Michael got to be a man he could call it his father's watch.

Most people forgot that Michael ever had a father; the memory of Gerry O'Sullivan faded. And for Maura the memory began to fade too. Days passed when she didn't think of the handsome fellow with the dark eyes who had cared enough to marry her, but hadn't got the strength to stay when he knew his child was handicapped. She had never hated him, sometimes she even pitied him that he didn't know the great hugs and devotion of Michael his son, who grew in size but not greatly in achievement.

Maura had got glances and serious invitations out from other men in the town, but she had always told them simply that she wasn't free to accept any invitation. She had a husband living in England and really there could be no question of anything else.

Her dream remained constant. A proper little home, not the broken-down cottage where only the hopeless and the helpless lived, as where she had grown up and from which she wanted to flee.

Then the Darcys came to Shancarrig. They bought a small grocery shop like the one Nellie Dunne ran, and they put in all kinds of newfangled things. The world was changing, even in places like Shancarrig. Mike and Gloria Darcy were new people who livened the place up. No one had ever met anyone called Gloria before and she lived up to her name. Lots of black curly hair like a gypsy, and she must have known this because she often wore a red scarf knotted around her neck and a full-colored skirt, as if she was going to break into a gypsy dance any moment.

Mike Darcy was easygoing and got on with everyone. Even old Nellie Dunne who looked on them as rivals liked Mike Darcy. He had a laugh and a word for anyone he met on the road. Mrs. Ryan in the Commercial Hotel felt they were a bit brash for the town, but when Mike said he'd buy for her at the market as well as for himself she began to change her tune.

It was good to see such energy about the place, she said, and it wasn't long before she had the front of the hotel painted to make it the equal of the new shopfront in Darcy's. Mike's brother, Jimmy Darcy, had come with them. He was a great housepainter and Mrs. Ryan claimed that even the dozy fellows from down in the cottages, who used to paint a bit when the humor took them, seemed to think Jimmy did a good job. Mike and Gloria had children, two tough dark little boys who used to get up to all kinds of devilment in the school.

Maura didn't wait to see whether the town liked the Darcys or not, she presented herself on the doorstop the moment they arrived.

"You'll be needing someone to work for you," she said to Gloria.

Gloria glanced at the round eager face of Michael, who stood holding his mother's hand. "Will you be able to make yourself free?" she asked.

"Michael would come with me. He's the greatest help you could imagine," she said, and Michael beamed at the praise.

"I'm not sure if we really *do* need anyone . . ." Gloria was polite but unsure.

"You do need someone, but take your time. Ask around a bit

about me. Maura O'Sullivan is the name, Mrs. Maura O'Sullivan."

"Well, yes, Mrs. O'Sullivan . . ."

"No, I just wanted you to know, because you're new. Michael's daddy had to go and live in England. You'd call me Maura if you had me in the house."

"And you'd call me Michael," the boy said, putting both his arms around Gloria's small waist.

"I don't need to ask around. When will you start?"

The Darcys were better payers than anyone else in the town. They seemed to have no end of money. The children's clothes were all good quality, their shoes were new, not mended. The furniture they had was expensive, not lovely old wood which Maura would have enjoyed polishing, but dear modern furniture. She knew the prices of all these things from her trips to the big town, and her dreams of furnishing the house that she'd buy.

Back in the cottage she had hardly anything worth speaking of. The small slow savings were being kept for the day she moved into the place she wanted. Only the glass-fronted cabinet with its small trove of treasures showed any sign of the gracious living that Maura yearned for. Otherwise it was converted boxes and broken secondhand furniture.

The Darcys had been in lots of places. Maura marveled at how quickly the children could adapt.

They were warmhearted too. They didn't like to come across Michael cleaning their shoes. "He doesn't have to do that, missus" said Kevin Darcy, who was nine.

"I'm doing them great," Michael protested.

"Don't worry, Kevin, that's Michael's and my job. All we ask you to do is not to leave everything on the floor of your bedroom so as we have to bend and pick it up."

It worked. Gloria Darcy said that Maura and her son had managed to put manners on her children, something no one in any house had ever done before.

"Don't you find it hard, Mam, all the moving from place to place?"

Gloria looked at her. "No, it's interesting. You meet new people, and in each place we better ourselves. We sell the place at a profit and then move on."

"And will you be moving on from here, too, do you think?" Maura was disappointed. She wouldn't ever get the kind of hours and payments that the Darcys gave her from anyone else. Gloria Darcy said not for a while. She thought they would stay in Shancarrig until the children got a bit of an education before uprooting them.

And their business prospered. They built on a whole new section to the original building they had bought and they expanded their range of goods. Soon people didn't need to go into the big town for their shopping trips. You could buy nearly everything you needed in Darcy's.

"I don't know where they get the money," Mrs. Hayes said one day to Maura. "They can't be doing that much business, nothing that would warrant the kind of showing off they're doing."

Maura said nothing. She thought that Mrs. Hayes was the kind of wife who might well disapprove of Gloria's low-cut blouses and winning ways with the men of Shancarrig.

It was around this time that Maura became aware of financial problems in the Darcy household. There were bills that were being presented over and over to them. She could hear Mike Darcy's voice raised on the phone. But at the same time he had bought Gloria some marvelous jewelry that was the talk of Shancarrig.

"She has me broke," he'd say to anyone who came into the shop. "Go on, Gloria, show them that emerald."

And laughing, Gloria would wave the emerald on the chain. It had been bought in the big town in the jewelers'. She had always wanted one. And it was the same with the little diamond earrings. They were so small, they were only specks really, but the thought that they were real diamonds made Gloria shiver with excitement.

Shancarrig looked on with admiration. And the Darcys weren't blowing or boasting either. Nessa Ryan, who was married to Niall Hayes, had been in the big town and checked. They were the real thing. The Darcys were new rich, courageous and not afraid to spend. With varying degrees of envy the people of Shancarrig wished them good luck.

The tinkers came every year on the way to the Galway races. They didn't stay in Shancarrig. They stayed nearby. Maura was struck with how Gloria looked like the Hollywood version of a gypsy, not the real thing. The real women of the traveling people had a tired and weatherbeaten look, not the flashing eyes and colorful garb of Gloria Darcy, and certainly not the real diamonds in the ears and the real emerald around her neck.

But this particular year people said some tinker woman must be wearing the jewels because at the very time they were encamped outside Shancarrig, Gloria Darcy's jewelry case was stolen.

All hell broke loose. It could only be the tinkers.

Sergeant Keane was in charge of the search, and the ill will created was enormous. Nothing was found. No one was charged. Everyone was upset. Even Michael was interrogated and asked about what he had seen and what he had touched in his visits to the Darcy house. It was a frightening time in Shancarrig; there had never been a robbery like this before.

There had never been anything like this to steal before.

A lot of tut-tutting and head-shaking went on. It was vulgar of the Darcys to have displayed that jewelry; it made people envious. It put temptation in the way of others. But then, how had the gypsies known about it? They had only just come to camp. They hadn't been given dazzling displays of the glinting emerald on the chain around Gloria's throat.

"I'm sorry if the Guards frightened Michael," Gloria said to Maura.

"I don't mind about that. Sergeant Keane has known Michael since he was in a pram, he wouldn't frighten him," Maura said. "But I'm sorry for you, Mrs. Darcy. You put a lot of store by those jewels. It won't be the same without them."

"No, but there will be the insurance money . . . eventually." Gloria said. She said they weren't going to buy emeralds and diamonds again. Maybe put the money into paying off the extension and getting the place rewired and better stocked.

Maura remembered some of the conversations she had heard about the need to pay builders' bills. She went back over those financial difficulties she thought she had been aware of. Possibly the insurance money was exactly what the Darcys needed at this stage.

Indeed, it could be said to come at exactly the right time.

Maura had been used to keeping her own counsel for as long as she could remember. She had seen what the wild indiscretions of her own family had brought on themselves and everyone else around—her father's blustering revelations of any bit of gossip he knew, her mother's trying to play one member of the family off against the other.

Maura said very little.

She had sometimes suspected over the years that the envelope Father Gunn gave her each Christmas, saying that it was from Gerry O'Sullivan from no fixed address in England, actually came from the priest himself. But she never let Father Gunn know of her suspicions. She thanked him for acting as postman.

She sometimes wondered why she had become so secretive and close. When she was a youngster she had been open and would talk to everyone. Maybe it was just the whole business of Gerry and having to be protective of Michael. And because there had never been a real friend to talk to.

The robbery of the jewels had been a nine-day wonder. Soon people stopped talking about it. There were other things to occupy their minds.

There was always something happening in Shancarrig. Maura never knew why people called it sleepy or a backwater. Only people who didn't know the place would have used words like that. Maura and Michael helped at the Dramatic Society and there was a drama a week there from the time that Biddy who worked at The Glen started to dance and went on like something wound up until no one could drag her from the stage. And there was all the business about Father Barry not being well, and then going off to the missions.

There was Richard, that handsome cousin of Niall Hayes, who had come to The Terrace and broken a few hearts—Nessa's maybe—and Maura thought there might be a bit of electricity between him and Mrs. Darcy, not that she would ever mention a word of it. Yet Nellie Dunne hinted of it too, so that rumor might well be going around the place. Eddie Barton had opened all their eyes with his unexpected romance, and the news of Foxy Dunne from London was always worth people pausing to discuss.

There was plenty to distract the minds of Shancarrig from the missing emeralds and diamonds.

Maura O'Sullivan and her son, Michael, went from house to house—the ironing for Miss Ross, who had lines set in her face now, and had begun to look like a waxwork image of her old mother—there was the silver polishing for Mrs. Hayes—the cleaning for Mrs. Murphy—the two hours on a Saturday for Mrs. Barton—but mainly, the Darcys.

There was a lot to be done in a house where there were two boys and where the parents were hardly ever out of the shop. Maura didn't wait to be asked to do things. She had her own routine.

She was doing the master bedroom, as Gloria called it, when she found the jewelry. It was on top of the wardrobe in a big round hatbox. Maura had been dusting the top of the wardrobe with sheets of newspapers spread below to catch the falling dirt. She saw a neater way to stack the suitcases, but it involved lifting them down. Michael stood willingly to take them from her. And it was only because the hatbox rattled that she opened it. It was as if there was a big stone in it. She didn't want whatever it was to fall out.

It was a red silk scarf with two small black velvet bags wrapped up in it.

Michael saw her stop and hold the wardrobe top for support.

"Are you going to fall down?" he asked anxiously.

"No, love." Maura climbed down and sat on the bed. Her heart was racing dangerously.

There was no way that she could have accidentally discovered the lost and much mourned jewelry. There would be no cries of delight if the gems were recovered and the insurance claim had to be canceled.

She also knew that they had not got into the hatbox by accident. The description had been given over and over. The emerald on its chain had been in a box on the desk downstairs, and the little earrings in their black velvet bag beside them. The room they were in, the sitting room, had a pair of glass doors opening onto the small back garden. A light-fingered, light-footed tinker boy could have been in and out without anyone noticing.

That was how the story went.

In all her time cleaning in this house Maura had never known the valuables kept in this hatbox. It was not a place someone would have put them and forgotten about them.

"Why aren't you speaking?" Michael wanted to know.

"I'm trying to think about something," she said. She put her arm around his shoulder and drew him close.

She seemed to sit there for a long time, yellow duster in hand, her feet squarely on the spread newspaper, her son enclosed in her arm.

That evening Maura put the two little black velvet bags in her cabinet of treasures. She had to think it out very cleverly. She mustn't do the wrong thing and end up the worse for this great discovery.

Weeks went by before she brought up the subject of the lost jewels. She waited until she had Gloria in the house on her own. She had left Michael playing with the chickens outside.

"I was thinking, Mam, Mrs. Darcy . . . what would happen if someone found your emerald chain say . . . thrown in a hedge by the tinkers?"

"What do you mean?" Gloria's voice was sharp.

"Well, now that you've done all the renovations here . . .

and got used to not having it and wearing it round your neck
. . . wouldn't it be bad for you if it turned up?"

"It won't turn up. That lot have it well sold by now, you can
be sure."

"But where would they sell it? If they brought it into a jeweler's shop, Mrs. Darcy, wouldn't people know it was the one
that was stolen from you? They'd call the Guards, not give them
the money."

"That crowd travel far and wide. They could take it to a shop
miles from here."

There was a silence.

Then Gloria said: "Anyway, it hasn't been found."

"My head is full of dreams, Mrs. Darcy. I go walking by the
hedges. I often find things . . . what would happen if I were to
find it?"

"I don't know what you mean."

"Well, suppose I did find it, would I take it to Sergeant Keane
and say where I came across it, or would I give it to
you . . . ?"

Gloria's eyes were very narrow.

Maura saw her glance toward the stairs as if she were about
to run up and check the hatbox.

"This is fancy talk," she said eventually. "But I suppose the
best would be, if you *were* to find it, to give it to me quietly. As
you say, the insurance money was really more use to us than
the jewelry itself at this stage."

"What about a reward?" Maura looked confused and eager.

"We'd have to see."

Maura went out to the chickens to find Michael, but she
paused before she closed the door behind her and heard the
light sound of Gloria Darcy's feet running up the stairs, and the
sound of the suitcases being thrown from the high wardrobe to
the floor.

Nothing was said.

It wasn't as hard for Maura as it might have been for others,
because after a life of keeping her thoughts and opinions to
herself it was relatively easy to work on in the house where

Gloria and Mike Darcy obviously walked on a knife edge of anxiety around her.

They offered her cups of tea in the middle of her cleaning. They found things for Michael in the shop as gifts, but Maura said he mustn't be allowed to think of the shop as a wonderland where he could stroll and take whatever bar of chocolate he wanted. It would be very bad for him, and she had spent so much time trying to make him see what was his and what wasn't.

When she said this Maura O'Sullivan looked Mike and Gloria straight in the eye. She could see that she had them totally perplexed.

It was Gloria who broke eventually.

"Remember you were saying that you were a great one for finding things, Maura?"

"Yes indeed. I prayed to St. Anthony for that good Parker pen of Mr. Darcy's to turn up and didn't it roll out from behind where we keep the trays stacked in the kitchen." Maura was proud and pleased with the results of her prayers.

"I was thinking about what you said . . . and in our business, well . . . we get to know a lot of people. Now, suppose you were to find the stuff that the tinkers took somewhere . . . ?"

"Yes, Mrs. Darcy?"

"Do you know what the very best thing to do with it would be . . . ?"

"I do not. And I've been wondering and wondering."

"You see, the insurance money has been paid and spent improving the shop, providing work for people, even for you in the house." Maura held her head on one side, waiting. "So, if it did turn up and you were able to give it to me I could get it sold for you, and give you some of it . . ." Her voice trailed away.

"Ah, but if I knew the right place to sell it myself, then I could get plenty of money. Because, as you say yourself, you got the insurance money out of it already. You wouldn't want to be getting things twice over . . . it wouldn't be fair."

"But why would it be fair for *you* to get it all?"

"If I found it in a hedge, or wherever I found it, it's finders keepers, isn't it?"

"But no use of course if you didn't know where to sell it."

This was the deal. They both knew it.

"I'll be going to the big town next week, Mrs. Darcy."

"Yes, for your Christmas shopping. Of course."

"I get this envelope from Michael's father, through Father Gunn. I'll be spending whatever there is . . ."

"I know."

"And I was thinking, suppose I found the lost jewels by then, I'd be able to sell the emerald on the chain and I could give you back the diamonds, on account of you taking me straight to the right place, and that way . . ." She let the sentence hang there.

"That way would be better, I suppose, than any other way." Gloria's face was grim.

Niall Hayes was surprised when he heard that a Mrs. O'Sullivan wanted to see him particularly. People usually wanted to see his father, Mr. Hayes Senior, the real solicitor as he had heard him described.

He was more surprised when he discovered that it was Maura Brennan from the cottages. He welcomed the two of them into his office—hardly anyone in Shancarrig had ever seen them apart.

"How have you been keeping, Maura?" he said, always a kind open fellow, despite his sharp snobby mother.

"I couldn't be better, Niall," she said. "We've had a bit of good luck. Michael's father always sends a bit to help out at Christmastime, and this year he was able to send a lot more."

"Well, that's good, very good." Niall couldn't see where the conversation was leading.

"And I'll tell you what we'd love, Niall . . . you know the cottage at the gate of The Glen?"

"I do, indeed. And they're putting it up for sale."

"I'd like to buy it for Michael and myself. Would you act for us?"

Niall paused. How could Maura have enough to buy and renovate a place like that.

"I'll talk to Leo," he said.

"No, talk to me. Tell me what's fair to offer her. Fair to her, fair to me."

That was the way Niall Hayes liked to do business. There wasn't enough of it around. People were changing, attitudes were different. They wanted sharp dealings here and there.

He patted Maura's hand. It would be done.

Maura told Father Gunn that Michael's father had given them a great deal of money this year, much more than other times. If the priest was surprised, he didn't show it.

"I think that's the last payment, Father." She looked into the priest's eyes behind the thick round glasses. "I don't think you'll be getting any more envelopes to give out at Christmas."

He looked after them as they went down the road—Maura and Michael, soon to be householders, soon to go into a place of dreams and paint it and tidy it and fill it with treasures.

He knew that the longer he lived in this parish the less he would understand.

4

Eddie

Eddie Barton only had a birthday once every four years, which was highly unusual. In fact, he thought he was the only person in the world in this situation. It came as a shock to him that other children had been born on this day. He was ten before he accepted it properly. Up to that he had thought he was unique.

Miss Ross, who was so nice at school, had told them all about Leap Year. Mr. Kelly had frightened the wits out of him by saying that if a woman proposed to you on February twenty-ninth, you had to say yes, even if she was the most terrifyingly awful person in the world. Mr. Kelly had laughed as he said it, but Eddie wasn't sure if it was a real laugh or not. Mr. Kelly often looked sad.

"Did Mrs. Kelly propose to you on my birthday?" Eddie asked fearfully. If the answer was yes, then this indeed was another bad aspect of growing up.

But Mr. Kelly had put his finger on his lips in a jokey sort of way and said: "Nonsense and don't let Mrs. Kelly hear a whisper of this or there'd be trouble." It was to be a secret between them.

"I thought you said it was a well-known fact." Eddie was confused.

"I did." The teacher sighed. "I did but I keep forgetting, even after all my years in a classroom, how dangerous it is to say anything, anything at all, to children."

Eddie's ninth birthday was free from danger. It was his tenth one that was worrying him. His mother said he could be ten on the day before or the day after.

"I'd better wait until the day after," he told Leo Murphy, who walked home after school with him because she lived in the big house, The Glen, up the hill, and Eddie lived in the small pink house halfway up the road. Leo had said that Eddie's house reminded her of a child's drawing of a house. It had windows that looked as if they were painted on. Eddie didn't know whether this was praise or not.

"What's wrong with that?" he had asked ferociously.

"Nothing. It's nice. It looks safe and normal, not like a jungle," Leo had replied.

That meant she liked it. He was pleased.

Eddie liked Leo Murphy. If *she* were to ask him to marry her when he had a real birthday, he wouldn't say no. The Glen would be a great place to live, orchards and an old tennis court. Fantastic.

Leo took things seriously.

"Why wait until March first?" she asked Eddie about his birthday. "Suppose you died on the night of the twenty-eighth then you'd have missed your birthday altogether."

It was unanswerable.

Eddie's mother said she didn't mind which day he had it just so long as he knew there'd be a cake and an apple tart and no more. He could have ten people or he could have two.

Eddie measured the cake plate carefully. He'd have three and himself. That way they'd have lots. He invited Leo Murphy and Nessa Ryan and Maura Brennan. They were the people he sat beside at class and liked.

"No boys at all?" Eddie's mother was a dressmaker. She was rarely seen without pins in her mouth or a frown of concentration on her face.

"I don't sit near any boys," Eddie said.

His mother seemed to accept this. Una Barton was a small dark woman with worried eyes. She always walked very quickly, as if she feared people might stop her and detain her in conversation. She had a kind heart and a good eye for color and dress fabrics in the clothes she made for the women of Shancarrig and the farmers' wives from out the country. They said that Una Barton lived for her son, Eddie, and for him alone.

Eddie had hair that grew upward from his head. Foxy Dunne had said he looked like a lavatory brush. Eddie didn't know what a lavatory brush was. They didn't have one in their house, but when he saw one in Ryan's Hotel he was very annoyed. His hair wasn't as bad as that.

He liked doing things that the other boys didn't like doing at all. He liked going up to Barna Woods and collecting flowers. He sometimes pressed them and wrote their names underneath, and then stuck them on a card. His mother said that he was a real artist.

"Was my father artistic?" Eddie asked.

"The less said about your father's artistry the better." His mother's face was in that sharp straight line again. There would be no more said.

He had to make a wish when he cut the cake. He closed his eyes and wished that his father would come back, like he had wished last year and the year before.

Maybe if you wished it three times, it happened.

Ted Barton had left when his son was five. He had left in some spectacular manner, because Eddie had heard it mentioned several times when people didn't know he was listening. People would say about something *there was nearly as much noise as the night Ted Barton was thrown out.*

And once he heard the Dunnes in their shop say that if someone didn't mind himself, it would be another case of Ted Barton, with the suitcase flung down the stairs after him. Eddie couldn't imagine his mother shouting or throwing a suitcase. But then again she must have.

She told him everything else he asked, but never told him about his father. "Let's just agree that he didn't keep his part of the bargain. He didn't look after his wife and son. He doesn't deserve our interest."

It was easy for her to say that but hard for Eddie to agree. Every boy wanted to know where his father was, even if it was a terrible father like the Brennans' or a fierce one like Leo Murphy's, with his moustache and being called a Major and everything.

Sometimes Eddie saw people getting off the bus and dreamed that maybe it was his father coming for him—coming to take him on a long holiday, just the two of them, walking all round Ireland, staying where they felt like. And then he'd imagine his father saying, with his head on one side, *How about it, Eddie son, will I come home?* In the daydream Eddie's mother would always be smiling and welcoming and there would be less work to make her tired because his father would be looking after them now.

After tea they played games. They had to play on the floor of Eddie's bedroom, because Mrs. Barton needed to bring her sewing machine back onto the table downstairs.

They said if only Eddie had a birthday in the summer they could all have gone up to Barna Woods. Eddie showed them some of the pressed flowers.

"They're beautiful," Nessa Ryan said.

Nessa never said anything nice just to please you. If Nessa Ryan said they were good, then they must be.

"You could even do that for a living," she added.

At ten they usually didn't think as far ahead as that, but today there had been a talk on careers in school and an encouragement to think ahead and try to get trained for something rather than just gazing out the window and letting the time pass by.

"How could I get trained to press flowers?" Eddie was interested, but Nessa's momentary enthusiasm had passed.

"We'll have another go at blow football," she said.

It had been Eddie's birthday present. His one gift. He hadn't really wanted it, but his mother had heard from the Dunnes in the shop that it was what every child wanted this year and she had paid it off over five weeks. She was pleased the game was being used. Eddie secretly thought it was silly and tiring and that there was too much spit trying to blow a paper ball through paper tubes that got chewy and soggy.

When the party was over he stood at the door of the pink house in the moonlight and watched Leo skipping up the hill to her home. You could see the walls of The Glen from here. She waved when she reached the gate.

Nessa and Maura went downhill, Maura to the row of cottages where she lived. Eddie hoped that her father wouldn't be drunk tonight. Sometimes Paudie Brennan fell around the town shouting and insulting people.

Nessa Ryan had run on ahead. She lived in Ryan's Hotel. She could have anything she wanted to eat any time. She had told that to Eddie when he had explained about the cake and the apple tart. But there must have been something of an apology in his face because Nessa had said quickly that she didn't get as much *cake* as she liked. It was really only chips and sandwiches.

The moon was shining brightly, even though it was only seven o'clock. His mother's sewing machine was already whirring away. There she would sit surrounded by paper patterns and the big dummy which used to frighten him when he was a child, always draped with some nearly finished garment, as she listened to the radio. She would smile at him a lot, but when he came upon her alone he thought her face looked sad and tired. He wished she didn't have to work so hard. And it would keep whirring until he slept. It had been like that as long as he remembered. Eddie wondered was his father looking at the moon somewhere. Did he remember his son was ten years old today?

That night Eddie wrote a letter to his father.

He told him about the day and the pressed flowers that Nessa

Ryan had admired so much. Then he wondered would his father think that bit was sissy so he crossed it out. He told his
father that there was a big wedding in the next town and that
his mother had been asked to do not only the bride's dress but
the two bridesmaids and the mother and aunt of the bride as
well. The whole church nearly would be dressed by Mrs. Barton. And that his mother had said it came just in the nick of
time because something needed to be done to the roof and there
wasn't enough money to pay for it.

Then he read that last bit again and wondered would his
father think it was a complaint. He didn't want to annoy him
now that he had just found him.

With a jolt Eddie realized that he hadn't found his father; he
was only making it up. Still, it was kind of comforting. He
crossed out the bit about the roof costing money and left in the
good news about the wedding dresses. He told his father about
the careers lecture at school and about there being lots of jobs
for hardworking young fellows over in England when he got
old enough. He thought that maybe his father might be in England. Wouldn't it be marvelous if he met him by accident over
there in a good job with prospects.

He wrote often that year. He told his father that Bernard
Shaw had died, in case he might be somewhere where they
didn't get that kind of news. Mr. Kelly at school had said he
was a great writer but he had been a bit against the Church.
Eddie asked his father why people would be against the
Church.

His father didn't answer, of course, because the letters were
never sent. There was nowhere to send them to.

It wasn't that Eddie was all *that* lonely and friendless. He did
have friends, of course he did. He often went up to The Glen to
play with Leo Murphy. They used to hit the ball across the net
to each other on the tennis court, and Leo had a great swing on
a big oak tree. She hadn't known it was an oak tree until he told
her and showed her the leaves and the acorns. It was extraordinary to have all those trees and still not know what they were.

Eddie often took oak leaves and traced around them. He

loved the shape—there were so many more zigzags than in the leaves of the plane trees, or the poplar. He liked the chestnut leaves, too, and he never played the silly game that the others did at school—peeling away the green bits to see who could have the most perfect fillet, like a fish with no flesh, only bones. Eddie liked the texture of the leaves.

He didn't write any of this to his father, but he did tell him when de Valera got back again and Nessa Ryan had said there had been a terrible shouting match one night in the hotel and they had to send for the Guards because some people didn't agree that it was great he was back. He went on writing and told a lot of fairly private things.

Still, he didn't mention that he was afraid of someone proposing to him on his birthday when he was twelve. It seemed such a stupid thing to be afraid of. But Eddie had great fears of Eileen Dunne at school, who had a terribly loud laugh and about five brothers who would deal with him if he refused her.

"You weren't thinking of asking me to marry you on Friday, were you?" he asked Leo hopefully. She had just raised her head from a book.

"No," Leo said. "I was thinking about the king of England being dead and my father being all upset about it."

"Would you?" he asked.

"Would I what? Be all upset?"

"No. Ask me to marry you."

"Why should I? You never asked *me* to marry you."

"It's the day, you see. It's the day women can."

"Men can every other day of the year."

Eddie had worked that out. "Suppose I asked you now, and we were engaged, then if anyone asked me on Friday I could say that I wasn't free."

He looked very worried. Leo wasn't concentrating one bit. She was reading her book. She always had a book with her. This time it was *Good Wives*. It seemed a fine coincidence to Eddie.

"What *is* it, Eddie?"

"Just say yes. You don't have to."

"Yes, then."

Eddie was flooded with relief. He wasn't having a party for his twelfth birthday, he was too old. He was getting a bicycle, a secondhand bicycle. His mother had told him he could cycle to school on the day. He thought he'd keep it until next day, he said. His mother looked at him affectionately. He was such a funny little thing, quirky and complicated but never a moment's trouble to her, which was more than she could have hoped the day that bastard had left her doorstep.

People sometimes said it must be hard for her to bring a boy up all on her own. But Una Barton thought they had a reasonable life together. Her son told her long, rambling tales, he was interested in helping her cook what they ate, and would dry the dishes dutifully. She wished there was more money or time to take him to the seaside or to Dublin to the zoo. But that wasn't for their kind. That was for boys who had fathers that didn't run away.

Eddie didn't want to remind anyone it was his birthday, just in case Eileen Dunne might get it into her head, or Maura Brennan's young sister Geraldine. But nobody seemed to have realized the opportunity they had of proposing to Eddie, or to anyone. They were far more interested in Father Barry, who had come to give them a talk about the missions and to show them a missionary magazine which had competitions in it and a Penfriends Corner. There were people in every part of the world who wanted to exchange ideas with young Irish people, he said. They could have a great time writing to youngsters in different lands.

Father Barry was very nice. He seemed kind of dreamy when he spoke and he sometimes closed his eyes as if the place he was talking about was somehow nearer than the place where he was. Eddie liked that. He often thought about being out with trees and flowers when he should have been thinking about the sums on the blackboard. Father Barry pinned up the page with names of the boys and girls who wanted pen friends. They could all speak English. They lived in far lands. One of them said he liked botany, flowers, and plants. His name was Chris and he lived in Glasgow, Scotland.

"That's not very far to be writing," Niall Hayes said dismissively. He had picked a boy in Argentina.

"There's more chance he might write back if he's not too far away," Eddie said.

"That's stupid," said Niall.

In his heart Eddie agreed that it was. Maybe the boy in Scotland wanted someone more exotic, not from a small town in Ireland. But the real reason he had picked Chris Taylor was that Scotland wouldn't be too dear a stamp and because he had said he liked plant life. Eddie had always thought botany was a kind of wool. He checked with Miss Ross. He didn't want to get involved in writing about knitting or sheep or anything. Not that a boy would like knitting. Miss Ross said botany was plants and things that grew.

He wrote to Chris, a long letter. It was extraordinary to be writing one that would actually go into the postbox. Other twelve-year-olds might have had to suck their pens and think of something more to say to use up another sheet of paper, but not Eddie Barton. He was well used to writing long letters about the state of the world in general and Shancarrig in particular.

The letter came back very quickly, but it came addressed to Miss E. Barton. It had a Glasgow postmark on it. Eddie looked at it for a long time. It must be for him. His mother's name was Una. But why had Chris Taylor called him Miss? Burning with shame he opened the letter.

Dear Edith,

I couldn't read your name properly and maybe yours is an Irish name, but I hope I'm right in guessing Edith.

The letter went on, a friendly interesting letter, lots about Scottish fir trees and pine cones, a request to send some pressed flowers, an inquiry about whether it might be good to learn the Latin names of things in case it was going to be easier to find them when you looked them up—Chris had gone to the library and spent two hours looking up a very ordinary maple and couldn't find it because he didn't know it was called *acer.*

Eddie read on, delighted. It was nice of Chris to take so much trouble to write, especially since he obviously thought that Eddie was a girl, a girl called Edith. Ugh. He even asked what kind of a convent was it if the teachers were called Miss Ross and Mrs. Kelly and weren't nuns.

Then on the last page Eddie got an even worse shock. Chris was closing in hope that there would be a letter soon, and saying that he was delighted to find a kindred spirit on the other side of the sea, and then signed his name

Christine

Chris was a girl.

He went hot and cold thinking about the stupid mistake. She wouldn't write to him anymore once she knew he didn't go to a convent school like she did, once she knew he was a twelve-year-old boy with baggy trousers and spiky hair. It was a great pity because that was just the sort of person he would have liked to write to. And it was her fault. Not his. She was the one who had the name that could have been anything. He had a perfectly normal male name, Eddie. He could imagine what they'd say at school if they knew he had got himself a *girl* in Scotland as a pen friend when they were all finding fellows in India or South America.

Typical sissy Eddie Barton, they'd say.

He'd love to have sent Chris, whether it was a boy Chris or a girl Chris, some of the pressed flowers. All of a sudden Eddie realized that's what he'd do, he'd *pretend* to be a girl. Just get her not to put the Miss on the envelopes anymore.

And for four years Eddie Barton and Christine Taylor wrote to each other, long long letters, pouring out their hearts in a way that neither of them could to anyone else.

Chris told how her mother had this dream of moving out of the city and into a house on an estate, a place with a garden and a garage, even though they didn't have a car. Chris hated the idea, she would be miles from the library and the art gallery and the places she went to when school was over. The girls at school didn't want to do anything except go to the sweet shop and talk about the fellows. Chris sent a picture of herself in school uniform and wanted Edith to send one too. In desperation Eddie sent one of Leo which he stole from The Glen when he was visiting there.

Chris wrote and said she hadn't thought of him as tall like that. She had a feeling from what he wrote that he was short and stocky and had hair that stood up. Eddie trembled when he read this, as if she had found him out. He thanked the heavens that Scotland was so far away and that she would never visit. It would have been better still if she had been in Argentina, then the thought needn't have crossed his mind.

It was hard to keep up the fiction of school life when he had left Shancarrig school at the age of fourteen and now went to the Brothers in the big town every day on the bus. He told Chris that truly he wasn't happy at school and he preferred to talk about other things in his letters, like the rowan tree, like the fact that his mother was getting headaches from working too hard, like he wondered was there any way of finding out where his father was, so that he could just let him know what things were like.

He wrote about Father Barry and how he had been preaching about this village in Peru called Vieja Piedra and then had to stop, and people said the Bishop didn't like money going out of the diocese to foreign places instead of being spent at home. Chris seemed to understand. She asked him why didn't he help his mother with the sewing—it wasn't hard, they could share it.

Eddie burned with frustration over that. He realized he had made himself sound selfish and unhelpful while his only crime was that he was a boy. Everyone knew boys didn't do sewing.

He was getting on very badly at school, but he couldn't tell Chris. How could he tell of Brothers who were loud and rough with him, who often hit him a belt when he least expected it, and one who even mocked his stutter?

Chris asked him for another picture when he was sixteen. He

had none of Leo. He couldn't bear to ask her personally so he wrote her a note.

"For a long complicated reason which I'll explain to you sometime, I need a photograph of you. I want you to know that it has nothing at all to do with that promise of marriage I once forced you to give. You are free from that vow, but could I have a picture next week."

She didn't reply, but then just before his sixteenth birthday he met her unexpectedly in the middle of the town.

"Did you forget the picture?" he asked.

Leo looked distracted. She hadn't remembered.

"Please, Leo, it is very important. You know I wouldn't ask you unless it were. Can I come to the house and see if you have one?"

It *was* important. Chris had sent him a picture of herself on *her* sixteenth birthday a month back. A dark girl with big eyes and a nice smile.

"*No.*" He had never known her so adamant.

"Well then, will you bring me one?"

She looked at him, as if deciding what would be the way that would cause less interference in her life.

"Oh God, I'll bring you one," she said.

He looked hurt. "I thought we were friends in a sort of a way," he said.

"Yes, yes of course we are," she relented.

"So, don't bite my head off. It's got nothing to do with being engaged."

"What?"

Eddie decided that Leo Murphy never listened to anything anyone said. She wasn't like Chris Taylor who cared about everything.

Except, of course, that she thought Eddie was a girl, a fellow conspirator in life. Eddie had been forced to write and say that yes he had got his periods when he was eleven. He had managed to say that he fancied the film star Fernando Lamas and that he liked red tartan as a color for a winter skirt.

But mainly Chris wrote about interesting things—she only

descended into these female things every now and then. It always gave him a start.

He posted the photograph and waited.

He knew that she would write with a card for his birthday, usually flowers and bows and entirely unsuitable things he couldn't show to anyone. This year it was a small envelope.

Do not open until Wednesday 29th, it said.

Eddie took it away to read when he was on his own. He had explained to his mother that he had this pen friend, a boy in Scotland.

"What does the Scots boy say?" his mother asked him from time to time.

"Not much. All about flowers and trees," Eddie would say.

"Keeps you out of harm's way, I suppose," Mrs. Barton would say.

Eddie knew she sounded gruffer than she was.

In his bedroom he opened the letter from Chris and got such a shock that he had to sit down.

"I always told myself that when we were both sixteen I would tell you that I have known since the very beginning that you were a boy. I was afraid to tell you that I knew in case you'd stop writing. I *like* you being a boy. You're the nicest boy I ever met in my whole life. Happy birthday dear Eddie and thank you for your friendship."

His first feeling was shame. How dare she have made a fool of him for four years? Then bewilderment. *How* did she know? He had agreed to having periods, being at a convent, wearing a red plaid skirt. Then came an entirely different feeling. A feeling of excitement. She knew he was a boy, and she liked him. She was afraid she'd lose him. He went to the drawer where her letters were. He read bits over and over.

You are so easy to talk to. You really understand. You have a marvelous mind, people here are so ignorant.

Eddie Barton was sixteen years old and in love. He went to Barna Woods. It was icy cold but he didn't care. He found an old log which he sat on, and thought about the new turn of events in his life. He must put a letter in the post to her before six o'clock. There was no question of going to school, there was far too much to think about.

Through the day he felt overwhelming regret about some of the things he had written, whole paragraphs that she must have known were lies. Then he was swept with an irritation. Why had she asked him to help his mother with the sewing when she knew he was a boy? But he mainly wanted his letter to her to be perfect and to say what he felt without frightening her off. He took the picture out again. Huge dark eyes, like an Italian. Then his heart lurched. She had no idea what he looked like. She thought he looked like Leo Murphy. Well, no, she didn't, but she had no idea. Eddie wished he was tall and strong, that he looked like Niall Hayes's cousin Richard, who had come to visit. Everyone said he was so handsome. He wished more than ever that he could find his father and ask his advice.

But his father didn't turn up on Eddie's sixteenth birthday any more than he had on any other anniversary, so he knew he would have to write it alone.

He decided to go to Miss Ross and her mother and ask if he could write the letter there. It would be warm and dry. There would be no fear of his mother asking him what he was doing, saying something that was bound to irritate him. He often did some work on the garden for Miss Ross, who wouldn't mind him coming in on a wild cold day like this.

She was just coming back from the school for her lunch when he arrived. She wore a belted raincoat which swished as she walked along. Eddie wondered if Chris wore a raincoat like that. He might ask her but somehow it seemed a bit personal, that swishy sound. Something he didn't want her to know about, and the feeling it gave him.

Miss Ross looked tired and pale. She said he was an answer to prayer. If he would just chop a few logs for her, not only could he sit by the fire and write for the afternoon, she would give him a big bowl of soup as well.

"It's my birthday, Miss Ross. That's why," he said.

She seemed to find the explanation perfectly satisfactory, and asked nothing about why he had absented himself from the

Brothers without any permission. She couldn't imagine Brother O'Brien saying to a lad of sixteen that he should celebrate the day.

"What kind of a letter? Is it an application for a job?" Miss Ross asked.

"No. It's more a letter to a friend." He was scarlet as he spoke.

"Yes, well, if the friend's in a convent boarding school don't forget the nuns might read it." Miss Ross was full of wisdom.

"No, the friend's not in a boarding school." Eddie knew he sounded stiff.

"Well, you're all right then." Eddie thought Miss Ross sounded as if she was trying to be cheerful for his sake. And maybe a little envious.

Eddie looked around the room before he began his letter. He had never noticed the house very much before, thinking of it as a place to take off his shoes before he came in from the garden. He remembered that Maura Brennan, who had been his friend at Shancarrig School, had always said she loved this house and that when she got old she would have one just like it, with lovely pieces of furniture that she would polish until they shone and china ornaments on shelves and thick rich velvet curtains. Eddie admired the colors, everything seemed to match with everything else, not like in his own home where the carpet was brown and the curtains were yellow and the tablecloth was green; it looked as if everything was chosen to clash with everything else. He knew this was not the case, it was because they didn't have enough money to get things that would look nice. His mother had great taste in the clothes she made. She was always advising her customers what went well with their eyes or their complexion.

But still, that didn't help him to write to Chris Taylor.

He sat for a long time, the old grandfather clock ticking. Miss Ross had gone back to Shancarrig School, her mother was having her afternoon rest upstairs.

"Dearest Chris," Eddie wrote. "I can't tell you how good it is to be able to write as myself. I wanted to so often but once I had begun with the silly lie I had to keep it going in case you stopped writing. Your letters are the most important thing in my life. I couldn't bear them to stop."

And then it was easy. Page after page. He tried to imagine himself sitting in this small house in Glasgow. She called it a two-up-two-down, meaning the number of rooms. Her mother had never realized the dream of moving to an estate. Her father kept pigeons and hadn't much interest in anything else. Her two brothers were at sea and only came home for a very short visit now and then. She wanted to go to a School of Art but she wasn't good enough. Her mother said to get a job in the florist's and be grateful for it; most people had to do work they hated. At least Chris liked flowers, so she'd be ahead of the game.

What would this girl like to read from Eddie, now revealed as a man? He knew one thing. There must be no more pretense.

"I'm small and square and have hair that sticks up. I don't think I ever told you properly about school and how much I hate it, because when I was meant to be a girl I couldn't tell you how rough they are there and how they think I'm as thick as the wall. I don't think I am, and your letters make me think I have something."

There was no trouble finding the words. When he read it over he thought she would think it was a fair explanation for his years of deceit. Not too much apology, more setting the record straight.

He was surprised when Miss Ross came back from school.

"That's a letter and a half, Eddie," she said approvingly.

"Would you have said I was thick, Miss Ross?"

"No I wouldn't, and you're not," she said.

He grinned at her and ran off. She looked out the door and saw him heading for the post office. He skipped and jumped over puddles. He didn't even notice them.

The letters came fast and thick. They wrote to each other about hopes and fears, about books and paintings, about colors and designs. They kept nothing back.

"If we ever meet I must show you the ferns of Barna Woods," he wrote once.

"What do you mean 'if we ever meet'? It's 'when we meet'!" she wrote back, and his heart felt leaden because he knew he had made Shancarrig sound too beautiful, too exciting, too romantic for Christine Taylor.

"That boy must have nothing to do but write letters," his mother said one day when the usual fat envelope arrived from Scotland.

"It's not a boy, it's a girl." Eddie knew he'd have to explain sometime.

"What do you mean? Did he turn into a girl all of a sudden?" Mrs. Barton didn't like the sound of it being a girl.

"No, it's a different one." Eddie didn't feel that any further explanation would help.

"Why Scotland?" his mother said.

"It's nice and far away." He grinned. "If I have to be writing to a girl, Ma, isn't it better that I write to one in a far-off country?"

"At your age you shouldn't be writing to a girl at all. There'll be plenty of time for that later. Too much time if you're your father's son."

There had been much mention over the years of Ted Barton's interest in women, always vague and generalized, never specific and detailed. Eddie had long given up the hope of getting any more information than the sketchy amount he already had. His father had been thrown out because of a known association with another woman. When he had left Shancarrig that night the woman had not gone with him. She might for all he knew be someone he knew. Someone he had spoken to. If only it was someone nice like Miss Ross, then maybe she could have told him more about the man who had left their lives.

"Did my father ever like Miss Ross?" he asked his mother suddenly.

"Maddy Ross?" His mother looked at him in surprise.

"Yes. Could she have been his love?"

"Well, given that she was about twelve or thirteen when he

left town it isn't entirely likely, but that doesn't say it should be ruled out either." His mother had even managed a wry smile as she said this.

Eddie thought she was less bitter. He must remember to tell this to Chris when he wrote; they had no secrets. She told him about her father being laid off in the shipyard and her mother getting an extra shift in the factory. Chris was doing Saturdays in the local flower shop. It wasn't like she thought it would be, working with flowers. It was very mechanical, stiff little arrangements and awful cheaty ways of making the flowers look alive when they were almost dead.

They wrote to each other when they should have been trying a last desperate effort at their books. Christine said that they were snobby in her convent and didn't like the girls whose mothers worked in factories. Eddie wrote that the Brothers had a down on anyone with a bit of soul at all and that they had him written off as a no-hoper. The results of the exams were a foregone conclusion to them both.

In the summer of 1957 they wrote and told each other of poor results, bad marks, and limited futures.

••• •••

"I had a word with Brother O'Brien. He doesn't think it worth trying to repeat the year," Eddie's mother said glumly. She had taken the bus into the big town to buy materials, threads, zip fasteners, and spare pieces for the sewing machine. She had used the opportunity to visit the school.

It hadn't been a happy encounter.

"I told him that other boys had fathers who could pay for this kind of thing, but that we weren't in the lucky position to know where your father is or has been for the last dozen years." Her face had that old bitter look which Eddie hated.

"Ma, you threw him out. You asked him to go. You can't keep blaming him for everything after he went, only for what he did before he went."

"And that was plenty for one lifetime, let me assure you."

"You always *assure* me these things but you never explain them."

"Oh, you've words at will, just like him."

"And was Brother O'Brien sympathetic? I bet he wasn't. He couldn't care about anyone's father, or mother, or anyone at all."

His mother gave him an odd look.

"He wasn't sympathetic. Neither to you nor to me. But I think he does care about people. He said there was no point in my lamenting the absence of a husband, that it was mainly women who did all the consulting whether their husbands were alive or around or whatever."

"And what else?"

"He said that you had got it into your head you were too good for the school, above them and their plain ways. And that would have been fine if you were a real artist burning to paint or to write, but the way things were he didn't know what would become of you. He sounded sorry."

To Eddie it had the ring of truth. That was exactly the way Brother O'Brien would speak, and there was some truth in it. He could see the big man with his red face regretting that he couldn't find a place for the boy. Brother O'Brien loved his boys to get into banks and insurance offices, the civil service, and the very odd time even into a university.

There would be nowhere for Eddie Barton.

If he hadn't had his lifeline of letters to hold him together as support and strength, Eddie would have been very depressed that summer. But Chris wrote every day. She said they must get themselves out of this situation. She would not work in a factory like her mother, nor would she train to be a florist.

They had begun to talk of love now, they ended each letter with more and more yearning and wishes that they could meet. Eddie said that perhaps he had made Shancarrig sound too attractive. Maybe they could meet in some foreign land where there would be warm winds and palm trees. Chris said that nobody could love anybody if they met in the gray streets around her home. She was all for somewhere exotic too.

The world of fantasy became an important part of their letter writing. It almost took over from the practical side. Chris Taylor went to work in a department store in Glasgow. She hated it, she said. It was very tiring. Her legs ached more than usual. Eddie wrote and asked did her legs usually ache, she had never mentioned it before. But she didn't mention it again so he thought it must have been just a phrase.

Eddie Barton went to work in Dunne's Hardware. He hated it. He wrote to Chris about the days talking to farmers who came in to buy chicken wire and plow parts. He said he was sick of harrows and rakes and if he had to talk about linseed oil or red oxide for painting a barn again, he thought he might actually lie down and die. He wrote about how ignorant the Dunnes were. Their aunt, Nellie Dunne, ran a small grocery shop and she gave people credit, which was the only reason why anyone shopped there. Eddie worked for old Mr. Dunne and his sons Brian and Liam. Eileen, who was his own age, worked in Ryan's Hotel, but was always giving him the eye when she came in.

"I tell you this . . ." he wrote to Chris, "not to make myself sound great or to make you jealous, but to remind myself how lucky I am that stupid girls like Eileen with her forward pushy ways form no part of my life now that I know what love is. Now that I have you."

Sometimes she wrote about going to a dance, but she said she sat in a seat on the balcony most of the time and thought about what he had said in his last letter.

Sometimes Nessa Ryan and Leo Murphy came into the shop to talk to him. The Dunnes never minded him talking to them because they were as near to the Quality as Shancarrig possessed. If Maura Brennan came in, or anyone else from the cottages, it would be different. But old Mr. Dunne seemed to take positive pleasure out of a visit from young Miss Ryan of the hotel and young Miss Murphy from The Glen.

"And how goes the good Major?" he would ask Leo about her father.

"Talking to himself as usual," Leo muttered once, and they all giggled.

Mr. Dunne didn't like such disrespect.

"And how are they all in Ireland's leading hostelry?" he would ask Nessa Ryan about her family's hotel.

Nessa always said it was doing fine thank you, which they all knew wasn't true. Ryan's Hotel hadn't kept up with the times.

Eddie wrote to Chris about how strained and worried Leo Murphy looked when she should have had no worries in the world. She had got six honors in her Leaving Certificate. She had all the money in the world; she could have gone to university in Cork or Galway or Dublin, yet she always seemed to be biting her lip.

Chris wrote back and said you never knew what worries people had. Perhaps Leo wasn't well, maybe it was her health. What did she look like? In shame Eddie wrote and said that Leo looked like him, or rather, the pictures he had sent of him when he was meant to be a girl were of Leo.

"She's very good-looking," Chris wrote back anxiously.

"I never noticed it," he wrote. "Perhaps I should have stayed a girl."

"No. You're lovely as you are," she said in the next letter.

They knew that they must talk. Neither household had a phone, but Chris could use the public phone and Eddie could be in Ryan's Hotel waiting for the call. They rehearsed it in letters for some weeks.

"We mightn't like each others' voices," Chris wrote. "But it's important to remember that we like each other so the voice isn't important."

"What do you mean we *like* each other?" wrote Eddie. "We love each other. That's what we must remember on Saturday night."

They made it Saturday so that they could look forward to it all week.

He dressed himself up and put on a clean shirt.

"On the town again I suppose." His mother hardly seemed to look up, but she had taken in that he was smartly turned out.

"Aw, no Mam. There's nowhere much to go on the town in Shancarrig."

"Well, where are you going if I might ask?" Her tone wasn't as sharp as the words. She was aching to know.

"Just down to Ryan's Hotel, Mam, for a cup of coffee."

"Eddie . . . ?"

"Yes, Mam."

"Eddie, I know I'm nagging you but you won't . . ."

"Mam, I told you I don't drink. I didn't like the smell of it or the taste of it the once I tried."

"I don't mean drink." She looked him up and down, a boy setting out for a date, for romance.

"What do you mean?"

"You wouldn't get involved with that Eileen Dunne, now would you? They'd be bad people to get on the wrong side of . . ."

"Who are you telling! Don't I work for them?"

"But Eileen . . . ?"

He knelt beside his mother and looked up into her face.

"If she were the last woman in Ireland I wouldn't want her."

Anyone would have known that he was speaking the truth. Eddie's mother waved him off with a lighter heart.

Chris was to ring at eight. Eddie positioned himself in the hall. The telephone would ring at the reception desk, then whoever was on duty would look around and say "Eddie Barton, I don't know . . . Oh yes, *there* he is," and she'd motion Eddie to go into the booth. Then he would speak to her. To the girl he loved.

Another good thing about it being a Saturday was that awful Eileen Dunne wouldn't be working at the desk. She was in the dining room on Saturdays, a black dress tight across the bottom and the bosom, and a small white apron making no attempt to cover her at all.

Eddie's heart was beating so strongly, it reminded him of the big clock in Shancarrig School and the thudding sounds it made as the seconds ticked on.

Soon, soon. Ten minutes. Nine.

He jumped a foot in the air when he heard the phone ring. He hadn't noticed that Eileen Dunne *was* working at Reception tonight. Please may she not make any remark, may she not say something stupid that Chris would hear all the way away in Scotland.

"Yes, he's here. Hold on. *Edd* . . . *ie?*"

He was at the desk.

"Yes?"

"There's someone on the phone for you. Will you take it here at the desk? God, you're looking like a dog's dinner tonight."

"I'll go into the box," he said, his face red with fury.

"Right. Hold on till I get this bloody thing through. There's more plugs and wires than a hedgehog's backside. Are you going into town to the dance?"

He ran in to the dark phone booth, his hands trembling. Damn Eileen Dunne to hell. Please may Chris not have heard.

"Hello?" he said tentatively.

It must be the Scottish telephone operator on the line. He could hardly understand her. She was saying something about difficulty in getting through.

"Can you put me on to Chris, please?" He knew his voice was shaky, but it had been a bit of luck that she hadn't come straight through. She wouldn't have heard that stupid stupid Eileen. Any moment she'd talk to him.

"This *is* Chris," he'd managed to decipher from the strange speech. "Do you mean you canna hear me?"

It wasn't Chris's voice. It was like someone imitating a Scottish comedian. Every word was *canna* and *woudna*.

"That's never you, not you yourself, Chris?" he said. She must be playing a joke.

"Och, Eddie, stop putting on that Irish blarney bit. You're like the fellows they have at Christmas concerts in the church, with their afther doing this and afther doing that."

There was a silence. They realized that neither of them was putting on an act. This is the way they were. The silence was broken by their laughter.

"Oh God, Eddie . . . I forgot. I had you talking normally in my mind."

His heart was full of love. This strange way she spoke didn't matter a bit. "I thought you'd be like a real person too," he said.

Then it was back to the way they were in letters. Until the three minutes ran out.

"I love you, Chris, more than ever."

"And I love you too," she said.

··• •··

They lived for Saturdays, and yet as they wrote to each other the phone calls were never as good as they expected. Sometimes they literally didn't understand what the other was saying and they wasted precious time explaining.

They were desperate to meet. The time was very long.

"We'd better meet soon before we're too old to recognize each other," she wrote.

"While we still remember what we wrote to each other."

They each kept their letters in shoe boxes. It seemed a small thing but a bond . . . another bond. Yet they hesitated each to ask the other to their town. Eddie couldn't bear the explanations, the doing up of the spare room, the questioning from his mother, the eyes of Shancarrig.

Chris said that if he had found it hard to understand her voice, then her family and her neighbors in Glasgow would be incomprehensible.

She obviously yearned for Barna Woods and the hill with the big rock on it, the rock that gave its name to the town. She wanted to see Eddie's pink house and meet his mother.

He wanted her here and he didn't want her. He wanted to leave Shancarrig forever, and yet he couldn't. One man had left his mother already, Eddie couldn't go.

Then he heard at last he heard himself inviting her. He didn't really intend to, it just came out.

It had been a long hard day in Dunne's when nothing had gone right. Old Mr. Dunne was like a devil, Liam had been scornful, Brian had been giving him orders, and to make matters worse their cousin Foxy who had been in Eddie's class at school had come back for a visit.

Foxy worked on the buildings in England. He was doing well by all accounts. He had started by making billycans of tea for Irishmen working on the lump, building the big roads over in Britain. He came home every year, eyes bright and darting around him as usual.

Normally Eddie was pleased to see Foxy, he had a quick wit and was always ready with a joke.

Today it hadn't been like that. "Don't let him speak to you like that," Foxy said to Eddie when Mr. Dunne had called him "an ignorant bosthoon."

"Fine words, Foxy. He's only an uncle to you, but he pays my week's wages."

"Still and all, you're letting him walk over you. You'll be here for the rest of your life with a shop coat on you stuck behind a counter."

"And what are you going to be?" Eddie had flared back.

"I've got the hell out of here. I wouldn't sit here listening to my uncle mumbling and bumbling, and my aunt Nellie letting people run up bad debts because they're Quality. I'm in England and I'll make a pile of money. And then I'll come back and marry Leo Murphy."

It was the longest speech that Foxy had ever made. Eddie had been surprised.

"And will Leo marry *you*?"

"Not now, she won't. Not the way I am. No one would marry either of us, Eddie. We're eejits. We have only one good suit each with an arse in the trousers of it. We have to *do* something with our lives instead of standing round here like fools. What class of a woman would want the likes of us?"

"I don't know. We might have a charm of our own." Eddie was being lighthearted, but he felt that Foxy was right.

Foxy turned away impatiently. "I can see you in twenty years still saying that, Eddie. This place makes us all slow and stupid. It's like a muddy river dragging us down."

Eddie had been thinking about it all day. He didn't dress up for the phone call that night. It was his turn to call the Glasgow phone box.

"Come over to Ireland. Come to Shancarrig," he said when Chris answered the phone.

"When? When will I come?"

"As soon as you can. I'm sick of being without you," he said. "There's nothing at all else in my life except you."

··• •··

Their letters changed tone. It was confident now. It was "when" not "if." It was definite. The love was there, the need, the surprise that one other person could feel exactly the same about everything as another.

There were the details.

Chris would take her two-weeks holidays from the flower shop. Eddie could take his two weeks off from Dunne's. She would get the boat from Stranraer to Larne, and the train to Belfast maybe?

"Will I come to meet you there? I've never been to the North of Ireland. It'll be familiar to you, red buses, red pillar boxes. Like England."

"Like Scotland," she corrected him. She had never been to England in her life.

Or would she take a train to Wales, and get the boat from Holyhead? Maybe that would be a nicer way to go. She could see Dun Laoghaire and a bit of Dublin before taking the train to Shancarrig.

"I don't want you wandering around on your own, meeting Dublin fellows. I'll come and meet you off the boat," he suggested.

Chris said no, she wanted to arrive in Shancarrig on the train herself. She knew about the station, and the flowers that now spelled out the word *Shancarrig*. He had written that long ago to her.

Eddie could be on the platform.

He prayed that it would be a fine fortnight, that the sun

would shine into Barna Woods between the branches, that there would be a sparkle on the River Grane. He knew you shouldn't pray for something bad to happen to another human, but he hoped that somehow Eileen Dunne would be in hospital when Chris arrived, and that Nessa Ryan wouldn't be superior toward him, and that he'd be free of Brian and Liam Dunne and their bad-tempered father because he was on holidays.

He hoped most of all that his mother would be nice to Chris. They had never had anyone to stay, and Eddie had distempered the walls, and painted the woodwork in the small stuffy room they had called a box room up to now. His mother had been curiously quiet.

"What kind of a girl is she?" was all she had asked.

"A girl I write to, I write to her a lot. I like her through the post and on the telephone. I've asked her to come over here so that . . . well, so that I wouldn't be the one going off on you."

His mother looked away so that he wouldn't see the look of gratitude on her face. But he saw all the same.

"I'll make curtains for the room," his mother said.

Please let them like each other.

They had got ham for tea, cooked ham and tomatoes, and a Fullers chocolate cake with four chocolate buttons on the top.

His mother had cleared the sewing away so that the place would look like a normal house. There were blue curtains on the window of the box room, and a matching bedspread. On the makeshift dressing table there was a little blue cloth and Eddie had gathered a bunch of flowers.

It was nearly time. The train would be in at three. Only four hours. Three. Two. It was time.

••• •••

Liam Dunne was on the platform; there was a delivery coming down with the Guard on the train.

"What are you doing?" Liam asked. "Aren't you meant to be on your holidays? If you're doing nothing you could give me a hand . . ."

"I most definitely *am* on my holidays and I'm meeting a friend," Eddie said firmly.

The train whistled and came around the corner. She got off. She carried a big suitcase, square with little firm bits over the corners like leather triangles to preserve it.

She had a red jacket and a navy skirt, a navy shoulder bag and a huge bright smile.

He had been afraid for a moment that she might think Liam Dunne was him. Liam was taller and good-looking in a rangey sort of way. Eddie felt like a barrel. He wished his spine would shoot up and make him willowy.

He started to walk toward her and saw her foot. Chris Taylor had a big built-up shoe. He willed his eyes away from it, and onto her smiling eager face.

Liam was busy with the Guard, hauling things from the luggage van, and nobody was watching them.

Eddie had never kissed anyone in his life apart from fumbles at dances. He put his arms around Chris.

"Welcome to Shancarrig," he said first, then he kissed her very gently. She clung to him.

"I didn't tell you about my foot," she said, her face working anxiously.

"What about your foot?" He forced himself not to look at it again to see how bad it was. Could she walk? Did it drag? His head was whirling.

"I didn't want you to pity me," she said.

"Me? Pity *you*? You must be mad," he said.

"I can walk and everything, and I can keep up. I'll be able to see every bit of Barna Woods with you after tea."

She looked very young and frightened. She must have been worried about this for ages, like he worried about the place not being as nice as he described.

"I don't know what you're going on about." He tried to reassure her, but he knew it wasn't working.

"My leg, Eddie. I've got one shorter than the other you see, I wear a special shoe.

He could read how hard it was for her to say this. How often she must have rehearsed it. He urged himself to find the right words.

He looked down at her foot in its black shoe with the big thick raised sole and heel.

"Does it hurt?" he asked.

"No, of course not, but it's the way it looks."

He took both her hands in his. "Chris, are you mad?" he asked her. "Are you off your head? It's me. It's Eddie, your best friend. Your love. Do you think for a moment that it's part of the bargain that our legs had to be the same length?"

It was, as it happened, exactly the right thing to say. Chris Taylor burst into tears and hugged Eddie to her as if she was never going to let him go. "I love you Eddie."

"I love you too. Come on, let's go home." He carried her case and they walked to the gate of the station.

Chris was still wiping her eyes. Liam Dunne stood watching them.

"Don't mind him." He nodded in Eddie's direction. "That fellow's as thick as the wall. He's always upsetting people and making them cry. There's plenty of real men in Shancarrig."

She gave him a bright smile.

"I bet there are. I've come all the way from Scotland to investigate them." She tucked her arm into Eddie's and they went out the gate.

Eddie felt ten feet tall.

"Who was that?" she whispered.

"Liam Dunne. Desperate . . ."

"Don't tell me. I know all about him. The younger son, the one that'll take over if Brian goes to England and the old man dies."

"You know it all," he said in wonder.

"I feel like *I'm* coming home."

As they walked up the road and he pointed out Ryan's Hotel where he had sat waiting for the phone calls, and the church where Father Gunn waved to him cheerfully, the pubs and Nellie Dunne's grocery, he knew that in many ways she had come home. He knew that he had been right, she was the center of his life. It would be fine when he brought her home to his mother.

···•· ••··

Afterward nobody could ever tell you exactly how and why Chris Taylor came to live in Shancarrig. One day she had never been heard of and then the next there she was, as if she had been part of the place all her life.

If people asked Mrs. Barton about her, they were told that she was a marvelous girl altogether and a dab hand at the sewing. There was nothing she couldn't turn her hand to. Look at the way she had made them go into furnishings, for example. Chris Taylor had loved the curtains and bedspread in her little room the day she arrived. Her praise was unstinting. Mrs. Barton was a genius.

Eddie never thought of his mother's dressmaking as anything except a way to make a living; he knew she didn't particularly like some of the women whose dresses she made. He hadn't realized that the work was artistic in itself.

Chris opened his eyes for him. "Look at the way the ribbon falls, look at the colors she's put together . . . Eddie, it's easy to see where you got your artistic sense from. . . ."

His mother reddened with pleasure. There were no derisory remarks about his father. In fact, Chris was able to introduce the first reasonable conversation about the long-departed Ted Barton that had ever been held in this house.

"I suppose he was a restless kind of a man. Better for him to be gone in a lot of ways."

And to his surprise Eddie heard his mother agreeing. Things had really begun to change around here.

Chris was part of Shancarrig.

They knew her coming in and out of Dunne's to see Eddie or to give him a message, they knew her in the hotel where she became friendly with Nessa Ryan. No one ever spoke dismissively to Chris Taylor as people had been known to do to Eddie Barton. She talked furnishings and fabrics to Nessa's mother.

There was going to be a grant for the hotel to make it smarter, the kind of a place where tourist visitors might stay as well as commercial travelers.

They couldn't stay in Ryan's the way it was. Chris seemed to know the way it should be—pelmets, nice wooden pelmets covered in fabric, she had seen it all in an American magazine, you stuck the fabric to the plywood, and then the curtains draped properly down below. And, of course, bed covers to match.

Nessa Ryan and her mother were very excited.

"How would we get it started? Would we need to call someone in from Dublin? Who'd do it?"

"We would," Chris said simply.

"We?"

"Mrs. Barton and I. Let us do one room as a sample and see."

"Wooden pelmets . . . ? You couldn't do that . . . ?"

"Eddie could, he could get the plywood. Liam Dunne could help him. . . ."

The room was a huge success. The whole hotel would be done the same way. They had chosen a fabric which would tone in with Eddie's pressed flowers, with his large bold designs, flowers from Barna Woods, a place in the locality especially commissioned from a local artist.

"You can't call me a local artist," Eddie had protested.

"You are local. You live here, don't you?" she said simply.

The plans were afoot. Chris and Eddie's mother would be able to do it between them, but they needed someone to organize it, someone who would go and choose the right fabrics, someone with an eye for color, someone whose pictures were already on the wall.

Flushed and happy, Chris told Eddie the plan.

"You can leave Dunne's. We'll have a business, all of us . . ."

"I can't leave . . . if we get married I have to support you."

"What's this *if*? Are you changing your mind? I've come over here and lived with you, set myself up shamelessly in your house and you say 'if'?"

"I want to ask you something properly."

"Not here, Eddie. Let's go up to the woods."

Maeve Binchy

Eddie's mother stood by the window and watched the two of them walk together, the limping figure of this strange strong Scottish girl, the stocky figure of her own son, who had grown taller since Chris had arrived.

She knew nothing about the kind of family over in Scotland who let their daughter wander away to another land without seeming to care.

She cared little now about the past. Once she had lived in it and felt burdened by it, now she thought only about the future, the proposal that was going to be made in Barna Woods and accepted, the new life that was ahead of all of them.

5

Dr. Jims

In Shancarrig they only knew him as Dr. Blake for about six weeks. Then they all started to call him Dr. Jims. It had to do with Maisie, of course. Maisie who couldn't pronounce any name properly, not even one as ordinary as James. She had been asked to call Dr. James to the telephone and in front of the whole waiting room she had said that Dr. Jims was wanted. Somehow, the name had stuck. James Blake was too young a man to be given a full title, not while the great Dr. Nolan held sway in Shancarrig.

Jims Blake got very accustomed to people asking for the real doctor when they came to The Terrace, and if a call came in the night which Dr. Jims answered, the gravest doubts were expressed. He learned to say that he was only holding the fort for the real doctor, and Dr. Nolan would be along at a more convenient hour to give his approval.

But it was a good partnership—the wise old man who knew all the secrets of Shancarrig and the thin eager young man, son of a small farmer out the country. The old man who drank more brandy at night than was good for him and the young man who stayed up late reading the journals and reports . . . they lived together peaceably. They had Maisie doting on both of them and resenting the fact that people kept getting sick and needing to disturb the two men in her life, the great Dr. Nolan and poor young Dr. Jims.

Dr. Nolan was always saying that Jims Blake should find a wife for himself and Maisie was always saying that there was plenty of time.

Matters came to a head in 1940 when Dr. Nolan was seventy and Dr. Jims was thirty. It had been a busy time. There was a baby to be delivered in almost every house around them. A little girl Leonora up at The Glen, a first daughter to the Ryans at the hotel, another Dunne to the cottages, a son for the wife of wild Ted Barton, another Brennan to add to Paudie's brood.

Dr. Jims would come back tired to the big house in The Terrace—the tall house, one of a line facing the hotel. It formed the center of the town in a triangle with the row of shops. The bus stopped nearby and the movement of Shancarrig could be charted from any of the windows. Dr. Jims' work took him to the far outlying districts as well, but the center of life remained this small area around the place where he lived.

Even though it was comfortable, there were ways in which it was not a real life. Dr. Nolan was able to put it into words. "I'm not going to let you make the same mistake as I did," the old man said. "A doctor needs a wife, really and truly. I had my chances and my choices in the old days, like you do now. But I was both too set and too easy in my ways. I didn't want to disrupt everything by bringing a woman in. I didn't really need a woman, I thought."

"And you didn't either," Dr. Jims encouraged him. "Didn't you have a full life . . . where was there room for a wife? I've seen too many doctors' wives neglected, left out . . . maybe the medical profession should take a vow of celibacy, like the clerics. It might be something we could bring up at the Irish Medical Association."

"Don't make a jeer out of it, Jims. I'm serious."

"So am I. How could I marry? Where would I get the stake for a house? I still send a bit home to the farm. You know that. I have to be averting my eyes for a bit, in case I think I might want a wife."

"And who are you averting them from?" The old man drank his brandy, looking deep into the glass and not at his partner.

"Not anybody in particular."

"But Frances Fitzgerald, maybe?"

"Ah, come on out of that. What could I offer Frances Fitzgerald?"

But Jims Blake knew that the old man had seen through him. He most desperately wanted to advance things with Frances, to go further than the games of tennis with other people present, the card evenings at The Glen or in Ryan's Hotel.

He'd hoped it hadn't been as transparent to other people.

Yet again Dr. Nolan seemed to read his mind.

"Nobody would know but myself," he said reassuringly. "And you could offer her half a house here."

"It's your house."

"I won't be here forever. It's taking more of this stuff to ease the pain in my gut." He raised his brandy glass to show what he was referring to.

"The pain in your gut would be less if you had less of that stuff."

"So you say, with the arrogance of youth. . . . We'll get the top two floors done up for you. The Dunnes can come in on Monday and lean on their picks and shovels and we'll see what they can do. Frances will want her own kitchen . . . she won't want Maisie traipsing around after her."

"Charles, I can't . . . we don't even know if Frances is interested . . ."

"We do," said Dr. Nolan.

Jims Blake didn't even wait to let that sink in.

"But I can't afford—" he began.

Charles Nolan's face winced with pain and anger. "Stop being such a defeatist, such a sniveler. . . . I can't this, I can't that. . . . Is that how you made yourself a doctor . . . ?"

His face was red now proving his point.

"Listen here to me, Jims Blake, why do you think I took you on here? Think about it. It wasn't for your great moneyed connections and class. No. I took you on because you were a fighter, and a dogged little fellow. I liked your thin white face and your determination. I liked the way you forced them to let you study, and took jobs to make up the extra money that they couldn't give you. That's what people need in a doctor—someone who won't quit."

"I could pay you so much a month for it, I suppose. I could take on more of the work."

"Boy, aren't you doing almost all the work already. I'm only giving you what's fair. . . ."

And it was settled like that. Dr. Jims was to have the upstairs part of the house. Everyone said it was very sensible. After all, Dr. Nolan wasn't getting any younger. Wasn't it sensible that a bedroom be built for him on the ground floor?

Maisie sniffed a bit, especially since it became known that Dr. Jims was now courting Miss Fitzgerald.

The Dunne brothers were in regularly, wondering should the kitchen be facing the front or the back of the house. It might be good to have it looking out on the town. There was a nice view of Shancarrig from upstairs in The Terrace. But then, traditionally a kitchen was at the back. They puzzled at it.

Before they came to any solution their work was rendered unnecessary. Dr. Charles Nolan died of the liver complaint he had been ignoring for some years, and he willed his house to his partner Dr. Blake.

Before he died he spoke of it to Jims. "You're a good lad. You'll keep it all going fine here, if only you'd learn to. . . ."

"You've got years yet. Stop making a farewell speech," Jims Blake said to the dying man.

"What I was *going* to say, if only you'd learn that there are people, myself included, who are quite glad to be coming to the end of their lives, who don't *want* to be told that there are years of pain and confusion ahead of them. . . ."

Jims held his partner's hand—it was a simple gesture of solidarity where no words would have worked.

"That's more like it," said Dr. Nolan. "Now, will you promise me to have a family and a real life for yourself? Don't be forced to leave this place to some whippersnapper of a junior partner, like I am!"

"You can't leave it all to me . . ." He was aghast.

"I was hoping to leave it to Frances as well. Tell me you've made some move in that direction."

"Yes. We were hoping to marry. . . ." His voice choked, realizing that his benefactor wouldn't now be at the wedding.

"That's good, very good. I'm tired now. Get me into hospital tomorrow, Jims. I don't want to die in the house where she's coming as a bride."

"It's your house. Die wherever you want to," Jims blazed at him.

The old man smiled. "I like to hear you talk that way. And where I would like to die is the hospital. Tell that young Father Gunn to come up there to me, not to be upsetting Maisie by coming here. And move that brandy bottle back to my reach."

It didn't take Shancarrig long to recognize Dr. Jims as the real doctor. Everything had changed. There was no old Dr. Nolan anymore to know their secrets so they told them to Dr. Jims instead. He was a married man now, of course, and his wife a very gentle person—one of the Fitzgeralds who owned a big milling business.

It had been a good match—that's what outsiders thought. But they only knew the surface. They didn't know about passion and love and understanding. Frances, with her gentle solemn face transformed so often with a quick smile that lit up her whole being was a wife that he never dreamed possible.

She would creep up behind him and lock her arms around his neck. She would feed him pieces of food from her plate when Maisie wasn't looking. When he was called out at night Frances sometimes left a note on his pillow saying *Wake me up. I want to welcome you home properly.* In every way she made him grow in confidence. Jims Blake walked with a lighter step and a smile in his eyes.

The fact that Dr. Nolan had left him the house made Dr. Jims even more respected in the community. If the old doctor had thought so much of him, then this must be a good man. Sometimes Jims Blake felt unworthy of all the respect he got in Shancarrig.

When he visited his dour family on their small bleak farm and saw the life-style that he would have been condemned to had he not fought so hard to study medicine, he felt guilty. He was saddened that they had so little, and even the money he gave them was stored under a mattress, not used to buy his mother and father a better standard of life.

He had tried to explain this guilt to Frances, but she calmed him down. He had done everything he could for the family. Surely that was as much as anyone was expected to do—he couldn't do any more.

Frances said that *they* were a family now, she and Jims and the baby they were expecting. There was no tie that bound them to the bleak family of Blakes in the small wet farm, or the distant, undemonstrative Fitzgeralds wrapped up in their business affairs. They were a little unit in themselves.

And so it was for a while.

Jims often thought that the spirit of old Dr. Nolan would have been pleased to hear the way that Number 3, The Terrace rang with laughter. First Eileen was born, then Sheila. No son and heir yet, but as people said, God would send the boy in His own good time.

There were many attempts for the boy—all ending in miscarriage.

Frances Blake was a frail woman—the efforts to hold a child to full term were taking a great toll on her health.

Several times Jims asked himself what would the old doctor have advised if he had been involved in a family where this had been the situation. He could almost hear Dr. Nolan's voice.

"This is a thing you could work out between the pair of you

. . . now the good God up in heaven doesn't have a book of rules saying you must do this or that, and so many times . . . the good God expects us to use our intelligence . . ."

And he might go on to explain some of the most elemental details of times of high fertility and low fertility, suggesting the latter as the wiser time to indulge in what he called the business of marriage.

But always he would urge the couple to talk to each other.

Jims Blake somehow found it hard to talk to his own wife.

The problem was all the greater because he loved her so much. He desired her *and* he wanted to protect her. A combination of that was hard to rationalize. He had worked out her ovulation as carefully as he could, they had tried to make love at the times she was least likely to conceive. He had held her face in his hands and assured her that his two little girls were plenty, they didn't need to try for a son. Let them live their lives without putting her to any additional strain, without placing her health in danger.

Sometimes she looked sad, he didn't know if it was because she feared that he didn't desire her as much as he once had. Perhaps it was because she really did yearn to give him a son. He found it impossible to believe that two people who loved each other so much could still have areas of misunderstanding. And yet, whenever he approached her she seemed so receptive and willing that he had to believe this was what she wanted too.

When Frances became pregnant again in 1946 the girls Eileen and Sheila were five and four—two cherubs waiting in their Viyella nightdresses and red flannel dressing gowns while he read them stories. This time he hoped for a son to join them.

In the coldest winter that Ireland had ever known Frances Blake gave birth to her son. And in the house with log fires burning in every room, with a midwife from the hospital in the big town in attendance, as well as her husband who had, even at the age of thirty-seven, delivered thousands of children into the world . . . she died.

They had never even discussed what to call the baby. They

hadn't dared to hope it would live, nor had they dared to hope it would be a boy.

Father Gunn, arriving at the house to the news of the birth and death, inquired if the child was sickly, and whether there should be an emergency baptism.

"I think the child is healthy enough." Jims Blake's voice was empty.

"Well, we'll leave it for a while then. It'll bring some cheer to the household to have a baptism." Father Gunn was optimistic. He tried to see some light at the end of the seemingly endless dark tunnels of this particular winter. He had been burying far more than he baptized.

"Maybe you could get it over with, Father." The young doctor looked white and strained.

"Not now, Jims. Wait a bit. Give the lad a start, find godparents for him. Think of a name. He has a life to live, Frances would want that for him."

"He mightn't live, let's do it now."

Something about the face of Jims Blake made Father Gunn know that this was not so. But he couldn't close the doors of heaven to a little soul.

He still had his stole on.

"Bill Hayes is downstairs, he could be the godfather. What about a godmother?"

"Maisie will stand for him . . ."

"But later, the boy might like to—"

"It doesn't matter what the boy might like later on. Will we do it or will we not?"

Father Gunn said the words of baptism while pouring the Holy Water on the head of Declan Blake. He had asked was there to be any other name—people usually had two.

"Declan will do," said Jims Blake.

Maisie, her face red from crying, her voice almost inaudible from the heavy chest cold, made the vows together with Bill Hayes, the local solicitor—they would look after the spiritual welfare of this child.

Bill Hayes had children the same age as Jims Blake's, including a newly born baby girl, safely delivered from a living wife not four weeks previously.

Never short of the right word in terms of the law, Bill Hayes found himself totally unable to give any meaningful sympathy at a time like this.

"If you were a drinking man I'd get you drunk, Jims," he said.

"But you're not a drinking man either, Bill."

"Still, I could become one if it would help you."

The doctor shook his head.

He had seen too many people opting for this solution.

"Would I sit with you downstairs by the fire?"

Poor Bill Hayes was truly at a loss for the small talk that came to him so easily in his office when consoling those who had been cut out of wills or who had lost a court case. Nothing seemed appropriate to say.

"No. Go home, Bill. I beg you. I'll sit by myself. There's a doctor coming in from the town. He'll be staying in the spare room tonight . . . in case I get a call out. He'll do it for me tonight. I wouldn't be much good to anyone."

"Did Frances know she had a son?" Bill Hayes asked. He knew his wife would want to know—it wasn't the kind of question he would normally ask.

"No. She knew nothing at all."

"Well, well. He'll grow up a credit to you both. I know that."

Jims tried to remember that he had a son, a boy who would grow in this house, as the girls had grown. A baby who would be fed with a bottle, and who would cry in the night. A baby who would smile and flail with little fists. A baby boy who would sit in a dressing gown and want to hear stories read aloud to him.

Suddenly it was all too much for him. He could see other pictures crowding in. A little boy with a school satchel, struggling along the road to Shancarrig School. A boy with a hurley going to a match. He almost felt dizzy with the responsibility of it all.

A wave of loneliness swept over him. There would be no

Frances ever again. No Frances so proud of the girls in their little powder blue coats, going up the church with them at Mass. No Frances to talk to in the evening. She was lying ice-cold already. Tomorrow she would be taken to the church and then the whole of Shancarrig would process to the churchyard.

His father and mother would come, his sister and his brother, Rosary beads dangling from their hands, nudging each other, whispering. No help or support to anyone.

The Fitzgeralds would come, the women in hats looking down at the Blake women in head scarves. There would be stiff and stilted conversation in the house.

Not one of them knew how terrible it was that his wife had died, and that he felt responsible. If it hadn't been for that time . . . the time they must have conceived the child . . . Frances would be alive and well tonight.

He said goodbye to Bill Hayes, who left with some relief. And then Jims Blake sat down at his fire and tried to count his blessings, like he always urged his patients to do.

He listed a good marriage with Frances as a blessing. Nearly seven years of it. Great passion, great friendship, a happy time full of hope.

He listed his little girls, he listed the big house in The Terrace, left to him by his good, kind partner. And a big steady doctor's practice. He counted in having escaped from his own family as a blessing, and he added his own good health. He did not include his son, the baby not yet one day old.

Everyone said that it was the worst funeral they were ever at —the rain lashing against the church, the traces of old snow slippery on the ground, a freezing east wind as they walked to the cemetery.

Jims Blake insisted that the girls be taken home after the Mass. In fact, as he stood shaking hands with the congregation of sympathizers, many of them with heavy colds and flu, he begged them not to come to the grave.

"Things are bad enough already, don't get pneumonia," he urged them.

But in Shancarrig people felt it was only right and respectful to accompany a funeral to the final resting place. They stood, a wretched group, as the wind caught the coats of the gravediggers and blew the few flowers away from the top of the coffin, hurtling them in a macabre sort of dance around the gravestones.

Back in The Terrace they asked in hushed tones how he would manage. What was he going to do? The loss of Frances wasn't just that of a wife, it was the loss of the person who managed the home. Three little children. Every time they said three he got a shock.

He thought of Eileen and Sheila with their little faces. He had forgotten about the baby.

This wasn't at all healthy, he told himself. And as his relations and friends drank sherry and ate plates of sandwiches in the rooms downstairs, he went up wearily to look at his son.

The child was sleeping as he went into the room.

Tiny and red as all children, seemingly swamped and smothered by the bedding, the tiny perfect little fists with their minuscule nails were on the pillow. Was it his imagination or did the baby look more helpless and alone than any other child? As if he knew he was motherless from the moment he had come on earth.

"I'll do my best for you, Declan," he promised aloud. It was curiously formal and he felt himself remote as he said it. It was like a contract or a bargain between strangers, not a father to his infant son.

He hadn't heard anyone come into the room they called the nursery, but turned to find Nora Kelly, the young schoolmistress married to the Master.

"Can I pick him up?" she whispered softly, as if she were in a sickroom.

"Of course, Nora."

He saw the woman who had been aching to have her own child, lift the tiny baby and hold him to her breast.

She said nothing, just walked around the room.

Her stance was that of a woman who had always nursed a child. Her hold on the baby was sure, her love obvious. No one except Jims Blake would know the amount of examination she had undergone to try to discover why she could not conceive.

He watched, almost mesmerized, as she walked to and fro crooning a very soft sound to the baby boy.

He didn't know how long they were there—the strange tableau of the doctor, the teacher, and child. But he felt this slow urge coming over him to give away his baby son. He wanted more than anything in the world to say to Nora Kelly . . . Take him home, you have none, you never will have any. I don't want this child that killed Frances. . . . Bring him back home and rear him as your own.

In a more civilized society that's what people would have done. Why would it be the scandal of Shancarrig, the talk of the country, and, moreover, a crime against the law of the land, for someone to walk out of this room with the child they so desperately wanted, taking it from a home where he wasn't needed?

Then he pulled himself together.

"I'll go on down, Nora. Stay here a bit if you want to."

"No, I'd better come down too, Doctor," she said.

He knew that the same solution had crossed her mind, and she was banishing it, as he had.

It was on occasions like this that Mrs. Kennedy, the mournful, bleak-looking housekeeper to Father Gunn, came into her own. She slid almost invisibly into the house of the bereaved, suggesting, helping, and organizing. She would arrive with a supply of gleaming white tablecloths to hand them, then in a thrice sum up what the house would need in order to give hospitality to those who would come to sympathize. A quick word with the hotel across the road from The Terrace about extra cups, glasses, and plates while Maisie listened to it all wringing her hands. Mrs. Kennedy had the authority of the clergy because she had worked with them for so long.

She never interfered, she just guided.

Maisie wouldn't have known about the need for good hot

soup to serve with the sandwiches, nor that a room should be cleared for people's coats and umbrellas. Mrs. Kennedy managed to imply that she was the voice of order and sanity in sad circumstances like these. And in houses rich and poor all over Shancarrig people had gone along with her, feeling a sense of overpowering relief that someone was taking charge.

Jims Blake greeted people, accepted their condolences, poured them more drinks, inquired about their health, but he did so with only part of his brain. He was working out what arrangements he was going to make. He did so by elimination. He would not have either of his unmarried sisters to live in the house, and he must make that clear before any offer was made. He would not have anyone from the Fitzgerald side of the family either, though they were less likely to present themselves.

Maisie couldn't manage a baby. It would be too expensive to have a live-in nurse. What was he to do?

As he had done so often, he asked himself what old Charles Nolan would have done. Again the voice came to him, booming as it would have been. "Isn't the countryside crawling with young girls only dying to get out from under their parents? Any one of them will have brought up a rake of brothers and sisters. They'll be well able to look after one small baby."

He felt better then, and was even able to smile at Foxy Dunne, one of the boldest of the entire Dunne clan from the cottages—a red-haired boy in raggy trousers who had come to the door to sympathize.

"I'm sorry for your trouble," Foxy had said, standing confidently in the cold outside Number 3, The Terrace.

"Thank you, Foxy. It was good of you to call."

The boy was looking past him to the table where there was food and orange squash.

"Well then . . ." Foxy said.

"Would you like to come in and . . . sympathize inside?"

"That's very good of you, sir," said Foxy, and was past him and at the table in two seconds.

Maisie looked disapproving and was on the point of ejecting him. Mrs. Kennedy frowned heavily.

Dr. Jims shook his head.

"Mr. Dunne has come to sympathize, Maisie. Mrs. Kennedy, can you please give him a slice of cake?"

The nurse was booked to stay for a month and Jims Blake began his search for the girl who would bring up his son. It didn't take long.

He found Carrie, a big-boned, dark-haired girl of twenty-four, living on the side of a hill, deeply discontented with a life that involved cooking for six unappreciative brothers. He had been to the house on several occasions, usually to deal with injuries from threshing machines or otherwise around the farm. He had never treated the girl, but when he was called to their place to stitch the father's head after yet another violent altercation with some farm machinery, it occurred to Jims Blake that Carrie might be glad of the offer of a place, and a better situation.

They walked to the farmyard gate and he told her what he had in mind.

"Why me, Doctor? I'd be a bit ignorant for the kind of house you run."

"You'd be kind. You could manage a child. You managed all this lot." He jerked his head back at the house where she had looked after brothers, older and younger than herself, since her own mother died.

"I'm not very smart," she said.

"You're fine. But here's a few pounds anyway, in case you want to buy yourself some clothes to travel in."

It was a nice way to put it. He knew the traveling which meant taking a few belongings on the next lift she could get to the town wasn't important, but it covered the fact that she hadn't an outfit to wear.

Maisie sniffed a bit at the news of the new arrival, but not too much. After all, the poor young doctor was still in mourning, and mustn't be upset. And it had been very clear from the outset that Carrie would help Maisie in the house. There would be no question of meals on a tray for a fancy nurse.

Declan Blake was only ten days old when Carrie took him in her arms.

"He's a bit like my own," she said quietly to Dr. Blake.

"You had one of your own?" The world was full of surprises. She had never consulted him about the pregnancy.

"Up in Dublin. He's given away, it was for the best. He's three now, somewhere."

"As you say, it would have been hard to have reared him." His voice was its usual gentle sympathetic tone, but it came from the heart. This gawky girl wouldn't think it was at all for the best that her three-year-old had been given away.

"I'll do a good job minding this little fellow, Dr. Jims," she said.

It reminded him of his own vow to the child. Everyone was promising this tiny baby some kind of care, as if the baby feared he wouldn't get any.

The summer eventually came that year, and Dr. Jims took his little daughters by the hand up to Shancarrig School.

He walked around the three classrooms with them, and showed them the globe and the map of the world. He pointed out the inkwells in the desks and told them that soon they'd be dipping their own pens in there and doing their exercises. Solemnly they all studied the charts showing the Irish lettering for the alphabet.

"You'll be able to speak Irish when you leave here," he promised them.

"Who would we speak it to?" Eileen asked.

Mrs. Kelly was standing at the door and gave one of her rare smiles.

"It's a good question," she said ruefully.

Dr. Jims had sent her to Dublin again for further tests, none of the results being remotely helpful. There was no reason that specialists could find why the Kellys were not conceiving a child. He remembered his strange urge to bundle the baby into her arms on that unreal day back at The Terrace. He knew how near he had been to saying something so unsettling that it could never have been unsaid.

Again, this time she seemed to be thinking along the same lines.

"How is Declan?" she asked the children. "It won't be long now until you'll be bringing him along to school with you."

"Oh, he'd be useless. He never says anything at all," Eileen said.

"And he'd wet the floor," Sheila added, in case there was any question of enrolling the baby.

"Not now. The child's only ten weeks old on Friday. You were the same at that age." Mrs. Kelly spoke in her stern teacher's voice. Eileen and Sheila drew back in awe.

Jims Blake noted that Nora Kelly remembered the exact age of the baby boy he had wanted to give her.

If he had been asked, he couldn't have said without counting back to the April day when Frances had died.

"Come on now, girls. We mustn't delay Mrs. Kelly." He began to shepherd them home.

"I'm sure you're dying to be back to him," she said.

"Yes. Yes, of course." His voice sounded false and he knew it.

As they closed the school gate he wondered was he unnatural not to hurry home to see a sleeping infant? He didn't think so. When Eileen and Sheila were babies he didn't see them for hours on end, and then only when presented with them by Frances after bathtime. Surely that was the way most men felt?

He mustn't dwell on that one highly charged moment on the day of his wife's death. Rationally, of course, he had no intention of giving away the baby that she had died bringing into the world. It was foolish to keep harking back to it with guilt.

He had perfectly normal feelings toward this child, and the hiring of Carrie had been inspired. She had indeed a natural instinct of motherhood, and she seemed to know that they wanted as little sign of a baby about the house as possible.

The girls went to the nursery each evening to play with him and to hear stories of Carrie's wild brothers, and the desperate injuries they had endured. She told them nothing of the child born in Dublin and given away. She sat rocking the substitute baby Declan in her arms.

Jims Blake called in from time to time. Not every day.

He knew that Mrs. Kelly at the school would find this unbelievable.

That evening he went into the nursery.

Carrie was sitting at a table with pen and ink and several sheets of screwed-up paper.

"I was never one for writing, Doctor," she said.

"We're all good at different things. Aren't you marvelous with the child?"

"Anyone would love a baby." She shrugged it off.

"Yes," he said.

Something in his voice made her look up. "Well, it's different in your case . . . I mean, being a man and everything, and your poor wife dying giving birth to him."

"I don't blame him for that." It was true. Jims Blake blamed himself, not his son, for the death of Frances.

"You'll grow to love him. Wait till he starts to call you Daddy . . . and clings to your legs. They're lovely at that age."

She must have been thinking about her brothers, he realized. She didn't see her own child grow.

He changed the subject. "Could I help you at all with the writing . . . or is it private?" He saw Carrie look at him. In many ways he had the same status as Father Gunn, a man who knew secrets, a man who could be told things.

Carrie had a brother in jail. None of the rest of the family wrote to him. She wanted him to feel that he wasn't forgotten, that there'd be a place for him when he got out. It was told trustingly and simply.

He sat down at the table and took out his pen.

He wrote a letter to the boy, whose head he had stitched some years back, as if the letter came from Carrie. He told of the changes in the farm, the new barn, the way they had let the lower field go to grass. He told how Jacky Noone had got a new truck, and how Cissy had married. He said that Shancarrig looked fine in the summer sunshine and would be waiting to greet him when he came home.

Haltingly Carrie read it aloud, and tears came to her eyes. "You're such a good man, Doctor. You knew what I wanted to say, even though I didn't know myself."

"Here. You can have my fountain pen as a present. You'll get into less of a mess with it than trying to dip that thing there." The baby began to cry and the doctor stood up. He walked to the door without going to see the child. "Copy that out Carrie, yourself. It's no use sending the boy my letter. You copy it and next time I'll give you more ideas."

She picked the child up and looked at him with a face confused. A man so kind as to spend time writing a letter to her jailbird brother, a man who would give her his own good pen, but wouldn't pick up his son who was ten weeks old.

When Declan Blake was three Carrie had a cake for him with three candles and there was a party in the nursery. Maisie made special drop scones for the occasion. The girls got him presents of sweets and they all sang Happy Birthday before he blew the candles out.

Jims Blake looked at the small excited face of his son, the snub nose and the straight shiny hair washed especially for the day. He was wearing a new yellow jumper which Carrie must have bought in the town. He left money for the children's clothes with Carrie and for the food with Maisie. Together they ran his house very well for him.

He had a curious empty feeling when the birthday song was over, as if something were expected of him.

It was only ten years ago in this house that Charles Nolan had urged him to marry. Ten years of visiting people and hearing their troubles and learning their hopes, realistic or wildly beyond their reach. He didn't know what his own hopes were. He had never had time to work them out, he told himself.

The children were still looking at him.

In his mind he asked old Charles Nolan what to do and he heard himself saying . . .

"Why don't we sing 'For he's a jolly good fellow' . . . ?"

Their eyes lit up, Carrie's face softened, the girls shouted the chorus, and Declan clapped his hands to be the center of such attention. Jims Blake felt the moment frozen for a long time.

The day came sooner than he ever thought it would when Declan should be brought to school.

"A great day for you, Doctor, to see your son setting out with a satchel," Carrie had said.

Jims Blake looked at the child. "It's a great day all right. Isn't it, Declan?"

Declan looked up at him solemnly, as if he were a stranger. "It is, yes." He spoke shyly, and half hid himself behind Carrie, scuffing his new shoes a little on the ground, and seeming awkward.

Probably all children that age are awkward with their fathers, the doctor told himself. He watched from the window as his son went off to school on wobbly legs.

The doctor meant to ask how the day went, but he was out on calls when Declan came home, and the next morning there wasn't time to talk either. It was a week before he even knew that there was a problem about Carrie delivering Declan to the school.

"The other children call him a baby," Carrie explained.

"He's too young at five to walk all that way by himself," his father protested.

"Other children do. All the young Dunnes come up from the cottages on their own . . ."

"Those Dunnes aren't children at all, they're like monkeys. They were climbing trees barefoot when they were two years old."

Jims Blake was indignant that there should be any comparison.

"But it's terrible to have him made a jeer of. Maybe he could go with the girls . . . ?"

"The girls say they don't want him traipsing after them. They have their own friends . . ."

Carrie looked at him as if he had let her down. Jims Blake felt a wave of self-pity sweep over him. Why was he always made out to be in the wrong? He thought he was doing his best for all of them, not loading Eileen and Sheila down with dragging their baby brother, and now he was the worst in the world as a result.

None of his patients challenged what he said. They took their tablets, drank their medicine bottles, changed poultices and dressings, made journeys into hospitals for tests, without ever doubting him.

Only at home did his every action seem suspect.

Later, when he was helping Carrie with her letters, as he did every week, underlining a spelling mistake lightly in pencil, she looked at him troubled.

"You're a very good man, Doctor."

"Why do you say that?"

"You correct me without insulting me. I write 'yez' meaning 'you all' and you just say 'wouldn't it be better to put you all, it might be clearer.' . . . You don't say I'm pig ignorant!"

"But you're *not* pig ignorant."

"Maybe you shouldn't be teaching me all the time. Maybe you should be doing pothooks with Declan."

"Pothooks?"

"It's how they teach them to write."

"I don't want to be cutting across Mrs. Kelly and her ways."

He did look at Declan's copy book though, and asked him knowledgeably . . . "Are these pothooks, then?"

"Yes, Daddy."

"Very good. Very good, keep at them," he said. There was the familiar feeling that it hadn't been the right thing to say.

Since he had organized them all to sing "For he's a jolly good fellow" when Declan was three, there had hardly been a time when he was sure that the right thing had been said.

Eileen and Sheila always asked about his patients, ever since they had been very young.

"Is Mrs. Barton going to die?" They liked the quiet dressmaker who lived with her only son in the pink house on the hill.

"No, of course not. She's only got the flu."

"Is Miss Ross going to have a baby?" They had seen her knitting and thought the two went together.

"Was there much blood in the car crash?"

He parried their questions, kept the secrecy and diffused the sense of drama, and always he was aware that his son never asked him questions.

As the years went by he was even more aware of it. The girls left Shancarrig School and went to be boarders at a good convent school fifty miles away. There was now only the doctor and Maisie and Declan left in the house.

Carrie had given her own notice when Declan made his First Communion.

"He's seven now, Doctor. He's a grown lad. He can dress himself, keep his room tidy, do his homework and all. You don't need me."

"And maybe you're thinking of getting married?" There was nothing Dr. Jims didn't see or know.

"I'm not going to say much about it."

"And is it the father of the little lad?"

"Yes, it is. Thanks to you, Doctor, I was able to write to him a bit, tell him things, speak my mind. You're a great man for getting people to say things out. There's far too many round here who bottle it all up."

He was pleased at her praise. "You'll have another child. I know you'll never forget the first one, but you'll be a family now." He was full of happiness for this dark-haired angular girl, who had such a poor start in life.

"And you'll have a chance to get to know your son more, maybe, when I'm gone."

"Ah, that will come, that will come. I was thinking of getting a desk up here for him to do his homework."

"The girls always did it downstairs, you know, more in the hub of things."

"But he'd like it here. More independent. Wouldn't he?"

"He might feel a bit shut away." Her eyes were troubled.

"Not a bit of it, it would let him concentrate. Anyway, enough of such things. You'll come back and see us?"

"Of course I will. It was the best seven years of my life. I grew up properly in this house. I was very privileged." He tried to brush it away. "I mean it, Dr. Jims. I wouldn't even have been able to use a word like privileged when I came here. Isn't that living proof?"

When she was gone he made deliberate efforts to get involved in his son's world.

Always he seemed choked off.

Declan did his homework silently up in the room that used to be called the nursery, then he would come down and sit with Maisie in the kitchen while she prepared the supper. Dr. Jims was out so often, it seemed only sensible for the boy to eat with Maisie, after all he had eaten his meals with Carrie when she was there to look after him.

He tried to think of things to interest Declan. "Are you on to fractions yet, lad?"

"I don't know."

"You must know. Either you are or you aren't," his voice suddenly impatient.

"We might be. Sometimes you call things one thing and they call it another at school."

"And how's your friend, Dinnie?"

"Vinnie."

"Yes, Vinnie. How is he?"

"He's all right, I think, Dad."

"Well, surely you know whether he's all right or not?" Again the impatience arising without control, the tone of his voice changing.

"I mean, I haven't seen him for ages."

"Aren't you friends anymore?"

"I don't know. We might be. He's living in the town, I'm here."

Guilt then. Had he not listened? Had he ever been told? Surely other parents had this confusion about their children's friends.

And, of course, girls were easier too, anyone knew that. There had never been any trouble about Eileen and Sheila. He knew who their friends were. They talked about them, they brought them to The Terrace. When they came home from boarding school they always sought out Nessa Ryan from the hotel, and Leo Murphy, the daughter of Major Murphy up at The Glen.

Boys were hard to fathom. They lived in a secretive world of their own, it seemed. Jims Blake looked back on his own childhood, on the small bleak farm with the dour uncommunicative father who had hardly ever thrown him a word. He was behaving so differently from that silent man, and still meeting rebuff it seemed.

The girls talked to him very easily. Eileen came and sat on a footstool in his study, hugging her knees. "Leo Murphy's got all odd and snooty this year," she complained.

"Is that a fact?" Jims Blake had his own worries about the mental health of Miriam Murphy, the girl's mother.

"Yes. She wouldn't let me in when I went up to The Glen, just said she couldn't play today. *Play*, as if I was a child or she was a child."

"I know, I know." He was soothing.

"And Nessa Ryan says the same thing about her, snooty as anything. She won't let you into her house, as if anyone wanted to go."

"Maybe Maisie could make you a nice tea here . . ."

"She doesn't want to go to anyone else's house either, Nessa says."

"At least you have Nessa," he said consolingly.

Eileen flounced: "Yes, and who needs Leo Murphy and her big house. Ours is much smarter than theirs anyway."

"Don't be boasting about our good fortune in having a nice house," he said.

He had tried to tell them all about the good fortune in being given a house of such quality by the late Dr. Nolan, but his loyal daughters dismissed it. They thought their father was worth it and more, they said.

Eileen was going to go to university if she got a lot of honors in her Leaving Certificate. She would be an architect. She would love that. The nuns said she had all the brains in the world and by the time she was qualified the world, and indeed Ireland, would be moving to the point where women architects would be quite acceptable. It would be the 1960s, after all. Imagine.

And Sheila wanted to do nursing, so he was already sending out feelers for her to the better training hospitals in Dublin.

Declan would do medicine, of course, so the main thing was to get him into a good boarding school. He had spoken to the Jesuits, the Benedictines, the Vincentians, and the Holy Ghost Fathers. There were advantages and drawbacks in all of them. He checked the records, the achievements, the teaching records, and he chose the one that came out best overall. The bad side was that it was further away than any other school.

"You won't be able to go and see him much there," Eileen said.

"He'll come home in the holidays." Dr. Jims knew he was being defensive. Again.

"But it's lovely to have visitors at school. We loved you coming on Sundays."

He used to go every second week, a long, wet drive in winter. He had never taken Declan. At first he would have been too young and restless for the drive, and the girls would have hated him to be troublesome when he arrived in the parlor. Then later, it didn't seem the right thing to suggest.

A ten-year-old boy wouldn't *want* to be dragged off to a girls' school of a Sunday even if he had been invited. It would be a sissy sort of thing for a boy.

He intended to spend more time with the boy during the summer before Declan went to boarding school, but there was so much to do. There was the whole business of Maura Brennan's child for one thing.

He had always liked Maura, the only Brennan girl to stay in Shancarrig. The others had long gone to unsatisfactory posts in

England. Maura had a dreamy quality about her, an acceptance of what life had to offer. He remembered the day he had confirmed her pregnancy.

"He'll never marry me, Dr. Jims," she had said, big tears waiting to fall from her eyes.

"I wouldn't be sure of that. Aren't you a great catch for any man?" He had said it, but his heart wasn't in the words. He had thought Gerry O'Sullivan would disappear, but he had been wrong, Gerry stayed. There had been a wedding, he had gone into Johnny Finn's to drink their health.

And then when he had delivered her child it was he who saw the epicanthic folds around the eyes. It was he who had to tell Maura O'Sullivan, as she so proudly called herself, about her son, a child with Down syndrome.

He remembered how he had held the girl in his arms and told her it would all be all right. Even when Father Gunn had told him that Gerry O'Sullivan, father of the boy, had taken the train from Shancarrig station and was gone before the baptism, he remembered the sense of hearing his own voice mouth the words of comfort, telling Maura that everything would be fine.

And he had been right to say that she would always love young Michael with an overpowering love. That much had been true even if Gerry O'Sullivan was never seen in the streets of Shancarrig again.

There was a human story everywhere he turned . . . in the small houses and in the big ones.

There was something seriously wrong up at The Glen and he didn't know how to cope with it. Frank Murphy, a quiet man who bore his war injuries bravely, had something much more serious on his mind than the bad leg he dragged after him so uncomplainingly.

Jims Blake thought it had to do with his wife. But Miriam Murphy was someone he had never examined. She assured him she was as strong as a horse. An attractive woman with a dismissive manner if crossed, he had liked her red-gold hair and her effortless way of looking elegant while walking around the big gardens with a shallow basket and an old silk scarf draped over her shoulders.

People in Shancarrig had long grown accustomed to the fact that Mrs. Murphy never came down to the shops. There were accounts in the shops and the delivery boys who called on bicycles always got a friendly wave from the mistress of The Glen. They would deal with Biddy the maid, or with the Major himself.

But this summer there was something different about Miriam. A vacancy in her eyes that was more than disturbing. And a cautious protective look in Frank's that hadn't been there before. Charles Nolan had told him often enough about families who guarded their secrets, who kept their unstable people hidden. Often it was better not to pry.

Jims Blake wondered what old Charles would have made of the situation in The Glen. Not only was the Major in a state of distress, but their daughter, Leo, who had been such a close friend of his daughters, had also begun to show signs of strain. He met the girl when driving past Barna Woods.

"Do you want a lift back up to the house, Leo?"

"Are you going that way?"

"A car goes whatever way you point it."

"Thanks, Doctor."

"Have you lots of new friends for yourself this summer, Leo?"

She was surprised. No, it turned out she hadn't any. Why did he ask? Without putting his own children in the role of complainers he hinted that she hadn't been around.

"We went on a bit of a holiday, you see, to the seaside."

That was true. He had heard Bill Hayes say that the Major had packed dogs and all into the car and driven off without warning.

"Ah, but you're back now, and still no one ever sees you. I thought you'd gone off with the gypsies." They had just driven in the gate of The Glen as he said this. She looked at him, as white as a sheet. "It's all right, Leo. I was only joking."

"I hate jokes about the gypsies," she said.

He wondered had they frightened her in the woods. Dark, suspicious, they were always on guard. He had delivered a child for them once; they had given him a pheasant. Unsmiling and proud, they had handed him the bird, wrapped in grass, to thank him for the skill they hadn't sought, but had used because he was passing near during a difficult birth.

The Major appeared at the door. "I won't ask you in," he said.

"No, no." His reputation as a discreet man who could be told anything rested on ending conversations when others wanted to. He never probed a step further, but his face was always open and ready to hear when others wanted to tell.

His son, Declan, never wanted to tell anything.

"Will you like being at the school do you think, Declan?"

"I won't know, not really, until I get there."

Had there ever been a boy so pedantic, so unwilling to talk?

Maisie wanted to know had he settled in? Was the bed aired? Were there any other boys from this part of the world there?

Dr. Jims Blake could answer none of this. His only memory was his son's hand waving goodbye. He wasn't clinging, like one or two other lads were, loath to let mothers go. Nor was he chatting and making friends as some of the more outgoing boys seemed to be doing.

They had to write letters home every Sunday. Declan wrote of saints' days, and walks, and doing a play, making a relief map. Jims Blake knew that these letters were supervised by the priests, that they were intended to give a good impression of the school and all its activities. Sometimes the letter lay unopened on the hall table along with the advertising literature from pharmaceutical companies that was sent to all doctors on a mailing list.

Declan didn't write to Eileen, now in a hostel in Dublin while she studied architecture in University College. He didn't write to Sheila, now nursing in one of Dublin's best hospitals. He sent a birthday card to Maisie, but they knew very little about his world at school.

The reports said that he was satisfactory, his marks were average, his place in the class was in the top end of the lower half.

His school holidays seemed long and formless. The doctor got the impression that he was dying to be back at school.

"Would you like to ask any of your friends to stay?"

"Here?" Declan had been surprised.

"Well, there's plenty of room. They might like it."

"What would they do, Daddy?"

"I don't know. Whatever they do, whatever you do anywhere." He was irritated now. It was this habit of answering one question with another that he found hard to take.

It never came to anything, that suggestion. Nor the invitation to go to Dublin.

"What would I do in Dublin for two days?"

"What does anyone do in Dublin? We could see your sisters, take them out to lunch. That would be nice, wouldn't it?" He realized he sounded as if he was talking to a five-year-old, not a boy of fifteen. A boy who had grown apart from Eileen, now nearly qualified as an architect, from Sheila, now almost a qualified nurse.

The visit never happened. Neither did the outing to the Galway races, which had been long spoken of as a reward when Declan's Leaving Certificate was over.

Jims Blake said he could put his hand on his heart and swear that he had made every move to try to get close to his son, and that at every turn he was repelled.

It wasn't a thing that he would normally talk to another man about, but he did mention it to Bill Hayes. "Do you find it like plowing a hard field trying to get a word out of your fellow Niall, or does he talk to you?"

"Niall would talk to the birds in the trees if he thought they'd listen. He has a yarn for every moment of the day. Not much of a knack of dealing with clients, though."

Bill Hayes shook his head gloomily. His son too seemed a slight disappointment to him. Although a qualified solicitor, he showed no signs of being able to attract new business or, indeed, cope with the business that was already there.

"And does he talk to *you*?" Dr. Jims persisted.

"When he can get me to listen, which isn't often. I don't want to hear rambling tales about the mountains and the lakes when he goes out to make some farmer's will for him. I want to hear that it's been done properly, the man's affairs are settled and everything's in order."

Dr. Jims sighed. "With me it's just the opposite. I can't even get him to talk about enrolling up at the university. He keeps making excuses."

"Talk to him at a meal. Don't serve him until he answers your question. . . . That'll get an answer out of him. Boys love their food."

Jims Blake was ashamed to say why this wouldn't work, to admit that his son still ate meals in the kitchen with Maisie, out of habit, out of tradition. No point in laying up two places in the dining room. Who knew when the poor doctor would have to be called out?

But the summer of 1965 was moving on. Arrangements would have to be made, fees must be paid, places in the Medical School reserved, living quarters booked.

"Declan? No one would ever think we lived in the same house, lad . . ."

"I'm always here," the boy said. It wasn't mutinous or defensive, it was said as a simple fact.

Jims Blake was annoyed by it.

"I'm always here too," he said. "Except when I'm out working, as you will be."

"I'm not going to do medicine, Dad."

Somehow, it came as no surprise. He must have been expecting it.

"When did you decide against it?" His voice was cold.

"I never decided *for* it, it was only in your mind. It wasn't in mine."

They talked like strangers, polite but firm.

Declan would like to join an auctioneering firm. His friend

Vinnie O'Neill's father would take him on. He'd like the life. It was the kind of thing that appealed to him, looking at places, showing them to customers. He was good at talking to people, telling them the good points of a place. There'd be a very good living in it for him. Vinnie was going off to be a priest. There was no other boy in the family, only girls. Mr. O'Neill liked him, got on well with him.

Jims Blake listened bleakly to the story of a man he didn't know, a man called Gerry O'Neill, whose estate agent's signs he had seen around the place. A man who got on well with Declan Blake and regarded him as a kind of son now that his own was going to enter the priesthood. Silently he accepted the plans, plans that involved Declan going to live in the big town. He could have Vinnie's room, apparently. It would be easier to have him on the spot, and the sooner the better.

Vinnie was going to the seminary next week. Declan thought he'd move in at the weekend.

Jims Blake heard that Maisie wouldn't miss him because so much of her life was now centered around the church. And she had got used to him being away at school.

"And what about me?" Jims Blake said. "What about my missing you?"

"Aw Dad, you're your own person. You wouldn't miss me."

It was said with total sincerity, and when the boy realized that there actually was loneliness in his father's face, he seemed distressed.

"But even if I were going to be doing medicine, wouldn't I be away all the time?"

"You'd be coming back to help me in the practice, and take over. That's what I thought."

There was a silence. A long silence.

"I'm sorry," Declan said.

Later Jims wondered should he have put his arm around the boy's shoulder. Should he have made some gesture to apologize for the coldness and distance of eighteen years, to hope that the next years would be better. But he shrugged. "You must do as you want to," he said. And then he heard himself saying, "It's what you've always done."

He knew it was the most final goodbye he could ever have said.

Sometimes when he was in the town Jims Blake called in to O'Neills. Like someone probing a sore tooth he was anxious to see the man and the home where Declan Blake felt he belonged. Gerry O'Neill, a florid man with a fund of anecdotes about people and places, regarded himself as a great raconteur. Jims Blake found him a boring and opinionated man. He sat and watched unbelievingly while the man's wife and daughters and Declan laughed and encouraged him in these tales.

The eldest girl was Ruth, a good-looking girl, her Daddy's pet. She was doing a commercial course in the local secretarial college so that she could help in the business. They talked of O'Neills Auctioneers as if it was a long-established and widely respected family firm, instead of a Mickey Mouse operation set up by Gerry O'Neill himself on the basis of being a fast talker.

"Invite Ruth to The Terrace sometime, won't you?" Jims asked his son.

He could see that Declan was very attracted to the dark-eyed girl in his new family.

"I don't think so . . ."

"I'm not asking you to live there, I'm just asking you to bring the girl to Sunday lunch, for God's sake." Again, the harsh ungracious words that he didn't mean to speak. His son looked taken aback.

"Yes, well. Of course . . . sometime."

Jims Blake contemplated getting an assistant. He realized now how the lonely old Charles Nolan must have relished him coming to stay in that house all those years ago. How he had felt able to will him the place, as well as the practice. Jims had thought the same thing would have happened with Declan. He had foreseen evenings like those with Charles, discussing articles in the *Lancet* and the *Irish Medical Times*, wondering about a new cure-all cream, with apparently magical qualities, that had come from one of the drug firms.

There was a phone call every week from Sheila in her Dublin hospital, and a letter every week from Eileen, now working in an architect's practice in England.

He had almost forgotten what Frances had looked like, or felt like in his arms. He should not have felt like an old man, after all he was only in his late fifties, yet he had the distinct feeling that his life, such as it was, was over.

Declan did bring Ruth to lunch eventually. And the girl chattered easily and eagerly, as she did in her own home. She asked questions, seemed interested in the answers. She asked Maisie about doing the flowers for the altar. Maisie said she was a girl of great breeding, and that Declan was very lucky to have met her and not some foolish fast girl, like he might well have met in the town.

On her third visit she took the initiative and leaned over to kiss him goodbye.

"Thank you, Dr. Jims," she said. She smelled of Knight's Castile soap, fresh and lovely. He was not surprised his son was so taken by her.

He was horrified when he saw Declan some weeks later. The boy arrived on a Thursday afternoon, Maisie's half day. He was ashen white, but the circles under his eyes were deep purple shadows.

He paced the house until the last patient left. "Will there be any more?"

"I have to go out the country. One of Carrie's brothers. Do you remember Carrie?"

"Of course I do. Can I come with you?"

Somehow Jims Blake found the right silences and didn't choose the wrong words. He didn't ask what had the boy out on a working day, and looking so terrible. Instead he smiled and opened the hall door for him. They walked together to the car, father and son, down the steps of Number 3, The Terrace, as he had always wanted to walk with a son.

They talked of nothing during the drive out to the farm where one of Carrie's brothers had impaled himself on yet another piece of rusting machinery. Declan watched wordlessly as his father cleaned the wound and stitched it.

The talk came on the way back.

They stopped under the shadow of the Old Rock, the big craggy monument from which Shancarrig got its name. They walked a little in the crisp afternoon with the shadows of the trees lengthening.

Jims Blake heard the story. The terrible tale of a boy invited into a good man's house. How Gerry O'Neill would die down dead when he knew Ruth was pregnant. How her brother, Vinnie, studying to be a priest, would never forgive such a betrayal.

The boy had not slept or eaten for a week, and presumably neither had the girl. It was the end of the road. Declan wanted them to run away, but Ruth wouldn't go, and in his saner moments he realized that she was right.

"You realize how bad things are, if I had to tell you," he said to his father.

Jims Blake bit back the retort. At another time he might have made the remark that would drive the boy back into the shell from which he had painfully dragged himself. He didn't ask what Declan wanted of him. He knew that Declan himself barely knew. So instead he did what he had been intending to do all his life, he put his arm around his son's shoulder.

He pretended not to notice the flinching in surprise. "I'll tell you what I think," he said. His voice was calm, almost cheerful. He could feel his son's shoulders relaxing under his arm. "I have this friend up in Dublin, we did our training together. He's in gynecology and obstetrics. A specialist now. Quite a well-known man . . . I'll recommend that young Ruth go to see him for a D and C . . . Oh, don't worry, these names are always very alarming. It's called a dilatation and curettage, just an examination under anesthetic of the neck of the womb. Clears up any disorders. A lot of girls have them. . . ."

Declan turned to look at him.

"Is that . . . ? I mean is that the same as . . . ?"

Jims Blake had decided how to play it. "As I was saying to you, there's no knowing what names all these things go by, the main thing is that Ruth will go in there and be out in a day or two and it can all go through this house and this address without having to bother anyone else."

They walked back to the car and drove to Shancarrig. The mood was not broken.

His son came in to Number 3, The Terrace and sat with him as they lit a fire, because the evening was getting chilly. Declan had a small brandy and some of the color had returned to his face.

Jims Blake remembered how old Dr. Nolan had often said to him that the ways of the world were stranger than anyone would ever believe. Dr. Jims Blake agreed with him as he sat there and realized that the only companionable evening he had ever had with his son was the evening he had arranged to abort his own grandchild.

6

Nora Kelly

Nora and Jim Kelly had no pictures of their wedding. The cousin with the camera had been unreliable. There was something wrong with the film, he told them afterward.

It didn't matter, they told him.

But to Nora it did. There was nothing to mark the day their marriage began. It hadn't been a very fancy wedding. During the Emergency, of course, people didn't go in for big flashy do's, not even people with more class and style than Nora and Jim. But theirs had been particularly quiet.

It took place in Lent, because they wanted to have a honeymoon in the Easter holidays, the two young teachers starting out life together. Nora's mother had been tight-lipped. A Lenten wedding often meant one thing and one thing only, that the privileges of matrimony had been anticipated and that an unexpected pregnancy had resulted.

But this was not the case, Nora and Jim had anticipated nothing. And the pregnancy that her mother feared might disgrace the whole family did not result, even after many years of marriage.

Month after month Nora Kelly reported to her husband that there was no reason to hope for a conception this time either. They shrugged and said it would happen sooner or later. That was for the first three years. Then they consoled each other in a brittle way. Why would two schoolteachers who had the entire child population of Shancarrig to cope with want to bring any more children into the world?

Then they decided to ask for help.

It was not easy for Nora Kelly to approach Dr. Jims. He was a courteous man and kind to everyone. She knew that he would not be coy, or too inquisitive. He would reach for his pad and write, as he nodded thoughtfully.

Nora Kelly was pale at the best of times and this was not the best of times. She was a slight young woman with flyaway fair hair. She did it in a braid, which she rolled loosely at the back of her neck.

Nobody in Shancarrig had seen her with hair loose and flowing. They thought her expression a little stern, but that was appropriate for the schoolmistress. Her big husband looked more like a local farmer than the Master—it was good to have some authority written on the face of the family.

Someone who had known Nora before she married said she was one of three young girls always dashing about and riding precarious bicycles, in a town some sixty miles away. They were three young harem-scarums, it was said. But it didn't sound likely.

She had no relations there now, she had no identity or past. She was just the schoolmistress—a sensible woman, not given to fancy dressing or notions. Not too fancy a cook either, to judge by what she bought in the butcher's, but a perfectly qualified woman to be teaching their children. It was, of course, a terrible cross to bear that the Lord hadn't given her children, but who ever knew the full story in these cases?

As she had expected, Dr. Jims was kindness itself. The examination was swift and impersonal, the advice gentle and practical—some very simple, maybe even folk, remedies. Dr. Jims said that he never despised wisdom handed down through the generations. He had got a cure from the tinkers once, he told her. They knew a lot of things that modern medicine hadn't discovered yet. But they were a people who kept their ways to themselves.

The old wives' advice hadn't worked. There were tests in the hospital in the big town. Jim had to give samples of his sperm. It was wearying, embarrassing, and ultimately depressing. The Kellys were told that, as far as medical science could determine in 1946, there was no reason why they should not conceive. They must live in hope.

Nora Kelly knew that Dr. Jims found it hard to deliver this news to her, in an autumn where his own wife was pregnant again. Their little girls were already up at the school, this was another family starting. She saw his sympathy and appreciated it all the more because he didn't speak it aloud. It wasn't easy to be a childless woman in a small town, she had been aware of the sideways glances for a long time. Nora knew that the ways of God were strange and past understanding by ordinary people, but it did seem hard to understand why he kept giving more and more children to the Brennans and the Dunnes in the cottages, families who couldn't feed or care for the children they already had, and passing her by.

Sometimes when she saw the little round faces coming in to start a new life at school, the pain she felt in her heart was as real as if it had been a physical one. She watched their little wobbly legs and the way the poorest of them came in shoes that were too big and clothes that were too long. If she and Jim had a child of their own, they would look after it so well. It seemed every other woman in the village only had to think about conception to become pregnant—women who claimed to have enough already, women who sighed and said *here we go again*.

When the doctor's baby son was born in the coldest winter that Shancarrig ever knew, the year that the River Grane had frozen solid for three long months, his wife died at the birth.

Nora Kelly held the infant child in her arms and wished that she could take the little boy home. She and Jim would rear him so well. They would take out the baby clothes, bought and made many years ago, now smelling of mothballs. He would grow up in their school. He would not be overfavored in front of the others just because he was the teachers' son.

For a wild moment that day in the doctor's nursery, when she had come to sympathize at the funeral, she thought that the doctor was going to give her the baby. But of course it was fantasy.

Nora had heard that couples who didn't have children often grew very close to each other. It was as if the disappointment had united them and the shared life-style, without the distractions of a family, made it easier for them to establish an intimacy.

She wished it had happened in her case, but in honesty she couldn't say that it had.

Jim grew more aloof. His walks of an evening became longer and longer. She found herself sitting alone by the fire, or even returning to the schoolroom to draw maps for the next day.

By the time she was twenty-eight years old her husband reached toward her to make love very rarely.

"Sure what's the point?" he said to her one night as she snuggled up to him. And after that she kept very much to her own side of the bed.

They had agreed not to say it was anyone's fault, but Nora looked to her side of the family. Her own two sisters had given birth to small families; one had only two, the other had an only child, while the sisters and sisters-in-law of Jim Kelly seemed to breed like rabbits.

Her sister Kay, who lived in Dublin, had two little boys. Sometimes they came to stay. Nora would feel her heart lurch when she saw how eagerly Jim reached for them and how happily he took them on walks. It was different entirely to the way he taught the children in the school. In the classroom he was patient and fair, but he was formal; there was no happy wildness like with her nephews. He used to take the small boys by the hand, and let them wade through the shallows of the River Grane and bring them to pick mushrooms up near the Old Rock, or to prowl through Barna Woods looking for bears and tigers.

Nora's sister never failed to say: "He's a born father, isn't he?" Nora's teeth never failed to be set on edge.

She had more contact with her twin sister, Helen, even though Helen lived on the other side of the world in Chicago.

She had sent grainy photographs of the baby, little Maria. Helen had gone to Chicago when Nora went to the Training College. She didn't have the brains, she said, and she wanted no more studying. She wanted to see the world and make sure she didn't end up in some one-horse town like the one they'd come from.

In fact, Shancarrig was a much smaller one-horse town than their native place. Nora was sure that Helen must pity her. What had she got with all her brains? Marriage, to the increasingly silent Jim, schoolmistress in a tiny backwater, and no children.

Helen's life had been much more exciting. She had worked as a waitress in Stouffer's. It was a coffeehouse—one of the many coffeehouses of that name—and they had restaurants as well. She met Lexi when he was delivering the meat from the yards.

Big, blond, handsome Lexi, Polish Catholic, silent, whose dark blue eyes followed her everywhere she went. Helen had written about how he asked her out, how she had been taken to meet his family. They spoke Polish in the home, but in broken English told Helen she was welcome.

When they married in one of the big Polish churches in Chicago no one of Helen's family was there to give her courage. Who could afford a journey halfway across the world in 1942, when that world was at war?

And then Maria was born in 1944, baptized by a Polish priest. There were potato cakes served at the christening party, except they called them *latkes,* and there was a terrible soup called *polewka,* which they all drank at the drop of a hat.

Maria was beautiful. Helen wrote this over and over. Nora knew from experience that there wasn't much point in believing old wives' tales—they certainly hadn't been much use in her predicament—but she did believe that twins sort of knew about each other, even when they were almost five thousand miles apart.

She read and reread Helen's letters for some hint of what was troubling her, because Nora Kelly knew that life on Chicago's South Side was not as it was described in the very frequent letters.

On an impulse she wrote to her one spring day in 1948.

"I know it sounds like a tall order, but why don't you bring Maria over to see us in the summer? When the school closes Jim and I have all the time in the world and there's nothing that would please us more."

Nora wrote warmly inviting Lexi too, but the implication was that he would not be able to take the time. Helen, working only part time in the restaurant now, could arrange leave.

Nora described the flowers and the hedges around Shancarrig. She made the river sound full of sparkle and the woods as if they were on the lid of a box of chocolates.

Helen replied by return of post. Lexi wouldn't be able to make the trip, but she and Maria would come to Shancarrig.

Nora could hardly wait. Their elder sister, Kay, said that Helen must have money to burn if she could just leap on a plane and fly off to Dublin on the spur of the moment. But Nora felt that it might well have taken a lot of explanations and excuses, as well as unimaginable scrimping and saving. She kept quiet about this. She would hear everything when Helen came home.

It was a relief to the twins when, after the big reunion in Dublin, they were able to leave Kay and travel together on the train to Shancarrig. They held hands and talked to each other, words tumbling and falling, finishing each other's sentences and beginning new ones . . . and mainly they said that the camera had not done the little girl justice.

Maria was beautiful.

She was four and a half, with a smile that went all the way around her face. She sang and hummed to herself, and was happy with the piece of cardboard and coloring pencils which Nora had brought to greet her.

"Aren't you great!" Helen exclaimed. "Everyone else gives her these ridiculous ornaments or lacy things that she breaks or tears up."

"Everyone else?"

"The Poles," confessed Helen, and they giggled like the children they had been when they said goodbye so many years ago.

··· •··

The sun shone as the train pulled into Shancarrig. There on the platform stood the Master, Jim Kelly, waiting to meet his sister-in-law and little niece.

Maria took to him straightaway. She reached up with her small chubby hand and he held it firmly while carrying the heavy suitcase in the other.

"Oh Nora." Helen's eyes were full of tears. "Oh Nora, you're so lucky."

As they left the station and walked along past Ryan's Commercial Hotel, past the elegant houses in The Terrace and the row of shops where of late she had felt that she had been an object of pity, the childless schoolteacher, Nora *did* feel lucky.

Nellie Dunne looked out of her door.

"Aren't you looking well today, Mrs. Kelly!" she said.

"This is my sister, Miss Dunne."

"And you have a little girl, do you?" Nellie Dunne asked. She wanted to have all the news for whoever came in next.

"That's my Maria," said Helen proudly.

When Nellie was out of hearing, Nora said: "It'll be a nine days' wonder in the place that someone belonging to me produced a child."

Helen laid her hand on her twin sister's arm.

"Shush now. We'll have weeks on end to talk about all that."

They walked companionably through Shancarrig, and home to make the tea.

But Nora Kelly did not have weeks on end to talk to her twin sister about life in Chicago and life in Shancarrig. Five days after she arrived Helen was killed when a runaway horse and cart went across the path of the bus which, swerving to avoid them, hit Helen, killing her outright.

Nora Kelly was in Nellie Dunne's with Maria when it happened. The child was trying to decide between a red and a green lollipop, holding them up against her yellow Viyella dress with the smocking on it, as if somehow one would look better with the outfit than the other.

The sounds were never to leave Nora's mind. She could hear them over and over, each one separate, the wheels of the cart, the whinnying of the horse, the irregular sound of the bus scraping the wrong way, and the long scream. Then silence, before the cries and shouts and everyone running to see what could be done.

Afterward people said there was no scream, that Helen made no sound.

But Nora heard it.

They took her into Ryan's Hotel. She was given brandy, people's arms were around her, everywhere there were running footsteps. Someone had been sent up to the schoolhouse for Jim. There was Major Murphy from The Glen, a military man trying to organize things on some kind of military lines.

There was Father Gunn with his stole around his neck. He had run from the church to say the Act of Contrition into the lifeless ear of the dead woman.

"She's in heaven now," Father Gunn told Nora. "She's there, praying for us all."

A great sense of the unfairness of it all rose in Nora. Helen didn't want to be in heaven praying for them all, she wanted to be here in Shancarrig telling the long, complicated tale of a strange marriage to a silent man who drank, not like the Irish people drink, but differently. She wanted to arrange that her daughter come to Ireland regularly rather than grow up speaking Polish, hardly noticed amid the great crowds of other children in the family. Lexi's brothers and sisters had produced great numbers of new Chicagoans, apparently. Helen had begun to fear that Maria might get lost and never know a life of her own, be a personality and character in her own right like all the children in Shancarrig were. Nora had told her about the children who filled the classrooms during term time, each one with a history and a future.

Nora could not take it in. It couldn't have happened. Every minute seemed like half an hour as she sat in the lounge and a procession advanced and retired.

The voice of Sergeant Keane seemed a hundred miles away when he spoke of the telegram to Chicago, or the possibility of a phone call.

"We can't wire that man and say Helen is dead." She heard her own voice as if it were someone else's. The words sounded unreal. The Sergeant explained that they could send a telegram asking him to phone Ryan's Hotel and someone would be here to give the message.

"I'll stay," said Nora Kelly.

No one could dissuade her. It was not three o'clock in the afternoon in Chicago, it was early morning. Lexi was on his meat delivery rounds. It might be many hours before he got the telegram. She would be in the hotel, whatever time he phoned. Mrs. Ryan organized a bed to be brought to the Commercial Room; the commercial travelers would understand that this was an emergency, that Mrs. Kelly had to be near the phone, day or night.

She drank tea and they brought jelly for Maria. Red jelly, with the top of the milk. Every spoonful seemed to be in slow motion.

Then, at ten o'clock at night, she heard them coming to tell her that the call had been put through. She spoke to the man with the broken English. She had lain on the bed with the curtains pulled to keep out the evening sunlight of Shancarrig.

And now it was almost dark. She spoke as she had drilled herself to speak, without tears, trying to give him all the information as calmly as possible.

"Why do you not weep for your sister?" He had a broken English accent, like a foreigner in a film.

"Because my sister would want me to be strong for you," she said simply.

She asked did he want to speak to Maria, but he said no. She told him that Helen's body would be brought to Shancarrig church the next night, and the funeral would be on the following day, and that Mr. Hayes had found out about flights. He had been on the phone to Shannon Airport all day—

She was cut short. Lexi would not come to the funeral.

Nora was literally unable to speak.

The slow voice spoke on. It would not be possible, they were not people who had unlimited money. Who would he know to walk with him behind his wife's coffin? There would be prayers said for her in his own parish, in his church. He returned again to the accident and how it had happened. Who was at fault? What part of Helen had been hurt to kill her?

The nightmare continued for what Nora Kelly thought was an endless time. It was only when the operator said six minutes that she realized how little time had actually passed.

"Will you ring again tomorrow?" she said.

"To say what?"

"To talk."

"There is nothing to talk about," he said.

"And Maria . . . ?"

"Will you look after her until we can come for her?"

"Of course . . . but if you are going to come for her, could you not come for Helen's funeral?"

"It will be later."

The day of the funeral passed without Nora being really aware of what was going on. Always she saw Jim, his big hand stretched out to little Maria, whose crying for her Mama grew less and less. They told her Mama was with the angels in heaven, and showed her the holy pictures on the wall and in the church to identify where her mother had gone.

And as the days passed Nora went through her sister's possessions, while Jim took little Maria up to Barna Woods to pick flowers.

Nora sat on her bed and looked at her sister's passport and official-looking cards for work and insurance. She could find no return air ticket. Was it possible that Helen had intended to stay here and not to return? There were letters from a solicitor "regarding the matter we spoke of." Could this solicitor have been arranging an American divorce? Did the strange tone of voice mean that Lexi was too upset to talk? or that all love and feeling had gone from his marriage with Helen? Her head was whirling. Why had they not talked at once, she and Helen? It had been part of the slow getting back to know each other, the delighted realization that each had only to begin a thought and the other could finish it.

What a cruel God to have taken this away from them five days after they had found it.

Kay, the eldest sister, was as usual practical.

"Don't grow too fond of the child," she warned Nora. "That unfeeling lout will be back for her the day it suits him."

What did people mean . . . don't grow too fond of? How could anyone put a limit to the love she felt for this little girl with the big dark blue eyes, the head of curls, and the endearing habit of stroking her cheek?

After a week Nora found herself saying to Jim: "Is the child asleep yet?" and realized she was certainly coming to regard Maria as her child.

His reply was tender. "I read her a story but she wants another from No, she says No has better stories."

He was smiling at her affectionately, like before. He didn't turn away from her in bed anymore, he reached for her like before. It was as if Maria had made their life complete.

"I suppose Kay's right about not getting too fond of her," Nora said one summer evening, as they sat watching Maria play with the three baby chickens that Mrs. Barton, the dressmaker, had brought along in a box as something to entertain the little girl.

"I keep hoping he won't want her back," Jim said. It was the first time in four weeks it had been mentioned.

"We shouldn't get up our hopes . . . any man would want his only child."

"Any man would have come to his wife's funeral," Jim said.

Nora wrote letters regularly. She described the funeral, the flowers, the sermon. She told about the grave under a tree in the churchyard, and how on Sundays she went there with Maria to lay flowers on it. In a year a stone would be put up, Lexi must let her know what he would like written on the tombstone.

She told him about the bus driver who would never be the same again after the accident; the man who walked alone up to Shancarrig Rock. Everyone had told him that it had not been his fault. No one could have faulted him, it was an Act of God that the horse had shied at that very time. But he said that he would never drive again, and had come with flowers to the grave when he thought no one was looking.

She wrote that Maria said God Bless Daddy and a lot of other names every night, so she assumed that these were grandparents or relations. She didn't want him to think that that side of the family had been forgotten. She said that when the term started in September, Maria would join the Mixed Infants. She was almost five—five was the age the children began coming to school.

She wrote and told him about the place, the huge big copper beech tree in the playground, and the maps on the schoolroom walls. She stopped saying "Until you come for her" and "for the present time." Instead she just wrote as if it was all agreed that Maria would stay here for an unspecified amount of time.

The children accepted her totally. They never thought it odd that she called Mrs. Kelly "No." They thought it was just because she was babyish and younger than they were. Geraldine Brennan from the cottages decided to be her protector. Nora

Kelly had to watch carefully in case part of the protecting might also mean eating Maria's little sandwich lunch.

The communications from Lexi were minimal. He wrote to say that he was grateful for her letters. His hand was not educated, and his grasp of grammar poor. He told her little or nothing about his intentions. He asked many times about the accident, what court case had resulted, and whether the compensation had arrived. Once he inquired whether Helen had any valuables with her that needed to be looked after.

In Shancarrig, too, people began to think of Maria as belonging to Jim and Nora. She was even called by their name.

"Hey, Maria Kelly, come over here and see the tadpoles!" Nora heard one day during dinner hour, when they played in the yard. Her heart soared with pleasure.

By accident she did have a child, a child of her own.

A child who had a fifth birthday party with a cake and candles. A child who had her first Christmas in Shancarrig and sang carols by the crib in the church.

"Do you remember the church back in Chicago at Christmas?" Nora asked as she wrapped the child up in a warm scarf before taking her across the bridge and back up the road home from the church.

Maria shook her curly head. "I can't think," she said, and Nora smiled in the dark. The less Maria thought, the greater seemed the likelihood of her remaining with them.

Mr. Hayes, father of Niall, an easygoing boy often put upon by the others, came to see her.

"My wife says he's being bullied by the other boys. Your husband will probably say it'll make a man of him. I wonder would you and I be better able to reach some kind of consensus?" he asked.

Nora Kelly smiled at him. It was typical of the way he did things, seeing was there a gentle way around things before you went in guns blazing.

"I think he needs to make a friend of Foxy Dunne," she said after some thought.

"Foxy? That little divil from the cottages?"

"He's as smart as paint, that Foxy. He'll get himself out of that place, and away from the mess he's growing up in."

"How should he make a friend of this fellow, so?"

"You could ask him up to the house?"

"Ethel'll be afraid he'll lift the silver." Bill Hayes looked rueful.

"He won't. He'd be a good ally for Niall. Niall's gentle. He doesn't need another gentle friend like Eddie, he needs a fighter in his court."

"You can solve it all, Mrs. Kelly."

"I wish I could. I wish I knew how to keep my sister's child. I wish I believed that possession is nine tenths of the law."

"You're too honorable for that."

"I think my sister was going to leave her husband. I have letters from a solicitor . . . they don't say much, though."

"They never do," Bill Hayes admitted ruefully.

She sighed. He was telling her what Father Gunn and Dr. Jims were telling her. Do nothing. Live in hope. If the man hadn't come over in six months, it was a good sign.

When a year had passed it was even better.

When the time came for the Holy Year ceremonies at the school and the big dedication ceremony Maria Kelly was part of their family and part of Shancarrig. She called Jim "Daddy" and she called Nora "Mama No."

"It sounds like something from Japan, or from *Madame Butterfly*!" Jim said to Nora. He was always good-natured these days.

"She can't call me Mother, she remembers her mother," Nora said.

"She seems to have forgotten her father though." Jim spoke in a whisper.

At night Maria's prayers included a litany of friends at school, and the chickens—now hens—that Mrs. Barton had given her. She prayed for all kinds of unlikely people, like little Declan Blake, who was pushed in his pram by that strange, abstracted maid, Carrie. Maria loved Carrie and Declan, and often asked Mama No if they could have a baby like Declan to play with. She prayed for Leo Murphy's dog, Jessica, which had broken its paw, and she prayed that Foxy Dunne would give her one of his worms in a jam jar. But the Polish names and her father's name had gone from the list.

It didn't take her long to realize she was in a privileged position being the daughter of the school.

"What would happen if you didn't know your tables?" Geraldine Brennan asked with great interest. "Would you get your hand slapped like the rest of us?"

"No, she wouldn't." Catherine Ryan from the hotel knew everything. "She can grow up knowing nothing if she likes."

"That's very unfair," Geraldine Brennan complained. "Just because my Mam and Dad aren't teachers I can get belted to bits, but you can do what you like."

Maria Kelly didn't like Dad and Mama No being criticized. She worked harder than ever.

"Go to bed, child. You'll hurt your eyes," Jim Kelly said as Maria was learning her poem by the light of the oil lamp.

"I have to know it, I *have* to. It's much worse on me than any of the others. If I'm not word perfect I *must* be beaten, or else they'll be giving out about you and Mama No."

Jim and Nora Kelly spoke in whispers that night. No child of their own could have brought them greater pleasure and happiness. It was literally as if she had been given to them as a gift from God in 1948, five long years ago.

Mattie the postman had delivered good and bad news to every house in Shancarrig. He knew when the emigrants' remittances arrived, he knew when a letter was unwelcome. He always hesitated slightly before handing Mrs. Kelly any letter with a Chicago postmark.

When he was delivering an envelope with American stamps that was bigger and bulkier than usual, and looked more serious than the short scrappy-looking ones which had come be-

fore, Mattie asked if he could come in for a drop of wa[...]
Kelly poured him a cup of tea.

"I don't want to be in the way or anything . . . it's [...]
case it was bad news. I know that you're on your own [...]
Hasn't the Master taken the children up to the Old Rock [...]

It was true. Early in each summer term Jim organize[...]
outing. The whole school would go—all fifty-six children. [...]
ther Gunn used to go too, and bring the elderly Monsig[...]
O'Toole when he felt able. The old Monsignor liked to kn[...]
that the children didn't think of the Old Rock as some kind [...]
pagan place. That was the trouble with ancient monuments tha[...]
dated back to before St. Patrick . . . people didn't relate them
to God.

Nora Kelly had decided not to go today, and here, as ill luck
would have it, was the news from Chicago. Could they be legal
papers? Her hand trembled. She opened it. There were newspaper cuttings, a description of how Maria's father, Lexi, had
opened his own shop, his own butcher's place, a beautiful meat
shop. He wanted his daughter to know this, to be proud of him.

Would Nora please show them to Maria? And perhaps she
might write. She is a big girl now, it is strange that she does not
write. Nora Kelly put her head in her hands and wept at her
kitchen table.

Mattie, who bitterly regretted not dropping the letter on the
table as he would have done ordinarily, reached out and patted
her heaving shoulders.

"It'll be all right, Mrs. Kelly. You were meant to have her," he
kept saying, over and over.

Nora Kelly pulled herself together, washed her face, and
combed her hair. She put on her summer hat, a black straw one,
and set off down the road to The Terrace, the row of houses in
Shancarrig where Dr. Jims Blake and Mr. Bill Hayes, the solicitor, lived.

Nellie Dunne, looking out her open door over her counter,
saw the schoolmistress walking briskly, cheeks flushed, face determined. Maybe she was heading for the doctor's? She might
have news for him. They often said when you stopped worry-

ing about having a child of your own that was the very time you conceived.

But Nora Kelly went up the steps to the Hayes household. Her business was legal, not medical.

Mr. Hayes seemed to notice a change in her, a determination to have the compensation settled and done with.

"Has anything happened, Mrs. Kelly?" he asked gently. "It's just that up to now you were the one to put it on the long finger, saying that money couldn't bring your sister back and that the child lacked for nothing." He was polite but questioning.

"I know," Nora Kelly agreed. "That's what I did think. But now I think my only hope is to get the compensation, whatever it is, and give it to him."

"Him?"

"Her father. He's not interested in anything else, believe me."

"But the compensation is for Maria as well as for him."

"We'll give it all to him if he'll let us keep the child."

"Ah Nora, Nora . . ." Normally Niall Hayes's father didn't call her by her first name. He seemed upset.

"What are you trying to say to me, Mr. Hayes?"

"I suppose I'm saying that you can't buy the child."

"And I'm saying that that's exactly what I'm going to do," she said, face flushed and eyes bright, much too bright.

Wearily Bill Hayes took out the file and together they went through the letters from CIE—the transport company—the solicitors for the insurance, and copies of his own to them. There was a sum. It would be agreed eventually. At most it would be £2,000, at the least £1,200. If they agreed to take something nearer the lower figure, it would be sooner rather than later. But perhaps, after all this time, they should hold out for more.

"Take whatever you can get, Mr. Hayes."

"Forgive me, but should your husband perhaps . . . ?"

"Jim is as desperate to keep her as I am. More so, if that's possible."

"There is absolutely no guarantee—"

"I know, but I have to have *something* to offer him. He's written to say he owns a shop. He's as proud as punch of it. Now he's started wanting her to write to him . . ." Her lip was trembling.

"Perhaps this is the first time he feels able to. You know Americans, they set a lot of store about having their own business. . . ."

"Please don't stand up for him. I could have borne it if he had come over and taken her away at once. Not now. Not all those years of ignoring and neglect and now . . ."

"She might come for holidays . . ."

Nora Kelly's mouth was a thin line. "You mean very well, Mr. Hayes, but it's not a help."

"Fine, Mrs. Kelly. I'll get it moving in as much as anything ever moves in the law." Bill Hayes waved his hand around shelves filled with envelopes and documents tied up in pale pink tape.

••• •••

"Will you write a little note to your father?" Nora asked Maria that night.

"What for? To thank him for the day up at the Old Rock?" She looked surprised.

Nora swallowed, and could hardly speak. Maria thought of Jim as her father. The man who was so proud of the new shop selling best meats in Chicago didn't even exist for her.

••• •••

A few days later she brought it up again.

"We've had a letter from your Papa Lexi in Chicago. He wanted you to see the pictures of his new meat shop."

Maria took the newspaper cutting.

"Ugh! Look at the dead animals hanging there," she said, handing it back.

"That's his job. Like Jimmy Morrissey's father." Nora wished she could leave it, but she knew that she dare not. "Anyway, Maria, it would be good to write him a letter and say the shop looks very nice."

"It doesn't!" Maria said, giggling her infectious laugh.

Her hair, long now but still curly, was tied with a colored ribbon. She always had her head in a book—the early years of long bedtime-story sessions had paid off. She was tall and suntanned and strong. She was nearly ten years old, a girl that anyone would love to claim as a daughter.

"But he'd like to hear," Nora insisted.

"It would only be pretending." She pulled the newspaper cutting toward her again and looked, as Nora knew she must, at the picture of the tall, handsome man standing beside his shop.

"Is this him?" she asked.

"Yes."

She looked uneasy, her dark blue eyes seeming troubled.

"What will I say?"

"Oh. Whatever you think. Whatever comes into your mind to say. I can't be dictating it for you."

"But nothing comes into my mind to say. I don't like thinking about it, it makes me feel . . . I don't know. I don't feel safe when I think about . . . all this."

Nora Kelly put her arms around Maria. "We'll make you safe, pet. Believe me, we will."

Maria wriggled away. It was too emotional.

"Yes. Fine. Okay, I'll say something. Will I say 'you look fine and rich'?"

"*No,* Maria. Whatever else you say, I beg you not to say that."

"Ah, Mama No, I don't know what to say. I think you are going to have to dictate it to me."

"I think I am," agreed Nora.

They kept the letters respectful and distant, telling little about life in Shancarrig, mentioning nothing of the Kellys who were her real parents, but giving vague sentiments of goodwill to a stranger in Chicago.

Nora noticed with delight how briefly and casually Maria read the stilted letters which came back, each one beginning "My dear daughter Maria."

The man had little to say, and said it badly.

"He's not much at spelling is Papa Lexi," Maria said.

"Now, now!" Jim corrected her.

"Is he a secret? Do people know about him?"

"Of course he's not a secret, love. Why do you think that?"

"Because we don't talk about him. And nobody else has another Papa miles away."

"We do talk about him, and you write to him. Of course he's not a secret." Nora was very anxious to take any glamour or mystery away.

"Do you write to him, Mama No?"

"I do, love. But about business."

"The meat business?" She was genuinely puzzled.

"No. Legal things, you know, after your mother's accident . . ."

"Why do you have to write about that?"

"Oh, you know. Red tape. Formalities. All that." Nora was vague.

Maria lost interest. Instead she wanted to tell Mama No about Miss Ross.

"I saw her climbing the tree this morning," she said, giggling at the thought of the elegant Miss Ross actually getting her leg up on the lower branch and hauling herself up into the higher parts of the tree.

"Nonsense! You imagined it."

"No, I didn't. I was looking out my window at six o'clock this morning, and she came into the school yard. I swear she did."

"What on earth could she have been doing at that hour?"

"Well, I saw her. She'd been up all night. She was coming back from Barna Woods."

"I think you've been reading too many stories—you can't tell what's true from what's made up."

Nora shook her head. The very idea of Miss Ross climbing the beech tree. Really.

"Miss Ross?"

"Yes, Maria."

"Miss Ross, did you climb the beech tree yesterday morning?"

Miss Ross's face was red. "Did I what, child?"

"It's just . . . it's just, I told Mama No, and she said 'nonsense.' "

"That's what it is too, Maria. Nonsense."

Miss Ross turned and walked away.

Nora heard the conversation. There was something about the way the young teacher spoke that didn't ring true.

"I was wrong about Miss Ross," Maria said.

"Maybe it was the light. It's full of odd shadows at that time of morning." Nora spoke kindly.

They exchanged a glance and somehow Maria seemed to know that Nora knew it wasn't something that had been made up. That it was something which might indeed have happened.

"I never thanked you properly for putting us right about that young divil Foxy Dunne," Mr. Hayes said to Nora Kelly when she called to see him next time. "It was absolutely the right thing for young Niall. Foxy taught him to catch rabbits—we have six of them out in the back. All male. Foxy taught him how to work that out too."

Nora laughed. "There's not much that fellow doesn't know."

Bill Hayes looked out his window at the back garden. "Look at that. He showed Niall how to build a proper little house for them, and put up a wire run from the hutch. It's very professional, and he's only a child."

"He'll go far," Nora said. She knew too that visiting The Terrace had a civilizing effect on Foxy Dunne. He combed his hair and washed his hands without being asked to. He ate slowly, like his hosts. He was a fast learner.

Nora liked talking to Bill Hayes, he was a quiet man and people who didn't know him well might think he was a little too precise and fussy. But nobody's life was easy. Nora Hayes knew it was not a bed of roses living with the gloomy Ethel Hayes who hadn't smiled for a long time. She knew that every-

one's business was safe and secret in Number 5, The Terrace.
And that she would get the best advice that she could be given.

"Well now, you didn't come to talk to me about rabbits and
hutches. I'm being very remiss." He moved back to his desk
and picked up some papers. "We do have an offer now . . .
they're delighted to be able to close the file after five and a half
years."

"How much?"

"Thirteen hundred. Now we could get—"

"That's fine, and here's a note from Jim saying he agrees too,
in case you think I'm doing all this on my own."

"No, no . . ." But he took the note.

"I'll write tonight. When would we have the money?"

"Oh, in a week or two."

"And would there be a certain percentage legally for him and
for Maria?"

"I'd advise that half be for her, to be invested . . ."

"You do know what we are going to do with her portion,
don't you?"

"Yes, and I must say again how very unwise it is from every
point of view. Suppose the child does stay with you, will she
thank you for handing away what is her legal inheritance?"

Nora Kelly wasn't listening . . . she would write tonight.

She went to the post office to get a stamp, and Katty Morrissey looked up from behind the grille.

"Well, isn't that the coincidence! There was a telegram for
you half an hour ago. I was going to get Mattie to go out with
it."

Nora felt cold. Her hand trembled as she opened the envelope, and in full view of Katty Morrissey and Nellie Dunne,
who had materialized as usual when any drama was about to
unfold, she read that Lexi was arriving in Shannon Airport on
Friday morning and would be with them on Friday afternoon.

"Would you like a glass of water, Mrs. Kelly?"

"No, Miss Dunne, thank you very much. I would like nothing
of the sort." Nora Kelly gathered every ounce of strength and
walked out of the post office, leaving Nellie and Katty to say to

each other, before they said it to the rest of Shancarrig, that the schoolteacher's time was up. The real father was on his way from the United States to take his child home.

"You don't look well, Mrs. Kelly." Maddy Ross had come up behind her as she crossed the bridge on the way back up home.

"Neither do you, Miss Ross," Nora countered. There would be no sympathy from this young teacher who had her life before her—a life with marriage and children in it.

"I'm fine. A little tired. I don't sleep at night. I walk a lot in the woods—it clears my head." She had a strange, almost wild, look about her.

Jim had said, over and over, that it was essential for Shancarrig School to keep Miss Ross. Her salary was small, as the department would only pay the minimum. And only Maddy Ross, who had a house, and a mother with private means of a sort, would be able to live on what went into her envelope every month.

But sometimes Nora thought that Miss Ross had a giddiness and light-headedness that none of their silliest fourteen-year-old girls had ever managed to reach. And more than once she thought, God forgive her, that Miss Ross was almost flirting with young Father Barry. Nora kept her own counsel about this, not even confiding to Jim.

"Do you sometimes feel the world is bursting with happiness?" Maddy Ross asked her as they walked together up the road.

Nora Kelly, who could well have done without this feverish conversation, replied tersely that she didn't think that at all, and particularly not today. So if Miss Ross would excuse her, she would like to be left to her own thoughts.

She saw Maddy Ross shrink away like an animal that has received a blow.

Still, there was no time to think about that now, the young teacher's nonsense could be dealt with later. Right now she had to cope with the event that she had dreaded since the week after her sister died—the arrival of her brother-in-law in Shancarrig to take his daughter home.

She walked like a woman in a dream. Not since the time of Helen's death had Nora felt this sensation of being outside her body, as if she were watching another being going through the motions—of filling a kettle, of setting a table.

When Jim came in she was sitting motionless at the table. He saw the telegram and needed to ask very little.

"When is he coming?" he said.

"Friday."

"Nora. Oh Nora, my love. What are we going to do?"

He put his hands over his face and wept like a baby.

She sat there stroking his arm, listing the possibilities. Could they leave Shancarrig and hide somewhere? No, that was ridiculous, he would get the Guards. Could they pretend that Maria was too sick to travel? Could they get Mr. Hayes to brief a barrister in Dublin who would fight a case against her being taken away from them? Each solution was more unlikely than the one which had gone before.

They could ask Maria to beg him. No. They must never do that.

Perhaps for the child it *was* the best. A comfortable living in the New World. A whole lot of cousins, a ready made family, a welcome home as if the five years since she left the Chicago airport in 1948 were just a pause in her real life.

Nora and Jim Kelly realized that this was one occasion when they could do absolutely nothing. They would have to wait for Friday and all it would bring.

By the time they showed Maria the telegram they had calmed each other sufficiently to speak without letting their emotions show.

"Is he going to take me away from here?" Maria asked.

"Well, we don't know what he plans, do we? After all, he just says 'arriving to visit you.' He doesn't say anything about . . . anything after that."

"I don't want to go."

"Now, that's not the way to start," Jim Kelly said.

"Well, what *is* the way to start . . . ?" Maria was flushed. They hadn't realized how independent she had become, how strong in her own views. "This is my home. You are my parents. I don't want to go away with someone I don't remember, someone who didn't come for me when my real mother died."

"He couldn't. And you mustn't begin by making him an enemy."

"He *is* an enemy. I don't want to meet him, I'll run away."

"No Maria, please. Please, that would be the worst thing."

"What would be the best thing?"

"I suppose it would be to reason with him, tell him how much you think of Shancarrig as your home, and of us as your . . . well, your people."

"My parents," Maria said stubbornly.

"He won't want to hear that," Nora said.

"I don't care what he wants to hear. Why should I have to beg him to let me stay in my own home?"

"Because life isn't fair, and you're only ten years of age."

Maria ran out the door through the yard, and across the fields toward Barna Woods.

When she came home later that night, she was very silent. And pale. Nora, who knew every heartbeat of this child, knew that it was something else, something not to do with what was going to happen on Friday.

"Did something happen to frighten you?"

"You know everything, Mama No."

"Was it something you saw?"

"Yes." She hung her head.

Nora's cheeks burned. How could life be so cruel, that someone must have exposed himself to the little girl on this of all days.

"You can tell me," she said.

"Not really. It's really very bad. You won't believe me."

"I will. I always do."

"I saw Miss Ross and Father Barry kissing each other." She blurted it out.

Immediately Nora knew she was telling the truth. Without a shadow of a doubt she realized that this was indeed what had been going on under her eyes.

A priest of God and their Junior Assistant Mistress.

But even the scandal, and the need to tell Father Gunn tactfully, and the whole attendant list of complications, faded away compared to the shock that it had all given to Maria.

"Do you remember when you told me Miss Ross had climbed the tree? I didn't really believe you, but I did later. And I most certainly believe you now. But Maria, we have so much to worry about, you and I. Let us put this to the very back of our minds, right back behind everything, and later we'll talk about it. Just you and I. It's best to tell nobody, nobody at all. These things have explanations."

"Don't send me to Papa Lexi."

"You'll be strong and good when he comes. I'll help you every step of the way. We'll ask him can you share your time between us. Hey, wouldn't that be great? Two countries. Two continents. And we all want you. Not everyone has that."

"Will it work?"

"Yes," said Nora Kelly, knowing that she had never spoken such an untruth in her whole life.

They survived the four days to Friday.

People were very kind, which they expected, but also very tactful, which they hadn't expected. They did practical things.

Mrs. Ryan in the hotel looked up the time of the flight, and since it would be arriving in the early hours of the morning worked out what time he could be expected in Shancarrig. Maybe lunchtime. If it would be easier, they could have lunch at Ryan's Commercial Hotel, she suggested, a private room.

Mr. Hayes, the solicitor, offered to take him through the steps of the settlement one by one, pointing out how it had been the best thing to do.

Dr. Jims dropped by with sleeping tablets in case they were finding the nights long.

Leo Murphy, daughter of the Major up at The Glen, said that Maria could come up and hit a ball around on the tennis court if she liked. Even though she was four years younger, it would be all right, because of things being difficult.

Young Father Barry said, with eyes of blazing sincerity, that God was a God of Love above all, and that he would open this man's heart to see the love the Kellys had for Maria.

Nora Kelly preferred not to think too deeply about the God of Love that Father Barry interpreted, but she thanked him all the same.

Father Gunn said that Polish Catholics were very devoted to Our Lady, and that Mrs. Kelly should show him the plaque on the wall, where the school had been dedicated to the Blessed Virgin.

Foxy Dunne said he had heard there was a bit of a problem, and he knew some very tough people, or his brothers did, if reinforcements were called for. Jim Kelly put on his sternest face when refusing this offer, but gripped Foxy by the arm and told him he was a great fellow for all that.

Eddie Barton told his mother that the gypsies were coming again, wouldn't it be great if they were to kidnap Maria and then for her to be found and brought back after the man had gone back to Chicago.

Mrs. Barton was altering Nora Kelly's best dress for her, with a trim of lace down the front, and on the collar and cuffs. She wanted to look the equal of anyone in Chicago for the visit. "I only tell you what Eddie said, just in case. It might work," she said, mouth full of pins.

"God bless you both," Nora Kelly said, looking at her pale reflection in the mirror.

In many ways it was like a western where they are all waiting for the gunmen to come to town. Down by the station Mattie the postman happened to be waiting with his bicycle, just waiting, looking into the middle distance as it were. Sergeant Keane was sitting on a windowsill by the bus stop, throwing the odd word to Nellie Dunne, who had come out from behind her counter to stand at her doorway.

The Morrisseys in the butcher's shop were making frequent sorties out onto the street, and Mrs. Breda Ryan from the hotel seemed to find a lot of activity that took her to the entrance porch of their premises.

Although none of them would have admitted it, and no one pretended to see the curtains of the presbytery move as Mrs. Kennedy watched from one window and Father Gunn from another . . . they were all waiting.

Someone would let the Kellys know the moment the man came into the town. They never thought he would arrive by car, and because it was an ordinary car, not a big American Cadillac, nobody knew it was Lexi when he drove into Shancarrig and looked around him to see where the schoolhouse was.

Not seeing it in the center or near the church, he took the road over the Grane and arrived at a huge copper beech tree, where the one-story building had the notice SHANCARRIG NATIONAL SCHOOL.

Behind was the small stone house of Jim and Nora Kelly. They were sitting waiting for the message that would tell them by which route he had arrived. They certainly had not expected the man himself.

He was big and handsome, fair curly hair around his ears, eyes dark blue. He must be thirty-six or thirty-seven—the same age as Jim. He looked years younger—he looked like a film star.

Nora and Jim stood in their doorway, their sides touching for strength. She longed to hold her husband's hand, but it would look too girlish. It wasn't in their manner to do a thing like that, hip to hip was enough.

"I am Alexis," he said. "You are Nora and Jim?"

"You're very welcome to Shancarrig," Nora said, the untruthfulness of the words hidden she hoped by the smile she had nailed on her face.

"My daughter Maria?" he said.

"We thought it best that she go to a friend's house. We will take you to her whenever you like." Jim spoke loudly to try to hide the shake in his voice.

"This house of her friend?" he asked.

"It's ten minutes walk, maybe two or three minutes in your car. Don't worry. She's there, she knows you're coming," Jim said. He thought he could sense suspicion in Lexi's voice.

"We felt it would be more fair on you not to have to tell her in her own home . . . what she thinks of as her own home." Nora looked around the kitchen of the small house where she had spent all her married life.

"Tell her?"

"Well, talk to her. Meet her, get to know her. Whatever it is you want to do." Jim knew his voice was trailing lamely. These monosyllables from Lexi were hard to cope with. Somehow he had expected something totally different.

"It is good that she is not here for the moment. May I sit down?"

They rushed to get him a chair, and offer him tea, or whiskey.

"Do you have poitin?" he asked.

Nora's warning bells sounded. She remembered her sister Helen telling of this morose drinking, this silent swallowing of neat alcohol.

"No. The local teacher has to set a good example, I'm afraid. But I *do* have a bottle of Irish whiskey that I bought in a bar, if that would do."

He smiled. Lexi, the man who had come to take their daughter, smiled as if he was a friend: "I need a drink for what I am to tell you."

Their hearts were like lead as they poured the *three* little glasses, lest he think them aloof. They proposed no toast.

"I am going to marry again," Lexi told them. "I am to marry a girl, Karina, who is also Polish. Her father owns a butcher's shop too, and we are going to combine the two. She is much more young than I am, Karina. She is twenty-two years of age."

"Yes, yes." Nora was holding her breath to know what would come next.

"I tell you the truth. It would be much more easy for our

marriage if Karina and I were to start our own family . . . to begin like any other couple. To get to know each other, to make our own children . . ."

Nora felt the breath hissing between her teeth. She gripped her small glass so hard, she feared it might shatter in her hands. "And you were wondering . . . ?" she said.

"And I thought that perhaps, if my daughter Maria is happy here . . . then perhaps this is where she might like to be . . . but, you see, it is not fair that I leave her with you . . . you have your life. You have been so good to her for so long . . ."

The tears were running down Nora's face. She didn't even try to wipe them away.

Lexi continued: "I have made many inquiries about the finances because I want you to have the money to do so. But always when I talk of the money you do not reply. I fear there may be no money. I fear to give you money in case you think I am trying to give you a bribe . . ."

Jim Kelly was on his feet. "Oh Lexi, sir, we'd *love* to keep her here. She'll always be your daughter. Whenever you want her she'll go on a holiday to you . . . but it's our hearts' desire that she stay with us."

Nora spoke very calmly: "And maybe she would see you as Uncle Lexi more than Papa Lexi, don't you think?" She didn't know where she found the strength to say the words that Lexi wanted to hear. She didn't dare to believe that she had got them right until she saw his face light up.

"Yes, yes. This would be much better for Karina, that she think of her as a niece, not a daughter. Because, in many ways now, that is what she is."

Nora saw, out of the corner of her eye, a shadow move on the beech tree in the school yard. It was Foxy Dunne, hovering. He had seen the car and guessed the driver.

"Foxy!" she called. He came swaggering in. This man was an enemy, he wouldn't be civil to him. "Foxy, could you do us a favor? Maria is over at The Glen with Leo Murphy. Would you go over and tell her to come home, and tell her everything's fine."

"It's a long journey over to the The Glen," Foxy said unexpectedly.

"It's ten minutes, you little pup," said Jim Kelly.

"It'd be easier if you let me drive over for her." He looked at the car keys on the table.

"Hey, how old are you?" Lexi asked.

"I've driven everything. That's dead easy."

"He's thirteen and a half," said Nora.

"That's a grown man," said Lexi. "But don't you put a scratch on it. I have to take it back to Shannon Airport tonight." He threw him the keys.

Tonight. The man was going back to his new life tonight. Without Maria.

The sunlight streamed into the kitchen as they talked, as they sat as friends and spoke of the past and the future, until Maria arrived, white-faced from the journey. Foxy had driven her three times around Shancarrig to get value from the drive, and then spotted Sergeant Keane so had put his foot down to get her back to the schoolhouse.

Nora put her arms around the girl.

"We've had a great chat, my love," she said. "This is Lexi, maybe even Uncle Lexi. He'll be going back to America tonight, and he wants to meet you and get to know you a little bit before he goes."

Maria's eyes were wide trying to take it in.

"Before he goes off and leaves you here with us. Which is what we all agreed is where you want to be," said Nora Kelly, who had told her daughter Maria that everything would be all right, and had now delivered on her promise.

7

Nessa

It was Mrs. Ryan who wore
the trousers in Ryan's Commercial Hotel. Everyone knew that.
And just as well, because if Conor Ryan had married a mouse
the place would have gone to the wall years ago.

Conor Ryan certainly hadn't married a mouse when he wed
Breda O'Connor. A small, thin girl with restless eyes and
straight black shiny hair, she was a distant cousin of the Ryans.
They met at a family wedding. Conor Ryan told her that he was
thinking of going off to England and joining the British Army.
Anything to get out from under his parents' feet—they ran this
hole-in-the-wall hotel in a real backward town.

"What do you want going into the army? There might be a
war and you'd get killed," she said.

Conor Ryan implied that it mightn't be a huge choice between that and staying put with his parents.

"They can't be *that* bad," Breda said.

"They are. The place is like the ark. No, the ark was safe and
dry and people wanted to get into it. This is like a morgue."

"Why don't you improve it?"

"I'm only twenty-three, they'd never let me," he said.

Breda O'Connor decided there and then that she would marry him. By the time Britain declared war on Germany they were already engaged.

"*Now*, aren't you glad I didn't let you join the army?" Breda said.

"You haven't lived with my father and mother yet," he said, with a look of defeat and resignation that she was determined to take out of him.

"Nor will I," she said with spirit. "We'll build a place of our own."

Conor Ryan's father said that he had picked a wastrel, a girl who thought they were made of money, when the outbuilding was converted into a small dwelling for the newlyweds.

Conor Ryan's mother said there would be no interfering from a fancy young one who thought she was the divil an' all because she had a Domestic Science diploma. Conor reported none of these views to the bride-to-be. Breda would find out soon enough what they were like. She had assured him that she had been given fair warning.

As it happened she never really found out how much they had resented her coming to their house, and marrying their only son while he was still a child.

Breda never heard how *his* parents prophesied that when she had a few children out in that cement hut she was getting built for herself in the yard it would soften her cough.

The Ryan parents fell victim to a bad flu that swept the countryside in the winter of 1939.

Two weeks after the winter wedding of Conor and Breda the same congregation stood in the church for the double funeral of the groom's parents.

There was a lot of headshaking. How hard it was for a young girl to step in like that. It would be too much for her. She was only a little bit of a thing. And you'd need to light a bonfire under Conor Ryan to get any kind of action out of him. It was the end of Ryan's Commercial Hotel for Shancarrig.

Never were people so wrong.

Breda Ryan took control at once. Even on the very day of that funeral. She assured the mourners that they would be very welcome to come back to the hotel bar for drinks rather than going up to Johnny Finn's pub, as they thought they should do out of some kind of respect.

"The best respect that you could give my parents-in-law is to come to their hotel," Breda Ryan said.

Within a week she made it known that she didn't like to be referred to as the *young* Mrs. Ryan.

"My husband's mother has gone to her reward, and the Lord have mercy on her she is no longer here to need her name. I am Mrs. Ryan now," she said.

And so she was. Mrs. Ryan of Shancarrig's only hotel, a part of the triangle that people called the heart of the town—one side The Terrace where the rich people like the doctor and Mr. Hayes the solicitor lived, one side the row of shops—Nellie Dunne's grocery, Mr. Connors the chemist, the other Dunnes who ran the hardware business, the butcher, the draper—the few small places that got a meager living from Shancarrig and its outlying farms. The third side of the triangle was Ryan's Hotel.

Not very prepossessing, dark brown throughout, floors covered in linoleum. The rooms all had heavy oak fireplaces, the pictures on the walls were in dark heavy frames. Most of them were of unlikely romantic scenes with men in frock coats, never seen in Shancarrig or even in the county, offering their arms to ladies in outfits similarly unknown.

There were some religious pictures in the hall . . . the one of the Sacred Heart had a small red lamp burning in front of it. The sideboards in the hall and dining room were stuffed with glass never used on the table, and Belleek china.

Mrs. Ryan had plans to change and improve it all, but first she must see that people came to it as it was.

She made sure that the smell of cooking didn't meet guests at the hall door by putting heavy curtains outside the kitchen doors. She installed a glass-fronted notice board near the reception desk and put up details of concerts, hunt balls, or other high-class events in neighboring towns.

She intended to make the hotel the very center of Shancarrig, the place where people would come to look for information. The bus and train times were there too for all to see, in the hopes that it would encourage travelers to come and have a drink or a coffee as they waited. Her plans had only just begun when she realized she was pregnant.

Her first child was born in 1940, a little girl, delivered by young Dr. Jims because the baby arrived in the middle of the night and Dr. Nolan was getting too old to come out at all hours.

"A lovely daughter," he said. "Is that what you wanted?"

"Indeed it's not. I wanted a strong son to run the hotel for me." She was laughing as she held the baby.

"Well, maybe she'll run it till she gets a brother." Dr. Jims had a warm way with him.

"It's no life for a woman. We'll find a better job for Vanessa." She held the child close.

"Vanessa! Now there's a name."

"Oh, think big, Doctor. That's what I always believed."

Conor Ryan poured a brandy for the doctor, and the two men sat companionably in the bar at 4:30 a.m. to drink to the new life in Shancarrig.

"May Vanessa live to see the year 2000," said Dr. Jims.

"Won't Nessa only be a young one of sixty then! Why are you wishing her a short life?" said the new father.

She was Nessa from the start. Even her strong-willed mother was not able to impose her will on the people of Shancarrig on this point. And when her sister was born the baby was Catherine, and the third girl Nuala. There were no strong sons to run the hotel. But by the time they realized there never would be, the women were so well established in Ryan's that the absence of a boy wasn't even noticed.

Nessa always thought she had got the worst possible combination of looks from her parents.

She had her mother's dead-straight hair. No amount of pipe cleaners would put even the hint of a wave or a kink in it. And she inherited her father's broad shoulders and big feet. Why could she not have got his curly hair and her mother's tiny proportions? Life was very unfair. Everyone admired people with curly hair.

Like Leo's hair.

Since Nessa could remember she had been best friends with Leo Murphy. Leo was the girl who lived up at The Glen. She was almost an only child. Lucky thing. Not a real only child like Eddie Barton, the son of the dressmaker, but Leo's two brothers were very old and didn't live at home.

Nessa had even known Leo before the day they both started at Shancarrig School. Leo had been invited to come and play with her. Mrs. Ryan had said she wanted Vanessa to have a proper friend before she started in there and had to consort with the Dunnes and the Brennans.

"What's consorting?" Nessa asked her mother.

"Never mind, but you won't be doing it anyway."

"That's why you're off to school, to learn things like that," said Conor Ryan, folding back the paper at the race card to see could he pick a likely winner in the afternoon races.

The first day at school Nessa Ryan sat beside Maura Brennan. Together they learned to do pothooks.

"Why are they called pothooks?" Nessa asked as the two girls slowly traced the S shapes in their headline copybooks.

"They look a bit like the hooks that hang over the fire. You know . . . to hold the pots," Maura explained.

Nessa told this information proudly to her mother.

"What! They have you sitting next to one of the Brennans from the cottages?" she said crossly.

"Don't be putting notions into her head. Isn't the poor Brennan child entitled to sit beside someone? Isn't she a human being?" Nessa's father was defending Maura Brennan for something. Her mother was still in a bad temper about it, whatever it was.

"That's not what you say when her father comes in here breaking all before him, and swearing like a soldier."

"He takes his trade to Johnny Finn's after what you said to him that time . . ."

"You sound as if you're sorry, as if you miss that good-for-nothing drunk. It was a fine day for this house when I shifted him out. You agreed yourself."

"I did, I did."

"So what are you going on about?"

"I don't know, Breda . . ." He shook his head. Nessa realized whatever it was . . . her Daddy really didn't know. He didn't know about things like her mother did. About running a hotel, and being in charge.

"Will I not sit beside her?" Nessa asked.

Her mother's face softened. "Don't mind me, your father is right. The child's not to be blamed."

"We don't have pothooks, do we?"

"No. We have a range, like any normal person would. The Brennans cook over an open fire, I expect. Did you not see Leo Murphy at school today?"

"She was sitting beside Eddie. They got told off for talking."

"What else happened? Tell me all about it."

"We played a game around the tree, you know, like a big ring o' roses."

"I did that myself," said her father.

She saw her mother going over and putting her arm around his shoulder. They were smiling. She felt safe. Maybe her mother *did* love her father even if he didn't know how to run a hotel. When anyone came to the hotel they asked for Mrs. Ryan, not for Mr., that's if they knew the place. Otherwise it was a delay while Mr. Ryan sent for his wife.

Nessa grew up knowing that she should get her mother not her father in any crisis. At the start she thought this was the same in all families.

But she learned it wasn't always the case. She discovered that

Leo Murphy's mother didn't know where anything was, that Major Murphy and Biddy the maid ran The Glen between them. Leo never had to consult her mother about anything. It was a huge freedom.

She learned that Maura Brennan's mother had to go out begging because Mr. Brennan drank whatever money he got. When Nessa wondered why Mrs. Brennan didn't stop him with a word or a glance as her mother would have, Maura shrugged. Women weren't like that, she said.

Niall Hayes said that his mother didn't have any say in the house. His father paid all the bills, and dealt with things that happened. Foxy Dunne said that his mother hadn't been known to open her mouth on any subject, but of course his father had never been known to close his, so that made up a pair of them.

Only Eddie, whose father was dead or had gone away or something, said that his mother was in charge. But she didn't like being in charge, he said. She kept thinking there should be a man around the place.

Sometimes they even made jokes about Nessa's mother, about how different she was to the other women in Shancarrig. Nessa didn't like that very much, but in her heart she had to admit it was true. Her mother was rather too interested in her for her liking. She wanted to know everything that happened.

"Why do you want to know so much?" Nessa asked her once.

"I want to make sure you don't make the same mistakes that I made. I want to try and help your childhood." Her mother had seemed very simple and direct in that answer, as if she were talking to someone her own age, not talking down.

"Leave the child alone," her father said, as he said so often. "Aren't they only children for a very short time? Let them enjoy it."

"I don't know about the very short time," Nessa's mother said. "There are quite a few people around here who never grew up."

When people stopped to admire young Nessa Ryan on the street they often asked: "And whose pet are you?" It was only a greeting, not a question, but Nessa took it seriously.

"Nobody's," she would say firmly. "There's so much work in a hotel there's no time to have pets." People laughed at the solemn way the child spoke, in the parrot fashion she must have heard at home.

Her mother didn't approve. "You're the most petted child in the country. Stop telling people that there's no one spoiling you," she said.

But Nessa didn't think this was so. She wondered was she a foundling. Had the dark gypsies, the families who came through every year, left her on the hotel doorstep? Had she been found up at the Old Rock, left there by a wonderful kind noblewoman with long hair—someone who was in great secret trouble and left her baby while she escaped?

Nessa didn't know exactly what she wanted, but she knew very definitely that it was something different to what she had got. She would never be able to please her mother, no matter what she did, and her father was too soft and easygoing for his views to count.

Sometimes when she was feeling particularly religious and near to God she used to ask *Him* to make her popular and loved.

"I'm not asking to be pretty, God, I know we're not meant to pray for good looks. But I am asking to be liked more. People that are popular are very very happy. They can go around doing good all the time. Honestly, God, even children. I'd be a great child and a great grown-up. Just try it and see."

The years of Nessa Ryan's childhood saw a great change in Ryan's Commercial Hotel.

After endless rationing and petrol shortages brought about by the war in Europe, suddenly cars appeared on the road again. Instead of the hotel's visitors arriving at Shancarrig railway station and walking across to where Ryan's stood taking up one side of the three-cornered green that formed the center and heart of the place . . . they now drew up outside the door. Most people were loath to leave their cars in the street, even though this was the best part of Shancarrig. Visitors didn't know that The Terrace where Dr. Nolan and then Dr. Jims lived in Number 3 and where the Hayes family lived in Number 5 was about the best address in the county. They wanted safe parking for their cars.

The hotel was no longer dark brown. The dark colors had been replaced by cream and what Breda called a lovely restful *eau de nil*. She had toured other, smarter hotels and discovered that this pale greenish shade was high fashion.

The more sober of the heavy framed pictures had been relegated to the master bedroom, out of view of any visitors.

More bathrooms had been installed, chamber pots were hidden discreetly in bedside cupboards rather than being placed expectantly under beds.

The women who served in the dining room of Ryan's Commercial Hotel wore smart green dresses now, with their white aprons and little white half caps. The days of black outfits were over. There were comfortable chairs in the entrance hall encouraging guests to think of it as it used to be.

When Nessa and her sisters, Catherine and Nuala, were young they were kept well out of sight of the hotel visitors, but were trained to say Good Morning or Good Evening to anyone they encountered, even scarlet-faced drunks who might not be able to reply.

Nessa's mother had cleared up the hotel yard. Old and broken machinery was removed, outbuildings were painted. No longer was the place used as a dumping ground. Guests were told that ample parking facilities existed.

And the visitors changed too.

A trickle of American servicemen who had got to know Europe during the days of war, returned again in peacetime bringing their wives, particularly if there was any Irish heritage in the family tree. They would stay in hotels around the country and try to find it out. They became a familiar sight, sometimes still in uniform, and looking very dashing as they would book into Ryan's Commercial Hotel.

Father Gunn said he was worn out tracing roots from old church records.

There were the commercial travelers too. The same people coming regularly, once a month—once a fortnight sometimes. Usually two or three rooms would be booked by the various representatives coming to take orders in Shancarrig and outlying areas.

Nessa's mother treated them with great respect. They would be the backbone of their business, she told her husband. Conor Ryan shrugged. He often thought them a dull crowd, abstemious, too, no bar profit from them. Pale tired men, anxious about their sales, restless, uneasy.

It was Nessa's mother who insisted on the Commercial Room, and lighting a fire there. There were a few tables strewn around, they could fill their order books and smoke there. They could bring in a cup of tea or coffee.

Conor Ryan thought it a waste. Why couldn't they sit in the bar like any other person? He had noted that few of them followed either horses or dogs, there was little conversation with them at the best of times.

At school everyone was always interested in the hotel, and its goings-on. They always asked about what the farmers ate for breakfast on the fair days once a month, and whether any of the beasts had ever backed into the windows and broken them, as happened once down in Nellie Dunne's grocery when she forgot to put up the barriers.

Nessa told of the huge breakfasts served all morning, and of how fathers and sons would take turns, one to mind the animals while the other would eat bacon and eggs heaped high on plates.

"Who was your best friend when you were young?" Nessa asked her mother when Breda Ryan was brushing the dark shiny hair which she persisted on admiring so much despite all Nessa's complaints.

"We didn't have time for best friends then. Stay still, Vanessa."

"Why do you call me Vanessa? Nobody else does."

"It's your name. There, that looks great."

"I look like the witch in the school play."

"Why are you always saying such awful things about yourself, child? If you think these stupid things other people will too."

"That's funny. That's what Leo said too."

"She's got her head screwed on her shoulders, that one," Mrs. Ryan said approvingly.

"We'll be going into the convent together next year, every day on the bus. Maybe she'll be more my friend then."

In a rare moment of affection Nessa's mother held her eldest daughter close.

"You'll have plenty of friends. Wait and see!" her mother said.

"It had better start soon. I'm nearly fourteen," Nessa said glumly.

In magazine stories Nessa had read of girls whose mothers were like friends. She wished she had a mother like that, not one so brisk and so sure of everything. Nessa had never known an occasion when her mother had been wrong, or at a loss for a word. Her father, now, that was different, he was always scratching his head and saying he hadn't a clue about things. But Nessa felt her mother was born knowing all the answers.

On their last day at Shancarrig School, Nessa Ryan stood between Niall Hayes and Foxy Dunne during the school photograph. Mrs. Kelly always liked to have a picture taken on that day, and they were urged to dress themselves up well so that future generations could see how respectable had been the classes that had gone through these schoolrooms.

It had become a tradition now. The formal photograph taken under the tree outside the schoolhouse door. The very last moment of the year, organized to calm them down after the other tradition of name carving and the boisterous racing around the classroom collecting the books and pencils while singing:

> *No more Irish, no more French*
> *No more sitting on a hard school bench*
> *Kick up tables, kick up chairs*
> *Kick the Master and the Mistress down the stairs.*

That there had been no French ever learned in Shancarrig and that there were no stairs in the schoolhouse were details that didn't concern them. All over the world children sang that song on the last day.

Those who were only thirteen, and would have to return to school after the summer, looked on enviously. This was the day when they wrote their names on the tree. The boys had brought penknives. Everyone was busy digging at the wood of the old beech tree.

Nessa wished she could enjoy this like the others did. They all seemed very intense. Maura Brennan had been planning for weeks where she would put her name. Eddie Barton said he was going to carve his in a drawing of a flower so that it would look special in years to come. Foxy was saying nothing, but looked knowing all the same.

Nessa took the extra knife from Master Kelly and wrote *Vanessa Ryan, June 1954*. She felt there was more to say, but she didn't know what it was.

The sun was in their eyes as they squinted at Mrs. Kelly's camera.

"Stand up straight! Stop fidgeting there!" She spoke, knowing these were the last commands she would ever give them.

Foxy Dunne stroked Nessa's hair, which hung loose on her shoulders. "Very nice," he said.

"Take your hands off me, Foxy Dunne," she snapped.

"Just admiring, Miss Bossy Boots. Admiring, that's all." He didn't look the slightest bit put out.

Imagine Foxy, from that desperate house of Dunnes, daring to touch her hair.

"It is very nice, your hair," Niall Hayes said. Square, dependable, dull Niall, who had never had an original thought. He said it as if he were trying to curry favor with Foxy and excuse him for his views.

"Well," she said, at a loss for words. To her surprise she felt her face and neck redden at the praise. Nessa Ryan hadn't known a compliment from a boy before. She put her hand up to her face so that they wouldn't see her flush.

"Smile, everyone. Nessa, take your hand away from your face at once. Leo, if I see you put your tongue out once more there's going to be trouble. Great trouble."

Everyone laughed, and it was a happy picture for the schoolhouse wall.

As they walked together for the last time from Shancarrig School, Nessa and Leo were arm in arm and Maura Brennan walked with them. Maura would get a job as a maid or in a factory, she had said she didn't want to go to England like her sisters. Nessa felt a flash of sympathy for the girl who hadn't the same chances as she had. Nessa's father had said about the Brennans and the Dunnes from the cottages that they had a poor hand dealt to them, very few aces there.

"Don't describe everything in terms of cards," Mrs. Ryan corrected him.

"Right. Then I'd say that the bookies' odds against the Brennans and Dunnes were fixed," he said, grinning.

But Maura Brennan never complained.

She was always very agreeable and quiet, as if she had accepted long ago that her father was a disgrace and her mother was always asking for handouts. Foxy Dunne was different, he behaved as if his family were dukes and earls instead of drunks and layabouts. You'd never know from looking at Foxy Dunne that his father and brothers were barred from almost every establishment in the town. They weren't even allowed into their Uncle Jimmy's, who ran the hardware shop.

Foxy neither apologized for them nor defended them. It was as if he regarded them as separate people.

Nessa wished she could be like that sometimes. It hurt her when her mother was sharp to her easygoing father. It annoyed her when her father just shrugged and took none of the responsibility.

"There's a gypsy telling fortunes. They say she's terrific," Maura said.

"Will we get our fortunes told?" Leo's eyes were sparkling.

Nessa knew that her mother would be very cross indeed if they went anywhere near the tinkers' camp. So would Leo's mother, but Leo didn't care. It would be wonderful to be as free as that.

"She'd only tell you back what you'd tell her," Foxy said. "That's what they do. They ask you what you want to be and then they tell you two minutes later that this is what's going to happen to you."

"But that's dishonest," Niall Hayes objected.

"That's life, Niall." Foxy spoke as if he knew much more of the world from his broken-down cottage than did Niall Hayes, the lawyer's son who lived in The Terrace.

"So? Will we go?" Leo was on for any excitement.

"We could read palms to know what's going to happen to us," Eddie said suddenly.

That seemed much safer to Nessa. Her mother need never know of this. "How could we do it?" she asked.

"It's easy. There's a life line and a love line, and a whole lot of ridges for children." Eddie sounded very confident.

"Where did you learn all this?" Foxy asked.

"I got interested in it through a friend," he said.

"Is that your pen friend?" Leo asked. He nodded.

A wave of jealousy flooded over Nessa. How did Leo know everything about everyone else and hardly anything about Nessa, who was meant to be her best friend.

"If we're going to do it, let's do it." Nessa spoke sharply.

They crossed the bridge into Shancarrig and walked along past the cottages up toward the Old Rock.

No one needed to lead the way or decide where they were going. Once anything of importance had to be done, it was always at the Old Rock.

Eddie showed them their life lines. Everyone seemed to have a long one.

"How many years to the inch, do you think?" Foxy asked.

"I don't know," Eddie admitted.

"Lots, I'd say." Maura wanted to believe the best.

"Now. This is the heart line." These varied. Nessa's seemed to have a break in hers.

"That means you'll have two loves," Eddie explained.

"Or maybe love the same person twice. You know. Get your heart broken in the middle and then he'd come back to you," Maura suggested.

"I might break *his* heart, whoever he is." Nessa tossed her head.

"Yeah, sure. It doesn't say. Back to the lines." Eddie moved away from troubled waters.

Foxy's heart line was faint.

So was Leo's. "Is that good or bad?" Leo asked.

"It's good." Foxy was firm. "It means that neither of us will have much romance until it's time for us to marry each other."

They all laughed.

Eddie moved to children. You'd know how many you were going to have by the number of tiny lines that went sideways at the base of your little finger. Maura was going to have six. She giggled. She'd be like her mother, she said, not knowing when to stop. Leo was going to have two. So was Foxy. He nodded approvingly. Eddie and Niall didn't look as if they were going to have any. They kept searching their hands and uttering great mock wails of despair.

Nessa had three little lines.

"That's three fine little Ryans to bring into the hotel with you," Foxy said approvingly. He had already pointed out to Leo that they each had a matching score of two on their hands.

"Not Ryans," Nessa corrected him sharply. "They'll be my husband's name."

"Yeah, but if you're anything like your ma they'll be thought of as Ryans," Foxy said.

Nessa wouldn't let him see how annoyed she was. She fought back the tears of rage at his mockery.

"Don't let him upset you," Leo said. "Let it roll off."

"It's all right for you. You don't care about your family," Nessa snapped.

The others were still counting their future children. Leo and Nessa sat apart.

Although Nessa's eyes were bright, she would not allow herself to cry. She felt she had to keep talking, it might stop her starting to weep. "If anyone says anything about your mother or father, Leo Murphy, you just laugh."

"It wouldn't matter *what* they say, Nessa you eejit. It's only important if it upsets you, otherwise it's just words floating around in the air."

Leo had lost interest as usual.

She went off to join the others, who had discovered the line in your hand that meant money. It looked as if the only one who would have any wealth to speak of was Maura Brennan from the cottages, the least likely one of them all.

Nessa didn't wait around to hear how her own future was mapped out in terms of wealth. Maybe Foxy would make some joke about her father's love of horses and greyhounds. It was so unfair, she raged. You couldn't answer back. You couldn't say that Foxy Dunne's father was even barred from Johnny Finn's, which meant he must have done something spectacular in terms of drunkenness.

Nor could you say that Foxy had one brother in jail, and one who had got on the boat to England an hour ahead of the posse before *he* was in jail too. It seemed that by being so really desperate Foxy's family had put themselves above being spoken badly of.

And yet she got annoyed at home when her mother would say those very things about the Dunnes. She found herself defending her friends in her home and defending her family when she was with her friends.

She couldn't bear it when Maura Brennan wiped her nose on

her sleeve, because she knew her mother would sigh and shake her head.

But it was just as bad and even worse if Eddie and Niall were around when her mother would speak sharply to Dad, and tell him to clear the papers away, put on his jacket, and make some pretense of running a hotel. She had seen them exchange glances once or twice at her mother's sharpness of tongue.

She longed to explain that it was needed, that Dad would sit there forever telling long pedigrees of dogs and horses in far-away racetracks, while people waited to be served. She wished they knew that her father didn't take offense like other men might.

Nessa wanted her friends to be interested in tales she told about what her parents discussed over supper at home, but no one could care less. She wanted her mother and father to listen to stories about Foxy being mad enough to fancy Leo, without sniffing and saying something dismissive about both of them.

Up to now, she had felt safe in her family. It was one of the many bad things about growing up that you began to feel it wasn't as safe as it used to be.

A few days after the end of term the convent where Nessa would go to school sent a message saying that they would like to see the new pupils in advance.

"We'll dress you up smartly. It's important to make a good impression," her mother said.

"But they're not going to refuse me, are they?"

"Will you ever learn? You want them to treat you as someone important, then *look* like someone important."

"They're nuns, Mam. They don't look at things in that snobby way."

"They don't, my foot." Her mother was adamant.

They had a good outing. Leo went in her ordinary clothes, she hadn't dressed up at all.

"She doesn't need to," Nessa's mother had said when they saw Leo arriving in her ordinary pink cotton frock, with its faded flower pattern and frayed collar.

"Why?"

"Because she is who she is."

It was a mystery.

Leo was in great form that day, she and Nessa laughed and giggled at everything. They laughed all the more because they had to keep such solemn faces in the convent.

The corridors were long and smelled of floor polish. Little red lights burned in front of statues and pictures of the Sacred Heart, little blue lights in front of Our Lady.

Mother Dorothy, the Principal, spoke to them very earnestly about the need to behave well in school uniform. She told them that it would all be very very different from Shancarrig. She made Shancarrig sound as if it were on the back of the moon.

"Are you two great friends?" Mother Dorothy asked.

"Everyone's friends in our school." Leo shrugged.

The nun's bright eyes seemed to take it all in.

Leo was all for exploring the town.

"We'd better go back," Nessa said. "They'll be wondering where we are."

Leo looked at her in surprise. "We're nearly fifteen, we've gone to see the convent where we are going to be imprisoned for the next three years. What can they be worried about?" she asked.

"They'll find something," Nessa said.

"You're a scream." Leo was affectionate.

And then, about three weeks later, Leo became almost a different person as far as Nessa was concerned. She was never around, and seemed unwilling to stir from The Glen at all. She'd gone off mysteriously for a holiday with her mother and father and the two great stupid dogs without even telling anyone where she was going.

The summer was endless. There was nobody to play with. Maura Brennan had gone around asking everyone could she be a maid in their house, and eventually Nessa's mother had given her a job, as a chambermaid in the hotel. Maura slept in, which was stupid because it was only ten minutes walk to the cottages. But then again, Mother had said would Maura want to sleep in that place, and would you want to have her sleeping there?

Eddie Barton was lost in his old pressed flowers, and writing letters. Niall Hayes was complaining all the time about the school he was going to start in next September. He seemed to want reassurance that it was going to be all right.

Nessa wished that Leo was more like Niall, dependent on her, asking for advice. She thought Niall should be more like that tough little girl up in The Glen, able to survive on her own, fight her own battles.

Her mother noticed, like she always did.

"I've told you a dozen times, lead and they'll follow."

"I could lead a thousand miles and Leo would never follow." Nessa wished she hadn't admitted it, but it was out before she knew it. Breda Ryan sighed, she looked disappointed. "I'm sorry, Mam, but it's different for you. You were always a born leader. Some people just have it in them."

Her mother looked at her thoughtfully.

"I've been thinking about your hair," she said unexpectedly.

"Well, don't think about it," Nessa cried. "Don't always think about how everyone else could do things better if only they did them like you."

"Nessa!" Her mother was shocked at the outburst.

"I mean it. I'm nearly grown up. In some countries I could be married and have my own family. *You* always know best. *You* know Dad can't talk about greyhounds. You know that we can't call anyone a fella because you think it's vulgar, we have to say boy or man or something that no one else says."

"I try to give you some manners. Style, that's all."

"No. That's not all. You don't let us be normal. Maura is below us for some reason. Leo Murphy's family is above us because they live in a big house. You're *so* sure of everything, you just *know* you're right." Nessa's face was red and angry.

"What brought this on, may I ask?"

"My hair. I was having an ordinary conversation with you and suddenly you said you wanted to talk to me about my hair.

I don't care *what* you want, I won't do it. I won't do it. I'll go and tell Dad you want me to cut it or dye it or put it in an awful bun like yours. Whatever you want I won't do it."

"Fine, fine . . . if that's the way you feel." Her mother stood up to leave the sitting room.

Nessa was still in a temper. "That's right. You'll go down now to Daddy and frighten him. You'll tell him I'm being so difficult you don't know how to handle me, and then poor Dad will come and plead with me, and ask me to apologize."

"Is that what you think I'm going to do?" Her mother looked distant and surprised.

"It's what you've done for years." She was in so far now, it didn't matter what she said.

"As it happens I was *going* to tell you about your hair. That it never looked better, that you should get a good cut. I was going to suggest that we went to Dublin together and I took you to a good place that I asked about."

"I don't believe you!"

"Well, believe what you like. The address is here on a piece of paper. I was going to say we could go on the cheap excursion on Wednesday. But go on your own."

"How can I go on my own? I've no money."

"I was going to ask your father to give you the money."

"But you're not now. I see. You mean I lost it all by being badly behaved." Nessa gave a mirthless laugh to show she knew the ways of adults.

"Ask him yourself, Nessa. You're too tiresome to talk to anymore."

Nessa didn't ask her father, so he mentioned it on Tuesday night. Why didn't she take the day trip up to Dublin and have a nice haircut. She said she didn't want to go, she said her mother hated her, she said her mother was only making her feel guilty, she said her hair was horrible, that it was like a horse's tail.

She said she wouldn't go to Dublin on her own.

"Take Leo. I'll stand you both," he said.

"You can't, Dad."

"Yes, I can. I make some of the decisions around here."

"No, you don't."

"I do, Nessa. I make the ones I want to." There was something about his voice. She believed him utterly.

Leo went to Dublin with her.

The hairdresser spent ages cutting and styling. "You should come back every three months."

"What about in five years?" Nessa said.

"Don't mind her," Leo interrupted. "She looks so great now, they'll have her up every week."

"Do I really?" Nessa asked.

"Do you really what?"

"Look great? Were you just saying it to be polite to her?"

"But you're terrific-looking. You *must* know that. You're like Jean Simmons or someone." Leo said this as if it was as obvious as the day is from night.

"How would I know? No one ever told me."

"I'm telling you."

"You're just my friend. You could be telling me just to keep me quiet," Nessa complained.

"Ah God, Nessa. You can be very tiresome sometimes," Leo said.

It was the same word as her mother had used. She had better watch it.

It was an up-and-down relationship with her mother all the years that Nessa Ryan went to school every day in the big town.

It was no use talking to Leo because Leo didn't seem to consider her own mother as any part of her life. If Nessa couldn't go to the pictures, it was because her mother wanted her to clean the silver. If Leo couldn't go to the pictures, it was only because Lance and Jessica—the dogs—needed to go for a run, or because her father wanted help with something.

Mrs. Murphy was never mentioned.

Nessa heard that Mrs. Murphy of The Glen was not a strong woman and possibly suffered from her nerves, but this wasn't talked about much in front of children. Leo seemed very distracted, as if there was something wrong at home, but even in the coziest of chats she couldn't be persuaded to talk about it.

And there were so few other people to talk to.

She wasn't encouraged to talk to Maura Brennan who worked as a chambermaid in the hotel. Every time she stopped in a corridor to speak to Maura, Maura looked around nervously.

"No, Nessa. Your mother wouldn't like us to be chatting."

"That's bull, Maura. Anyway, I don't care what she wants."

"I do. It's my bread and butter."

And there was no answer to that.

Sometimes Mrs. Ryan was terrific, like when she got them all dancing lessons—Leo, Nessa and her young sisters Catherine and Nuala, the two Blake girls. It had been the greatest of fun.

Sometimes Mother was horrible—when she had asked Father to leave the bar the night he won eighty-five pounds on a greyhound. "I just didn't want to lose *two hundred* and eighty-five pounds, Nessa," she had explained afterward. "He was going out into the streets looking for greyhounds, or anything that approached them in shape, to buy them drinks."

Nessa had fumed over it. Her father should have been allowed his dignity. He should have had his night of celebration.

Her mother had been wonderful about the record player, and Nessa built up her own collection—"Three Coins in the Fountain," "Rock Around the Clock," "Whatever Will Be, Will Be." But by the time she bought Tab Hunter's "Young Love," her mother had become horrible again, saying that Nessa was now leaving school with a very poor Leaving Certificate.

There was no question of university, no plan for a career, nothing except the usual refuge of those who couldn't think what to do—the secretarial course in the town.

Nessa became very mulish that summer. Several times her father asked her for the sake of peace to try and ensure they had a happy house.

"You're so weak, Daddy," she snapped at him one day. She

was sorry instantly. It was so like something she felt her mother would have said.

"No, I'm not weak actually. I just like a quiet life without the people I love fighting like tinkers, that's all." He spoke mildly.

"Why do you nag me so much?" she asked her mother. "I mean, it's not going to make either of us happier, and it's upsetting Daddy."

"I don't think of it as nagging. I think of it as giving you courage and strength to live your own life. To be full of courage. Honestly." She believed her mother too when she said that.

"Did you always have courage?"

"No I did not. I learned it when I came to this house. When I had to cope with the pair on the wall."

"The what?"

"Your sainted grandparents," her mother said crisply.

Nessa looked up in shock at the elderly Ryans who had always been spoken of with such admiration and respect in this house.

"Why did it need courage to cope with them?" she asked.

"They would have liked your father to live in a glass case and they could have thrown sugar at him," Mrs. Ryan said.

When she said a thing like this she seemed very normal, like someone you could talk to, but she didn't say them often enough.

So, the summer she was eighteen Nessa began her course in shorthand and typewriting with a very bad grace.

Leo Murphy wouldn't come with her, a series of vague and unsatisfactory excuses about being needed up at The Glen. It was a confused time in Shancarrig.

Eddie Barton was so depressed working in Dunne's that he could hardly raise his eyes when you went in to talk to him. Niall Hayes was in Dublin setting up his plans to study law. Foxy was in England on the building sites. The Blake girls were at university in Dublin. She wasn't meant to talk to Maura. Her mother asked so many questions about who she went to the pictures with in the big town, it sometimes seemed hardly worth the whole business of going.

She was ready for something exciting to happen the weekend Richard Hayes came to town.

He was very handsome, not square like Niall. He was tall and slim and very grown up, seven or eight years older than Nessa —twenty-five or twenty-six. He had been sent away from Dublin because of some disgrace with a girl.

Everyone knew that.

He had been banished to Shancarrig. Where apparently there would be no girls. Or no girls worth looking at.

Nessa dressed herself very very carefully until she caught his eye.

"Things *are* looking up," he said. "I'm Richard Hayes."

"Hello, Richard," Nessa said in a voice she had been practicing for weeks.

His smile was warm but it made her nervous. She longed to run away and ask someone for advice, and as it happened at that very moment her mother called for her.

"Now I know your name," he said.

"Only my mother calls me Vanessa," she said.

But she was glad to escape.

Her mother had seen it all. "What a handsome young man," she said.

"Yes." Nessa bit her lip.

"You have absolutely no competition," her mother assured her. "That's a man who likes pretty girls, and you are the prettiest girl in Shancarrig."

··• •··

The next time he met her he suggested that she take him for a walk.

"I'd love to do that but I'm practicing my awful gramma-logues," said Nessa.

"Shorthand is going out of fashion, it'll all be machines soon," he said.

"You may very well be right, but not before I do my certificate exams. So maybe I'll see you later in the evening," she said. She could see by his eyes that she had done the right thing. He was more interested than ever before.

"Absolutely, Vanessa," he said with a mock bow.

She took him for long walks around her country.

She brought him up to the Old Rock and told him all its legends. She brought him to the school and showed him the tree where they had carved their names. She took him to the graveyard and pointed out the oldest tombstones to him. She showed him the children fishing in the river, and explained how you caught little fish with your hands if you could trap them in the stones.

She told him about Mattie the postman, who didn't go to Mass but could deliver any letter to anyone if it just had their name and Shancarrig on it. She brought him to meet Father Gunn and Father Barry, saying that she was being a guide. Mrs. Kennedy, the priests' housekeeper, looked very disapproving so Nessa just laughed and sat up on her table, saying that she had brought Richard Hayes here especially to taste one of Mrs. Kennedy's scones. They were legendary.

Privately she told Richard they were legendary because they were as heavy as stones.

Nessa took Richard Hayes to visit Miss Ross in her cottage, she brought him to Nellie Dunne's shop, she took him to every nook and cranny in about three days.

"It's your introduction," she said to him cheerfully. "So that you'll never say you weren't shown the place properly." She could sense that he was delighted with her, that he thought her a confident, bright young woman.

And indeed, that is what she was.

She was proud of her dark thick hair, her clear skin, her bright yellow and red blouses, and most proud of all that she wasn't silly and giggling like so many others were with him. Her mother had given her this gift, this belief that she was the equal of any Adonis who came to Shancarrig.

But Nessa would not settle for a weaker man like her mother had done. She wouldn't take second best, which was obviously how her mother must regard her father. There would be no dull, plodding, average fellow for Nessa. Not now. Not now that she had seen the admiring glance of a man like Richard.

He was the kind of man who came through a town like this once every fifty years. She was lucky to have caught his eye, she must be absolutely certain not to lose it again. This was the kind of man you could dream about night and day, someone that would occupy all your thoughts. But for some reason she didn't really allow herself to think about what she felt for him, this charming attentive Richard Hayes, who seemed to want to spend every free minute he had in her company. Yes of course she wanted to think that he really liked her, but some warning voice made her think that she could only keep his attention if she didn't seem to care.

It was an act.

Life shouldn't be an act. Yet she felt that they were unequal somehow. She must play this one very carefully.

Of course, she heard a lot of stories about why he had come to help his uncle Bill in the office. Some people said that Mr. Hayes was getting too busy to manage on his own and that he had little hopes of his son Niall ever learning enough about the business. Niall was off to university in Dublin where he would serve his time in a solicitor's office as well. It would be four or five years before he'd qualify—old Bill Hayes was quite right to take this bright young man into his firm.

There were others who said that Richard had been sent to Shancarrig to cool his heels—there had been talk of an incident in Dublin, an incident involving a judge's daughter. There was another story about a broken engagement and a breach of promise action settled at the last moment.

In the stories Richard Hayes, cousin of the solid Niall, was always shown as a playboy.

The feeling was that Shancarrig would be very small potatoes indeed for someone who had seen and done as much as this handsome young man of twenty-five or so who had taken the place by storm.

"Isn't he fantastic?" Leo had said when she saw him for the first time.

"He's very easy to talk to." Nessa was quick to let her best friend know just how far she was ahead in the race which every woman in Shancarrig seemed to have joined.

"I wish he'd come into the bar more," Nessa's mother said. "He's such an attractive kind of fellow he'd be a great draw."

"I'd say that boyo has been asked to leave more bars than a few," Conor Ryan said with the voice of a man who has seen it all and knew it all.

Unexpectedly Gerry O'Sullivan, their personable young barman, agreed.

"Real ladykiller," he said. "The kind they'd go for each others' throats over."

"That's what we don't need," Mrs. Ryan said firmly. "Maybe it's just as well he's not in here every night."

"Who is there in Shancarrig that would cut anyone's throat over a fellow. There's not that kind of passion and spark around the place at all." Conor Ryan was back reading the forecasts for race meetings in towns he would never visit, on courses he would never walk.

Breda Ryan looked thoughtfully out at the front desk where Nessa was painstakingly practicing her typing. They were meant to do an hour a day of homework, and she had covered up the keys of the hotel machine with adhesive tape so that she couldn't see the letters.

Nessa's hair was shiny, her eyes were bright, her neckline low. They didn't have to look far for any passion and spark as far as Richard Hayes was concerned.

Nessa fought off three attempts by her mother to talk about sex.

"I *know* all that, didn't you tell me that years ago when I got my periods first."

"It's a different kind of telling now, there are other things to be taken into consideration . . . please, Nessa."

"There are no other things, I don't want to talk about it." She wriggled away.

She didn't want to hear her mother say anything coarse or frightening. She was terrified enough already. These were problems that no mother could solve.

Richard Hayes told Nessa that she was beautiful. He called into the hotel and sat up on the reception desk to talk to her. It was the middle of the afternoon, a time when hotel business was slack and when Richard very probably should have been in his uncle's office.

He told Nessa that she had wonderful dark looks and she reminded him of Diana the huntress.

"Was she good or bad?"

"She was beautiful. Don't you know about her?"

"No, the nuns sort of dwelt more on the New Testament. She was the one that was extremely chaste, wasn't she?"

"That's her story and she's sticking to it." He laughed, and she reddened. It seemed to her that he was eyeing her as if he was thinking along those lines himself.

He stroked her cheek thoughtfully.

"What happens if a girl is less than extremely chaste here?" he asked.

"They go to their grannies or to England." She hoped that her cheeks didn't still look so red. It was just that he was looking at her breasts and appreciating her in a way that a man might if he wanted to make love.

Or maybe she was just fancying it. Nessa didn't know these days if anything was real or whether she was imagining a whole series of looks and gestures and feelings that didn't exist at all.

"I'd be very careful if we were . . . to do anything that might cause a trip to your granny's," he said. "You know, really careful. There would be no danger at all."

From somewhere she found a confident answer.

"Ah but there wouldn't be any question of that, Richard," she said.

He was more interested than ever.

"Are you afraid?"

"No. There could be other reasons why people might say no to you."

"But you do like me, that I know." He was playful.

"But do I *love* you, and do you love *me*? That's what you'd have to ask yourself before going wherever people go."

"Like up to the Old Rock?"

He had only been in Shancarrig ten days and already he knew where the lovers went. To the little hollow in Barna Woods where the road to the Old Rock began.

"If only we knew what love is, Vanessa Mary Ryan, then we could rule the world." He sighed a heavy mock sigh.

"And would we rule it well, Richard Aloysius Hayes?" she laughed.

"How did you know that?"

"I asked Niall what the RAH stood for on your tennis bag."

"And he told you? The swine!"

They were fencing now, and laughing. He caught her by the wrist.

"I'm not joking, you're the loveliest girl for miles around."

"You haven't seen any others."

"Excuse me but I have. I went on a tour of inspection, brought my tennis bag up to The Glen, got no game, and no great joy out of your so-called best friend, little bag of nerves with a frizzy head she is."

"Don't speak like that about Leo."

"And I studied Madeleine Ross."

"She's ancient."

"She's three years older than I am. And let me see who else. Pretty little Maura Brennan who works in Ryan's Ritz, but I think she's been to the Old Rock with a young Mr. O'Sullivan. We'll have wedding bells there if I'm not greatly mistaken."

"Maura? Pregnant! I don't believe it."

He held up his hands defensively.

"I could be wrong," he said.

"She's a fool. Gerry O'Sullivan will never marry her . . ." Nessa had let it slip out.

"Aha . . . so it's not just a question of loving each other. It's a question of the chap marrying the girl is it?"

Nessa had lost that one. "I must be off," she said.

She barely made it upstairs on shaking legs and went into her room. There she found her sisters Catherine and Nuala starting up guiltily from the dressing table where they had been reading her diary.

"I thought you were meant to be at the reception desk," Catherine said, flying immediately to the attack.

"We hadn't read anything private really," begged Nuala, who was younger and more frightened.

Frightened she had reason to be.

Nessa Ryan, eighteen and desired by the most handsome man in Ireland, drew herself up to her full height.

"You can explain all that later," she said, taking the key out of the inside of the door. "I'm locking you in until I find Mother."

"Don't tell Mam," roared Nuala.

"Mam won't like what you've been up to," Catherine threatened.

But Nessa had the upper hand. She had written nothing in her diary, it was all in the back of her shorthand notebook which never left her side.

She had been coming up to write more, to tell herself of the passion in his voice, the tingles she had felt when he held her wrist, how he had said that he could love her.

She ignored the pleas and lamentations from her room and set off to find her mother.

In the corridor she met Maura Brennan carrying sheets.

"Is everything all right, Maura?" she asked.

"Why do you ask?"

"Well, I don't know. You look different."

"I *am* different. I'm getting married next week to Gerry. I haven't told everyone else. It was only just arranged."

"Married?"

"I know. Isn't it great!"

Nessa was dumbfounded. Perhaps there was a different set of rules, perhaps fellows *did* marry you if you went to the Old Rock with them. Maybe her mother and the nuns and Catholic Truth Society pamphlets had it all wrong. She pulled herself together.

"That's great, Maura," she said. "Congratulations."

Nessa found her mother, and told her of the two criminals locked in the bedroom.

"Give them a very bad punishment," she ordered.

"Did they find anything to read, anything they shouldn't have?" Her mother's eyes were anxious.

"If I have to say to you once more that there is nothing to find, nothing to discuss, I will go *mad*." The words were almost shouted.

To her surprise her mother looked at her admiringly.

"You know I think Richard may be good for you after all. You're getting to be confident at last. You'll be a leader yet."

It was true. She did feel more in control. She was delighted to find that her mother took such a strong stand with Catherine and Nuala. And so, unexpectedly, did her father.

"A person must be allowed to have their private life and their dreams," he told the two sulking girls, who were allowed no outings for a week. "It's a monstrous thing to invade someone's life of dreams."

"There was nothing there," Catherine said.

"To say that is making it worse still."

The two girls were startled.

There was Nessa, usually the one in trouble, Nessa who had been making calf's eyes at Niall Hayes's cousin, and all she was getting was praise for doing something as dangerous as locking them in a bedroom.

"Suppose there had been a fire?" Catherine even suggested it as a possibility.

She got little support.

"Then you would have burned to death," said their mother.

Eddie Barton came in sometimes for a chat.

"Are you seeing Richard Hayes?" he asked Nessa.

"How do you mean?"

"I don't know. Are you?"

"No I'm not. He comes in and out. He's very handsome, probably too handsome for me."

"I know what you mean," Eddie said unflatteringly.

"Thanks a lot, friend."

"No, I didn't mean that. You're fine-looking and you've got much better-looking than when we were all young, honestly . . ." Eddie was flustered now and he saw he was making gestures to show how much better-looking Nessa had got. Gestures that indicated a bosom and a small waist. But she didn't seem offended. "Looks are important, aren't they?" He seemed anxious.

"I suppose so, though people keep saying they're not."

Eddie was running his hand through his spiky hair. "I wish fellows improved, all fellows, like all girls seem to."

"Aren't you a grand-looking fellow, Eddie?" Her voice was encouraging and light she thought.

"Don't make fun of me." His face was red.

"I'm not."

"Yes you are. I've hair like God knows what, I'm pushing a brush around bloody Dunne's all day. Who'd look at me?"

He banged out of the hotel leaving Nessa mystified. As far as she knew, Eddie had never asked any girl in Shancarrig out, and had shown no interest at all in any of the females around the place. He did come in from time to time to make mysterious phone calls to Scotland. It was too hard to understand, and anyway she had far more important things on her mind.

••• •••

Richard took Nessa to the pictures in the town in his uncle's car.

"He lets you drive this?"

"He doesn't go out at night."

"Niall never drove it."

"Niall never asked."

Niall Hayes was staying with a school friend of his. Together they were going to a three-week course in bookkeeping. They hated it. Niall had sent several letters and postcards to Nessa saying how dreary it was. He hoped university would be better.

"I think Niall fancies you desperately," Richard said as he kissed Nessa in his uncle's car.

She drew away.

"I don't think so," she said, cool, ungiggly. Her mother was right. She had grown up a lot since Richard had come to Shancarrig.

"Oh I think he does. Doesn't he take you to the pictures? Doesn't Niall plan journeys to the Old Rock with you like I do?" He repeated his own words about his younger cousin.

"Niall never asked," said Nessa.

"Niall will be back tomorrow Ethel was telling me," Mrs. Ryan said to Nessa.

"That should shake the town to its foundations," Nessa said.

"You and he were always good friends." Her mother's voice was mild so Nessa became contrite.

"That's true, we were. He's got very mopey though, Mam. Not easy to talk to."

"Everyone doesn't have the charm of his cousin Richard."

"Richard's normal. He's nice to people, he's pleasant. He's not always grousing and groaning about things the way Niall is."

"Maybe Niall has something to grouse and groan about."

"What? What any more than the rest of us?"

"Well, his best girl is starry-eyed about his cousin, his place in the firm isn't nearly as secure as it used to be . . . *and* he doesn't have a wonderful understanding mother like you do. He has dreary old Ethel."

They laughed as they sometimes could nowadays like sisters, like friends.

"What would *you* do for Niall if you were his friend?" Nessa asked. She thought she saw her mother watching her very carefully, but she couldn't be sure.

"I'd encourage him to fight for his place over there. He's Bill's son. It's *his* business. I'd tell him that there are only a few chances and you should take them. Oh, I suppose I'd go on a bit about letting grass grow under your feet."

"He mightn't listen to me."

"No. People often don't listen when others are out for their good."

"Did Dad listen to you?"

"Ah, yes. But that was different, I loved your father. Still do."

"I don't *love* Niall, but I am very fond of him."

"Then don't let him get walked on," said Breda Ryan.

Nessa invited Niall to come over to the hotel and have a drink with her. It felt very grown up.

"You look great," he said.

"Thanks, Niall. You look fine too."

"I meant *pretty* like . . ." he said.

"What work are you doing in the office?" She changed the subject.

"Filing! Taking things out of torn envelopes and putting them into nontorn envelopes. God, Dinny Dunne could do that on one of his good days."

Niall was full of misery and Nessa was full of impatience. Why hadn't he the fire to get up and go, the sheer charm of his cousin. They were the sons of brothers after all. Richard's father must have been the one with the spirit.

Richard had told his uncle that a younger man should go around on home visits, which meant that he had the use of the car and could be out all day. Who knew how long it took to make a will or to get the details in a right-of-way claim. Who could measure how many hours it might involve talking to a publican about the extinguishing of a license or to a woman about a marriage settlement involving a farm.

Richard was sunny and cheerful to everyone.

If he had been asked to do the files, he would have made it into the most prestigious job in the office. Why could Niall not see this? Why did he hunch his shoulders and look defeated? Why didn't he throw back his head and laugh?

"Did you see much of Richard while I was away?" Niall asked, cutting across her thoughts.

"He's been around, he's been very lively."

"He's not reliable, of course," Niall said.

"Don't be such a telltale, Niall." Her lightness of voice hid her annoyance. She wanted to hear nothing that would puncture her idea of Richard Hayes, no silly family story of shame or disgrace.

"It's just that you should know."

"Oh, I know all about him," she said airily.

"You do?" Niall seemed relieved.

"A girl in every town. We even had that Judy down from Dublin last week. No, there are no secrets."

"Judy was here? After all that happened!"

"Right in front of your house. Dropped him off from a real posh car."

"There'll be hell to pay if anyone knows that. She was the one."

"The one?"

"The one that had the . . . the one who got into . . . the one."

"Oh yes, I supposed she was." Nessa's heart was leaden. Niall didn't have to finish any of his sentences. The stories had gone before, the judge's daughter who was reported to have been pregnant.

Imagine her coming down to Shancarrig, pursuing Richard after all that.

She must be pretty desperate.

"So that's all right." Niall looked at Nessa protectively, as if he was relieved that he didn't have to rescue her from a quagmire of misunderstanding.

"We're all fine here, it was a lovely summer. *You* sound as if you had a terrible time." She led him into a further catalogue of his woes so that she could follow her own line of thought. Surely Richard couldn't still be involved with this girl. Then, of course, it was known that this girl, unlike Nessa, would go to bed with him. And had.

Is this all he wanted? Surely he wanted other things—fun and chat, and kissing, and a girl who was seven years younger than him who looked like Diana the huntress?

If only there was someone to ask. But there was no one.

••• •••

On Maura Brennan's wedding day Leo suggested they go to the church.

"Maura won't like it. She doesn't want to mix because of working in the hotel."

"That's pure rubbish," Leo said. "It's just your mother who doesn't want her to mix. Let's go."

As they sat waiting for the sad little ceremony to begin Nessa was pleased to see Niall Hayes and Eddie Barton come in as well.

"I got an hour off from the desperate Dunnes," Eddie whispered—he worked for the more respectable branch of the family in Foxy's uncle's hardware shop. He seemed very miserable about it.

"I'm allowed out from sticking labels on envelopes," Niall said.

"I'm meant to be at the typing course but I told my mother we had a day off. I'm watched like a hawk," Nessa complained.

"We weren't the most successful class ever to come out of Shancarrig School, were we?" asked Leo with a little laugh.

"Well, at least the rest of us—" Nessa stopped. She remembered before that Leo had looked very upset when she had been referred to as a lady of leisure.

Leo flashed her a smile of gratitude. They sat in supportive silence, the four of them, as they watched their school friend Maura, pregnant and happy, marry Gerry O'Sullivan, small, handsome with one best man but no other friend or family in the church.

"He doesn't look very reliable," whispered Niall.

"Jesus, Mary, and Holy Saint Joseph who do you think *is* reliable these days?" Nessa hissed.

"*I* am, for what it's worth." He looked at her and suddenly she saw that he did like her, much more than in the sort of hangdog dependent way she had thought. Niall Hayes was keen on her. It didn't give her the kind of boost that she had thought it might. In the days when nobody fancied her she would have loved to have a few notches on her gun, affections to play with, hearts to break.

But Niall was too much of a friend for that.

"Thank you," she said very simply in a whisper.

Maura was delighted with the present they bought her, a little glass-fronted cabinet. Leo had remembered Maura saying that she would love to collect treasures and display them in a cabinet. There were tears of joy in her eyes when they delivered it to the cottage where she would be living—only a stone's throw from where her father still fell home drunk every night.

"You're great friends," she said, her voice choked.

Nessa felt a blanket of guilt almost suffocate her. For years Maura had been working in Ryan's Hotel and hardly a sentence exchanged between them. If only she had the courage of a Leo Murphy, she would have taken no heed of offending her mother, of crossing boundaries of familiarity between staff and owners.

But she *did* have courage these days and she would show it, use it. When she got back to the hotel her mother asked where the festivities were going to be held.

"You know that it will be a few drinks in Johnny Finn's and whatever bit of cold chicken poor Maura managed to put out on plates for those that will drag themselves back to her cottage for it."

"Well, she should have thought of all that . . ." her mother began.

"No she shouldn't, she should be having a reception here by right. She was my school friend, she and Gerry both work here. Anyone with a bit of decency would have given them that at least."

Breda Ryan was taken aback.

"You don't understand . . ."

"I don't like what I do understand. It's so snobby, so ludicrous. Does it make us better people to be seen to be superior to Maura Brennan from the cottages? Is this what you always wanted, a place on some kind of ladder?"

"No. That's not what I always wanted." Her mother was calm and didn't show the expected anger at being shouted at in the front hall of the hotel.

"Well, what did you want, then?"

"I'll tell you if you take that puss off your face . . . and stop shouting like a fishwife. Come on." Her mother was talking to her like an equal. They walked into the bar. "Conor, why don't you take a fiver from the till and go up to Johnny Finn's to buy a few drinks for Gerry and Maura?"

Nessa's father looked up pleased.

"Didn't I only suggest . . . ?"

"And you were right. Go on now while they're still sober enough to know you're treating them. Nessa and I'll look after the bar."

They watched as Conor Ryan moved eagerly across to the festivities, hardly daring to believe his good luck. Nessa sat still and waited to be told. Mrs. Ryan poured two small glasses of cream sherry, something that had never happened before. Nessa decided to make no comment, she raised the glass to her lips as if she and her mother had been knocking back drinks for years.

"People want things at different times. I wanted a man called Teddy Burke. I wanted him from the moment I saw him when I was sixteen until I was twenty-one. Five long years." Nessa looked at this stranger sipping the sherry, she was afraid to speak. "Teddy Burke had a word for everyone, but that's all it was . . . a word . . . I thought it was more. I thought I was special. I built a life of dreams on it. I couldn't eat. I lost my health and my looks, such as they were. They sent me away to do a Domestic Science course.

"Do you know, I can't really remember those years. I suppose

I must have followed the course—I got my exams and certificates—but I only thought of Teddy Burke." She paused for such a long time that Nessa felt able to speak.

She spoke as a friend, as an equal. "And did he know, did he have any idea . . . ?"

"I don't think so, truly. He was so used to everyone admiring, I was just one more." Her mother's eyes were far away as she sat there in the empty hotel bar, her dark hair back on a loose coil with a mother-of-pearl clasp on it. Her pale pink blouse had its neat collar out over her dark pink cardigan—she looked every inch the successful businesswoman. This story of a thin frightened girl loving a man for five years—a man who didn't know she existed—was hard to believe.

"So anyway, one day I was told that Teddy Burke was going to marry Annie Lynch, the plainest girl for three parishes, with a bad temper and a cast in her eye. Everything changed. He was marrying her for her land, for her great acres running down to the lakes and over green valleys, for the fishing rights for the stock. A man as handsome and loving as Teddy Burke could trade everything for land.

"It made me wonder what I really wanted.

"And I went to a cousin's wedding and met your father and I decided that I wanted to go far from where I lived, where I would remember Teddy Burke's laugh and his way with people. I decided that I wanted to make your father strong and confident like Teddy was when he got the land, like Annie Lynch always was because she had the land . . . I put my mind to it."

There was a long silence. Nessa was taking it in.

"Were you ever sorry?"

"Not a day, not once I decided. And hasn't it turned out well? The hotel has survived, the pair out in the pictures in the hall would have let it run into the ground, and they'd have let your father go off to the British Army."

"Why are you telling me this now?"

"Because you thought that all I wanted was to put ourselves

above other people. I may have done that by accident but it wasn't what I set out to do."

"Does Dad know about Teddy Burke?"

"There was nothing for him to know but a young girl's silliness and dreams."

Mattie came in, his sack of letters delivered.

"This town is going to hell, Mrs. Ryan," he said. "A wedding party bawling "Bless This House" above in Johnny Finn's and the women of the house sipping sherry in Ryan's."

"And no one to pour a pint for the postman," laughed Nessa's mother.

The moment was over, it might never come again.

Nessa began to look at other people in a new light after this. Perhaps everyone had a huge love in their life, or something they thought was a huge love. Maybe Mr. Kelly up at the school had fancied a nightclub singer before he settled for Mrs. Kelly. Maybe Nellie Dunne had once been head over heels in love with some traveling salesman that had come many years ago to Ryan's Commercial Hotel, but who had married someone else. Maybe one of those old men in the Commercial Room had been Nellie's heart's desire.

It wasn't so impossible.

Look at Eddie Barton, falling in love with someone in Scotland. It had never been exactly clear how he had got in touch with her in the first place, but apparently he had been writing to Christine Taylor for ages, and phoning her from the hotel.

And then she had arrived over and was living with his mother. Nessa was amazed at the change in Eddie. He was speaking to the Dunnes, cousins of Foxy, as if he was their equal. He was in the hotel with Christine discussing improvements and ways to decorate the bedrooms.

Love did extraordinary things to people.

There was a picture of Richard Hayes at the races in the paper that week, with a girl on his arm. Eileen Blake from The Terrace said that she was stopping for a coffee in Portlaoise on her way back from Dublin and who was there but Richard Hayes and a girl, and they were booking in. As man and wife.

Young Maria Kelly from Shancarrig schoolhouse was reported to have been at a dance with him in the big town, but her parents didn't know because she had climbed in and out her window through the branches of the old copper beech tree that grew in the yard.

Nessa Ryan heard all these facts in the space of three days. She came across them accidentally, they were not brought in as deliberate bad news to her door.

She felt—not as she had feared she might—no sense of cold betrayal, no rage that a man should tell her she was special and he wanted her to be his girl, and yet behave the same way with half the country. Very clearly and deliberately she felt her infatuation with him end. Perhaps she *was* her mother's daughter much more than she had ever believed. She was not ready to give him up, but she would have him in her life under different terms.

Richard came into the Commercial Room of the hotel. There were no travelers staying and so Nessa was using the room to do her shorthand homework.

"I have to go into town tomorrow. I could pick you up outside your college," he offered.

She could imagine the eyes of her classmates when Richard Hayes leaned across to open the door of the car for her.

"And where would we go then?" she asked.

"I'm sure we'd find somewhere," he said.

Nessa looked back into the bar where her mother and father were standing, well out of earshot.

"They're not listening." Richard was impatient. But that wasn't what concerned Nessa. She looked at them and saw her mother stroke Dad's face gently, lovingly.

She saw that it really never mattered who talked to the men from the brewery, the biscuit salesmen, who hired or fired the barmen. It wasn't important that Sergeant Keane dealt with her mother over the licensing laws, not her father. Mother had forgotten Teddy whatever he was, he'd have been no good to her.

She had found what she really wanted, someone she could share her own strength with. Nessa saw for the first time that her mother had got what she wanted. It wasn't a case of settling for second best.

And with a shock of recognition she felt that she was going to follow exactly the same path. It wouldn't be a question of aiming high and searching for fireworks. There might be an entirely different way to live your life. Unbidden, Niall's worried face came to mind. She longed to calm him and tell him it would all be all right.

She looked straight at Richard, right into his eyes.

"No thanks," she said. "No to everything. Thank you all the same."

It wasn't at all easy to do.

But she would not live in fear of him and how he would react. Nothing was worth that.

"Well, well, well." He looked around the room scornfully. "So *this* is all you are ever going to amount to. A second-rate shabby hotel . . . a grown woman still a prisoner to her mother." He looked very angry and put out. People didn't usually speak to Richard Hayes like this. Girls certainly didn't.

Nessa was furious.

"It is *not* a shabby hotel. It's my home. *My* home. I live here and I choose to live here. You can't even live where you want to because they run you out of town. Don't come down here and start criticizing us. It doesn't sit well on you. And answer me one thing, how would I amount to any more if I were to go off to the glen with you and roll around for five minutes on the ground?"

"It would be longer than five minutes," he said mischievously. She hadn't lost him. He fancied her all the more because she was refusing him.

What a wonderful power.

It was the making of Nessa Ryan.

She didn't flirt with him like every other woman within a

hundred-mile radius seemed to. She did not want to be known as his girl.

It was as if she had turned around the relationship, made it businesslike, affectionate but in no way exclusive. She teased him about his latest conquests, real and supposed, she knew that her very lack of jealousy was driving him wild. She was happy in the knowledge that he desired her. When she met him it was always with other people.

She finished her course at the college and went to work full-time for her mother and father.

It was she who decided to lift the hotel onto a higher level. She contacted the Tourist Board about grants, and organized that they got money advanced to improve their facilities. She asked visiting Americans to write letters to their local papers praising Ryan's so as to get them further custom.

She told her mother to drop the word *Commercial* from the title.

"Ryan's makes it sound like a pub," her mother complained.

"Call it Ryan's Shancarrig Hotel," said Nessa.

A few eyebrows were raised. Nellie Dunne presided over several conversations about the Ryans having notions.

"That young one is the cut of her mother," said Nellie. "I remember when Breda O'Connor came in and took the whole establishment from Conor's mother and father. That Nessa will do the same."

But Nessa Ryan showed no signs of friction with her mother and father. She would laugh with her mother about the sainted grandparents who glared from the picture on the wall. She told her father that he looked handsome in a jacket and begged him to have nice framed pictures of racehorses on the wall, so that they might attract a few of the horsey set and give some legitimacy to her father's constant topic of conversation.

Catherine and Nuala were mystified by her. The most handsome man around seemed to be waiting on their sister Nessa and she barely gave him the time of day. They watched uncomprehending as Nessa became more and more attractive-looking, her dark shiny hair always loose and cut with a fringe. A style that owed nothing to the hairdresser but a lot to a picture in a book she had seen, a picture of Diana the huntress.

Nessa got on well with her mother. The two of them often drove to Dublin to look for fittings and fabrics. At an early age she seemed to have their trust, and to be allowed a lot of freedom that was later denied to the more spirited Catherine and Nuala.

"Why can't we go to Galway on our own? Nessa did." Catherine complained.

"Because you're both so unreliable and untrustworthy you'd probably go under a hedge with the first pair of tinker boys you met," Nessa said cheerfully to them. They felt it a great betrayal, there should be *some* solidarity between sisters. Imagine mentioning going under hedges in front of their mother, putting ideas in her mind.

"I have no solidarity with you," Nessa said. "You steal my makeup, you wear my nylons, you spray yourself with *my* perfume. You don't wash the bath, you do nothing to help in the hotel . . . you can't wait to get away from here. . . . *Why* should I help you?"

Put like that it was hard to know why.

"Flesh and blood," Catherine suggested.

"Overrated," Nessa told her.

"Would you try for hotel management do you think?" her mother suggested. "It would teach you so much. There's a great course in Dublin."

"I'm happy here," Nessa said.

"I don't ask you about Richard . . ." her mother began.

"I know, Mother. It's one of the things I love about you." Nessa headed her off before she could start.

She wondered how long would be his exile in Shancarrig, and on Niall's behalf she worried lest he had made too permanent and important a niche for himself with his uncle Bill.

Mr. Hayes came in to drink in Ryan's Shancarrig Bar with Major Murphy, Leo's father, sometimes. Nessa served behind the bar from time to time. She said it helped her to know what the customers wanted. Mr. Hayes dropped no hint of how long his nephew would stay, but to Nessa's distress he showed little enthusiasm about his son's return.

"Hard to know what he learned up there, you couldn't get a word out of him," she heard him say to Dr. Jims Blake one evening. She didn't want to join in the conversation, but later she brought up the subject.

"Niall seems to be enjoying university and studying hard," she said.

"Divil a bit of a sign he gives of either."

"Oh now. All fathers are the same. Still, business is good. There'll be plenty for Niall to take on when he comes back."

"Oh, I don't know. What with Richard . . ." He let his voice trail away.

"But Richard won't be here forever?" Her voice was clear and without guile.

Bill Hayes looked at her directly. "There's something keeping him here. I had a notion it might be yourself?" he said.

"No, Mr. Hayes, I'm not the girl for Richard." There was no playacting, nothing wistful—she seemed to be stating a fact.

"Well, something's keeping him here, Nessa. It's not the pay, and it's not the social life."

"I expect he'll move on one day, like he moved in." Her voice was bland, expressionless.

"I expect so." He sounded troubled.

Niall was home the following week.

"I hear they're giving you a car for your twenty-first birthday," he said to Nessa.

"It's meant to be a surprise, shut up about it," she hissed.

"I didn't know it was a secret. Isn't it great though? A car of your own."

"You could have one too."

"How, might I ask? I'm not the doted-on daughter of the house."

"No, but you're the eldest son of the house, and you never show the slightest interest in your father's business."

"I'm only qualifying as a bloody solicitor, that's all." Niall was offended.

"But what kind of a solicitor? You don't even ask him what's going on. You don't know about the competition."

"Richard, I suppose."

"No, you fool. He's the family, he's on your team. The competition. You know Gerry O'Neill the auctioneer in the town? Well, he has a brother who's taking a lot of the conveyancing, even out this way. They have to fight back."

"I didn't know that."

"You don't ask."

"When I do ask can I help I'm told to tear up files and put labels on envelopes."

"That was three years ago, silly." She put her arm around his shoulder. "Bring your father in here for a pint, treat him as an equal."

"He wouldn't like that."

"I used to be like that, I spent my whole childhood thinking my mother wouldn't like this or that. I was wrong. They want us to have minds of our own."

"No. They want us to be reliable," Niall insisted.

"Yes, well. You and I *are* reliable, so they've got that much. Now they want us to have views, opinions, be out for the common good."

He looked at her with great admiration.

"Have you . . . ?" he began.

She knew he wanted to say something about Richard.

"Yes?" her voice stopped him asking.

"Nothing," Niall said.

"See you and your father tonight."

When Nessa Ryan got her car for her twenty-first birthday she first took her mother and father for a drive around Shancarrig waving to everyone they passed. She caught her mother's eye in the driving mirror more than once and they smiled. Friends. People who understood each other. She was doing the right thing. Thanking them publicly, showing Shancarrig that

Breda O'Connor had come here twenty-two years ago and made a triumph of her life.

It was six o'clock and the Angelus was ringing as she headed back home. People would be coming into Ryan's Shancarrig now for a drink. There would be autumn tourists to check in—the coach buses arrived in the evening.

As they passed Eddie Barton's house Eddie and his Scottish Christine were in the garden. Nessa screeched to a halt.

"I'll come back for you later. I'll pick up Leo, Niall, and Maura and take you all for a spin," she called.

"Just Eddie," Christine said. "So it will be like old times."

"You too."

"No. Thanks, but no."

"She knows what she's doing," Nessa's mother said approvingly.

"Like all women, it seems to me," Conor Ryan said. His sigh was happy, not resigned. Nessa knew this now. Once she thought he was yearning to be free, now she believed that her father had the life he wanted.

Maura wouldn't come, Nessa knew that, but she would love to be asked. She would be so pleased for the car to pull up at her cottage and a group of the nobs, as Mrs. Brennan would call them, to get out and beg her to join them.

But she would stay and mind Michael—her little boy, two and a half years old, a loving child, a Mongol child who never knew his father. Gerry O'Sullivan the handsome barman had been reliable enough to marry Maura, but not reliable enough to stay when the child had been born handicapped.

Nessa ran up the steps of Number 5, The Terrace. The door was never locked.

"Hello, Mr. Hayes. I've come to take your right-hand man out for a drive in my new car," she said.

"Congratulations, Nessa. I heard of the birthday and the car. Richard should be with you in a minute," he said.

"I meant Niall," she answered.

"Oh yes," he said.

"I don't know *why* you're not out playing golf yourself, Mr.

Hayes, with all the help you have in here." She was playful, confident, she knew he liked her. Three years ago she wouldn't have raised her glance to him, let alone her voice.

"Oh my wife wouldn't like that," he said.

Nessa thought of Niall's mother, a solid glum-looking woman, dressed always in browns or olive green. No spark, no life. Mr. Hayes would have been better with a woman like Nessa's mother, or Nessa herself.

Niall had heard her voice. "Did the car arrive?"

"It did. And I've come to drive you off in it." She linked her arm in his and appeared not to notice as Richard arrived out of the other door, straightening his tie and assuming that all the fuss in the hall meant someone had called for him.

Richard Hayes was standing at the top of the steps as Nessa ushered Niall into the front seat.

"Didn't you want . . . ?" Niall began.

"Yeah. I wanted you but I waited till after six not to annoy your father. Let's pick up Eddie."

If Niall had been going to say anything about Richard, he didn't now. He settled back happily in the front seat. Eddie came, on his own. Chris had things to discuss with his mother. They drove up the long drive of The Glen. Leo was at the door waiting to meet them.

"Will I show the car to your parents?" Nessa asked.

"No. No, I'd rather not," Leo said.

Possibly Leo's mother and father might not have been able to afford a car for her. Or maybe her mother wasn't well. Nobody had seen Mrs. Murphy in ages, and Leo's brothers never came home from wherever they were. Biddy their maid was as silent as the grave, as if she were defending the family. Perhaps they had their secrets. Nessa didn't mind.

Not nowadays.

And she was right about Maura. Maura wouldn't come out with them, but she had a cake and they ate it together companionably in her cottage. The glass-fronted cabinet had a few items in it—a spoon in a purple velvet box, a piece of Connemara marble, and one of Eddie's pressed flowers that he had done under glass as a christening present for the baby Michael.

There was a picture of Gerry O'Sullivan in a small frame on the mantelpiece.

"Isn't it great how we all stuck together," said Maura. And they nodded, unable to speak. "All we need is Foxy to come home and we'd be complete."

"He's doing very well," Leo said unexpectedly. "He'll be able to buy the town the way things are going."

"Does he want to buy the town?" Niall asked.

"Well, he'd like to be a person of importance here, that's for certain," Leo said.

"Wouldn't we all?" Niall said.

"You *are*, Niall. You're a solicitor. If ever I have any business I'll bring it to you," Maura said.

They laughed good-naturedly, Maura most of all.

"But remember when we did our fortunes *you* were going to be the one who was going to be wealthy, not Foxy. Maybe you *will* have business," Eddie Barton said. They all remembered the day they left Shancarrig School. It was seven years ago—it seemed a lifetime.

Nessa drove them up to the base of the Old Rock. They left the car and scampered up as they had done so often before.

It was hard to read their faces, but Nessa thought that Eddie's future seemed certain, bound up with the Scottish Chris who had come in some unexplained way into his life.

She knew that Maura would never consider herself unlucky. She would like a better house, maybe she was saving for one— there was no sign of her hard-earned wages in the cottage they had visited.

Leo would always be unfathomable, but it was Niall, good dependable Niall, that Nessa was thinking about today. Leo and Eddie wandered off to stand on the stone where you were meant to be able to view four counties. Sometimes it was easier in this evening light. You could see a steeple that was in one county, a mountain that was in another.

Niall sat beside her, his jacket too small for him, his shirt crumpled. His hair was the same soft brown-black as his cousin Richard's, but jagged and not lying right. His eyes were troubled as he looked at her.

"We'll be very happy, Niall," she said to him, patting his hand.

"I hope you will." His voice was gruff with generosity and wishing her well, and loneliness. She could hear it, as her mother must have heard the eagerness in Conor Ryan's voice all those years ago and coped with it.

"You and I," Nessa said. "We will get married, won't we? You will ask me eventually?"

"Don't make fun of me, Nessa."

"I was never more serious in my life."

"But Richard?"

"What about him?"

"Don't you . . . ?"

"No."

"Well, didn't you . . . ?"

"No."

"I thought that you didn't even *see* me," he said.

"I've always seen you. Since the day you told me my hair was nice, the day we left Shancarrig School."

"I wrote your name on the tree," he said.

"You what?"

"I wrote JNH loves VR, very low down near a root. I did then, and I do now."

"John Niall Hayes, Vanessa Ryan. You never did!"

"Will we go and see it?" he said. "As proof."

They had their first kiss in the sunset on her twenty-first birthday, on the hill that looked down over the town. Nessa knew that there would be a lot of work ahead. She would have to fight the apathy of his glum mother, the refusal to relinquish power by his father. She would have to decide where they would live and how they would live. Richard would move on sooner or later. Possibly sooner, now that this had all been planned.

Over the years she would reassure Niall Hayes that there had never been anything to fear from Richard, he was not a lover, nor even a love. He was someone who came in when she needed it and gave her the surge of confidence that her mother had never been given.

And yet, the reason that she felt so sure had a lot to do with being her mother's daughter.

8

Richard

Richard hated the sight of the Old Rock. It meant that they were back in Shancarrig for their miserable summer holiday. Back in Uncle Bill and Auntie Ethel's dark gloomy house, with the solicitor's office on the ground floor and the living quarters upstairs. Bedrooms with heavy furniture, nothing to see, nothing to do. A one-horse town and a pretty poor horse at that.

For as long as he could remember they had come here for a week in July. All through the war years, or the Emergency as it was called, they had traveled down from Dublin on a train fueled by turf. If the weather was any way bad, the turf was bad and the journey was endless.

Richard's father would walk every night for miles with Uncle Bill. They both carried blackthorn sticks and pointed happily to places they had played when they were children—the gravelly shallows of the River Grane where they had caught their fish, the great Barna Woods which had got so small since they were young, the huge ugly heap of stones they called the Old Rock.

They would stand outside Shancarrig School and marvel at the old copper beech where they had carved their initials in 1914, twin boys aged fourteen, KH and WH—Kevin and William. It made Richard sick to see them so full of happy memories over nothing.

He was a handsome boy and a restless one. He thought this week of enforced idleness in his father's old village a waste of time. Even when he was only eight he had tugged at his mother's skirts and asked if they really needed to go.

"Yes of course we need to go. It's only one week out of fifty-two," his mother had said.

It gave him hope that she didn't like it either. But she wasn't the soft touch on this as she was on other things. She was adamant.

"Your father doesn't ask much from us. Just this one week. We will do it and do it with a good grace."

"But it's so boring, and Aunt Ethel is so awful."

"She's not awful, she's just quiet. Bring something to entertain yourself—books, games."

He noted his mother brought knitting. She usually managed to get two jumpers finished in their week in Shancarrig.

"You're a powerful knitter," Aunt Ethel had said once.

"I love it. It's so restful," his mother had murmured. Richard noticed that she didn't say that she hardly produced the needles and wool at all when she was in Dublin, she regarded Shancarrig as her knitting time—her purgatory on earth.

Uncle Bill's children were all very young, the eldest boy, Niall, was a whole seven years younger than Richard, a child of five when Richard was twelve and looking for company.

By the year 1950 Richard was seventeen. It would be his last holiday in this terrible place.

As he stood at an endless school dedication with bishop and priest and self-important people from around he vowed he would never come back. It made him feel claustrophobic, as if he were being choked.

Richard Hayes was leaving his Jesuit boarding school that year. He would get his Leaving Certificate and Matriculation and go to university to study, not medicine like his father, but law. Next summer he could legitimately be away on some study course or be abroad.

They would never drag him to this village again. Let his sisters come, they seemed perfectly happy to play with the village children and run free. Richard Hayes had done his stint.

There was only one good-looking girl at the ceremony, in a blue and white dress, and a straw hat with the same material around the brim. She was shading her eyes from the sun and listening intently to the speeches. She was slim with a tiny waist and a pretty if pale face.

"Who's that, Uncle Bill?" he asked.

"Madeleine Ross, she's going to be the JAM here."

"The what?"

"Junior Assistant Mistress. Nice girl, a bit under her mother's thumb though."

"She's going to stay here all her life?" Richard was horrified.

"Some of us do that willingly." His uncle sounded huffy.

"Oh I know, Uncle Bill, I meant she seems so young."

"I was young when I decided to come back here to live, all those years ago. If old Dr. Nolan had wanted someone in the practice at that time, then your father would have come back too. It's home, you see."

Richard shuddered at the very thought.

The Dublin Hayeses lived in Waterloo Road, which was ideal for anyone with children at university. Richard was within walking distance of his lectures and, even more useful, within walking distance of all the nighttime activities that went with being a student. The pubs in Leeson Street were literally on his way home, the student dances nearby, the parties in Baggot Street where fellows had flats only a stone's throw away.

Richard Hayes offered to do up the disused basement of his

parents' house so that he could live there. To study, he said. To be out of their way.

His father and mother never heard or saw any sign of anything untoward. They were pleased with their son who was unfailingly charming as he came to sit at their table for supper at six and for weekend lunches. He was always smiling politely as he passed his bag of laundry to Lizzie to wash, and managed to make his own part of the house off limits.

"You've enough to do up here, honestly. I'll keep my own place tidy down below," he had said with his boyish smile. So without anyone realizing it he had got his own little self-contained flat down in the basement. At eighteen years of age he had a freedom undreamed of by other undergraduates.

His parents had no idea that their son brought a series of girlfriends home and that not all of them left before morning. He had posters on his walls, Chianti bottles that had been turned into lamps, colored Indian bedspreads over chairs and sofas and his own bed.

There were never noisy parties with loud songs and crashers. The kind of parties that Richard Hayes gave were usually for two people, and sometimes for four. There were two rooms in his little basement flat, and all you had to do was to leave confidently and authoritatively, as if you had every right to be there.

"Don't slink in and out," Richard warned one girl. "Walk out the gate as if you had been delivering a note in my door. They wouldn't in their wildest dreams believe anything else."

And he was totally correct in his belief that his parents knew nothing of his private life. They told their friends, and Richard's uncle Bill down in Shancarrig, that the law studies seemed to be going very well, and that unlike a lot of young tearaways their son seemed to be a homebird, which was all they could have wanted for him and more.

So it came as a complete shock when shortly before Richard's finals there was the unpleasant business of Olive Kennedy and her parents.

It appeared that Olive was pregnant and that Richard Hayes was to blame.

Richard felt that the scene was like a play, a film of a court case. Nobody seemed to be speaking the truth.

Not Olive, who was crying and saying that she had thought it would be all right because Richard loved her and they were getting married. Not the Kennedy parents, who said their daughter had been ruined. Not his own parents, who kept protesting that their son could never have done anything like this. He lived at home, for heavens' sake, he was under their watchful eye.

Olive made no mention of the many nights she had spent in the basement in Waterloo Road—perhaps she didn't want her family to know that. The location of the conception was not discussed, only the responsibility for it. And what was to be done now. Richard spoke clearly. He was very very sorry. He denied nothing, but he said that he and Olive were far too young to consider marriage. They had never committed themselves to it. He seemed to think that this was all that was needed.

His manner, respectful and firm, won the day. It now became a matter of negotiation, Olive was to go to England and have the child, she would return having given the baby for adoption and resume her studies. Some financial contribution should be expected for this. It was agreed between the fathers.

"Olive, I wouldn't have had this happen for the world," Richard said as they left.

"Thank you, Richard." She lowered her eyes, pleased that he still respected her and loved her even if they were too young to marry.

That was when Richard Hayes, as he let his breath out slowly in relief, began to realize that he must be by some kind of an accident a bit of a ladykiller.

Richard kept his head down and studied hard for months after this event. He invited his parents down to his flat on several occasions so that they could see every sign of a blameless life and a hardworking son.

Bit by bit, without his having to tell any story, they began to see this Olive as a scheming wanton girl who had set out to get their Richard. They began to think he had behaved decently in the face of such temptation.

They watched proudly as he received his parchment, was admitted to practice as a solicitor, and got a job in a first-rate office in Dublin. Even before his first month's salary they gave him money for clothes—he went to a tailor and his real good looks were obvious to everyone he met.

Particularly Judy, one of the apprentices in the office. She was a niece of the senior partner, and the daughter of a judge. She wore the most expensive of twin sets, her string of pearls was real, her handbags and silk scarves came from Paris. They looked a very elegant couple when they were seen together.

But they were rarely seen together because Richard said he wasn't a suitable escort for her. A penniless young solicitor starting off . . .

"You're not penniless, my uncle pays you a fortune . . ." She used to cling to his arm as if she never wanted him out of her sight.

"But we're too young, you and I . . ." he begged, knowing that she found him all the more irresistible the more he protested.

"We could grow up," she said looking at him directly.

So Richard Hayes saw a lot of Judy the judge's daughter, but always in his flat where nobody else saw them.

For three years they lived a hidden life, behaving perfectly correctly to each other in the office, wrapped around each other passionately all night. It amazed him how easily she was able to tell her parents that she was staying with girlfriends.

As she stood in the sunlight bare-bottomed, wearing only the top of his pajamas and frying eggs for their breakfast, he marveled at his luck, that such a beautiful and clever girl should make him her choice in this way.

"Do you love me at all, Richard?" she asked as she turned the eggs in the pan.

He lay back on his bed, luxuriating and waiting for the breakfast that would be brought to him on a tray before they got up and dressed and made their separate ways to the office. He loved the very clandestine nature of it all, the fact that nobody in the office knew.

"What an extraordinary question! Why do you ask?" he said.

"It's always dangerous when people answer questions with another question." She laughed, pretty Judy with the golden hair and the expensive clothes thrown on the floor of his flat.

"No seriously, we loved each other twice last night and once this morning . . . and you ask me an odd thing like that?" He seemed puzzled.

"No, I meant real love."

"That's real love. It seemed pretty real to me."

"I'm pregnant," she said.

"Oh shit," he said.

"I see where we stand." Judy threw the plate of fried eggs into the sink and picked up her clothes.

"Judy wait . . . I didn't mean . . ."

From the bathroom he heard over the running water her voice call back.

"You're so right, you didn't mean it. You didn't mean any bloody word you said."

She was out of the bathroom, dressed and furious. He came toward her.

"Don't touch me. You've said what you wanted to say."

"I've said nothing. We have to talk."

"You've talked. You said 'shit.' That's what you said."

It was awkward in the office. She wouldn't catch his eye or agree to meet. Then she went missing for four days.

At home alone Richard didn't dare to let his thoughts follow the train they were heading down. Was it possible that she could have gone to have an abortion?

In the Dublin of 1958 such things were not unknown. There had been stories, none of them pleasant, of a nurse . . . he headed away from that thought. Judy wouldn't have done that on her own.

But then, had he not shown how he didn't want to be involved? He telephoned her house; when he gave his name to the maid he was told that Judy didn't want to speak to him.

This time there was no carpeting, no council of war as there had been in the case of Olive Kennedy. This time he was told by the senior partner that his position with the firm was now being terminated.

"But why?" Richard cried.

"I think you know." The older man, Judy's uncle, stood up and turned away.

It was the coldest gesture that Richard had ever seen. Now to explain to his parents.

He decided to try to get another job first: to tell his parents that he had decided to change offices. This way it might not appear so bald. He had reckoned without the power of the senior partner, brother of the judge, and the smallness of Dublin legal circles. The word was out about him. He didn't know which word it was, but it must have had something to do with being unreliable, a seducer of young women, someone unwilling to pay for his pleasure.

There were no jobs for Richard Hayes whose record in the law was not so staggering that it would override the other considerations.

He told his parents.

It was not an easy conversation. There were very few solutions, and to his horror he realized that the only one which seemed possible was Shancarrig.

In July of 1958 he installed himself in Number 5, The Terrace. He wandered disconsolately around the village, looking without interest at the church with its notices of upcoming events, like whist drives in aid of some villagers in South America who apparently needed a church . . . just like this one.

He walked hands in pockets across the River Grane and up toward the school where he remembered going to some tedious ceremony years ago. The place hadn't changed at all. Nor had the ill-kept riverbank with its row of shabby dwellings, nor the clumps of trees they so proudly called Barna Woods. He couldn't bear to make the climb he had done so often as a child to the Old Rock. He came home shoulders hunched wearily and crossed the bridge back into the town.

A group of youngsters were playing on the bridge and turned to look at him as he passed. He realized that whatever he did in this village would be under the scrutiny of hundreds of eyes. It was an appalling thought.

Everything about Shancarrig depressed him.

The small fat beady-eyed priest welcoming him, and saying it would be a pleasure to have him in the congregation—what could he mean? And the wraithlike priests' housekeeper with a face like the Queen of Spades—a sour woman called Mrs. Kennedy who looked straight through him and seemed to read his inner soul. She nodded dryly on being introduced, as if to say she knew his type and didn't like it.

His uncle's home offered little joy to him. Although Uncle Bill was a pleasant enough man and an efficient solicitor, he had managed to encumber himself with such a mournful wife. Aunt Ethel saw little to celebrate in the world. And the children were not going to rate high on any ladder of companionship.

Niall was now about eighteen and at an age when he should have been full of the joys of spring, but he appeared disconsolate and without any fire. It didn't occur to Richard that his cousin Niall might merely be lacking in self-confidence; Richard had never known that state. He wondered why the boy didn't ask to borrow his father's Ford which was parked outside The Terrace. That way he could have toured the countryside and found wider horizons. There must be *some* social life for a boy in this place, but Niall had seemingly never found it; he stayed around the house moving between The Terrace and Ryan's Hotel.

Richard looked at the bedroom he had been given—a huge heavy dark mahogany wardrobe which despite its great size found it difficult to hold the suits and coats of the young solicitor down from the city. His aunt Ethel had proudly shown him the hot and cold running water; he had the only room with a handbasin. The bed would never welcome a companion. To maneuver a girl up those stairs past offices, kitchens, sitting rooms, and bedrooms would be a feat that few would undertake. It would be celibacy, or else find someone with a place of their own, which didn't look at all likely in Shancarrig.

There were, of course, pretty children.

Like Nessa from the hotel. He saw the huge interest in her eyes, the eagerness and shyness, the trying to please, the fear she was boring him.

He was not arrogant, he was realistic about this kind of response. If you were nice to girls, if you smiled at them and listened to them and just *liked* them, they opened up like flowers.

He supposed it helped being reasonably good-looking, but he truly thought it was a matter of liking them. Many a man in Dublin who had envied Richard's success had been so anxious for the conquest that he forgot to enjoy the chase. That must be where the secret, if there was a secret, lay.

He spent a lot of time wooing Vanessa Ryan. She was the best in town. He had been on an exploratory mission.

There was Madeleine Ross the schoolteacher, very intense and spiritual, deeply caught up in this attempt to convert some Spanish-named place that apparently meant Shancarrig in Peruvian or whatever. He suspected that she might harbor longings for the rather fey-looking priest, but he was very sure that neither of them had done anything about this hothouse passion if it existed.

There was a tough little girl who came from a falling-down Georgian mansion called The Glen, frizzy hair, good legs, strong face. There was some secret there too. Money maybe, or a mad relative. He had called and been discouraged from calling again.

There were a few others, unsatisfactory.

Nessa with her clear eyes and dark good looks was the only one. To his surprise he didn't wear her down. He must be losing his touch, he thought. His winning Dublin ways didn't work here.

He threatened her that they wouldn't see each other anymore . . . gentle loving threats, of course, but she got the message. . . . She said no.

And continued to say no.

It was a constant irritant to see her across the road in her parents' hotel, growing more attractive and confident by the week. Her dark hair shining as if hung framing her face, she wore clear yellows and reds that set off her coloring. She laughed and joked with the customers, he had even seen American men look at her approvingly.

The years passed slowly.

They were not as bad as he feared his years of exile would be, but still he yearned to be back in Dublin.

Judy came to visit him.

"I'm getting married," she told him.

"Do you love him?" he asked.

"You'd never have asked that question a few years ago. You didn't think love existed."

"I know it exists. I haven't come across it, that's all."

"You will." She was gentle.

"About the baby . . . ?"

"There never was a baby," she said.

"*What?*"

"There never was. I made it up."

The color drained from his face.

"You sent me here, you got me drummed out of Dublin on a lie."

"There *could* have been a child, and your response would have been exactly the same. 'Oh shit.' That's all you would have said if we had created a child between us."

"But *you* . . . why did you let yourself be seen in that light by everyone . . . tell your father and your uncle . . . and let people think . . . ?"

"It seemed worth it at the time. It's a long time ago."

"And why are you telling me *now*? Is the interdict lifted? Is the barring order called off? Can I crawl back to Dublin and they'll give me a job?"

"No, it's much more selfish. I wanted to tell you so that you'd know there never had been a child, no child born, no child aborted. I wanted you to know that in case . . ."

"In case what?"

"In case . . ." She seemed lost for words. He thought she was going to tell him that she worried lest he was thinking about this child, in case he felt ashamed. He had never thought of it as a child, real or imaginary as it now proved to be.

"In case Gerald ever heard. In case you might ever say . . ."

He realized she was more afraid of Gerald knowing about her past than anything to do with him.

"Tell Gerald you're white as the driven snow," he said. He had been so right not to marry this devious lady.

It was around this time that his young cousin Niall asked him for advice.

"You sort of know everything, Richard."

"Oh yeah?"

"Well, I know you're good-looking and everything but you know how to be nice to people and make them like you. Is there a trick?"

Richard looked at him, his hair unkempt, the jacket expensive but out of fashion, the trousers baggy. Mainly the boy's stance was what held him back, his shoulders were rounded, he looked down and not at the people he was talking to; it came from a natural diffidence, but it made him look feeble and untrustworthy.

At another time and in another place Richard might have given the boy some brotherly advice, after all Niall *had* asked, which could not have been easy.

But this was the wrong time.

The business with Judy had ruffled him. He began to doubt his own success with women, and there was also the fact that that little madam, Nessa Ryan across the road in the hotel, had become altogether too pert and self-confident. Richard Hayes didn't feel in the mood to give out advice.

"There's no trick," he said gruffly. "People either like you or they don't. That's the way it goes through life." He looked away from the naked disappointment on the boy's face.

"You mean people can't get better, more popular, or successful?"

Richard shrugged. "I never saw anyone change, did you?"

Niall had said nothing.

He looked increasingly mopey at meals in The Terrace. Richard wondered what work they would find for the lad to do when he came back to Shancarrig full-time, as he undoubtedly would. It might make more sense for him to cut his teeth in a solicitor's office somewhere else. But this was his father's firm. He should come back and claim his inheritance lest Richard take it over from him. Not that Richard was going to stay here forever. After Judy's revelations he thought that it might well be time for him to go back to Dublin.

But that was when he got to know Gloria Darcy.

The Darcys were newcomers. This meant they hadn't been born and raised here for three generations like everyone else. They had been considered fly-by-nights when they came first, but that was before their small grocery shop became a larger grocery shop, and before they started selling light bulbs, saucepans, and cutlery and began to bite into the profits of Dunne's Hardware. Mike and Gloria Darcy always smiled cheerfully in the face of any muttering.

"Isn't there plenty for everyone?" Mike would say with his big broad smile.

"This place is only starting out, it'll be a boom town in the middle sixties," Gloria would say with a toss of her long dark curly hair and her gypsy smile.

She often wore a handkerchief tied around her neck so that she looked like a picture of a gypsy girl—not like the tall silent tinker girls who came into Shancarrig when they camped each year at Barna Woods, more like an illustration from a child's storybook.

Bit by bit they were accepted.

Gloria was flashy, the women all agreed on this. Richard heard his aunt Ethel tut-tutting about her to Nellie Dunne and to Mrs. Ryan, but there was nothing they could put their finger on. Her neckline wasn't so low as to raise a comment, nor were her skirts too short. It was just that she walked with a swish and a certainty. Her eyes roamed around and lit up when they caught other eyes. There was nothing demure about Mrs. Gloria Darcy.

Richard met her first when he bought a packet of razor blades. He didn't like the fussy Mr. Connors the chemist—a small man with bad breath who was inclined to keep you half the day. When he saw packets of razor blades in the window of Darcys he regarded it as a merciful escape.

"Anything else?" Gloria asked him, her smile wide and generous, her tongue moving slightly over her lower lip.

If it weren't for the fact that her husband stood not a foot away, Richard would have thought she was flirting, being suggestive.

"Not for the moment," he said in exactly the same tone, and their eyes met.

He warned himself not to be stupid as he walked back to The Terrace. This would be the silliest thing that a human could do.

What he must do now is sort out a new job in Dublin, and leave this town without having committed any major misdemeanor. He had been saving his salary quite methodically over the three years of his exile in the sticks. There was no point in buying finery to be paraded here, there were no places for meals, no going to the races. He had learned a lot about the rural practice, for all the use it would be to him in the future. But human nature was the same everywhere, perhaps his stay here might have been a better apprenticeship than he had ever thought possible.

It was early closing, the day his uncle Bill usually walked up to The Glen and went for a stroll with old Major Murphy. What the two of them talked about it would be hard to know. But today Bill Hayes was still in his office.

"I'm in a quandary," he said to Richard.

"Tell me about it." Richard sat down, legs stretched, face enthusiastic and receptive. He knew his uncle was pleased to be able to talk.

There was no one else in the house, not dour Aunt Ethel nor sulky Niall.

"It's up at The Glen. Miriam Murphy keeps telephoning me, saying she wants to set her affairs in order."

"Well?"

"Well, Frank says not to take any notice of her—she's rambling."

"She is a bit daft, isn't she?" Richard encouraged his uncle to speak.

"I suppose so, I mean it's not the kind of thing you'd ask a man. Not something that you'd talk about to a friend." Bill Hayes looked troubled.

Richard thought that it should be the most important thing you might talk to a friend about, whether your wife was going off her head or not, but the more he heard of marriage the less likely anyone seemed to do anything normal within its bonds.

"So what do you think you should do?" he asked, expert as always in finding out what the other man wanted before giving his own view.

"You see, I think she has something pressing on her mind, some crime even . . . imaginary, of course."

"Well, if it's imaginary . . ."

"But suppose it's not, suppose it's something she wants to make restitution for?"

"You're not Father Gunn, Uncle Bill. You're not Sergeant Keane, all you have to do is make her will, or not be free to make it if that's what you'd prefer for Major Frank's sake."

"It's worrying me."

"Why don't I go and see her? Then you won't have failed either of them."

"Would you, Richard?"

"I'll go today while you and Major Murphy take your constitutional." His smile was bright.

"I don't know what I'd do without you, Richard."

"You'll have a son of your own to help you in no time. You won't need me, I'll head off to Dublin soon."

"Not too soon."

"All right, not too soon, but soonish." He stood up and clapped his uncle on the shoulder.

What was one more mad old bat of a woman confessing to the Lord knew what!

He had his lunch in the dark dining room of The Terrace, they talked of other things and he waited until his uncle and the Major would be well clear before he went to The Glen.

He didn't even have to go into the house to find her. Mrs. Miriam Murphy half lay, half sat across the rockery. She was wearing a long white dress, possibly a nightgown, her hair streaked with gray was loose on her shoulders.

She was crying.

There was some garden furniture strewn about. Richard Hayes pulled up a chair for himself.

"I'm from Bill Hayes's office, I'm his nephew. He says you're anxious for us to sort something out for you."

"You're too young," she said.

"Ah no, Mrs. Murphy, I'm older than I look. I'm twenty-eight, well on my way to thirty." His smile would have broken down the reserve of any woman in Ireland, but Miriam Murphy's mind was miles away.

"That's what he was, twenty-eight, if you could believe him," she said.

Richard was nonplussed. "Well, what do you think we should do?" he said.

He knew his uncle wanted the woman to say that she had

changed her mind, that she wanted no will made, no affairs sorted out. He must try to lead her in that direction.

"It's too late to do anything. It was done," she said. He nodded uncomprehendingly.

There was a long silence between them, she seemed quite at ease lounging, half lying over the rock plants and the jagged edges of the stones that made up their rockery. He didn't suggest that she sit somewhere more comfortable—he knew that this was irrelevant.

"So perhaps we should leave things as they are?" He looked at her, pouring out reassurance.

"Is that enough?" she asked.

"I think it is."

"You don't think we should leave them the place, The Glen, for themselves whenever they come this way?"

"Leave it to who exactly?"

"The gypsies."

"No, no. Definitely not. People are always trying to leave them places. They want to be free," he said.

"Free?"

"Yes, that's what they like best." He stood up, anxious to be away from the mad staring eyes. It wasn't healthy for that girl Leo to stay here all the time. Why didn't she get a training, a job?

"If you think so." Mrs. Miriam Murphy didn't look relieved, she looked only resigned.

He walked down the long drive and was about to head down the hill to Shancarrig. God, the sooner he was out of a place like this the better. Walking along the road toward him was Gloria Darcy.

"Well, well, well. You had a shave, I see." She looked directly at his face.

"What do you mean?"

"I sold you razor blades this morning, don't tell me you've forgotten me already?" She was most definitely leading him on. Her laugh was unaffected, she could see the impression that she was making on him.

"No, Mrs. Darcy, I imagine that very few people forget you," he said. He was being equally gallant and flattering, giving as good as he got.

"And were you going to walk straight home down the hill or go the better way through the woods?"

He knew he stood at a crossroads. He could have said that he was needed back at the office, that he had work to catch up with, that he had to make a phone call to Dublin. He might have said anything.

But he said: "I was hoping to find some attractive company to walk me through Barna Woods, and now I have."

They laughed as they walked. She teased him about his city suit, he said she was dressing deliberately like a pantomime gypsy. She asked what he had been doing at The Glen, he said that there was a secrecy like the seal of confession about matters between lawyer and client. He asked if the Darcys had a proper title to their shop, they hadn't bought it through his uncle's firm . . . she said the same seal of confession applied to business deals.

By the time they came out into the sunshine again, and walked by the cottages to the bridge, they were well aware of each other. Much more than attractive faces and winning ways. They were people who could talk and play. They were a match for each other.

So when he went to buy things there he went knowing that it was a move, a degree of courtship. He bought more razor blades.

"My, what a strong beard we must have," she said. Again within her husband's hearing.

When he bought a pound of tomatoes she asked him was he going on a picnic in the woods. Mike Darcy was serving another customer.

"No, my aunt wants some more, that's all."

"No, she was in this morning and bought plenty," said Gloria, eyes dancing and full of mischief.

The teasing visits and banter went on for some days.

"It's lovely of you to come and see me so often," she said,

pressing her body toward the counter. She wore a chain around her neck, the pendant was between her breasts, the eye followed it down as it was intended to.

"Yes, it's lovely of me, you never come to call on me," Richard said.

"Ah, but I can't make excuses about civil bills and statements of claim," she said. "You can invent all the tomatoes and razor blades in the world."

"So we'll have to meet on neutral ground," he suggested.

They met two days later at the church when they both attended the funeral of Mrs. Miriam Murphy.

It was pneumonia, Dr. Jims Blake had said. Brought on by exposure, someone else had said, Mrs. Murphy had taken to sleeping out on the rockery of their garden. It was a sure fact that money and position didn't bring you happiness.

Richard Hayes looked at the small wiry Leo as she walked down the church supporting her father. Two strange men, the brothers from abroad, had come for the funeral. They looked military, they knew hardly anyone.

There was a gathering in Ryan's Hotel. Young Nessa had done up one of the downstairs rooms as a special function room. It was exactly what was needed for this occasion. Coffee and sandwiches and some drinks. Those who wished to adjourn to the bar could do so. It had never been done before in Shancarrig, you either went back to someone's house or you went to the pub. This was a new respectability.

"Very clever of you to have thought this up, Nessa," he said admiringly. Genuinely so.

"Leo is my friend. It's not easy for her to have people at the house." Nessa hadn't time to talk to him—these days she was great with young Niall, and already the boy was beginning to look the better for it. His hair was smarter, he had got a new jacket. Somehow he even seemed to walk taller.

Gloria and Mike Darcy were in the gathering, though somehow Richard wondered had they been invited in the strict sense of the word.

As people moved around offering sympathy and trying to

place Harry and James who had long left Shancarrig, Gloria found herself beside Richard.

"So now we're on neutral ground," she said.

"Yes, but very crowded neutral ground," he said, shaking his head in exaggerated sorrow.

"Have you any suggestions for somewhere that's not crowded?" She couldn't have been more direct. Had she asked him to make love to her she could not have said it more clearly.

"Well, since your place, my place, and this hotel are out of the question let's think of somewhere that might be deserted at this moment." He wasn't serious. There was nowhere they could go in Shancarrig, literally nowhere.

"There's The Glen," she said. She saw the look of revulsion on his face. They were sympathizing over the death of the woman who had lived all her life in The Glen, Gloria could not possibly be considering going there to use the empty house. "Not the house, the gate lodge," she said.

"How would we get in?" Already he had bypassed any moral objections to a place in the grounds. That was different.

"The back window is open, I checked."

"Twenty minutes?" he asked. It would take him ten to say his goodbyes, two to go back to his room for condoms.

"Fifteen," she said, and again she ran her tongue along her lower lip. His goodbyes were courteous and very swift.

There was a crotchety old farmer who lived out that direction. If he was asked, he could say he got a message to visit him but then he had turned out not to be there. But why was he making these kinds of precautions? No one would ask him. Nobody would dream he was about to do what he was about to do.

She was there before him, lying on a divan covered with a rug. The place smelled musty but not of damp.

"Did you bring anything?"

"Yes, that's what delayed me. I had to go back to my room for them. I don't carry them always just in case." He laughed, patting his pocket.

"Now don't be so unromantic. I meant champagne, something like that."

"No, I'm afraid not." He looked crestfallen.

"Never mind, I did." Her white teeth flashed as she bit the foil from the top of the bottle, there were cups on the dresser. They laughed as they drank it too quickly so that the fizzy liquid went up their noses. And they kissed.

"Did you go back to the shop for this?" He marveled at her speed.

"No. I had it with me in my big shoulder bag." She laughed at her own wickedness and the confidence that it would have needed.

"Let me take off these dark respectable clothes. They don't suit you," he said.

"Well, it was a funeral. I couldn't wear my red skirt but . . ." She was wearing a red petticoat, trimmed with white lace, she wore no brassiere, just a gold chain around her throat. She looked so abandoned and wild as she lay there laughing up at him, he could scarcely bear the moments of waiting.

"I've longed for you, Richard Hayes," she said. And he sank into her as if he had known her all his life.

After that it was always urgent and never easy. If only the Murphys lived a more regular life, Richard groaned to himself. If he could know they would stay in the big house, or stay out of it, then the gate lodge would have been the ideal place for his meetings with Gloria. But they could never be sure, they would have no excuse if they were seen going in and out of the window.

It took them weeks to work out some kind of a pattern to the curious ways of Leo and her father.

Leo eventually started a secretarial course which involved going to the town on the bus. This gave her day a shape. The Major, who walked the long avenue with his old dogs, which he kept calling Lance and Jessie, was less predictable. Richard tried to find out more of his movements by asking his uncle, but it seemed that a friendship of twenty-five years was based on

Bill Hayes knowing nothing whatsoever about Frank Murphy. It was hard to believe, but that was the way it was.

And there was the time that Hayes and Son, Solicitors were asked to see to a property. Richard and Gloria had many happy meetings there in the guise of showing it to clients.

Gloria could get away so easily it was almost frightening.

"Does Mike never ask where you're going?"

"Lord no. Why should he?"

"Well, if I had a beautiful wife like you I wouldn't let her wander off . . . to do the devil knows what . . ." He squeezed her and held her to him again.

"Then you wouldn't be a husband, you'd be a jailer," she laughed. He thought about it.

There was some truth in what she said. If you married someone just to guard her like a possession, it was like an imprisonment. But look at it the other way, if Mike was more careful and caring about his wife, then surely Gloria wouldn't wander free as she was.

Sometimes he spoke about her children, her little boys, Kevin and Sean.

"What is there to say?"

"Aren't you afraid they'll find out, that they'd hate you for this?"

"Darling Richard, you are riddled with guilt. I think we should make a regular thing of visiting Father Gunn together after we meet."

"Don't tease me, I only say these things because I love you."

"No, you don't."

"I do. I never said it to anyone before."

"We say it at the moment we make love, because at that moment everyone loves. But you don't love me in an everyday sort of way."

"I could."

"No, Richard." She put her finger on his lips and then into his mouth, and then she kissed him and soon the words were forgotten.

She was the ideal lover. He could never have dreamed of anyone so passionate and responsive, a beautiful woman who found him desirable and wasn't afraid to say so. A witty flowing secret love whose dark eyes flashed at him when they met in Ryan's Hotel, in the shops, or at the church.

After years of girls wanting more from Richard here was someone who wanted no more at all. Not public recognition, not a commitment, and obviously because of the heavy band she already wore on her finger . . . not an engagement ring. For quite a time it was the perfect romance.

And then he began to notice small changes in his own attitude. He couldn't say that Gloria had changed, she had always been lighthearted in their daring and the fear of discovery . . . and enthusiastic about the pleasure they gave each other.

No. It was Richard who changed.

He couldn't bear to see her holding her little boys by the hand. He thought back to his own mother and father, the respectable Dublin doctor and his busy bridge-playing wife. Theirs had been a house of stability as he grew up in Waterloo Road. His mother had always been there for them. Suppose she had been someone who sneaked out to the arms of a lover while his father worked. He dismissed the thought as some kind of guilty fantasy.

There had been no ways in which he had compared his life with that of his parents before, why was he holding up their staid and plodding existence as some kind of example now? Gloria was a wonderful mother to Kevin and Sean. What she had with Richard was something totally different, something separate entirely.

Then Richard found himself uneasy about Mike, big handsome Mike Darcy with his teeth as white and even as his wife's, who stood long hours in the grocery shop they were so busy building up together. Mike, who would go to endless trouble to find something Richard ordered, furrowing his brow to think where they might get that particular chamois leather Richard wanted. He didn't like the man being so generous with his time and help for him. Mike's innocent face was a reproach to Richard Hayes.

Gloria only laughed when he mentioned it. "What Mike and I have is different to what you and I have . . . let's keep them separate," she said.

"But I know about him, he doesn't know about me."

"Why do men have to think everything's a game, with rules?" she laughed.

And then there were times when he wondered if he *did* know about Mike and Gloria and what they had together. He would see the way they leaned toward each other in the shop when they thought no one was looking. He saw the way Mike Darcy sometimes stroked his wife's body.

A very unfamiliar feeling of raging jealousy came over him when he saw them touch.

"You don't do this with Mike, do you?" he begged her one afternoon in their gate lodge.

"Nobody could do what you and I do. This is ours."

"But does he want to . . . ? I mean do you and he . . . ?"

"You're so handsome when you look worried, Richard," she said.

"I must know."

Suddenly she sat up, eyes flashing. "No you must not know. There is no must about it. We are not master and slave . . . you have no right to know anything that I do not wish to tell you. Do I ask you any such questions . . . ?"

"But there's nothing to know about me." He was wretched.

"That's because this is the way I choose to see things. I am not curious, suspicious, asking where I should ask nothing." Her voice held an ultimatum.

Accept things as they were or there would be no more to accept. He longed to know if she had known other men since her marriage to Mike, if they had failed at this test and been sent away.

He would have killed any man, any traveler who walked into Ryan's Hotel, if he had said he shared a bed with Gloria Darcy. Yes, he would have taken this man by the throat and shaken him to squeeze out his life, uncaring about what onlookers or the law would say or do. Why then was Mike able to stand and fill bags with sugar and other bags with potatoes and not wonder where his beautiful wife went to in the afternoons?

It was becoming more difficult too for Richard to be free in the afternoons since young Niall had joined the firm. The boy had definitely gained a new confidence, which Richard suspected was due to the blossoming of a friendship and even courtship with the glossy young Nessa Ryan from the hotel.

Gone were the days when Niall Hayes was happy with the menial jobs, the work of a glorified clerk. Now he wanted to learn, to share, to study Richard's ways with clients. "Can I come with you to that place that there's all the fuss about the title?" he would ask.

This was one of Richard's mythical excuses for being out of the office. He had described a difficult old farmer set in his ways who had to be cajoled and flattered into revealing his documents.

"No, Niall. It wouldn't work out . . . this fellow is as mad as a wasps' nest. You wouldn't know what he'd do if I brought anyone else. I've only got as far as I have because I go on my own and put in endless bloody hours with him."

"Well, can I see the file on him?" Niall asked.

"Why? What do you want to bother yourself with that old fart for, there's plenty of other work to do . . ."

"But won't we need to know when . . . ?"

The words remained unfinished, the sentence hung in the air. When . . . Richard went back to Dublin—something they all knew would happen. There wasn't room for two partnerships in the firm. The business simply wasn't there, even two salaries was beginning to strain Bill Hayes. Niall was the son of the family.

Surely Richard would be going back any day now.

Only Richard knew that he could never leave Shancarrig and the woman he loved.

"I *do* love you," he said defensively to Gloria, as they sat smoking a cigarette by their little oil stove one cold evening in the gate lodge.

"I know." She sat hugging her knees.

"No you don't know, you said we shouldn't talk of love, that I only felt it at the moment of taking you. That's what you said."

"Stop sounding like a schoolboy, Richard." She looked beautiful as she sat there in the flickering light.

"What are you thinking about?" he asked.

"About you and how good you make me feel."

"What are we going to do, Gloria?"

"Well, get dressed and go home, I imagine."

"About everything?"

"We can't solve everything, we can only solve things like not letting the light be seen through the windows and not getting our death of cold in all the rain."

"What will you say . . . about where you've been."

"That's not your concern."

"But it is, you are my concern."

"Then let me handle it." Again he saw the warning in her eyes, and he felt frightened.

They had met in late summer and continued through autumn and a cold wet winter, soon it would be spring. Surely some solution would have to be found.

But for Gloria spring meant that she could wear fresh yellow and white flowery dresses, and white sandals, and take her lover to hidden parts of Barna Woods, to dells with bluebells and soft springy grass. Again an ache came over him. How did she know where to find such places? She hadn't grown up in this place, had other men taken her here? Not only could he never ask, he must never think about it. He hated that the shop was doing so well, he wanted to be her provider and give her things, but she would never take them.

"What would I say, Richard? I mean I could hardly say that the handsome young solicitor who drops in to buy an inordinate amount of razor blades bought me a silver bracelet, now could I?"

But with increased prosperity Mike Darcy bought his wife jewelry. There was an emerald pendant, there were diamonds. Nobody in Shancarrig had ever known such an extravagance. Quite unsuitable, Richard's aunt Ethel had said, shaking her head about it.

Richard agreed from the bottom of his heart but was careful not to express this.

To his surprise young Niall had the opposite view.

"What do people work for if it isn't to get themselves what they want?" he asked.

"I hope you wouldn't throw your money away on emeralds for Gloria Darcy and her like," his father said in ritual dismissive vein to his son.

These days Niall Hayes answered back. "I'm not sure what you mean by 'her like,' but if I loved someone and I earned my money lawfully I would feel very justified in spending it on presents for her," he said.

Suddenly the room was silent and drab. Aunt Ethel looked at her son in some surprise. On her cardigan there was no jewelry, there never had been any except the engagement ring, wedding ring, and good watch. Perhaps life might have been better if Bill Hayes had visited a shop and looked at jewels.

··• •··

"Let's celebrate our anniversary," Richard said to Gloria.

"Like what? Dinner for two in Ryan's Shancarrig Hotel, a bottle of wine?"

"No, but let's do something festive."

"I find what we do is fairly festive already," she laughed at him.

"You must want more, you must want more than creeping around."

She sighed. It was the weary sigh of a mother who can't explain to a toddler how to tie his shoelaces. "No, I don't want any more," she said resignedly. "But you do, so we'll do whatever you like for the anniversary."

It was hard to think what they could do. The mystery was

that they had spent a year as lovers without being discovered. In a place of this size and curiosity it was a miracle.

Perhaps they could go to Dublin. He would find an excuse and she would surely be able to think of some reason to go away as well.

Before he suggested it he would plan what they would do, otherwise she would shrug and say that they might as well stay here. He wanted to take her into Dublin bars, restaurants, he wanted people to admire her and be attracted by her beautiful face and sparkling laugh. He wanted to see her against some other background, not just the gray shapeless forms of Shancarrig. In all his years there Richard had never been able to like the place, it was lit up only by Gloria and he wanted to take her away from it.

He planned the visit to Dublin, how he would meet her off the train in Kingsbridge in his car—he would have gone up the day before so that there would be even less suspicion—how he would show her the sights—she didn't know Dublin well, she had told him. He would be her guide.

They would check into one of the better hotels. He would check out the room first, make sure it was perfect . . . they would walk arm in arm down Grafton Street. If they met anyone from Shancarrig, they would all laugh excitedly and say wasn't it great coming to Dublin how you ran into everyone from home.

The more he thought about it the more Richard realized that he did not want Gloria in Dublin just for one night, he wanted her there always. He didn't want them in a furtive hotel room, he wanted them in a home of their own. Together always.

There were the most enormous difficulties in the way. The biggest, most handsome, and innocent was Mike Darcy, smiling and welcoming with no idea that his wife loved another.

There were the children. Richard loved the look of them, dark boys with enormous eyes like Gloria. They had their father's slow lopsided grin too, but it was silly to work out characteristics and assign them to one parent or the other.

He wished he could get to know the children, but it had been impossible. If he could get to know them, then they would find it easier to come as a little family to Dublin to live with him. Richard realized suddenly that he was no longer planning an illicit trip to celebrate an anniversary, he was planning a new life. He must take it more slowly.

He must not rush things and risk losing her.

The anniversary was all that he could have wanted and more.

The hotel welcomed them as Mr. and Mrs. Hayes with no difficulty. Gloria's large rings did not look as if they had been put on for the occasion, they had a right to sit on her hand.

They had champagne in their room, they walked the city. He showed her places that he had loved when he was a boy, the canal bank from Baggot Street to Leeson Street. It thrilled him to be so near Waterloo Road. It was quite possible that his father could walk by on his way to the bookshop on Baggot Street Bridge, or his mother going to the butcher's shop to say that last Sunday's joint had not been as tender as they would have expected and the Doctor had been very disappointed.

He didn't see his parents but he did see Judy, pregnant and contented-looking, getting out of her mother's car. She hadn't seen him, and under normal circumstances he would have let her go on without stopping her. But these were not normal times. He wanted so show her Gloria, he wanted her to see the magnificent woman on his arm.

He called and she waddled over.

"Oh, Mummy will be sorry to have missed you," she said. He had waited carefully until her mother had driven off. He didn't think his name was held in any favor in that family.

"I'd like you to meet Gloria Darcy." The pride in his voice was overpowering.

They talked easily, Gloria asked her was it the first baby. Looking Richard straight in the eye, Judy said yes it was, she was very excited.

Gloria said she had two little boys of her own, and that you wished they'd never grow up and yet you were so proud of every little thing they did. She was saying all the things that Judy wanted to hear. She also told her that the old wives' tales about labor were greatly exaggerated—it was probably to put people off having children before they were married.

"Oh, very few of us would be foolish enough to do that," Judy said, looking again at Richard.

He realized with a shock that he had been a monster of self-ishness. Suppose Judy *had* gone to England and given birth to their child. Where was this child now? A boy or girl in an or-phanage, in a foster family, adopted. A child of four. The age of Gloria's little boy Sean.

How could he have not cared before? He felt his eyes water.

They had drinks in the Shelbourne Bar, and lunch in a small restaurant near Grafton Street that he had heard was very good.

He managed to meet three people he knew slightly. That wasn't bad for a man four years in exile from the capital city. He had chosen the place well.

"Did you love that girl Judy a lot?" Gloria asked.

"No, I have never loved anyone except you," he said simply.

"I thought you looked sad when you left, your eyes were full of tears . . . but it's not my business. I'd be very cross with you for asking prying questions," she said, squeezing his hand warmly.

He could barely speak.

"I'll die if I can't be with you always, Gloria," he said.

"Shush now." She put her finger in the little glass of Irish Mist that she was drinking and offered it to him to suck. Soon the familiar desire returned, banishing for the moment the sense of loss and anxiety about returning her to real life in Shancarrig. They went back to their hotel and celebrated their anniversary well and truly.

He never asked what excuse she had made to Mike, whether it was shopping, or a visit to a hospital, or seeing an old friend. He knew she didn't want him to be a party to her lies. It could not have been hard to lie to Mike, his enthusiasm and simplicity wouldn't take into account the deviousness of the world around him, a wife who would betray him, a casual friend Richard Hayes walking in and out of his shop not for the errands he pretended but to feast his eyes on Gloria, to remind himself of the last time and look forward to the next time.

Kevin Darcy was at Shancarrig School. Sometimes Richard stopped him on the road just for the excuse to talk to him.

"How's your Mammy and Daddy?" he'd say.

"They're all right." Kevin hadn't much interest.

"What did you learn at school?" he might ask.

"Not much," Kevin would say.

One day Richard saw him with a cut head. He fell off the tree, Christy Dunne explained. Richard went to the shop to sympathize. Mike was out in the yard supervising the building of the new extension. Darcys was now almost three times the size it was when when they had bought it first.

"Oh, for God's sake Richard it's only a scrape. Don't be such a clucking hen," she said.

"He was bleeding a lot, I was worried."

"Well, don't worry, he's fine. I put a big plaster on him, and gave him two chocolate bars, one for him and one for Christy. There wasn't a bother out of him." He looked at her with admiration. How was she so calm, so good and wise a mother as well as everything else?

He was still more admiring when the burglars came the following week and stole all the jewelry that Mike Darcy had bought for his wife.

Sergeant Keane was in and out of the place, inquiries were made everywhere, tinkers had been in Johnny Finn's pub, you couldn't watch the place all the time.

Gloria was philosophical. It was terrible, particularly the little emerald, she loved the way it glowed. But then what was the alternative. You watched them day and night, you made the place into something like Fort Knox. It would be like living in a prison. She shivered. Richard remembered how she had once said that to be married to a suspicious husband who checked up on her would be like living with a jailer. She needed to be free.

Maura O'Sullivan, who minded the Darcy children and cleaned the house for them, also worked in his aunt's house. He tried to find out more about the household, but Maura, unlike the rest of Shancarrig, was not inclined to gossip.

"What was it exactly you wanted to know?" she would say in a way that ended all inquiries.

"I was just wondering how the family were getting over the loss," he said lamely.

Maura nodded, satisfied. She always brought her son with her, an affectionate boy called Michael who had Down syndrome. Richard liked him and the way he would run toward whoever came into the room.

"Daddy?" he said hopefully to Richard.

The first time he had said this Maura explained that the child's father had had to go to England, and that consequently he thought everyone he met was his father.

"Daddy, my Daddy?" he asked Richard again and again.

"Sort of, we're all Daddys and Mammys to other people," Richard said to him.

Niall had heard him.

"You're very kind, Richard. It comes naturally to you. I mean it, you're terribly nice to people, that's why you're so successful." Richard was surprised, the boy had never made a speech like this.

"No I'm not. I'm quite selfish really. I'm surprised it doesn't show."

"I never saw it. I was jealous of you of course with women, but I didn't think you were selfish."

"Not jealous of me anymore?"

"Well, I only like one person and she assures me that she's not under your spell . . . so . . ." Niall Hayes looked happy.

"She never was. I thought she was lovely like anyone would, but it was admiration from afar, I assure you."

"That's what she says." Niall sounded smug and content.

"I'm not cramping your style in work here, am I?" Richard wanted to have it out. This seemed a good time.

"No. No of course not, it's just that I suppose we expected . . . everyone thought that sooner or later . . ."

"Yes, and one day I will but . . . not just yet."

"You're saving I know." Niall was understanding.

"How do you know?"

"Well, you never go anywhere, you only have a shabby car. You don't buy jazzy suits."

"That's right," Richard admitted. "I'm saving." This was his cover, he realized. He was putting together a stake to buy into a practice in Dublin.

The months went on. Gloria bought him a silk tie.

"You said no presents." he fingered the cream and gold tie lovingly.

"I said you weren't to buy *me* any, that's all."

"I want to buy you a piece of jewelry. Not an emerald, a ruby —a very small ruby. Let me," he begged.

"No, Richard. Seriously, when could I wear it? Be sensible."

He bought it anyway. He gave it to her in the gate lodge.

Their Wednesday afternoons there were totally secure. Major Murphy walked with his uncle rain or shine, and Leo had got a job working in the office of one of the building contractor's firms in the town. It seemed an unlikely job, but Gloria told him that she heard Leo was still in touch with that mad Foxy Dunne, who was going from strength to strength on the building sites in England. The word was that he would come back and set up his own firm. The word was that he and Leo had an understanding.

"Foxy Dunne, son of Dinny Dunne?"

"Oh, Foxy Dunne is like the papal nuncio in terms of respectability compared to his father. You know him falling out of Johnny Finn's most nights."

"Well, well, well." He realized he was getting a small-town mentality, he was finding serious difficulty in believing that Major Murphy of The Glen would let his daughter contemplate one of the Dunnes from the cottages. He was glad, however, that it meant Leo worked far away. It left the coast much more clear.

Gloria looked at the ruby for a long time.

"You're not angry?"

"How could I be angry that you spent so much on me? I'm touched, but I'll never wear it."

"Couldn't you say . . . ?"

"We both know there's nothing I could say."

"You could wear it here with me."

"Yes, I will."

She took the ruby away and had it made into a tie pin, then she gave it back to him. "I'll put on a chain to wear it when I am with you, but for the rest of the time you keep it. Wear it on the tie that I gave you, then you'll think of me."

"I think of you always," he said.

Too much perhaps.

It was the beginning of the withdrawal. He saw it and blinded himself to it. He feared that someone else had come to town, but he knew there could be no one. She didn't dream up schemes to meet him for five minutes anymore, and although she lay and took his loving she didn't implore him to love her as she once had, begging, encouraging, and exciting him to performances that he had thought impossible.

He felt it was the place, it was getting too much for them. There had been endless complications about builders' suppliers, and the building of the extension, and the hostility of the Dunnes who said that they weren't anxious to build the place that was going into direct competition with them. There had been delays over the insurance money for the jewelry. There was a problem about the newspaper delivery they planned, Nellie Dunne had created difficulties.

In his uncle's office Niall was restless and urging that he be involved in more cases, have consultations with clients and barristers, and in general learn his trade. Richard felt he was putting him off at every turn.

It was time to take Gloria away.

He began to explain it and for once he wouldn't listen when she tried to stop him. "No, I've shushed enough. We have to think. It's been nearly two years. We must have our own home, our own life together. I don't wish Mike any harm but he has to know, he has to be told. He's a decent man, he'll agree to whatever we suggest. Whatever's for the best . . . he can come to Dublin and see the boys, we'll never hide from them who their real father is . . . he'd prefer to be taken into our confidence from the start . . . well, not exactly from the start but from now . . ." His voice trailed away as he looked at her face.

They sat in the gate lodge. They hadn't undressed. Their cigarettes and the little tin they used as an ashtray and cleaned after each visit sat between them on the table. It was an odd place to be talking about their future. It was an odd expression on her face as she listened. It showed utter bewilderment and shock.

He thought first it was the enormity of what they were about to do . . . coupled with the disruption for the children. He must reassure her. "I've been looking at houses in Dublin, a little out of the city so that we could have privacy and so that Kevin and Sean would have a local-type school, not somewhere huge like the big Christian Brothers in the city—" He stopped. He had not read her look right.

She didn't want reassurance, she wanted him to stop talking straightaway. "None of this is going to happen, you must know this. Richard, you *must* know."

"But you love me . . ."

"Not like this, not to run away with you. . . ."

"Why have we been doing all this . . . ?" He waved his hand wildly around the room where they had made love so often.

"It had nothing whatsoever to do with my leaving here. That was never promised, never on the cards."

He was the one bewildered now, and confused. "What was it all about . . . ?" he asked, begging to be told.

She stood up and walked around the room as she spoke. She had never looked more beautiful, she spoke of a happy time with Richard, how he had made her feel wonderful and needed, how she had given him no undertaking, no looking ahead.

She said that her future was here in Shancarrig or very possibly another small town. They might sell up to the Dunnes and move. She and Mike liked starting a place from scratch. They had done that in other places. It was a challenge, it kept everything exciting, new.

Richard Hayes listened amazed as she spoke of Mike with this respect and love.

She was totally enmeshed with him in a way he had never understood. Her concern had nothing to do with a fear that he might be hurt or made to suffer. It was much more an involvement, a caring what he would do and decide and where he would want to go.

"But you don't love him!" he gasped.

"Of course I love him, I've never loved anyone else."

"But why . . . ?" He couldn't even finish the sentence.

"He couldn't give me everything I wanted. No one can do that for anybody. I love him because he lets me be free."

Richard realized she spoke the utter truth. "And does he know . . . ?"

"Know what?"

"About me, about us. Do you tell him?" His voice grew angry and loud. "Is this what gets him excited, your coming home and telling him what you and I did together?"

"Don't be disgusting," she said.

"You're the one who is disgusting, out like an alley cat and then pretending that you're the model wife and mother."

She looked at him reproachfully. He knew it was over.

In the years when he had wriggled out of relationships and escaped from affairs he had not been as honest as she was being, he had been devious and avoided face-to-face contact except when it was utterly necessary. His heart was heavy when he thought of Olive Kennedy, and the way he had disowned her in front of her parents.

If only he could have his time all over again. He hung his head.

"Richard?" she said.

"I didn't mean it about the alley cat."

"I know you didn't."

"I don't know what to do, darling Gloria. I don't know what to do."

"Go away and leave this place, have a good life in Dublin. One day I'll meet you there, we will talk in a civilized way like you and that girl in Baggot Street, the one who was having the baby."

"No."

"That's what you'll do." She spoke soothingly.

"And if you go to another town will you find someone new?"

"I won't go out looking for anyone, that I assure you."

"And will he . . . will he put up with it, turn the other way . . . ?" He couldn't even bear to speak Mike Darcy's name.

"He'll know I love him and will never leave him."

There was nothing more to say.

There was a lot to be done.

He would go back to the office and telephone some solicitors' offices in Dublin. He would ask his mother if he could go back to the basement flat in Waterloo Road. He would work day and night to clear his files, and leave everything shipshape for Niall. He could shake off his years here and start again.

They tidied the little house that they were visiting for the last time. As usual they emptied the cigarette butts and ash into an envelope. They straightened the furniture to the way it had been when they first found the place. They left by the window as they had always done. They rearranged the branches that hung to hide it.

She wouldn't bring anyone here after he had gone, he felt sure of that. With a little lurch he wondered had she ever brought anyone before.

But that was useless speculation.

"Now that we're legitimate we can walk home together," he said.

"Why not?" She was easy and affectionate, as she was with everyone.

"The long way or the short way?" He offered her the choice.

"The scenic route," she decided.

They went up past the open ground that led to the Old Rock, and back through the woods, past Maddy Ross's cottage where she sat at her little desk, maybe writing letters to that priest who had gone to the missions, the one that she might have fancied. Richard felt a huge wave of sympathy for her. What a wasted love that must have been. Compared to his own great passion.

They came to the bridge, children still playing there as they had been the day Richard Hayes had come to town five long years ago.

Different children, same game.

Imagine, only an hour ago he had been planning for Gloria's children to go to school in Dublin. He thought he had taken over a family.

And now everything was over.

Now they were free to talk to each other there was nothing to say. His thoughts went up the road to the old schoolhouse, to the big beech tree which was covered with people's initials and their names.

In the first weeks of loving Gloria he had gone there secretly and carved GLORIA IN EXCELSIS.

It didn't seem blasphemous, it seemed a celebration. If anyone saw it in years to come, they would think it was a hymn of praise to God. They might think a priest had put it there. He would not go and score it out. That would be childish. He could finish the story, of course. He could say that the glory of the world passed by, SIC TRANSIT GLORIA MUNDI. Only a few would understand it and when they did they would never connect it with Gloria Darcy, loving wife of Mike Darcy, shopkeeper.

But that would be childish too.

Maura O'Sullivan and her son, Michael, passed them by as they stood on the bridge, Gloria and Richard who would never speak again.

"Good day Mrs. Darcy, Mr. Hayes," she said.

"My Daddy?" Michael ran up to him and hugged his leg.

Richard knelt down to return the hug properly.

"Go home, Gloria," he said.

She went without a word. He could hear the sound of her high red heels tapping down the road toward the center of Shancarrig.

"How are you Michael? You're getting to be a very big fellow altogether," he said, and buried his head in the boy's shoulder so that no one would see his tears.

9

$\mathcal{L}eo$

When Leonora Murphy was a toddler, her father used to sit her on his knee and tell her about the little girl who had a little curl *right* in the middle of her forehead. He would poke Leo's forehead on the word *right* to show her where the curl was. Then he would go on, *And when she was good she was very very good, but when she was bad she was* HORRID. At the last word he would make a terrible face and roar at her HORRID HORRID. It was always frightening, even though Leo knew it would end well with a big hug, and sometimes his throwing her up in the air.

She wasn't frightened of Daddy, just the rhyme. It seemed menacing, as if someone else was saying it.

Anyway it wasn't even suitable for her because she was a girl with much more than one little curl. She had a headful of them, brown-gold curls. They got tangled when anyone tried to brush her hair. Her mother gave up in despair several times. "Like a furze bush, like something you'd see on a tinker child." Leo knew this was an insult. People were half afraid of the tinkers, who camped behind Barna Woods sometimes when they were on the way to the Galway races.

If Leo ever was bad and wouldn't eat her rice or fasten her shoes properly, Biddy would say that she'd be given to the tinkers next time one of them passed the door. It seemed a terrible fate.

But later when she was older, when she could go exploring, Leo Murphy thought that it might be exciting to go and live with the tinkers. They had open fires. The children ran around half dressed. They went through the woods finding rabbits.

She used to creep around with her friends from school, Nessa Ryan and Niall Hayes and Eddie Barton. Not daring to move, they'd peep through the trees and the bushes and watch the marvelous free life-style of people who had no rules or no laws to tie them down.

Leo couldn't remember why she had been so afraid.

But then, that was when she was a child. Once she was eleven and grown up things could be viewed differently. She realized that there were a lot of things she hadn't understood properly while she was young.

She hadn't realized that she lived in the biggest house in Shancarrig, for one thing. The Glen was a Georgian house, with a wide hall leading back to the kitchen and pantry. On either side of the hall door were big beautifully proportioned rooms— the dining room where the table was covered with papers and books, since they rarely had anyone to dine—the drawing room where the old piano had not been tuned for many a year, and where the dogs slept on cushions behind the big baskets of logs for the fire.

There was a breakfast room behind, where they ate their meals, and a sports room which had wellingtons and guns, and fishing tackle. This is where Leo kept her bicycle when she remembered, but often she left it outside the kitchen door. Sometimes the wild cats that Biddy loved to feed at the kitchen window came and perched on the bicycle. There was a time when a cat brought all her little kittens one by one and left them in the bicycle basket, thinking it might be a safe haven for them.

That was the day that Leo had watched stony-faced as her father drowned them in the rain barrel.

"It's for the best," her father said. "Life is about doing things for the best, things you don't like."

Leo's father was Major Murphy. He had been in the British Army. In fact, he had been away at the war when Leo was born. She knew that because every birthday he told her how he had been in Dunkirk and hadn't known if the new baby was a boy or a girl. Since there had been two boys already the news, when it did arrive, was great news.

Leo's brothers were away at school. They didn't go to Shancarrig School like other boys did, they were sent to a boarding school from the time they were very young. The school was in England, where Grandfather lived. Grandfather wanted some of his family near him and he paid the school fees, which were enormous. It was a famous school, where prime ministers had gone.

Leo knew that it wasn't a Catholic school, but that Harry and James did go to Mass on Sundays. She also knew that, for some reason, she wasn't to talk about this to her friend Nessa Ryan, or to Miss Ross, or Mrs. Kelly, or especially not to Father Gunn. It was all perfectly right and good, but not something you went on about.

She knew there were other ways in which she was different. Major Murphy didn't go out to work like other people's fathers did. He didn't have a business or a farm, just The Glen. He didn't go down to Ryan's Hotel in the evening like other men, or pop into Johnny Finn's Noted for Best Drinks. He sometimes went for a walk with Niall Hayes's father, and he went to Dublin on the train for the day. But he didn't have a job.

Her mother didn't go shopping every morning. She didn't call to Dunne's or to the butcher's. She didn't get a blouse and skirt made with Eddie Barton's mother. She didn't get involved with arranging flowers on the altar for Father Gunn, or helping with the sale of work at the school. Leo's mother was very beautiful and gave the air of having a lot to do as she floated from room to room. She really was a very beautiful woman, everyone always said so. Mrs. Murphy had red-gold hair like her daughter, but not those unruly curls. It was smooth and shiny and turned in naturally, as if it had always been like that. Once a month Mother went to Dublin and she had it trimmed then, in a place in St. Stephen's Green.

Somehow Leo knew that Harry and James weren't going to come back to Shancarrig when they left school. They had been talking about Sandhurst for as long as she could remember. They were both accepted. Her father was delighted.

"We must tell everyone," he said when the letter arrived.

"Who can we tell?" His wife looked at him almost dreamily across the breakfast table.

Father looked disappointed. "Hayes will be pleased."

"Your friend Bill Hayes is the only one who's heard of Sandhurst." Miriam Murphy spoke sharply.

"Ah come on. They're not as bad as that."

"They are, Frank. I've been the one who's always lived here, you're only the newcomer."

"Eighteen years, and still a newcomer . . ." He smiled at her affectionately.

Leo's mother had been born in The Glen, and had played as a child in Barna Woods herself. She had gone fishing down at the River Grane, and taken picnics up the Old Rock, from which Shancarrig got its name. She had been here all through the troubles after the Easter Rising, and through the Civil War. In fact, because there were so many upheavals at that time her parents had sent her off to a convent school in England.

Shortly after she left it she had met Frank Murphy and as two Irish amid the croquet and tennis parties of the South of England in the early 1930s they had been drawn together. Frank's knowledge of Ireland was sketchy, but romantic. He always hoped to settle there one day. Miriam Moore had been more practical. She had a falling-down home, she said. It needed much more money than they would ever have to turn it into a dream.

Miriam's parents were old. They welcomed the bright son-in-law with open arms. They hoped he would be able to manage their beautiful but neglected house and estate. They hoped he would be able to keep their beautiful but restless daughter contented.

They died before they could judge whether he had been able to do either.

"Is Sandhurst on the sea?" Leo asked interestedly. If Harry and James were going to a beach next year, instead of back to school, she was very jealous indeed.

Her parents smiled indulgently at her. They told her it was in Surrey, nothing to do with sand as in Sandycove or Sandymount or any other seaside place she had been to. It was a great honor to get in there. They would be officers of the highest kind.

"Will they be a higher rank than Daddy if there's another war?" Leo asked.

"There won't be another war, not after the last one."

He looked sad when he said that. Leo wished she hadn't brought the subject up. Her father walked with a stick and he had a lot of pain. She knew this because she could hear him groaning sometimes if he thought he was alone. Perhaps he didn't like being reminded of the war, which had damaged his spine.

"You should write to them, Leo," her mother said. "They'd like to get a letter from their little sister."

It was like writing to strangers, but she wrote. She told them that she was sitting in the drawing room, and that Lance and Jessie were stretched in front of the fire. She told them about the school concert where they all wanted to sing "I've got a lovely bunch of coconuts" and Mrs. Kelly had said it was a filthy song.

She told them how Eddie Barton had taught her how to draw different kinds of leaves, fishes, and birds, and said she might do them a special drawing for Christmas if they ordered it.

She said she was glad they were going to be high-class officers in the army, even if there was never going to be another war. She said they would be glad to know that Daddy was walking a bit better and Mother looking a lot less sad.

To her surprise they both wrote almost by return and said that they loved her news. It was strange not being one thing or the other, they wrote.

Leo had a big bedroom that looked out over the garden. It was one of four large rooms around the big square landing. Nessa Ryan was always admiring the upstairs.

"It's like a room in itself, this landing," she said in admiration. "It's so pokey in the hotel, and all the rooms have numbers on them."

Leo said that when her mother was young in The Glen there was breakfast on the landing. Imagine, people bringing all the food upstairs to save the family going down. Sometimes they used to eat in their dressing gowns, Mother had told her.

Nessa was very interested that Major and Mrs. Murphy had different bedrooms, her parents slept in the same bed.

"Do they really?" Leo was fascinated. She broached the subject with Biddy.

Somehow, it didn't seem right to ask directly.

"Don't go inquiring about where and how people sleep. Nothing but trouble comes out of that."

"But *why*, Biddy?"

"Ah, people sleep where they want to sleep. Your parents sleep at each end of the house, that's what they want. Leave it at that."

"But where did your parents sleep?"

"With all of us, in one room." So it wasn't much help.

When Harry and James came home for a very quick visit she decided to ask them. They looked at each other.

"Well, you see. With Papa being wounded and everything . . ."

"All that sort of thing changed," James finished.

"What sort of thing?" Leo asked.

They looked at each other in despair.

"All sorts of things. No sorts of things," Harry said. And she knew the subject was over.

Mother never told Leo anything about the facts of life. If it hadn't been for Biddy and Nessa, she should have been astonished by her first period. Although she knew how kittens, puppies, and rabbits, and therefore babies, were born, she had no idea how they were conceived. She very much hoped that it was nothing to do with the behavior of the dogs and cats at certain times. She didn't see how such a thing would be possible for humans anyway, even if any of them would agree to do it. She hated Nessa Ryan being so knowing so she didn't ask her, and she knew that Biddy in the kitchen flushed a dark red when the matter was mentioned. . . .

When Leo Murphy was fourteen such matters had been sorted out, if not exactly satisfactorily, at least she felt that she had mastered whatever technical information there was about it from reading pamphlets and magazines.

She had agreed with Nessa and Maura Brennan that it was quite impossible to believe that your own parents could ever have done it, but then the living proof that they must have was all around.

Maura Brennan was able to add the information that a lot of it happened when the man was drunk, and Leo said it was very unfair that the woman shouldn't be allowed to get drunk as well, because it was bound to be so awful.

Maura was very nice. She never pushed herself on anyone. In ways Leo liked her better than she liked Nessa Ryan, who could be moody if she didn't get her own way. But Maura lived in the poorest of the cottages. Her father, Paudie, was often to be seen sitting on someone's steps with a bottle in his hand, having been out drinking all night.

Maura wouldn't go on to the convent with them next year when she and Nessa went into town on the bus to secondary school. And yet at fourteen Maura seemed to know a lot more about life than the rest of them did.

It seemed very unfair to Leo that families like Maura Brennan's and Foxy Dunne's had to live in the falling-down cottages by the river and had such shabby clothes. Foxy Dunne was much brighter than Niall Hayes, much quicker when it came to giving answers in school, but Foxy had no bicycle, no proper clothes, and had never been known to wear shoes that fitted him. Maura Brennan was much kinder and more gentle than Nessa Ryan, but she never got a dress like Nessa got for her birthday and she hadn't a winter coat.

Leo knew she wasn't meant to go into the cottages and so she didn't. No one ever said not to, it was something that was unspoken.

Only Foxy ever challenged it.

"Aren't you coming in to see the Dunne family at leisure . . . ?" he asked.

They had learned the word *leisure* at school today, Mrs. Kelly had written it on the board and talked about what it meant. . . .

"No thanks. I've got to go home today," Leo would say.

"But *I'm* allowed to come and see the Murphy family at leisure," he would say.

Leo was able to handle him. "Yes you are, and very welcome too, when you want to. . . ."

It was a standoff.

They admired each other . . . it had always been like that, since they were in Mixed Infants together. . . .

After the end of the summer term Leo and Nessa traveled on the bus to the convent school. They would meet the Reverend Mother, get a list of books and other items they would need, details of the school uniform, and probably a string of rules as well. They thought that they would also be shown around the convent, but this did not materialize. They were tempted to spend the time idling around and sampling the pleasures and freedom of a place ten times the size of Shancarrig, but they felt that somehow they would be found out. It would be told back in Ryan's Hotel that they had been seen skitting and laughing on a corner with an idling lad, or licking ice creams in the street.

Better by far to get the early bus home and be shown to be reliable.

Nessa went into the hotel, where she felt they weren't nearly grateful enough to see her.

"Are you back already?" Mrs. Ryan said without enthusiasm.

"I hope you did everything you were meant to do," her father said.

Leo grinned at her. "It'll be the same at my place," she said companionably. "They'll have fed the dogs and won't have kept anything for me."

She strolled up the hill, pausing to talk to Eddie Barton and tell him about the convent. He would be going to the Brothers. He said he wasn't looking forward to it. It was only games they cared about.

"In this place it's only prayers they care about," Leo grumbled. "There're statues leaping at you out of every wall."

She trailed her shoulder bag behind her as she passed the old gate lodge that had been let once to people, who had left it like a pigsty. Now it was all boarded up in case any intruders got in.

It was a Thursday, and as soon as she was home Leo remembered that it was, of course, Biddy's half day. There would be food left under the meat safe. They usually had something cold for supper on a night when Biddy wasn't there. Leo knew that she should help herself because there was no one to greet her. Major Murphy had gone to Dublin that morning. He had caught the early train. Her mother must have gone walking in Barna Woods. Leo planned to take her food up to her bedroom and listen to her gramophone. She had written to James and Harry about the song "I love Paris in zee springtime." She could play it over and over. Someday she would go to Paris in "zee springtime or zee fall" with someone who would sing that to her. She thought it would never go out of fashion. She closed herself into her room and before she even started on her milk and chicken sandwich she put on the record.

She threw herself on her windowseat and was singing along with it when, to her surprise, she heard a door bang and footsteps running up or down the stairs, she couldn't tell which.

Thinking she might be playing the machine too loudly, she went to take off its handle and as she did so her eye caught sight of a young man fleeing across the grass and into the shrubbery. As he ran he was pulling on a shirt.

Leo was very frightened. It must have been a robber. Could there be more of them downstairs? She didn't know whether to shout for help or pretend that she wasn't there.

Her mind raced. They must know she was there if they had heard the music playing. Perhaps one was waiting for her outside her bedroom door. She could feel her heart thumping. In the silence of the house she heard a door creak open. She had been right. There *was* someone else lying in wait for her. She prayed as she had never prayed before.

As if in direct answer to her, God had managed to make her mother's voice call out: "Leo. Leo. Is that you?"

Mother was standing outside her bedroom door, flushed-looking and confused.

Leo ran to her. "Mother. There were robbers . . . are you all right?"

"Shush, shush. Of course I am . . . what are you talking about?"

"I heard them running down the stairs . . . they went through the garden."

"Nonsense, Leo. There were no robbers."

"There *were*, Mother. I heard them, I saw them . . . I saw one of them."

"What did you see?"

"I saw him pulling off or putting on a shirt. Mother, he ran over there behind the lilacs, over the back fence."

"What on earth are you doing home anyway . . . weren't you meant to be on a tour of that school . . . ?"

"Yes, but they didn't show us. I saw him, Mother. There might be others in the house."

Leo had never seen her mother so full of purpose. "Come downstairs with me this moment and we'll put an end to this foolishness." She flung open the doors of all the rooms. "What burglar was here if he didn't take the silver, the glass. Or here, in the sports room, all your father's guns. Each one intact. Look, they didn't even take our supper, so let's have no chats about burglars and robbers."

"But the feet on the stairs?" She was less sure of the figure now.

"I went downstairs myself and came back up to my room. I didn't know you were back . . ."

"But I was playing the record player . . ."

"Yes. That's what made me come out and look for you. To know what you were doing blasting it out and then turning it off . . ."

Mother looked excited. Different to the way she was normally.

Leo didn't know what made her think that it was dangerous, but that is exactly what she felt it was. She had to walk just as delicately here as if there really were a robber hiding in the house.

She spoke nothing of the incident to her father, nor to Biddy. When Nessa Ryan asked whether Leo's welcome home had been any more cordial than the one that Nessa had got herself in the hotel Leo said that she had made a sandwich and listened to "I Love Paris."

Nessa Ryan said that life was very unfair. She had been roped in to help polish silver since she was back.

Imagine having all the freedom in the world in a big house like that.

Imagine. She didn't notice Leo shiver as she realized that she had denied the fright, and that, somehow, made the fright much bigger than it had been before.

Foxy Dunne came up the drive next day. His swagger showed a confidence that many of those twice his age might not have felt approaching The Glen.

But Foxy didn't push his luck; he went to the back door.

Biddy was most disapproving.

"Yes?" she said coldly.

"Ah, thank you, Biddy. It's good to get a real traditional Irish welcome everywhere, that's what I always say."

"You and your breed never say anything except to make a jeer of other people who put their minds to work."

Foxy looked at her without flinching.

"*I'm* different to my breed, as you call it, Biddy. I have every intention of putting my mind to work."

"You'll be the first of the Dunnes who did, then." She was still annoyed to see him sitting so confidently in her kitchen.

"There always has to be the first of some family who does. Where's Leo?"

"What's that to you?"

At that moment Leo came into the kitchen. She was pleased to see Foxy Dunne. She offered him one of Biddy's scones that were cooling on a wire tray.

"Will you like the place inside?" He was speaking about the secondary school.

"I think so. A bit Holy Mary, but you know."

"A lot of people around here could do with being Holy Mary," Biddy said.

Leo laughed. Everything seemed to be back to normal again.

"You'll work hard, won't you?" Foxy was concerned.

"Imagine one of Dinny Dunne's lads laying down the law on working hard," Biddy snorted.

Foxy ignored her. "It's important that you work as hard as I do," he said to Leo. "I have to, because I come from nothing. You have to because you come from everything."

"I don't know what you mean," Leo said.

"It would be dead easy for you to do nothing, for you to just drift about without doing anything, and end up just marrying someone."

"Not for ages." Leo was indignant.

"Not anytime. You should get a job."

"I might *want* to marry someone."

"Yes, yes. But you'd be better off with a job, whether you married anyone or not."

"I never heard such nonsensical talk." Biddy was banging the saucepans around to show her disapproval.

"Come on, Foxy. We'll go out to the orchard," Leo said.

They picked small gooseberries and put them in a basket that Leo's mother had left under a tree.

"It won't always be like this here, you know," Foxy said.

"No. It'll be term time, and a list of books as long as your arm."

"I meant this house, this way of going on."

She looked at him, alarmed. The anxiety of the other night came back; things changing, not being safe anymore.

"What do you mean?"

She looked very startled suddenly, and he didn't like the way her face got so alarmed, so he reassured her. He told her that if he could pretend to be sixteen or over, he could get taken on by a man who was raising a crew for a builder—all fellows from around here, fellow countymen . . . he'd start just doing odd jobs, but he'd work his way up.

"I wish you weren't going away," Leo said. "I know it's crazy, but I have this stupid feeling that something awful is going to happen."

It was three weeks later that it happened. On a warm summer evening. Leo had just finished her letter to Harry and James, she had written how Daddy's back seemed much better and that Dr. Jims had said that walking couldn't do him any harm— it couldn't hurt him any more than he had been hurt in the war —and that if he sat in a chair like an old man with a rug over his knees then he'd turn into one.

So he went off for long walks with Mr. Hayes, even up as far as the Old Rock. That's where they had gone today. Leo decided to walk down to the town to post the letter. Once it was written she liked it to be on its way. It could sit on the hall table for days, with Biddy dusting around it. She found a stamp and headed off. Mrs. Barton was ironing, Leo could see her through the window. She never went out to sit in her little garden. Surely she could have brought some of her sewing out-of-doors on a beautiful evening like this. Leo looked up to see if she could see Eddie's face at his window. He wrote almost as many letters as she did. She met him sometimes at the post office and Katty Morrissey said that between them they kept the whole of P & T going.

But there was no sign of Eddie. Maybe he was off finding odd shapes of wood and clumps of flowers to draw. She did meet Niall Hayes, however, walking disconsolately up and down The Terrace.

"God, that school *I'm* going to is like a prison," Niall said. "It's like the Count of Monte Cristo."

"The convent's all right. It's choked with statues, though, all of them with cross faces."

"Oh, I wouldn't mind if it was only the statues. You should see the faces on these fellows. All of them in long black dresses, and looking desperate."

"Sure doesn't Father Gunn wear a long dress, and Father Barry. You're used to them." Leo thought Niall Hayes was making heavy weather out of it all.

"They don't have faces like lighting devils."

"Did your father go to school there?"

"Of course he did, and all my uncles. And they've forgotten how awful it is. They keep telling me of all the fun they had there."

"Your father's gone for a walk with my father." Leo was tired of all the gloom.

"Well, it must have been a short one then. My father's back in the house there, making some farmer's will I don't know. Leo, I don't think I could *bear* to be a solicitor here in Shancarrig."

"You could always go somewhere else," Leo said. There seemed to be no cheering Niall today.

She was sorry her father's walk had been canceled, but

maybe he was sitting with Mother in the orchard. She had seen sometimes they had a big jug of homemade lemonade, and they looked as if they were a bit happy.

She met Father Gunn, who said wasn't it amazing the way the time raced by. There was another whole class ready to leave Shancarrig and go out into the wide world. It was extraordinary how grown-ups thought time raced by. Leo found it went very slowly indeed.

As she came in the gate of The Glen she heard the cries coming from the gate lodge, and at the same moment she saw her father hastening as fast as he was able down the drive. Leo shrank away from the sound of crashing furniture and screams.

But she knew without a shadow of a doubt that it was her mother's voice she heard screaming: "No. No. You can't. No," and a great long wail.

"Oh. My God, my God. Miriam. Miriam."

Her father was stumbling. He had dropped his stick, and had to bend down for it.

Leo watched as if it were slow motion.

Then they heard the shots. Three of them. And at that moment Leo's mother came staggering to the door. Her blouse was covered with blood. Her hair and her eyes were wild.

"My God . . . He tried to . . . he was trying to . . . he would have killed me," she cried. She kept looking behind her where they could see a shape on the ground.

"Frank!" screamed Leo's mother. "Oh, do something, Frank. For God's sake! He would have killed me."

Leo shrank still further away from the scene which she could see unfolding, but yet could not take in.

Her father walked in exaggeratedly slow motion toward the door and took her mother in his arms.

He soothed her like a baby.

"It's over, Miriam, it's over," he said.

"Is he dead?" Leo's mother didn't want to look.

Horrified, Leo saw her father bend to the shape on the floor and turn it over. Leo could see a man with dark hair, lying on the floor of the gate lodge. There was a big red stain all over the front of his shirt.

It was the man she had seen running toward the lilacs in the shrubbery three weeks ago, the day that she thought there had been robbers.

And now both her father and mother were crying.

"It's all right, Miriam darling. It's over. He's dead." Her father was saying this over and over again.

Later they gave Leo a brandy too. With a little water in it. But that was well after they had come back to the house.

The door of the gate lodge had been closed. They all walked up the drive arm in arm and Mother had gone up to wash herself.

"You might need to, you know, not change anything," Leo heard Daddy say, but Mother had looked at him wildly.

"You mean . . . wear this? Wear *this* on my body? All this blood? What for? Frank, use your head. What for?" She was near hysteria.

"I'll wash you," he offered.

"No. Please let me be on my own for a few moments."

Mother had a handbasin in her room, with a mirror and light over it, and little pink floral curtains.

Leo didn't want to be alone, so she followed her mother into the room.

"You're saying nothing." Their eyes met in the mirror.

"Are you all right, Mummy?" She rarely used that word.

Mother's face softened. "It's all right, Leo. It's over." She said Father's words like a parrot.

"What are we going to do? What's going to happen?"

"Shush. Let me get rid of all this. We'll put it out of our minds. It'll be like a bad dream."

"But . . ."

"That's for the best, Leo, believe me." Mother looked very young as she stood there just in her slip and skirt. She rubbed her neck and arms with a soapy flannel and warm water, even though there was no trace of blood. That was all streaked and hardening on the yellow blouse she had thrown into the waste-paper basket.

Mother was brushing her teeth, then she shook her tin of Tweed talcum powder into her hand and rubbed it into her skin.

"Go on, darling. Go down to your father. I want to finish dressing."

Leo thought Mother only had to put on a blouse. And of course a brassiere. She had only just realized that for some reason Mother hadn't been wearing one as she stood beside the handbasin. Just the slip. Her silky peach-colored one.

Everything was so strange and unreal. The fact that Mother had asked her to leave the room now was only one tiny fragment more in the whole thing.

Leo went into the drawing room. She felt something like this should not be discussed in the breakfast room where they lived on ordinary days. Her father must have felt the same thing. He had put a match to the fire and the two dogs, Lance and Jessie, seemed pleased. They stretched their big cream limbs in front of the grate.

Leo thought to herself suddenly that Lance and Jessie didn't know what had happened. Then she remembered that nobody knew—not Niall Hayes, whom she had been talking to half an hour ago—nor Mrs. Barton, who had waved from her ironing—nor Father Gunn, who had said that time passed so quickly.

Father Gunn? Why wasn't he here?

The moment someone died you sent for the priest. And Dr. Jims, Eileen and Sheila's father, he should be here. That's what happened when people got sick or died, Father Gunn and Dr. Jims arrived in the cars.

Mother was at the door. She shivered and hugged herself.

"That's lovely of you to light the fire," she said.

They both looked up, Leo and her father. Mother sounded so ordinary—so normal. As if it all hadn't happened out there. Down in the gate lodge.

That was when Father poured the brandy for the two of them.

"Give Leo a little too." Mother sounded as if she were offering more soup at lunchtime.

"Come up here to the fire. Warm your hands. I'll phone Sergeant Keane. He'll be up in five minutes."

"No." It was like a whiplash.

"We have to call him, we should have phoned immediately."

Leo was sipping the horrible and unfamiliar brandy. She didn't know how people like Maura Brennan's father wanted to drink alcohol all the time. It was disgusting.

"My nerves won't stand it, Frank. I've been through enough already."

"Sergeant Keane's very gentle. He'll make it as quick as possible. It's just the formalities."

"I won't *have* the formalities. There's no point in asking me to."

"A man tried to kill you, he had one of my guns. He *could* have killed you." Father's voice broke with emotion at the thought of it.

Mother became even more icily calm.

"But he didn't. What happened was that I killed him."

"You defended yourself against him . . . the gun went off. He killed himself."

"No. I picked up the gun and shot him."

"You don't know *what* happened. You're in shock."

Major Murphy made a move as if to go out to the hall to the telephone.

Mother didn't even need to raise her voice to make her seriousness felt.

"If you ring him, Frank, *I'm* walking out that door and you'll never see me again. Either of you."

He put out his arms as if to hold her again, support her as he had up the drive, console her as he had done when he was holding her, telling her it was over.

Mother really seemed to believe that it *was* over.

Leo kept moving the glass around between her hands as she

listened to her parents talking about the man who lay dead in their gate lodge.

Her mother's voice was strange and unnatural. It didn't sound like a voice, it sounded like a noise, a thin even noise, with no highs and lows.

She spoke as one who is being perfectly reasonable.

Frank had told her it was over, finished. So let it be forgotten. Why drag heavy-footed policemen in, and go over it and over it, and ask questions and give answers? The man had threatened her. He had got killed himself. It was an eye for an eye. Justice had been done. Let it be left as it was.

At every interruption she gave her strange disembodied threat: "Or else I will disappear from this house and you will never see me again."

It was as if they had forgotten she was here. Leo watched mesmerized as her mother, by sheer force of repetition, began to beat down the rational arguments. She saw her father change from the strong man comforting his wife caught in a terrible accident and become someone hunted and unsure. She saw him bite his lip and watched his eyes widen with fear at every repeated threat that Miriam Murphy would walk out the door and never be seen again.

She wanted to interrupt to ask Mother where she would go. Why she would leave them, her home and her family?

But Leo didn't dare to move.

It was almost an eternity before they remembered she was there.

It was when her father had said: "I couldn't *live* without you, Miriam, you couldn't leave knowing that . . ."

"Please . . ." She looked across at her fourteen-year-old daughter, as if a lapse of taste had been committed. A man shouldn't speak of his need, of his weakness, not in front of a child.

Major Murphy came over to the window seat where Leo was sitting.

"Leo, dearest child."

"What's going to happen, Daddy?"

"It's going to be all right. As your mother says, it's over, it's over. We mustn't—"

"Will we get Dr. Jims . . . Father Gunn . . . ?"

"Leo, come with me. I'll bring you up to bed. . . ."

"I want to stay here, Daddy, please . . ."

"You want to help us, you want to be big and brave and do the right thing. . . ."

"No. I want to stay here. I'm afraid."

Outside in the big garden darkness had fallen. The bushes were big shapes, not colors as they had been when the three of them walked back up, huddled together from the horrors they had left in the gate lodge.

He propelled her out the door and to the kitchen, where he warmed some milk in a saucepan. He took the big silver pepperpot and sprinkled some over the top of the milk when it was poured into a mug.

He walked up the stairs with her and led her to the room.

"Put on your nightie, like a good girl," he said.

He turned his back as Leo slipped out of her green cotton dress and her summer vest and knickers, and pulled the pink brushed cotton nightdress that was in the nightdress case shaped like a rabbit. Leo remembered with a shock that when she had stuffed her nightie in there this morning nothing had happened. None of this nightmare had begun.

She got into bed and sipped the milk.

Her father sat on the bed and stroked her forehead. "It will be all right, Leo," he said.

"How can it be all right, Daddy?"

"I don't know. I used to wonder that in the war, but it was."

"It wasn't really. You got wounded and you can't walk properly."

"Yes, I can." He stood up.

His face was so sad, Leo wanted to cry aloud. She wanted to open the window in her room, kneel upon the window seat, and cry out for someone in Shancarrig to help them all.

But she bit her lip.

"I have to go down now, Leo," he said.

It was as if they were allies. Allies to protect a strange silent mother downstairs who wasn't speaking in her ordinary voice.

She used to play that game of "if."

If I get up the stairs before the grandfather clock in the hall stops striking, then Mrs. Kelly won't be in a bad mood tomorrow. If the crocuses come up in front of the house by Tuesday, I'll get a letter from Harry and James.

Now she sat in the dark bedroom with her arms around her knees. If I don't get out of bed, it will all be all right. Dr. Jims will come and say he wasn't dead at all. If he is really dead, then Father Gunn will say it wasn't Mother's fault.

If I don't get out of bed at all and if I sit like this all night without moving, then it'll turn out not to have happened at all.

She woke in the morning stiff and awkward. She hadn't managed to stay awake. Now the charm wouldn't work. It *had* happened, all of it.

There was no point in holding her knees anymore. None of it was going to work.

How could it be an ordinary day? A sunny day with Lance and Jessie rushing around outside, with Mattie the postman cycling up the drive, with smells of breakfast coming from downstairs.

Leo got out of bed and looked at her face in the wardrobe mirror. It was gray-white and there were shadows under her frightened gray-green eyes. Her curly hair stood upright over her head.

She pulled on the clothes she had thrown on the floor last night, last night when Daddy had been standing with his frightened face.

At that moment the door opened and Mother came in. A different Mother to last night. Mother was dressed in a blue linen suit, her hair was combed, she wore her pink lipstick, and she looked bright and enthusiastic.

"I have the most wonderful news," she said.

Leo felt the color rushing to her cheeks. The man wasn't dead. Dr. Jims had cured him.

Before she could speak Mother had opened the wardrobe door and started to take out some of Leo's frocks.

"We're going on a holiday, all three of us," she said. "Your father and I suddenly decided that this was what we all needed. Now, isn't that a lovely surprise . . . ?"

"But . . ." Leo's voice dried in her throat.

"But we have to get going just after breakfast, it's a long drive. . . ."

"Are we running away?" Leo's voice was a whisper.

"For a whole week we are. . . . Now, where are your bathing togs? We're going to a lovely hotel on a cliff, and we'll be able to run down and have a swim before breakfast every day. Imagine."

Her father didn't catch her eye at breakfast, and Leo knew that she must not mention the events of last night. Her father had somehow bought the right for both of them to run away with Mother. That's what was happening.

They heard a knock at the back door. All three of them looked at each other in alarm, but it was Ned, who did the garden. Leo heard her father explaining about the sudden holiday . . . and giving instructions.

The glasshouses were in a terrible state, if Ned could concentrate entirely on clearing them, and sorting out what was to be done.

"And what about the rockery, Major, sir?"

"It's very important that you leave that. There's a man coming down from the Botanic Gardens to have a look at it. He said nothing was to be touched until he came. . . ."

"I'm glad of that." Ned sounded relieved. "Will I fill in the hole we dug?"

"Oh, we've done that already. . . ."

If Ned was surprised that a man with war injuries, and his frail wife, had covered in a pit that it had taken him two days to dig, he showed no sign of it.

"I'll leave it as it is then, Major, sir?"

"Just as it is, Ned. No disturbing it at all."

Leo felt a cold horror spread all over her.

The memory of last night, hugging her knees in the dark. The sound of footsteps, of low urgent voices, of dragging and pulling. But her mother was calm as she listened to the conversation at the back door, and even laughed when Daddy came back into the room.

"Well, I expect that was welcome news for our Ned. Anything that he hasn't to do must come as a pleasant surprise."

Leo beat back the wild fears.

Often her dreams seemed real to her . . . more real than ordinary life. This is what must be happening now. There was another knock at the door. Again the look of alarm exchanged.

This time it was Foxy Dunne.

"Yes, Foxy?" Leo's father was unenthusiastic.

"How are you?" Foxy never addressed people by title. He wouldn't greet the priest as Father and he certainly wouldn't call Leo's father Major.

"I'm fine thank you, Foxy. How are you?"

"Great altogether. I came to say goodbye to Leo."

Suddenly her father's voice sounded wary. "And how, might I ask, did you know that she was going away?"

"I didn't." Foxy was cheerful. "I'm going away myself, that's why I came to say goodbye."

"Well, I suppose you'd better come in."

Foxy walked easily through the scullery and the kitchen and into the breakfast room.

"How're ya?" he said, nodding easily at Leo's mother.

She smiled at the small boy with the freckles and the red hair, the one Dunne boy that poverty and neglect had never managed to defeat.

"And where are you off to?" she asked politely.

Foxy ignored her and addressed Leo. "I'm off to London, Leo. I didn't think I'd ever be able to do it. I thought I'd be hanging around here like an eejit, dragging a brush around someone's shop."

"You're too young to go to England."

"They won't ask. All they want is someone to make tea on a site."

"Will you be frightened?"

"After my old fellow and Maura Brennan's old fellow? Both of them coming home drunk and both of them trying to beat me up . . . how could I be frightened?"

He talked as if Leo's parents weren't there. It wasn't deliberately rude, it was just that he didn't see them.

"Will you ever come back to Shancarrig again?"

"I'll come home every Christmas with fistfuls of pound notes, like everyone else on the buildings."

Major Murphy asked whether Foxy would learn a trade.

"I'll learn everything," Foxy told him.

"No, I mean a skilled trade, you know, an honorable trade, like a bricklayer. . . . It would be very good to serve your time, to do an apprenticeship."

"It'll be that all right." Foxy didn't even look at the man, let alone heed him.

"Will you write and tell what it's like?" Leo knew her voice sounded shaky and not full of interest as Foxy would have liked.

"I was never one for the writing, but as I say, I'll see you every Christmas. I'll tell you then."

"Good luck to you over there." Leo's mother was standing up from the breakfast table. She was bringing the conversation to a close.

Foxy gave her a long look.

"Yeah. I suppose I'll need a bit of luck all right. But it's more a matter of working and letting them know you can work."

"You're only a child. Don't let them ruin your health, tell them you're not able for heavy work." The Major was kind.

But Foxy was having none of it. "I'll tell them I'm seventeen. That's how I'll get on. Seventeen, and a bit stunted." He was going in his own time, not in Mrs. Murphy's. "I'll see you at Christmas, Leo," he said.

Leo saw him fondling the ears of Lance, and throwing a stick for Jessie.

Other people were in awe of the two loudly barking Labradors. Not Foxy Dunne.

She thought of him a few times during their holiday, that strange time in a faraway hotel, where there was nothing whatsoever for her to do except read the books that were in the library. Sometimes she walked with her father and mother along the sandy beaches, collecting cowrie shells. But usually she left Mother and Father to walk alone, with the dogs. They seemed very close together, sometimes even holding hands as Father limped along, and Mother sometimes bent to pick up some driftwood and throw it out into the sea so that Lance and Jessie could struggle to bring it back.

She didn't sleep too well at night in the small room with the diamond-shaped panes of glass in the window. The roar of the Atlantic Ocean down below the cliffs was very insistent. The stars looked different here to the way they looked in Shancarrig when she'd sit on her window seat and watch at night—the familiar gardens of The Glen, the lilacs, the shrubbery down to the big iron gates and the gate lodge.

She shivered when she thought of the gate lodge. She had not been able to look at it as they had driven past on the morning they left home. She dreaded seeing it again when she went back, but she wanted to be away from this strange dreamlike place too, this holiday that never should have been.

Biddy would be at home now in The Glen. What might have happened? What might have been found? Yet neither Father nor Mother telephoned her or seemed remotely worried.

Leo felt a constriction in her throat. She couldn't eat the food that was put in front of her.

"My daughter hasn't been well. It has nothing to do with your lovely food."

Leo looked at her mother in disbelief. How could she lie so easily and in such a matter-of-fact voice? If she could do that, she could lie about anything. Nothing was as it used to be anymore.

Leo was very afraid. She wanted a friend. Not Nessa whose

eyes would widen with horror. Not Eddie Barton who would retreat into his woods, and his flowers, and his drawings. Not Niall Hayes who would say it was typical of grown-ups—they never did anything you could rely on.

She couldn't tell Father Gunn, not even in Confession. Maura Brennan would be more frightened than she was herself.

For a moment she thought of Foxy Dunne, but even if he were at home he wasn't the kind of person you could tell. She wondered how he was standing up to life on a big building site in London. Did he seriously think that people would believe he was seventeen? But he was always so cocky, so confident, maybe they would.

She looked away to the other side of the car as they drove back in through the gates of The Glen. It was as if she was afraid that the door of the gate lodge would be swinging wide open and that Sergeant Keane and a lot of Guards would be there waiting for them.

But everything was as it always had been. The dogs raced around, happy to be home and no longer cooped up in the station wagon. Biddy was bustling around full of interest in their sudden holiday. Old Ned who was sitting smoking in the glasshouse busied himself suddenly.

There had been no news, Biddy said. Everything had gone fine. There was a letter from Master Harry and Master James, and some other parcel that didn't have enough stamps on it and Mattie wanted money paid.

There had been cross words with the butchers because they had delivered the Sunday joint of beef as usual and been annoyed when told that the family were on holidays. Sergeant Keane had been up to know if there was any word of one of the tinkers who had gone missing.

Biddy had given them all short shrift.

She had told Mattie that enough money had been spent on stamps to and from this house for him to feel embarrassed even mentioning the question of underpayment. He had slunk away, as well he might. The butchers had felt the lash of Biddy's tongue as she told them that the new frontage on the shop had been paid for with money that Major Murphy and his family had spent on the best of meat, they should be ashamed to grumble.

She asked Sergeant Keane what he could have been thinking of to imagine that a tinker boy could even have crossed the lawns of The Glen.

At first Leo didn't want to meet anyone. She wanted to stay half sitting, half kneeling on her window seat, looking out to where the dogs played, and old Ned made halfhearted attempts at hoeing, to where her father walked with his halting movements out to meet Mr. Hayes, and where Mother drifted, her straw hat in her hand, through the shrubbery and past the lilacs.

No man came from the Botanic Gardens to deal with the rockery that they had planned on top of the great pit that had been filled in.

When Mr. O'Neill, the auctioneer from the big town, came to inquire whether they would be interested in letting the gate lodge, Leo's father and mother said not just now, sometime certainly, but at the moment everything was quite undecided, perhaps one of the boys might come home and live in it.

There had never been any question of Harry or James coming back. Leo realized it was one more of these easy lies her mother told, the way she had told the people at the hotel that Leo had been unwell and that was why she hadn't been able to eat her meals.

One day Maura Brennan from school came and asked for a job as a maid in the house. She said she had to work somewhere and why not for someone like Leo, whom she liked. Leo had been awkward and frightened that day. It seemed another example of the world going mad. Maura, who had sat beside her at school, wanting to come and scrub floors in their house because that was the way things were.

But as the days turned into weeks Leo got the courage to leave The Glen. She called on Eddie Barton and his mother. They spoke to her as if things were normal. She began to believe they were. There was an ill-written postcard from London saying *Wish you were here*. She knew it was from Foxy, though it didn't say. And one Saturday at Confession, Father Gunn had asked her was there anything troubling her.

Leo's heart leaped into her throat.

"Why do you ask that, Father?" she said in a whisper.

"You seem nervous, my child. If there's anything you want to say to me, remember you're saying it to God through me."

"I know, Father."

"So, if there is any worry . . ."

"I am worried about something, but it's not my worry, it's someone else's worry."

"Is it your sin, my child?"

"No, Father. No. Not at all. It's just that I can't understand it. You see, it has to do with grown-ups."

There was a silence.

Father Gunn was digesting this. He assumed that it was to do with a child's perception of adult sexuality and all the loathing and embarrassment that this could bring.

"Perhaps all these things will become clear later," he said soothingly.

"So, I shouldn't worry, do you think, Father?"

"Not if it's something you have no control over, my child, something where it would not be appropriate for you to be involved," said the priest.

Leo felt much better. She said her three Hail Marys, penance for her other small sins, and put the biggest thing as far to the back of her mind as possible. After all, the priest had said that God would make it all clear later, now was not the appropriate time to worry about it.

As she prepared for her years in the convent school in the town she tried to make life in The Glen seem normal. She had joined their game. She was pretending that nothing had ever happened on that summer evening when the world stopped.

Leo started to go down the hill to meet the people she had been at school with once more—her friend Nessa Ryan in the hotel, whose mother always found work for idle hands—Sheila and Eileen Blake, who were home from a posh boarding school and kept asking could they come and play tennis at The Glen. Leo told them the court needed a lot of work. She realized she was lying as smoothly as her mother these days. She met Niall Hayes, who told Leo that he thought he was in love.

"Everyone's doing everything too young," Leo said reprovingly. "Foxy's too young to be going to England to work, you're too young to be in love. Who is it anyway?"

He didn't say. Leo thought it might be Nessa. But no, surely not? He lived across the road from Nessa, he had known her all his life. That couldn't be what falling in love was like. It was too confusing.

She met Nancy Finn from the pub. Nancy was what they called a "bold strap" in Shancarrig. She was fifteen and had been accused of being forward and giving people the eye. Sometimes she helped serve behind the counter. It was a rough sort of place.

Nancy said she'd really love to go to America and work as a cocktail waitress. That was her goal, but her father said it was lunacy. Nancy said that her father, Johnny Finn Noted for Best Drinks, was fed up. The Guards had been in every night for three weeks asking was there any brawl between tinkers and anyone, and her father said he wouldn't let a bloody tinker in the door. Sergeant Keane said that was a very unchristian attitude, and Nancy's father had said the Guards would have another tune to play if he *did* let the tinkers in and took their money, so there had been hard words and the upshot was that the Guards were watching Johnny Finn's pub night after night, ready to pounce if anyone was left with a drink in front of them for thirty seconds beyond the licensing hours.

The summer ended and a new life began, a life of getting the bus every day into school in the big town. The bus bounced along the roads through villages and woods, and stopped at junctions and crossroads where people came down long narrow tracks to the main road. Leo and Nessa Ryan learned their homework to the rhythm of the bus crossing the countryside. They heard each other's poems, they puzzled out theorems and algebra. Often they didn't even look out the window at the countryside passing by.

Sometimes Leo seemed as if she was looking out at the scenery. Anyone watching her would think that there was a dreamy schoolgirl looking out at the fields with the cattle grazing, the colors changing from season to season in the hedges and clusters of bushes that they passed.

But Leo Murphy's eyes might not have been focusing on these things at all. Her thoughts were often on her mother. Her pale delicate mother, who wandered more often through the gardens of The Glen no matter what the weather, with empty eyes, talking softly to herself.

Leo had seen her mother sit under the lilac tree picking the great purple flowers apart absently in her lap and crooning to herself, "You had lilac eyes, Danny. Your eyes were like deep lilac. Your eyes are closed now."

She spoke of Danny too when she half sat and half lay over the rockery. Every day, rain or shine, she tended it, and a weed could hardly put its head out before Mrs. Murphy had snapped it away.

"At least I kept your grave for you, Danny boy," she would cry. "You can never say I didn't put flowers on your grave. No man in Ireland got more flowers."

The first time Leo heard her mother speak like this she was frozen with horror. It was a known fact that the missing tinker was Danny. His family had told people that he must have had a girl in Shancarrig. He used to be gone from the camp for long periods, and when he'd come back he was always smiling and saying nothing. There was the question he might have run off with someone from the locality. Sergeant Keane had assured the travelers that there were no unexplained disappearances of any of the girls of the village; he had made inquiries and there was no one missing from the area.

"No one except Danny," said Mrs. McDonagh, the sad-looking woman with the dark, lined face who was Danny's mother.

Leo heard all this from other people. Nessa Ryan heard it discussed a lot in the hotel, and reported it word for word. It was the only exciting thing that had happened in their lives. She couldn't understand why her friend Leo wasn't interested in it, and wouldn't speculate like everyone else about what might have happened.

The months went by and Leo's mother became less in touch with reality.

Leo had stopped trying to talk to her about school, and everyday things. Instead she spoke as if her mother was an invalid.

"How do you feel today, Mother?"

"Well . . . I don't know, I really don't know." She spoke in a dull voice. The woman who used to be so elegant and graceful, the mother who would plan a picnic, correct bad grammar or a mispronounced word with cries of horror . . . that had all gone.

She barely touched her food, just smiled vaguely at Father, at Leo, and at Biddy as if they were people she used to know. She spoke to the dogs, Lance and Jessie, no longer the big gamboling pups, but more stately with years. She reminded them of how they had known Danny, and they would stand guard over his grave.

Biddy *must* have heard it. She would have had to be deaf not to have known what she was talking about.

But the conspiracy continued.

Mrs. Murphy had been feeling under the weather, surely now the longer days, or the bright weather, or the good crisp winter without any damp . . . whichever season . . . she would show an improvement.

Old Ned had been pensioned off. Eddie Barton came and cut the grass sometimes, but there was nobody coming to do the gardens as they should have been done. Sometimes Leo and her father would struggle, but it was beyond them. Only the rockery bloomed. Mrs. Murphy wandered outside The Glen with her secateurs in her pocket and took cuttings for it, or even dug up little plants that she thought might flourish.

In the increasingly jungle-like gardens of The Glen the rockery bloomed as a monument, as a memorial.

In her efforts to keep her mother out of anyone else's sight and hearing Leo pieced together the story of horror, of what had happened in those weeks when she was fourteen and had understood nothing of the world. Those weeks before her world changed.

Mother remembered not only Danny's lilac eyes but his strong arms, and his young body. She remembered his laughter and his impatience and greed to have her, over and over. With a sick stomach Leo listened to her mother remembering and crying for a lost love. She hated the childlike coquettish enthusiasm in her mother's face when she spoke of the man she had welcomed on the mossy earth, in her bedroom on the rug, under the lilac trees, and in the gate lodge.

But it was when she mentioned the gate lodge that her face would harden and her questioning take a different turn. Why did he have to be so greedy? What did he need with silver? Why had he demanded to take their treasures? What did he mean that he needed something to trade, some goods to deal in as they went toward Galway? Had he not taken her, was that not the greatest treasure of all? Miriam Murphy's eyes were like stone when she went through that part of the story of the last time they had met . . . of the silver he had wrapped in a tablecloth as he had roamed through the house, touching things, taking this, leaving that. She had begged him and pleaded.

"Say there was a robbery . . . say you came back and found it all gone." His lilac eyes had laughed at her.

"I told him he must not go, he had been sent to me, and he could not leave."

Leo knew the chant off by heart, she could say it with her mother as the woman stroked the earth of the rockery.

"You wouldn't listen, Danny. You called me old. You said

you had given me my fun and my loving and that I should be grateful.

"You said you'd take some guns, that we had no need of them, but in your life you'd need to hunt in the forest . . . I asked you to take me with you . . . and you laughed, and you called me old. I couldn't let you leave, I had to keep you here, and that was why . . ." Her mother would smile then, and stroke the earth again. "And you are here, Danny Boy. You'll never leave me now."

Leo had known for years why her father had struggled that night, dragging and pulling with his wounds aching and his useless leg trailing behind. He knew why this woman had to be protected from telling this singsong tale to the law. And Leo knew too.

At school they thought her a tense child. They spoke to her father about her since Mrs. Murphy, the mother, never made any appearance.

Mother Dorothy, who was wise in the ways of the world, decided that the mother might have a drink problem. It had to be. Otherwise she'd have come in sometime. Very tough on the child, a nice girl, but with a shell on her as hard as rock.

Leo told Father Gunn that Mother wasn't all that well, and that if they didn't see her at Mass he wasn't to take any wrong meaning out of it.

Father Gunn asked would she like the Sacraments brought up to The Glen.

"I'm not too sure, Father." Leo bit her lip.

Father Gunn also knew the ways of the world.

"Why don't we leave it for the moment?" he suggested. "And if there's any change in that department then all you have to do is ask me."

Leo thought to herself that in Shancarrig it was really quite easy to hide anything from anybody.

Or maybe it was only if you happened to live in The Glen, a

big house surrounded by high walls, with its own gardens and shrubberies and gate lodge.

It might be different trying to keep your secrets if you lived in the cottages down by the river, or in The Terrace with everyone seeing your front entrance, or in the hotel with half of Shancarrig in and out your doors every day.

She felt watchful about her mother, but not always on edge. No long-term anxiety like that can be felt at the pain level all the time. There were many hours when Leo didn't even think about her mother's telling and retelling the story. There were the school outings, there were the parties, the times when Niall Hayes kissed her and their noses kept bumping, and later when quite suddenly Richard Hayes, who was Niall's older cousin, kissed her and there was no nose bumping at all.

Richard Hayes was very handsome, he had stirred the place up since he arrived. Leo felt sorry for Niall because deep in her heart she thought Niall still had a very soft spot for Nessa, and Nessa was of course crazy about the new arrival in town.

And it had to be said that Richard was paying a lot of attention to Nessa. There were walks, drives, and trips to the pictures in the town. Leo thought he was rather dangerous, but then she shrugged. Who was she to know? Her views on love and attraction were extremely suspect.

Some of the girls at school were going to be nurses, they had applied to hospitals in Dublin and in Britain for places.

"Should I be a nurse, Daddy?" she asked.

They were walking, as they often did in the evening. Mother was safely talking to the rockery, and if you counted Biddy as the silent rock she had been for five long years, then there was no one around to hear the chant that had begun again.

"Would you *like* to be a nurse?"

"Only if it would help."

Her father looked old and gray. Much of his time was spent persuading his sons not to come back to Shancarrig, and telling them that their mother was in poor mental health.

Naturally they had written and asked why was nothing being done about this. They had written also to Dr. Jims, which Major

Murphy thought an outrageous interference. But fortunately Jims Blake had agreed with him that arrogant young men thought they knew everything. If Frank Murphy said there was nothing wrong with Miriam, then that was that. The doctor had seen the thin pale face and the overbrilliant eyes of Miriam Murphy, always a fairly obsessional person he would have thought, checking light switches, refusing to throw out old papers. This is what he had noticed on his visits to The Glen, and assumed that as with many a nervy woman there was nothing asked and therefore nothing that could be answered. This was not a household where he would be asked to refer her to a psychiatrist in order to work out the cause of the unease. At least he wasn't being asked for ever-increasing prescriptions of tranquilizers or sleeping pills. That in itself was something to be thankful for.

Foxy Dunne came home every Christmas as he had promised. When he arrived on his first visit home, wearing a new zippered jacket with a tartan lining, at the back door of The Glen, he was surprised at the frostiness of his reception. Not that he had ever been warmly welcomed there, but this was out of that league. . . . "Well, tell my friend Leo. She knows where I live," he said haughtily to Biddy.

"And I'm sure, like everyone, she knows only too well where the Dunnes live and would want to avoid it," Biddy said.

Leo had heard. She called at the Dunnes' cottage that afternoon.

"I came to ask if you'd like to go for a walk in Barna Woods," she said.

Foxy looked very pleased. He was at a loss for words. The quick shrugging reaction or the smart joke deserted him.

"Well, I won't ask you into my house either," he said. "Let's go and be babes in the wood."

He told her of living in a house with eleven men from their own county. He told her of the drinking and how so many of them spent everything they had nearly killed themselves earning.

"Why do you stay there?" she asked.

"To learn . . . to save. But mainly to learn."

"What can you learn from old men like that drinking their lives away?"

"I can learn what not to do, I suppose, or how it could have been done right."

Foxy sat on a fallen tree and told her about the chances, the men who had made it, the small contractors who did things right and did them quickly. He told her how you had to watch out for the fellow who was a great electrician, a good plumber, a couple of bright brickies, a class carpenter. Then all you needed was someone to get them together and you had your own team—someone who had a head for figures, someone who could cost a job and make the contacts.

"And who would you get to do that?" She was genuinely interested.

"God, Leo, that's what *I'm* going to do. That's what it's all about," he said.

She felt ashamed that she hadn't the confidence in him.

"Did you know my father was in jail?" he asked defensively.

"I heard. I think Biddy told me."

"She would have."

She was torn between being sympathetic and telling him it didn't matter.

"Did he hate it?" she asked.

"I don't know, he doesn't talk to me. He should have been there longer. He hit a fellow with a plank that had nails in it. He's dangerous."

"You're not like that," she said suddenly.

"I know, but I didn't want you to forget where I come from."

"You are what you are, so am I."

"And do you have any tales to tell me?" he asked.

"No. Why?" Her voice was clipped.

He shrugged. It was as if he had been offering her the chance to trade confessions.

But he didn't know they were not equal confessions. What his father had done was known the length and breadth of the county. What her mother had done was known by only three people.

He looked at her for a while, as if waiting.

Then he said: "No reason, no reason at all."

She saw him looking at her, with her belted raincoat, hands stuck deep in her pockets. The wind made her cheeks red. Her brown-gold curls stood out around her head like furze. She felt he was looking straight through her, that he could see everything, knew everything.

"I hate my hair," she said suddenly.

"It's like a halo," he said.

And she grinned.

Every Christmas he came home. He called at The Glen and she would take him walking. For the week that he was home they would meet every day.

Nessa Ryan was very disapproving. "You *do* know his father was in jail," she told Leo.

"I do," Leo sighed. She had heard it all from Biddy, over and over.

"I'd be surprised you'd go walking with him, then."

"I know you would." Leo had heard the same thing from her father. But that particular time she had answered back. "Well, if everyone knew about us, Daddy, maybe people wouldn't want to go walking with us either." Her father looked as if she had struck him. Immediately she had repented. "I'm so sorry, I didn't mean it . . . I just think that Foxy is lonely when he comes home. I don't ask him in here. I'm seventeen, nearly eighteen, Daddy. Why can't we let people alone? We, of all people?"

Her father had tears in his eyes. "Go and walk with whoever you like in the woods," he had said, his voice choked.

That was the Christmas when Foxy told her that he was on the way to the big time. He was working with two others. They were setting up their own contracts, they would hire men, get a team together. No more working for cheats and fellows who took all the profit.

"I'll soon have enough saved to come back a rich man," he said. "Then I'll drive up your avenue in a big car, hand my coat and gloves to Biddy, and ask your father for your hand in marriage. Your mother will take out the sherry and plan your wedding dress."

"I'll never marry," Leo told him.

"You sure as anything didn't take my advice about getting trained for a career or a job," he said.

"I can't leave The Glen."

"Will you tell me why?" His eyes still had that power to look as if they could see right through her, and know everything.

"I will, one day," she promised, and she knew she would.

This year at least she had an address for Foxy. She wrote to him, he sent a very short note back.

"Why don't you learn to type, Leo? Your writing is worse than my own. We can't have that when we're in the big time, neither of us able to write a letter."

She laughed.

She didn't tell Nessa Ryan that she had just got a sort of proposal from Foxy Dunne.

She didn't tell her parents.

Her mother died on an autumn night. They said it was of exposure. Her lungs filled up with the damp night air and, added to a chest infection . . . there was no hope for a woman whose health had always been so frail.

She had been found in her nightdress, lying over the rockery in the garden.

The church was crowded. Major Murphy asked people to come back to Ryan's Hotel for a drink and some sandwiches afterward. This was very unusual and had never been known in

Shancarrig. But he said that The Glen was too sad for him and for Leo just now. He was sure people would understand.

Then Leo went to the town every day on the bus and learned to type in the big secretarial college where Nessa had done a course.

"Why couldn't you have done it with me?" Nessa grumbled.

"It wasn't the right time."

There had been no note from Foxy Dunne about her mother's death.

She didn't write to tell him. Surely some member of his awful family was in touch, surely there would have been a mention that Mrs. Murphy of The Glen had been found dead in her nightdress, and that her wits must have been astray. Everyone else knew about it.

When he came back at Christmas it was clear that he hadn't known. He was sympathetic and sad.

She asked him in, not to the breakfast room but to the drawing room. Together they lit the fire.

The old dogs lay down, pleased that the room was being opened up.

Biddy was beyond complaining now. Too much had happened in this house. That Foxy Dunne be invited into the Major's drawing room seemed minor these days.

He told her of his plans. He had seen so much in England of how places could be developed. Take The Glen. They could sell off most of the land, build maybe eight houses, and still keep their own home.

"I expect your father would like that," he said.

Outside they could see the sad lonely figure of Major Murphy walking up and down to the gate and back in the darkening evening.

"We can never sell the land," Leo said.

"Is this part of what you told me you'd tell me one day?"

"Yes."

"Are you ready to tell me now?"

"No. Not yet, Foxy."

"Does your mother's death not make it different?" Again that feeling that he knew everything.

"No. You see, Daddy still lives here. Nothing could be . . . interfered with."

She thought of the big diggers, the excavators, the rockery going, as it would one day, when The Glen would disappear like so much of Ireland, and make way for houses for the Irish who were coming back to live in their own land, having worked hard in other countries.

People like Foxy coming back to their inheritances.

The body of Danny McDonagh which had lain so long under its mausoleum of flowers would be disturbed. The questions would be asked.

"We're over twenty-one. We can do what we like," he said.

"I could always do what I liked, for all the good it did me."

"So could I," he answered her with spirit. "And it did me a lot of good. I never wanted anyone else but you, not since we were children. What did you want?"

"I wanted to be safe," she said.

He promised her that was exactly what he would do for her. They talked a little that night, and more the next day in Barna Woods. He left her at the gate of The Glen, and saw her look away from the gate house.

"Something happened here," he said.

"I always knew you had second sight."

"Tell me, Leo. We're not people to have secrets from each other."

Through the window of The Glen they could see her father sitting at the drawing room fire. He must have got the idea of sitting in that room after seeing them there yesterday. She told Foxy the story.

"Let's get the key," he said.

She went through the kitchen and took it from the rack in the hall. Together, with candles, they walked through the gate lodge, a blameless place that didn't know what had happened there.

He raised her face toward him and looked into her eyes.

"Your hair is like a halo again. You're doing it to drive me mad," he said.

"Don't you see all the problems, all the terrible problems?"

"I see nothing that won't be solved by a load of concrete on where that rockery stands now," Foxy Dunne said.

10

A Stone House and a Big Tree

The decision to close the school was known in 1969, but still it was a shock to see the building advertised for sale in the summer of 1970.

FOR SALE

TRADITIONAL STONE SCHOOLHOUSE. BUILT 1899. SCHOOL ACCOMMODATION COMPRISES THREE LARGE CLASSROOMS, TOILET FACILITIES, AND OUTHALL. ACCOMPANYING COTTAGE: TWO BEDROOMS, ONE LIVING ROOM/KITCHEN WITH STANLEY RANGE.

FOR SALE BY PUBLIC AUCTION JUNE 24TH IF NOT DISPOSED OF BY PRIVATE TREATY.

AUCTIONEERS: O'NEILL AND BLAKE.

Nessa and Niall Hayes read it over breakfast.
From their dining room they could look over at Ryan's Shan-

carrig Hotel and see the early tour buses leaving on their excursions. Nessa worked flexible hours across the road in her family business. Neither of her sisters had shown any interest in hotel work.

"They will when they see there's money in it," her mother had said darkly.

"Imagine the school for sale. We'd never have thought that possible." Niall was thirty now. Nobody ever referred to him as young Mr. Hayes anymore, in fact his father took the backseat in almost every aspect of the business nowadays.

"What's not possible?" Danny Hayes was four, and very inquisitive. He loved long words and would pronounce them carefully.

"That you're not going to go to the same school we went to." Nessa wiped his chin expertly of the runny bits of egg. "You'll go on a big yellow bus to school. You won't walk over the bridge like we did."

"Can I go today?" Danny asked.

"After Christmas," Nessa promised.

"Won't he be a bit young?" Niall looked worried.

"If *your* mother had had her way you wouldn't have been allowed up the road to Shancarrig School until you were twenty." There was a laugh in Nessa's voice, but also a tinge of bitterness.

It had not been quite as simple moving into The Terrace as she had thought it would be. Although her father-in-law had handed over the reins quite willingly to his son, Ethel Hayes had been less anxious to let go the gloomy reign over the family.

There were dire warnings of pneumonia, rheumatic fever, spoiled children, temper tantrums, all directed at Nessa. Danny and Breda would suffer for it all later, was Mrs. Hayes's prediction—the children were allowed too much freedom, too little discipline, and a severe absence of cod liver oil.

"Would we buy it?" Nessa asked suddenly.

"What on earth for?" Niall was genuinely surprised.

"To live in. It would be a great place for the children to play . . . the tree and everything. It would be lovely."

"I don't know." Niall bit his lip. It was his usual reaction to a new idea, to something totally unexpected.

Nessa knew him well enough.

"Well, let's not think about it now. It's a month to the auction," she said.

Deftly she forced Danny to finish egg and toast by cutting it into tiny cubes and eating one alternately with him. She settled Breda into her carry-cot. Niall was still sitting at his place pondering the bombshell.

"It's only an idea," Nessa said airily. "But if you're talking to Declan Blake at all, ask him how much he thinks they'll get for it."

Niall looked out the window, and saw Nessa moving into her parents' hotel. The carry-cot was taken from her at the door by the porter. Danny had run to the hotel backyard where Nessa and her mother had built a sandpit, and swings and a seesaw to entertain the children who came to stay.

It had been yet one more excellent marketing notion for Ryan's Shancarrig Hotel.

••• •••

Jim and Nora Kelly read it in Galway. They were staying with Maria and Hugh. They had wanted to be away when it was announced and by wonderful chance it coincided with the very time they were badly needed. Maria's first baby was due. She wanted her parents to be with her.

"It's the end of an era," Maria said. "There must be people all over Ireland saying that."

"Not only Ireland, didn't our people go all over the world?" Jim Kelly said.

He was fifty years of age, and had been reemployed in the school in the town. It wasn't the same, of course, nothing would ever be the same. But he knew a great number of the children, and he came trailing clouds of respect. A man who had run his own show, even in a small village, was a man to be reckoned with.

Nora had taken early retirement. And taken many a train to visit Maria over on the Atlantic coast. They walked along the beach together, the pregnant girl and the woman who was as good as her mother, with so much to say. Jim was pleased that his wife had taken the closing of the school so well. It might have been too much of a change for her to have gone to teach in the town.

Maria patted her stomach. "It'll be so strange that she won't know the place as a school," she said wonderingly.

"Or he. Remember, you could have a boy." Jim Kelly knew that none of them minded whether it was boy or girl.

They were so happy that Maria had found the steady Hugh after a series of wilder boyfriends had broken their hearts. Hugh seemed to know how much Maria needed her background in Shancarrig, he was always finding excuses to bring her there.

"Still, when the baby's born I'll wheel her . . . or him . . . up to the school and say that this is where Grandpa or Grandma used to live . . . live, where every child lived for a while." Maria looked sad. "Oh, come on. I'm being stupidly sentimental," she said with a little shake. "And anyway, aren't you better off by far living in that fine house near everything, instead of having to toil up and down the hill?"

The Kellys had settled in one of the cottages that had been vastly changed and upgraded. The row of houses by the Grane that had once held the most unruly Brennans and Dunnes were now what young Declan Blake called Highly Des. Res. material.

"I wish there were going to be children there," Nora Kelly said. "I suppose it's unlikely that anyone who has children could afford to buy it, but somehow the place cries out for them. Or am I the one being sentimental now?"

"There'd be nobody local who could think of it." Jim was ticking off people in his mind.

"Maybe when Hugh makes a fortune we'll buy it ourselves . . . and let little Nora play under the copper beech like I did."

There was a lump in their throats. It hadn't been said that Maria was going to call her child after Nora Kelly.

"I thought maybe Helen after your mother." Nora felt she should say it anyway.

"The second one will be Helen!" said Maria.

And the matter was left there.

••• •••

Chris Barton read the notice out to her mother-in-law. She always called Eddie's mother Una. It was yet another bond between them, the fact that she thought of the older woman as her sister.

"Well, Una. Is this our big chance?" Chris asked. "Is this the famous opportunity that is meant to present itself to people? A readymade craft center . . . get Foxy to build a few more outbuildings that we could rent out as studios . . . is this it or is it madness?"

"You're the one with the courage. I'd still be turning up hems for people and letting out their winter skirts if you hadn't come along." Mrs. Barton declared that she said an extra decade of the rosary every single night of her life to thank the Lord and His Mother for sending Chris to Shancarrig.

"I don't know, I really don't know. I'll ask Eddie. He has a great instinct for these things. We might be running before we can walk, or we might regret it all our lives. I trust his nose for this sort of thing."

It was true. Mrs. Barton realized that her daughter-in-law really did defer to Eddie's instincts and tastes. It wasn't a case of pretending to take his advice like Mrs. Ryan in the hotel did, and indeed her daughter young Nessa, who was busy pushing Niall Hayes into some kind of confidence. Chris genuinely thought Eddie the brains of the outfit. It made Una Barton's heart soar.

She thought less and less about the husband who had left her all those years ago—a quarter of a century—but sometimes she wished that Ted Barton could know how well his son had done and how splendidly they had managed without him.

Eddie came in holding the twins by the hand. He laughed as he saw his wife and his mother automatically reach to protect everything on the table that was in danger of being pulled to the floor.

"Can we leave them with you, Una? I want to talk to Eddie in Barna Woods."

"The last time you did that you proposed to me. I hope this doesn't mean you're going to leave." He laughed confidently. He didn't think it was likely.

The children were strapped into their high chairs, and fussed over by their grandmother. Chris and Eddie walked as they so often walked together, shoulders touching, talking so that they finished each other's sentences, at ease with each other and the world. There was nobody in Shancarrig who noticed that Chris had a Scottish accent now, any more than they saw that she had a lame leg and a built-up shoe. She had been there since she was eighteen or nineteen. Part of the scenery.

They sat in the wood and she asked him about the center. Was it exactly the right time? Or was this folly? Her eyes looked at him for an answer and she saw his face light up. He would never have thought of it, he said . . . to him it would always have been the school, the place that he had gone, rain or shine, where he had played and studied. Of course it was the answer.

"Would we live there, or just work there?" Chris wondered.

"It would be great for the children . . . it's a bit isolated for the twins in our house."

"We could sell the pink house." Chris had always called it that, since the moment she had arrived.

"But my mother?"

"She said she'd leave it to us."

"Where would she go? She's so used to being beside us . . ." Mrs. Barton lived in her own little wing of the pink house, beside them but not on top of them.

"She'd come with us, you big nellie. We'd be building a whole lot of places and she could choose the kind of place she'd like. It's no bigger a hill for her to climb than the one that she's been on all her life."

Eddie's eyes were dancing. "We could invite people in . . . like the pottery couple, or the weavers . . ."

"We could have a small shop there, selling everyone's work. Not only ours, but everyone's."

"Nessa would get them up there from the hotel for a start, and Leo's got all sorts of contacts all over the place."

"Will we do it?"

They embraced, as they had embraced in these woods years ago at the thought of being married and living happily ever after.

••• •••

Richard saw the advertisement.

He wondered would whoever bought it cut down the tree in the yard. What would they make of the things that were written on it? He was prepared to bet that his wasn't the only carving that told a story.

He thought about the school all day in the office.

It was a tiring journey home, a lot of traffic. He was hot and tired. He hoped that Vera hadn't arranged anything for tonight. What he really would like to do was . . . he paused. He didn't know what he would really like to do. It had been so long since he had allowed himself a thought like that.

He knew what he would really *not* like to do, and that would be to go to the club. Vera might have set up a little evening, a few drinks at the bar, dinner. He would know when he got in. If she had been to the hairdresser, this is what she had planned.

He nosed the car into the garage beside Vera's.

Jimmy the gardener was edging the lawn. "Good evening, Mr. Hayes," he said, touching his forehead.

"That looks great, Jimmy. Great work." Richard knew his voice was automatic, he didn't see what the man had done or what needed to be done. He thought that a full-time gardener was a bit excessive in a Dublin garden.

Still, it was Vera's decision. It was after all she who had bought the house, and filled it with valuable things. It was Vera who made the day-to-day decisions about how they spent the money which was mainly her money.

She was sitting in the conservatory. He noticed sadly that she had been to the hairdresser.

"You look lovely," he said.

"Thank you, darling. I thought we might meet some of the others at the club . . . you know, rather than just sitting looking at each other all night?" She smiled.

She was very attractive in her lemon-colored dress, her blond upswept hair, and her even suntan.

She did not look in her late thirties any more than he did. But unlike him she never seemed to find their life empty. She filled it with acquaintances, parties given, parties attended, a group of what she called "like-minded people" at the golf club.

Vera had taken their childlessness with what Richard considered a disturbing lack of concern. If the question was ever raised either between themselves or when other people were present, she always said the same thing. She said that if it happened it did, and if it didn't it didn't. No point in having all those exhaustive tests to discover whose *fault* it was, as if someone was to blame.

Since Richard knew from the past, only too well from his dramas with Olive and Judy, that there could be nothing lacking on his side, he wished that Vera would go for an examination. But she refused.

She had the newspaper open in front of her.

"Look! There's a simply lovely place for sale, in that Shancarrig where you spent all those years."

"I know. I saw it."

"Should we buy it, do you think? It has tons of potential. It would make a nice weekend place, we could have people to stay. You know, it might be fun."

"No."

"What do you mean *no*?"

"I mean *no*, Vera," he said.

Her face flushed. "Well, I don't know what you're turning on *me* for, I only thought *you'd* like it. I do everything that I think *you'd* like. It's becoming impossible to please you."

He moved over to reach for her, but she stood up and pulled away.

"Seriously, Richard. Nobody could please you. There isn't a woman on earth that could hold you. Maybe you should never have married, just been a desirable bachelor all your life." She was very hurt, he could see.

"Please. Please forgive me, I've had a horrible day. I'm tired, that's all. Please, I'm a pig."

She was softening. "Have a bath and a drink and we'll go out. You'll feel much better then."

"Yes. Yes, of course. I'm sorry for snapping." His voice was dead, he could hear it in his own ears.

"And you really don't think we should pick up this little house as a weekend place?"

"No, Vera. No, I wasn't happy there. It wouldn't make me happy to go back."

"Right. It will never be mentioned again," she said.

And he knew that she would look for somewhere else, a place where they could invite people for the weekend—fill their life with even more half strangers. Maybe she might even pick on whatever town Gloria had settled in. He knew the Darcys had left Shancarrig not long after he had.

··• •··

Leo sat in the kitchen of The Glen making a very unsuccessful effort to comb Moore's hair. He had inherited the frizz from his mother and the color from his father. He was six years old and in the last pageant that Shancarrig School had put on he had been asked to play the Burning Bush. This was apparently his own choice.

Foxy was delighted. Leo was less sure.

Moore Dunne was turning out to be a bigger handful than anyone could have believed. Foxy had insisted on the name. While he worked in England he said that he had discovered it was very classy to use one family name added to another. Leo's mother had been Miriam Moore, this had been the Moore household.

Moore's younger sister, Frances, was altogether more tractable. "We'll liven her up yet," Foxy had said ominously.

Unlike many of the builders who had returned from England in the prosperous sixties with their savings and their ideas of a quick killing, Foxy Dunne had decided to go the route of befriending rather than alienating architects.

The eight small houses he had built within the grounds of The Glen had a style and a character that was noticeably missing in such similar small developments in other towns. A huge row of semimature trees had been planted to give the new houses privacy, but also to maintain the long sweep of The Glen's avenue.

Major Murphy had lived to see his grandchildren but was buried now in the graveyard beside his wife.

From the big drawing room of The Glen, Leo ran the ever-increasing building empire that Foxy had set up. All his cousins in the town now worked for him, the cousins who had once barred his father from crossing the doors of their shops. His cousins Brian and Liam waited on his every word and his uncle treated him with huge respect.

Foxy's father was not around to see the fruits of having totally ignored his son. Old Dinny had died in the county home some years previously. Foxy's own brothers, never men to have held down jobs for any notable length of time, most of them with some kind of prison record, were now regarded as remittance men. Small allowances were paid as long as they stayed far away from Shancarrig.

The main alterations that had put Ryan's Shancarrig Hotel on the map for tourism had been done by Foxy Dunne. It was he who had transformed the cottages by the River Grane, his only concession to any sentimentality or revenge having been his own personal presence as they leveled to the ground the house he grew up in.

The church hall, which was the pride of Father Gunn's life,

was built by Foxy at such a reduced rate that it might even have been called his gift to the parish.

Foxy kept proper accounts. The books that Leo kept were regularly audited. The leases to the property he bought and sold were handled by his friend Niall Hayes. Maura came up from the gate lodge every day to do some of the housework and to mind the children. As always, her son Michael came with her. Michael was growing up big and strong but with the mind and loving heart of a small child.

Moore Dunne was particularly fond of him. "He's much more interesting than other big people," Moore pronounced.

Leo made sure she told that to Maura.

"I've always thought that myself," Maura agreed.

Leo and Maura had a cup of tea together every morning before both went to their work—Leo to cope with Foxy's deals and Maura to polish and shine The Glen. Together they looked at the advertisement offering their old school for sale.

"Who would buy it, unless to set up another school?" Maura wondered.

"I'm very much afraid Foxy wants to," said Leo. He hadn't said it yet, but she knew it was on his mind. It was as if he could never burn out the memory of the way things used to be. Not until he owned the whole town.

They heard the sound of his car outside the door. "How's Squire Dunne?" he said to his son.

"I'm all *right*," said Moore doubtfully.

"Only *all right*. You should be tip-top," Foxy said.

"Well yes, but I think there's another cat growing inside Flossie." Moore was troubled.

"That's great," said Foxy. "It'll be a kitten, or maybe five kittens even."

"But how are they going to get out?" Moore was puzzled. Maura giggled.

"That's your mother's department," said Foxy, heading for the office. "I have to think of other things like planning permissions, son."

"For the school?" Leo asked.

"Aha, you're there before me," he said.

She looked at him, small and quick and eager as ever, nowadays dressed in clothes that were made to measure, but still the endearing Foxy of their childhood. She followed him into the room that was once their drawing room, where her father had paced, and her mother had sat distracted, and Lance and Jessie had slept uncaring by the fire.

"Do we need it, Foxy?" she asked.

"What's need?" He put his arms around her shoulders and looked into her eyes.

"Haven't we enough?" she said.

"Love, it's a gold mine. It's *made* for us. The right kind of cottages, classy stuff, the kind rich Dubliners might even have as a summer place, or for visiting at the weekends. Do them up really well, let Chris and Eddie loose on them. Slate floors . . . you know the kind of thing." He looked so eager. He would love the challenge.

Perhaps he was right it *was* made for them. Why did she keep thinking he was doing everything just to show? To show some anonymous invisible people who didn't care.

••• •••

Maddy Ross thought it was wonderful that God moved so mysteriously. Look at how He had closed the school just at exactly the right time for Maddy.

Now she could be quite free to spend all her time with the Family. The wonderful Family of Hope. Madeleine Ross had been a member of the Family of Hope for three years. And it had not been easy.

For one thing there had been all that adverse publicity in the papers about the castle they had been given, and the misunderstanding over the deeds.

There had been no intention at all to defraud or deceive, but the way the papers wrote it all up you'd think that the Family of Hope was some kind of international confidence tricksters' organization.

And there had been the whole attitude of Father Gunn.

Maddy had never really liked Father Gunn, not since that time long long ago when he had been so patronizing and so judgmental about her friendship with Father Barry. If Father Gunn had been more understanding or open and liberal about the place of Love in God's scheme of things, then a lot of events would have worked out differently.

Still, that was water under the bridge. The big problem was Father Gunn's attitude today.

He had said that the Family of Hope was not a wonderful way of doing God's work on earth, that it was a dangerous cult, that it was brainwashing people like Maddy, that God wanted love and honor to be shown to Him through the conventional channels of the Church.

It was just exactly what you would have expected him to say. It was what people had said to Our Lord when he went to the Temple to drive out the scribes and the pharisees. They had said to Him that this wasn't the way. They had been wrong, just as Father Gunn was wrong. But it didn't matter. Father Gunn couldn't rule her life for her. It was 1970 now, it wasn't the bad old days when poor Father Barry could be sent away before he knew his mind to a missionary place where they weren't ready for him.

And Father Barry didn't know about the insurance policy that Mother had left her. The money she had been going to give to the people of Vieja Piedra before they had been abandoned and the work stopped in midstream.

Maddy Ross still walked by herself in Barna Woods and hugged herself thinking of the money she could give to the Family of Hope.

They wanted to buy a place to be their center.

She had wondered for a long time if there might be anywhere near here. She wanted to live on in Mother's house and near the woods and river that were so dear to her, and held so many memories. And now at last she had found the very place.

The schoolhouse was for sale.

··• •··

Maura showed the picture of the school to Michael that evening in their little home—the gate lodge of The Glen.

"Do you know where that is, Michael?" she asked.

He held it in both his hands. "Is my school," he said.

"That's right, Michael. It's your school," she said, and she stroked his head.

Michael had never attended a lesson inside the school, but he had gone sometimes to play with the children in the yard. Maura had often stood, lump in throat, watching him pick up the beech leaves as she had done before him, and all his uncles and aunts—the Brennans who had gone away.

"We might walk up there tonight, Michael, and have a look at it again. Would you like that?"

"Will we have tea early so?" He looked at her anxiously.

"We'll have tea early so," she agreed.

He got his own plate and mug, made of Bakelite that wouldn't crack. Michael dropped things sometimes. His mother's china he never touched. Some of it was in a little cabinet that hung on the wall, other pieces were wrapped in tissue paper.

Maura O'Sullivan went to local auctions, always buying bargains in bone china. She never had a full set, or even a half set, but it didn't matter since she didn't ever invite anyone to dine. It was all for her.

They walked past the pink house and waved to the Bartons.

"Can I go in and play with the twins?" Michael said.

"Aren't we going to look at your old school?" They crossed the bridge where the children called out a greeting to Michael, as they had done for many years. And would always do. As long as Maura was there to look after him. Suppose Maura weren't there?

She gave a little shudder.

At the school she saw Dr. Jims and his son, Declan. The FOR SALE sign was there in the sunset. It would look big in other places, under the copper beech it looked tiny.

"Good evening, Doctor." She was formal.

"Hello Declan . . ." Michael embraced the doctor's son, whom he had known since he was a boy in his pram.

"Changing times," Dr. Jims said. "Lord, I never thought I'd see this day."

"Don't be denying me my bit of business, Dad . . ." Declan laughed.

They got on so well these days, Maura realized. It must have been that nice girl Ruth that Declan had married. Some people had great luck altogether out of their marriages. But hadn't she got as much love and happiness as anyone had ever got in the whole world.

Michael was looking at the names on the tree. "Is my name there, Mammy?" he asked.

"If it's not it should be," Dr. Jims said. "Weren't you here as much as any child in Shancarrig?"

"I'll write it if you like," Declan offered.

"What will you put?"

"Let's see. I'll put it near my initials. There, see D.B. 1961? That's me."

"You've no heart drawn," Michael complained.

"I didn't love anyone then," Declan said. His voice seemed full of emotion. The two of them made a great production of getting out Declan's penknife and choosing a spot.

Dr. Jims said to Maura: "Are you feeling all right? You're a bit pale."

"You know me, I worry about things. Nothing maybe . . ."

"It's a while since you've been to see me . . . ?"

"No, Doctor. Not my health, the future."

"Ah. There's divil a thing you can do about the future." Jims Blake smiled at her.

"It's like . . . I wonder sometimes in case something happened to me, what would happen . . . you know." Maura looked over at Michael.

"Child, you're not thirty years of age!"

"I am that. Last week."

"Maura, all I can say is that every mother in Ireland worries abut her child. It's both a wonder and a waste. Life goes on."

"For ordinary people yes."

Michael gave a cry of pleasure, and came to tug at her.

"Look at what he's written. Look Mammy."

Declan Blake had drawn a heart, and on one side he had M o's. On the other he said he was going to put *All his friends in Shancarrig.*

"See what I mean?" said Dr. Jims.

··· ···

Maddy Ross invited Sister Judith of the Family of Hope to come to see the schoolhouse. Sister Judith said it was perfect. She asked how much would it cost. Maddy said she had heard in the area of five thousand pounds. With her mother's insurance policy, Maddy explained, there would be that and plenty more. She would get the deeds drawn up with a solicitor. Not with Niall Hayes and Son. After all she had taught Niall Hayes at school, it wouldn't be appropriate.

··· ···

Maria's child was born in Galway. It was a girl. She was to be called Nora. The Kellys were going to wait for the baptism, but Nora Kelly telephoned Una Barton with the good news. The old habits die hard and they still addressed each other formally.

"Mrs. Kelly, I'm so *very* pleased. I'll make the baby a little dress with smocking on it," she said.

"Maria'll bring her back to Shancarrig on a triumphal tour, and you'll be the first port of call, Mrs. Barton," she cried. The Kellys inquired about the school and was there any word about buyers.

Mrs. Barton paused. She didn't know whether the children wanted it known or not. Still, she couldn't lie to a woman like Mrs. Kelly.

"Between ourselves, Eddie and Chris are trying to get the money together, with grants and everything. They hope to turn it into an Arts Center." There was a silence. "Aren't you pleased to hear that?"

"Yes, yes. It's just I suppose we were hoping there would be children there."

"But there will. They're going to live there with the twins, and me as well. That's the hope, Mrs. Kelly, but it may come to nothing."

"That would be great, Mrs. Barton. I'll say a prayer to St. Anne for you. I'd love to think of your grandchildren and mine playing under that tree."

••• •••

The Dixons were just driving through when they saw the schoolhouse. They were enchanted by it, and called in to Niall Hayes to inquire more about it.

They found him singularly unhelpful.

"There's an auctioneer's name and telephone number on the sign," he said brusquely.

"But seeing that you are the local solicitor we thought you'd know, might shortcut it a bit." The Dixons were wealthy Dublin people looking for a weekend home, they were used to shortcutting things a bit.

"There could be a conflict of interests," Niall Hayes said.

"If you want to buy it, then why is the board still up?" asked Mr. Dixon.

"Good afternoon," Niall Hayes said.

"Terrifying, these country bumpkins," said Mrs. Dixon, well within his hearing.

••• •••

"We've never fought about anything, Foxy, have we?" Leo said to him in bed.

"What do you mean? Our life is one long fight!" he said.

"I don't want us to buy the school."

"Give me one good reason."

"We don't need it, Foxy. Truly we don't. It'd be a hassle."

He stroked her face, but she got up and sat on the edge of the bed reaching for a cigarette.

"Things are always a hassle, love. That's the fun. That's what it was always about. *You* know that."

"No. This time it's different. Lots of others want it too."

"So? *We* get it."

"No, not just rivals, real people. Chris and Eddie, Nessa and Niall, Miss Ross, and I think Maura has hopes of it."

"Miss Ross!" He laughed and rolled around the bed. "Miss Ross is away with the fairies. It would be a *kindness* not to let her have it."

"But the others! I'm serious."

"Look. Niall and Nessa are business people, they know about deals. That's what Niall does all day. Same with Chris and Eddie, they'd understand. Some things you go for, some you get."

Leo began to pace around the room. She reminded herself of her parents. They had paced in this house too.

She shivered at the thought. He was out of bed concerned. He put a dressing gown around her shoulders.

"I told you. Give me one good reason, one *real* reason, and I'll stop."

"Maura."

"Aw, come on, Leo, give me a break! Maura hasn't a penny, we practically *gave* her the gate lodge. Where would she get the money? What would she want it for?"

"I don't know, but she has Michael up there every evening, the two of them staring at it. She wants it for something."

··· ···

"Nessa, come in to me a moment will you?"

"Why do I always feel like a child, instead of the best help you ever had in this hotel, when you use that tone of voice?" Nessa laughed at her mother.

Breda Ryan poured them a glass of sherry each, always a sign of something significant.

"Has Daddy gone on the tear?"

"No, cynical child." They sat companionably. Nessa waited. She knew her mother had something to say.

She was right. Her mother said she was going to give her one piece of advice and then withdraw and let Nessa think about it. She had heard that Nessa and Niall were thinking of buying the schoolhouse as a place to live. Now, there was no way she was going to say how she had heard, nor any need for Nessa to bridle and say it was her own business. But all Breda Ryan wanted to put on the table, for what it was worth, was the following:

It would be an act of singular folly to leave The Terrace, to abandon that beautiful house just because old Ethel was a lighting devil and Nessa didn't feel mistress of her own home. The solution was a simple matter of relocation, banishing both parents to the basement.

But not, of course, describing it as that. Describing it in fact as Foxy Dunne and his architect having come up with this amazing idea about making a totally self-contained flat for the older folk.

Nessa fidgeted as she listened.

"It's only a matter to time," her mother told her. "Suppose you went up to the schoolhouse and his parents were dead next year, think how cross you'd be. Losing the high ground like that. Keep the place, don't let them divide it up with his sisters. It's the best house in the town."

"I wonder are you right." Nessa spoke thoughtfully, as to an equal.

"I'm right," said her mother.

··• •··

Eddie came back from his travels. He had found enough people to make the whole center work. Exactly the kind of people they had always wanted to work with, some of whom had known their work too. It was flattering how well Chris and Eddie Barton were becoming known in Ireland.

The next thing was to visit the bank manager.

And the projections.

Eddie had asked the potential tenants to write their stories so that he and Chris could work out the costings. He also asked them to tell what had been successful or unsatisfactory in the previous places they had been.

He and Chris together read the stories.

They read of places where no visitors came because it wasn't near enough to the town, places that the tour buses passed by because there was no time on the itinerary. They learned that it was best to be part of a community, not outside it. They sat together and realized that in many ways the schoolhouse was not the dream location they had thought.

"That's if we take notice of them," Chris said.

"We *have* to take notice of them. That's our research." Eddie's face was sad.

"Aren't we better to know now than after," Chris said. "Though it's awful to see a dream to go up like that."

"What do you mean a dream go up like that? Haven't we our eye on Nellie Dunne's place after her time. That place is like a warren at the back."

She saw Eddie smile again and that pleased her. "Come on, let's tell Una." She leaped up and went to Eddie's mother's quarters.

"I don't mind *where* I am as long as I'm with the pair of you," said Mrs. Barton. She also told them that she heard that both Foxy Dunne *and* Niall Hayes were said to have their eye on the school.

"Then we're better off not alienating good friends who happen to be good customers as well," said Chris. The two women laughed happily like conspirators.

··• •··

Father Gunn twisted and turned in his narrow bed. In his mind he was trying to write the letter to the Bishop, the letter that would get him a ruling about the Family of Hope. It now seemed definite that Madeleine Ross had given these sinister people the money to set up a center in Shancarrig schoolhouse. They would be here in the midst of his parish, taking away his flock, preaching to them, in long robes, by the river.

Please let the Bishop know what to do.

Why had he made all those moves years ago to prevent a scandal? Wouldn't God and the parish have been far better served if that half-cracked Father Brian Barry and that entirely cracked Maddy Ross had been encouraged to run away with each other? None of this desperate mess about the Family of Bloody Hope would ever have happened.

••• •••

Terry and Nancy Dixon called in to Vera and Richard Hayes's house on their way back home after their ramble.

"We saw the most perfect schoolhouse, I think we should buy it together," Terry said. "It's in that place you worked for a while, Shancarrig."

"We saw it advertised," Vera said, glancing at Richard.

"And?" The Dixons looked from one to the other. Richard's eyes were far away.

"Richard said he wasn't happy in Shancarrig." Vera spoke for him.

"I'm not surprised," said Nancy Dixon. "But you wouldn't have to mix all that much. It would be just the perfect place to get away from it all. There's a really marvelous tree."

"A copper beech," Richard said.

"Yes, that's right. It should go for a song. We talked to the solicitor but he wasn't very forthcoming."

"That's my uncle," Richard said.

The Dixons looked embarrassed. They said it was a younger man, must have been his son. Not someone who was going to set the world on fire? they ventured.

Richard wasn't responding. "They all wrote their names on that tree," he said.

"Aha! Perhaps you wrote *your* name on the tree, that's why we can't go back there." Vera was coquettish.

"No. I never wrote my name there," Richard said. His eyes were still very far away.

••• •••

"Is there much interest from Dublin?" Dr. Jims asked his son.

"No, I thought there'd be more. Maybe if we advertised it again."

The two men walked regularly together in Shancarrig. Declan and Ruth were having a house built there now. They didn't want the place in The Terrace. They wanted somewhere with more space, space for rabbits and a donkey, for the children they would have. Ruth was pregnant. They also felt that it was time to have a suboffice of O'Neill and Blake Estate Agents in Shancarrig. Many of the visitors who came to Ryan's Shancarrig Hotel now wanted to buy sites. Foxy Dunne was only too ready to build on them.

"What will it go for?" Dr. Jims had the school on his mind a lot.

"We've an offer of five. You know that." Declan Blake jerked his head across at Maddy Ross's cottage.

"We don't want them, Declan."

"I can't play God, Dad. I have to get the best price for my client."

"Your client is only the old Department of Education, son. They're being done left, right, and center, or making killings all over the place. They don't count."

"You're honorable in your trade. I have to be in mine."

"I'm also human in mine." There was a silence.

If either of them was remembering how Dr. Jims had bent the rules to help his son all those years ago neither of them said it.

"Perhaps they'll get outbidden." Declan didn't seem very hopeful.

"Has Niall Hayes dropped out?"

"Yes. And Foxy Dunne—that's a relief in a way. And so has Eddie. I wouldn't want them raising the price on each other."

"There. You do have a heart." Dr. Jims seemed pleased.

"And nobody else?"

"Nobody serious."

"Who knows what's serious?"

"All right, Dad. Maura. Michael's mother. She says that she wants the place to be a home, a home for children like Michael, with someone to run it. And she'd help in it too. People like Michael who have no mothers . . . that's what she wants."

"Well, isn't that what we'd all want?" said Dr. Jims. "And if we want it, it can be done."

···•·••·

Nobody ever knew what negotiation went on behind the scenes, how the Family of Hope were persuaded that it would be very damaging publicity to cross swords with a community which wanted to provide a home for Down syndrome children —and raised the money for it. Maddy Ross was heard to say that she was just as glad that Sister Judith hadn't been forced to meet the collective ignorance, superstition, and bigotry of Shancarrig.

···•·••·

Foxy and Leo had provided a sister for Moore and Frances— Chris and Eddie a brother for the twins—Nessa and Niall a brother for Danny and Breda—Mr. and Mrs. Hayes had decided of their own volition to move downstairs to the basement of The Terrace and had their own front door by which they came and went—Declan and Ruth Blake had built their house and had their son called James—the Kellys' granddaughter, Nora, was walking—when the Shancarrig Home was opened.

There were photographs of it in all the papers and nice little pieces describing it.

But it was hard to do it justice, because all anyone could see was a stone house and a big tree.